6-
CGF

DATE DUE

		PRINTED IN U.S.A.

ADA

Books by Vladimir Nabokov

Bend Sinister, a novel
The Defense, a novel
Despair, a novel
Eugene Onegin, by Alexander Pushkin,
    translated from the Russian, with a Commentary
The Eye, a novel
The Gift, a novel
Invitation to a Beheading, a novel
Laughter in the Dark or *Camera Obscura,* a novel
Lolita, a novel
Nabokov's Dozen, a collection of short stories
Nabokov's Quartet, a collection of short stories
Nikolai Gogol, a critical biography
Pale Fire, a novel
Pnin, a novel
Poems
The Real Life of Sebastian Knight, a novel
The Song of Igor's Campaign, Anon.,
    translated from Old Russian
Speak, Memory or *Conclusive Evidence,* a memoir
Spring in Fialta and Other Stories
Three Russian Poets, verse translation from the Russian
The Waltz Invention, a drama
Ada, a novel

VLADIMIR NABOKOV

ADA

OR ARDOR: A FAMILY CHRONICLE

McGraw-Hill Book Company · New York · Toronto

To Véra

FAMILY TREE

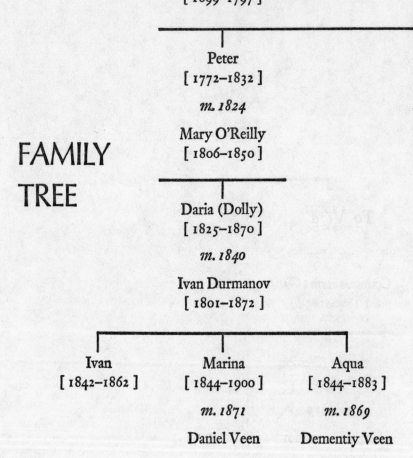

Prince Vseslav Zemski
[1699–1797]   *m. 1770*

Peter
[1772–1832]

m. 1824

Mary O'Reilly
[1806–1850]

Daria (Dolly)
[1825–1870]

m. 1840

Ivan Durmanov
[1801–1872]

Ivan	Marina	Aqua
[1842–1862]	[1844–1900]	[1844–1883]
	m. 1871	*m. 1869*
	Daniel Veen	Dementiy Veen

Princess Sofia Temnosiniy
[1755–1809]

Olga
[1773–1814]

m. 1793

Erasmus Veen
[1760–1852]

Dedalus
[1799–1883]

m. 1837

Countess Irina Garin
[1820–1838]

Ardelion
[1800–1848]

m.

Mary Trumbell
[?–1849]

Dementiy (Demon)
[1838–1905]

m. 1869

Aqua Durmanov

Daniel
[1838–1893]

m. 1871

Marina Durmanov

Ivan (Van)
[1870–]

Adelaida (Ada)
[1872–]

Lucinda [Lucette]
[1876–1901]

m. 1893

Andrey Vinelander
[1865–1922]

With the exception of Mr. and Mrs. Ronald Oranger,
a few incidental figures,
and some non-American citizens, all the persons
mentioned by name in this book are dead.

[Ed.]

ADA

PART ONE

PART ONE

1

"All happy families are more or less dissimilar; all unhappy ones are more or less alike," says a great Russian writer in the beginning of a famous novel (*Anna Arkadievitch Karenina*, transfigured into English by R. G. Stonelower, Mount Tabor Ltd., 1880). That pronouncement has little if any relation to the story to be unfolded now, a family chronicle, the first part of which is, perhaps, closer to another Tolstoy work, *Detstvo i Otrochestvo* (*Childhood and Fatherland*, Pontius Press, 1858).

Van's maternal grandmother Daria ("Dolly") Durmanov was the daughter of Prince Peter Zemski, Governor of Bras d'Or, an American province in the Northeast of our great and variegated country, who had married, in 1824, Mary O'Reilly, an Irish woman of fashion. Dolly, an only child, born in Bras, married in 1840, at the tender and wayward age of fifteen, General Ivan Durmanov, Commander of Yukon Fortress and peaceful country gentleman, with lands in the Severn Tories (Severnïya Territorii), that tesselated protectorate still lovingly called "Russian" Estoty, which commingles, granoblastically and organically, with "Russian"

Canady, otherwise "French" Estoty, where not only French, but Macedonian and Bavarian settlers enjoy a halcyon climate under our Stars and Stripes.

The Durmanovs' favorite domain, however, was Raduga near the burg of that name, beyond Estotiland proper, in the Atlantic panel of the continent between elegant Kaluga, New Cheshire, U.S.A., and no less elegant Ladoga, Mayne, where they had their town house and where their three children were born: a son, who died young and famous, and a pair of difficult female twins. Dolly had inherited her mother's beauty and temper but also an older ancestral strain of whimsical, and not seldom deplorable, taste, well reflected, for instance, in the names she gave her daughters: Aqua and Marina ("Why not Tofana?" wondered the good and sur-royally antlered general with a controlled belly laugh, followed by a small closing cough of feigned detachment—he dreaded his wife's flares).

On April 23, 1869, in drizzly and warm, gauzy and green Kaluga, Aqua, aged twenty-five and afflicted with her usual vernal migraine, married Walter D. Veen, a Manhattan banker of ancient Anglo-Irish ancestry who had long conducted, and was soon to resume intermittently, a passionate affair with Marina. The latter, some time in 1871, married her first lover's first cousin, also Walter D. Veen, a quite as opulent, but much duller, chap.

The "D" in the name of Aqua's husband stood for Demon (a form of Demian or Dementius), and thus was he called by his kin. In society he was generally known as Raven Veen or simply Dark Walter to distinguish him from Marina's husband, Durak Walter or simply Red Veen. Demon's twofold hobby was collecting old masters and young mistresses. He also liked middle-aged puns.

Daniel Veen's mother was a Trumbell, and he was prone

to explain at great length—unless sidetracked by a bore-baiter—how in the course of American history an English "bull" had become a New England "bell." Somehow or other he had "gone into business" in his twenties and had rather rankly grown into a Manhattan art dealer. He did not have—initially at least—any particular liking for paintings, had no aptitude for any kind of salesmanship, and no need whatever to jolt with the ups and down of a "job" the solid fortune inherited from a series of far more proficient and venturesome Veens. Confessing that he did not much care for the countryside, he spent only a few carefully shaded summer weekends at Ardis, his magnificent manor near Ladore. He had revisited only a few times since his boyhood another estate he had, up north on Lake Kitezh, near Luga, comprising, and practically consisting of, that large, oddly rectangular though quite natural body of water which a perch he had once clocked took half an hour to cross diagonally and which he owned jointly with his cousin, a great fisherman in his youth.

Poor Dan's erotic life was neither complicated nor beautiful, but somehow or other (he soon forgot the exact circumstances as one forgets the measurements and price of a fondly made topcoat worn on and off for at least a couple of seasons) he fell comfortably in love with Marina, whose family he had known when they still had their Raduga place (later sold to Mr. Eliot, a Jewish businessman). One afternoon in the spring of 1871, he proposed to Marina in the Up elevator of Manhattan's first ten-floor building, was indignantly rejected at the seventh stop (Toys), came down alone and, to air his feelings, set off in a counter-Fogg direction on a triple trip round the globe, adopting, like an animated parallel, the same itinerary every time. In November 1871, as he was in the act of making his evening plans with the same smelly but nice cicerone in a *café-au-lait* suit whom he had hired already twice at the same Genoese hotel, an aerocable from Marina (forwarded with a whole week's delay via his Manhattan office which had filed it away through a new girl's oversight in a dove hole marked RE AMOR) arrived on a silver salver telling him she would marry him upon his return to America.

According to the Sunday supplement of a newspaper that had just begun to feature on its funnies page the now long defunct Goodnight Kids, Nicky and Pimpernella (sweet siblings who shared a narrow bed), and that had survived with other old papers in the cockloft of Ardis Hall, the Veen-Durmanov wedding took place on St. Adelaida's Day, 1871. Twelve years and some eight months later, two naked children, one dark-haired and tanned, the other dark-haired and milk-white, bending in a shaft of hot sunlight that slanted through the dormer window under which the dusty cartons stood, happened to collate that date (December 16, 1871) with another (August 16, same year) anachronistically scrawled in Marina's hand across the corner of a professional photograph (in a raspberry-plush frame on her husband's kneehole library table) identical in every detail—including the commonplace sweep of a bride's ectoplasmic veil, partly blown by a parvis breeze athwart the groom's trousers —to the newspaper reproduction. A girl was born on July 21, 1872, at Ardis, her putative father's seat in Ladore County, and for some obscure mnemonic reason was registered as Adelaida. Another daughter, this time Dan's very own, followed on January 3, 1876.

Besides that old illustrated section of the still existing but rather gaga *Kaluga Gazette*, our frolicsome Pimpernel and Nicolette found in the same attic a reel box containing what turned out to be (according to Kim, the kitchen boy, as will be understood later) a tremendous stretch of micro-film taken by the globetrotter, with many of its quaint bazaars, painted cherubs and pissing urchins reappearing three times at different points, in different shades of helio-color. Naturally, at a time one was starting to build a family one could not display very well certain intérieurs (such as the group scenes in Damascus starring him and the steadily cigar-smoking archeologist from Arkansas with the fasci-nating scar on his liver side, and the three fat whores, and old Archie's premature squitteroo, as the third male member of the party, a real British brick, drolly called it); yet most of the film, accompanied by purely factual notes, not always easy to locate—because of the elusive or misleading book-marks in the several guidebooks scattered around—was run by Dan many times for his bride during their instructive honeymoon in Manhattan.

The two kids' best find, however, came from another carton in a lower layer of the past. This was a small green album with neatly glued flowers that Marina had picked or otherwise obtained at Ex, a mountain resort, not far from Brig, Switzerland, where she had sojourned before her marriage, mostly in a rented chalet. The first twenty pages were adorned with a number of little plants collected at random, in August, 1869, on the grassy slopes above the chalet, or in the park of the Hotel Florey, or in the garden of the sanatorium near it ("my nusshaus," as poor Aqua dubbed it, or "the Home," as Marina more demurely identified it in her locality notes). Those introductory pages did not present much botanical or psychological interest; and the fifty last pages or so remained blank; but the middle part, with a conspicuous decrease in number of specimens, proved to be a regular little melodrama acted out by the ghosts of dead flowers. The specimens were on one side of the folio, with Marina Dourmanoff (*sic*)'s notes *en regard*.

Ancolie Bleue des Alpes, Ex en Valais, i.ix.69. From Englishman in hotel. "Alpine Columbine, color of your eyes."

Epervière auricule. 25.x.69, Ex, *ex* Dr. Lapiner's walled alpine garden.

Golden [ginkgo] leaf: fallen out of a book "The Truth about Terra" which Aqua gave me before going back to her Home. 14.xii.69.

Artificial edelweiss brought by my new nurse with a note from Aqua saying it came from a "*mizernoe* and bizarre" Christmas Tree at the Home. 25.xii.69.

Petal of orchid, one of 99 orchids, if you please, mailed to me yesterday, Special Delivery, *c'est bien le cas de le dire*, from Villa Armina, Alpes Maritimes. Have laid aside ten for Aqua to be taken to her at her Home. Ex en Valais, Switzerland. "Snowing in Fate's crystal ball," as he used to say. (Date erased.)

Gentiane de Koch, rare, brought by *lapochka* [darling] Lapiner from his "mute gentiarium" 5.i. 1870.

[blue-ink blot shaped accidentally like a flower, or improved felt-pen deletion] *Compliquaria compliquata* var. *aquamarina*. Ex, 15.i.70.

Fancy flower of paper, found in Aqua's purse. Ex, 16.ii. 1870, made by a fellow patient, at the Home, which is no longer hers.

Gentiana verna (*printanière*). Ex, 28.iii.1870, on the lawn of my nurse's cottage. Last day here.

The two young discoverers of that strange and sickening treasure commented upon it as follows:

"I deduce," said the boy, "three main facts: that not yet

married Marina and her married sister hibernated in my *lieu de naissance*; that Marina had her own Dr. Krolik, *pour ainsi dire*; and that the orchids came from Demon who preferred to stay by the sea, his dark-blue great-grandmother.

"I can add," said the girl, "that the petal belongs to the common Butterfly Orchis; that my mother was even crazier than her sister; and that the paper flower so cavalierly dismissed is a perfectly recognizable reproduction of an early-spring sanicle that I saw in profusion on hills in coastal California last February. Dr. Krolik, our local naturalist, to whom you, Van, have referred, as Jane Austen might have phrased it, for the sake of rapid narrative information (you recall Brown, don't you, Smith?), has determined the example I brought back from Sacramento to Ardis, as the Bear-Foot, B,E,A,R, my love, not my foot or yours, or the Stabian flower girl's—an allusion, which your father, who, according to Blanche, is also mine, would understand like this (American finger-snap). "You will be grateful," she continued, embracing him, "for my not mentioning its scientific name. Incidentally the other foot—the *Pied de Lion* from that poor little Christmas larch, is by the same hand—possibly belonging to a very sick Chinese boy who came all the way from Barkley College."

"Good for you, Pompeianella (whom *you* saw scattering her flowers in one of Uncle Dan's picture books, but whom *I* admired last summer in a Naples museum). Now don't you think we should resume our shorts and shirts and go down, and bury or burn this album at once, girl. Right?"

"Right," answered Ada. "Destroy and forget. But we still have an hour before tea."

Re the "dark-blue" allusion, left hanging:

A former viceroy of Estoty, Prince Ivan Temnosiniy, father of the children's great-great-grandmother, Princess

Sofia Zemski (1755–1809), and a direct descendant of the Yaroslav rulers of pre-Tartar times, had a millennium-old name that meant in Russian "dark blue." While happening to be immune to the sumptuous thrills of genealogic awareness, and indifferent to the fact that oafs attribute both the aloofness and the fervor to snobbishness, Van could not help feeling esthetically moved by the velvet background he was always able to distinguish as a comforting, omnipresent summer sky through the black foliage of the family tree. In later years he had never been able to reread Proust (as he had never been able to enjoy again the perfumed gum of Turkish paste) without a roll-wave of surfeit and a rasp of gravelly heartburn; yet his favorite purple passage remained the one concerning the name "Guermantes," with whose hue his adjacent ultramarine merged in the prism of his mind, pleasantly teasing Van's artistic vanity.

Hue or who? Awkward. Reword! (marginal note in Ada Veen's late hand).

2

Marina's affair with Demon Veen started on his, her, and Daniel Veen's birthday, January 5, 1868, when she was twenty-four and both Veens thirty.

As an actress, she had none of the breath-taking quality that makes the skill of mimicry seem, at least while the show lasts, worth even more than the price of such footlights as insomnia, fancy, arrogant art; yet on that particular night, with soft snow falling beyond the plush and the paint, *la Durmanska* (who paid the great Scott, her impresario, seven thousand gold dollars a week for publicity alone, plus a bonny bonus for every engagement) had been from the start of the trashy ephemeron (an American play based by some pretentious hack on a famous Russian romance) so dreamy, so lovely, so stirring, that Demon (not *quite* a gentleman in amorous matters) made a bet with his orchestra-seat neighbor, Prince N., bribed a series of green-room attendants, and then, in a *cabinet reculé* (as a French writer of an earlier century might have mysteriously called that little room in which the broken trumpet and poodle hoops of a forgotten clown, besides many dusty pots of colored grease, happened to be stored) proceeded to possess her between two scenes (Chapter Three and Four of the martyred novel). In the first of these she had undressed in graceful silhouette behind a semitransparent screen, reappeared in a flimsy and fetching nightgown, and spent the rest of the wretched scene discussing a local squire, Baron d'O., with an old nurse in Eskimo boots. Upon the infinitely wise countrywoman's suggestion, she goosepenned, from the edge of her bed, on a side table with cabriole legs, a love letter and took five minutes to reread it in a languorous but loud voice for nobody's benefit in particular since the nurse sat dozing on a kind of sea chest, and the spectators were mainly concerned with the artificial moonlight's blaze upon the lovelorn young lady's bare arms and heaving breasts.

Even before the old Eskimo had shuffled off with the message, Demon Veen had left his pink velvet chair and proceeded to win the wager, the success of his enterprise being assured by the fact that Marina, a kissing virgin, had been in love with him since their last dance on New Year's Eve. Moreover, the tropical moonlight she had just bathed in, the penetrative sense of her own beauty, the ardent pulses of the imagined maiden, and the gallant applause of an almost full house made her especially vulnerable to the tickle of Demon's moustache. She had ample time, too, to change for the next scene, which started with a longish intermezzo staged by a ballet company whose services Scotty had engaged, bringing the Russians all the way in two sleeping cars from Belokonsk, Western Estoty. In a splendid orchard several merry young gardeners wearing for some reason the garb of Georgian tribesmen were popping raspberries into their mouths, while several equally implausible servant girls in sharovars (somebody had goofed—the word "samovars" may have got garbled in the agent's aerocable) were busy plucking marshmallows and peanuts from the branches of fruit trees. At an invisible sign of Dionysian origin, they all plunged into the violent dance called *kurva* or "ribbon boule" in the hilarious program whose howlers almost caused Veen (tingling, and light-loined, and with Prince N.'s rose-red banknote in his pocket) to fall from his seat.

His heart missed a beat and never regretted the lovely loss, as she ran, flushed and flustered, in a pink dress into the orchard, earning a claque third of the sitting ovation that greeted the instant dispersal of the imbecile but colorful transfigurants from Lyaska—or Iveria. Her meeting with Baron O., who strolled out of a side alley, all spurs and green tails, somehow eluded Demon's consciousness, so struck was he by the wonder of that brief abyss of absolute reality between two bogus fulgurations of fabricated life. Without waiting for the end of the scene, he hurried out of the theater into the crisp crystal night, the snowflakes star-spangling his top hat as he returned to his house in the next block to arrange a magnificent supper. By the time he went to fetch his new mistress in his jingling sleigh, the last-act ballet of Caucasian generals and metamorphosed Cinderellas had come to a sudden close, and Baron d'O., now in black tails and white gloves, was kneeling in the middle of an empty stage, holding the glass slipper that his fickle lady had left him when eluding his belated advances. The claqueurs were getting tired and looking at their watches when Marina in a black cloak slipped into Demon's arms and swan-sleigh.

They reveled, and traveled, and they quarreled, and flew back to each other again. By the following winter he began to suspect she was being unfaithful to him, but could not determine his rival. In mid-March, at a business meal with an art expert, an easy-going, lanky, likeable fellow in an old-fashioned dress-coat, Demon screwed in his monocle, unclicked out of its special flat case a small pen-and-wash and said he thought (did not doubt, in fact, but wished his certitude to be admired) that it was an unknown product of Parmigianino's tender art. It showed a naked girl with a peach-like apple cupped in her half-raised hand sitting sideways on a convolvulus-garlanded support, and had for its discoverer the additional appeal of recalling Marina when, rung out of a hotel bathroom by the phone, and perched on the arm of a chair, she muffled the receiver while asking her lover something that he could not make out because the bath's voice drowned her whisper. Baron d'Onsky had only to cast one glance at that raised shoulder and at certain vermiculated effects of delicate vegetation to confirm Demon's guess. D'Onsky had the reputation of not showing one sign of esthetic emotion in the presence of the loveliest masterpiece; this time, nonetheless, he laid his magnifier aside as he would a mask, and allowed his undisguised gaze to caress the velvety apple and the nude's dimpled and mossed parts with a smile of bemused pleasure. Would Mr. Veen consider selling it to him there and then, Mr. Veen, please? Mr. Veen would not. Skonky (a one-way nickname) must content himself with the proud thought that, as of today, he and the lucky owner were the sole people to have ever admired it *en connaissance de cause*. Back it went into its special integument; but after finishing his fourth cup of cognac, d'O. pleaded for one last peep. Both men were a little drunk, and Demon secretly wondered if the rather banal resemblance of that Edenic girl to a young actress, whom his visitor had no doubt seen on the stage in "Eugene and Lara" or "Lenore Raven" (both painfully panned by a "disgustingly incorruptible" young critic), should be, or would be, commented upon. It was not: such nymphs were really very much alike because of their elemental limpidity since the similarities of young bodies of water are but murmurs of natural innocence and double-talk mirrors, that's my hat, his is older, but we have the same London hatter.

Next day Demon was having tea at his favorite hotel with a Bohemian lady whom he had never seen before and was never to see again (she desired his recommendation for a job in the Glass Fish-and-Flower department in a Boston museum) when she interrupted her voluble self to indicate Marina and Aqua, blankly slinking across the hall in modish sullenness and bluish furs with Dan Veen and a *dackel* behind, and said:

"Curious how that appalling actress resembles 'Eve on the Clepsydrophone' in Parmigianino's famous picture."

"It is anything but famous," said Demon quietly, "and you can't have seen it. I don't envy you," he added; "the naïve stranger who realizes that he or she has stepped into the mud of an alien life must experience a pretty sickening feeling. Did you get that small-talk information directly from a fellow named d'Onsky or through a friend of a friend of his?"

"Friend of his," replied the hapless Bohemian lady.

Upon being questioned in Demon's dungeon, Marina, laughing trillingly, wove a picturesque tissue of lies; then broke down, and confessed. She swore that all was over; that the Baron, a physical wreck and a spiritual Samurai, had gone to Japan forever. From a more reliable source Demon learned that the Samurai's real destination was smart little Vatican, a Roman spa, whence he was to return to Aardvark, Massa, in a week or so. Since prudent Veen preferred killing his man in Europe (decrepit but indestructible Gamaliel was said to be doing his best to forbid duels in the Western Hemisphere —a canard or an idealistic President's instant-coffee caprice, for nothing was to come of it after all), Demon rented the fastest petroloplane available, overtook the Baron (looking very fit) in Nice, saw him enter Gunter's Bookshop, went in after him, and in the presence of the imperturbable and rather bored English shopkeeper, back-slapped the astonished Baron across the face with a lavender glove. The challenge was accepted; two native seconds were chosen; the Baron plumped for swords; and after a certain amount of good blood (Polish and Irish—a kind of American "Gory Mary" in barroom parlance) had bespattered two hairy torsoes, the white-washed terrace, the flight of steps leading backward to the walled garden in an amusing Douglas d'Artagnan arrangement, the apron of a quite accidental milkmaid, and the shirtsleeves of both seconds, charming Monsieur de Pastrouil and Colonel St. Alin, a scoundrel, the latter gentlemen separated the panting combatants, and Skonky died, not "of his wounds" (as it was viciously rumored) but of a gangrenous afterthought on the part of the least of them, possibly self-inflicted, a sting in the groin, which caused circulatory trouble, notwithstanding quite a few surgical interventions during two or three years of protracted stays at the Aardvark Hospital in Boston—a city where, incidentally, he married in 1869 our friend the Bohemian lady, now keeper of Glass Biota at the local museum.

Marina arrived in Nice a few days after the duel, and tracked Demon down in his villa Armina, and in the ecstasy of reconciliation neither remembered to dupe procreation, whereupon started the extremely *interesnoe polozhenie* ("interesting condition") without which, in fact, these anguished notes could not have been strung.

(Van, I trust your taste and your talent but are we *quite sure* we should keep reverting so *zestfully* to that wicked world which after all may have existed only oneirologically, Van? Marginal jotting in Ada's 1965 hand; crossed out lightly in her latest wavering one.)

That reckless stage was not the last but the shortest—a matter of four or five days. He pardoned her. He adored her. He wished to marry her very much—on the condition she dropped her theatrical "career" at once. He denounced the mediocrity of her gift and the vulgarity of her entourage, and she yelled he was a brute and a fiend. By April 10 it was Aqua who was nursing him, while Marina had flown back to her rehearsals of "Lucile," yet another execrable drama heading for yet another flop at the Ladore playhouse.

"Adieu. Perhaps it is better thus," wrote Demon to Marina in mid-April, 1869 (the letter may be either a copy in his calligraphic hand or the unposted original), "for whatever bliss might have attended our married life, and however long that blissful life might have lasted, one image I shall not forget and will not forgive. Let it sink in, my dear. Let me repeat it in such terms as a stage performer can appreciate. You had gone to Boston to see an old aunt—a cliché, but the truth for the nonce—and I had gone to *my* aunt's ranch near Lolita, Texas. Early one February morning (around noon *chez vous*) I rang you up at your hotel from a roadside booth of pure crystal still tear-stained after a tremendous thunderstorm to ask you to fly over at once because I, Demon, rattling my crumpled wings and cursing the automatic dorophone, could not live without you and because I wished you to see, with me holding you, the daze of desert flowers that the rain had brought out. Your voice was remote but sweet; you said you were in Eve's state, hold the line, let me put on a *penyuar*. Instead, blocking my ear, you spoke, I suppose, to the man with whom you had spent the night (and whom I would have dispatched, had I not been overeager to castrate him). Now *that* is the sketch made by a young artist in Parma, in the sixteenth century, for the fresco of *our* destiny, in a prophetic trance, and coinciding, except for the apple of terrible knowledge, with an image repeated in two men's minds. Your runaway maid, by the way, has been found by the police in a brothel here and will be shipped to you as soon as she is sufficiently stuffed with mercury."

3

The details of the L disaster (and I do not mean Elevated)
in the *beau milieu* of last century, which had the singular
effect of both causing and cursing the notion of "Terra," are
too well-known historically, and too obscene spiritually, to
be treated at length in a book addressed to young laymen
and lemans—and not to grave men or gravemen.

Of course, today, after great anti-L years of reactionary
delusion have gone by (more or less!) and our sleek little
machines, Faragod bless them, hum again after a fashion, as
they did in the first half of the nineteenth century, the mere
geographic aspect of the affair possesses its redeeming comic
side, like those patterns of brass marquetry, and bric-à-
Braques, and the ormolu horrors that meant "art" to our hu-
morless forefathers. For, indeed, none can deny the presence
of something highly ludicrous in the very configurations that
were solemnly purported to represent a varicolored map of
Terra. *Ved'* ("it is, isn't it") sidesplitting to imagine that
"Russia," instead of being a quaint synonym of Estoty, the
American province extending, from the Arctic no longer vicious Circle to the United States proper, was on Terra the

name of a country, transferred as if by some sleight of *land* across the ha-ha of a doubled ocean to the opposite hemisphere where it sprawled over all of today's Tartary, from Kurland to the Kuriles! But (even more absurdly), if, in Terrestrial spatial terms, the Amerussia of Abraham Milton was split into its components, with tangible water and ice separating the political, rather than poetical, notions of "America" and "Russia," a more complicated and even more preposterous discrepancy arose in regard to time—not only because the history of each part of the amalgam did not quite match the history of each counterpart in its discrete condition, but because a gap of up to a hundred years one way or another existed between the two earths; a gap marked by a bizarre confusion of directional signs at the crossroads of passing time with not *all* the no-longers of one world corresponding to the not-yets of the other. It was owing, among other things, to this "scientifically ungraspable" concourse of divergences that minds *bien rangés* (not apt to unhobble hobgoblins), rejected Terra as a fad or a fantom, and deranged minds (ready to plunge into any abyss) accepted it in support and token of their own irrationality.

As Van Veen himself was to find out, at the time of his passionate research in terrology (then a branch of psychiatry) even the deepest thinkers, the purest philosophers, Paar of Chose and Zapater of Aardvark, were emotionally divided in their attitude toward the possibility that there existed "a distortive glass of our distorted glebe" as a scholar who desires to remain unnamed has put it with such euphonic wit. (Hm! Kveree-kveree, as poor Mlle L. used to say to Gavronsky. In Ada's hand.)

There were those who maintained that the discrepancies and "false overlappings" between the two worlds were too numerous, and too deeply woven into the skein of successive events, not to taint with trite fancy the theory of essential sameness; and there were those who retorted that the dissimilarities only confirmed the live organic reality pertaining to the other world; that a perfect likeness would rather suggest a specular, and hence speculatory, phenomenon; and that two chess games with identical openings and identical end moves might ramify in an infinite number of variations, on *one* board and in *two* brains, at any middle stage of their irrevocably converging development.

The modest narrator has to remind the rereader of all this, because in April (my favorite month), 1869 (by no means a mirabilic year), on St. George's Day (according to Mlle Larivière's maudlin memoirs) Demon Veen married Aqua Veen—out of spite and pity, a not unusual blend.

Was there some additional spice? Marina, with perverse vainglory, used to affirm in bed that Demon's senses must have been influenced by a queer sort of "incestuous" (whatever that term means) pleasure (in the sense of the French *plaisir*, which works up a lot of supplementary spinal vibrato), when he fondled, and savored, and delicately parted and defiled, in unmentionable but fascinating ways, flesh (*une chair*) that was both that of his wife and that of his mistress, the blended and brightened charms of twin peris, an Aquamarina both single and double, a mirage in an emirate, a geminate gem, an orgy of epithelial alliterations.

Actually, Aqua was less pretty, and far more dotty, than Marina. During her fourteen years of miserable marriage she spent a broken series of steadily increasing sojourns in sanatoriums. A small map of the European part of the British Commonwealth—say, from Scoto-Scandinavia to the Riviera, Altar and Palermontovia—as well as most of the U.S.A., from Estoty and Canady to Argentina, might be quite thickly prickled with enameled red-cross-flag pins, marking, in her

War of the Worlds, Aqua's bivouacs. She had plans at one time to seek a modicum of health ("just a little grayishness, please, instead of the solid black") in such Anglo-American protectorates as the Balkans and Indias, and might even have tried the two Southern Continents that thrive under our joint dominion. Of course, Tartary, an independent inferno, which at the time spread from the Baltic and Black seas to the Pacific Ocean, was touristically unavailable, though Yalta and Altyn Tagh sounded strangely attractive . . . But her real destination was Terra the Fair and thither she trusted she would fly on libellula long wings when she died. Her poor little letters from the homes of madness to her husband were sometimes signed: Madame Shchemyashchikh-Zvukov ("Heartrending-Sounds").

After her first battle with insanity at Ex en Valais she returned to America, and suffered a bad defeat, in the days when Van was still being suckled by a very young wet nurse, almost a child, Ruby Black, born Black, who was to go mad too: for no sooner did all the fond, all the frail, come into close contact with him (as later Lucette did, to give another example) than they were bound to know anguish and calamity, unless strengthened by a strain of his father's demon blood.

Aqua was not quite twenty when the exaltation of her nature had begun to reveal a morbid trend. Chronologically, the initial stage of her mental illness coincided with the first decade of the Great Revelation, and although she might have found just as easily another theme for her delusion, statistics shows that the Great, and to some Intolerable, Revelation caused more insanity in the world than even an over-preoccupation with religion had in medieval times.

Revelation can be more perilous than Revolution. Sick minds identified the notion of a Terra planet with that of another world and this "Other World" got confused not only with the "Next World" but with the Real World in us and beyond us. *Our* enchanters, *our* demons, are noble iridescent creatures with translucent talons and mightily beating wings; but in the eighteen-sixties the New Believers urged one to imagine a sphere where our splendid friends had been utterly degraded, had become nothing but vicious monsters, disgusting devils, with the black scrota of carnivora and the fangs of serpents, revilers and tormentors of female souls; while on the opposite side of the cosmic lane a rainbow mist of angelic spirits, inhabitants of sweet Terra, restored all the stalest but still potent myths of old creeds, with rearrangement for melodeon of all the cacophonies of all the divinities and divines ever spawned in the marshes of this our sufficient world.

Sufficient for your purpose, Van, *entendons-nous*. (Note in the margin.)

Poor Aqua, whose fancies were apt to fall for all the fangles of cranks and Christians, envisaged vividly a minor hymnist's paradise, a future America of alabaster buildings one hundred stories high, resembling a beautiful furniture store crammed with tall white-washed wardrobes and shorter fridges; she saw giant flying sharks with lateral eyes taking barely one night to carry pilgrims through black ether across an entire continent from dark to shining sea, before booming back to Seattle or Wark. She heard magic-music boxes talking and singing, drowning the terror of thought, uplifting the lift girl, riding down with the miner, praising beauty and godliness, the Virgin and Venus, in the Wellings of the lonely and the poor. The unmentionable magnetic power denounced by evil lawmakers in this our shabby country—oh, everywhere, in Estoty and Canady, in "German" Mark Kennensie, as well as in "Swedish" Manitobogan, in the workshop of the red-shirted Yukonets as well as in the kitchen of the red-

kerchiefed Lyaskanka, and in "French" Estoty, from Bras
d'Or to Ladore—and very soon throughout both our Americas, and all over the other stunned continents—was used on
Terra as freely as water and air, as bibles and brooms. Two or
three centuries earlier she might have been just another con-
sumable witch.

In her erratic student years Aqua had left fashionable
Brown Hill College, founded by one of her less reputable
ancestors, to participate (as was also fashionable) in some
Social Improvement project or another in the Severnïya Territorii. She organized with Milton Abraham's invaluable help
a Phree Pharmacy in Belokonsk, and fell grievously in love
there with a married man, who after one summer of parvenu
passion dispensed to her in his Camping Ford *garçonnière*
preferred to give her up rather than run the risk of endanger-
ing his social situation in a philistine town where businessmen played "golf" on Sundays and belonged to "lodges." The
dreadful sickness, roughly diagnosed in her case, and in that
of other unfortunate people, as an "extreme form of mystical mania combined with existalienation" (otherwise plain
madness), crept over her by degrees, with intervals of ecstatic
peace, with skipped areas of precarious sanity, with sudden
dreams of eternity-certainty, which grew ever rarer and
briefer.

After her death in 1883, Van computed that in the course
of thirteen years, counting every presumed moment of presence, counting the dismal visits to her various hospitals, as
well as her sudden tumultuous appearances in the middle of
the night (wrestling with her husband or the frail but agile
English governess all the way upstairs, wildly welcomed by
the old *appenzeller*—and finally making the nursery, wigless,
slipperless, with bloodied fingernails), he had actually seen

her, or been near her, all in all, for a length of time hardly exceeding that of human gestation.

The rosy remoteness of Terra was soon veiled for her by direful mists. Her disintegration went down a shaft of phases, every one more racking than the last; for the human brain can become the best torture house of all those it has invented, established and used in millions of years, in millions of lands, on millions of howling creatures.

She developed a morbid sensitivity to the language of tap water—which echoes sometimes (much as the bloodstream does predormitarily) a fragment of human speech lingering in one's ears while one washes one's hands after cocktails with strangers. Upon first noticing this immediate, sustained, and in her case rather eager and mocking but really quite harmless replay of this or that recent discourse, she felt tickled at the thought that she, poor Aqua, had accidentally hit upon such a simple method of recording and transmitting speech, while technologists (the so-called Eggheads) all over the world were trying to make publicly utile and commercially rewarding the extremely elaborate and still very expensive, hydrodynamic telephones and other miserable gadgets that were to replace those that had gone *k chertyam sobach'im* (Russian "to the devil") with the banning of an unmentionable "lammer." Soon, however, the rhythmically perfect, but verbally rather blurred volubility of faucets began to acquire too much pertinent sense. The purity of the running water's enunciation grew in proportion to the nuisance it made of itself. It spoke soon after she had listened, or been exposed, to somebody talking—not necessarily to her—forcibly and expressively, a person with a rapid characteristic voice, and very individual or very foreign phrasal intonations, some compulsive narrator's patter at a horrible party, or a liquid soliloquy in a tedious play, or Van's lovely voice, or a bit of poetry heard at a lecture, my lad, my pretty, my love, take pity, but especially the more fluid and *flou* Italian verse, for instance that ditty recited between knee-knocking and palpebra-lifting, by a half-Russian, half-dotty old doctor, doc, toc, ditty, dotty, ballatetta, deboletta . . . tu, voce sbigottita . . . spigotty e diavoletta . . . de lo cor dolente . . . con ballatetta va . . . va . . . della strutta, destruttamente . . . mente . . . mente . . . stop that record, or the guide will go on demonstrating as he did this very morning in Florence a silly pillar commemorating, he said, the "elmo" that broke into leaf when they carried stone-heavy-dead St. Zeus by it through the gradual, gradual shade; or the Arlington harridan talking incessantly to her silent husband as the vineyards sped by, and even in the tunnel (they can't do this to you, you tell them, Jack Black, you just tell them . . .). Bathwater (or shower) was too much of a Caliban to speak distinctly—or perhaps was too brutally anxious to emit the hot torrent and get rid of the infernal ardor—to bother about small talk; but the burbly flowlets grew more and more ambitious and odious, and when at her first "home" she heard one of the most hateful of the visiting doctors (the Cavalcanti quoter) garrulously pour hateful instructions in Russian-lapped German into her hateful bidet, she decided to stop turning on tap water altogether.

But that phase elapsed too. Other excruciations replaced her namesake's loquacious quells so completely that when, during a lucid interval, she happened to open with her weak little hand a lavabo cock for a drink of water, the tepid lymph replied in its own lingo, without a trace of trickery or mimicry: *Finito!* It was now the forming of soft black pits (*yamī, yamishchi*) in her mind, between the dimming sculptures of thought and recollection, that tormented her phenomenally; mental panic and physical pain joined black-ruby hands, one making her pray for sanity, the other, plead for death. Man-made objects lost their significance or grew monstrous con-notations; clothes hangers were really the shoulders of decapitated Tellurians, the folds of a blanket she had kicked off her bed looked back at her mournfully with a stye on one drooping eyelid and dreary reproof in the limp twist of a livid lip. The effort to comprehend the information conveyed somehow to people of genius by the hands of a timepiece, or piece of time, became as hopeless as trying to make out the sign language of a secret society or the Chinese chant of that young student with a non-Chinese guitar whom she had known at the time she or her sister had given birth to a mauve baby. But her madness, the majesty of her madness, still re-tained a mad queen's pathetic coquetry: "You know, Doctor, I think I'll need glasses soon, I don't know" (lofty laugh), "I just can't make out what my wrist watch says . . . For heav-en's sake, tell me what it says! Ah! Half-past for—for what? Never mind, never mind, 'never' and 'mind' are twins, I have a twin sister and a twin son. I know you want to examine my pudendron, the Hairy Alpine Rose in *her* album, collected ten years ago" (showing her ten fingers gleefully, proudly, ten is ten!).

Then the anguish increased to unendurable massivity and nightmare dimensions, making her scream and vomit. She wanted (and was allowed, bless the hospital barber, Bob Bean) to have her dark curls shaved to an aquamarine prickle, because they grew *into* her porous skull and curled inside. Jigsaw pieces of sky or wall came apart, no matter how deli-cately put together, but a careless jolt or a nurse's elbow can disturb so easily those lightweight fragments which became incomprehensible blancs of anonymous objects, or the blank backs of "Scrabble" counters, which she could not turn over sunny side up, because her hands had been tied by a male nurse with Demon's black eyes. But presently panic and pain, like a pair of children in a boisterous game, emitted one last shriek of laughter and ran away to manipulate each other behind a bush as in Count Tolstoy's *Anna Karenina*, a novel, and again, for a while, a little while, all was quiet in the house, and their mother had the same first name as hers had.

At one time Aqua believed that a stillborn male infant half a year old, a surprised little fetus, a fish of rubber that she had produced in her bath, in a *lieu de naissance* plainly marked X in her dreams, after skiing at full pulver into a larch stump, had somehow been saved and brought to her at the Nusshaus, with her sister's compliments, wrapped up in blood-soaked cotton wool, but perfectly alive and healthy, to be registered as her son Ivan Veen. At other moments she felt convinced that the child was her sister's, born out of wedlock, during an exhausting, yet highly romantic blizzard, in a mountain refuge on Sex Rouge, where a Dr. Alpiner, general practitioner and gentian-lover, sat providentially waiting near a rude red stove for his boots to dry. Some confusion ensued less than two years later (September, 1871—her proud brain still retained dozens of dates) when upon escaping from *her* next refuge and somehow reaching her husband's unforgettable country house (imitate a foreigner: "*Signor Konduktor, ay vant go Lago di Luga, hier geld*") she took advantage of his being massaged in the solarium, tiptoed into their former bedroom—and experienced a delicious shock: *her* talc powder in a half-full glass container marked colorfully Quelques Fleurs still stood on *her* bedside table; *her* favorite flame-colored nightgown lay rumpled on the bedrug; to her it meant that only a brief black nightmare had obliterated the radiant fact of her having slept with her husband all along—ever since Shakespeare's birthday on a green rainy day, but for most other people, alas, it meant that Marina (after

G. A. Vronsky, the movie man, had left Marina for another long-lashed *Khristosik* as he called all pretty starlets) had conceived, *c'est bien le cas de le dire*, the brilliant idea of having Demon divorce mad Aqua and marry Marina who thought (happily and correctly) she was pregnant again. Marina had spent a *rukuliruyushchiy* month with him at Kitezh but when she smugly divulged her intentions (just before Aqua's arrival) he threw her out of the house. Still later, on the last short lap of a useless existence, Aqua scrapped all those ambiguous recollections and found herself reading and rereading, busily, blissfully, her son's letters in a luxurious "sanastoria" at Centaur, Arizona. He invariably wrote in French calling her *petite maman* and describing the amusing school he would be living at after his thirteenth birthday. She heard his voice through the nightly tinnitus of her new, planful, last, last insomnias and it consoled her. He called her usually mummy, or mama, accenting the last syllable in English, the first, in Russian; somebody had said that triplets and heraldic draconculi often occurred in trilingual families; but there was absolutely no doubt *whatsoever* now (except, perhaps, in hateful long-dead Marina's hell-dwelling mind) that Van was *her, her*, Aqua's, beloved son.

Being unwilling to suffer another relapse after this blessed state of perfect mental repose, but knowing it could not last, she did what another patient had done in distant France, at a much less radiant and easygoing "home." A Dr. Froid, one of the administerial centaurs, who may have been an émigré brother with a passport-changed name of the Dr. Froit of Signy-Mondieu-Mondieu in the Ardennes or, more likely, the same man, because they both came from Vienne, Isère, and were only sons (as her son was), evolved, or rather revived, the therapistic device, aimed at establishing a "group" feeling, of having the finest patients help the staff if "thusly inclined." Aqua, in her turn, repeated exactly clever Eleonore Bonvard's trick, namely, opting for the making of beds and the cleaning of glass shelves. The astorium in St. Taurus, or whatever it was called (who cares—one forgets little things very fast, when afloat in infinite non-thingness) was, perhaps, more modern, with a more refined desertic view, than the Mondefroid bleakhouse horsepittle, but in both places a demented patient could outwit in one snap an imbecile pedant.

In less than a week Aqua had accumulated more than two hundred tablets of different potency. She knew most of them —the jejune sedatives, and the ones that knocked you out from eight P.M. till midnight, and several varieties of superior soporifics that left you with limpid limbs and a leaden head after eight hours of non-being, and a drug which was in itself delightful but a little lethal if combined with a draught of the cleansing fluid commercially known as Morona; and a plump purple pill reminding her, she had to laugh, of those with which the little gypsy enchantress in the Spanish tale (dear to Ladore schoolgirls) puts to sleep all the sportsmen and all their bloodhounds at the opening of the hunting season. Lest some busybody resurrect her in the middle of the float-away process, Aqua reckoned she must procure for herself a maximum period of undisturbed stupor elsewhere than in a glass house, and the carrying out of that second part of the project was simplified and encouraged by another agent or double of the Isère Professor, a Dr. Sig Heiler whom everybody venerated as a great guy and near-genius in the usual sense of near-beer. Such patients who proved by certain twitchings of the eyelids and other semi-private parts under the control of medical students that Sig (a slightly deformed but not unhandsome old boy) was in the process of being dreamt of as a "papa Fig," spanker of girl bottoms and spunky spittoon-user, were assumed to be on the way to haleness and permitted, upon awakening, to participate in normal out-door activities such as picnics. Sly Aqua twitched, simulated a yawn, opened her light-blue eyes (with those startlingly contrasty jet-black pupils that Dolly, her mother, also had), put on yellow slacks and a black bolero, walked through a little pinewood, thumbed a ride with a Mexican truck, found a suitable gulch in the chaparral and there, after writing a short note, began placidly eating from her cupped palm the multicolored contents of her handbag, like any Russian coun-try girl *lakomyashchayasya yagodami* (feasting on berries) that she had just picked in the woods. She smiled, dreamily enjoying the thought (rather "Kareninian" in tone) that her extinction would affect people about as deeply as the abrupt, mysterious, never explained demise of a comic strip in a Sunday paper one had been taking for years. It was her last smile. She was discovered much sooner, but had also died much faster than expected, and the observant Siggy, still in his baggy khaki shorts, reported that Sister Aqua (as for some reason they all called her) lay, as if buried prehistorically, in a *fetus-in-utero* position, a comment that seemed relevant to his students, as it may be to mine.

Her last note, found on her and addressed to her husband and son, might have come from the sanest person on this or that earth.

Aujourd'hui (*heute*-toity!) I, this eye-rolling toy, have earned the psykitsch right to enjoy a landparty with Herr Doktor Sig, Nurse Joan the Terrible, and several "patients," in the neighboring *bor* (piney wood) where I noticed ex-actly the same skunk-like squirrels, Van, that your Darkblue ancestor imported to Ardis Park, where you will ramble one day, no doubt. The hands of a clock, even when out of order, must know and let the dumbest little watch know where they stand, otherwise neither is a dial but only a white face with a trick mustache. Similarly, *chelovek* (human being) must know where he stands and let others know, otherwise he is not even a *klok* (piece) of a *chelovek*, neither a he, nor she, but "a tit of it" as poor Ruby, my little Van, used to say of her scanty right breast. I, poor *Princesse Lointaine, très lointaine* by now, do not know where I stand. Hence I must fall. So adieu, my dear, dear son, and farewell, poor Demon, I do not know the date or the season, but it is a reasonably, and no doubt seasonably, fair day, with a lot of cute little ants queuing to get at my pretty pills.

> [Signed]   My sister's sister who *teper'*
> *iz ada* ("now is out of hell")

"If we want life's sundial to show its hand," commented Van, developing the metaphor in the rose garden of Ardis Manor at the end of August, 1884, "we must always remember that the strength, the dignity, the delight of man is to spite and despise the shadows and stars that hide their secrets from us. Only the ridiculous power of pain made her surrender. And I often think it would have been so much more plausible, esthetically, ecstatically, Estotially speaking —if she were really my mother."

4

When, in the middle of the twentieth century, Van started to reconstruct his deepest past, he soon noticed that such details of his infancy as really mattered (for the special purpose the reconstruction pursued) could be best treated, could not seldom be *only* treated, when reappearing at various later stages of his boyhood and youth, as sudden juxtapositions that revived the part while vivifying the whole. This is why his first love has precedence here over his first bad hurt or bad dream.

He had just turned thirteen. He had never before left the comforts of the paternal roof. He had never before realized that such "comforts" might not be taken for granted, only occurring in some introductory ready-made metaphor in a book about a boy and a school. A few blocks from the schoolgrounds, a widow, Mrs. Tapirov, who was French but spoke English with a Russian accent, had a shop of objets d'art and more or less antique furniture. He visited it on a bright winter day. Crystal vases with crimson roses and golden-brown asters were set here and there in the fore part of the shop—on a gilt-wood console, on a lacquered chest, on the shelf of a cabinet, or simply along the carpeted steps leading to the next floor where great wardrobes and flashy dressers semiencircled a singular company of harps. He satisfied himself that those flowers were artificial and thought it puzzling that such imitations always pander so exclusively to the eye instead of also copying the damp fat feel of live petal and leaf. When he called next day for the object (unremembered now, eighty years later) that he wanted repaired or duplicated, it was not ready or had not been obtained. In passing, he touched a half-opened rose and was cheated of the sterile texture his fingertips had expected when cool life kissed them with pouting lips. "My daughter," said Mrs. Tapirov, who saw his surprise, "always puts a bunch of real ones among the fake *pour attraper le client*. You drew the joker." As he was leaving she came in, a schoolgirl in a gray coat with brown shoulder-length ringlets and a pretty face. On another occasion (for a certain part of the thing—a frame, perhaps—took an infinite time to heal or else the entire article proved to be unobtainable after all) he saw her curled up with her schoolbooks in an armchair—a domestic item among those for sale. He never spoke to her. He loved her madly. It must have lasted at least one term.

That was love, normal and mysterious. Less mysterious and considerably more grotesque were the passions which several generations of schoolmasters had failed to eradicate, and which as late as 1883 still enjoyed an unparalleled vogue at Riverlane. Every dormitory had its catamite. One hysterical lad from Upsala, cross-eyed, loose-lipped, with almost abnormally awkward limbs, but with a wonderfully tender skin texture and the round creamy charms of Bronzino's Cupid (the big one, whom a delighted satyr discovers in a lady's bower), was much prized and tortured by a group of foreign boys, mostly Greek and English, led by Cheshire, the rugby ace; and partly out of bravado, partly out of curiosity, Van surmounted his disgust and coldly watched their rough orgies. Soon, however, he abandoned this surrogate for a more natural though equally heartless divertissement.

The aging woman who sold barley sugar and Lucky Louse magazines in the corner shop, which by tradition was not strictly out of bounds, happened to hire a young helper, and Cheshire, the son of a thrifty lord, quickly ascertained that this fat little wench could be had for a Russian green dollar. Van was one of the first to avail himself of her favors. These were granted in semi-darkness, among crates and sacks at the back of the shop after hours. The fact of his having told her he was sixteen and a libertine instead of fourteen and a virgin proved a source of embarrassment to our hell-raker when he tried to bluster his inexperience into quick action but only succeeded in spilling on the welcome mat what she would have gladly helped him to take indoors. Things went better six minutes later, after Cheshire and Zographos were through; but only at the next mating party did Van really begin to enjoy her gentleness, her soft sweet grip and hearty joggle. He knew she was nothing but a fubsy pig-pink whorelet and would elbow her face away when she attempted to kiss him after he had finished and was checking with one quick hand, as he had seen Cheshire do, if his wallet was still in his hip pocket; but somehow or other, when the last of some forty convulsions had come and gone in the ordinary course of collapsing time, and his train was bowling past black and green fields to Ardis, he found himself endowing with unsuspected poetry her poor image, the kitchen odor of her arms, the humid eyelashes in the sudden gleam of Cheshire's lighter and even the creaky steps of old deaf Mrs. Gimber in her bedroom upstairs.

In an elegant first-class compartment, with one's gloved

hand in the velvet side-loop, one feels very much a man of the world as one surveys the capable landscape capably skimming by. And every now and then the passenger's roving eyes paused for a moment as he listened inwardly to a nether itch, which he supposed to be (correctly, thank Log) only a minor irritation of the epithelium.

5

In the early afternoon he descended with his two suitcases into the sunny peace of the little rural station whence a winding road led to Ardis Hall, which he was visiting for the first time in his life. In a miniature of the imagination, he had seen a saddled horse prepared for him; there was not even a trap. The station master, a stout sunburnt man in a brown uniform, was sure they expected him with the evening train which was slower but had a tea car. He would ring up the Hall in a moment, he added as he signaled to the anxious engine driver. Suddenly a hackney coach drove up to the platform and a red-haired lady, carrying her straw hat and laughing at her own haste, made for the train and just managed to board it before it moved. So Van agreed to use the means of transportation made available to him by a chance crease in the texture of time, and seated himself in the old calèche. The half-hour drive proved not unpleasant. He was taken through pinewoods and over rocky ravines, with birds and other animals singing in the flowering undergrowth. Sunflecks and lacy shadows skimmed over his legs and lent a green twinkle to the brass button deprived of its twin on the back of the coachman's coat. They passed through Torfyanka, a dreamy hamlet consisting of three or four log izbas, a milkpail repair shop and a smithy smothered in jasmine. The driver waved to an invisible friend and the sensitive runabout swerved slightly to match his gesture. They were now spinning along a dusty country road between fields. The road dipped and humped again, and at every ascent the old clockwork taxi would slow up as if on the brink of sleep and reluctantly overcome its weakness.

They bounced on the cobblestones of Gamlet, a half-Russian village, and the chauffeur waved again, this time to a boy in a cherry tree. Birches separated to let them pass across an old bridge. Ladore, with its ruinous black castle on a crag, and its gay multicolored roofs further downstream were glimpsed—to be seen again many times much later in life.

Presently the vegetation assumed a more southern aspect as the lane skirted Ardis Park. At the next turning, the romantic mansion appeared on the gentle eminence of old novels. It was a splendid country house, three stories high, built of pale brick and purplish stone, whose tints and substance seemed to interchange their effects in certain lights. Notwithstanding the variety, amplitude and animation of great trees that had long replaced the two regular rows of stylized saplings (thrown in by the mind of the architect rather than observed by the eye of a painter) Van immediately recognized Ardis Hall as depicted in the two-hundred-year-old aquarelle that hung in his father's dressing room: the mansion sat on a rise overlooking an abstract meadow with two tiny people in cocked hats conversing not far from a stylized cow.

None of the family was at home when Van arrived. A servant in waiting took his horse. He entered the Gothic archway of the hall where Bouteillan, the old bald butler who unprofessionally now wore a mustache (dyed a rich gravy brown) met him with gested delight—he had once been the valet of Van's father—"*Je parie*," he said, "*que Monsieur ne me reconnaît pas*," and proceeded to remind Van of what Van had already recollected unaided, the farmannikin (a special kind of box kite, untraceable nowadays even in the greatest museums housing the toys of the past) which Bouteillan had helped him to fly one day in a meadow dotted with buttercups. Both looked up: the tiny red rectangle hung for an instant askew in a blue spring sky. The hall was famous for its painted ceilings. It was too early for tea: Would Van like him or a maid to unpack? Oh, one of the maids, said Van, wondering briefly what item in a schoolboy's luggage might be supposed to shock a housemaid. The picture of naked Ivory Revery (a model)? Who cared, now that he was a man?

Acting upon the butler's suggestion he went to make a *tour du jardin*. As he followed a winding path, soundlessly stepping on its soft pink sand in the cloth gumshoes that were part of the school uniform, he came upon a person whom he recognized with disgust as being his former French governess (the place swarmed with ghosts!). She was sitting on a green bench under the Persian lilacs, a parasol in one hand and in the other a book from which she was reading aloud to a small girl who was picking her nose and examining with dreamy satisfaction her finger before wiping it on the edge of the bench. Van decided she must be "Ardelia," the eldest of the two little cousins he was supposed to get acquainted with. Actually it was Lucette, the younger one, a neutral child of eight, with a fringe of shiny reddish-blond hair and a freckled button for nose: she had had pneumonia in spring and was still veiled by an odd air of remoteness that children, especially impish children, retain for some time after brushing through death. Mlle Larivière suddenly looked at Van over her green spectacles—and he had to cope with another warm welcome. In contrast to Albert, she had not changed at all since the days she used to come three times a week to Dark Veen's house in town with a bagful of books and the tiny, tremulous poodlet (now dead) that could not be left behind. It had glistening eyes like sad black olives.

Presently they all strolled back, the governess shaking in reminiscent grief her big-chinned, big-nosed head under the moiré of her parasol; Lucy gratingly dragging a garden hoe she had found, and young Van in his trim gray suit and flowing tie, with his hands behind his back, looking down at his neatly stepping mute feet—trying to place them in line, for no special reason.

A victoria had stopped at the porch. A lady, who resembled Van's mother, and a dark-haired girl of eleven or twelve, preceded by a fluid dackel, were getting out. Ada carried an untidy bunch of wild flowers. She wore a white frock with a black jacket and there was a white bow in her long hair. He never saw that dress again and when he mentioned it in retrospective evocation she invariably retorted that he must have dreamt it, she never had one like that, never could have put on a dark blazer on such a hot day, but he stuck to his initial image of her to the last.

Some ten years ago, not long before or after his fourth birthday, and toward the end of his mother's long stay in a sanatorium, "Aunt" Marina had swooped upon him in a public park where there were pheasants in a big cage. She advised his nurse to mind her own business and took him to a booth near the band shell where she bought him an emerald stick of peppermint candy and told him that if his father wished she would replace his mother and that you could not feed the birds without Lady Amherst's permission, or so he understood.

They now had tea in a prettily furnished corner of the otherwise very austere central hall from which rose the grand staircase. They sat on chairs upholstered in silk around a pretty table. Ada's black jacket and a pink-yellow-blue nosegay she had composed of anemones, celandines and columbines lay on a stool of oak. The dog got more bits of cake than it did ordinarily. Price, the mournful old footman who brought the cream for the strawberries, resembled Van's teacher of history, "Jeejee" Jones.

"He resembles my teacher of history," said Van when the man had gone.

"I used to love history," said Marina, "I loved to identify myself with famous women. There's a ladybird on your plate, Ivan. Especially with famous beauties—Lincoln's second wife or Queen Josephine."

"Yes, I've noticed—it's beautifully done. We've got a similar set at home."

"*Slivok* (some cream)? I hope you speak Russian?" Marina asked Van, as she poured him a cup of tea.

"*Neohotno no sovershenno svobodno* (reluctantly but quite fluently)," replied Van, *slegka ulibnuvshis'* (with a slight smile). "Yes, lots of cream and three lumps of sugar."

"Ada and I share your extravagant tastes. Dostoevski liked it with raspberry syrup."

"Pah," uttered Ada.

Marina's portrait, a rather good oil by Tresham, hanging above her on the wall, showed her wearing the picture hat she had used for the rehearsal of a Hunting Scene ten years ago, romantically brimmed, with a rainbow wing and a great drooping plume of black-banded silver; and Van, as he recalled the cage in the park and his mother somewhere in a cage of her own, experienced an odd sense of mystery as if the commentators of his destiny had gone into a huddle. Marina's face was now made up to imitate her former looks, but fashions had changed, her cotton dress was a rustic print, her auburn locks were bleached and no longer tumbled down her temples, and nothing in her attire or adornments echoed the dash of her riding crop in the picture and the tegular pattern of her brilliant plumage which Tresham had rendered with ornithological skill.

There was not much to remember about that first tea. He noticed Ada's trick of hiding her fingernails by fisting her hand or stretching it with the palm turned upward when helping herself to a biscuit. She was bored and embarrassed by everything her mother said and when the latter started to talk about the Tarn, otherwise the New Reservoir, he noted that Ada was no longer sitting next to him but standing a little way off with her back to the tea table at an open casement with the slim-waisted dog on a chair peering over splayed front paws out into the garden too, and she was asking it in a private whisper what it was it had sniffed.

"You can see the Tarn from the library window," said Marina. "Presently Ada will show you all the rooms in the house. Ada?" (She pronounced it the Russian way with two deep, dark "*a*"s, making it sound rather like "ardor.")

"You can catch a glint of it from here too," said Ada, turning her head and, *pollice verso*, introducing the view to Van who put his cup down, wiped his mouth with a tiny embroidered napkin, and stuffing it into his trouser pocket, went up to the dark-haired, pale-armed girl. As he bent toward her (he was three inches taller and the double of that when she married a Greek Catholic, and his shadow held the bridal crown over her from behind), she moved her head to make him move his to the required angle and her hair touched his neck. In his first dreams of her this re-enacted contact, so light, so brief, invariably proved to be beyond the dreamer's endurance and like a lifted sword signaled fire and violent release.

"Finish your tea, my precious," called Marina.

Presently, as Marina had promised, the two children went upstairs. "Why do stairs creak so desperately, when two children go upstairs," she thought, looking up at the balustrade along which two left hands progressed with strikingly similar flips and glides like siblings taking their first dancing lesson. "After all, we were twin sisters; everybody knows that." The same slow heave, she in front, he behind, took them over the last two steps, and the staircase was silent again. "Old-fashioned qualms," said Marina.

6

Ada showed her shy guest the great library on the second floor, the pride of Ardis and her favorite "browse," which her mother never entered (having her own set of a Thousand-and-One Best Plays in her boudoir), and which Red Veen, a sentimentalist and a poltroon, shunned, not caring to run into the ghost of his father who had died there of a stroke, and also because he found nothing so depressing as the collected works of unrecollected authors, although he did not mind an occasional visitor's admiring the place's tall bookcases and short cabinets, its dark pictures and pale busts, its ten chairs of carved walnut, and two noble tables inlaid with ebony. In a slant of scholarly sunlight a botanical atlas upon a reading desk lay open on a colored plate of orchids. A kind of divan or daybed covered in black velvet, with two yellow cushions, was placed in a recess, below a plate-glass window which offered a generous view of the banal park and the man-made lake. A pair of candlesticks, mere phantoms of metal and tallow, stood, or seemed to stand, on the broad window ledge.

A corridor leading off the library would have taken our

silent explorers to Mr. and Mrs. Veen's apartments in the west wing, had they pursued their investigations in that direction. Instead, a semi-secret little staircase spiraled them from behind a rotatory bookcase to the upper floor, she, pale-thighed, above him, taking longer strides than he, three steep steps behind.

The bedchambers and adjacent accommodations were more than modest, and Van could not help regretting he was too young, apparently, to be assigned one of the two guest rooms next to the library. He recalled nostalgically the luxuries of home as he considered the revolting objects that would close upon him in the solitude of summer nights. Everything struck him as being intended for a cringing cretin, the dismal poorhouse bed with a medieval headboard of dingy wood, the self-creaking wardrobe, the squat commode of imitation mahogany with chain-linked knobs (one missing), the blanket chest (a sheepish escape from the linen room), and the old bureau whose domed front flap was locked or stuck: he found the knob in one of its useless pigeonholes and handed it to Ada who threw it out of the window. Van had never encountered a towel horse before, never seen a washstand made specially for the bathless. A round looking-glass above it was ornamented with gilt gesso grapes; a satanic snake encircled the porcelain basin (twin of the one in the girls' washroom across the passage). An elbow chair with a high back and a bedside stool supporting a brass candlestick with a greasepan and handle (whose double he had seemed to have seen mirrored a moment ago—where?) completed the worst and main part of the humble equipment.

They went back to the corridor, she tossing her hair, he clearing his throat. Further down, a door of some playroom or nursery stood ajar and stirred to and fro as little Lucette peeped out, one russet knee showing. Then the doorleaf flew open—but she darted inside and away. Cobalt sailing boats adorned the white tiles of a stove, and as her sister and he passed by that open door a toy barrel organ invitingly went into action with a stumbling little minuet. Ada and Van returned to the ground floor—this time all the way down the sumptuous staircase. Of the many ancestors along the wall, she pointed out her favorite, old Prince Vseslav Zemski (1699–1797), friend of Linnaeus and author of *Flora Ladorica*, who was portrayed in rich oil holding his barely pubescent bride and her blond doll in his satin lap. An enlarged photograph, soberly framed, hung (rather incongruously, Van thought) next to the rosebud-lover in his embroidered coat. The late Sumerechnikov, American precursor of the Lumière brothers, had taken Ada's maternal uncle in profile with upcheeked violin, a doomed youth, after his farewell concert.

On the first floor, a yellow drawing room hung with damask and furnished in what the French once called the Empire style opened into the garden and now, in the late afternoon, was invaded across the threshold by the large leaf shadows of a paulownia tree (named, by an indifferent linguist, explained Ada, after the patronymic, mistaken for a second name or surname of a harmless lady, Anna Pavlovna Romanov, daughter of Pavel, nicknamed Paul-minus-Peter, why she did not know, a cousin of the non-linguist's master, the botanical Zemski, I'm going to scream, thought Van). A china cabinet encaged a whole zoo of small animals among which the oryx and the okapi, complete with scientific names, were especially recommended to him by his charming but impossibly pretentious companion. Equally fascinating was a five-fold screen with bright paintings on its black panels reproducing the first maps of four and a half continents. We now pass into the music room with its little-used piano, and a corner room called the Gun Room containing a stuffed Shetland pony which an aunt of Dan Veen's, maiden name forgotten, thank Log, once rode. On the other, or some other, side of the house was the ballroom, a glossy wasteland with wallflower chairs. "Reader, ride by" (*"mimo, chitatel'*," as Turgenev wrote). The "mews," as they were improperly called in Ladore County, were architecturally rather confusing in the case of Ardis Hall. A latticed gallery looked across its garlanded shoulder into the garden and turned sharply toward the drive. Elsewhere, an elegant loggia, lit by long windows, led now tonguetied Ada and intolerably bored Van into a bower of rocks: a sham grotto, with ferns clinging to it shamelessly, and an artificial cascade borrowed from some brook or book, or Van's burning bladder (after all that confounded tea).

The servants' quarters (except those of two painted and powdered maids who had rooms upstairs) were on the courtyard side of the ground floor and Ada said she had visited them once in the explorative stage of her childhood but all she remembered was a canary and an ancient machine for grinding coffee beans which settled the matter.

They zoomed upstairs again. Van popped into a watercloset—and emerged in much better humor. A dwarf Haydn again played a few bars as they walked on.

The attic. This is the attic. Welcome to the attic. It stored a great number of trunks and cartons, and two brown couches one on top of the other like copulating beetles, and lots of pictures standing in corners or on shelves with their faces against the wall like humiliated children. Rolled up in its case was an old "jikker" or skimmer, a blue magic rug with Arabian designs, faded but still enchanting, which uncle Daniel's father had used in his boyhood and later flown when drunk. Because of the many collisions, collapses and other accidents, especially numerous in sunset skies over idyllic fields, jikkers were banned by the air patrol; but four years later Van who loved that sport bribed a local mechanic to clean the thing, reload its hawking-tubes, and generally bring it back into magic order and many a summer day would they spend, his Ada and he, hanging over grove and river or gliding at a safe ten-foot altitude above surfaces of roads or roofs. How comic the wobbling, ditch-diving cyclist, how weird the arm-flailing and slipping chimney sweep!

Vaguely impelled by the feeling that as long as they were inspecting the house they were, at least, doing *something*—keeping up a semblance of consecutive action which, despite the brilliant conversational gifts both possessed, would degenerate into a desperate vacuum of self-conscious loafing with no other resource than affected wit followed by silence, Ada did not spare him the basement where a big-bellied robot throbbed, manfully heating the pipes that meandered to the huge kitchen and to the two drab bathrooms, and did their poor best to keep the castle habitable on festive visits in winter.

"You have not seen anything yet!" cried Ada. "There is still the roof!"

"But that is going to be our last climb today," said Van to himself firmly.

Owing to a mixture of overlapping styles and tiles (not easily explainable in non-technical terms to non-roof-lovers), as well as to a haphazard continuum, so to speak, of renovations, the roof of Ardis Manor presented an indescribable confusion of angles and levels, of tin-green and fin-gray surfaces, of scenic ridges and wind-proof nooks. You could clip and kiss, and survey in between, the reservoir, the groves, the meadows, even the incline of larches that marked the boundary of the nearest estate miles away, and the ugly little shapes of more or less legless cows on a distant hillside. And one could easily hide behind some projection from inquisitive skimmers or picture-taking balloons.

A gong bronzily boomed on a terrace.

For some odd reason both children were relieved to learn that a stranger was expected to dinner. He was an Andalusian architect whom Uncle Dan wanted to plan an "artistic" swimming pool for Ardis Manor. Uncle Dan had intended to come, too, with an interpreter, but had caught the Russian "hrip" (Spanish flu) instead, and had phoned Marina asking her to be very nice to good old Alonso.

"You must help me!" Marina told the children with a worried frown.

"I could show him a copy, perhaps," said Ada, turning to Van, "of an absolutely fantastically lovely *nature morte* by Juan de Labrador of Extremadura—golden grapes and a strange rose against a black background. Dan sold it to Demon, and Demon has promised to give it to me on my fifteenth birthday."

"We also have some Zurbarán fruit," said Van smugly. "Tangerines, I believe, and a fig of sorts, with a wasp upon it. Oh, we'll dazzle the old boy with shop talk!"

They did not. Alonso, a tiny wizened man in a double-breasted tuxedo, spoke only Spanish, while the sum of Spanish words his hosts knew scarcely exceeded half a dozen. Van had *canastilla* (a little basket), and *nubarrones* (thunderclouds), which both came from an *en regard* translation of a lovely Spanish poem in one of his schoolbooks. Ada remembered, of course, *mariposa*, butterfly, and the names of two or three birds (listed in ornithological guides) such as *paloma*, pigeon, or *grevol*, hazel hen. Marina knew *aroma* and *hombre*, and an anatomical term with a "j" hanging in the middle. In consequence, the table-talk consisted of long lumpy Spanish phrases pronounced very loud by the voluble architect who thought he was dealing with very deaf people, and of a smatter of French, intentionally but vainly italianized by his victims. Once the difficult dinner over, Alonso investigated by the light of three torches held by two footmen a possible site for an expensive pool, put the plan of the grounds back into his brief-case, and after kissing by mistake Ada's hand in the dark, hastened away to catch the last southbound train.

7

Van had gone to bed, sandpaper-eyed, soon after "evening tea," a practically tea-less summertime meal which came a couple of hours after dinner and the occurrence of which seemed to Marina as natural and inevitable as that of a sunset before night. This routine Russian feast consisted in the Ardis household of *prostokvasha* (translated by English governesses as curds-and-whey, and by Mlle Larivière as *lait caillé*, "curdled milk"), whose thin, cream-smooth upper layer little Miss Ada delicately but avidly (Ada, those adverbs qualified many actions of yours!) skimmed off with her special Ѵ monogrammed silver spoon and licked up, before attacking the more amorphous junkety depths of the stuff; with this came coarse black peasant bread; dusky *klubnika* (*Fragaria elatior*), and huge, bright-red garden strawberries (a cross between two other *Fragaria* species). Van had hardly laid his cheek on his cool flat pillow than he was violently aroused by a clamorous caroling—bright warbles, sweet whistles, chirps, trills, twitters, rasping caws and tender chew-chews—which he assumed, not without a non-Audubon's apprehension, Ada could, and would, break up into the right voices of the right birds. He slipped into loafers, collected soap, comb and towel, and, containing his nudity in a terry-cloth robe, left his bedroom with the intention of going for a dip in the brook he had observed on the eve. The corridor clock tocked amid an auroral silence broken indoors only by the snore coming from the governess' room. After a moment of hesitation he visited the nursery water closet. There, the mad aviary and rich sun got at him through a narrow casement. He was quite well, quite well! As he descended the grand staircase, General Durmanov's father acknowledged Van with grave eyes and passed him on to old Prince Zemski and other ancestors, all as discreetly attentive as those museum guards who watch the only tourist in a dim old palace.

The front door proved to be bolted and chained. He tried the glassed and grilled side door of a blue-garlanded gallery; it, too, did not yield. Being still unaware that under the stairs an inconspicuous recess concealed an assortment of spare keys (some very old and anonymous, hanging from brass hooks) and communicated through a toolroom with a secluded part of the garden, Van wandered through several reception rooms in search of an obliging window. In a corner room he found, standing at a tall window, a young chambermaid whom he had glimpsed (and promised himself to investigate) on the preceding evening. She wore what his father termed with a semi-assumed leer "soubret black and frissonet frill"; a tortoiseshell comb in her chestnut hair caught the amber light; the French window was open, and she was holding one hand, starred with a tiny aquamarine, rather high on the jamb as she looked at a sparrow that was hopping up the paved path toward the bit of baby-toed biscuit she had thrown to him. Her cameo profile, her cute pink nostril, her long, French, lily-white neck, the outline, both full and frail, of her figure (male lust does not go very far for descriptive felicities!), and especially the savage sense of opportune license moved Van so robustly that he could not resist clasping the wrist of her raised tight-sleeved arm. Freeing it, and confirming by the coolness of her demeanor that she had sensed his approach, the girl turned her attractive, though almost eyebrowless, face toward him and asked him if he would like a cup of tea before breakfast. No. What was her name? Blanche—But Mlle Larivière called her "Cendrillon" because her stockings got so easily laddered, see, and because she broke and mislaid things, and confused flowers. His loose attire revealed his desire; this could not escape a girl's notice, even if color-blind, and as he drew up still closer, while looking over her head for a suitable couch to take shape in some part of this magical manor—where *any* place, as in Casanova's remembrances could be dream-changed into a sequestered seraglio nook—she wiggled out of his reach completely and delivered a little soliloquy in her soft Ladoran French:

"*Monsieur a quinze ans, je crois, et moi, je sais, j'en ai dix-neuf. Monsieur* is a nobleman; I am a poor peat-digger's daughter. *Monsieur a tâté, sans doute, des filles de la ville; quant à moi, je suis vierge, ou peu s'en faut. De plus,* were I to fall in love with you—I mean really in love—and I might, alas, if you possessed me *rien qu'une petite fois*—it would be, for me, only grief, and infernal fire, and despair, and even death, *Monsieur. Finalement,* I might add that I have the whites and must see *le Docteur Chronique,* I mean Crolique, on my next day off. Now we have to separate, the sparrow has disappeared, I see, and Monsieur Bouteillan has entered the next room, and can perceive us clearly in that mirror above the sofa behind that silk screen."

"Forgive me, girl," murmured Van, whom her strange,

tragic tone had singularly put off, as if he were taking part in a play in which he was the principal actor, but of which he could only recall that one scene.

The butler's hand in the mirror took down a decanter from nowhere and was withdrawn. Van, reknotting the cord of his robe, passed through the French window into the green reality of the garden.

8

On the same morning, or a couple of days later, on the terrace:

"*Mais va donc jouer avec lui*," said Mlle Larivière, pushing Ada, whose young hips disjointedly jerked from the shock. "Don't let your cousin *se morfondre* when the weather is so fine. Take him by the hand. Go and show him the white lady in your favorite lane, and the mountain, and the great oak."

Ada turned to him with a shrug. The touch of her cold fingers and damp palm and the self-conscious way she tossed back her hair as they walked down the main avenue of the park made him self-conscious too, and under the pretext of picking up a fir cone he disengaged his hand. He threw the cone at a woman of marble bending over a stamnos but only managed to frighten a bird that had perched on the brim of her broken jar.

"There is nothing more banal in the world," said Ada, "than pitching stones at a hawfinch."

"Sorry," said Van, "I did not intend to scare that bird. But then, I'm not a country lad, who knows a cone from a stone. What games, *au fond*, does she expect us to play?"

"*Je l'ignore*," replied Ada. "I really don't care very much how her poor mind works. *Cache-cache*, I suppose, or climbing trees."

"Oh, I'm good at that," said Van, "in fact, I can even brachiate."

"No," she said, "we are going to play *my* games. Games I have invented all by myself. Games Lucette, I hope, will be able to play next year with me, the poor pet. Come, let us start. The present series belongs to the shadow-and-shine group, two of which I'm going to show you."

"I see," said Van.

"You will in a moment," rejoined the pretty prig. "First of all we must find a nice stick."

"Look," said Van, still smarting a bit, "there goes another haw-haw finch."

By then they had reached the *rond-point*—a small arena encircled by flowerbeds and jasmine bushes in heavy bloom. Overhead the arms of a linden stretched toward those of an oak, like a green-spangled beauty flying to meet her strong father hanging by his feet from the trapeze. Even then did we both understand that kind of heavenly stuff, even then.

"Something rather acrobatic about those branches up there, no?" he said, pointing.

"Yes," she answered. "I discovered it long ago. The teil is the flying Italian lady, and the old oak aches, the old lover aches, but still catches her every time" (impossible to reproduce the right intonation while rendering the entire sense —after eight decades!—but she did say something extravagant, something quite out of keeping with her tender age as they looked up and then down).

Looking down and gesturing with a sharp green stake borrowed from the peonies, Ada explained the first game.

The shadows of leaves on the sand were variously interrupted by roundlets of live light. The player chose his roundlet—the best, the brightest he could find—and firmly outlined it with the point of his stick; whereupon the yellow round light would appear to grow convex like the brimming surface of some golden dye. Then the player delicately scooped out the earth with his stick or fingers within the roundlet. The level of that gleaming *infusion de tilleul* would magically sink in its goblet of earth and finally dwindle to one precious drop. That player won who made the most goblets in, say, twenty minutes.

Van asked suspiciously if that was all.

No, it was not. As she dug a firm little circle around a particularly fine goldgout, Ada squatted and moved, squatting, with her black hair falling over her ivory-smooth moving knees while her haunches and hands worked, one hand holding the stick, the other brushing back bothersome strands of hair. A gentle breeze suddenly eclipsed her fleck. When that occurred, the player lost one point, even if the leaf or the cloud hastened to move aside.

All right. What was the other game?

The other game (in a singsong voice) might seem a little more complicated. To play it properly one had to wait for P.M. to provide longer shadows. The player—

"Stop saying 'the player.' It is either you or me."

"Say, you. You outline my shadow behind me on the sand. I move. You outline it again. Then you mark out the next boundary (handing him the stick). If I now move back—"

"You know," said Van, throwing the stick away, "personally I think these are the most boring and stupid games anybody has ever invented, anywhere, any time, A.M. or P.M."

She said nothing but her nostrils narrowed. She retrieved the stick and stuck it back, furiously, where it belonged, deep into the loam next to a grateful flower to which she looped it with a silent nod. She walked back to the house. He wondered if her walk would be more graceful when she grew up.

"I'm a rude brutal boy, please forgive me," he said.

She inclined her head without looking back. In token of partial reconciliation, she showed him two sturdy hooks passed into iron rings on two tulip-tree trunks between which, before she was born, another boy, also Ivan, her mother's brother, used to sling a hammock in which he slept in midsummer when the nights became really sultry—this was the latitude of Sicily, after all.

"A splendid idea," said Van. "By the way, do fireflies burn one if they fly into you? I'm just asking. Just a city boy's silly question."

She showed him next where the hammock—a whole set of hammocks, a canvas sack full of strong, soft nets—was stored: this was in the corner of a basement toolroom behind the lilacs, the key was concealed in this hole here which last year was stuffed by the nest of a bird—no need to identify it. A pointer of sunlight daubed with greener paint a long green box where croquet implements were kept; but the balls had been rolled down the hill by some rowdy children, the little Erminins, who were now Van's age and had grown very nice and quiet.

"As we all are at that age," said Van and stooped to pick up a curved tortoiseshell comb—the kind that girls use to hold up their hair behind; he had seen one, exactly like that, quite recently, but when, in whose hairdo?

"One of the maids," said Ada. "That tattered chapbook must also belong to her, *Les Amours du Docteur Mertvago,* a mystical romance by a pastor."

"Playing croquet with you," said Van, "should be rather like using flamingoes and hedgehogs."

"Our reading lists do not match," replied Ada. "That *Palace in Wonderland* was to me the kind of book everybody so often promised me I would adore, that I developed an insurmountable prejudice toward it. Have you read any of Mlle Larivière's stories? Well, you will. She thinks that in some former Hindooish state she was a boulevardier in Paris; and writes accordingly. We can *squirm* from here into the front hall by a secret passage, but I think we are supposed to go and look at the *grand chêne* which is really an elm." Did he like elms? Did he know Joyce's poem about the two washerwomen? He did, indeed. Did he like it? He did. In fact he was beginning to like very much arbors and ardors and Adas. They rhymed. Should he mention it?

"And now," she said, and stopped, staring at him.

"Yes?" he said, "and now?"

"Well, perhaps, I ought not to try to divert you—after you trampled upon those circles of mine; but I'm going to relent and show you the real marvel of Ardis Manor; my larvarium, it's in the room next to mine" (which he never saw, never—how odd, come to think of it!).

She carefully closed a communicating door as they entered into what looked like a glorified rabbitry at the end of a marble-flagged hall (a converted bathroom, as it transpired). In spite of the place's being well aired, with the heraldic stained-glass windows standing wide open (so that one heard the screeching and catcalls of an undernourished and horribly frustrated bird population), the smell of the hutches—damp earth, rich roots, old greenhouse and maybe a hint of goat—was pretty appalling. Before letting him come nearer, Ada fiddled with little latches and grates, and a sense of great emptiness and depression replaced the sweet fire that had been consuming Van since the beginning of their innocent games on that day.

"*Je raffole de tout ce qui rampe* (I'm crazy about everything that crawls)," she said.

"Personally," said Van, "I rather like those that roll up in a muff when you touch them—those that go to sleep like old dogs."

"Oh, they don't go to *sleep, quelle idée,* they *swoon,* it's a little syncope," explained Ada, frowning. "And I imagine it may be quite a little shock for the younger ones."

"Yes, I can well imagine that, too. But I suppose one gets used to it, by-and-by, I mean."

But his ill-informed hesitations soon gave way to esthetic empathy. Many decades later Van remembered having much admired the lovely, naked, shiny, gaudily spotted and streaked sharpmoth caterpillars, as poisonous as the mullein flowers clustering around them, and the flat larva of a local catocalid whose gray knobs and lilac plaques mimicked the knots and lichens of the twig to which it clung so closely as to practically lock with it, and, of course, the little Vaporer fellow, its black coat enlivened all along the back with painted tufts, red, blue, yellow, of unequal length, like those of a fancy toothbrush treated with certified colors. And that kind of simile, with those special trimmings, reminds me today of the entomological entries in Ada's diary—which we must have somewhere, mustn't we, darling, in that drawer there, no? you don't think so? Yes! Hurrah! Samples (your round-cheeked script, my love, was a little larger, but otherwise nothing, nothing, nothing has changed):

"The retractile head and diabolical anal appendages of the garish monster that produces the modest Puss Moth belong to a most uncaterpillarish caterpillar, with front segments shaped like bellows and a face resembling the lens of a folding camera. If you gently stroke its bloated smooth body, the

sensation is quite silky and pleasant—until the irritated creature ungratefully squirts at you an acrid fluid from a slit in
its throat."

"Dr. Krolik received from Andalusia and kindly gave me
five young larvae of the newly described very local Carmen
Tortoiseshell. They are delightful creatures, of a beautiful
jade nuance with silvery spikes, and they breed only on a
semi-extinct species of high-mountain willow (which dear
Crawly also obtained for me)."

(At ten or earlier the child had read—as Van had—*Les
Malheurs de Swann*, as the next sample reveals):

"I think Marina would stop scolding me for my hobby
('There's something indecent about a little girl's keeping
such revolting pets . . . ,' 'Normal young ladies should
loathe snakes and worms,' et cetera) if I could persuade her
to overcome her old-fashioned squeamishness and place
simultaneously on palm and pulse (the hand alone would
not be roomy enough!) the noble larva of the Cattleya Hawk-
moth (mauve shades of Monsieur Proust), a seven-inch-
long colossus, flesh colored, with turquoise arabesques,
rearing its hyacinth head in a stiff 'Sphinxian' attitude."

(Lovely stuff! said Van, but *even* I did not quite assimilate
it, when I was young. So let us not bore the boor who flips
through a book and thinks: "what a hoaxer, that old V.V.!")

At the end of his so remote, so near, 1884 summer Van,
before leaving Ardis, was to make a visit of adieu to Ada's
larvarium.

The porcelain-white, eye-spotted Cowl (or "Shark") larva,

[61]

a highly prized gem, had safely achieved its next metamorphosis, but Ada's unique Lorelei Underwing had died, paralyzed by some ichneumon that had not been deceived by those clever prominences and fungoid smudges. The multicolored toothbrush had comfortably pupated within a shaggy cocoon, promising a Persian Vaporer later in the autumn. The two Puss Moth larvae had assumed a still uglier but at least more vermian and in a sense venerable aspect: their pitchforks now limply trailing behind them, and a purplish flush dulling the cubistry of their extravagant colors, they kept "ramping" rapidly all over the floor of their cage in a surge of prepupational locomotion. Aqua had walked through a wood and into a gulch to do it last year. A freshly emerged *Nymphalis carmen* was fanning its lemon and amber-brown wings on a sunlit patch of grating, only to be choked with one nip by the nimble fingers of enraptured and heartless Ada; the Odettian Sphinx had turned, bless him, into an elephantoid mummy with a comically encased trunk of the guermantoid type; and Dr. Krolik was swiftly running on short legs after a very special orange-tip above timberline, in another hemisphere, *Antocharis ada* Krolik (1884)—as it was known until changed to A. *prittwitzi* Stümper (1883) by the inexorable law of taxonomic priority.

"But, afterwards, when all these beasties have hatched," asked Van, "what do you do with them?"

"Oh," she said, "I take them to Dr. Krolik's assistant who sets them and labels them and pins them in glassed trays in a clean oak cabinet, which will be mine when I marry. I shall then have a big collection, and continue to breed all kinds of leps—my dream is to have a special Institute of Fritillary larvae and violets—all the special violets they breed on. I would have eggs or larvae rushed to me here by plane from all

[62]

over North America, with their foodplants—Redwood Violets from the West Coast, and a Pale Violet from Montana, and the Prairie Violet, and Egglestone's Violet from Kentucky, and a rare white violet from a secret marsh near an unnamed lake on an arctic mountain where Krolik's Lesser Fritillary flies. Of course, when the things emerge, they are quite easy to mate by hand—you hold them—for quite a while, sometimes—like this, in folded-wing profile" (showing the method, ignoring her poor fingernails), "male in your left hand, female in your right, or vice versa, with the tips of their abdomens touching, but they must be quite fresh and *soaked* in their favorite violet's reek."

9

Was she really pretty, at twelve? Did he want—would he ever want to caress her, to really caress her? Her black hair cascaded over one clavicle and the gesture she made of shaking it back and the dimple on her pale cheek were revelations with an element of immediate recognition about them. Her pallor shone, her blackness blazed. The pleated skirts she liked were becomingly short. Even her bare limbs were so free from suntan that one's gaze, stroking her white shins and forearms, could follow upon them the regular slants of fine dark hairs, the silks of her girlhood. The iridal dark-brown of her serious eyes had the enigmatic opacity of an Oriental hypnotist's look (in a magazine's back-page advertisement) and seemed to be placed higher than usual so that between its lower rim and the moist lower lid a cradle crescent of white remained when she stared straight at you. Her long eyelashes seemed blackened, and in fact were. Her features were saved from elfin prettiness by the thickish shape of her parched lips. Her plain Irish nose was Van's in miniature. Her teeth were fairly white, but not very even.

Her poor pretty hands—one could not help cooing with

pity over them—rosy in comparison to the translucent skin of
the arm, rosier even than the elbow that seemed to be blushing for the state of her nails: she bit them so thoroughly that
all vestige of free margin was replaced by a groove cutting
into the flesh with the tightness of wire and lending an additional spatule of length to her naked fingertips. Later,
when he was so fond of kissing her cold hands she would
clench them, allowing his lips nothing but knuckle, but he
would fiercely pry her hand open to get at those flat blind
little cushions. (But, oh my, oh, the long, languid, rose-and-
silver, painted and pointed, delicately stinging onyxes of her
adolescent and adult years!)

What Van experienced in those first strange days when she
showed him the house—and those nooks in it where they
were to make love so soon—combined elements of ravishment and exasperation. Ravishment—because of her pale,
voluptuous, impermissible skin, her hair, her legs, her angular
movements, her gazelle-grass odor, the sudden black stare of
her wide-set eyes, the rustic nudity under her dress; exasperation—because between him, an awkward schoolboy of
genius, and that precocious, affected, impenetrable child
there extended a void of light and a veil of shade that no
force could overcome and pierce. He swore wretchedly in
the hopelessness of his bed as he focused his swollen senses
on the glimpse of her he had engulfed when, on their second
excursion to the top of the house, she had mounted upon a
captain's trunk to unhasp a sort of illuminator through
which one acceded to the roof (even the dog had once gone
there), and a bracket or something wrenched up her skirt
and he saw—as one sees some sickening miracle in a Biblical
fable or a moth's shocking metamorphosis—that the child
was darkly flossed. He noticed that she seemed to have
noticed that he had or might have noticed (what he not only

noticed but retained with tender terror until he freed himself of that vision—much later—and in strange ways), and an odd, dull, arrogant look passed across her face: her sunken cheeks and fat pale lips moved as if she were chewing something, and she emitted a yelp of joyless laughter when he, big Van, slipped on a tile after wriggling in his turn through the skylight. And in the sudden sun, he realized that until then, he, small Van, had been a blind virgin, since haste, dust and dusk had obscured the mousy charms of his first harlot, so often possessed.

His sentimental education now went on fast. Next morning, he happened to catch sight of her washing her face and arms over an old-fashioned basin on a rococo stand, her hair knotted on the top of her head, her nightgown twisted around her waist like a clumsy corolla out of which issued her slim back, rib-shaded on the near side. A fat snake of porcelain curled around the basin, and as both the reptile and he stopped to watch Eve and the soft woggle of her bud-breasts in profile, a big mulberry-colored cake of soap slithered out of her hand, and her black-socked foot hooked the door shut with a bang which was more the echo of the soap's crashing against the marble board than a sign of pudic displeasure.

10

Weekday lunch at Ardis Hall. Lucette between Marina and the governess; Van between Marina and Ada; Dack, the golden-brown stoat, under the table, either between Ada and Mlle Larivière, or between Lucette and Marina (Van secretly disliked dogs, especially at meals, and especially that smallish longish freak with a gamey breath). Arch and grandiloquent, Ada would be describing a dream, a natural history wonder, a special belletristic device—Paul Bourget's *"monologue intérieur"* borrowed from old Leo—or some ludicrous blunder in the current column of Elsie de Nord, a vulgar literary demimondaine who thought that Lyovin went about Moscow in a *nagol'nïy tulup*, "a muzhik's sheepskin coat, bare side out, bloom side in," as defined in a dictionary our commentator produced like a conjurer, never to be procurable by Elsies. Her spectacular handling of subordinate clauses, her parenthetic asides, her sensual stressing of adjacent monosyllables ("Idiot Elsie simply *can't read*")—all this somehow finished by acting upon Van, as artificial excitements and exotic torture-caresses might have done, in an aphrodisiac sinistral direction that he both resented and perversely enjoyed.

"My precious" her mother called her, punctuating Ada's discourse with little ejaculations: "Terribly funny!" "Oh, I adore that!" but also indulging in more admonitory remarks, such as "Do sit a wee bit straighter" or "*Eat*, my precious" (accenting the "eat" with a motherly urge very unlike the malice of her daughter's spondaic sarcasms).

Ada, now sitting straight, incurving her supple spine in her chair, then, as the dream or adventure (or whatever she was relating) reached a climax, bending over the place from which Price had prudently removed her plate, and suddenly all elbows, sprawling forward, invading the table, then leaning back, extravagantly making mouths, illustrating "long, long" with both hands up, up!

"My precious, you haven't tried the—oh, Price, bring the—"

The what? The rope for the fakir's bare-bottomed child to climb up in the melting blue?

"It was sort of long, long. I mean (interrupting herself) . . . like a tentacle . . . no, let me see" (shake of head, jerk of features, as if unknotting a tangled skein with one quick tug).

No: enormous purple pink plums, one with a wet yellow burst-split.

"And so there I was—" (the tumbling hair, the hand flying to the temple, sketching but not terminating the brushing-off-strand stroke; then a sudden peal of rough-rippled laughter ending in a moist cough).

"No, but seriously, Mother, you must imagine me utterly speechless, *screaming* speechlessly, as I realized—"

At the third or fourth meal Van also realized something. Far from being a bright lass showing off for the benefit of a newcomer, Ada's behavior was a desperate and rather clever attempt to prevent Marina from appropriating the conversation and transforming it into a lecture on the theater. Marina, on the other hand, while awaiting a chance to trot out her troika of hobby horses, took some professional pleasure in playing the hackneyed part of a fond mother, proud of her daughter's charm and humor, and herself charmingly and humorously lenient toward their brash circumstantiality: *she* was showing off—not Ada! And when Van had understood the true situation, he would take advantage of a pause (which Marina was on the point of filling with some choice Stanislavskiana) to launch Ada upon the troubled waters of Botany Bay, a voyage which at other times he dreaded, but which now proved to be the safest and easiest course for his girl. This was particularly important at dinner, since Lucette and her governess had an earlier evening meal upstairs, so that Mlle Larivière was not there, at those critical moments, and could not be relied on to take over from lagging Ada with a breezy account of her work on a new novella of her composition (her famous *Diamond Necklace* was in the last polishing stage) or with memories of Van's early boyhood such as those eminently acceptable ones concerning his beloved Russian tutor, who gently courted Mlle L., wrote "decadent" Russian verse in sprung rhythm, and drank, in Russian solitude.

Van: "That yellow thingum" (pointing at a floweret prettily depicted on an Eckercrown plate) "—is it a buttercup?"

Ada: "No. That yellow flower is the common Marsh Marigold, *Caltha palustris*. In this country, peasants miscall it 'Cowslip,' though of course the true Cowslip, *Primula veris*, is a different plant altogether."

"I see," said Van.

"Yes, indeed," began Marina, "when I was playing Ophelia, the fact that I had once collected flowers—"

"Helped, no doubt," said Ada. "Now the Russian word for

marsh marigold is *Kuroslep* (which muzhiks in Tartary misapply, poor slaves, to the buttercup) or else *Kaluzhnitsa*, as used quite properly in Kaluga, U.S.A."

"Ah," said Van.

"As in the case of many flowers," Ada went on, with a mad scholar's quiet smile, "the unfortunate French name of our plant, *souci d'eau*, has been traduced or shall we say transfigured—"

"Flowers into bloomers," punned Van Veen.

"Je vous en prie, mes enfants!" put in Marina, who had been following the conversation with difficulty and now, through a secondary misunderstanding, thought the reference was to the undergarment.

"By chance, this very morning," said Ada, not deigning to enlighten her mother, "our learned governess, who was also yours, Van, and who—"

(First time she pronounced it—at that botanical lesson!)

"—is pretty hard on English-speaking transmongrelizers—monkeys called 'ursine howlers'—though I suspect her reasons are more chauvinistic than artistic and moral—drew my attention—my wavering attention—to some really gorgeous bloomers, as you call them, Van, in a Mr. Fowlie's *soi-disant* literal version—called 'sensitive' in a recent Elsian rave—sensitive!—of *Mémoire*, a poem by Rimbaud (which she fortunately—and farsightedly—made me learn by heart, though I suspect she prefers Musset and Coppée)"—

". . . *les robes vertes et déteintes des fillettes* . . ." quoted Van triumphantly.

"Egg-zactly" (mimicking Dan). "Well, Larivière allows me to read him only in the Feuilletin anthology, the same you have apparently, but I shall obtain his *oeuvres complètes* very soon, oh very soon, much sooner than anybody thinks. Incidentally, she will come down after tucking in Lucette, our darling copperhead who by now should be in her green nightgown—"

"*Angel moy*," pleaded Marina, "I'm sure Van cannot be interested in Lucette's nightdress!"

"—the nuance of willows, and counting the little sheep on her *ciel de lit* which Fowlie boy turns into 'the *sky's bed*' instead of 'bed ceiler.' But, to go back to our poor flower. The forged *louis d'or* in that collection of fouled French is the transformation of *souci d'eau* (our marsh marigold) into the asinine 'care of the water'—although he had at his disposal dozens of synonyms, such as mollyblob, marybud, maybubble, and many other nicknames associated with fertility feasts, whatever those are."

"On the other hand," said Van, "one can well imagine a similarly bilingual Miss Rivers checking a French version of, say, Marvell's *Garden*—"

"Oh," cried Ada, "I can recite 'Le jardin' in my own transversion—let me see—

> *En vain on s'amuse à gagner*
> *L'Oka, la Baie du Palmier . . .*"

". . . to win the Palm, the Oke, or Bayes!" shouted Van.

"You know, children," interrupted Marina resolutely with calming gestures of both hands, "when I was your age, Ada, and my brother was *your* age, Van, we talked about croquet, and ponies, and puppies, and the last *fête-d'enfants*, and the next picnic, and—oh, millions of nice normal things, but never, never of old French botanists and God knows what!"

"But you just said you collected flowers?" said Ada.

"Oh, just one season, somewhere in Switzerland. I don't remember when. It does not matter now."

The reference was to Ivan Durmanov: he had died of lung cancer years ago in a sanatorium (not far from Ex, somewhere in Switzerland, where Van was born eight years later). Marina often mentioned Ivan who had been a famous violinist at eighteen, but without any special show of emotion, so that Ada now noted with surprise that her mother's heavy make-up had started to thaw under a sudden flood of tears (maybe some allergy to flat dry old flowers, an attack of hay fever, or gentianitis, as a slightly later diagnosis might have shown retrospectively). She blew her nose, with the sound of an elephant, as she said herself—and here Mlle Larivière came down for coffee and recollections of Van as a *bambin angélique* who adored *à neuf ans*—the precious dear!—Gilberte Swann *et la Lesbie de Catulle* (and who had learned, all by himself, to release the adoration as soon as the kerosene lamp had left the mobile bedroom in his black nurse's fist).

11

A few days after Van's arrival Uncle Dan came by the morning train from town for his habitual weekend stay with his family.

Van happened to run into him as Uncle Dan was crossing the hall. The butler very charmingly (thought Van) signaled to his master *who* the tall boy was by setting one hand three feet from the ground and then notching it up higher and higher—an altitudinal code that our young six-footer alone understood. Van saw the little red-haired gentleman glance with perplexity at old Bouteillan, who hastened to whisper Van's name.

Mr. Daniel Veen had a curious manner, when advancing toward a guest, of dipping the fingers of his stiffly held right hand into his coat pocket and holding them there in a kind of purifying operation until the exact moment of the handshake came.

He informed Van that it was going to rain in a few minutes "because it had started to rain at Ladore," and the rain, he said, "took about half-an-hour to reach Ardis." Van thought this was a quip and chuckled politely but Uncle Dan looked perplexed again and, staring at Van with pale fish-eyes, inquired if he had familiarized himself with the environs, how many languages he knew, and would he like to buy for a few kopecks a Red Cross lottery ticket?

"No, thank you," said Van, "I have enough of my own lotteries"—and his uncle stared again, but sort of sideways.

Tea was served in the drawing room, and everybody was rather silent and subdued, and presently Uncle Dan retired to his study, pulling a folded newspaper out of an inner pocket, and no sooner had he left the room than a window flew open all by itself, and a powerful shower started to drum upon the lirodendron and imperialis leaves outside, and the conversation became general and loud.

Not long did the rain last—or rather stay: it continued on its presumable way to Raduga or Ladoga or Kaluga or Luga, shedding an uncompleted rainbow over Ardis Hall.

Uncle Dan in an overstuffed chair was trying to read, with the aid of one of the dwarf dictionaries for undemanding tourists which helped him to decipher foreign art catalogues, an article apparently devoted to oystering in a Dutch-language illustrated paper somebody on the train had abandoned opposite him—when an abominable tumult started to spread from room to room through the whole house.

The sportive dackel, one ear flapping, the other upturned and showing its gray-mottled pink, rapidly moving his comical legs, and skidding on the parquetry as he executed abrupt turns, was in the act of carrying away, to a suitable hiding place where to worry it, a sizable wad of blood-soaked cottonwool, snatched somewhere upstairs. Ada, Marina and two maids were pursuing the merry animal but he was impossible to corner among all the baroque furniture as he tore through innumerable doorways. Suddenly the whole chase veered past Uncle Dan's armchair and shot out again.

"Good Lord!" he exclaimed, on catching sight of the gory trophy, "somebody must have chopped off a thumb!" Patting his thighs and his chair, he sought and retrieved—from under the footstool—the vestpocket wordbook and went back to his paper, but a second later had to look up "*groote*," which he had been groping for when disturbed.

The simplicity of its meaning annoyed him.

Through an open french door Dack led his pursuers into the garden. There, on the third lawn, Ada overtook him with the flying plunge used in "American football," a kind of Rugby game cadets played at one time on the wet turfy banks of the Goodson River. Simultaneously, Mlle Larivière rose from the bench where she had been paring Lucette's fingernails, and pointing her scissors at Blanche who had rushed up with a paper bag, she accused the young slattern of a glaring precedent—namely of having once dropped a hairpin in Lucette's cot, *un machin long comme ça qui faillit blesser l'enfant à la fesse*. Marina, however, who had a Russian noblewoman's morbid fear of "offending an inferior," declared the incident closed.

"*Nehoroshaya, nehoroshaya sobaka*," crooned Ada with great aspiratory and sibilatory emphasis as she gathered into her arms the now lootless, but completely unabashed, "bad dog."

12

Hammock and honey: eighty years later he could still recall
with the young pang of the original joy his falling in love
with Ada. Memory met imagination halfway in the hammock
of his boyhood's dawns. At ninety-four he liked retracing
that first amorous summer not as a dream he had just had
but as a recapitulation of consciousness to sustain him in
the small gray hours between shallow sleep and the first pill
of the day. Take over, dear, for a little while. Pill, pillow, bil-
low, billions. Go on from here, Ada, please!

(She). Billions of boys. Take one fairly decent decade. A
billion of Bills, good, gifted, tender and passionate, not only
spiritually but physically well-meaning Billions, have bared
the jillions of their no less tender and brilliant Jills during
that decade, at stations and under conditions that have to
be controlled and specified by the worker, lest the entire
report be choked up by the weeds of statistics and waist-
high generalizations. No point would there be, if we left
out, for example, the little matter of prodigious individual
awareness and young genius, which makes, in some cases, of
this or that particular gasp an *unprecedented and unrepeat-*

able event in the continuum of life or at least a thematic anthemia of such events in a work of art, or a denouncer's article. The details that shine through or shade through: the local leaf through the hyaline skin, the green sun in the brown humid eye, *tout ceci, vsyo eto*, in tit and toto, must be taken into account, now prepare to take over (no, Ada, go on, *ya zaslushalsya*: I'm all enchantment and ears), if we wish to convey the fact, the fact, the fact—that among those billions of brilliant couples in one cross section of what you will allow me to call spacetime (for the convenience of reasoning), one couple is a unique super-imperial couple, *sverhimperatorskaya cheta*, in consequence of which (to be inquired into, to be painted, to be denounced, to be put to music, or to the question and death, if the decade has a scorpion tail after all), the particularities of their love-making influence in a special unique way two long lives and a few readers, those pensive reeds, and their pens and mental paintbrushes. Natural history indeed! Unnatural history—because that precision of senses and sense must seem unpleasantly peculiar to peasants, and because the detail is all: The song of a Tuscan Firecrest or a Sitka Kinglet in a cemetery cypress; a minty whiff of Summer Savory or Yerba Buena on a coastal slope; the dancing flitter of a Holly Blue or an Echo Azure— combined with other birds, flowers and butterflies: *that* has to be heard, smelled and seen through the transparency of death and ardent beauty. And the most difficult: beauty itself as perceived through the there and then. The males of the firefly (now it's really your turn, Van).

The males of the firefly, a small luminous beetle, more like a wandering star than a winged insect, appeared on the first warm black nights of Ardis, one by one, here and there, then in a ghostly multitude, dwindling again to a few individuals as their quest came to its natural end. Van watched them with the same pleasurable awe he had experienced as a child, when, lost in the purple crepuscule of an Italian hotel garden, in an alley of cypresses, he supposed they were golden ghouls or the passing fancies of the garden. Now as they softly flew, apparently straight, crossing and recrossing the darkness around him, each flashed his pale-lemon light every five seconds or so, signaling in his own specific rhythm (quite different from that of an allied species, flying with *Photinus ladorensis*, according to Ada, at Lugano and Luga) to his grass-domiciled female pulsating in photic response after taking a couple of moments to verify the exact type of light code he used. The presence of those magnificent little animals delicately illuminating, as they passed, the fragrant night, filled Van with a subtle exhilaration that Ada's entomology seldom evoked in him—maybe in result of the abstract scholar's envy which a naturalist's immediate knowledge sometimes provokes. The hammock, a comfortable oblong nest, reticulated his naked body either under the weeping cedar that sprawled over one corner of a lawn, and granted a partial shelter in case of a shower, or, on safer nights, between two tulip trees (where a former summer guest, with an opera cloak over his clammy nightshirt, had awoken once because a stink-bomb had burst among the instruments in the horsecart, and striking a match, Uncle Van had seen the bright blood blotching his pillow).

The windows in the black castle went out in rows, files, and knight moves. The longest occupant of the nursery water closet was Mlle Larivière, who came there with a rose-oil lampad and her *buvard*. A breeze ruffled the hangings of his now infinite chamber. Venus rose in the sky; Venus set in his flesh.

All that was a little before the seasonal invasion of a certain interestingly primitive mosquito (whose virulence the not-too-kind Russian contingent of our region attributed to the diet of the French winegrowers and bogberry-eaters of Ladore); but even so the fascinating fireflies, and the still more eerie pale cosmos coming through the dark foliage, balanced with new discomforts the nocturnal ordeal, the harassments of sweat and sperm associated with his stuffy room. Night, of course, *always* remained an ordeal, throughout the near-century of his life, no matter how drowsy or drugged the poor man might be—for genius is not all gingerbread even for Billionaire Bill with his pointed beardlet and stylized bald dome, or crusty Proust who liked to decapitate rats when he did not feel like sleeping, or *this* brilliant or obscure V.V. (depending on the eyesight of readers, also poor people despite our jibes and their jobs); but at Ardis, the intense life of the star-haunted sky troubled the boy's night so much that, on the whole, he felt grateful when foul weather or the fouler gnat—the *Kamargsky Komar* of our *muzhiks* and the *Moustique moscovite* of their no less alliterative retaliators—drove him back to his bumpy bed.

In this our dry report on Van Veen's early, too early love, for Ada Veen, there is neither reason, nor room for metaphysical digression. Yet, let it be observed (just while the lucifers fly and throb, and an owl hoots—also most rhythmically—in the nearby park) that Van, who at the time had still not really tasted the Terror of Terra—vaguely attributing it, when analyzing his dear unforgettable Aqua's torments, to pernicious fads and popular fantasies—even then, at fourteen, recognized that the old myths, which willed into helpful being a whirl of worlds (no matter how silly and mystical) and situated them within the gray matter of the star-suffused heavens, contained, perhaps, a glowworm of strange truth. His nights in the hammock (where that other poor youth had cursed his blood cough and sunk back into dreams of prowling black spumas and a crash of symbols in an orchal orchestra—as suggested to him by career physicians) were now haunted not so much by the agony of his desire for Ada, as by that meaningless space overhead, underhead, everywhere, the demon counterpart of divine time, tingling about him and through him, as it was to retingle—with a little more meaning fortunately—in the last nights of a life, which I do not regret, my love.

He would fall asleep at the moment he thought he would never sleep again, and his dreams were young. As the first flame of day reached his hammock, he woke up another man—and very much of a man indeed. "Ada, our ardors and arbors"—a dactylic trimeter that was to remain Van Veen's only contribution to Anglo-American poetry—sang through his brain. Bless the starling and damn the stardust! He was fourteen and a half; he was burning and bold; he would have her fiercely some day!

One such green resurrection he could particularize when replaying the past. Having drawn on his swimming trunks, having worked in and crammed in all that intricate, reluctant multiple machinery, he had toppled out of his nest and forthwith endeavored to determine whether her part of the house had come alive. It had. He saw a flash of crystal, a fleck of color. She was having *sa petite collation du matin* alone on a private balcony. Van found his sandals—with a beetle in one and a petal in the other—and, through the toolroom, entered the cool house.

Children of her type contrive the purest philosophies. Ada had worked out her own little system. Hardly a week had elapsed since Van's arrival when he was found worthy of being initiated in her web of wisdom. An individual's life consisted of certain classified things: "real things" which were unfrequent and priceless, simply "things" which formed the routine stuff of life; and "ghost things," also called "fogs," such as fever, toothache, dreadful disappointments, and death. Three or more things occurring at the same time formed a "tower," or, if they came in immediate succession, they made a "bridge." "Real towers" and "real bridges" were the joys of life, and when the towers came in a series, one experienced supreme rapture; it almost never happened, though. In some circumstances, in a certain light, a neutral "thing" might look or even actually become "real" or else, conversely, it might coagulate into a fetid "fog." When the joy and the joyless happened to be intermixed, simultaneously or along the ramp of duration, one was confronted with "ruined towers" and "broken bridges."

The pictorial and architectural details of her metaphysics made her nights easier than Van's, and that morning—as on most mornings—he had the sensation of returning from a much more remote and grim country than she and her sunlight had come from.

Her plump, stickily glistening lips smiled.

(When I kiss you *here*, he said to her years later, I always remember that blue morning on the balcony when you were eating a *tartine au miel*; so much better in French.)

The classical beauty of clover honey, smooth, pale, translucent, freely flowing from the spoon and soaking my love's bread and butter in liquid brass. The crumb steeped in nectar.

"Real thing?" he asked.

"Tower," she answered.

And the wasp.

The wasp was investigating her plate. Its body was throbbing.

"We shall try to eat one later," she observed, "but it must be *gorged* to taste good. Of course, it can't sting your

[81]

tongue. No animal will touch a person's tongue. When a lion has finished a traveler, bones and all, he *always* leaves the man's tongue lying like that in the desert" (making a negligent gesture).

"I doubt it."

"It's a well-known mystery."

Her hair was well brushed that day and sheened darkly in contrast with the lusterless pallor of her neck and arms. She wore the striped tee shirt which in his lone fantasies he especially liked to peel off her twisting torso. The oilcloth was divided into blue and white squares. A smear of honey stained what remained of the butter in its cool crock.

"All right. And the third Real Thing?"

She considered him. A fiery droplet in the wick of her mouth considered him. A three-colored velvet violet, of which she had done an aquarelle on the eve, considered him from its fluted crystal. She said nothing. She licked her spread fingers, still looking at him.

Van, getting no answer, left the balcony. Softly her tower crumbled in the sweet silent sun.

13

For the big picnic on Ada's twelfth birthday and Ida's forty-second *jour de fête*, the child was permitted to wear her lolita (thus dubbed after the little Andalusian gipsy of that name in Osberg's novel and pronounced, incidentally, with a Spanish "t," not a thick English one), a rather long, but very airy and ample, black skirt, with red poppies or peonies, "deficient in botanical reality," as she grandly expressed it, not yet knowing that reality and natural science are synonymous in the terms of this, and only this, dream.

(Nor did you, wise Van. Her note.)

She had stepped into it, naked, while her legs were still damp and "piney" after a special rubbing with a washcloth (morning baths being unknown under Mlle Larivière's regime) and pulled it on with a brisk jiggle of the hips which provoked her governess's familiar rebuke: *mais ne te trémousse pas comme ça quand tu mets ta jupe! Une petite fille de bonne maison*, etc. Per contra, the omission of panties was ignored by Ida Larivière, a bosomy woman of great and repulsive beauty (in nothing but corset and gartered stockings at the moment) who was not above making secret con-

cessions to the heat of the dog-days herself; but in tender
Ada's case the practice had deprecable effects. The child
tried to assuage the rash in the soft arch, with all its accompaniment of sticky, itchy, not altogether unpleasurable sensations, by tightly straddling the cool limb of a Shattal apple
tree, much to Van's disgust as we shall see more than once.
Besides the lolita, she wore a short-sleeved white black-
striped jersey, a floppy hat (hanging behind her back from
an elastic around her throat), a velvet hairband and a pair
of old sandals. Neither hygiene, nor sophistication of taste,
were, as Van kept observing, typical of the Ardis household.

She tumbled out of her tree like a hoopoe when they all
were ready to start. Hurry, hurry, my bird, my angel. The
English coachman, Ben Wright, was still stone-sober (having had for breakfast only one pint of ale). Blanche, who
had been to a big picnic at least once (when rushed to Pine-
glen to unlace Mademoiselle, who had fainted), now performed the less glamorous duty of carrying away snarling and
writhing Dack to her little room in the turret.

A charabanc had already conveyed two footmen, three armchairs and a number of hampers to the site of the picnic.
The novelist, wearing a white satin dress (made by Vass of
Manhattan for Marina who had lately lost ten pounds),
with Ada sitting beside her, and Lucette, *très en beauté*
in a white sailor blouse, perched next to sullen Wright, drove
there in the *calèche*. Van rode behind on one of his uncle's
or grand-uncle's bicycles. The forest road remained reasonably smooth if you kept to its middle run (still sticky and
dark after a rainy dawn) between the sky-blue ruts, speckled
with the reflections of the same birch leaves whose shadows
sped over the taut nacrine silk of Mlle Larivière's open sun-
shade and the wide brim of Ada's rather rakishly donned
white hat. Now and then Lucette from beside blue-coated

Ben looked back at Van and made slacken-speed little signals with the flat of one hand as she had seen her mother do to Ada when fearing she would crash with her pony or bicycle into the back of the carriage.

Marina came in a red motorcar of an early "runabout" type, operated by the butler very warily as if it were some fancy variety of corkscrew. She looked unwontedly smart in a man's gray flannels and sat holding the palm of her gloved hand on the knob of a clouded cane as the car, wobbling a little, arrived to the very edge of the picnic site, a picturesque glade in an old pinewood cut by ravishingly lovely ravines. A strange pale butterfly passed from the opposite side of the woods, along the Lugano dirt road, and was followed presently by a landau from which emerged one by one, nimbly or slowly, depending on age and condition, the Erminin twins, their young pregnant aunt (narrationally a great burden), and a governess, white-haired Mme Forestier, the school friend of Mathilde in a forthcoming story.

Three adult gentlemen, moreover, were expected but never turned up: Uncle Dan, who missed the morning train from town; Colonel Erminin, a widower, whose liver, he said in a note, was behaving like a *pecheneg*; and his doctor (and chess partner), the famous Dr. Krolik, who called himself Ada's court jeweler, and indeed brought her his birthday present early on the following day—three exquisitely carved chrysalids ("Inestimable gems," cried throatily Ada, tensing her brows), all of which were to yield, before long, specimens of a disappointing ichneumon instead of the Kibo Fritillary, a recently discovered rarity.

Stacks of tender crustless sandwiches (perfect rectangles five inches by two), the tawny corpse of a turkey, black Russian bread, pots of Gray Bead caviar, candied violets, little raspberry tarts, half a gallon of Goodson white port, another of ruby, watered claret in thermos flasks for the girls, and the cold sweet tea of happy childhoods—all this is more readily imagined than described. One found it instructive [thus in the ms. Ed.].

One found it instructive to place side by side Ada Veen and Grace Erminin: the skimmed-milk pallor of Ada and her coeval's healthy hot flush; the straight black witchwench-hair of the one and the brown bob of the other; my love's lackluster grave eyes and the blue twinkle behind Grace's horn-rimmed glasses; the former's naked thigh and the latter's long red stockings; the gipsy skirt and the sailor suit. Still more instructive, perhaps, was to note how Greg's plain features had been transposed practically intact into his sister's aura where they acquired a semblance of girlish "good looks" without impairing the close resemblance between sailor boy and maiden.

The ruins of the turkey, the port wine which only the governesses had touched, and a broken Sèvres plate were quickly removed by the servants. A cat appeared from under a bush, stared in a shock of intense surprise, and, despite a chorus of "kitty-kitty," vanished.

Presently Mlle Larivière asked Ada to accompany her to a secluded spot. There, the fully clad lady, with her voluminous dress retaining its stately folds but grown as it were an inch longer so that it now hid her prunella shoes, stood stock-still over a concealed downpour and a moment later reverted to her normal height. On their way back, the well-meaning pedagogue explained to Ada that a girl's twelfth birthday was a suitable occasion to discuss and foresee a thing which, she said, was going to make a *grande fille* of Ada any day now. Ada, who had been sufficiently instructed about it by a schoolteacher six months earlier, and who in fact had had it already twice, now astounded her poor governess (who could never cope with Ada's sharp and strange mind) by declaring that it was all bluff and nuns' nonsense; that those things hardly ever happened to normal girls today and would certainly not occur in her case. Mlle Larivière, who was a remarkably stupid person (in spite or perhaps because of her propensity for novelizing), mentally passed in review her own experience and wondered for a few dreadful minutes if perhaps, while she indulged in the arts, the progress of science had not changed that of nature.

The early afternoon sun found new places to brighten and old places to toast. Aunt Ruth dozed with her head on an ordinary bed pillow provided by Mme Forestier, who was knitting a tiny jersey for her charges' future half-sibling. Lady Erminin, through the bothersome afterhaze of suicide, was, reflected Marina, looking down, with old wistfulness and an infant's curiosity, at the picnickers, under the glorious pine verdure, from the Persian blue of her abode of bliss. The children displayed their talents: Ada and Grace danced a Russian fling to the accompaniment of an ancient music box (which kept halting in mid-bar, as if recalling other shores, other, radial, waves); Lucette, one fist on her hip, sang a St. Malô fisher-song; Greg put on his sister's blue skirt, hat and glasses, all of which transformed him into a very sick, mentally retarded Grace; and Van walked on his hands.

Two years earlier, when about to begin his first prison term at the fashionable and brutal boarding school, to which other Veens had gone before him (as far back as the days "when Washingtonias were Wellingtonias"), Van had resolved to study some striking stunt that would give him an immediate and brilliant ascendancy. Accordingly, after a conference with Demon, King Wing, the latter's wrestling master, taught the strong lad to walk on his hands by means of a special play of the shoulder muscles, a trick that necessitated for its acquirement and improvement nothing short of a dislocation of the caryatics.

What pleasure (thus in the MS.). The pleasure of suddenly discovering the right knack of topsy-turvy locomotion was rather like learning to man, after many a painful and ignominious fall, those delightful gliders called Magicarpets (or "jikkers") that were given a boy on his twelfth birthday in the adventurous days before the Great Reaction—and then what a breathtaking long neural caress when one became airborne for the first time and managed to skim over a haystack, a tree, a burn, a barn, while Grandfather Dedalus Veen, running with upturned face, flourished a flag and fell into the horsepond.

Van peeled off his polo shirt and took off his shoes and socks. The slenderness of his torso, matching in tint if not in texture, the tan of his tight shorts, contrasted with the handsome boy's abnormally developed deltoids and sinewy forearms. Four years later Van could stun a man with one blow of either elbow.

His reversed body gracefully curved, his brown legs hoisted like a Tarentine sail, his joined ankles tacking, Van gripped with splayed hands the brow of gravity, and moved to and fro, veering and sidestepping, opening his mouth the wrong way, and blinking in the odd bilboquet fashion peculiar to eyelids in his abnormal position. Even more extraordinary than the variety and velocity of the movements he made in imitation of animal hind legs was the effortlessness of his stance; King Wing warned him that Vekchelo, a Yukon professional, lost it by the time he was twenty-two; but that summer afternoon, on the silky ground of the pineglade, in the magical heart of Ardis, under Lady Erminin's blue eye, fourteen-year-old Van treated us to the greatest performance we have ever seen a brachiambulant give. Not the faintest flush showed on his face or neck! Now and then, when he detached his organs of locomotion from the lenient ground, and seemed actually to clap his hands in midair, in a miraculous parody of a ballet jump, one wondered if this dreamy indolence of levitation was not a result of the earth's canceling its pull in a fit of absentminded benevolence. Incidentally, one curious consequence of certain muscular changes and osteal "reclicks" caused by the special training with which Wing had racked him was Van's inability in later years to shrug his shoulders.

Questions for study and discussion:

1. Did *both* palms leave the ground when Van, while reversed, seemed actually to "skip" on his hands?

2. Was Van's adult incapacity to "shrug" things off only physical or did it "correspond" to some archetypal character of his "undersoul"?

3. Why did Ada burst into tears at the height of Van's performance?

Finally Mlle Larivière read her *La Rivière de Diamants*, a story she had just typed out for *The Quebec Quarterly*. The pretty and refined wife of a seedy clerk borrows a necklace from a wealthy woman friend. On the way home from the office party she loses it. For thirty or forty horrible years the unfortunate husband and wife labor and economize to repay the debts they accumulated in the purchase of a half-million-franc necklace which they had secretly substituted for the lost one when returning the jewelbox to Mme F. Oh, how Mathilde's heart fluttered—would Jeanne open the box? She did not. When decrepit but victorious (he, half-paralyzed by a half-century of *copie* in their *mansarde*, she, unrecognizably coarsened by the washing of floors *à grand eau*), they confess everything to a white-haired but still young-looking Mme F. the latter tells them, in the last phrase of the tale: "But, my poor Mathilde, the necklace was false: it cost only five hundred francs!"

Marina's contribution was more modest, but it too had its charm. She showed Van and Lucette (the others knew all about it) the exact pine and the exact spot on its rugged red trunk where in old, very old days a magnetic telephone nested, communicating with Ardis Hall. After the banning of "currents and circuits," she said (rapidly but freely, with an actress's *désinvolture* pronouncing those not quite proper words—while puzzled Lucette tugged at the sleeve of Van, of Vanichka, who could explain everything), her husband's grandmother, an engineer of great genius, "tubed" the Redmont rill (running just below the glade from a hill above Ardis). She made it carry vibrational *vibgyors* (prismatic pulsations) through a system of platinum segments. These produced, of course, only one-way messages, and the installation and upkeep of the "drums" (cylinders) cost, she said, a Jew's eye, so that the idea was dropped, however tempting the possibility of informing a picnicking Veen that his house was on fire.

As if to confirm many people's discontent with national and international policies (old Gamaliel was by now pretty gaga), the little red car came chugging back from Ardis Hall and the butler jumped out with a message. Monsieur had just arrived with a birthday present for Mademoiselle Ada, but nobody could figure out how the complicated object worked, and Madame must help. The butler had brought a letter which he now placed on a pocket tray and presented to Marina.

We cannot reconstitute the exact wording of the message, but we know it said that this thoughtful and very expensive gift was a huge beautiful doll—unfortunately, and strangely, more or less naked; still more strangely, with a braced right leg and a bandaged left arm, and a boxful of plaster jackets and rubber accessories, instead of the usual frocks and frills. Directions in Russian or Bulgarian made no sense because they were not in the modern Roman, but in the old Cyrillitsa, a nightmare alphabet which Dan had never been able to master. Could Marina come over at once to have suitable doll clothes cut out of some nice silk discards her maid had collected in a drawer he had discovered and wrap the box again in fresh tissue paper?

Ada, who had been reading the note over her mother's shoulder, shuddered and said:

"You tell him to take a pair of tongs and carry the whole business to the surgical dump."

"*Bednyachok!* Poor, poor little man," exclaimed Marina, her eyes brimming with pity. "Of course I'll come. Your cruelty, Ada, is sometimes, sometimes, I don't know—satanic!"

Briskly walking her long cane, her face twitching with nervous resolution, Marina marched toward the vehicle, which presently moved, turning and knocking over an empty half-gallon bottle as its fender leafed through an angry burnberry bush in order to avoid the parked *calèche*.

But whatever wrath there hung in the air, it soon subsided. Ada asked her governess for pencils and paper. Lying on his stomach, leaning his cheek on his hand, Van looked at his love's inclined neck as she played anagrams with Grace, who had innocently suggested "insect."

"Scient," said Ada, writing it down.

"Oh no!" objected Grace.

"Oh yes! I'm sure it exists. He is a great scient. Dr. Entsic was scient in insects."

Grace meditated, tapping her puckered brow with the eraser end of the pencil, and came up with:

"Nicest!"

"Incest," said Ada instantly.

"I give up," said Grace. "We need a dictionary to check your little inventions."

But the glow of the afternoon had entered its most oppressive phase, and the first bad mosquito of the season was resonantly slain on Ada's shin by alert Lucette. The charabanc had already left with the armchairs, the hampers and the munching footmen, Essex, Middlesex and Somerset; and now Mlle Larivière and Mme Forestier were exchanging melodious adieux. Hands waved, and the twins with their ancient governess and sleepy young aunt were carried away in the landau. A pale diaphanous butterfly with a very black body followed them and Ada cried "Look!" and explained it was closely related to a Japanese Parnassian. Mlle Larivière said suddenly she would use a pseudonym when publishing the story. She led her two pretty charges toward the calèche and poked *sans façons* in his fat red neck with the point of her parasol Ben Wright, grossly asleep in the back under the low-hanging festoons of foliage. Ada tossed her hat into Ida's lap and ran back to where Van stood. Being unfamiliar with the itinerary of sun and shade in the clearing, he had left his bicycle to endure the blazing beams for at least three hours. Ada mounted it, uttered a yelp of pain, almost fell off, googled, recovered—and the rear tire burst with a comic bang.

The discomfitured machine was abandoned under a shrub to be fetched later by Bouteillan Junior, yet another household character. Lucette refused to give up her perch (accepting with a bland little nod the advice of her drunken boxfellow who was seen to touch her bare knees with a good-natured paw); and there being no *strapontin*, Ada had to content herself with Van's hard lap.

It was the children's first bodily contact and both were em-

barrassed. She settled down with her back to Van, resettled
as the carriage jerked, and wriggled some more, arranging her
ample pine-smelling skirt, which seemed to envelop him air-
ily, for all the world like a barber's sheet. In a trance of
awkward delight he held her by the hips. Hot gouts of
sun moved fast across her zebra stripes and the backs of her
bare arms and seemed to continue their journey through the
tunnel of his own frame.

"Why did you cry?" he asked, inhaling her hair and the
heat of her ear. She turned her head and for a moment
looked at him closely, in cryptic silence.

(Did I? I don't know—it upset me somehow. I can't
explain it, but I felt there was something dreadful, brutal,
dark, and, yes, dreadful, about the whole thing. A later
note.)

"I'm sorry," he said as she looked away, "I'll never do it
again in your presence."

(By the way, that "for all the world," I detest the phrase.
Another note in Ada's late hand.)

With his entire being, the boiling and brimming lad relished her weight as he felt it responding to every bump of the
road by softly parting in two and crushing beneath it the
core of the longing which he knew he had to control lest a
possible seep perplex her innocence. He would have yielded
and melted in animal laxity had not the girl's governess saved
the situation by addressing him. Poor Van shifted Ada's
bottom to his right knee, blunting what used to be termed in
the jargon of the torture house "the angle of agony." In the
mournful dullness of unconsummated desire he watched a
row of izbas straggle by as the *calèche* drove through Gamlet,
a hamlet.

"I can never get used (*m'y faire*)" said Mlle Laparure,
"to the contrast between the opulence of nature and the

squalor of human life. See that old moujik *décharné* with that rent in his shirt, see his miserable *cabane*. And see that agile swallow! How happy, nature, how unhappy, man! Neither of you told me how you liked my new story? Van?"

"It's a good fairytale," said Van.

"It's a fairytale," said careful Ada.

"*Allons donc!*" cried Mlle Larivière. "On the contrary—every detail is realistic. We have here the drama of the petty bourgeois, with all his class cares and class dreams and class pride."

(True; that might have been the intent—apart from the *pointe assassine*; but the story lacked "realism" *within its own terms*, since a punctilious, penny-counting employee would have found out, first of all, no matter how, *quitte à tout dire à la veuve*, what exactly the lost necklace had cost. *That* was the fatal flaw in the Larivière pathos-piece, but at the time young Van and younger Ada could not quite grope for that point although they felt instinctively the falsity of the whole affair.)

A slight commotion took place on the box. Lucette turned around and spoke to Ada.

"I want to sit with you. *Mne tut neudobno, i ot nego nehorosho pakhnet* (I'm uncomfortable here, and he does not smell good)."

"We'll be there in a moment," retorted Ada, "*poterpi* (have a little patience)."

"What's the matter?" asked Mlle Larivière.

"Nothing. *Ile pue.*"

"Oh dear! I doubt strongly he ever was in that Rajah's service."

14

Next day, or the day after the next, the entire family was having high tea in the garden. Ada, on the grass, kept trying to make an anadem of marguerites for the dog while Lucette looked on, munching a crumpet. Marina remained for almost a minute wordlessly stretching across the table her husband's straw hat in his direction; finally he shook his head, glared at the sun that glared back and retired with his cup and the *Toulouse Enquirer* to a rustic seat on the other side of the lawn under an immense elm.

"I ask myself who can that be," murmured Mlle Larivière from behind the samovar (which expressed fragments of its surroundings in demented fantasies of a primitive genre) as she slitted her eyes at a part of the drive visible between the pilasters of an open-work gallery. Van, lying prone behind Ada, lifted his eyes from his book (Ada's copy of *Atala*).

A tall rosy-faced youngster in smart riding breeches dismounted from a black pony.

"It's Greg's beautiful new pony," said Ada.

Greg, with a well-bred boy's easy apologies, had brought Marina's platinum lighter which his aunt had discovered in her own bag.

"Goodness, I've not even had time to miss it. How is Ruth?"

Greg said that both Aunt Ruth and Grace were laid up with acute indigestion—"not because of your wonderful sandwiches," he hastened to add, "but because of all those burnberries they picked in the bushes."

Marina was about to jingle a bronze bell for the footman to bring some more toast, but Greg said he was on his way to a party at the Countess de Prey's.

"Rather soon (*skorovato*) she consoled herself," remarked Marina, alluding to the death of the Count killed in a pistol duel on Boston Common a couple of years ago.

"She's a very jolly and handsome woman," said Greg.

"And ten years older than me," said Marina.

Now Lucette demanded her mother's attention.

"What are Jews?" she asked.

"Dissident Christians," answered Marina.

"Why is Greg a Jew?" asked Lucette.

"Why-why!" said Marina; "because his parents are Jews."

"And his grandparents? His *arrière* grandparents?"

"I really wouldn't know, my dear. Were your ancestors Jews, Greg?"

"Well, I'm not sure," said Greg. "Hebrews, yes—but not Jews in quotes—I mean, not comic characters or Christian businessmen. They came from Tartary to England five centuries ago. My mother's grandfather, though, was a French marquis who, I know, belonged to the Roman faith and was crazy about banks and stocks and jewels, so I imagine people may have called him *un juif*."

"It's not a very old religion, anyway, as religions go, is it?" said Marina (turning to Van and vaguely planning to steer the chat to India where she had been a dancing girl long before Moses or anybody was born in the lotus swamp).

[96]

"Who cares—" said Van.

"And Belle" (Lucette's name for her governess), "is she also a dizzy Christian?"

"Who cares," cried Van, "who cares about all those stale myths, what does it matter—Jove or Jehovah, spire or cupola, mosques in Moscow, or bronzes and bonzes, and clerics, and relics, and deserts with bleached camel ribs? They are merely the dust and mirages of the communal mind."

"How did this idiotic conversation start in the first place?" Ada wished to be told, cocking her head at the partly ornamented dackel or *taksik*.

"*Mea culpa*," Mlle Larivière explained with offended dignity. "All I said, at the picnic, was that Greg might not care for ham sandwiches, because Jews and Tartars do not eat pork."

"The Romans," said Greg, "the Roman colonists, who crucified Christian Jews and Barabbits, and other unfortunate people in the old days, did not touch pork either, but I certainty do and so did my grandparents."

Lucette was puzzled by a verb Greg had used. To illustrate it for her, Van joined his ankles, spread both arms horizontally, and rolled up his eyes.

"When I was a little girl," said Marina crossly, "Mesopotamian history was taught practically in the nursery."

"Not all little girls can learn what they are taught," observed Ada.

"Are we Mesopotamians?" asked Lucette.

"We are Hippopotamians," said Van. "Come," he added, "we have not yet ploughed today."

A day or two before, Lucette had demanded that she be taught to hand-walk. Van gripped her by her ankles while she slowly progressed on her little red palms, sometimes falling with a grunt on her face or pausing to nibble a daisy. Dack barked in strident protest.

"*Et pourtant*," said the sound-sensitive governess, wincing, "I read to her twice Ségur's adaptation in fable form of Shakespeare's play about the wicked usurer."

"She also knows my revised monologue of his mad king," said Ada:

> *Ce beau jardin fleurit en mai,*
> *Mais en hiver*
> *Jamais, jamais, jamais, jamais, jamais*
> *N'est vert, n'est vert, n'est vert, n'est vert,*
> *n'est vert.*

"Oh, that's good," exclaimed Greg with a veritable sob of admiration.

"Not so *energichno*, children!" cried Marina in Van-and-Lucette's direction.

"*Elle devient pourpre*, she is getting crimson," commented the governess. "I sustain that these indecent gymnastics are no good for her."

Van, his eyes smiling, his angel-strong hands holding the child's cold-carrot-soup legs just above the insteps, was "ploughing around" with Lucette acting the sullow. Her bright hair hung over her face, her panties showed from under the hem of her skirt, yet she still urged the ploughboy on.

"*Budet, budet*, that'll do," said Marina to the plough team.

Van gently let her legs down and straightened her dress. She lay for a moment, panting.

"I mean, I would love lending him to you for a ride any time. For any amount of time. Will you? Besides, I have another black."

But she shook her head, she shook her bent head, while still twisting and twining her daisies.

"Well," he said, getting up, "I must be going. Good-bye, everybody. Good-bye, Ada. I guess it's your father under that oak, isn't it?"

"No, it's an elm," said Ada.

Van looked across the lawn and said as if musing—perhaps with just a faint touch of boyish show-off:

"I'd like to see that Two-Lice sheet too when Uncle is through with it. I was supposed to play for my school in yesterday's cricket game. Veen sick, unable to bat, River-lane humbled."

15

One afternoon they were climbing the glossy-limbed shattal tree at the bottom of the garden. Mlle Larivière and little Lucette, screened by a caprice of the coppice but just within earshot, were playing grace hoops. One glimpsed now and then, above or through foliage, the skimming hoop passing from one unseen sending stick to another. The first cicada of the season kept trying out its instrument. A silver-and-sable skybab squirrel sat sampling a cone on the back of a bench.

Van, in blue gym suit, having worked his way up to a fork just under his agile playmate (who naturally was better acquainted with the tree's intricate map) but not being able to see her face, betokened mute communication by taking her ankle between finger and thumb as *she* would have a closed butterfly. Her bare foot slipped, and the two panting youngsters tangled ignominiously among the branches, in a shower of drupes and leaves, clutching at each other, and the next moment, as they regained a semblance of balance, his expressionless face and cropped head were between her legs and a last fruit fell with a thud—the dropped dot of an inverted exclamation point. She was wearing his wristwatch and a cotton frock.

("Remember?"

"Yes, of course, I remember: you kissed me here, on the inside—"

"And you started to strangle me with those devilish knees of yours—"

"I was seeking some sort of support.")

That might have been true, but according to a later (considerably later!) version they were still in the tree, and still glowing, when Van removed a silk thread of larva web from his lip and remarked that such negligence of attire was a form of hysteria.

"Well," answered Ada, straddling her favorite limb, "as we all know by now, Mlle La Rivière de Diamants has nothing against a hysterical little girl's not wearing pantalets during *l'ardeur de la canicule*."

"I refuse to share the ardor of your little canicule with an apple tree."

"It is really the Tree of Knowledge—this specimen was imported last summer wrapped up in brocade from the Eden National Park where Dr. Krolik's son is a ranger and breeder."

"Let him range and breed by all means," said Van (her natural history had long begun to get on his nerves), "but I swear no apple trees grow in Iraq."

"Right, but that's not a true apple tree."

("Right and wrong," commented Ada, again much later: "We did discuss the matter, but you could not have permitted yourself such vulgar repartees then. At a time when the chastest of chances allowed you to snatch, as they say, a first shy kiss! Oh, for shame. And besides, there was no National Park in Iraq eighty years ago." "True," said Van. "And no caterpillars bred on that tree in our orchard." "True,

[101]

my lovely and larveless." Natural history was past history by that time.)

Both kept diaries. Soon after that foretaste of knowledge, an amusing thing happened. She was on her way to Krolik's house with a boxful of hatched and chloroformed butter-flies and had just passed through the orchard when she suddenly stopped and swore (*chort!*). At the same moment Van, who had set out in the opposite direction for a bit of shooting practice in a nearby pavilion (where there was a bowling alley and other recreational facilities, once much used by other Veens), also came to an abrupt standstill. Then, by a nice coincidence, both went tearing back to the house to hide their diaries which both thought they had left lying open in their respective rooms. Ada, who feared the curiosity of Lucette and Blanche (the governess presented no threat, being pathologically unobservant), found out she was wrong—she had put away the album with its latest entry. Van, who knew that Ada was a little "snoopy," discovered Blanche in his room feigning to make the made bed, with the unlocked diary lying on the stool beside it. He slapped her lightly on the behind and removed the shagreen-bound book to a safer place. Then Van and Ada met in the passage, and would have kissed at some earlier stage of the Novel's Evolution in the History of Literature. It might have been a neat little sequel to the Shattal Tree incident. Instead, both resumed their separate ways—and Blanche, I suppose, went to weep in her bower.

16

Their first free and frantic caresses had been preceded by a brief period of strange craftiness, of cringing stealth. The masked offender was Van, but her passive acceptance of the poor boy's behavior seemed tacitly to acknowledge its disreputable and even monstrous nature. A few weeks later both were to regard that phase of his courtship with amused condescension; at the time, however, its implicit cowardice puzzled her and distressed him—mainly because he was keenly conscious of her being puzzled.

Although Van had never had the occasion to witness anything close to virginal revolt on the part of Ada—not an easily frightened or overfastidious little girl (*"Je raffole de tout ce qui rampe"*), he could rely on two or three dreadful dreams to imagine her, in real, or at least responsible, life, recoiling with a wild look as she left his lust in the lurch to summon her governess or mother, or a gigantic footman (not existing in the house but killable in the dream—punchable with sharp-ringed knuckles, puncturable like a bladder of blood), after which he knew he would be expelled from Ardis—

(In Ada's hand: I vehemently object to that "not over-fastidious." It is unfair in fact, and fuzzy in fancy. Van's marginal note: Sorry, puss; that must stay.)

—but even if he were to will himself to mock that image so as to blast it out of all consciousness, he could not feel proud of his conduct: in those actual undercover dealings of his with Ada, by doing what he did and the way he did it, with that unpublished relish, he seemed to himself to be either taking advantage of her innocence or else inducing her to conceal from him, the concealer, her awareness of what he concealed.

After the first contact, so light, so mute, between his soft lips and her softer skin had been established—high up in that dappled tree, with only that stray ardilla daintily leaves-dropping—nothing seemed changed in one sense, all was lost in another. Such contacts evolve their own texture; a tactile sensation is a blind spot; we touch in silhouette. Henceforth, at certain moments of their otherwise indolent days, in certain recurrent circumstances of controlled madness, a secret sign was erected, a veil drawn between him and her—

(Ada: They are now practically extinct at Ardis. Van: Who? Oh, I see.)

—not to be removed until he got rid of what the necessity of dissimulation kept degrading to the level of a wretched itch.

(Och, Van!)

He could not say afterwards, when discussing with her that rather pathetic nastiness, whether he really feared that his *avournine* (as Blanche was to refer later, in her bastard French, to Ada) might react with an outburst of real or well-feigned resentment to a stark display of desire, or whether a glum, cunning approach was dictated to him by considerations of pity and decency toward a chaste child, whose charm

[104]

was too compelling not to be tasted in secret and too sacred to be openly violated; but something went wrong—that much was clear. The vague commonplaces of vague modesty so dreadfully in vogue eighty years ago, the unsufferable banalities of shy wooing buried in old romances as arch as Arcady, those moods, those modes, lurked no doubt behind the hush of his ambuscades, and that of her toleration. No record has remained of the exact summer day when his wary and elaborate coddlings began; but simultaneously with her sensing that at certain moments he stood indecently close behind her, with his burning breath and gliding lips, she was aware that those silent, exotic approximations must have started long ago in some indefinite and infinite past, and could no longer be stopped by her, without her acknowledging a tacit acceptance of their routine repetition in that past.

On those relentlessly hot July afternoons, Ada liked to sit on a cool piano stool of ivoried wood at a white-oilcloth'd table in the sunny music room, her favorite botanical atlas open before her, and copy out in color on creamy paper some singular flower. She might choose, for instance, an insect-mimicking orchid which she would proceed to enlarge with remarkable skill. Or else she combined one species with another (unrecorded but possible), introducing odd little changes and twists that seemed almost morbid in so young a girl so nakedly dressed. The long beam slanting in from the french window glowed in the faceted tumbler, in the tinted water, and on the tin of the paint-box—and while she delicately painted an eyespot or the lobes of a lip, rapturous concentration caused the tip of her tongue to curl at the corner of her mouth, and as the sun looked on, the fantastic, black-blue-brown-haired child seemed in her turn to mimic the mirror-of-Venus blossom. Her flimsy, loose frock hap-

pened to be so deeply cut out behind that whenever she concaved her back while moving her prominent scapulae to and
fro and tilting her head—as with air-poised brush she sur-
veyed her damp achievement, or with the outside of her left
wrist wiped a strand of hair off her temple—Van, who had
drawn up to her seat as close as he dared, could see down
her sleek *ensellure* as far as her coccyx and inhale the warmth
of her entire body. His heart thumping, one miserable hand
deep in his trouser pocket—where he kept a purse with
half a dozen ten-dollar gold pieces to disguise his state—he
bent over her, as she bent over her work. Very lightly he let
his parched lips travel down her warm hair and hot nape. It
was the sweetest, the strongest, the most mysterious sensation that the boy had ever experienced; nothing in his sordid
venery of the past winter could duplicate that downy tenderness, that despair of desire. He would have lingered forever
on the little middle knob of rounded delight on the back of
her neck, had she kept it inclined forever—and had the unfortunate fellow been able to endure much longer the ecstasy
of its touch under his wax-still mouth without rubbing
against her with mad abandon. The vivid crimsoning of an
exposed ear and the gradual torpor invading her paintbrush
were the only signs—fearful signs—of her feeling the increased pressure of his caress. Silently he would slink away to
his room, lock the door, grasp a towel, uncover himself, and
call forth the image he had just left behind, an image still as
safe and bright as a hand-cupped flame—carried into the
dark, only to be got rid of there with savage zeal; after
which, drained for a while, with shaky loins and weak calves,
Van would return to the purity of the sun-suffused room
where a little girl, now glistening with sweat, was still painting her flower: the marvelous flower that simulated a bright
moth that in turn simulated a scarab.

If the relief, any relief, of a lad's ardor had been Van's sole concern; if, in other words, no love had been involved, our young friend might have put up—for one casual summer—with the nastiness and ambiguity of his behavior. But since Van loved Ada, that complicated release could not be an end in itself; or, rather, it was only a dead end, because unshared; because horribly hidden; because not liable to melt into any subsequent phase of incomparably greater rapture which, like a misty summit beyond the fierce mountain pass, promised to be the true pinnacle of his perilous relationship with Ada. During that midsummer week or fortnight, notwithstanding those daily butterfly kisses on that hair, on that neck, Van felt even farther removed from her than he had been on the eve of the day when his mouth had accidentally come into contact with an inch of her skin hardly perceived by him sensually in the maze of the shattal tree.

But nature is motion and growth. One afternoon he came up behind her in the music room more noiselessly than ever before because he happened to be barefooted—and, turning her head, little Ada shut her eyes and pressed her lips to his in a fresh-rose kiss that entranced and baffled Van.

"Now run along," she said, "quick, quick, I'm busy," and as he lagged like an idiot, she anointed his flushed forehead with her paintbrush in the semblance of an ancient Estotian "sign of the cross." "I have to finish this," she added, pointing with her violet-purple-soaked thin brush at a blend of *Ophrys scolopax* and *Ophrys veenae*, "and in a minute we must dress up because Marina wants Kim to take our picture—holding hands and grinning" (grinning, and then turning back to her hideous flower).

17

The hugest dictionary in the library said under Lip: "Either of a pair of fleshy folds surrounding an orifice."

Mileyshiy Emile, as Ada called Monsieur Littré, spoke thus: "*Partie extérieure et charnue qui forme le contour de la bouche . . . Les deux bords d'une plaie simple*" (we simply speak with our wounds; wounds procreate) ". . . *C'est le membre qui lèche.*" Dearest Emile!

A fat little Russian encyclopedia was solely concerned with *guba*, lip, as meaning a district court in ancient Lyaska or an arctic gulf.

Their lips were absurdly similar in style, tint and tissue. Van's upper one resembled in shape a long-winged sea bird coming directly at you, while the nether lip, fat and sullen, gave a touch of brutality to his usual expression. Nothing of that brutality existed in the case of Ada's lips, but the bow shape of the upper one and the largeness of the lower one with its disdainful prominence and opaque pink repeated Van's mouth in a feminine key.

During our children's kissing phase (a not particularly healthy fortnight of long messy embraces), some odd pudibund screen cut them off, so to speak, from each other's raging bodies. But contacts and reactions to contacts could not help coming through like a distant vibration of desperate signals. Endlessly, steadily, delicately, Van would brush his lips against hers, teasing their burning bloom, back and forth, right, left, life, death, reveling in the contrast between the airy tenderness of the open idyll and the gross congestion of the hidden flesh.

There were other kisses. "I'd like to taste," he said, "the inside of your mouth. God, how I'd like to be a goblin-sized Gulliver and explore that cave."

"I can lend you my tongue," she said, and did.

A large boiled strawberry, still very hot. He sucked it in as far as it would go. He held her close and lapped her palate. Their chins got thoroughly wet. "Hanky," she said, and informally slipped her hand into his trouser pocket, but withdrew it quickly, and had him give it himself. No comment.

("I appreciated your tact," he told her when they recalled, with amusement and awe that rapture and that discomfort. "But we lost a lot of time—irretrievable opals.")

He learned her face. Nose, cheek, chin—all possessed such a softness of outline (associated retrospectively with keepsakes, and picture hats, and frightfully expensive little courtesans in Wicklow) that a mawkish admirer might well have imagined the pale plume of a reed, that unthinking man—*pascaltrezza*—shaping her profile, while a more childish and sensual digit would have liked, and did like, to palpate that nose, cheek, chin. Remembrance, like Rembrandt, is dark but festive. Remembered ones dress up for the occasion and sit still. Memory is a photo-studio de luxe on an infinite Fifth Power Avenue. The fillet of black velvet binding her hair that day (the day of the mental picture) brought out its sheen at the silk of the temple and along the chalk of the parting. It hung lank and long over the neck, its flow disjoined by the shoulder; so that the mat white of her neck through the black bronze stream showed in triangular elegancy.

Accentuating her nose's slight tilt turned it into Lucette's; smoothing it down, into Samoyed. In both sisters, the front teeth were a trifle too large and the nether lip too fat for the ideal beauty of marble death; and because their noses were permanently stuffed, both girls (especially later, at fifteen and twelve) looked a little dreamy or dazed in profile. The lusterless whiteness of Ada's skin (at twelve, sixteen, twenty, thirty-three, et cetera) was incomparably rarer than Lucette's golden bloom (at eight, twelve, sixteen, twenty-five, finis). In both, the long pure line of the throat, coming straight from Marina, tormented the senses with unknown, ineffable promises (not kept by the mother).

The eyes. Ada's dark brown eyes. What (Ada asks) are eyes anyway? Two holes in the mask of life. What (she asks) would they mean to a creature from another corpuscle or milk bubble whose organ of sight was (say) an internal parasite resembling the written word "deified"? What, indeed, would a pair of beautiful (human, lemurian, owlish) eyes mean to anybody if found lying on the seat of a taxi? Yet I have to describe yours. The iris: black brown with amber specks or spokes placed around the serious pupil in a dial arrangement of identical hours. The eyelids: sort of pleaty, *v skladochku* (rhyming in Russian with the diminutive of her name in the accusative case). Eye shape: languorous. The procuress in Wicklow, on that satanic night of black sleet, at the most tragic, and almost, fatal point of my life (Van, thank goodness, is ninety now—in Ada's hand) dwelt with peculiar force on the "long eyes" of her pathetic and adorable grandchild. How I used to seek, with what tenacious anguish, traces and tokens of my unforgettable love in all the brothels of the world!

He discovered her hands (forget that nail-biting business). The pathos of the carpus, the grace of the phalanges demanding helpless genuflections, a mist of brimming tears, agonies of unresolvable adoration. He touched her wrist, like a dying doctor. A quiet madman, he caressed the parallel strokes of the delicate down shading the brunette's forearm. He went back to her knuckles. Fingers, please.

"I am sentimental," she said. "I could dissect a koala but not its baby. I like the words damozel, eglantine, elegant. I love when you kiss my elongated white hand."

She had on the back of her left hand the same small brown spot that marked his right one. She was sure, she said—either disingenuously or giddily—it descended from a birthmark Marina had had removed surgically from that very place years ago when in love with a cad who complained it resembled a bedbug.

On very still afternoons one could hear the pre-tunnel toot of the two-two to Toulouse from the hill, where that exchange can be localized.

"Cad is too strong," remarked Van.

"I used it fondly."

"Even so. I think I know the man. He has less heart than wit, that's a fact."

As he looks, the palm of a gipsy asking for alms fades into that of the almsgiver asking for a long life. (When will filmmakers reach the stage *we* have reached?) Blinking in the green sunshine under a birch tree, Ada explained to her passionate fortuneteller that the circular marblings she shared with Turgenev's Katya, another innocent girl, were called "waltzes" in California ("because the señorita will dance all night").

On her twelfth birthday, July 21, 1884, the child had stopped biting her fingernails (but not her toenails) in a grand act of will (as her quitting cigarettes was to be, twenty years later). True, one could list some compensations—such as a blessed lapse into delicious sin at Christmas, when *Culex chateaubriandi* Brown does not fly. A new and conclusive resolution was taken on New Year's Eve after Mlle Larivière had threatened to smear poor Ada's fingertips with French mustard and tie green, yellow, orange, red, pink riding hoods of wool around them (the yellow index was a *trouvaille*).

Soon after the birthday picnic, when kissing the hands of his little sweetheart had become a tender obsession with Van, her nails, although still on the squarish side, became strong enough to deal with the excruciating itch that local children experienced in midsummer.

During the last week of July, there emerged, with diabolical regularity, the female of Chateaubriand's mosquito. Chateaubriand (Charles), who had not been the first to be bitten by it . . . but the first to bottle the offender, and with cries of vindictive exultation to carry it to Professor Brown who wrote the rather slap-bang Original Description ("small black palpi . . . hyaline wings . . . yellowy in certain lights . . . which should be extinguished if one keeps open the kasements [German printer!] . . ." The *Boston Entomologist* for August, quick work, 1840) was not related to the great poet and memoirist born between Paris and Tagne (as he'd better, said Ada, who liked crossing orchids).

> *Mon enfant, ma soeur,*
> *Songe à l'épaisseur*
> *Du grand chêne à Tagne;*
> *Songe à la montagne,*
> *Songe à la douceur—*

—of scraping with one's claws or nails the spots visited by that fluffy-footed insect characterized by an insatiable and reckless appetite for Ada's and Ardelia's, Lucette's and Lucile's (multiplied by the itch) blood.

The "pest" appeared as suddenly as it would vanish. It settled on pretty bare arms and legs without the hint of a hum, in a kind of *recueilli* silence, that—by contrast—caused the sudden insertion of its absolutely hellish proboscis to resemble the brass crash of a military band. Five minutes after the attack in the crepuscule, between porch step and cricket-crazed garden, a fiery irritation would set in, which the strong and the cold ignored (confident it would last a mere hour) but which the weak, the adorable, the voluptuous took advantage of to scratch and scratch and scratch scrumptiously (canteen cant). "*Sladko!* (Sweet!)" Pushkin used to exclaim in relation to a different species in Yukon. During the week following her birthday, Ada's unfortunate fingernails used to stay garnet-stained and after a particularly ecstatic, lost-to-the-world session of scratching, blood literally streamed down her shins—a pity to see, mused her distressed admirer, but at the same time disgracefully fascinating—for we are visitors and investigators in a strange universe, indeed, indeed.

The girl's pale skin, so excitingly delicate to Van's eye, so vulnerable to the beast's needle, was, nevertheless, as strong as a stretch of Samarkand satin and withstood all self-flaying attempts whenever Ada, her dark eyes veiled as in the erotic trances Van had already begun to witness during their immoderate kissing, her lips parted, her large teeth lacquered with saliva, scraped with her five fingers the pink mounds caused by the rare insect's bite—for it *is* a rather rare and interesting mosquito (described—not quite simultaneously—by two angry old men—the second was Braun, the Philadelphian dipterist, a much better one than the Boston professor), and rare and rapturous was the sight of my beloved trying to quench the lust of her precious skin, leaving at first pearly, then ruby, stripes along her enchanting leg and briefly attaining a drugged beatitude into which, as into a vacuum, the ferocity of the itch would rush with renewed strength.

"Look here," said Van, "if you do not stop *now* when I say one, two, three, I shall open this knife" (opening the knife) "and slash my leg to match yours. Oh, please, devour your fingernails! Anything is more welcome."

Because, perhaps, Van's lifestream was too bitter—even in those glad days—Chateaubriand's mosquito never cared much for him. Nowadays it seems to be getting extinct, what with the cooler climate and the moronic draining of the lovely rich marshes in the Ladore region as well as near Kaluga, Conn., and Lugano, Pa. (A short series, all females, replete with their fortunate captor's blood, has recently been collected, I am told, in a secret habitat quite far from the above-mentioned stations. Ada's note.)

18

Not only in ear-trumpet age—in what Van called their dot-dot-dotage—but even more so in their adolescence (summer, 1888), did they seek a scholarly excitement in establishing the past evolution (summer, 1884) of their love, the initial stages of its revelations, the freak discrepancies in gappy chronographies. She had kept only a few—mainly botanical and entomological—pages of her diary, because on rereading it she had found its tone false and finical; he had destroyed his entirely because of its clumsy schoolboyish style combined with heedless, and false, cynicism. Thus they had to rely on oral tradition, on the mutual correction of common memories. "And do you remember, *a ti pomnish', et te souviens-tu*" (invariably with that implied codetta of "and," introducing the bead to be threaded in the torn necklace) became with them, in their intense talks, the standard device for beginning every other sentence. Calendar dates were debated, sequences sifted and shifted, sentimental notes compared, hesitations and resolutions passionately analyzed. If their recollections now and then did not tally, this was often owing to sexual differences rather than to individual temperament. Both were diverted by life's young fumblings, both saddened by the wisdom of time. Ada tended to see those initial stages as an extremely gradual and diffuse growth, possibly unnatural, probably unique, but wholly delightful in its smooth unfolding which precluded any brutish impulses or shocks of shame. Van's memory could not help picking out specific episodes branded forever with abrupt and poignant, and sometimes regrettable, physical thrills. She had the impression that the insatiable delectations she arrived at, without having expected or summoned them, were experienced by Van only by the time she attained them: that is, after weeks of cumulative caresses; her first physiological reactions to them she demurely dismissed as related to childish practices which she had indulged in before and which had little to do with the glory and tang of individual happiness. Van, on the contrary, not only could tabulate every informal spasm he had hidden from her before they became lovers, but stressed philosophic and moral distinctions between the shattering force of self-abuse and the overwhelming softness of avowed and shared love.

When we remember our former selves, there is always that little figure with its long shadow stopping like an uncertain belated visitor on a lighted threshold at the far end of an impeccably narrowing corridor. Ada saw herself there as a wonder-eyed waif with a bedraggled nosegay; Van saw himself as a nasty young satyr with clumsy hooves and an ambiguous flue pipe. "But I was only twelve," Ada would cry when some indelicate detail was brought up. "I was in my fifteenth year," sadly said Van.

And did the young lady recall, he asked, producing metaphorically some notes from his pocket, the very first time she guessed that her shy young "cousin" (their official relationship) was physically excited in her presence, though decently swathed in layers of linen and wool and not in contact with the young lady?

She said, frankly no, she did not—indeed, could not—because at eleven, despite trying numberless times to unlock with every key in the house the cabinet in which Walter Daniel Veen kept "Jap. & Ind. erot. prints" as seen distinctly labeled through the glazed door (the key to which Van found for her in a twinkle—taped to the back of the pediment), she had still been rather hazy about the way human beings mated. She was very observant, of course, and had closely examined various insects *in copula,* but at the period discussed clear examples of mammalian maleness had rarely come to her notice and had remained unconnected with any idea or possibility of sexual function (such as for example the time she had contemplated the soft-looking beige beak of the Negro janitor's boy who sometimes urinated in the girls' water closet at her first school in 1883).

Two other phenomena that she had observed even earlier proved ridiculously misleading. She must have been about nine when that elderly gentleman, an eminent painter whom she could not and would not name, came several times to dinner at Ardis Hall. Her drawing teacher, Miss Wintergreen, respected him greatly, though actually her *natures mortes* were considered (in 1888 and again 1958) incomparably superior to the works of the celebrated old rascal who drew his diminutive nudes invariably from behind—fig-picking, peach-buttocked nymphets straining upward, or else rock-climbing girl scouts in bursting shorts—

"I know exactly," interrupted Van angrily, "whom you mean, and would like to place on record that even if his delicious talent is in disfavor today, Paul J. Gigment had every right to paint schoolgirls and poolgirls from any side he pleased. Proceed."

Every time (said unruffled Ada) Pig Pigment came, she cowered when hearing him trudge and snort and pant upstairs, ever nearer like the Marmoreal Guest, that immemorial ghost, seeking her, crying for her in a thin, querulous voice not in keeping with marble.

"Poor old chap," murmured Van.

His method of contact, she said, "*puisqu'on aborde ce thème-là,* and I'm certainly *not* making offensive comparisons," was to insist, with maniacal force, that he help her reach for something—anything, a little gift he had brought, bonbons, or simply some old toy that he'd picked up from the floor of the nursery and hung up high on the wall, or a pink candle burning blue that he commanded her to blow out on an arbre de Noël, and despite her gentle protests he would raise the child by her elbows, taking his time, pushing, grunting, saying: ah, how heavy and pretty she was—this went on and on until the dinner gong boomed or Nurse entered with a glass of fruit juice and what a relief it was, for everybody concerned, when in the course of that fraudulent ascension her poor little bottom made it *at last* to the crackling snow of his shirtfront, and he dropped her, and buttoned his dinner jacket. And she remembered—

"Stupidly exaggerated," commented Van. "Also, I suppose, artificially recolored in the lamplight of later events as revealed still later."

And she remembered blushing painfully when somebody said poor Pig had a very sick mind and "a hardening of the artery," that is how she heard it, or perhaps "heartery"; but she also knew, even then, that the artery could become awfully long, for she had seen Drongo, a black horse, looking, she must confess, most dejected and embarrassed by what was happening to it right in the middle of a rough field with all the daisies watching. She thought, arch Ada said (how truthfully, was another question), that a foal was dangling, with one black rubber leg free, out of Drongo's belly because she did not understand that Drongo was not a mare at all and had not got a pouch as the kangaroo had in an illustration she worshipped, but then her English nurse explained that Drongo was a very sick horse and everything fell into place.

"Fine," said Van, "that's certainly fascinating; but I was thinking of the first time you might have suspected I was also a sick pig or horse. I am recalling," he continued, "the round table in the round rosy glow and you kneeling next to me on a chair. I was perched on the chair's swelling arm and you were building a house of cards, and your every movement was magnified, of course, as in a trance, dream-slow but also tremendously vigilant, and I positively reveled in the girl odor of your bare arm and in that of your hair which now is murdered by some popular perfume. I date the event around June 10—a rainy evening less than a week after my first arrival to Ardis."

"I remember the cards," she said, "and the light and the noise of the rain, and your blue cashmere pullover—but nothing else, nothing odd or improper, *that* came later. Besides, only in French love stories *les messieurs hument* young ladies."

"Well, I did while you went on with your delicate work. Tactile magic. Infinite patience. Fingertips stalking gravity. Badly bitten nails, my sweet. Forgive these notes, I cannot really express the discomfort of bulky, sticky desire. You see I was hoping that when your castle toppled you would make a Russian splash gesture of surrender and sit down on my hand."

"It was not a castle. It was a Pompeian Villa with mosaics and paintings inside, because I used only court cards from

Grandpa's old gambling packs. Did I sit down on your hot hard hand?"

"On my open palm, darling. A pucker of paradise. You remained still for a moment, fitting my cup. Then you rearranged your limbs and reknelt."

"Quick, quick, quick, collecting the flat shining cards again to build again, again slowly? We were abominably depraved, weren't we?"

"All bright kids are depraved. I see you do recollect—"

"Not that particular occasion, but the apple tree, and when you kissed my neck, *et tout le reste*. And then—*zdravstvuyte: apofeos*, the Night of the Burning Barn!"

19

A sort of hoary riddle (*Les Sophismes de Sophie* by Mlle Stopchin in the Bibliothèque Vieux Rose series): did the Burning Barn come before the Cockloft or the Cockloft come first. Oh, first! We had long been kissing cousins when the fire started. In fact, I was getting some Château Baignet cold cream from Ladore for my poor chapped lips. And we both were roused in our separate rooms by her crying *au feu!* July 28? August 4?

Who cried? Stopchin cried? Larivière cried? Larivière? Answer! Crying that the barn *flambait?*

No, she was fast ablaze—I mean, asleep. I know, said Van, it was she, the hand-painted handmaid, who used your watercolors to touch up her eyes, or so Larivière said, who accused her and Blanche of fantastic sins.

Oh, of course! But not Marina's poor French—it was our little goose Blanche. Yes, she rushed down the corridor and lost a miniver-trimmed slipper on the grand staircase, like Ashette in the English version.

"And do you remember, Van, how warm the night was?"

"*Eshcho bï!* (as if I did not!). That night because of the blink—"

That night because of the bothersome blink of remote sheet lightning through the black hearts of his sleeping-arbor, Van had abandoned his two tulip trees and gone to bed in his room. The tumult in the house and the maid's shriek interrupted a rare, brilliant, dramatic dream, whose subject he was unable to recollect later, although he still held it in a saved jewel box. As usual, he slept naked, and wavered now between pulling on a pair of shorts, or draping himself in his tartan lap robe. He chose the second course, rattled a match-box, lit his bedside candle, and swept out of his room, ready to save Ada and all her larvae. The corridor was dark, somewhere the dachshund was barking ecstatically. Van gleaned from subsiding cries that the so-called "baronial barn," a huge beloved structure three miles away, was on fire. Fifty cows would have been without hay and Larivière without her midday coffee cream had it happened later in the season. Van felt slighted. They've all gone and left me behind, as old Fierce mumbles at the end of the *Cherry Orchard* (Marina was an adequate Mme Ranevski).

With the tartan toga around him, he accompanied his black double down the accessory spiral stairs leading to the library. Placing a bare knee on the shaggy divan under the window, Van drew back the heavy red curtains.

Uncle Dan, a cigar in his teeth, and kerchiefed Marina with Dack in her clutch deriding the watchdogs, were in the process of setting out between raised arms and swinging lanterns in the runabout—as red as a fire engine!—only to be overtaken at the crunching curve of the drive by three English footmen on horseback with three French maids *en croupe*. The entire domestic staff seemed to be taking off to enjoy the fire (an infrequent event in our damp windless region), using every contraption available or imaginable: telegas, teleseats, roadboats, tandem bicycles and even the clockwork luggage carts with which the stationmaster supplied the family in memory of Erasmus Veen, their inventor. Only the governess (as Ada, not Van, had by then discovered) slept on through everything, snoring with a wheeze and a harkle, in the room adjacent to the old nursery where little Lucette lay for a minute awake before running after her dream and jumping into the last furniture van.

Van, kneeling at the picture window, watched the inflamed eye of the cigar recede and vanish. That multiple departure . . . Take over.

That multiple departure really presented a marvelous sight against the pale star-dusted firmament of practically subtropical Ardis, tinted between the black trees with a distant flamingo flush at the spot where the Barn was Burning. To reach it one had to drive round a large reservoir which I could make out breaking into scaly light here and there every time some adventurous hostler or pantry boy crossed it on water skis or in a Rob Roy or by means of a raft—typical raft ripples like fire snakes in Japan; and one could now follow with an artist's eye the motorcar's lamps, fore and aft, progressing east along the AB bank of that rectangular lake, then turning sharply upon reaching its B corner, trailing away up the short side and creeping back west, in a dim and diminished aspect, to a middle point on the far margin where they swung north and disappeared.

As two last retainers, the cook and the night watchman, scurried across the lawn toward a horseless trap or break, that stood beckoning them with erected thills (or was it a rickshaw? Uncle Dan once had a Japanese valet), Van was delighted and shocked to distinguish, right there in the inky shrubbery, Ada in her long nightgown passing by with a lighted candle in one hand and a shoe in the other as if stealing after the belated ignicolists. It was only her reflection in the glass. She dropped the found shoe in a wastepaper basket and joined Van on the divan.

"Can one see anything, oh, can one see?" the dark-haired child kept repeating, and a hundred barns blazed in her amber-black eyes, as she beamed and peered in blissful curiosity. He relieved her of her candlestick, placing it near his own longer one on the window ledge. "You are naked, you are dreadfully indecent," she observed without looking and without any emphasis or reproof, whereupon he cloaked himself tighter, Ramses the Scotsman, as she knelt beside him. For a moment they both contemplated the romantic night piece framed in the window. He had started to stroke her, shivering, staring ahead, following with a blind man's hand the dip of her spine through the batiste.

"Look, gipsies," she whispered, pointing at three shadowy forms—two men, one with a ladder, and a child or dwarf—circumspectly moving across the gray lawn. They saw the candle-lit window and decamped, the smaller one walking *à reculons* as if taking pictures.

"I stayed home on purpose, because I hoped you would too—it was a contrived coincidence," she said, or said later she'd said—while he continued to fondle the flow of her hair, and to massage and rumple her nightdress, not daring yet to go under and up, daring, however, to mold her nates until, with a little hiss, she sat down on his hand and her heels, as the burning castle of cards collapsed. She turned to him and next moment he was kissing her bare shoulder, and pushing against her like that soldier behind in the queue.

First time I hear about him. I thought old Mr. Nymphobottomus had been my only predecessor.

Last spring. Trip to town. French theater matinée. Made-

moiselle had mislaid the tickets. The poor fellow probably
thought "Tartuffe" was a tart or a stripteaser.

Ce qui n'est pas si bête, au fond. Which was not so dumb
after all. Okay. In that scene of the Burning Barn—

Yes?

Nothing. Go on.

Oh, Van, that night, that moment as we knelt side by
side in the candlelight like Praying Children in a very bad
picture, showing two pairs of soft-wrinkled, once arboreal-
animal, soles—not to Grandma who gets the Xmas card but
to the surprised and pleased Serpent, I remember wanting
so badly to ask you for a bit of purely scientific information,
because my sidelong glance—

Not now, it's not a nice sight right now and it will be
worse in a moment (or words to that effect).

Van could not decide whether she really was utterly
ignorant and as pure as the night sky—now drained of its
fire color—or whether total experience advised her to indulge
in a cold game. It did not really matter.

Wait, not right now, he replied in a half-muffled mutter.

She insisted: I wannask, I wannano—

He caressed and parted with his fleshy folds, *parties très
charnues*, in the case of our passionate siblings, her lank
loose, nearly lumbus-length (when she threw back her head
as now) black silks as he tried to get at her bed-warm
splenius. (It is not necessary, here or elsewhere, there was
another similar passage, to blotch a reasonably pure style
with vague anatomical terms that a psychiatrist remembers
from his student days. In Ada's late hand.)

"I wannask," she repeated as he greedily reached his hot
pale goal.

"I want to ask you," she said quite distinctly, but also
quite beside herself because his ramping palm had now

worked its way through at the armpit, and his thumb on a nipplet made her palate tingle: ringing for the maid in Georgian novels—inconceivable without the presence of elettricità—

(I protest. You cannot. It is banned even in Lithuanian and Latin. Ada's note.)

"—to ask you . . ."

"Ask," cried Van, "but don't spoil everything" (such as feeding upon you, writhing against you).

"Well, why," she asked (demanded, challenged, one flame crepitated, one cushion was on the floor), "why do you get so fat and hard there when you—"

"Get where? When I what?"

In order to explain, tactfully, tactually, she belly-danced against him, still more or less kneeling, her long hair getting in the way, one eye staring into his ear (their reciprocal positions had become rather muddled by then).

"Repeat!" he cried as if she were far away, a reflection in a dark window.

"You will show me at once," said Ada firmly.

He discarded his makeshift kilt, and her tone of voice changed immediately.

"Oh, dear," she said as one child to another. "It's all skinned and raw. Does it hurt? Does it hurt horribly?"

"Touch it quick," he implored.

"Van, poor Van," she went on in the narrow voice the sweet girl used when speaking to cats, caterpillars, pupating puppies, "yes, I'm sure, it smarts, would it help if I'd touch, are you sure?"

"You bet," said Van, "on n'est pas bête à ce point" ("there are limits to stupidity," colloquial and rude).

"Relief map," said the primrose prig, "the rivers of Africa." Her index traced the blue Nile down into its jungle and traveled up again. "Now what's this? The cap of the Red Bolete is not half as plushy. In fact" (positively chattering), "I'm reminded of geranium or rather pelargonium bloom."

"God, we all are," said Van.

"Oh, I like this texture, Van, I like it! Really I do!"

"Squeeze, you goose, can't you see I'm dying."

But our young botanist had not the faintest idea how to handle the thing properly—and Van, now in extremis, driving it roughly against the hem of her nightdress, could not help groaning as he dissolved in a puddle of pleasure.

She looked down in dismay.

"Not what you think," remarked Van calmly. "This is *not* number one. Actually it's as clean as grass sap. Well, now the Nile is settled stop Stanley."

(I wonder, Van, *why* you are doing your best to transform our poetical and unique past into a dirty farce? Honestly, Van! Oh, I *am* honest, that's how it went. I wasn't sure of my ground, hence the sauciness and the simper. *Ah, parlez pour vous:* I, dear, can affirm that those famous fingertrips up your Africa and to the edge of the world came considerably later when I knew the itinerary by heart. Sorry, no—if people remembered the same they would not be different people. That's-how-it-went. But we are not "different"! Think and dream are the same in French. Think of the *douceur*, Van! Oh, I am thinking of it, of course, I am—it was all *douceur*, my child, my rhyme. That's better, said Ada.)

Please, take over.

Van stretched himself naked in the now motionless candlelight.

"Let us sleep here," he said. "They won't be back before dawn relights Uncle's cigar."

"My nightie is *trempée*," she whispered.

"Take it off, this plaid sleeps two."

"Don't look, Van."

"That's not fair," he said and helped her to slip it up and over her hair-shaking head. She was shaded with a mere touch of coal at the mystery point of her chalk-white body. A bad boil had left a pink scar between two ribs. He kissed it, and lay back on his clasped hands. She was inspecting from above his tanned body the ant caravan to the oasis of the navel; he was decidedly hirsute for so young a boy. Her young round breasts were just above his face. I denounce the philistine's postcoital cigarette both as a doctor and an artist. It is, however, true that Van was not unaware of a glass box of Turkish Traumatis on a console too far to be reached with an indolent stretch. The tall clock struck an anonymous quarter, and Ada was presently watching, cheek on fist, the impressive, though oddly morose, stirrings, steady clockwise launch, and ponderous upswing of virile revival.

But the shag of the couch was as tickly as the star-dusted sky. Before anything new happened, Ada went on all fours to rearrange the lap robe and cushions. Native girl imitating rabbit. He groped for and cupped her hot little slew from behind, then frantically scrambled into a boy's sandcastle-molding position; but she turned over, naively ready to embrace him the way Juliet is recommended to receive her Romeo. She was right. For the first time in their love story, the blessing, the genius of lyrical speech descended upon the rough lad, he murmured and moaned, kissing her face with voluble tenderness, crying out in three languages—the three greatest in all the world—pet words upon which a dictionary of secret diminutives was to be based and go through many revisions till the definitive edition of 1967. When he grew too loud, she shushed, shushingly breathing into his mouth, and now her four limbs were frankly around him as if she had been love-making for years in all our dreams —but impatient young passion (brimming like Van's overflowing bath while he is reworking this, a crotchety gray old wordman on the edge of a hotel bed) did not survive the first few blind thrusts; it burst at the lip of the orchid, and a bluebird uttered a warning warble, and the lights were now stealing back under a rugged dawn, the firefly signals were circumscribing the reservoir, the dots of the carriage lamps became stars, wheels rasped on the gravel, all the dogs returned well pleased with the night treat, the cook's niece Blanche jumped out of a pumpkin-hued police van in her stockinged feet (long, long after midnight, alas)—and our two naked children, grabbing lap robe and nightdress, and giving the couch a parting pat, pattered back with their candlesticks to their innocent bedrooms.

"And do you remember," said gray-moustached Van as he took a Cannabina cigarette from the bedside table and rattled a yellow-blue matchbox, "how reckless we were, and how Larivière stopped snoring but a moment later went on shaking the house, and how cold the iron steps were, and how disconcerted I was—by your—how shall I put it?—lack of restraint."

"Idiot," said Ada, from the wall side, without turning her head.

Summer 1960? Crowded hotel somewhere between Ex and Ardez?

Ought to begin dating every page of the manuscript: Should be kinder to my unknown dreamers.

20

Next morning, his nose still in the dreambag of a deep pillow contributed to his otherwise austere bed by sweet Blanche (with whom, by the parlor-game rules of sleep, he had been holding hands in a heartbreaking nightmare—or perhaps it was just her cheap perfume), the boy was at once aware of the happiness knocking to be let in. He deliberately endeavored to prolong the glow of its incognito by dwelling on the last vestiges of jasmine and tears in a silly dream; but the tiger of happiness fairly leaped into being.

That exhilaration of a newly acquired franchise! A shade of it he seemed to have kept in his sleep, in that last part of his recent dream in which he had told Blanche that he had learned to levitate and that his ability to tread air with magic ease would allow him to break all records for the long jump by strolling, as it were, a few inches above the ground for a stretch of say thirty or forty feet (too great a length might be suspicious) while the stands went wild, and Zambovsky of Zambia stared, arms akimbo, in consternation and disbelief.

Tenderness rounds out true triumph, gentleness lubricates

genuine liberation: emotions that are not diagnostic of glory or passion in dreams. One half of the fantastic joy Van was to taste from now on (forever, he hoped) owed its force to the certainty that he could lavish on Ada, openly and at leisure, all the puerile petting that social shame, male selfishness, and moral apprehension had prevented him from envisaging before.

On weekends, all three meals of the day were heralded by three gongs, small, medium and big. The first now announced breakfast in the dining room. Its vibration suscitated the thought that in twenty-six steps Van would join his young accomplice, whose delicate musk he still preserved in the hollow of his hand—and affected Van with a kind of radiant amazement: Had it *really* happened? Are we *really* free? Certain caged birds, say Chinese amateurs shaking with fatman mirth, knock themselves out against the bars (and lie unconscious for a few minutes) every blessed morning, right upon awakening, in an automatic, dream-continuing, dreamlined dash—although they are, those iridescent prisoners, quite perky and docile and talkative the rest of the time.

Van thrust his bare toe into a sneaker, retrieving the while its mate from under the bed; he hurried down, past a pleased-looking Prince Zemski and a grim Vincent Veen, Bishop of Balticomore and Como.

But she was not down yet. In the bright dining room, full of yellow flowers in drooping clusters of sunshine, Uncle Dan was feeding. He wore suitable clothes for a suitably hot day in the country—namely, a candy-striped suit over a mauve flannel shirt and piqué waistcoat, with a blue-and-red club tie and a safety-goldpinned very high soft collar (all his trim stripes and colors were a little displaced, though, in the process of comic strip printing, because it was Sunday).

He had just finished his first buttered toast, with a dab of ye-old Orange Marmalade and was making turkey sounds as he rinsed his dentures orally with a mouthful of coffee prior to swallowing it and the flavorous flotsam. Being, as I had reason to believe, plucky, I could make myself suffer a direct view of the man's pink face with its (rotating) red "tashy," but I was not obliged (mused Van, in 1922, when he saw those *baguenaudier* flowers again) to stand his chinless profile with its curly red sideburn. So Van considered, not without appetite, the blue jugs of hot chocolate and baton-segments of bread prepared for the hungry children. Marina had her breakfast in bed, the butler and Price ate in a recess of the pantry (a pleasing thought, somehow) and Mlle Larivière did not touch any food till noon, being a doom-fearing *"midinette"* (the sect, not the shop) and had actually made her father confessor join her group.

"You could have taken us to see the fire, Uncle dear," remarked Van, pouring himself a cup of chocolate.

"Ada will tell you all about it," replied Uncle Dan, lovingly buttering and marmalading another toast. "She greatly enjoyed the excursion."

"Oh, she went with you, did she?"

"Yes—in the black charabanc, with all the butlers. Jolly good fun, rally" (pseudo-British pronunciation).

"But that must have been one of the scullery maids, not Ada," remarked Van. "I didn't realize," he added, "we had several here—I mean, butlers."

"Oh, I imagine so," said Uncle Dan vaguely. He repeated the internal rinsing process, and with a slight cough put on his spectacles, but no morning paper had come—and he took them off again.

Suddenly Van heard her lovely dark voice on the staircase saying in an upward direction, "*Je l'ai vu dans une des*

[132]

corbeilles de la bibliothèque"—presumably in reference to some geranium or violet or slipper orchid. There was a "bannister pause," as photographers say, and after the maid's distant glad cry had come from the library Ada's voice added: "*Je me demande,* I wonder *qui l'a mis là,* who put it there." *Aussitôt après* she entered the dining room.

She wore—though not in collusion with him—black shorts, a white jersey and sneakers. Her hair was drawn back from her big round brow and thickly pigtailed. The rose of a rash under her lower lip glistened with glycerine through the patchily dabbed-on powder. She was too pale to be really pretty. She carried a book of verse. My eldest is rather plain but has nice hair, and my youngest is pretty, but foxy red, Marina used to say. Ungrateful age, ungrateful light, ungrateful artist, but *not* ungrateful lover. A veritable wave of adoration buoyed him up from the pit of the stomach to heaven. The thrill of seeing her, and knowing she knew, and knowing nobody else knew what they had so freely, and dirtily, and delightfully indulged in, less than six hours ago, turned out to be too much for our green lover despite his trying to trivialize it with the moral corrective of an opprobrious adverb. Fluffing badly a halfhearted "hello," not a habitual morning greeting (which, besides, she ignored), he bent over his breakfast while watching with a secret polyphemic organ her every movement. She slapped lightly Mr. Veen's bald head with her book in passing behind him and noisily moved the chair next to him on the other side from Van. Blinking, doll-lashing daintily, she poured herself a big cup of chocolate. Though it had been thoroughly sweetened, the child placed a lump of sugar on her spoon and eased it into the cup, relishing the way the hot brown liquid suffused and dissolved one crystal-grained crumbling corner and then the entire piece.

Meanwhile, Uncle Dan, in delayed action, chased an imaginary insect off his pate, looked up, looked around, and at last acknowledged the newcomer.

"Oh yes, Ada," he said, "Van here is anxious to know something. What were you doing, my dear, while he and I were taking care of the fire?"

Its reflection invaded Ada. Van had never seen a girl (as translucently white-skinned as she), or indeed anybody else, porcelain or peach, blush so substantially and habitually, and the habit distressed him as being much more improper than any act that might cause it. She stole a foolish glance at the somber boy and began saying something about having been fast ablaze in her bedroom.

"You were not," interrupted Van harshly, "you were with me looking at the blaze from the library window. Uncle Dan is all wet."

"*Ménagez vos américanismes*," said the latter—and then opened his arms wide in paternal welcome as guileless Lucette trotted into the room with a child's pink, stiff-bagged butterfly net in her little fist, like an oriflamme.

Van shook his head disapprovingly at Ada. She showed him the sharp petal of her tongue, and with a shock of self-indignation her lover felt himself flushing in his turn. So much for the franchise. He ringed his napkin and retired to the *mestechko* ("little place") off the front hall.

After she too had finished breakfasting, he waylaid her, gorged with sweet butter, on the landing. They had one moment to plan things, it was all, historically speaking, at the dawn of the novel which was still in the hands of parsonage ladies and French academicians, so such moments were precious. She stood scratching one raised knee. They agreed to go for a walk before lunch and find a secluded place. She had to finish a translation for Mlle Larivière. She showed him her draft. François Coppée? Yes.

> Their fall is gentle. The woodchopper
> Can tell, before they reach the mud,
> The oak tree by its leaf of copper
> The maple by its leaf of blood.

"*Leur chute est lente,*" said Van, "*on peut les suivre du regard en reconnaissant*—that paraphrastic touch of 'chopper' and 'mud' is, of course, pure Lowden (minor poet and translator, 1815–1895). Betraying the first half of the stanza to save the second is rather like that Russian nobleman who chucked his coachman to the wolves, and then fell out of his sleigh."

"I think you are very cruel and stupid," said Ada. "This is not meant to be a work of art or a brilliant parody. It is the ransom exacted by a demented governess from a poor overworked schoolgirl. Wait for me in the Baguenaudier Bower," she added. "I'll be down in exactly sixty-three minutes."

Her hands were cold, her neck was hot; the postman's boy had rung the doorbell; Bout, a young footman, the butler's bastard, crossed the resonant flags of the hall.

On Sunday mornings the mail came late, because of the voluminous Sunday supplements of the papers from Balticomore, and Kaluga, and Luga, which Robin Sherwood, the old postman, in his bright green uniform, distributed on horseback throughout the somnolent countryside. As Van, humming his school song—the only tune he could ever carry—skipped down the terrace steps, he saw Robin on his old bay holding the livelier black stallion of his Sunday helper, a handsome English lad whom, it was rumored behind the rose hedges, the old man loved more vigorously than his office required.

Van reached the third lawn, and the bower, and carefully inspected the stage prepared for the scene, "like a provincial come an hour too early to the opera after jogging all day along harvest roads with poppies and bluets catching and twinkle-twining in the wheels of his buggy (Floeberg's *Ursula*)."

Blue butterflies nearly the size of Small Whites, and likewise of European origin, were flitting swiftly around the shrubs and settling on the drooping clusters of yellow flowers. In less complex circumstances, forty years hence, our lovers were to see again, with wonder and joy, the same insect and the same bladder-senna along a forest trail near Susten in the Valais. At the present moment he was looking forward to collecting what he would recollect later, and watched the big bold Blues as he sprawled on the turf, burning with the evoked vision of Ada's pale limbs in the variegated light of the bower, and then coldly telling himself that fact could never quite match fancy. When he returned from a swim in the broad and deep brook beyond the bosquet, with wet hair and tingling skin, Van got the rare treat of finding his foreglimpse of live ivory accurately reproduced, except that she had loosened her hair and changed into the curtal frock of sunbright cotton that he was so fond of and had so ardently yearned to soil in the so recent past.

He had resolved to deal first of all with her legs which he felt he had not feted enough the previous night; to sheathe them in kisses from the A of arched instep to the V of velvet; and this Van accomplished as soon as Ada and he got sufficiently deep in the larchwood which closed the part on the steep side of the rocky rise between Ardis and Ladore.

Neither could establish in retrospect, nor, indeed, persisted in trying to do so, how, when and where he actually "deflowered" her—a vulgarism Ada in Wonderland had happened to find glossed in *Phrody's Encyclopedia* as: "to break a virgin's vaginal membrane by manly or mechanical means," with the example: "The sweetness of his soul was deflowered (Jeremy Taylor)." Was it that night on the lap robe? Or that day in the larchwood? Or later in the shooting gallery, or in the attic, or on the roof, or on a secluded balcony, or in the bathroom, or (not very comfortably) on the Magic Carpet? We do not know and do not care.

(You kissed and nibbled, and poked, and prodded, and worried me there so much and so often that my virginity was lost in the shuffle; but I do recall definitely that by midsummer the machine which our forefathers called "sex" was working as smoothly as later, in 1888, etc., darling. Marginal note in red ink.)

21

Ada was denied the free use of the library. According to the latest list (printed May 1, 1884), it contained 14,841 items, and even that dry catalogue her governess preferred not to place in the child's hands—"*pour ne pas lui donner des idées.*" On her own shelves, to be sure, Ada had taxonomic works on botany and entomology as well as her schoolbooks and a few innocuous popular novels. But not only was she not supposed to browse in the library unsupervised, but every book she took out to read in bed or bower had to be checked by her mentor and charged "*en lecture*" with name and stamped date in the index-card files kept in a careful mess by Mlle Larivière and in a kind of desperate order (with the insertion of queries, calls of distress, and even imprecations, on bits of pink, red or purple paper) by a cousin of hers, Monsieur Philippe Verger, a diminutive old bachelor, morbidly silent and shy, who moused in, every other week, for a few hours of quiet work—so quiet, in fact, that one afternoon when a tallish library ladder suddenly went into an eerie backward slow-motion swoon with him high up on it embracing a windmill of volumes, he reached the floor, supine, with his ladder and books, in such a hush that guilty Ada, who had thought she was alone (pulling out and scanning the utterly unrewarding *Arabian Nights*), mistook his fall for the shadow of a door being stealthily opened by some soft-fleshed eunuch.

Her intimacy with her *cher, trop cher René,* as she sometimes called Van in gentle jest, changed the reading situation entirely—whatever decrees still remained pinned up in midair. Soon upon his arrival at Ardis, Van warned his former governess (who had reasons to believe in his threats) that if he were not permitted to remove from the library at any time, for any length of time, and without any trace of *"en lecture,"* any volume, collected works, boxed pamphlets or incunabulum that he might fancy, he would have Miss Vertograd, his father's librarian, a completely servile and infinitely accommodative spinster of Verger's format and presumable date of publication, post to Ardis Hall trunkfuls of eighteenth-century libertines, German sexologists, and a whole circus of Shastras and Nefsawis in literal translation with apocryphal addenda. Puzzled Mlle Larivière would have consulted the Master of Ardis, but she never discussed with him anything serious since the day (in January, 1876) when he had made an unexpected (and rather halfhearted, really—let us be fair) pass at her. As to dear, frivolous Marina, she only remarked, when consulted, that at Van's age she would have poisoned her governess with anti-roach borax if forbidden to read, for example, Turgenev's *Smoke.* Thereafter, anything Ada wanted or might have wanted to want was placed by Van at her disposal in various safe nooks, and the only visible consequence of Verger's perplexities and despair was an increase in the scatter of a curious snow-white dust that he always left here and there, on the dark carpet, in this or that spot of plodding occupation—such a cruel curse on such a neat little man!

At a nice Christmas party for private librarians arranged under the auspices of the Braille Club in Raduga a couple of years earlier, empathic Miss Vertograd had noticed that she and giggling Verger, with whom she was in the act of sharing a quiet little cracker (tugged apart with no audible result—nor did the gold paper frilled at both ends yield any bonbon or breloque or other favor of fate), shared also a spectacular skin disease that had been portrayed recently by a famous American novelist in his *Chiron* and described in side-splitting style by a co-sufferer who wrote essays for a London weekly. Very delicately, Miss Vertograd would transmit through Van library slips to the rather unresponsive Frenchman with this or that concise suggestion: "Mercury!" or "*Höhensonne* works wonders." Mademoiselle, who was in the know, too, looked up "Psoriasis" in a one-volume medical encyclopedia, which her late mother had left her and which had not only helped her and her charges on various minor occasions but had suggested suitable illnesses for the characters in the stories she contributed to the *Québec Quarterly*. In the present case, the cure optimistically advised was to "take a warm bath at least twice a month and avoid spices"; this she typed out and passed on to her cousin in a Get-Well envelope. Finally, Ada showed Van a letter from Dr. Krolik on the same subject; it said (English version): "Crimson-blotched, silver-scaled, yellow-crusted wretches, the harmless psoriatics (who cannot communicate their skin trouble and are otherwise the healthiest of people —actually, their *bobo*'s protect them from bubas and buboes, as my teacher used to observe) were confused with lepers— yes, lepers—in the Middle Ages, when thousands if not millions of Vergers and Vertograds crackled and howled bound by enthusiasts to stakes erected in the public squares of Spain and other fire-loving countries." But this note they decided not to plant in the meek martyr's index under PS as they had first intended: lepidopterists are overeloquent on lepidosis.

Novels, poems, scientific and philosophical works wandered out unnoticed after the poor librarian gave his *démission éplorée* on the first of August, 1884. They crossed lawns and traveled along hedges somewhat in the manner of the objects carried away by the Invisible Man in Wells' delightful tale, and landed in Ada's lap wherever she and Van had their trysts. Both sought excitement in books as the best readers always do; both found in many renowned works pretentiousness, tedium and facile misinformation.

In a story by Chateaubriand about a pair of romantic siblings, Ada had not quite understood when she first read it at nine or ten the sentence *"les deux enfants pouvaient donc s'abandonner au plaisir sans aucune crainte."* A bawdy critic in a collection of articles which she now could gleefully consult (*Les muses s'amusent*) explained that the *"donc"* referred both to the infertility of tender age and to the sterility of tender consanguinity. Van said, however, that the writer and the critic erred, and to illustrate his contention, drew his sweetheart's attention to a chapter in the opus "Sex and Lex" dealing with the effects on the community of a disastrous caprice of nature.

In those times, in this country "incestuous" meant not only "unchaste"—the point regarded linguistics rather than legalistics—but also implied (in the phrase "incestuous cohabitation," and so forth) interference with the continuity of human evolution. History had long replaced appeals to "divine law" by common sense and popular science. With those considerations in mind, "incest" could be termed a crime only inasmuch as inbreeding might be criminal. But as Judge Bald pointed out already during the Albino Riots of 1835, practically all North American and Tartar agriculturists and animal farmers used inbreeding as a method of propagation that tended to preserve, and stimulate, stabilize and even create anew favorable characters in a race or strain unless practiced too rigidly. If practiced rigidly incest led to various forms of decline, to the production of cripples, weaklings, "muted mutates" and, finally, to hopeless sterility. Now *that* smacked of "crime," and since nobody could be supposed to control judiciously orgies of indiscriminate inbreeding (somewhere in Tartary fifty generations of ever woolier and woolier sheep had recently ended abruptly in one hairless, five-legged, impotent little lamb—and the beheading of a number of farmers failed to resurrect the fat strain), it was perhaps better to ban "incestuous cohabitation" altogether. Judge Bald and his followers disagreed, perceiving in "the deliberate suppression of a possible benefit for the sake of avoiding a probable evil" the infringement of one of humanity's main rights—that of enjoying the liberty of its evolution, a liberty no other creature had even known. Unfortunately after the rumored misadventure of the Volga herds and herdsmen a much better documented *fait divers* happened in the U.S.A. at the height of the controversy. An American, a certain Ivan Ivanov of Yukonsk, described as an "habitually intoxicated laborer" ("a good definition," said Ada lightly, "of the true artist"), managed somehow to impregnate—in his sleep, it was claimed by him and his huge family—his five-year-old great-granddaughter, Maria Ivanov, and, then, five years later, also got Maria's daughter, Daria, with child, in another fit of somnolence. Photographs of Maria, a ten-year-old granny with little Daria and baby Varia crawling around her, appeared in all the newspapers, and all kinds of amusing puzzles were provided by the genealogical farce that the relationships between the numerous living—and not always clean-living—members of the Ivanov clan had become in angry Yukonsk. Before the sixty-year-old somnambulist could go on procreating, he was clapped into a monastery for fifteen years as required by an ancient Russian law. Upon his release he proposed to make honorable amends by marrying Daria, now a buxom lass with problems of her own. Journalists made a lot of the wedding, and the shower of gifts from well-wishers (old ladies in New England, a progressive poet in residence at Tennessee Waltz College, an entire Mexican high school, et cetera), and on the same day Gamaliel (then a stout young senator) thumped a conference table with such force that he hurt his fist and demanded a retrial and capital punishment. It was, of course, only a temperamental gesture; but the Ivanov affair cast a long shadow upon the little matter of "favorable inbreeding." By mid-century not only first cousins but uncles and grandnieces were forbidden to intermarry; and in some fertile parts of Estoty the izba windows of large peasant families in which up to a dozen people of different size and sex slept on one *blin*-like mattress were ordered to be kept uncurtained at night for the convenience of petrol-torch-flashing patrols—"Peeping Pats," as the anti-Irish tabloids called them.

Another hearty laugh shook Van when he unearthed for entomologically-minded Ada the following passage in a reliable *History of Mating Habits*. "Some of the perils and ridicule which attend the missionary position adopted for mating purposes by our puritanical intelligentsia and so justly derided by the 'primitive' but healthy-minded natives of the Begouri Islands are pointed out by a prominent French orientalist [thick footnote, skipped here] who describes the mating habits of the fly *Serromyia amorata* Poupart. Copulation takes place with both ventral surfaces pressed together and the mouths touching. When the last throb (*frisson*) of intercourse is terminated the female sucks out the male's body content through the mouth of her impassioned partner. One supposes (see Pesson *et al.*) [another copious footnote] that the titbits, such as the juicy leg of a bug enveloped in a webby substance, or even a mere token (the frivolous dead end or subtle beginning of an evolutionary process—*qui le sait!*) such as a petal carefully wrapped up and tied up with a frond of red fern, which certain male flies (but apparently not the *femorata* and *amorata* morons) bring to the female before mating, represent a prudent guarantee against the misplaced voracity of the young lady."

Still more amusing was the "message" of a Canadian social worker, Mme de Réan-Fichini, who published her treatise, *On Contraceptive Devices,* in Kapuskan patois (to spare the blushes of Estotians and United Statians; while instructing hardier fellow-workers in her special field). "*Sole sura metoda,*" she wrote, "*por decevor natura, est por un strong-guy de contino-contino-contino jusque le plesir brimz; et lors, a lultima instanta, svitchera a l'altra gropa* [groove]; *ma perquoi una femme ardora andor ponderosa ne se retorna kvik enof, la transita e facilitata per positio torovago*"; and that term an appended glossary explained in blunt English as "the posture generally adopted in rural communities by all classes, beginning by the country gentry and ending with the lowliest farm animals throughout the United Americas from Patagony to Gasp." *Ergo*, concluded Van, our missionary goes up in smoke.

"Your vulgarity knows no bounds," said Ada.

"Well, I prefer to burn than to be slurped up alive by the

Cheramie—or whatever you call her—and have my widow lay a lot of tiny green eggs on top of it!"

Paradoxically, "scient" Ada was bored by big learned works with woodcuts of organs, pictures of dismal medieval whorehouses, and photographs of this or that little Caesar in the process of being ripped out of the uterus as performed by butchers and masked surgeons in ancient and modern times; whereas Van, who disliked "natural history" and fanatically denounced the existence of physical pain in all worlds, was infinitely fascinated by descriptions and depictions of harrowed human flesh. Otherwise, in more flowery fields, their tastes and titters proved to be much the same. They liked Rabelais and Casanova; they loathed le sieur Sade and Herr Masoch and Heinrich Müller. English and French pornographic poetry, though now and then witty and instructive, sickened them in the long run, and its tendency, especially in France before the invasion, of having monks and nuns perform sexual feats seemed to them as incomprehensible as it was depressing.

The collection of Uncle Dan's Oriental Erotica prints turned out to be artistically second-rate and inept calisthenically. In the most hilarious, and expensive, picture, a Mongolian woman with an inane oval face surmounted by a hideous hair-do was shown communicating sexually with six rather plump, blank-faced gymnasts in what looked like a display window jammed with screens, potted plants, silks, paper fans and crockery. Three of the males, contorted in attitudes of intricate discomfort, were using simultaneously three of the harlot's main orifices; two older clients were treated by her manually; and the sixth, a dwarf, had to be contented with her deformed foot. Six other voluptuaries were sodomizing her immediate partners, and one more had got stuck in her armpit. Uncle Dan, having patiently disentangled all those limbs and belly folds directly or indirectly connected with the absolutely calm lady (still retaining somehow parts of her robes), had penciled a note that gave the price of the picture and identified it as: "Geisha with 13 lovers." Van located, however, a fifteenth navel thrown in by the generous artist but impossible to account for anatomically.

That library had provided a raised stage for the unforgettable scene of the Burning Barn; it had thrown open its glazed doors; it had promised a long idyll of bibliolatry; it might have become a chapter in one of the old novels on its own shelves; a touch of parody gave its theme the comic relief of life.

22

My sister, do you still recall
The blue Ladore and Ardis Hall?

Don't you remember any more
That castle bathed by the Ladore?

Ma soeur, te souvient-il encore
Du château que baignait la Dore?

My sister, do you still recall
The Ladore-washed old castle wall?

Sestra moya, ti pomnish' goru,
I dub visokiy, i Ladoru?

My sister, you remember still
The spreading oak tree and my hill?

Oh! qui me rendra mon Aline
Et le grand chêne et ma colline?
Oh, who will give me back my Jill
And the big oak tree and my hill?

Oh! qui me rendra, mon Adèle,
Et ma montagne et l'hirondelle?

Oh! qui me rendra ma Lucile,
La Dore et l'hirondelle agile?

Oh, who will render in our tongue
The tender things he loved and sung?

They went boating and swimming in Ladore, they followed the bends of its adored river, they tried to find more rhymes to it, they walked up the hill to the black ruins of Bryant's Castle, with the swifts still flying around its tower. They traveled to Kaluga and drank the Kaluga Waters, and saw the family dentist. Van, flipping through a magazine, heard Ada scream and say *"chort"* (devil) in the next room, which he had never heard her do before. They had tea at a neighbor's, Countess de Prey—who tried to sell them, unsuccessfully, a lame horse. They visited the fair at Ardisville where they especially admired the Chinese tumblers, a German clown, and a sword-swallowing hefty Circassian Princess who started with a fruit knife, went on to a bejeweled dagger and finally engulfed, string and all, a tremendous salami sausage.

They made love—mostly in glens and gullies.

To the average physiologist, the energy of those two youngsters might have seemed abnormal. Their craving for each other grew unbearable if within a few hours it was not satisfied several times, in sun or shade, on roof or in cellar, anywhere. Despite uncommon resources of ardor, young Van could hardly keep pace with his pale little *amorette* (local French slang). Their immoderate exploitation of physical joy amounted to madness and would have curtailed their young lives had not summer, which had appeared in prospect as a boundless flow of green glory and freedom, begun to hint hazily at possible failings and fadings, at the fatigue of its fugue—the last resort of nature, felicitous alliterations (when flowers and flies mime one another), the coming of a first pause in late August, a first silence in early September. The orchards and vineyards were particularly picturesque that year; and Ben Wright was fired after letting winds go free while driving Marina and Mlle Larivière home from the *Vendange* Festival at Brantôme near Ladore.

Which reminds us. Catalogued in the Ardis library under "Exot Lubr" was a sumptuous tome (known to Van through Miss Vertograd's kind offices) entitled "Forbidden Masterpieces: a hundred paintings representing a private part of Nat. Gal. (Sp. Sct.), printed for H.R.M. King Victor." This was (beautifully photographed in color) the kind of voluptuous and tender stuff that Italian masters allowed themselves to produce in between too many pious Resurrections during a too long and lusty Renaissance. The volume itself had been either lost or stolen or lay concealed in the attic among Uncle Ivan's effects, some of them pretty bizarre. Van could not recollect whose picture it was that he had in mind, but thought it might have been attributed to Michelangelo da Caravaggio in his youth. It was an oil on unframed canvas depicting two misbehaving nudes, boy and girl, in an ivied or vined grotto or near a small waterfall overhung with bronze-tinted and dark, emerald leaves, and great bunches of translucent grapes, the shadows and limpid reflections of fruit and foliage blending magically with veined flesh.

Anyway (this may be purely a stylistic transition), he felt himself transferred into that forbidden masterpiece, one afternoon, when everybody had gone to Brantôme, and Ada and he were sunbathing on the brink of the Cascade in the larch plantation of Ardis Park, and his nymphet had bent over him and his detailed desire. Her long straight hair that seemed of a uniform bluish-black in the shade now revealed, in the gem-like sun, strains of deep auburn alternating with dark amber in lanky strands which clothed her hollowed cheek or were gracefully cleft by her raised ivory shoulder.

The texture, gloss and odor of those brown silks had once inflamed his senses at the very beginning of that fatal summer, and continued to act upon him, strongly and poignantly, long after his young excitement had found in her other sources of incurable bliss. At ninety, Van remembered his first fall from a horse with scarcely less breathlessness of thought than that first time she had bent over him and he had possessed her hair. It tickled his legs, it crept into his crotch, it spread all over his palpitating belly. Through it the student of art could see the summit of the *trompe-l'oeil* school, monumental, multicolored, jutting out of a dark background, molded in profile by a concentration of caravagesque light. She fondled him; she entwined him: thus a tendril climber coils round a column, swathing it tighter and tighter, biting into its neck ever sweeter, then dissolving strength in deep crimson softness. There was a crescent eaten out of a vine leaf by a sphingid larva. There was a well-known microlepidopterist who, having run out of Latin and Greek names, created such nomenclatorial items as Marykisme, Adakisme, Ohkisme. She did. Whose brush was it now? A titillant Titian? A drunken Palma Vecchio? No, she was anything but a Venetian blonde. Dosso Dossi, perhaps? Faun Exhausted by Nymph? Swooning Satyr? Doesn't that new-filled molar hurt your own tongue? It bruised me. I'm joking, my circus Circassian.

A moment later the Dutch took over: Girl stepping into a pool under the little cascade to wash her tresses, and accompanying the immemorial gesture of wringing them out by making wringing-out mouths—immemorial too.

> My sister, do you recollect
> That turret, "Of the Moor" yclept?
>
> My sister, do you still recall
> The castle, the Ladore, and all?

23

All went well until Mlle Larivière decided to stay in bed for
five days: she had sprained her back on a merry-go-round at
the Vintage Fair, which, besides, she needed as the setting
for a story she had begun (about a town mayor's strangling
a small girl called Rockette), and knew by experience that
nothing kept up the itch of inspiration so well as *la chaleur
du lit*. During that period, the second upstairs maid, French,
whose moods and looks did not match the sweet temper and
limpid grace of Blanche, was supposed to look after Lucette,
and Lucette did her best to avoid the lazy servant's surveillance in favor of her cousin's and sister's company. The ominous words: "Well, if Master Van lets you come," or "Yes,
I'm sure Miss Ada won't mind your mushroom-picking with
her," became something of a knell in regard to love's freedom.

While the comfortably resting lady was describing the bank
of a brook where little Rockette liked to frolic, Ada sat reading on a similar bank, wistfully glancing from time to time
at an inviting clump of evergreens (that had frequently
sheltered our lovers) and at brown-torsoed, barefooted Van,
in turned-up dungarees, who was searching for his wristwatch that he thought he had dropped among the forget-me-

nots (but which Ada, he forgot, was wearing). Lucette had abandoned her skipping rope to squat on the brink of the brook and float a fetus-sized rubber doll. Every now and then she squeezed out of it a fascinating squirt of water through a little hole that Ada had had the bad taste to perforate for her in the slippery orange-red toy. With the sudden impatience of inanimate things, the doll managed to get swept away by the current. Van shed his pants under a willow and retrieved the fugitive. Ada, after considering the situation for a moment, shut her book and said to Lucette, whom usually it was not hard to enchant, that she, Ada, felt she was quickly turning into a dragon, that the scales had begun to turn green, that now she *was* a dragon and that Lucette must be tied to a tree with the skipping rope so that Van might save her just in time. For some reason, Lucette balked at the notion but physical strength prevailed. Van and Ada left the angry captive firmly attached to a willow trunk, and, "prancing" to feign swift escape and pursuit, disappeared for a few precious minutes in the dark grove of conifers. Writhing Lucette had somehow torn off one of the red knobbed grips of the rope and seemed to have almost disentangled herself when dragon and knight, prancing, returned.

She complained to her governess who, completely misconstruing the whole matter (which could also be said of her new composition), summoned Van and from her screened bed, through a reek of embrocation and sweat, told him to refrain from turning Lucette's head by making of her a fairytale damsel in distress.

On the following day Ada informed her mother that Lucette badly needed a bath and that she would give it to her, whether her governess liked it or not. "*Horosho*," said

Marina (while getting ready to receive a neighbor and his protégé, a young actor, in her best Dame Marina style), "but the temperature should be kept at exactly twenty-eight (as it had been since the eighteenth century), and don't let her stay in it longer than ten or twelve minutes."

"Beautiful idea," said Van as he helped Ada to heat the tank, fill the old battered bath and warm a couple of towels.

Despite her being only in her ninth year and rather underdeveloped, Lucette had not escaped the delusive pubescence of red-haired little girls. Her armpits showed a slight stipple of bright floss and her chub was dusted with copper.

The liquid prison was now ready and an alarm clock given a full quarter of an hour to live.

"Let her soak first, you'll soap her afterwards," said Van feverishly.

"Yes, yes, yes," cried Ada.

"I'm Van," said Lucette, standing in the tub with the mulberry soap between her legs and protruding her shiny tummy.

"You'll turn into a boy if you do that," said Ada sternly, "and that won't be very amusing."

Warily, the little girl started to sink her buttocks in the water.

"Too hot," she said, "much too horribly hot!"

"It'll cool," said Ada, "plop down and relax. Here's your doll."

"Come on, Ada, for goodness' sake, let her soak," repeated Van.

"And remember," said Ada, "don't you dare get out of this nice warm water until the bell rings or you'll die, because that's what Krolik said. I'll be back to lather you, but don't call me; we have to count the linen and sort out Van's hankies."

The two elder children, having locked the door of the L-shaped bathroom from the inside, now retired to the seclusion of its lateral part, in a corner between a chest of drawers and an old unused mangle, which the sea-green eye of the bathroom looking-glass could not reach; but barely had they finished their violent and uncomfortable exertions in that hidden nook, with an empty medicine bottle idiotically beating time on a shelf, when Lucette was already calling resonantly from the tub and the maid knocking on the door: Mlle Larivière wanted some hot water too.

They tried all sorts of other tricks.

Once, for example, when Lucette had made of herself a particular nuisance, her nose running, her hand clutching at Van's all the time, her whimpering attachment to his company turning into a veritable obsession, Van mustered all his persuasive skill, charm, eloquence, and said with conspiratory undertones: "Look, my dear. This brown book is one of my most treasured possessions. I had a special pocket made for it in my school jacket. Numberless fights have been fought over it with wicked boys who wanted to steal it. What we have here" (turning the pages reverently) "is no less than a collection of the most beautiful and famous short poems in the English language. This tiny one, for example, was composed in tears forty years ago by the Poet Laureate Robert Brown, the old gentleman whom my father once pointed out to me up in the air on a cliff under a cypress, looking down on the foaming turquoise surf near Nice, an unforgettable sight for all concerned. It is called 'Peter and Margaret.' Now you have, say" (turning to Ada in solemn consultation), "forty minutes" ("Give her a full hour, she can't even memorize *Mironton, mirontaine*")—"all right, a full hour to learn these eight lines by heart. You and I" (whispering) "are going to prove to your nasty arrogant sister that stupid little Lucette can do anything. If" (lightly brushing her bobbed hair with his lips), "if, my sweet, you can recite it and confound Ada by not making one single slip—you must be careful about the 'here-there' and the 'this-that,' and every other detail—*if* you can do it then I shall give you this valuable book for keeps." ("Let her try the one about finding a feather and seeing Peacock plain," said Ada drily—"it's a bit harder.") "No, no, she and I have already chosen that little ballad. All right. Now go in here" (opening a door) "and don't come out until I call you. Otherwise, you'll forfeit the reward, and will regret the loss all your life."

"Oh, Van, how lovely of you," said Lucette, slowly entering her room, with her bemused eyes scanning the fascinating flyleaf, his name on it, his bold flourish, and his own wonderful drawings in ink—a black aster (evolved from a blot), a doric column (disguising a more ribald design), a delicate leafless tree (as seen from a classroom window), and several profiles of boys (Cheshcat, Zogdog, Fancytart, and Ada-like Van himself).

Van hastened to join Ada in the attic. At that moment he felt quite proud of his stratagem. He was to recall it with a fatidic shiver seventeen years later when Lucette, in her last note to him, mailed from Paris to his Kingston address on June 2, 1901, "just in case," wrote:

"I kept for years—it must be in my Ardis nursery—the anthology you once gave me; and the little poem you wanted me to learn by heart is still word-perfect in a safe place of my jumbled mind, with the packers trampling on my things, and upsetting crates, and voices calling: time to go, time to go. Find it in Brown and praise me again for my eight-year-old intelligence as you and happy Ada did that distant day, that day somewhere tinkling on its shelf like an empty little bottle. Now read on:

"Here, said the guide, was the field,
There, he said, was the wood.
This is where Peter kneeled,
That's where the Princess stood.

No, the visitor said,
You are the ghost, old guide.
Oats and oaks may be dead,
But she is by my side."

24

Van regretted that because Lettrocalamity (Vanvitelli's old joke!) was banned all over the world, its very name having become a "dirty word" among upper-upper-class families (in the British and Brazilian sense) to which the Veens and Durmanovs happened to belong, and had been replaced by elaborate surrogates only in those very important "utilities"—telephones, motors—what else?—well a number of gadgets for which plain folks hanker with lolling tongues, breathing faster than gundogs (for it's quite a long sentence), such trifles as tape recorders, the favorite toys of his and Ada's grandsires (Prince Zemski had one for every bed of his harem of schoolgirls) were not manufactured any more, except in Tartary where they had evolved *"minirechi"* ("talking minarets") of a secret make. Had our erudite lovers been allowed by common propriety and common law to knock into working order the mysterious box they had once discovered in their magic attic, they might have recorded (so as to replay, eight decades later) Giorgio Vanvitelli's arias as well as Van Veen's conversations with his sweetheart. Here, for example, is what they might have heard today—with amusement, embarrassment, sorrow, wonder.

(Narrator: on that summer day soon after they had entered the kissing phase of their much too premature and in many ways fatal romance, Van and Ada were on their way to the Gun Pavilion *alias* Shooting Gallery, where they had located, on its upper stage, a tiny, Oriental-style room with bleary glass cases that had once lodged pistols and daggers—judging by the shape of dark imprints on the faded velvet—a pretty and melancholy recess, rather musty, with a cushioned window seat and a stuffed Parluggian Owl on a side shelf, next to an empty beer bottle left by some dead old gardener, the year of the obsolete brand being 1842.)

"Don't jingle them," she said, "we are watched by Lucette, whom I'll strangle some day."

They walked through a grove and past a grotto.

Ada said: "Officially we are maternal cousins, and cousins can marry by special decree, *if* they promise to sterilize their first five children. But, moreover, the father-in-law of my mother was the brother of your grandfather. Right?"

"That's what I'm told," said Van serenely.

"Not sufficiently distant," she mused, "or is it?"

"Far enough, fair enough."

"Funny—I saw that verse in small violet letters before you put it into orange ones—just one second before you spoke. Spoke, smoke. Like the puff preceding a distant cannon shot.

"Physically," she continued, "we are more like twins than cousins, and twins or even siblings can't marry, of course, or will be jailed and 'altered,' if they persevere."

"Unless," said Van, "they are specially decreed cousins."

(Van was already unlocking the door—the green door against which they were to bang so often with boneless fists in their later separate dreams.)

Another time, on a bicycle ride (with several pauses) along wood trails and country roads, soon after the night of the

Burning Barn, but before they had come across the herbarium in the attic, and found confirmation of something both had forefelt in an obscure, amusing, bodily rather than moral way, Van casually mentioned he was born in Switzerland and had been abroad twice in his boyhood. She had been once, she said. Most summers she spent at Ardis; most winters in their Kaluga town home—two upper stories in the former Zemski *chertog* (palazzo).

In 1880, Van, aged ten, had traveled in silver trains with showerbaths, accompanied by his father, his father's beautiful secretary, the secretary's eighteen-year-old white-gloved sister (with a bit part as Van's English governess and milkmaid), and his chaste, angelic Russian tutor, Andrey Andreevich Aksakov ("AAA"), to gay resorts in Louisiana and Nevada. AAA explained, he remembered, to a Negro lad with whom Van had scrapped, that Pushkin and Dumas had African blood, upon which the lad showed AAA his tongue, a new interesting trick which Van emulated at the earliest occasion and was slapped by the younger of the Misses Fortune, put it back in your face, sir, she said. He also recalled hearing a cummerbunded Dutchman in the hotel hall telling another that Van's father, who had just passed whistling one of his three tunes, was a famous "camler" (camel driver—shamoes having been imported recently? No, "gambler").

Before his boarding-school days started, his father's pretty house, in Florentine style, between two vacant lots (5 Park Lane in Manhattan), had been Van's winter home (two giant guards were soon to rise on both sides of it, ready to frog-march it away), unless they journeyed abroad. Summers in Radugalet, the "other Ardis," were so much colder and duller than those here in *this*, Ada's, Ardis. Once he even spent both winter *and* summer there; it must have been in 1878.

Of course, of course, because that was the first time, Ada recalled, she had glimpsed him. In his little white sailor suit and blue sailor cap. (*Un régulier angelochek*, commented Van in the Raduga jargon.) He was eight, she was six. Uncle Dan had unexpectedly expressed the desire to revisit the old estate. At the last moment Marina had said she'd come too, despite Dan's protests, and had lifted little Ada, hopla, with her hoop, into the calèche. They took, she imagined, the train from Ladoga to Raduga, for she remembered the way the station man with the whistle around his neck went along the platform, past the coaches of the stopped local, banging shut door after door, all six doors of every carriage, each of which consisted of six one-window carrosses of pumpkin origin, fused together. It was, Van suggested, a "tower in the mist" (as she called any good recollection), and then a conductor walked on the running board of every coach with the train also running and opened doors all over again to give, punch, collect tickets, and lick his thumb, and change money, a hell of a job, but another "mauve tower." Did they hire a motor landaulet to Radugalet? Ten miles, she guessed. Ten versts, said Van. She stood corrected. He was out, he imagined, *na progulke* (promenading) in the gloomy firwood with Aksakov, his tutor, and Bagrov's grandson, a neighbor's boy, whom he teased and pinched and made horrible fun of, a nice quiet little fellow who quietly massacred moles and anything else with fur on, probably pathological. However, when they arrived, it became instantly clear that Demon had not expected ladies. He was on the terrace drinking goldwine (sweet whisky) with an orphan he had adopted, he said, a lovely Irish wild rose in whom Marina at once recognized an impudent scullery maid who had briefly worked at Ardis Hall, and had been ravished by an unknown gentleman—who was now well-known. In those days Uncle Dan wore a monocle in gay-dog copy of his cousin, and this he screwed in to view Rose, whom perhaps he had also been promised (here Van interrupted his interlocutor telling her to mind her vocabulary). The party was a disaster. The orphan languidly took off her pearl earrings for Marina's appraisal. Grandpa Bagrov hobbled in from a nap in the boudoir and mistook Marina for a *grande cocotte* as the enraged lady conjectured later when she had a chance to get at poor Dan. Instead of staying for the night, Marina stalked off and called Ada who, having been told to "play in the garden," was mumbling and numbering in raw-flesh red the white trunks of a row of young birches with Rose's purloined lipstick in the preamble to a game she now could not remember—what a pity, said Van—when her mother swept her back straight to Ardis in the same taxi leaving Dan—to his devices and vices, inserted Van—and arriving home at sunrise. But, added Ada, just before being whisked away and deprived of her crayon (tossed out by Marina *k chertyam sobach'im*, to hell's hounds—and it did remind one of Rose's terrier that had kept trying to hug Dan's leg) the charming glimpse was granted her of tiny Van, with another sweet boy, and blond-bearded, white-bloused Aksakov, walking up to the house, and, oh yes, she had forgotten her hoop—no, it was still in the taxi. But, personally, Van had not the slightest recollection of that visit or indeed of that particular summer, because his father's life, anyway, was a rose garden all the time, and he had been caressed by ungloved lovely hands more than once himself, which did not interest Ada.

Now what about 1881, when the girls, aged eight-nine and five, respectively, had been taken to the Riviera, to Switzerland, to the Italian lakes, with Marina's friend, the theatrical big shot, Gran D. du Mont (the "D" also stood for Duke, his mother's maiden name, *des hobereaux irlandais*, *quoi*), traveling discreetly on the next Mediterranean Express or next Simplon or next Orient, or whatever other *train de luxe* carried the three Veens, an English governess, a Russian nurse and two maids, while a semi-divorced Dan went to some place in equatorial Africa to photograph tigers (which he was surprised not to see) and other notorious wild animals, trained to cross the motorist's path, as well as some plump black girls in a traveling-agent's gracious home in the wilds of Mozambique. She could recollect, of course, when she and her sister played "note-comparing," much better than Lucette such things as itineraries, spectacular flora, fashions, the covered galleries with all sorts of shops, a handsome suntanned man with a black mustache who kept staring at her from his corner in the restaurant of Geneva's Manhattan Palace; but Lucette, though so much younger, remembered heaps of bagatelles, little "turrets" and little "barrels," *biryul'ki proshlago*. She was, *cette Lucette*, like the girl in *Ah, cette Line* (a popular novel), "a macédoine of intuition, stupidity, naïveté and cunning." By the way, she had confessed, Ada had *made* her confess, that it was, as Van had suspected, the other way round—that when they returned to the damsel in distress, she was in all haste, not freeing herself, but actually trying to tie herself up again after breaking loose and spying on them through the larches. "Good Lord," said Van, "that explains the angle of the soap!" Oh, what did it matter, who cared, Ada only hoped the poor little thing would be as happy at Ada's age as Ada was now, my love, my love, my love, my love. Van hoped the bicycles parked in the bushes did not show their sparkling metal through the leaves to some passenger on the forest road.

After that, they tried to settle whether their ways had merged somewhere or run closely parallel for a bit that year in Europe. In the spring of 1881, Van, aged eleven, spent a few months with his Russian tutor and English valet at his grandmother's villa near Nice, while Demon was having a much better time in Cuba than Dan was at Mocuba. In June, Van was taken to Florence, and Rome, and Capri, where his father turned up for a brief spell. They parted again, Demon sailing back to America, and Van with his tutor going first to Gardone on Lake Garda, where Aksakov reverently pointed out Goethe's and d'Annunzio's marble footprints, and then staying for a while in autumn at a hotel on a mountain slope above Leman Lake (where Karamzin and Count Tolstoy had roamed). Did Marina suspect that Van was somewhere in the same general area as she throughout 1881? Probably no. Both girls had scarlet fever in Cannes, while Marina was in Spain with her Grandee. After carefully matching memories, Van and Ada concluded that it was not impossible that somewhere along a winding Riviera road they passed each other in rented victorias that both remembered were green, with green-harnessed horses, or perhaps in two different trains, going perhaps the same way, the little girl at the window of one sleeping car looking at the brown sleeper of a parallel train which gradually diverged toward sparkling stretches of sea that the little boy could see on the other side of the tracks. The contingency was too mild to be romantic, nor did the possibility of their having walked or run past each other on the quay of a Swiss town afford any concrete thrill. But as Van casually directed the searchlight of backthought into that maze of the past where the mirror-lined narrow paths not only took different turns, but used different levels (as a mule-drawn cart passes under the arch of a viaduct along which a motor skims by), he found himself tackling, in still vague and idle fashion, the science that was to obsess his mature years—problems of space and time, space versus time, time-twisted space, space as time, time as space—and space breaking away from time, in the final tragic triumph of human cogitation: I am because I die.

"But *this*," exclaimed Ada, "is certain, this is reality, this is pure fact—this forest, this moss, your hand, the ladybird on my leg, this cannot be taken away, can it? (it will, it was). *This* has all come together *here*, no matter how the paths twisted, and fooled each other, and got fouled up: they inevitably met here!"

"We must now find our bicycles," said Van, "we are lost 'in another part of the forest.'"

"Oh, let's not return yet," she cried, "oh, wait."

"But I want to make sure of our whereabouts and whenabouts," said Van. "It is a philosophical need."

The day was darkening; a beaming vestige of sunlight lingered in a western strip of the overcast sky: we have all seen the person who after gaily greeting a friend crosses the street with that smile still fresh on his face—to be eclipsed by the stare of the stranger who might have missed the cause and mistaken the effect for the bright leer of madness. Having worked out that metaphor, Van and Ada decided it was really time to go home. As they rode through Gamlet, the sight of a Russian *traktir* gave such a prod to their hunger that they dismounted and entered the dim little tavern. A coachman drinking tea from the saucer, holding it up to his loud lips in his large claw, came straight from a pretzel-string of old novels. There was nobody else in the steamy hole save a kerchiefed woman pleading with (*ugovarivayushchaya*) a leg-dangling lad in a red shirt to get on with his fish soup. She proved to be the *traktir*-keeper and rose, "wiping her hands on her apron," to bring Ada (whom she recognized at once) and Van (whom she supposed, not incorrectly, to be the little chatelaine's "young man") some small Russian-type "hamburgers" called *bitochki*. Each devoured half a dozen of them—then they retrieved their bikes from under the jasmins to pedal on. They had to light their carbide lamps. They made a last pause before reaching the darkness of Ardis Park.

By a kind of lyrical coincidence they found Marina and Mlle Larivière having evening tea in the seldom-used Russian-style glassed-in veranda. The novelist, who was now quite restored, but still in flowery négligé, had just finished reading her new story in its first fair copy (to be typed on the morrow) to Tokay-sipping Marina, who had *le vin triste* and was much affected by the suicide of the gentleman "*au cou rouge et puissant de veuf encore plein de sève*" who, frightened by his victim's fright, so to speak, had compressed too hard the throat of the little girl he had raped in a moment of "*gloutonnerie impardonnable.*"

Van drank a glass of milk and suddenly felt such a wave of delicious exhaustion invading his limbs that he thought he'd go straight to bed. "*Tant pis,*" said Ada, reaching voraciously for the *keks* (English fruit cake). "Hammock?" she inquired; but tottering Van shook his head, and having kissed Marina's melancholy hand, retired.

"*Tant pis,*" repeated Ada, and with invincible appetite started to smear butter all over the yolk-tinted rough surface and rich incrustations—raisins, angelica, candied cherry, cedrat—of a thick slice of cake.

Mlle Larivière, who was following Ada's movements with awe and disgust, said:

"*Je rêve. Il n'est pas possible qu'on mette du beurre par-dessus toute cette pâte britannique, masse indigeste et immonde.*"

"*Et ce n'est que la première tranche,*" said Ada.

"Do you want a sprinkle of cinnamon on your *lait caillé?*"

asked Marina. "You know, Belle" (turning to Mlle Larivière), "she used to call it 'sanded snow' when she was a baby."

"She was never a baby," said Belle emphatically. "She could break the back of her pony before she could walk."

"I wonder," asked Marina, "how many miles you rode to have our athlete drained so thoroughly."

"Only seven," replied Ada with a munch smile.

25

On a sunny September morning, with the trees still green, but the asters and fleabanes already taking over in ditch and dalk, Van set out for Ladoga, N.A., to spend a fortnight there with his father and three tutors before returning to school in cold Luga, Mayne.

Van kissed Lucette on each dimple and then on the neck—and winked to prim Larivière who looked at Marina.

It was time to go. They saw him off: Marina in her *shlafrok*, Lucette petting (substitutionally) Dack, Mlle Larivière who did not know yet that Van had left behind an inscribed book she had given him on the eve, and a score of copiously tipped servants (among whom we noticed kitchen Kim with his camera)—practically the entire household, except Blanche who had the headache, and dutiful Ada who had asked to be excused, having promised to visit an infirm villager (she had a heart of gold, that child, really—as Marina so willingly, so wisely used to observe).

Van's black trunk and black suitcase, and black king-size dumbbells, were heaved into the back of the family motorcar; Bouteillan put on a captain's cap, too big for him, and grape-blue goggles; *"remouvez votre* bottom, I will drive," said Van—and the summer of 1884 was over.

"She rolls sweetly, sir," remarked Bouteillan in his quaint old-fashioned English. *"Tous les pneus sont neufs,* but, alas, there are many stones on the way, and youth drives fast. Monsieur should be prudent. The winds of the wilderness are indiscreet. *Tel un lis sauvage confiant au désert—"*

"Quite the old comedy retainer, aren't you?" remarked Van drily.

"Non, Monsieur," answered Bouteillan, holding on to his cap. *"Non. Tout simplement j'aime bien Monsieur et sa demoiselle."*

"If," said Van, "you're thinking of little Blanche, then you'd better quote Delille not to me, but to your son, who'll knock her up any day now."

The old Frenchman glanced at Van askance, *pozheval gubami* (chewed his lips), but said nothing.

"One will stop here for a few minutes," said Van, as they reached Forest Fork, just beyond Ardis. "I intend to pick some boletes for Father to whom I shall certainly (Bouteillan having sketched a courteous gesture) transmit your salute. This handbrake must have been—damn it—in use before Louis the Sixteenth migrated to England."

"It needs to be greased," said Bouteillan and consulted his watch; "yes, we have ample time to catch the 9:04."

Van plunged into the dense undergrowth. He wore a silk shirt, a velvet jacket, black breeches, riding boots with star spurs—and this attire was hardly convenient for making *klv zdB AoyvBno wkh gwzxm dqg kzwAAqvo* a *gwttp vq wjfhm* Ada in a natural bower of aspens; *xlic mujzikml,* after which she said:

"Yes—so as not to forget. Here's the formula for our correspondence. Learn this by heart and then eat it up like a good little spy."

"*Poste restante* both ways; and I want at least three letters a week, my white love."

It was the first time he had seen her in that luminous frock nearly as flimsy as a nightgown. She had braided her hair, and he said she resembled the young soprano Maria Kuznetsova in the letter scene in Tschchaikow's opera *Onegin and Olga*.

Ada, doing her feminine best to restrain and divert her sobs by transforming them into emotional exclamations, pointed out some accursed insect that had settled on an aspen trunk.

(Accursed? *Accursed?* It was the newly described, fantastically rare vanessian, *Nymphalis danaus* Nab., orange-brown, with black-and-white foretips, mimicking, as its discoverer Professor Nabonidus of Babylon College, Nebraska, realized, not the Monarch butterfly directly, but the Monarch *through* the Viceroy, one of the Monarch's best known imitators. In Ada's angry hand.)

"Tomorrow you'll come here with your green net," said Van bitterly, "my butterfly."

She kissed him all over the face, she kissed his hands, then again his lips, his eyelids, his soft black hair. He kissed her ankles, her knees, her soft black hair.

"When, my love, when again? In Luga? Kaluga? Ladoga? Where, when?"

"That's not the point," cried Van, "the point, the point, the point is—will you be faithful, will you be faithful to me?"

"You spit, love," said wan-smiling Ada, wiping off the P's and the F's. "I don't know. I adore you. I shall never love anybody in my life as I adore you, never and nowhere, neither in eternity, nor in terrenity, neither in Ladore, nor on Terra, where they say our souls go. But! But, my love, my Van, I'm physical, horribly physical, I don't know, I'm frank, *qu'y puis-je?* Oh dear, don't ask me, there's a girl in my school who is in love with me, I don't know what I'm saying—"

"The girls don't matter," said Van, "it's the fellows I'll kill if they come near you. Last night I tried to make a poem about it for you, but I can't write verse; it begins, it only begins: Ada, our ardors and arbors—but the rest is all fog, try to fancy the rest."

They embraced one last time, and without looking back he fled.

Stumbling on melons, fiercely beheading the tall arrogant fennels with his riding crop, Van returned to the Forest Fork. Morio, his favorite black horse, stood waiting for him, held by young Moore. He thanked the groom with a handful of stellas and galloped off, his gloves wet with tears.

26

For their correspondence in the first period of separation,
Van and Ada had invented a code which they kept perfect-
ing during the next fifteen months after Van left Ardis. The
entire period of that separation was to span almost four
years ("our black rainbow," Ada termed it), from September,
1884 to June, 1888, with two brief interludes of intolerable
bliss (in August, 1885 and June, 1886) and a couple of
chance meetings ("through a grille of rain"). Codes are a
bore to describe; yet a few basic details must be, reluctantly, given.

One-letter words remained undisguised. In any longer
word each letter was replaced by the one succeeding it in the
alphabet at such an ordinal point—second, third, fourth,
and so forth—which corresponded to the number of letters in
that word. Thus "love," a four-letter word, became "*pszi*"
("p" being the fourth letter after "l" in the alphabetic series,
"s" the fourth after "o," et cetera), whilst, say, "lovely" (in
which the longer stretch made it necessary, in two instances,
to resume the alphabet after exhausting it) became
"*ruBkrE,*" where the letters overflowing into the new alpha-

betic series were capitalized: B, for instance, standing for
"v" whose substitute had to be the sixth letter ("lovely" consists of six letters) coming after it: *wxyzAB*, and "y" going
still deeper into that next series: *zABCDE*. There is an awful
moment in popular books on cosmic theories (that breezily
begin with plain straightforward chatty paragraphs) when
there suddenly start to sprout mathematical formulas,
which immediately blind one's brain. We do not go as far as
that here. If the description of our lovers' code (the "our"
may constitute a source of irritation in its own right, but
never mind) with a little more attention and a little less an-
tipathy, the simplest-minded reader will, one trusts, understand that "overflowing" into the next ABC business.

Unfortunately, complications arose. Ada suggested certain
improvements, such as beginning every message in ciphered
French, then, switching to ciphered English after the first
two-letter word, switching back to French after the first
three-letter word, and reshuffling the shuttle with additional
variations. Owing to these improvements the messages became even harder to read than to write, especially as both
correspondents, in the exasperation of tender passion, inserted afterthoughts, deleted phrases, rephrased insertions
and reinstated deletions with misspellings and miscodings,
owing as much to their struggle with inexpressible distress as
to their overcomplicating its cryptogram.

In the second period of separation, beginning in 1886, the
code was radically altered. Both Van and Ada still knew by
heart the seventy-two lines of Marvell's "The Garden" and
the forty lines of Rimbaud's "Mémoire." It was from those
two texts that they chose the letters of the words they
needed. For example, l2.11. l1.2.20. l2.8 meant "love," with "l"
and the number following it denoting the line in the Marvell
poem, and the next number giving the position of the letter

in that line, l2.11, meaning "eleventh letter in second line," I hold this to be pretty clear; and when, for the sake of misleading variety, the Rimbaud poem was used, the letter denoting the line would simply be capitalized. Again, this is a nuisance to explain, and the explanation is fun to read only for the purpose (thwarted, I am afraid) of looking for errors in the examples. Anyway, it soon proved to have defects even more serious than those of the first code. Security demanded they should not possess the poems in print or script for consultation and however marvelous their power of retention was, errors were bound to increase.

They wrote to each other in the course of 1886 as often as before, never less than a letter per week; but, curiously enough, in their third period of separation, from January, 1887, to June, 1888 (after a very long long-distance call and a very brief meeting), their letters grew scarcer, dwindling to a mere twenty in Ada's case (with only two or three in the spring of 1888) and about twice as many coming from Van. No passages from the correspondence can be given here, since all the letters were destroyed in 1889.

(I suggest omitting this little chapter altogether. Ada's note.)

27

"Marina gives me a glowing account of you and says *uzhe chuvstvuetsya osen'*. Which is very Russian. Your grandmother would repeat regularly that 'already-is-to-be-felt-autumn' remark every year, at the same time, even on the hottest day of the season at Villa Armina: Marina never realized it was an anagram of the sea, not of her. You look splendid, *sïnok moy*, but I can well imagine how fed up you must be with her two little girls. Therefore, I have a suggestion—"

"Oh, I liked them enormously," purred Van. "Especially dear little Lucette."

"My suggestion is, come with me to a cocktail party today. It is given by the excellent widow of an obscure Major de Prey—obscurely related to our late neighbor, a fine shot but the light was bad on the Common, and a meddlesome garbage collector hollered at the wrong moment. Well, that excellent and influential lady who wishes to help a friend of mine" (clearing his throat) "has, I'm told, a daughter of fifteen summers, called Cordula, who is sure to recompense you for playing Blindman's Buff all summer with the babes of Ardis Wood."

"We played mostly Scrabble and Snap," said Van. "Is the needy friend also in my age group?"

"She's a budding Duse," replied Demon austerely, "and the party is strictly a 'prof push.' You'll stick to Cordula de Prey, I, to Cordelia O'Leary."

"D'accord," said Van.

Cordula's mother, an overripe, overdressed, overpraised comedy actress, introduced Van to a Turkish acrobat with tawny hairs on his beautiful orang-utan hands and the fiery eyes of a charlatan—which he was not, being a great artist in his circular field. Van was so taken up by his talk, by the training tips he lavished on the eager boy, and by envy, ambition, respect and other youthful emotions, that he had little time for Cordula, round-faced, small, dumpy, in a turtle-neck sweater of dark-red wool, or even for the stunning young lady on whose bare back the paternal hand kept resting lightly as Demon steered her toward this or that useful guest. But that very same evening Van ran into Cordula in a bookshop and she said, "By the way, Van—I can call you that, can't I? Your cousin Ada is my schoolmate. Oh, yes. Now, explain, please, what did you do to our difficult Ada? In her very first letter from Ardis, she positively gushed—our Ada gushed!—about how sweet, clever, unusual, irresistible—"

"Silly girl. When was that?"

"In June, I imagine. She wrote again later, but her reply—because I was quite jealous of you—really I was!—and had fired back lots of questions—well, her reply was evasive, and practically void of Van."

He looked her over more closely than he had done before. He had read somewhere (we might recall the precise title if we tried, not Tiltil, that's in Blue Beard . . .) that a man can recognize a Lesbian, young and alone (because a tailored old pair can fool no one), by a combination of three characteristics: slightly trembling hands, a cold-in-the-head voice, and that skidding-in-panic of the eyes if you happen to scan with obvious appraisal such charms as the occasion might force her to show (lovely shoulders, for instance). Nothing whatever of all that (yes—*Mytilène, petite isle,* by Louis Pierre) seemed to apply to Cordula, who wore a "garbotosh" (belted mackintosh) over her terribly unsmart turtle and held both hands deep in her pockets as she challenged his stare. Her bobbed hair was of a neutral shade between dry straw and damp. Her light blue iris could be matched by millions of similar eyes in pigment-poor families of French Estoty. Her mouth was doll-pretty when consciously closed in a mannered pout so as to bring out what portraitists call the two "sickle folds" which, at their best, are oblong dimples and, at their worst, the creases down the well-chilled cheeks of felt-booted apple-cart girls. When her lips parted, as they did now, they revealed braced teeth, which, however, she quickly remembered to shutter.

"My cousin Ada," said Van, "is a little girl of eleven or twelve, and much too young to fall in love with anybody, except people in books. Yes, I too found her sweet. A trifle on the blue-stocking side, perhaps, and, at the same time, impudent and capricious—but, yes, sweet."

"I wonder," murmured Cordula, with such a nice nuance of pensive tone that Van could not tell whether she meant to close the subject, or leave it ajar, or open a new one.

"How could I get in touch with you?" he asked. "Would you come to Riverlane? Are you a virgin?"

"I don't date hoodlums," she replied calmly, "but you can always 'contact' me through Ada. We are not in the same class, in more ways than one" (laughing); "she's a little genius, I'm a plain American ambivert, but we are enrolled in the same Advanced French group, and the Advanced French group is assigned the same dormitory so that a dozen blondes, three brunettes and one redhead, la Rousse, can whisper French in their sleep" (laughing alone).

"What fun. Okay, thanks. The even number means bunks, I guess. Well, I'll be seeing you, as the hoods say."

In his next coded letter to Ada Van inquired if Cordula might not be the *lezbianochka* mentioned by Ada with such unnecessary guilt. I would as soon be jealous of your own little hand. Ada replied, "What rot, leave what's-her-name out of it"; but even though Van did not know yet how fiercely untruthful Ada could be when shielding an accomplice, Van remained unconvinced.

The rules of her school were old-fashioned and strict to the point of lunacy, but they reminded Marina nostalgically of the Russian Institute for Noble Maidens in Yukonsk (where she had kept breaking them with much more ease and success than Ada or Cordula or Grace could at Brownhill). Girls were allowed to see boys at hideous teas with pink cakes in the headmistress's Reception Room three or four times per term, and any girl of twelve or thirteen could meet a gentleman's son in a certified milk-bar, just a few blocks away, every third Sunday, in the company of an older girl of irreproachable morals.

Van braced himself to see Ada thus, hoping to use his magic wand for transforming whatever young spinster came along into a spoon or a turnip. Those "dates" had to be approved by the victim's mother at least a fortnight in advance. Soft-toned Miss Cleft, the headmistress, rang up Marina who told her that Ada could not possibly need a chaperone to go out with a cousin who had been her sole companion on daylong rambles throughout the summer. "That's exactly it,"

Cleft rejoined, "two young ramblers are exceptionally prone to intertwine, and a thorn is always close to a bud."

"But they are practically brother and sister," ejaculated Marina, thinking as many stupid people do that "practically" works both ways—reducing the truth of a statement and making a truism sound like the truth. "Which only increases the peril," said soft Cleft. "Anyway, I'll compromise, and tell dear Cordula de Prey to make a third: she admires Ivan and adores Ada—consequently can only add zest to the zipper" (stale slang—stale even then).

"Gracious, what *figli-migli*" (mimsey-fimsey), said Marina, after having hung up.

In a dark mood, unwarned of what to expect (strategic foreknowledge might have helped to face the ordeal), Van waited for Ada in the school lane, a dismal back alley with puddles reflecting a sullen sky and the fence of the hockey ground. A local high-school boy, "dressed to kill," stood near the gate, a little way off, a fellow waiter.

Van was about to march back to the station when Ada appeared—with Cordula. *La bonne surprise!* Van greeted them with a show of horrible heartiness ("And how goes it with you, sweet cousin? Ah, Cordula! Who's the chaperone, you, or Miss Veen?"). The sweet cousin sported a shiny black raincoat and a down-brimmed oilcloth hat as if somebody was to be salvaged from the perils of life or sea. A tiny round patch did not quite hide a pimple on one side of her chin. Her breath smelled of ether. Her mood was even blacker than his. He cheerily guessed it would rain. It did—hard. Cordula remarked that his trench coat was chic. She did not think it worth while to go back for umbrellas—their delicious goal was just round the corner. Van said corners were never round, a tolerable quip. Cordula laughed. Ada did not: there were no survivors, apparently.

The milk-bar proved to be so crowded that they decided to walk under The Arcades toward the railway station café. He knew (but could do nothing about it) that all night he would regret having deliberately overlooked the fact—the main, agonizing fact—that he had not seen his Ada for close to three months and that in her last note such passion had burned that the cryptogram's bubble had burst in her poor little message of promise and hope, baring a defiant, divine line of uncoded love. They were behaving now as if they had never met before, as if this was but a blind date arranged by their chaperone. Strange, malevolent thoughts revolved in his mind. What exactly—not that it mattered but one's pride and curiosity were at stake—what exactly had they been up to, those two ill-groomed girls, last term, this term, last night, every night, in their pajama-tops, amid the murmurs and moans of their abnormal dormitory? Should he ask? Could he find the right words: not to hurt Ada, while making her bed-filly know he despised her for kindling a child, so dark-haired and pale, coal and coral, leggy and limp, whimpering at the melting peak? A moment ago when he had seen them advancing together, plain Ada, seasick but doing her duty, and Cordula, apple-cankered but brave, like two shackled prisoners being led into the conqueror's presence, Van had promised himself to revenge deceit by relating in polite but minute detail the latest homosexual or rather pseudo-homosexual row at his school (an upper-form boy, Cordula's cousin, had been caught with a lass disguised as a lad in the rooms of an eclectic prefect). He would watch the girls flinch, he would demand some story from them to match his. That urge had waned. He still hoped to get rid for a moment of dull Cordula and find something cruel to make dull Ada dissolve in bright tears. But that was prompted by his *amour-propre*, not by their *sale amour*. He would die with an old pun on his lips. And why "dirty"? Did he feel any Proustian pangs? None. On the contrary: a private picture of their fondling each other kept pricking him with perverse gratification. Before his inner bloodshot eye Ada was duplicated and enriched, twinned by entwinement, giving what he gave, taking what he took: Corada, Adula. It struck him that the dumpy little Countess resembled his first whorelet, and that sharpened the itch.

They talked about their studies and teachers, and Van said:

"I would like your opinion, Ada, and yours, Cordula, on the following literary problem. Our professor of French literature maintains that there is a grave philosophical, and hence artistic, flaw in the entire treatment of the Marcel and Albertine affair. It makes sense if the reader *knows* that the narrator is a pansy, and that the good fat cheeks of Albertine are the good fat buttocks of Albert. It makes none if the reader cannot be supposed, and should not be required, to know *anything* about this or any other author's sexual habits in order to enjoy to the last drop a work of art. My teacher contends that if the reader knows nothing about Proust's perversion, the detailed description of a heterosexual male jealously watchful of a homosexual female is preposterous because a normal man would be only amused, tickled pink in fact, by his girl's frolics with a female partner. The professor concludes that a novel which can be appreciated only by *quelque petite blanchisseuse* who has examined the author's dirty linen is, artistically, a failure."

"Ada, what on earth is he talking about? Some Italian film he has seen?"

"Van," said Ada in a tired voice, "you do not realize that the Advanced French Group at my school has advanced no farther than to Racan and Racine."

"Forget it," said Van.

"But *you*'ve had too much Marcel," muttered Ada.

The railway station had a semi-private tearoom supervised by the stationmaster's wife under the school's idiotic auspices. It was empty, save for a slender lady in black velvet, wearing a beautiful black velvet picture hat, who sat with her back to them at a "tonic bar" and never once turned her head, but the thought brushed him that she was a cocotte from Toulouse. Our damp trio found a nice corner table and with sighs of banal relief undid their raincoats. He hoped Ada would discard her heavy-seas hat but she did not, because she had cut her hair because of dreadful migraines, because she did not want him to see her in the rôle of a moribund Romeo.

(On fait *son grand Joyce* after doing one's *petit Proust*. In Ada's lovely hand.)

(But read on; it is pure V.V. Note that lady! In Van's bed-buvard scrawl.)

As Ada reached for the cream, he caught and inspected her dead-shamming hand. We remember the Camberwell Beauty that lay tightly closed for an instant upon our palm, and suddenly our hand was empty. He saw, with satisfaction, that her fingernails were now long and sharp.

"Not too sharp, are they, my dear," he asked for the benefit of *dura* Cordula, who should have gone to the "powder room"—a forlorn hope.

"Why, no," said Ada.

"You don't," he went on, unable to stop, "you don't scratch little people when you stroke little people? Look at your little girl friend's hand" (taking it), "look at those dainty short nails (cold innocent, docile little paw!). *She* could not catch them in the fanciest satin, oh, no, could you, Ardula—I mean, Cordula?"

Both girls giggled, and Cordula kissed Ada's cheek. Van hardly knew what reaction he had expected, but found that simple kiss disarming and disappointing. The sound of the rain was lost in a growing rumble of wheels. He glanced at his watch; glanced up at the clock on the wall. He said he was sorry—that was his train.

"Not at all," wrote Ada (paraphrased here) in reply to his abject apologies, "we just thought you were drunk; but I'll never invite you to Brownhill again, my love."

28

The year 1880 (Aqua was still alive—somehow, somewhere!) was to prove to be the most retentive and talented one in his long, too long, never too long life. He was ten. His father had lingered in the West where the many-colored mountains acted upon Van as they had on all young Russians of genius. He could solve an Euler-type problem or learn by heart Pushkin's "Headless Horseman" poem in less than twenty minutes. With white-bloused, enthusiastically sweating Andrey Andreevich, he lolled for hours in the violet shade of pink cliffs, studying major and minor Russian writers—and puzzling out the exaggerated but, on the whole, complimentary allusions to his father's volitations and loves in another life in Lermontov's diamond-faceted tetrameters. He struggled to keep back his tears, while AAA blew his fat red nose, when shown the peasant-bare footprint of Tolstoy preserved in the clay of a motor court in Utah where he had written the tale of Murat, the Navajo chieftain, a French general's bastard, shot by Cora Day in his swimming pool. What a soprano Cora had been! Demon took Van to the world-famous Opera House in Telluride in West Colorado and there he enjoyed (and sometimes detested) the greatest international shows—English blank-verse plays, French tragedies in rhymed couplets, thunderous German musical dramas with giants and magicians and a defecating white horse. He passed through various little passions—parlor magic, chess, fluff-weight boxing matches at fairs, stunt-riding—and of course those unforgettable, much too early initiations when his lovely young English governess expertly petted him between milkshake and bed, she, petticoated, petititted, half-dressed for some party with her sister and Demon and Demon's casino-touring companion, bodyguard and guardian angel, monitor and adviser, Mr. Plunkett, a reformed card-sharper.

Mr. Plunkett had been, in the summer of his adventurous years, one of the greatest *shuler*'s, politely called "gaming conjurers," both in England and America. At forty, in the middle of a draw-poker session he had been betrayed by a fainting fit of cardiac origin (which allowed, alas, a bad loser's dirty hands to go through his pockets), had spent several years in prison, had become reconverted to the Roman faith of his forefathers and, upon completing his term, had dabbled in missionary work, written a handbook on conjuring, conducted bridge columns in various papers and done some sleuthing for the police (he had two stalwart sons in the force). The outrageous ravages of time and some surgical tampering with his rugged features had made his gray face not more attractive but at least unrecognizable to all but a few old cronies, who now shunned his chilling company, anyway. To Van he was even more fascinating than King Wing. Gruff but kindly Mr. Plunkett could not resist exploiting that fascination (we all like to be liked) by introducing Van to the tricks of an art now become pure and abstract, and therefore genuine. Mr. Plunkett considered the use of all mechanical media, mirrors and vulgar "sleeve rakes" as leading inevitably to exposure, just as jellies, muslin, rubber hands and so on sully and shorten a professional medium's career. He taught Van what to look for when suspecting the cheater with bright objects around him ("Xmas tree" or "twinkler," as those amateurs, some of them respectable clubmen, are called by professionals). Mr. Plunkett believed only in sleight-of-hand; secret pockets were useful (but could be turned inside out and against you). Most essential was the "feel" of a card, the delicacy of its palming, and digitation, the false shuffle, deck-sweeping, pack-roofing, prefabrication of deals, and above all a finger agility that practice could metamorphose into veritable vanishing acts or, conversely, into the materialization of a joker or the transformation of two pairs into four kings. One absolute requisite, if using privately an additional deck, was memorizing discards when hands were not prearranged. For a couple of months Van practiced card tricks, then turned to other recreations. He was an apprentice who learned fast, and kept his labeled phials in a cool place.

In 1885, having completed his prep-school education, he went up to Chose University in England, where his fathers had gone, and traveled from time to time to London or Lute (as prosperous but not overrefined British colonials called that lovely pearl-gray sad city on the other side of the Channel).

Sometime during the winter of 1886–7, at dismally cold Chose, in the course of a poker game with two Frenchmen and a fellow student whom we shall call Dick, in the latter's smartly furnished rooms in Serenity Court, he noticed that the French twins were losing not only because they were happily and hopelessly tight, but also because *milord* was that "crystal cretin" of Plunkett's vocabulary, a man of many mirrors—small reflecting surfaces variously angled and shaped, glinting discreetly on watch or signet ring, dissimulated like female fireflies in the undergrowth, on table legs, inside cuff or lapel, and on the edges of ashtrays, whose position on adjacent supports Dick kept shifting with a negligent air—all of which, as any cardsharper might tell you, was as dumb as it was redundant.

Having bided his time, and lost several thousands, Van decided to put some old lessons into practice. There was a pause in the game. Dick got up and went to a speaking-tube in the corner to order more wine. The unfortunate twins were passing to each other a fountain pen, thumb-pressing and re-pressing it in disastrous transit as they calculated their losses, which exceeded Van's. Van slipped a pack of cards into his pocket and stood up rolling the stiffness out of his mighty shoulders.

"I say, Dick, ever met a gambler in the States called Plunkett? Bald gray chap when I knew him."

"Plunkett? Plunkett? Must have been before my time. Was he the one who turned priest or something? Why?"

"One of my father's pals. Great artist."

"Artist?"

"Yes, artist. I'm an artist. I suppose *you* think you're an artist. Many people do."

"What on earth is an artist?"

"An underground observatory," replied Van promptly.

"That's out of some modern novel," said Dick, discarding his cigarette after a few avid inhales.

"That's out of Van Veen," said Van Veen.

Dick strolled back to the table. His man came in with the wine. Van retired to the W.C. and started to "doctor the deck," as old Plunkett used to call the process. He remembered that the last time he had made card magic was when showing some tricks to Demon—who disapproved of their poker slant. Oh, yes, and when putting at ease the mad conjurer at the ward whose pet obsession was that gravity had something to do with the blood circulation of a Supreme Being.

Van felt pretty sure of his skill—and of *milord*'s stupidity —but doubted he could keep it up for any length of time. He was sorry for Dick, who, apart from being an amateur rogue, was an amiable indolent fellow, with a pasty face and a flabby body—you could knock him down with a feather, and he frankly admitted that if his people kept refusing to pay his (huge and trite) debts, he would have to move to Australia to make new ones there and forge a few checks on the way.

He now *constatait avec plaisir*, as he told his victims, that only a few hundred pounds separated him from the shoreline of the minimal sum he needed to appease his most ruthless creditor, whereupon he went on fleecing poor Jean and Jacques with reckless haste, and then found himself with three honest aces (dealt to him lovingly by Van) against Van's nimbly mustered four nines. This was followed by a good bluff against a better one; and with Van's generously slipping the desperately flashing and twinkling young lord good but not good enough hands, the latter's martyrdom came to a sudden end (London tailors wringing their hands in the fog, and a moneylender, the famous St. Priest of Chose, asking for an appointment with Dick's father). After the heaviest betting Van had yet seen, Jacques showed a forlorn *couleur* (as he called it in a dying man's whisper) and Dick surrendered with a straight flush to his tormentor's royal one. Van, who up to then had had no trouble whatever in concealing his delicate maneuvers from Dick's silly lens, now had the pleasure of seeing him glimpse the second joker

[187]

palmed in his, Van's, hand as he swept up and clasped to his bosom the "rainbow ivory"—Plunkett was full of poetry. The twins put on their ties and coats and said they had to quit.

"Same here, Dick," said Van. "Pity you had to rely on your crystal balls. I have often wondered why the Russian for it—I think we have a Russian ancestor in common—is the same as the German for 'schoolboy,' minus the umlaut" —and while prattling thus, Van refunded with a rapidly written check the ecstatically astonished Frenchmen. Then he collected a handful of cards and chips and hurled them into Dick's face. The missiles were still in flight when he regretted that cruel and commonplace bewgest, for the wretched fellow could not respond in any conceivable fashion, and just sat there covering one eye and examining his damaged spectacles with the other—it was also bleeding a little—while the French twins were pressing upon him two handkerchiefs which he kept good-naturedly pushing away. Rosy aurora was shivering in green Serenity Court. Laborious old Chose.

(There should be a sign denoting applause. Ada's note.)

Van fumed and fretted the rest of the morning, and after a long soak in a hot bath (the best adviser, and prompter and inspirer in the world, except, of course, the W.C. seat) decided to pen—pen is the word—a note of apology to the cheated cheater. As he was dressing, a messenger brought him a note from Lord C. (he was a cousin of one of Van's Riverlane schoolmates), in which generous Dick proposed to substitute for his debt an introduction to the Venus Villa Club to which his whole clan belonged. Such a bounty no boy of eighteen could hope to obtain. It was a ticket to paradise. Van tussled with his slightly overweight conscience (both grinning like old pals in their old gymnasium)—and accepted Dick's offer.

(I think, Van, you should make it clearer why you, Van, the proudest and cleanest of men—I'm not speaking of abject physicalities, we are all organized that way—but why you, pure Van, could accept the offer of a rogue who no doubt continued to "flash and twinkle" after that fiasco. I think you should explain, *primo*, that you were dreadfully overworked, and *secundo*, that you could not bear the thought that the rogue knew, that he being a rogue, you could not call him out, and were safe, so to speak. Right? Van, do you hear me? I think—.)

He did not "twinkle" long after that. Five or six years later, in Monte Carlo, Van was passing by an open-air café when a hand grabbed him by the elbow, and a radiant, ruddy, comparatively respectable Dick C. leaned toward him over the petunias of the latticed balustrade:

"Van," he cried, "I've given up all that looking-glass dung, congratulate me! Listen: the only safe way is to mark 'em! Wait, that's not all, can you imagine, they've invented a microscopic—and I mean microscopic—point of euphorion, a precious metal, to insert under your thumbnail, you can't see it with the naked eye, but one minuscule section of your monocle is made to magnify the mark you make with it, like killing a flea, on one card after another, as they come along in the game, that's the beauty of it, no preparations, no props, nothing! Mark 'em! Mark 'em!" good Dick was still shouting, as Van walked away.

29

In mid-July, 1886, while Van was winning the table-tennis tournament on board a "luxury" liner (that now took a whole week to reach in white dignity Manhattan from Dover!), Marina, both her daughters, their governess, and two maids were shivering in more or less simultaneous stages of Russian *influentsa* at various stops on their way by train from Los Angeles to Ladore. A hydrogram from Chicago awaiting Van at his father's house on July 21 (her dear birthday!) said: "dadaist impatient patient arriving between twenty-fourth and seventh call doris can meet regards vicinity."

"Which reminds me painfully of the *golubyanki* (*petits bleus*) Aqua used to send me," remarked Demon with a sigh (having mechanically opened the message). "Is tender Vicinity some girl I know? Because you may glare as much as you like, but this is *not* a wire from doctor to doctor."

Van raised his eyes to the Boucher plafond of the breakfast room and, shaking his head in derisive admiration, commented on Demon's acumen. Yes, that was right. He had to travel incontinently to Garders (anagram of "regards," see?) to a hamlet the opposite way from Letham (see?) to see a mad girl artist called Doris or Odris who drew only gee-gees and sugar daddies.

Van rented a room under a false name (Boucher) at the only inn of Malahar, a miserable village on Ladore River, some twenty miles from Ardis. He spent the night fighting the celebrated mosquito, or its *cousin*, that liked him more than the Ardis beast had. The toilet on the landing was a black hole, with the traces of a fecal explosion, between a squatter's two giant soles. At 7 A.M. on July 25 he called Ardis Hall from the Malahar post office and got connected with Bout who was connected with Blanche and mistook Van's voice for the butler's.

"Dammit, Pa," he said into his bedside dorophone, "I'm busy!"

"I want Blanche, you idiot," growled Van.

"*Oh, pardon,*" cried Bout, "*un moment, Monsieur.*"

A bottle was audibly uncorked (drinking hock at seven in the morning!) and Blanche took over, but scarcely had Van begun to deliver a carefully worded message to be transmitted to Ada, when Ada herself who had been on the *qui vive* all night answered from the nursery, where the clearest instrument in the house quivered and bubbled under a dead barometer.

"Forest Fork in Forty-Five minutes. Sorry to spit."

"Tower!" replied her sweet ringing voice, as an airman in heaven blue might say "Roger."

He rented a motorcycle, a venerable machine, with a saddle upholstered in billiard cloth and pretentious false mother-of-pearl handlebars, and drove, bouncing on tree roots along a narrow "forest ride." The first thing he saw was the star gleam of her dismissed bike: she stood by it, arms akimbo, the black-haired white angel, looking away in a daze of shyness, wearing a terrycloth robe and bedroom slippers. As he carried her into the nearest thicket he felt the fever of her body, but only realized how ill she was when after two passionate spasms she got up full of tiny brown ants and tottered, and almost collasped, muttering about gipsies stealing their jeeps.

It was a beastly, but beautiful, tryst. He could not remember—

(That's right, I can't either. Ada.)

—one word they said, one question, one answer; he rushed her back as close to the house as he dared (having kicked her bike into the bracken)—and that evening when he rang up Blanche, she dramatically whispered that *Mademoiselle* had *une belle pneumonie, mon pauvre Monsieur.*

Ada was much better three days later, but he had to return to Man to catch the same boat back to England—and join a circus tour which involved people he could not let down.

His father saw him off. Demon had dyed his hair a blacker black. He wore a diamond ring blazing like a Caucasian ridge. His long, black, blue-ocellated wings trailed and quivered in the ocean breeze. *Lyudi oglyadivalis'* (people turned to look). A temporary Tamara, all kohl, kasbek rouge, and flamingo-boa, could not decide what would please her daemon lover more—just moaning and ignoring his handsome son or acknowledging bluebeard's virility as reflected in morose Van, who could not stand her Caucasian perfume, Granial Maza, seven dollars a bottle.

(You know, that's my favorite chapter up to now, Van, I don't know why, but I love it. And you can keep your Blanche in her young man's embrace, even that does not matter. In Ada's fondest hand.)

30

On February 5, 1887, an unsigned editorial in *The Ranter*
(the usually so sarcastic and captious Chose weekly) described Mascodagama's performance as "the most imagina-
tive and singular stunt ever offered to a jaded music-hall
public." It was repeated at the Rantariver Club several
times, but nothing in the programme or in publicity notices
beyond the definition "Foreign eccentric" gave any indica-
tion either of the exact nature of the "stunt" or of the performer's identity. Rumors, carefully and cleverly circulated
by Mascodagama's friends, diverted speculations toward his
being a mysterious visitor from beyond the Golden Curtain,
particularly since at least half-a-dozen members of a large
Good-will Circus Company that had come from Tartary
just then (i.e., on the eve of the Crimean War)—three dancing girls, a sick old clown with his old speaking goat, and
one of the dancers' husbands, a make-up man (no doubt, a
multiple agent)—had already defected between France and
England, somewhere in the newly constructed "Chunnel."
Mascodagama's spectacular success in a theatrical club that
habitually limited itself to Elizabethan plays, with queens

and fairies played by pretty boys, made first of all a great impact on cartoonists. Deans, local politicians, national statesmen, and of course the current ruler of the Golden Horde were pictured as mascodagamas by topical humorists. A grotesque imitator (who was really Mascodagama himself in an oversophisticated parody of his own act!) was booed at Oxford (a women's college nearby) by local rowdies. A shrewd reporter, who had heard him curse a crease in the stage carpet, commented in print on his "Yankee twang." Dear Mr. "Vascodagama" received an invitation to Windsor Castle from its owner, a bilateral descendant of Van's own ancestors, but he declined it, suspecting (incorrectly, as it later transpired) the misprint to suggest that his incognito had been divulged by one of the special detectives at Chose—the same, perhaps, who had recently saved the psychiatrist P. O. Tyomkin from the dagger of Prince Potyomkin, a mixed-up kid from Sebastopol, Id.

During his first summer vacation, Van worked under Tyomkin, at the Chose famous clinic, on an ambitious dissertation he never completed, "Terra: Eremitic Reality or Collective Dream?" He interviewed numerous neurotics, among whom there were variety artists, and literary men, and at least three intellectually lucid, but spiritually "lost," cosmologists who either were in telepathic collusion (they had never met and did not even know of one another's existence) or had discovered, none knew how or where, by means, maybe, of forbidden "ondulas" of some kind, a green world rotating in space and spiraling in time, which in terms of matter-and-mind was like ours and which they described in the same specific details as three people watching from three separate windows would a carnival show in the same street.

He spent his free time in gross dissipation.

Sometime in August he was offered a contract for a series

of matinées and nights in a famous London theater during the Christmas vacation and on weekends throughout the winter season. He accepted gladly, being badly in need of a strict distraction from his perilous studies: the special sort of obsession under which Tyomkin's patients labored had something about it that made it liable to infect its younger investigators.

Mascodagama's fame reached inevitably the backwoods of America: a photograph of him, masked, it is true, but unable to mislead a fond relative or faithful retainer, was reproduced by the Ladore, Ladoga, Laguna, Lugano and Luga papers in the first week of 1888; but the accompanying reportage was not. The work of a poet, and only a poet ("especially of the Black Belfry group," as some wit said), could have adequately described a certain macabre quiver that marked Van's extraordinary act.

The stage would be empty when the curtain went up; then, after five heartbeats of theatrical suspense, something swept out of the wings, enormous and black, to the accompaniment of dervish drums. The shock of his powerful and precipitous entry affected so deeply the children in the audience that for a long time later, in the dark of sobbing insomnias, in the glare of violent nightmares, nervous little boys and girls relived, with private accretions, something similar to the "primordial qualm," a shapeless nastiness, the swoosh of nameless wings, the unendurable dilation of fever which came in a cavern draft from the uncanny stage. Into the harsh light of its gaudily carpeted space a masked giant, fully eight feet tall, erupted, running strongly in the kind of soft boots worn by Cossack dancers. A voluminous, black shaggy cloak of the *burka* type enveloped his *silhouette inquiétante* (according to a female Sorbonne correspondent—we've kept all those cuttings) from neck to knee or what appeared to be those sections of his body. A Karakul cap surmounted his top. A black mask covered the upper part of his heavily bearded face. The unpleasant colossus kept strutting up and down the stage for a while, then the strut changed to the restless walk of a caged madman, then he whirled, and to a clash of cymbals in the orchestra and a cry of terror (perhaps faked) in the gallery, Mascodagama turned over in the air and stood on his head.

In this weird position, with his cap acting as a pseudopodal pad, he jumped up and down, pogo-stick fashion—and suddenly came apart. Van's face, shining with sweat, grinned between the legs of the boots that still shod his rigidly raised arms. Simultaneously his real feet kicked off and away the false head with its crumpled cap and bearded mask. The magical reversal "made the house gasp." Frantic ("deafening," "delirious," "a veritable tempest of") applause followed the gasp. He bounded offstage—and next moment was back, now sheathed in black tights, dancing a jig on his hands.

We devote so much space to the description of his act not only because variety artists of the "eccentric" race are apt to be forgotten especially soon, but also because one wishes to analyze its thrill. Neither a miraculous catch on the cricket field, nor a glorious goal slammed in at soccer (he was a College Blue in both those splendid games), nor earlier physical successes, such as his knocking out the biggest bully on his first day at Riverlane School, had ever given Van the satisfaction Mascodagama experienced. It was not directly related to the warm breath of fulfilled ambition, although as a very old man, looking back at a life of unrecognized endeavor, Van did welcome with amused delight—more delight than he had actually felt at the time—the banal acclaim and the vulgar envy that swirled around him for a short while in his youth.

The essence of the satisfaction belonged rather to the same order as the one he later derived from self-imposed, extravagantly difficult, seemingly absurd tasks when V.V. sought to express something, which *until* expressed had only a twilight being (or even none at all—nothing but the illusion of the backward shadow of its imminent expression). It was Ada's castle of cards. It was the standing of a metaphor on its head not for the sake of the trick's difficulty, but in order to perceive an ascending waterfall or a sunrise in reverse: a triumph, in a sense, over the ardis of time. Thus the rapture young Mascodagama derived from overcoming gravity was akin to that of artistic revelation in the sense utterly and naturally unknown to the innocents of critical appraisal, the social-scene commentators, the moralists, the idea-mongers and so forth. Van on the stage was performing organically what his figures of speech were to perform later in life— acrobatic wonders that had never been expected from them and which frightened children.

Neither was the sheer physical pleasure of maniambulation a negligible factor, and the peacock blotches with which the carpet stained the palms of his hands during his gloveless dance routine seemed to be the reflections of a richly colored nether world that he had been the first to discover. For the tango, which completed his number on his last tour, he was given a partner, a Crimean cabaret dancer in a very short scintillating frock cut very low on the back. She sang the tango tune in Russian:

> *Pod znóynïm nébom Argentínï,*
> *Pod strástnïy góvor mandolínï*

> 'Neath sultry sky of Argentina,
> To the hot hum of mandolina

Fragile, red-haired "Rita" (he never learned her real name), a pretty Karaite from Chufut Kale, where, she nostalgically said, the Crimean cornel, *kizil'*, bloomed yellow among the arid rocks, bore an odd resemblance to Lucette as she was to look ten years later. During their dance, all Van saw of her were her silver slippers turning and marching nimbly in rhythm with the soles of his hands. He recouped himself at rehearsals, and one night asked her for an assignation. She indignantly refused, saying she adored her husband (the make-up fellow) and loathed England.

Chose had long been as famous for the dignity of its regulations, as for the brilliancy of its pranksters. Mascodagama's identity could not escape the interest and then the knowledge of the authorities. His college tutor, a decrepit and dour homosexual, with no sense of humor whatever and an innate respect for all the conventions of academic life, pointed out to a highly irritated and barely polite Van that in his second year at Chose he was not supposed to combine his university studies with the circus, and that if he insisted on becoming a variety artist he would be sent down. The old gentleman also wrote a letter to Demon asking him to make his son forget Physical Stunts for the sake of Philosophy and Psychiatry, especially since Van was the first American to have won (at seventeen!) the Dudley Prize (for an essay on Insanity and Eternal Life). Van was not quite sure yet what compromise pride and prudence might arrive at, when he left for America early in June, 1888.

31

Van revisited Ardis Hall in 1888. He arrived on a cloudy June afternoon, unexpected, unbidden, unneeded; with a diamond necklace coiled loose in his pocket. As he approached from a side lawn, he saw a scene out of some new life being rehearsed for an unknown picture, without him, not for him. A big party seemed to be breaking up. Three young ladies in yellow-blue Vass frocks with fashionable rainbow sashes surrounded a stoutish, foppish, baldish young man who stood, a flute of champagne in his hand, glancing down from the drawing-room terrace at a girl in black with bare arms: an old runabout, shivering at every jerk, was being cranked up by a hoary chauffeur in front of the porch, and those bare arms, stretched wide, were holding outspread the white cape of Baroness von Skull, a grand-aunt of hers. Against the white cape Ada's new long figure was profiled in black—the black of her smart silk dress with no sleeves, no ornaments, no memories. The slow old Baroness stood groping for something under one armpit, under the other—for what? a crutch? the dangling end of tangled bangles?—and as she half-turned to accept the cloak (now taken from her grandniece by a belated new footman) Ada also half-turned, and her yet un-gemmed neck showed white as she ran up the porch steps.

Van followed her inside, in between the hall columns, and through a group of guests, toward a distant table with crystal jugs of cherry *ambrozia*. She wore, unmodishly, no stockings; her calves were strong and pale, and (I have a note here, for the ghost of a novel) "the low cut of her black dress allowed the establishment of a sharp contrast between the familiar mat whiteness of her skin and the brutal black horse-tail of her new hair-do."

Excluding each other, private swoons split him in two: the devastating certainty that as soon as he reached, in the laby-rinth of a nightmare, a brightly remembered small room with a bed and a child's washstand, she would join him there in her new smooth long beauty; and, on the shade side, the pang and panic of finding her changed, hating what he wanted, condemning it as wrong, explaining to him dreadful new cir-cumstances—that they both were dead or existed only as ex-tras in a house rented for a motion picture.

But hands offering him wine or almonds or their open selves, impeded his dream quest. He pressed on, notwith-standing the swoops of recognition: Uncle Dan pointed him out with a cry to a stranger who feigned amazement at the singularity of the optical trick—and, next moment, a re-painted, red-wigged, very drunk and tearful Marina was gluing cherry-vodka lips to his jaw and unprotected parts, with smothered mother-sounds, half-moo, half-moan, of Russian affection.

He disentangled himself and pursued his quest. She had now moved to the drawing room, but by the expression of her back, by the tensed scapulae, Van knew she was aware of him. He wiped his wet buzzing ear and acknowledged with a nod the raised glass of the stout blond fellow (Percy de

Prey? Or did Percy have an older brother?). A fourth maiden in the Canadian couturier's corn-and-bluet summer "creation" stopped Van to inform him with a pretty pout that he did not remember her, which was true. "I am exhausted," he said. "My horse caught a hoof in a hole in the rotting planks of Ladore Bridge and had to be shot. I have walked eight miles. I think I am dreaming. I think you are Dreaming Too." "No, I'm Cordula!" she cried, but he was off again.

Ada had vanished. He discarded the caviar sandwich that he found himself carrying like a ticket and, turning into the pantry, told Bout's brother, a new valet, to take him to his old room and get him one of those rubber tubs he had used as a child four years ago. Plus somebody's spare pajamas. His train had broken down in the fields between Ladoga and Ladore, he had walked twenty miles, God knows when they'd send up his bags.

"They have just come," said the real Bout with a smile both confidential and mournful (Blanche had jilted him).

Before tubbing, Van craned out of his narrow casement to catch sight of the laurels and lilacs flanking the front porch whence came the hubbub of gay departures. He made out Ada. He noticed her running after Percy who had put on his gray topper and was walking away across a lawn which his transit at once caused to overlap in Van's mind with the fleeting memory of the paddock where he and Van had once happened to discuss a lame horse and Riverlane. Ada overtook the young man in a patch of sudden sunlight; he stopped, and she stood speaking to him and tossing her head in a way she had when nervous or displeased. De Prey kissed her hand. That was French, but all right. He held the hand he had kissed while she spoke and then kissed it again, and that was not done, that was dreadful, that could not be endured.

Leaving his post, naked Van went through the clothes he had shed. He found the necklace. In icy fury, he tore it into thirty, forty glittering hailstones, some of which fell at her feet as she burst into the room.

Her glance swept the floor.

"What a shame—" she began.

Van calmly quoted the punchline from Mlle Larivière's famous story: "*Mais, ma pauvre amie, elle était fausse*"—which was a bitter lie; but before picking up the spilled diamonds, she locked the door and embraced him, weeping—the touch of her skin and silk was all the magic of life, but why does everybody greet me with tears? He also wanted to know was that Percy de Prey? It was. Who had been kicked out of Riverlane? She guessed he had. He had changed, he had grown swine-stout. He had, hadn't he just? Was he her new beau?

"And now," said Ada, "Van is going to stop being vulgar—I mean, stop forever! Because I had and have and shall always have only one beau, only one beast, only one sorrow, only one joy."

"We can collect your tears later," he said, "I can't wait."

Her open kiss was hot and tremulous, but when he tried to draw up her dress she flinched with a murmur of reluctant denial, because the door had come alive: two small fists could be heard drumming upon it from the outside, in a rhythm both knew well.

"Hi, Lucette!" cried Van: "I'm changing, go away."

"Hi, Van! They want Ada, not you. They want you downstairs. Ada!"

One of Ada's gestures—used when she had to express in a muted flash all the facets of her predicament ("See, I was right, that's how it is, *nichego ne podelaesh*'" (—consisted of rounding by means of both hands an invisible bowl from rim to base, accompanied by a sad bow. This is what she did now before leaving the room.

The situation was repeated in a much more pleasing strain a few hours later. For supper Ada wore another dress, of crimson cotton, and when they met at night (in the old toolroom by the glow of a carbide lantern) he unzipped her with such impetuous force that he nearly tore it in two to expose her entire beauty. They were still fiercely engaged (on the same bench covered with the same tartan lap robe— thoughtfully brought) when the outside door noiselessly opened, and Blanche glided in like an imprudent ghost. She had her own key, was back from a rendezvous with old Sore the Burgundian night watchman, and stopped like a fool gaping at the young couple. "Knock next time," said Van with a grin, not bothering to pause—rather enjoying, in fact, the bewitching apparition: she wore a miniver cloak that Ada had lost in the woods. Oh, she had become wonderfully pretty, and *elle le mangeait des yeux*—but Ada slammed the lantern shut, and with apologetic groans, the slut groped her way to the inner passage. His true love could not help giggling; and Van resumed his passionate task.

They stayed on and on, quite unable to part, knowing any explanation would do if anybody wondered why their rooms had remained empty till dawn. The first ray of the morning dabbed a toolbox with fresh green paint, when, at last moved by hunger, they got up and quietly repaired to the pantry.

"*Chto, vispalsya, Vahn* (well, slept your fill, Van)?" said Ada, beautifully mimicking her mother's voice, and she continued in her mother's English: "By your appetite, I judge. And, I think, it is only the first *brekfest*."

"Okh," grumbled Van, "my kneecaps! That bench was cruel. And I am *hongry*."

They sat, facing each other, at a breakfast table, munching black bread with fresh butter, and Virginia ham, and slices of genuine Emmenthaler cheese—and here's a pot of transparent honey: two cheerful cousins, "raiding the icebox" as children in old fairy tales, and the thrushes were sweetly whistling in the bright-green garden as the dark-green shadows drew in their claws.

"My teacher," she said, "at the Drama School thinks I'm better in farces than in tragedy. If they only knew!"

"There is nothing to know," retorted Van. "Nothing, nothing has changed! But that's the general impression, it was too dim down there for details, we'll examine them tomorrow on our little island: 'My sister, do you still recall . . .'"

"Oh shut up!" said Ada. "I've given up all that stuff— *petits vers, vers de soie* . . ."

"Come, come," cried Van, "some of the rhymes were magnificent arcrobatics on the part of the child's mind: 'Oh! *qui me rendra, ma Lucile, et le grand chêne and zee big hill.*' Little Lucile," he added in an effort to dissipate her frowns with a joke, "little Lucile has become so peachy that I think I'll switch over to her if you keep losing your temper like that. I remember the first time you got cross with me was when I chucked a stone at a statue and frightened a finch. That's memory!"

She was on bad terms with memory. She thought the servants would be up soon now, and then one could have something hot. That fridge was all fudge, really.

"Why, suddenly sad?"

Yes, she was sad, she replied, she was in dreadful trouble, her quandary might drive her insane if she did not know that her heart was pure. She could explain it best by a parable. She was like the girl in a film he would see soon, who is in the triple throes of a tragedy which she must conceal lest she lose her only true love, the head of the arrow, the point of the pain. In secret, she is simultaneously struggling with three torments—trying to get rid of a dreary dragging affair with a married man, whom she pities; trying to nip in the bud—in the sticky red bud—a crazy adventure with an attractive young fool, whom she pities even more; and trying to keep intact the love of the only man who is all her life and who is above pity, above the poverty of her feminine pity, because as the script says, his ego is richer and prouder than anything those two poor worms could imagine.

What had she actually done with the poor worms, after Krolik's untimely end?

"Oh, set them free" (big vague gesture), "turned them out, put them back onto suitable plants, buried them in the pupal state, told them to run along, while the birds were not looking—or alas, feigning not to be looking.

"Well, to mop up that parable, because you have the knack of interrupting and diverting my thoughts, I'm in a sense also torn between three private tortures, the main torture being ambition, of course. I know I shall never be a biologist, my passion for creeping creatures is great, but not all-consuming. I know I shall always adore orchids and mushrooms and violets, and you will still see me going out alone, to wander alone in the woods and return alone with a little lone lily; but flowers, no matter how irresistible, must be given up, too, as soon as I have the strength. Remains the great ambition and the greatest terror: the dream of the bluest, remotest, hardest dramatic climbs—probably ending as one of a hundred old spider spinsters teaching drama students, knowing, that, as you insist, sinister insister, we can't marry, and having always before me the awful example of pathetic, second-rate, brave Marina."

"Well, that bit about spinsters is rot," said Van, "we'll pull it off somehow, we'll become more and more distant relations in artistically forged papers and finally dwindle to mere namesakes, or at the worst we shall live quietly, you as my housekeeper, I as your epileptic, and then, as in your Chekhov, 'we shall see the whole sky swarm with diamonds.'"

"Did you find them all, Uncle Van?" she inquired, sighing, laying her dolent head on his shoulder. She had told him everything.

"More or less," he replied, not realizing she had. "Anyway, I made the best study of the dustiest floor ever accomplished by a romantic character. One bright little bugger rolled under the bed where there grows a virgin forest of fluff and fungi. I'll have them reassembled in Ladore when I motor there one of these days. I have lots of things to buy— a gorgeous bathrobe in honor of your new swimming pool, a cream called Chrysanthemum, a brace of dueling pistols, a folding beach mattress, preferably black—to bring you out not on the beach but on that bench, and on our *isle de Ladore*."

"Except," she said, "that I do not approve of your making a laughingstock of yourself by looking for pistols in souvenir shops, especially when Ardis Hall is full of old shotguns and rifles, and revolvers, and bows and arrows—you remember, we had lots of practice with them when you and I were children."

Oh, he did, he did. Children, yes. In point of fact, how puzzling to keep seeing that recent past in nursery terms. Because nothing had changed—you are with me, aren't you? —nothing, not counting little improvements in the grounds and the governess.

Yes! Wasn't that a scream? Larivière blossoming forth, bosoming forth as a great writer! A sensational Canadian best-selling author! Her story "The Necklace" (*La rivière de diamants*) had become a classic in girls' schools and her gorgeous pseudonym "Guillaume de Monparnasse" (the leaving out of the "t" made it more *intime*) was well-known from Quebec to Kaluga. As she put it in her exotic English: "Fame struck and the roubles rolled, and the dollars poured" (both currencies being used at the time in East Estotiland); but good Ida, far from abandoning Marina, with whom she had been platonically and irrevocably in love ever since she had seen her in "Bilitis," accused herself of neglecting Lucette by overindulging in Literature; consequently she now gave the child, in spurts of vacational zeal, considerably more attention than poor little Ada (said Ada) had received at twelve, after *her* first (miserable) term at school. Van had been such an idiot: suspecting Cordula! Chaste, gentle, dumb, little Cordula de Prey, when Ada had explained to him, twice, thrice, in different codes, that she had *invented* a nasty tender schoolmate, at a time when she had been literally *torn* from him, and only assumed—in advance, so to speak—such a girl's existence. A kind of blank check that she wanted from him; "Well, you got it," said Van, "but now it's destroyed and will not be renewed; but why did you run after fat Percy, what was so important?"

"Oh, very important," said Ada, catching a drop of honey on her nether lip, "his mother was on the dorophone, and he said please tell her he was on his way home, and I forgot all about it, and rushed up to kiss you!"

"At Riverlane," said Van, "we used to call that a Doughnut Truth: only the truth, and the whole truth, with a hole in the truth."

"I hate you," cried Ada, and made what she called a warning frog face, because Bouteillan had appeared in the doorway, his mustache shaved, coatless, tieless, in crimson braces that were holding up to his chest his well-filled black trousers. He disappeared, promising to bring them their coffee.

"But let me ask you, dear Van, let me ask you something.

How many times has Van been unfaithful to me since September, 1884?"

"Six hundred and thirteen times," answered Van. "With at least two hundred whores, who only caressed me. I've remained absolutely true to you because those were only 'obmanipulations' (sham, insignificant strokings by unremembered cold hands)."

The butler, now fully dressed, arrived with the coffee and toast. And the *Ladore Gazette*. It contained a picture of Marina being fawned upon by a young Latin actor.

"Pah!" exclaimed Ada. "I had quite forgotten. He's coming today, with a movie man, and our afternoon will be ruined. But I feel refreshed and fit," she added (after a third cup of coffee). "It is only ten minutes to seven now. We shall go for a nice stroll in the park; there are one or two places that you might recognize."

"My love," said Van, "my phantom orchid, my lovely bladder-senna! I have not slept for two nights—one of which I spent imagining the other, and this other turned out to be more than I had imagined. I've had enough of you for the time being."

"Not a very fine compliment," said Ada, and rang resonantly for more toast.

"I've paid you eight compliments, as a certain Venetian—"

"I'm not interested in vulgar Venetians. You have become so coarse, dear Van, so strange . . ."

"Sorry," he said, getting up. "I don't know what I'm saying, I'm dead tired, I'll see you at lunch."

"There will be no lunch today," said Ada. "It will be some messy snack at the poolside, and sticky drinks all day."

He wanted to kiss her on her silky head but Bouteillan at that moment came in and while Ada was crossly rebuking him for the meager supply of toast, Van escaped.

32

The shooting script was now ready. Marina, in dorean robe and coolie hat, reclined reading in a long-chair on the patio. Her director, G. A. Vronsky, elderly, baldheaded, with a spread of grizzled fur on his fat chest, was alternately sipping his vodka-and-tonic and feeding Marina typewritten pages from a folder. On her other side, crosslegged on a mat, sat Pedro (surname unknown, stagename forgotten), a repulsively handsome, practically naked young actor, with satyr ears, slanty eyes, and lynx nostrils, whom she had brought from Mexico and was keeping at a hotel in Ladore.

Ada, lying on the edge of the swimming pool, was doing her best to make the shy dackel face the camera in a reasonably upright and decent position, while Philip Rack, an insignificant but on the whole likable young musician who in his baggy trunks looked even more dejected and awkward than in the green velvet suit he thought fit to wear for the piano lessons he gave Lucette, was trying to take a picture of the recalcitrant chop-licking animal and of the girl's parted breasts which her half-prone position helped to disclose in the opening of her bathing suit.

If one dollied now to another group standing a few paces away under the purple garlands of the patio arch, one might take a medium shot of the young maestro's pregnant wife in a polka-dotted dress replenishing goblets with salted almonds, and of our distinguished lady novelist resplendent in mauve flounces, mauve hat, mauve shoes, pressing a zebra vest on Lucette, who kept rejecting it with rude remarks, learned from a maid but uttered in a tone of voice just beyond deafish Mlle Larivière's field of hearing.

Lucette remained topless. Her tight smooth skin was the color of thick peach syrup, her little crupper in willow-green shorts rolled drolly, the sun lay sleek on her russet bob and plumpish torso: it showed but a faint circumlocution of femininity, and Van, in a scowling mood, recalled with mixed feelings how much more developed her sister had been at not quite twelve years of age.

He had spent most of the day fast asleep in his room, and a long, rambling, dreary dream had repeated, in a kind of pointless parody, his strenuous "Casanovanic" night with Ada and that somehow ominous morning talk with her. Now that I am writing this, after so many hollows and heights of time, I find it not easy to separate our conversation, as set down in an inevitably stylized form, and the drone of complaints, turning on sordid betrayals that obsessed young Van in his dull nightmare. Or was he dreaming now that he had been dreaming? Had a grotesque governess really written a novel entitled *Les Enfants Maudits*? To be filmed by frivolous dummies, now discussing its adaptation? To be made even triter than the original Book of the Fortnight, and its gurgling blurbs? Did he detest Ada as he had in his dream? He did.

Now, at fifteen, she was an irritating and hopeless beauty; a rather unkempt one, too; only twelve hours ago, in the dim toolroom he had whispered a riddle in her ear: what begins with a "de" and rhymes more or less with a Silesian river ant? She was eccentric in habits and clothing. She cared nothing for sunbathing, and not a tinge of the tan that had californized Lucette could be traced on the shameless white of Ada's long limbs and scrawny shoulder blades.

A remote cousin, no longer René's sister, not even his half-sister (so lyrically anathematized by Monparnasse), she stepped over him as over a log and returned the embarrassed dog to Marina. The actor, who quite likely would run into somebody's fist in a forthcoming scene, made a filthy remark in broken French.

"*Du sollst nicht zuhören*," murmured Ada to German Dack before putting him back in Marina's lap under the "accursed children." "*On ne parle pas comme ça devant un chien*," added Ada, not deigning to glance at Pedro, who nevertheless got up, reconstructed his crotch, and beat her to the pool with a Nurjinski leap.

Was she really beautiful? Was she at least what they call attractive? She was exasperation, she was torture. The silly girl had heaped her hair under a rubber cap, and this gave an unfamiliar, vaguely clinical look to her neck, with its odd dark wisps and strags, as if she had obtained a nurse's job and would never dance again. Her faded, bluish-gray, one-piece swimsuit had a spot of grease and a hole above one hip—nibbled through, one might conjecture, by a tallow-starved larva—and seemed much too short for careless comfort. She smelled of damp cotton, axillary tufts, and nenuphars, like mad Ophelia. None of those minor matters would have annoyed Van, had she and he been alone together; but the presence of the all-male actor made everything obscene, drab and insupportable. We move back to the lip of the pool.

Our young man, being exceptionally *brezgliv* (squeamish,

easily disgusted), had no desire to share a few cubic meters of chlorinated celestino ("blues your bath") with two other fellows. He was emphatically not Japanese. He always remembered, with shudders of revulsion, the indoor pool of his prep school, the running noses, the pimpled chests, the chance contacts with odious male flesh, the suspicious bubble bursting like a small stink bomb, and especially, especially, the bland, sly, triumphant and absolutely revolting wretch who stood in shoulder-high water and secretly urinated (and, God, how he had beaten him up, though that Vere de Vere was three years older than he).

He now kept carefully out of reach of any possible splash as Pedro and Phil snorted and fooled in their foul bath. Presently the pianist, floating up and showing his awful gums in a servile grin, tried to draw Ada into the pool from her outstretched position on the tiled margin, but she evaded the grab of his despair by embracing the big orange ball she had just fished out and, pushing him away with that shield, she then threw it toward Van, who slapped it aside, refusing the gambit, ignoring the gambol, scorning the gambler.

And now hairy Pedro hoisted himself onto the brink and began to flirt with the miserable girl (his banal attentions were, really, the least of her troubles).

"Your leetle aperture must be raccommodated," he said.

"*Que voulez-vous dire*, for goodness sake?" she asked, instead of dealing him a backhand wallop.

"Permit that I contact your charming penetralium," the idiot insisted, and put a wet finger on the hole in her swimsuit.

"Oh *that*" (shrugging and rearranging the shoulder strap displaced by the shrug). "Never mind that. Next time, maybe, I'll put on my fabulous new bikini."

"Next time, maybe, no Pedro?"

"Too bad," said Ada. "Now go and fetch me a Coke, like a good dog."

"*E tu?*" Pedro asked Marina as he walked past her chair. "Again screwdriver?"

"Yes, dear, but with grapefruit, not orange, and a little *zucchero*. I can't understand" (turning to Vronsky), "why do I sound a hundred years old on this page and fifteen on the next? Because if it is a flashback—and it is a flashback, I suppose" (she pronounced it *fleshbeck*)," Renny, or what's his name, René, should not know what he seems to know."

"He does not," cried G.A., "it's only a half-hearted flashback. Anyway, this Renny, this lover number one, does not know, of course, that she is trying to get rid of lover number two, while she's wondering all the time if she can dare go on dating number three, the gentleman farmer, see?"

"*Nu, eto chto-to slozhnovato* (sort of complicated), Grigoriy Akimovich," said Marina, scratching her cheek, for she always tended to discount, out of sheer self-preservation, the considerably more *slozhnïe* patterns of her own past.

"Read on, read, it all becomes clear," said G.A., riffling through his own copy.

"Incidentally," observed Marina, "I hope dear Ida will not object to our making him not only a poet, but a ballet dancer. Pedro could do that beautifully, but he can't be made to recite French poetry."

"If she protests," said Vronsky, "she can go and stick a telegraph pole—where it belongs."

The indecent "telegraph" caused Marina, who had a secret fondness for salty jokes, to collapse in Ada-like ripples of rolling laughter (*pokativshis' so smehu vrode Adi*): "But let's be serious, I still don't see how and why his wife—I mean the second guy's wife—accepts the situation (*polozhenie*)."

Vronsky spread his fingers and toes.

"*Prichyom tut polozhenie* (situation-shituation)? She is blissfully ignorant of their affair and besides, she knows she is fubsy and frumpy, and simply cannot compete with dashing Hélène."

"I see, but some won't," said Marina.

In the meantime, Herr Rack swam up again and joined Ada on the edge of the pool, almost losing his baggy trunks in the process of an amphibious heave.

"Permit me, Ivan, to get you also a nice cold Russian *kok?*" said Pedro—really a very gentle and amiable youth at heart. "Get yourself a cocoanut," replied nasty Van, testing the poor faun, who did not get it, in any sense, and, giggling pleasantly, want back to his mat. Claudius, at least, did not court Ophelia.

The melancholy young German was in a philosophical mood shading into the suicidal. He had to return to Kalugano with his Elsie, who Doc Ecksreher thought "would present him with driplets in dry weeks." He hated Kalugano, his and her home town, where in a moment of "mutual aberration" stupid Elsie had given him her all on a park bench after a wonderful office party at Muzakovski's Organs where the oversexed pitiful oaf had a good job.

"When are you leaving?" asked Ada.

"Forestday—after tomorrow."

"Fine. That's fine. Adieu, Mr. Rack."

Poor Philip drooped, fingerpainting sad nothings on wet stone, shaking his heavy head, gulping visibly.

"One feels . . . One feels," he said, "that one is merely playing a role and has forgotten the next speech."

"I'm told many feel that," said Ada; "it must be a *furchtbar* feeling."

"Cannot be helped? No hope any more at all? I am dying, yes?"

"You are dead, Mr. Rack," said Ada.

She had been casting sidelong glances, during that dreadful talk, and now saw pure, fierce Van under the tulip tree, quite a way off, one hand on his hip, head thrown back, drinking beer from a bottle. She left the pool edge, with its corpse, and moved toward the tulip tree making a strategic detour between the authoress, who—still unaware of what they were doing to her novel—was dozing in a deckchair (out of whose wooden arms her chubby fingers grew like pink mushrooms), and the leading lady, now puzzling over a love scene where the young chatelaine's "radiant beauty" was mentioned.

"But," said Marina, "how can one act out 'radiant,' what does radiant beauty mean?"

"Pale beauty," said Pedro helpfully, glancing up at Ada as she passed by, "the beauty for which many men would cut off their members."

"Okay," said Vronsky. "Let us get on with this damned script. He leaves the pool-side patio, and since we contemplate doing it in color—"

Van left the pool-side patio and strode away. He turned into a side gallery that led into a grovy part of the garden, grading insensibly into the park proper. Presently, he noticed that Ada had hastened to follow him. Lifting one elbow, revealing the black star of her armpit, she tore off her bathing cap and with a shake of her head liberated a torrent of hair. Lucette, in color, trotted behind her. Out of charity for the sisters' bare feet, Van changed his course from gravel path to velvet lawn (reversing the action of Dr. Ero, pursued by the Invisible Albino in one of the greatest novels of English literature). They caught up with him in the Second

Coppice. Lucette, in passing, stopped to pick up her sister's cap and sunglasses—the sunglasses of much-sung lasses, a shame to throw them away! My tidy little Lucette (I shall never forget you . . .) placed both objects on a tree stump near an empty beer bottle, trotted on, then went back to examine a bunch of pink mushrooms that clung to the stump, snoring. Double take, double exposure.

"Are you furious, because—" began Ada upon overtaking him (she had prepared a sentence about her having to be polite after all to a piano tuner, practically a servant, with an obscure heart ailment and a vulgar pathetic wife—but Van interrupted her).

"I object," he said, expelling it like a rocket, "to two things. A brunette, even a sloppy brunette, should shave her groin before exposing it, and a well-bred girl does not allow a beastly lecher to poke her in the ribs even if she must wear a moth-eaten, smelly rag much too short for her charms." "Ach!" he added, "why the hell did I return to Ardis!"

"I promise, I promise to be more careful from now on and not let lousy Pedro come near," she said with happy rigorous nods—and an exhalation of glorious relief, the cause of which was to torture Van only much later.

"Oh, wait for me!" yelped Lucette.

(Torture, my poor love! Torture! Yes! But it's all sunk and dead. Ada's late note.)

The three of them formed a pretty Arcadian combination as they dropped on the turf under the great weeping cedar, whose aberrant limbs extended an oriental canopy (propped up here and there by crutches made of its own flesh like this book) above two black and one golden-red head as they had above you and me on dark warm nights when we were reckless, happy children.

Van, sprawling supine, sick with memories, put his hands

behind his nape and slit his eyes at the Lebanese blue of the sky between the fascicles of the foliage. Lucette fondly admired his long lashes while pitying his tender skin for the inflamed blotches and prickles between neck and jaw where shaving caused the most trouble. Ada, her keepsake profile inclined, her mournful magdalene hair hanging down (in sympathy with the weeping shadows) along her pale arm, sat examining abstractly the yellow throat of a waxy-white helleborine she had picked. She hated him, she adored him. He was brutal, she was defenseless.

Lucette, always playing her part of the clinging, affection-ately fussy lassy, placed both palms on Van's hairy chest and wanted to know why he was cross.

"I'm not cross with *you*," replied Van at last.

Lucette kissed his hand, then attacked him.

"Cut it out!" he said, as she wriggled against his bare thorax. "You're unpleasantly cold, child."

"It's not true, I'm hot," she retorted.

"Cold as two halves of a canned peach. Now, roll off, please."

"Why two? Why?"

"Yes, why," growled Ada with a shiver of pleasure, and, leaning over, kissed him on the mouth. He struggled to rise. The two girls were now kissing him alternately, then kiss-ing each other, then getting busy upon him again—Ada in perilous silence, Lucette with soft squeals of delight. I do not remember what *Les Enfants Maudits* did or said in Monparnasse's novelette—they lived in Bryant's château, I think, and it began with bats flying one by one out of a turret's *oeil-de-boeuf* into the sunset, but *these* children (whom the novelettist did not really know—a delicious point) might also have been filmed rather entertainingly had snoopy Kim, the kitchen photo-fiend, possessed the necessary apparatus. One hates to write about those matters, it all comes out so improper, esthetically speaking, in written description, but one cannot help recalling in this ultimate twilight (where minor artistic blunders are fainter than very fugitive bats in an insect-poor wilderness of orange air) that Lucette's dewy little contributions augmented rather than dampened Van's invariable reaction to the only and main girl's lightest touch, actual or imagined. Ada, her silky mane sweeping over his nipples and navel, seemed to enjoy doing everything to jolt my present pencil and make, in that ridiculously remote past, her innocent little sister notice and register what Van could not control. The crushed flower was now being merrily crammed under the rubber belt of his black trunks by twenty tickly fingers. As an ornament it had not much value; as a game it was inept and dangerous. He shook off his pretty tormentors, and walked away on his hands, a black mask over his carnival nose. Just then, the governess, panting and shouting, arrived on the scene. "*Mais qu'est-ce qu'il t'a fait, ton cousin?*" She kept anxiously asking, as Lucette, shedding the same completely unwarranted tears that Ada had once shed, rushed into the mauve-winged arms.

33

The following day began with a drizzle; but cleared up after lunch. Lucette had her last piano lesson with gloomy Herr Rack. The repetitive tinkle-thump-tinkle reached Van and Ada during a reconnaissance in a second-floor passage. Mlle Larivière was in the garden, Marina had fluttered away to Ladore, and Van suggested they take advantage of Lucette's being "audibly absent" by taking refuge in an upstairs dressing room.

Lucette's first tricycle stood there in a corner; a shelf above a cretonne-covered divan held some of the child's old "untouchable" treasures among which was the battered anthology he had given her four years ago. The door could not be locked, but Van was impatient, and the music would surely endure, as firm as a wall, for at least another twenty minutes. He had buried his mouth in Ada's nuque, when she stiffened and raised a warning finger. Heavy slow steps were coming up the grand staircase. "Send him away," she muttered. "*Chort* (hell)," swore Van, adjusting his clothes, and went out on the landing. Philip Rack was trudging up, Adam's apple bobbing, ill-shaven, livid, gums exposed, one hand on his chest, the other clutching a roll of pink paper while the music continued to play on its own as if by some mechanical device.

"There's one downstairs in the hall," said Van, assuming, or feigning to assume, that the unfortunate fellow had stomach cramps or nausea. But Mr. Rack only wanted "to make his farewells"—to Ivan Demonovich (accented miserably on the second "o"), to Fraülein Ada, to Mademoiselle Ida, and of course to Madame. Alas, Van's cousin and aunt were in town, but Phil might certainly find his friend Ida writing in the rose garden. Was Van sure? Van was damned well sure. Mr. Rack shook Van's hand with a deep sigh, looked up, looked down, tapped the banisters with his mysterious pink-paper tube, and went back to the music room, where Mozart had begun to falter. Van waited for a moment, listening and grimacing involuntarily, and presently rejoined Ada. She sat with a book in her lap.

"I must wash my right hand before I touch you or anything," he said.

She was not really reading, but nervously, angrily, absently flipping through the pages of what happened to be that old anthology—*she* who at any time, if she picked up a book, would at once get engrossed in whatever text she happened to slip into "from the book's brink" with the natural movement of a water creature put back into its brook.

"I have never clasped a wetter, limper, nastier forelimb in all my life," said Van, and cursing (the music downstairs had stopped), went to the nursery W.C. where there was a tap. From its window he saw Rack put his lumpy black briefcase into the front basket of his bicycle and weave away, taking his hat off to an unresponsive gardener. The clumsy cyclist's balance did not survive his futile gesture: he brushed harshly against the hedge on the other side of the path, and crashed. For a moment or two Rack remained in tangled communion with the privet, and Van wondered if he should not go down to his aid. The gardener had turned his back on the sick or drunken musician, who, thank goodness, was now getting out of the bushes and replacing his briefcase in its basket. He rode away slowly, and a surge of obscure disgust made Van spit into the toilet bowl.

Ada had left the dressing room by the time he returned. He discovered her on a balcony, where she was peeling an apple for Lucette. The kind pianist would always bring her an apple, or sometimes an inedible pear, or two small plums. Anyway, that was his last gift.

"Mademoiselle is calling you," said Van to Lucette.

"Well, she'll have to wait," said Ada, leisurely continuing her "ideal peel," a yellow-red spiral which Lucette watched with ritual fascination.

"Have some work to do," Van blurted out. "Bored beyond words. Shall be in the library."

"Okay," limpidly responded Lucette without turning—and emitted a cry of pleasure as she caught the finished festoons.

He spent half an hour seeking a book he had put back in the wrong place. When he found it at last, he saw he had finished annotating it and so did not need it any more. For a while he lay on the black divan, but that seemed only to increase the pressure of passionate obsession. He decided to return to the upper floor by the cochlea. There he recalled with anguish, as something fantastically ravishing and hopelessly irretrievable, her hurrying up with her candlestick on the night of the Burning Barn, capitalized in his memory forever—he with his dancing light behind her hurdies and calves and mobile shoulders and streaming hair, and the shadows in huge surges of black geometry overtaking them, in their winding upward course, along the yellow wall. He now found the third-floor door latched on the other side, and had to return down to the library (memories now blotted out by trivial exasperation) and take the grand staircase.

As he advanced toward the bright sun of the balcony door he heard Ada explaining something to Lucette. It was something amusing, it had to do with—I do not remember and cannot invent. Ada had a way of hastening to finish a sentence before mirth overtook her, but sometimes, as now, a brief burst of it would cause her words to explode, and then she would catch up with them and conclude the phrase with still greater haste, keeping her mirth at bay, and the last word would be followed by a triple ripple of sonorous, throaty, erotic and rather cosy laughter.

"And now, my sweet," she added, kissing Lucette on her dimpled cheek, "do me a favor: run down and tell bad Belle it's high time you had your milk and *petit-beurre*. *Zhivo* (quick)! Meanwhile, Van and I will retire to the bathroom—or somewhere where there's a good glass—and I'll give him a haircut; he needs one badly. Don't you, Van? Oh, I know where we'll go . . . Run along, run along, Lucette."

34

That frolic under the sealyham cedar proved to be a mistake. Whenever not supervised by her schizophrenic governess, whenever not being read to, or walked, or put to bed, Lucette was now a pest. At nightfall—if Marina was not around, drinking, say, with her guests under the golden globes of the new garden lamps that glowed here and there in the sudden greenery, and mingled their kerosene reek with the breath of heliotrope and jasmine—the lovers could steal out into the deeper darkness and stay there until the *nocturna*—a keen midnight breeze—came tumbling the foliage "*troussant la raimée*," as Sore, the ribald night watchman, expressed it. Once, with his emerald lantern, he had stumbled upon them and several times a phantom Blanche had crept past them, laughing softly, to mate in some humbler nook with the robust and securely bribed old glowworm. But waiting all day for a propitious night was too much for our impatient lovers. More often than not they had worn themselves out well before dinnertime, just as they used to in the past; Lucette, however, seemed to lurk behind every screen, to peep out of every mirror.

They tried the attic, but noticed, just in time, a rent in its floor through which one glimpsed a corner of the mangle room where French, the second maid, could be seen in her corset and petticoat, passing to and fro. They looked around—and could not understand how they had ever been able to make tender love among splintered boxes and projecting nails, or wriggle through the skylight onto the roof, which any green imp with coppery limbs could easily keep under surveillance from a fork of the giant elm.

There still was the shooting gallery, with its Orientally draped recess under the sloping roof. But it crawled now with bedbugs, reeked of stale beer, and was so grimy and greasy that one could not dream of undressing or using the little divan. All Van saw there of his new Ada were her ivorine thighs and haunches, and the very first time he clasped them she bade him, in the midst of his vigorous joy, to glance across her shoulder over the window ledge, which her hands were still clutching in the ebbing throbs of her own response, and note that Lucette was approaching—skipping rope, along a path in the shrubbery.

Those intrusions were repeated on the next two or three occasions. Lucette would come ever nearer, now picking a chanterelle and feigning to eat it raw, then crouching to capture a grasshopper or at least going through the natural motions of idle play and carefree pursuit. She would advance up to the center of the weedy playground in front of the forbidden pavilion, and there, with an air of dreamy innocence, start to jiggle the board of an old swing that hung from the long and lofty limb of Baldy, a partly leafless but still healthy old oak (which appeared—oh, I remember, Van! —in a century-old lithograph of Ardis, by Peter de Rast, as a young colossus protecting four cows and a lad in rags, one shoulder bare). When our lovers (you like the authorial possessive, don't you, Van?) happened to look out again, Lucette was rocking the glum dackel, or looking up at an imaginary woodpecker, or with various pretty contortions unhurriedly mounting the gray-looped board and swinging gently and gingerly as if never having done it yet, while idiot Dack barked at the locked pavilion door. She increased her momentum so cannily that Ada and her cavalier, in the pardonable blindness of ascending bliss, never once witnessed the instant when the round rosy face with all its freckles aglow swooped up and two green eyes leveled at the astounding tandem.

Lucette, the shadow, followed them from lawn to loft, from gatehouse to stable, from a modern shower booth near the pool to the ancient bathroom upstairs. Lucette-in-the-Box came out of a trunk. Lucette desired they take her for walks. Lucette insisted on their playing "leaptoad" with her —and Ada and Van exchanged dark looks.

Ada thought up a plan that was not simple, was not clever, and moreover worked the wrong way. Perhaps she did it on purpose. (Strike out, strike out, *please*, Van.) The idea was to have Van fool Lucette by petting her in Ada's presence, while kissing Ada at the same time, and by caressing and kissing Lucette when Ada was away in the woods ("in the woods," "botanizing"). This, Ada affirmed, would achieve two ends—assuage the pubescent child's jealousy and act as an alibi in case she caught them in the middle of a more ambiguous romp.

The three of them cuddled and cosseted so frequently and so thoroughly that at last one afternoon on the long-suffering black divan he and Ada could no longer restrain their amorous excitement, and under the absurd pretext of a hide-and-seek game they locked up Lucette in a closet used for storing bound volumes of *The Kaluga Waters* and

The Lugano Sun, and frantically made love, while the child knocked and called and kicked until the key fell out and the keyhole turned an angry green.

More objectionable yet than those fits of vile temper were, to Ada's mind, the look of stricken ecstasy that Lucette's face expressed when she would tightly cling to Van with arms and knees, and prehensile tail, as if he were a tree trunk, even an ambulating tree trunk, and could not be pried off him unless smartly slapped by big sister.

"I have to admit," said Ada to Van as they floated downstream in a red boat, toward a drape of willows on a Ladore islet, "I have to admit with shame and sorrow, Van, that the splendid plan is a foozle. I think the brat has a dirty mind. I think she is criminally in love with you. I think I shall tell her you are her uterine brother and that it is illegal and altogether abominable to flirt with uterine brothers. Ugly dark words scare her, I know; they scared me when I was four; but she is essentially a dumb child, and should be protected from nightmares and stallions. If she still does not desist, I can always complain to Marina, saying she disturbs us in our meditations and studies. But perhaps you don't mind? Perhaps she excites you? Yes? She excites you, confess?"

"This summer is so much sadder than the other," said Van softly.

35

We are now on a willow islet amidst the quietest branch of the blue Ladore, with wet fields on one side and on the other a view of Bryant's Castle, remote and romantically black on its oak-timbered hill. In that oval seclusion, Van subjected his new Ada to a comparative study; juxtapositions were easy, since the child he had known in minute detail four years before stood vividly illumined in his mind against the same backdrop of flowing blue.

Her forehead area seemed to have diminished, not only because she had become taller, but because she did her hair differently, with a dramatic swirl in front; its whiteness, now clear of all blemishes, had acquired a particularly mat tinge, and soft skinfolds crossed it, as if she had been frowning too much all those years, poor Ada.

The eyebrows were as regal and thick as ever.

The eyes. The eyes had kept their voluptuous palpebral creases; the lashes, their semblance of jet-dust incrustation; the raised iris, its Hindu-hypnotic position; the lids, their inability to stay alert and wide open during the briefest embrace; but those eyes' expression—when she ate an apple, or examined a found thing, or simply listened to an animal or a person—had changed, as if new layers of reticence and sadness had accumulated, half-veiling the pupil, while the glossy eyeballs shifted in their lovely long sockets with a more restless motion than of yore: Mlle Hypnokush, "whose eyes never dwell on you and yet pierce you."

Her nose had not followed Van's in the latter's thickening of Hibernian outline; but the bone was definitely bolder, and the tip seemed to turn up more strongly, and had a little vertical groove that he did not recall having seen in the twelve-year-old colleenette.

In a strong light, a suggestion of darkish silk down (related to that on her forearms) could be now made out between nose and mouth but was doomed, she said, to extinction at the first cosmetical session of the fall season. A touch of lipstick now gave her mouth an air of deadpan sullenness, which, by contrast, increased the shock of beauty when in gayety or greed she revealed the moist shine of her large teeth and the red riches of tongue and palate.

Her neck had been, and remained, his most delicate, most poignant delight, especially when she let her hair flow freely, and the warm, white, adorable skin showed through in chance separations of glossy black strands. Boils and mosquito bites had stopped pestering her, but he discovered the pale trace of an inch-long cut which ran parallel to her vertebrae just below the waist and which resulted from a deep scratch caused last August by an erratic hatpin—or rather by a thorny twig in the inviting hay.

(You are merciless, Van.)

On that secret islet (forbidden to Sunday couples—it belonged to the Veens, and a notice-board calmly proclaimed that "trespassers might get shot by sportsmen from Ardis Hall," Dan's wording) the vegetation consisted of three Babylonian willows, a fringe of alder, many grasses, cattails, sweet-flags, and a few purple-lipped twayblades, over which Ada crooned as she did over puppies or kittens.

Under the shelter of those neurotic willows Van pursued his survey.

Her shoulders were intolerably graceful: I would never permit my wife to wear strapless gowns with such shoulders, but how could she be my wife? Renny says to Nell in the English version of Monparnasse's rather comic tale: "The infamous shadow of our unnatural affair will follow us into the low depths of the Inferno which our Father who is in the sky shows to us with his superb digit." For some odd reason the worse translations are not from the Chinese, but from plain French.

Her nipples, now pert and red, were encircled by fine black hairs which would soon go, too, being, she said, *unschicklich*. Where had she picked up, he wondered, that hideous word? Her breasts were pretty, pale and plump, but somehow he had preferred the little soft swellings of the earlier girl with their formless dull buds.

He recognized the familiar, individual, beautiful intake of her flat young abdomen, its wonderful "play," the frank and eager expression of the oblique muscles and the "smile" of her navel—to borrow from the vocabulary of the belly dancer's art.

One day he brought his shaving kit along and helped her to get rid of all three patches of body hair:

"Now I'm Scheher," he said, "and you are his Ada, and that's your green prayer carpet."

Their visits to that islet remained engraved in the memory of that summer with entwinements that no longer could be untangled. They saw themselves standing there, embraced, clothed only in mobile leafy shadows, and watching the red rowboat with its mobile inlay of reflected ripples carry them off, waving, waving their handkerchiefs; and that mystery of mixed sequences was enhanced by such things as the boat's floating back to them while it still receded, the oars crippled by refraction, the sunflecks now rippling the other way like the strobe effect of spokes counterwheeling as the pageant rolls by. Time tricked them, made one of them ask a remembered question, caused the other to give a forgotten answer, and once in a small alder thicket, duplicated in black by the blue stream, they found a garter which was certainly hers, she could not deny it, but which Van was positive she had never worn on her stockingless summer trips to the magic islet.

Her lovely strong legs had, maybe, grown longer but they still preserved the sleek pallor and suppleness of her nymphet years. She could still suck her big toe. The right instep and the back of her left hand bore the same small not overconspicuous but indelible and sacred birthmark, with which nature had signed his right hand and left foot. She attempted to coat her fingernails with Scheherazade's Lacquer (a very grotesque fad of the 'eighties) but she was untidy and forgetful in matters of grooming, the varnish flaked off, leaving unseemly blotches, and he requested her to revert to her "lack-luster" state. In compensation, he bought her in the town of Ladore (that rather smart little resort) an ankle chain of gold but she lost it in the course of their strenuous trysts and unexpectedly broke into tears when he said never mind, another lover some day would retrieve it for her.

Her brilliance, her genius. Of course, she had changed in four years, but he, too, had changed, by concurrent stages, so that their brains and senses stayed attuned and were to stay thus always, through all separations. Neither had remained the brash *Wunderkind* of 1884, but in bookish knowledge both surpassed their coevals to an even more absurd extent than in childhood; and in formal terms Ada (born on July 21, 1872) had already completed her private school course while Van, her senior by two years and a half, hoped to get his master's degree at the end of 1889. Her conversation might have lost some of its sportive glitter, and the first faint shadows of what she would later term "my acarpous destiny" (*pustotsvetnost'*) could be made out—at least, in back view; but the quality of her innate wit had deepened, strange "metempirical" (as Van called them) undercurrents seemed to double internally, and thus enrich, the simplest expression of her simplest thoughts. She read as voraciously and indiscriminately as he, but each had evolved a more or less "pet" subject—he the terrological part of psychiatry, she the drama (especially Russian), a "pet" he found "pat" in her case but hoped would be a passing vagary. Her florimania endured, alas; but after Dr. Krolik died (in 1886) of a heart attack in his garden, she had placed all her live pupae in his open coffin where he lay, she said, as plump and pink as *in vivo*.

Amorously, now, in her otherwise dolorous and irresolute adolescence, Ada was even more aggressive and responsive than in her abnormally passionate childhood. A diligent student of case histories, Dr. Van Veen never quite managed to match ardent twelve-year-old Ada with a non-delinquent, non-nymphomaniac, mentally highly developed, spiritually happy and normal English child in his files, although many similar little girls had bloomed—and run to seed—in the old châteaux of France and Estotiland as portrayed in extravagant romances and senile memoirs. His own passion for her Van found even harder to study and analyze. When he recollected caress by caress his Venus Villa sessions, or earlier visits to the riverhouses of Ranta or Livida, he satisfied himself that his reactions to Ada remained beyond all that, since the merest touch of her finger or mouth following a swollen vein produced not only a more potent but essentially different *delicia* than the slowest "winslow" of the most sophisticated young harlot. What, then, was it that raised the animal act to a level higher than even that of the most exact arts or the wildest flights of pure science? It would not be sufficient to say that in his love-making with Ada he discovered the pang, the *ogon'*, the agony of supreme "reality." Reality, better say, lost the quotes it wore like claws—in a world where independent and original minds must cling to things or pull things apart in order to ward off madness or death (which is the master madness). For one spasm or two, he was safe. The new naked reality needed no tentacle or anchor; it lasted a moment, but could be repeated as often as he and she were physically able to make love. The color and fire of that instant reality depended solely on Ada's identity as perceived by him. It had nothing to do with virtue or the vanity of virtue in a large sense—in fact it seemed to Van later that during the ardencies of that summer he knew all along that she had been, and still was, atrociously untrue to him—just as she knew long before he told her that he had used off and on, during their separation, the live mechanisms tense males could rent for a few minutes as described, with profuse woodcuts and photographs, in a three-volume *History of Prostitution* which she had read at the age of ten or eleven, between *Hamlet* and Captain Grant's *Microgalaxies*.

For the sake of the scholars who will read *this* forbidden memoir with a secret tingle (they are human) in the secret chasms of libraries (where the chatter, the lays and the fannies of rotting pornographers are piously kept)—its author must add in the margin of galley proofs which a bedridden old man heroically corrects (for those slippery long snakes add the last touch to a writer's woes) a few more [the end of the sentence cannot be deciphered but fortunately the next paragraph is scrawled on a separate writing-pad page. Editor's Note].

. . . about the rapture of her identity. The asses who might really think that in the starlight of eternity, *my*, Van Veen's, and *her*, Ada Veen's, conjunction, somewhere in North America, in the nineteenth century represented but one trillionth of a trillionth part of a pinpoint planet's significance can bray *ailleurs, ailleurs, ailleurs* (the English word would not supply the onomatopoeic element; old Veen is kind), because the rapture of her identity, placed under the microscope of reality (which is the only reality), shows a complex system of those subtle bridges which the senses traverse—laughing, embraced, throwing flowers in the air —between membrane and brain, and which always was and is a form of memory, even at the moment of its perception. I am weak. I write badly. I may die tonight. My magic carpet no longer skims over crown canopies and gaping nestlings, and her rarest orchids. Insert.

36

Pedantic Ada once said that the looking up of words in a lexicon for any other needs than those of expression—be it instruction or art—lay somewhere between the ornamental assortment of flowers (which could be, she conceded, mildly romantic in a maidenly headcocking way) and making collage-pictures of disparate butterfly wings (which was always vulgar and often criminal). *Per contra*, she suggested to Van that verbal circuses, "performing words," "poodle-doodles," and so forth, might be redeemable by the quality of the brain work required for the creation of a great logogriph or inspired pun and should not preclude the help of a dictionary, gruff or complacent.

That was why she admitted "Flavita." The name came from *alfavit*, an old Russian game of chance and skill, based on the scrambling and unscrambling of alphabetic letters. It was fashionable throughout Estoty and Canady around 1790, was revived by the "Madhatters" (as the inhabitants of New Amsterdam were once called) in the beginning of the nineteenth century, made a great comeback, after a brief slump, around 1860, and now a century later seems to be again in vogue, so I am told, under the name of "Scrabble," invented by some genius quite independently from its original form or forms.

Its chief Russian variety, current in Ada's childhood, was played in great country houses with 125 lettered blocks. The object was to make rows and files of words on a board of 225 squares. Of these, 24 were brown, 12 black, 16 orange, 8 red, and the rest golden-yellow (i.e., flavid, in concession to the game's original name). Every letter of the Cyrillic alphabet rated a number of points (the rare Russian F as much as 10, the common A as little as 1). Brown doubled the basic value of a letter, black tripled it. Orange doubled the sum of points for the whole word, red tripled the sum. Lucette would later recall how her sister's triumphs in doubling, tripling, and even nonupling (when passing through two red squares) the numerical value of words evolved monstrous forms in her delirium during a severe streptococcal ague in September, 1888, in California.

For each round of the game each player helped himself to seven blocks from the container where they lay face down, and arrayed in turn his word on the board. In the case of the opening coup, on the still empty field, all he had to do was to align any two or all of his seven letters in such a way as to involve the central square, marked with a blazing heptagon. Subsequently, the catalyst of one of the letters already on the board had to be used for composing one's word, across or down. That player won who collected the greatest number of points, letter by letter and word by word.

The set our three children received in 1884 from an old friend of the family (as Marina's former lovers were known), Baron Klim Avidov, consisted of a large folding board of saffian and a boxful of weighty rectangles of ebony inlaid with platinum letters, only one of which was a Roman one, namely the letter J on the two joker blocks (as thrilling to get as a blank check signed by Jupiter or Jurojin). It was, incidentally, the same kindly but touchy Avidov (mentioned in many racy memoirs of the time) who once catapulted with an uppercut an unfortunate English tourist into the porter's lodge for his jokingly remarking how clever it was to drop the first letter of one's name in order to use it as a *particule*, at the Gritz, in Venezia Rossa.

By July the ten A's had dwindled to nine, and the four D's to three. The missing A eventually turned up under an Aproned Armchair, but the D was lost—faking the fate of its apostrophizable double as imagined by a Walter C. Keyway, Esq., just before the latter landed, with a couple of unstamped postcards, in the arms of a speechless multilinguist in a frock coat with brass buttons. The wit of the Veens (says Ada in a marginal note) knows no bounds.

Van, a first-rate chess player—he was to win in 1887 a match at Chose when he beat the Minsk-born Pat Rishin (champion of Underhill and Wilson, N.C.)—had been puzzled by Ada's inability of raising the standard of her, so to speak, damsel-errant game above that of a young lady in an old novel or in one of those anti-dandruff color-photo ads that shows a beautiful model (made for other games than chess) staring at the shoulder of her otherwise impeccably groomed antagonist across a preposterous traffic jam of white and scarlet, elaborately and unrecognizably carved, Lalla Rookh chessmen, which not even cretins would want to play with—even if royally paid for the degradation of the simplest thought under the itchiest scalp.

Ada did manage, now and then, to conjure up a combinational sacrifice, offering, say, her queen—with a subtle win after two or three moves if the piece were taken; but she saw only one side of the question, preferring to ignore, in the queer lassitude of clogged cogitation, the obvious counter combination that would lead inevitably to her defeat if the grand sacrifice were *not* accepted. On the Scrabble board, however, this same wild and weak Ada was transformed into a sort of graceful computing machine, endowed, moreover, with phenomenal luck, and would greatly surpass baffled Van in acumen, foresight and exploitation of chance, when shaping appetizing long words from the most unpromising scraps and collops.

He found the game rather fatiguing, and toward the end played hurriedly and carelessly, not deigning to check "rare" or "obsolete" but quite acceptable possibilities provided by a loyal dictionary. As to ambitious, imcompetent and temperamental Lucette, she had to be, even at twelve, discreetly advised by Van who did so chiefly because it saved time and brought a little closer the blessed moment when she could be bundled off to the nursery, leaving Ada available for the third or fourth little flourish of the sweet summer day. Especially boring were the girls' squabbles over the legitimacy of this or that word: proper names and place names were taboo, but there occurred borderline cases, causing no end of heartbreak, and it was pitiful to see Lucette cling to her last five letters (with none left in the box) forming the beautiful ARDIS which her governess had told her meant "the point of an arrow"—but only in Greek, alas.

A particular nuisance was the angry or disdainful looking up of dubious words in a number of lexicons, sitting, standing and sprawling around the girls, on the floor, under Lucette's chair upon which she knelt, on the divan, on the big round table with the board and the blocks and on an adjacent chest of drawers. The rivalry between moronic Ozhegov (a big, blue, badly bound volume, containing 52,872 words) and a small but chippy Edmundson in

Dr. Gerschizhevsky's reverent version, the taciturnity of abridged brutes and the unconventional magnanimity of a four-volume Dahl ("My darling dahlia," moaned Ada as she obtained an obsolete cant word from the gentle long-bearded ethnographer)—all this would have been insupportably boring to Van had he not been stung as a scientist by the curious affinity between certain aspects of Scrabble and those of the planchette. He became aware of it one August evening in 1884 on the nursery balcony, under a sunset sky the last fire of which snaked across the corner of the reservoir, stimulated the last swifts, and intensified the hue of Lucette's copper curls. The morocco board had been unfolded on a much inkstained, monogrammed and notched deal table. Pretty Blanche, also touched, on earlobe and thumbnail, with the evening's pink—and redolent with the perfume called Miniver Musk by handmaids—had brought a still unneeded lamp. Lots had been cast, Ada had won the right to begin, and was in the act of collecting one by one, mechanically and unthinkingly, her seven "luckies" from the open case where the blocks lay face down, showing nothing but their anonymous black backs, each in its own cell of flavid velvet. She was speaking at the same time, saying casually: "I would much prefer the Benten lamp here but it is out of *kerosin*. Pet (addressing Lucette), be a good scout, call her —Good Heavens!"

The seven letters she had taken, S,R,E,N,O,K,I, and was sorting out in her *spektrik* (the little trough of japanned wood each player had before him) now formed in quick and, as it were, self-impulsed rearrangement the key word of the chance sentence that had attended their random assemblage.

Another time, in the bay of the library, on a thundery evening (a few hours before the barn burned), a succession of Lucette's blocks formed the amusing VANIADA, and from this she extracted the very piece of furniture she was in the act of referring to in a peevish little voice: "But I, too, perhaps, would like to sit on the divan."

Soon after that, as so often occurs with games, and toys, and vacational friendships, that seem to promise an eternal future of fun, Flavita followed the bronze and blood-red trees into the autumn mists; then the black box was mislaid, was forgotten—and accidentally rediscovered (among boxes of table silver) four years later, shortly before Lucette's visit to town where she spent a few days with her father in mid-July, 1888. It so happened that this was to be the last game of Flavita that the three young Veens were ever to play together. Either because it happened to end in a memorable record for Ada, or because Van took some notes in the hope —not quite unfulfilled—of "catching sight of the lining of time" (which, as he was later to write, is "the best informal definition of portents and prophecies"), but the last round of that particular game remained vividly clear in his mind.

"*Je ne peux rien faire*," wailed Lucette, "*mais rien*—with my idiotic *Buchstaben*, REMNILK, LINKREM . . ."

"Look," whispered Van, "*c'est tout simple*, shift those two syllables and you get a fortress in ancient Muscovy."

"Oh, no," said Ada, wagging her finger at the height of her temple in a way she had. "Oh, no. That pretty word does not exist in Russian. A Frenchman invented it. There is no second syllable."

"Ruth for a little child?" interposed Van.

"Ruthless!" cried Ada.

"Well," said Van, "you can always make a little cream, KREM or KREME—or even better—there's KREMLI, which means Yukon prisons. Go through her ORHIDEYA."

"Through her silly orchid," said Lucette.

"And now," said Ada, "Adochka is going to do something

[239]

even sillier." And taking advantage of a cheap letter recklessly sown sometime before in the seventh compartment of the uppermost fertile row, Ada, with a deep sigh of pleasure, composed the adjective TORFYaNUYu which went through a brown square at F and through two red squares (37 x 9 = 333 points) and got a bonus of 50 (for placing all seven blocks at one stroke) which made 383 in all, the highest score ever obtained for one word by a Russian scrambler. "There!" she said, "Ouf! *Pas facile*." And brushing away with the rosy knuckles of her white hand the black-bronze hair from her temple, she recounted her monstrous points in a smug, melodious tone of voice like a princess narrating the poison-cup killing of a superfluous lover, while Lucette fixed Van with a mute, fuming appeal against life's injustice—and then looking again at the board emitted a sudden howl of hope:

"It's a place name! One can't use it! It's the name of the first little station after Ladore Bridge!"

"That's right, pet," sang out Ada. "Oh, pet, you are so right! Yes, Torfyanaya, or as Blanche says, *La Tourbière*, is, indeed, the pretty but rather damp village where our *cendrillon*'s family lives. But, *mon petit*, in our mother's tongue —*que dis-je*, in the tongue of a maternal grandmother we all share—a rich beautiful tongue which my pet should not neglect for the sake of a Canadian brand of French—this quite ordinary adjective means 'peaty,' feminine gender, accusative case. Yes, that one coup has earned me nearly 400. Too bad—*ne dotyanula* (didn't quite make it)."

"*Ne dotyanula!*" Lucette complained to Van, her nostrils flaring, her shoulders shaking with indignation.

He tilted her chair to make her slide off and go. The poor child's final score for the fifteen rounds or so of the game was less than half of her sister's last masterstroke, and Van had hardly fared better, but who cared! The bloom streaking

Ada's arm, the pale blue of the veins in its hollow, the charred-wood odor of her hair shining brownly next to the lampshade's parchment (a translucent lakescape with Japanese dragons), scored infinitely more points than those tensed fingers bunched on the pencil stub could ever add up in the past, present or future.

"The loser will go *straight* to bed," said Van merrily, "and *stay* there, and we shall go down and fetch her—in exactly ten minutes—a big cup (the dark-blue cup!) of cocoa (sweet, dark, skinless Cadbury cocoa!)."

"I'm not going anywhere," said Lucette, folding her arms. "First, because it is only half-past eight, and, second, because I know perfectly well *why* you want to get rid of me."

"Van," said Ada, after a slight pause, "will you please summon Mademoiselle; she's working with Mother over a script which cannot be more stupid than this nasty child is."

"I would like to know," said Van, "the meaning of her interesting observation. Ask her, Ada dear."

"She thinks we are going to play Scrabble without her," said Ada, "or, go through those Oriental gymnastics which, you remember, Van, you began teaching me, as you remember."

"Oh, I remember! You remember I showed you what my teacher of athletics, you remember his name, King Wing, taught me."

"You remember a lot, ha-ha," said Lucette, standing in front of them in her green pajamas, sun-tanned chest bare, legs parted, arms akimbo.

"Perhaps the simplest—" began Ada.

"The simplest answer," said Lucette, "is that you two *can't* tell me why exactly you want to get rid of me."

"Perhaps the simplest answer," continued Ada, "is for you, Van, to give her a vigorous, resounding spanking."

[241]

"I dare you!" cried Lucette, and veered invitingly.

Very gently Van stroked the silky top of her head and kissed her behind the ear; and, bursting into a hideous storm of sobs, Lucette rushed out of the room. Ada locked the door after her.

"She's an utterly mad and depraved gipsy nymphet, of course," said Ada, "yet we must be more careful than ever . . . oh terribly, terribly, terribly . . . oh, careful, my darling."

37

It was raining. The lawns looked greener, and the reservoir grayer, in the dull prospect before the library bay window. Clad in a black training suit, with two yellow cushions propped under his head, Van lay reading Rattner on Terra, a difficult and depressing work. Every now and then he glanced at the autumnally tocking tall clock above the bald pate of tan Tartary as represented on a large old globe in the fading light of an afternoon that would have suited early October better than early July. Ada, wearing an unfashionable belted macintosh that he disliked, with her handbag on a strap over one shoulder, had gone to Kaluga for the whole day—officially to try on some clothes, unofficially to consult Dr. Krolik's cousin, the gynecologist Seitz (or "Zayats," as she transliterated him mentally since it also belonged, as Dr. "Rabbit" did, to the leporine group in Russian pronunciation). Van was positive that not once during a month of love-making had he failed to take all necessary precautions, sometimes rather bizarre, but incontestably trustworthy, and had lately acquired the sheath-like contraceptive device that in Ladore county only barbershops, for some odd but ancient reason, were allowed to sell. Still he felt anxious—and was cross with his anxiety—and Rattner, who halfheartedly denied any objective existence to the sibling planet in his text, but grudgingly accepted it in obscure notes (inconveniently placed between chapters), seemed as dull as the rain that could be discerned slanting in parallel pencil lines against the darker background of a larch plantation, borrowed, Ada contended, from Mansfield Park.

At ten minutes to five, Bout quietly came in with a lighted kerosene lamp and an invitation from Marina for a chat in her room. As Bout passed by the globe he touched it and looked with disapproval at his smudged finger. "The world is dusty," he said. "Blanche should be sent back to her native village. *Elle est folle et mauvaise, cette fille.*"

"Okay, okay," muttered Van, going back to his book. Bout left the room, still shaking his silly cropped head, and Van, yawning, allowed Rattner to slide down from the black divan on to the black carpet.

When he looked up again at the clock, it was gathering its strength to strike. He hastily got up from his couch recalling that Blanche had just come in to ask him to complain to Marina that Mlle Ada had again refused to give her a lift to "Beer Tower," as local jokers called her poor village. For a few moments the brief dim dream was so closely fused with the real event that even when he recalled Bout's putting his finger on the rhomboid peninsula where the Allies had just landed (as proclaimed by the Ladore newspaper spread-eagled on the library table), he still clearly saw Blanche wiping Crimea clean with one of Ada's lost handkerchiefs. He swarmed up the cochlea to the nursery water-closet; heard from afar the governess and her wretched pupil recite speeches from the horrible "Berenice" (a contralto croak alternating with a completely expressionless little voice); and decided that Blanche or rather Marina probably wished to know if he had been serious when he said the other day he would enlist at nineteen, the earliest volunteer age. He also gave a minute's thought to the sad fact that (as he well knew from his studies) the confusion of two realities, one in single, the other in double, quotes, was a symptom of impending insanity.

Naked-faced, dull-haired, wrapped up in her oldest kimono (her Pedro had suddenly left for Rio), Marina reclined on her mahogany bed under a golden-yellow quilt, drinking tea with mare's milk, one of her fads.

"Sit down, have a spot of *chayku*," she said. "The cow is in the smaller jug, I *think*. Yes, it is." And when Van, having kissed her freckled hand, lowered himself on the *ivanilich* (a kind of sighing old hassock upholstered in leather): "Van, dear, I wish to say something to you, because I know I shall never have to repeat it again. Belle, with her usual flair for the right phrase, has cited to me the *cousinage-dangereux-voisinage adage*—I mean 'adage,' I always fluff that word—and complained *qu'on s'embrassait dans tous les coins*. Is that true?"

Van's mind flashed in advance of his speech. It was, Marina, a fantastic exaggeration. The crazy governess had observed it once when he carried Ada across a brook and kissed her because she had hurt her toe. I'm the well-known beggar in the saddest of all stories.

"*Erunda* (nonsense)," said Van. "She once saw me carrying Ada across the brook and misconstrued our stumbling huddle (*spotïkayushcheesya sliyanie*)."

"I do not mean Ada, silly," said Marina with a slight snort, as she fussed over the teapot. "Azov, a Russian humorist, derives *erunda* from the German *hier und da*, which is neither here nor there. Ada is a big girl, and big girls, alas, have their own worries. Mlle Larivière meant Lucette, of course. Van, those soft games must stop. Lucette is twelve, and naive, and I know it's all clean fun, yet (*odnako*) one can never behave too *delikatno* in regard to a budding little woman. A *propos de coins:* in Griboedov's *Gore ot uma,* 'How stupid to be so clever,' a play in verse, written, I think, in Pushkin's time, the hero reminds Sophie of their childhood games, and says:

> How oft we sat together in a corner
> And what harm might there be in that?

but in Russian it is a little ambiguous, have another spot, Van?" (he shook his head, simultaneously lifting his hand, like his father), "because, you see,—no, there is none left anyway—the second line, *i kazhetsya chto v etom,* can be also construed as 'And in *that* one, meseems,' pointing with his finger at a corner of the room. Imagine—when I was rehearsing that scene with Kachalov at the Seagull Theater, in Yukonsk, Stanislavski, Konstantin Sergeevich, actually wanted him to make that cosy little gesture (*uyutnen'kiy zhest*)."

"How very amusing," said Van.

The dog came in, turned up a brimming brown eye Vanward, toddled up to the window, looked at the rain like a little person, and returned to his filthy cushion in the next room.

"I could never stand that breed," remarked Van. "Dackelophobia."

"But girls—do you like girls, Van, do you have many girls? You are not a pederast, like your poor uncle, are you? We have had some dreadful perverts in our ancestry but—Why do you laugh?"

"Nothing," said Van. "I just want to put on record that I adore girls. I had my first one when I was fourteen. *Mais qui me rendra mon Hélène?* She had raven black hair and a skin like skimmed milk. I had lots of much creamier ones later. *I kazhetsya chto v etom?*"

"How strange, how sad! Sad, because I know hardly anything about your life, my darling (*moy dushka*). The Zemskis were terrible rakes (*razvratniki*), one of them loved small girls, and another *raffolait d'une de ses juments* and had her tied up in a special way—don't ask me how" (double-hand gesture of horrified ignorance) "—when he dated her in her stall. *Kstati* (*à propos*), I could never understand how heredity is transmitted by bachelors, unless genes can jump like chess knights. I almost beat you, last time we played, we must play again, not today, though—I'm too sad today. I would have liked so much to know everything, *everything*, about you, but now it's too late. Recollections are always a little 'stylized' (*stilizovanï*), as your father used to say, an irresistible and hateful man, and now, even if you showed me your old diaries, I could no longer whip up any real emotional reaction to them, though all actresses can shed tears, as I'm doing now. You see (rummaging for her handkerchief under her pillow), when children are still quite tiny (*takie malyutki*), we cannot imagine that we can go without them, for even a couple of days, and later we do, and it's a couple of weeks, and later it's months, gray years, black decades, and then the *opéra bouffe* of the Christians' eternity. I think even the shortest separation is a kind of training for the Elysian Games—who said that? I said that. And your costume, though very becoming, is, in a sense, *traurnïy* (funerary). I'm spouting drivel. Forgive me these idiotic tears

. . . Tell me, is there *anything* I could do for you? Do think up something! Would you like a beautiful, practically new Peruvian scarf, which he left behind, that crazy boy? No? It's not your style? Now go. And remember—not a word to poor Mlle Larivière, who means well!"

Ada came back just before dinnertime. Worries? He met her as she climbed rather wearily the grand staircase, trailing her vanity bag by its strap up the steps behind her. Worries? She smelled of tobacco, either because (as she said) she had spent an hour in a compartment for smokers, or had smoked (she added) a cigarette or two herself in the doctor's waiting room, or else because (and this she did not say) her unknown lover was a heavy smoker, his open red mouth full of rolling blue fog.

"Well? *Tout est bien?*" asked Van after a sketchy kiss. "No worries?"

She glared, or feigned to glare, at him.

"Van, you should not have rung up Seitz! He does not even know my name! You promised!"

Pause.

"I did not," answered Van quietly.

"*Tant mieux,*" said Ada in the same false voice, as he helped her out of her coat in the corridor. "*Oui, tout est bien.* Will you stop sniffing me over, dear Van? In fact the blessed thing started on the way home. Let me pass, please."

Worries of her own? Of her mother's automatic making? A casual banality? "We all have our troubles"?

"Ada!" he cried.

She looked back, before unlocking her (always locked) door. "What?"

"Tuzenbakh, not knowing what to say: 'I have not had coffee today. Tell them to make me some.' Quickly walks away."

"Very funny!" said Ada, and locked herself up in her room.

[248]

38

In mid-July Uncle Dan took Lucette to Kaluga where she was to stay, with Belle and French, for five days. The Lyaskan Ballet and a German circus were in town, and no child would want to miss the schoolgirls' field-hockey and swimming matches which old Dan, a child at heart, attended religiously at that time of the year; moreover she had to undergo a series of "tests" at the Tarus Hospital to settle what caused her weight and temperature to fluctuate so abnormally despite her eating so heartily and feeling so well.

On the Friday afternoon when her father planned to return with her, he also expected to bring a Kaluga lawyer to Ardis where Demon was to come too, an unusual occurrence. The business to be discussed was the sale of some "blue" (peat-bog) land which belonged to both cousins and which both, for different reasons, were anxious to get rid of. As usually happened with Dan's most carefully worked-out plans, something misfired, the lawyer could not promise to come till late in the evening, and just before Demon arrived, his cousin aerogrammed a message asking Marina to "dine Demon" without waiting for Dan and Miller.

That *kontretan* (Marina's humorous term for a not necessarily nasty surprise) greatly pleased Van. He had seen little of his father that year. He loved him with light-hearted devotion, had worshipped him in boyhood, and respected him staunchly now in his tolerant but better informed youth. Still later a tinge of repulsion (the same repulsion he felt in regard to his own immorality) became admixed to the love and the esteem; but, on the other hand, the older he grew the more firmly he felt that he would give his life for his father, at a moment's notice, with pride and pleasure, in any circumstance imaginable. When Marina, in the late Eighteen-Nineties, in her miserable dotage, used to ramble on, with embarrassing and disgusting details, about dead Demon's "crimes," he felt pity for him and her, but his indifference to Marina and his adoration for his father remained unchanged —to endure thus even now, in the chronologically hardly believable Nineteen-Sixties. No accursed generalizer, with a half-penny mind and dry-fig heart, would be able to explain (and this is my sweetest revenge for all the detractions my lifework has met with) the individual vagaries evolved in those and similar matters. No art and no genius would exist without such vagaries, and this is a final pronouncement, damning all clowns and clods.

When had Demon visited Ardis in recent years? April 23, 1884 (the day Van's first summer stay there had been suggested, planned, promised). Twice in the summer of 1885 (while Van was climbing mountains in the Western states, and the Veen girls were in Europe). A dinner in 1886, in June or July (where was Van?). In 1887 for a few days in May (Ada was botanizing with a German woman in Estotia or California. Van was whoring in Chose).

Taking advantage of Larivière's and Lucette's absence, Van had long dallied with Ada in the comfortable nursery, and was now hanging from the wrong window, which did not give a clear view of the drive, when he heard the rich purr of his father's motorcar. He dashed downstairs—the speed of his descent causing the heat of the banisters to burn the palm of his hand in a merry way remindful of similar occasions in his boyhood. There was nobody in the hall. Demon had entered the house from a side gallery and was now settled in the sun-dusted music room, wiping his monocle with a special *zamshinka* ("shammy") as he awaited his "prebrandial" brandy (an ancient quip). His hair was dyed a raven black, his teeth were hound-white. His smooth glossy brown face with its trimly clipped black mustache and humid dark eyes beamed at his son, expressing the radiant love which Van reciprocated, and which both vainly tried to camouflage with habitual pleasantry.

"Hullo, Dad."

"Oh, hullo, Van."

Très Américain. Schoolyard. There he slams the car door, there he comes through the snow. Always gloves, no overcoat ever. Want to go to the "bathroom," Father? My land, sweet land.

"D'you want to go to the 'bathroom'?" asked Van, with a twinkle.

"No thanks, I had my bath this morning." (Quick sigh acknowledging the passage of time: he, too, remembered every detail of those father-and-son dinners at Riverlane, the immediate dutiful offer of the W.C., the hearty masters, the ignoble meal, creamed hash, God save America, embarrassed sons, vulgar fathers, titled Britisher and Greek grandee matching yachts, and yacs, and yoickfests in the Bahamudas. May I transfer inconspicuously this delicious pink-frosted synthesis from my plate to yours, son? "You don't *like* it, Dad!" (acting horribly hurt). God save their poor little American tastebuds.

"Your new car sounds wonderful," said Van.

"Doesn't it? Yes." (Ask Van about that *gornishon*—Franco-Russian slang of the meanest grade for a cute *kameristochka*). "And how is everything, my dear boy? I saw you last the day you returned from Chose. We waste life in separations! We are the fools of fate! Oh let's spend a month together in Paris or London before the Michaelmas term!"

Demon shed his monocle and wiped his eyes with the modish lace-frilled handkerchief that lodged in the heart pocket of his dinner jacket. His tear glands were facile in action when no real sorrow made him control himself.

"You look quite satanically fit, Dad. Especially with that fresh oeillet in your lapel eye. I suppose you have not been much in Manhattan lately—where did you get its last syllable?"

Homespun pun in the Veenish vein.

"I offered myself *en effet* a trip to Akapulkovo," answered Demon, needlessly and unwillingly recollecting (with that special concussion of instant detail that also plagued his children) a violet-and-black-striped fish in a bowl, a similarly striped couch, the subtropical sun bringing out the veins of an onyx ashtray astray on the stone floor, a batch of old, orange-juice-stained *Povesa* (playboy) magazines, the jewels he had brought, the phonograph singing in a dreamy girl's voice "*Petit nègre, au champ qui fleuronne*," and the admirable abdomen of a very expensive, and very faithless, and altogether adorable young Créole.

"Did what's-her-name go with you?"

"Well, my boy, frankly, the nomenclature is getting more and more confused every year. Let us speak of plainer things. Where are the drinks? They were promised me by a passing angel."

(Passing angel?)

Van pulled a green bell-cord which sent a melodious message pantryward and caused the old-fashioned, bronze-framed little aquarium, with its lone convict cichlid, to bubble antiphonally in a corner of the music room (an eerie, perhaps self-aerating reaction, which only Kim Beauharnais, the kitchen boy, understood). "Should he ring her up after dinner," wondered Demon. What time would it be there? Not much use, bad for the heart.

"I don't know if you know," said Van, resuming his perch on the fat arm of his father's chair. "Uncle Dan will be here with the lawyer and Lucette only after dinner."

"Capital," said Demon.

"Marina and Ada should be down in a minute—*ce sera un dîner à quatre*."

"Capital," he repeated. "You look splendid, my dear, dear fellow—and I don't have to exaggerate compliments as some do in regard to an aging man with shoe-shined hair. Your dinner jacket is very nice—or, rather, it's very nice recognizing one's old tailor in one's son's clothes—like catching oneself repeating an ancestral mannerism—for example, this (wagging his left forefinger three times at the height of his temple), which my mother did in casual, pacific denial; that gene missed you, but I've seen it in my hairdresser's looking-glass when refusing to have him put Crêmlin on my bald spot; and you know who had it too—my aunt Kitty, who married the banker Bolenski after divorcing that dreadful old wencher Lyovka Tolstoy, the writer."

Demon preferred Walter Scott to Dickens, and did not think highly of Russian novelists. As usual, Van considered it fit to make a corrective comment:

"A fantastically artistic writer, Dad."

"You are a fantastically charming boy," said Demon, shedding another sweet-water tear. He pressed to his cheek Van's strong shapely hand. Van kissed his father's hairy fist which was already holding a not yet visible glass of liquor. Despite the manly impact of their Irishness, all Veens who had Russian blood revealed much tenderness in ritual overflows of affection while remaining somewhat inept in its verbal expression.

"I say," exclaimed Demon, "what's happened—your shaftment is that of a carpenter's. Show me your other hand. Good gracious" (muttering:) "Hump of Venus disfigured, Line of Life scarred but monstrously long . . ." (switching to a gipsy chant:) "You'll live to reach Terra, and come back a wiser and merrier man" (reverting to his ordinary voice:) "What puzzles me as a palmist is the strange condition of the Sister of your Life. And the roughness!"

"Mascodagama," whispered Van, raising his eyebrows.

"Ah, of course, how blunt (dumb) of me. Now tell me—you like Ardis Hall?"

"I adore it," said Van. "It's for me the *château que baignait la Dore*. I would gladly spend all my scarred and strange life here. But that's a hopeless fancy."

"Hopeless? I wonder. I know Dan wants to leave it to Lucile, but Dan is greedy, and my affairs are such that I can satisfy great greed. When I was your age I thought that the sweetest word in the language rhymes with 'billiard,' and now I know I was right. If you're really keen, son, on having this property, I might try to buy it. I can exert a certain pressure upon my Marina. She sighs like a hassock when you sit upon her, so to speak. Damn it, the servants here are not Mercuries. Pull that cord again. Yes, maybe Dan could be made to sell."

"That's very black of you, Dad," said pleased Van, using a slang phrase he had learned from his tender young nurse,

Ruby, who was born in the Mississippi region where most magistrates, public benefactors, high priests of various so-called "denominations," and other honorable and generous men, had the dark or darkish skin of their West-African ancestors, who had been the first navigators to reach the Gulf of Mexico.

"I wonder," Demon mused. "It would cost hardly more than a couple of millions minus what Cousin Dan owes me, minus also the Ladore pastures, which are utterly mucked up and should be got rid of gradually, if the local squires don't blow up that new kerosene distillery, the *stïd i sram* (shame) of our county. I am not *particularly* fond of Ardis, but I have nothing against it, though I detest its environs. Ladore Town has become very honky-tonky, and the gaming is not what it used to be. You have all sorts of rather odd neighbors. Poor Lord Erminin is practically insane. At the races, the other day, I was talking to a woman I preyed upon years ago, oh long before Moses de Vere cuckolded her husband in my absence and shot him dead in my presence—an epigram you've heard before, no doubt from these very lips—"

(The next thing will be "paternal repetitiousness.")

"—but a good son should put up with a little paternal repetitiousness—Well, she tells me her boy and Ada see a lot of each other, et cetera. Is that true?"

"Not really," said Van. "They meet now and then—at the usual parties. Both like horses, and races, but that's all. There is no et cetera, that's out of the question."

"Good! Ah, the portentous footfall is approaching, I hear. Prascovie de Prey has the worst fault of a snob: overstatement. *Bonsoir*, Bouteillan. You look as ruddy as your native vine—but we are not getting any younger, as the amerlocks say, and that pretty messenger of mine must have been waylaid by some younger and more fortunate suitor."

"*Proshu, papochka* (please, Dad)," murmured Van, who always feared that his father's recondite jests might offend a menial—while sinning himself by being sometimes too curt.

But—to use a hoary narrational turn—the old Frenchman knew his former master too well to be bothered by gentlemanly humor. His hand still tingled nicely from slapping Blanche's compact young bottom for having garbled Mr. Veen's simple request and broken a flower vase. After placing his tray on a low table he retreated a few steps, his fingers remaining curved in the tray-carrying position, and only then acknowledged Demon's welcome with a fond bow. Was Monsieur's health always good? Indeed it was.

"I'll want," said Demon, "a bottle of your Château Latour d'Estoc for dinner"; and when the butler, having removed *en passant* a crumpled little handkerchief from the piano top, had left the room with another salute: "How do you get along with Ada? She's what—almost sixteen now? Very musical and romantic?"

"We are close friends," said Van (who had carefully prepared his answer to a question he had expected to come in one form or another). "We have really more things in common than, for instance, ordinary lovers or cousins or siblings. I mean, we are really inseparable. We read a lot, she is spectacularly self-educated, thanks to her granddad's library. She knows the names of all the flowers and finches in the neighborhood. She is altogether a very amusing girl."

"Van . . . ," began Demon, but stopped—as he had begun and stopped a number of times before in the course of the last years. Some day it would have to be said, but this was not the right moment. He inserted his monocle and examined the bottles: "By the way, son, do you crave any of these aperitifs? My father allowed me Lilletovka and that Illinois Brat—awful bilge, *antranou svadi*, as Marina would say. I suspect your uncle has a cache behind the solanders in his study and keeps there a finer whisky than this *usque ad Russkum*. Well, let us have the cognac, as planned, unless you are a *filius aquae?*"

(No pun intended, but one gets carried away and goofs.)

"Oh, I prefer claret. I'll concentrate (*nalyagu*) on the Latour later on. No, I'm certainly no T-totaler, and besides the Ardis tap water is not recommended!"

"I must warn Marina," said Demon after a gum-rinse and a slow swallow, "that her husband should stop swilling tittery, and stick to French and Califrench wines—after that little stroke he had. I met him in town recently, near Mad Avenue, saw him walking toward me quite normally, but then as he caught sight of me, a block away, the clockwork began slowing down and he stopped—oh, helplessly!—before he reached me. That's hardly normal. Okay. Let our sweethearts never meet, as we used to say, up at Chose. Only Yukonians think cognac is bad for the liver, because they have nothing but vodka. Well, I'm glad you get along so well with Ada. That's fine. A moment ago, in that gallery, I ran into a remarkably pretty soubrette. She never once raised her lashes and answered in French when I—Please, my boy, move that screen a little, that's right, the stab of a sunset, especially from under a thunderhead, is not for my poor eyes. Or poor ventricles. Do you like the type, Van—the bowed little head, the bare neck, the high heels, the trot, the wiggle, you do, don't you?"

"Well, sir—"

(Tell him I'm the youngest Venutian? Does he belong, too? Show the sign? Better not. Invent.)

"—Well, I'm resting after my torrid affair, in London, with

my tango-partner whom you saw me dance with when you flew over for that last show—remember?"

"Indeed, I do. Curious, you calling it that."

"I think, sir, you've had enough brandy."

"Sure, sure," said Demon, wrestling with a subtle question which only the ineptitude of a kindred conjecture had crowded out of Marina's mind, granted it could have entered by some back door; for ineptitude is always synonymous with multitude, and nothing is fuller than an empty mind.

"Naturally," continued Demon, "there is a good deal to be said for a restful summer in the country . . ."

"Open-air life and all that," said Van.

"It is incredible that a young boy should control his father's liquor intake," remarked Demon, pouring himself a fourth shallow. "On the other hand," he went on, nursing the thin-stemmed, gold-rimmed cup, "open-air life may be pretty bleak without a summer romance, and not many decent girls haunt the neighborhood, I agree. There was that lovely Erminin girl, *une petite juive très aristocratique,* but I understand she's engaged. By the way, the de Prey woman tells me her son has enlisted and will soon be taking part in that deplorable business abroad which our country should have ignored. I wonder if he leaves any rivals behind?"

"Goodness no," replied honest Van. "Ada is a serious young lady. She has no beaux—except me, *ça va seins durs.* Now who, who, who, Dad, who said that for '*sans dire*'?"

"Oh! King Wing! When I wanted to know how he liked his French wife. Well, that's fine news about Ada. She likes horses, you say?"

"She likes," said Van, "what all our belles like—balls, orchids, and *The Cherry Orchard.*"

Here Ada herself came running into the room. Yes-yes-yes-yes, here I come. Beaming!

[258]

Old Demon, iridescent wings humped, half rose but sank back again, enveloping Ada with one arm, holding his glass in the other hand, kissing the girl in the neck, in the hair, burrowing in her sweetness with more than an uncle's fervor. "Gosh," she exclaimed (with an outbreak of nursery slang that affected Van with even more *umilenie, attendrissement,* melting ravishment, than his father seemed to experience). "How lovely to see you! Clawing your way through the clouds! Swooping down on Tamara's castle!"

(Lermontov paraphrased by Lowden).

"The last time I enjoyed you," said Demon "was in April when you wore a raincoat with a white and black scarf and simply reeked of some arsenic stuff after seeing your dentist. Dr. Pearlman has married his receptionist, you'll be glad to know. Now to business, my darling. I accept your dress" (the sleeveless black sheath), "I tolerate your romantic hairdo, I don't care much for your pumps *na bosu nogu* (on bare feet), your Beau Masque perfume—*passe encore,* but, my precious, I abhor and reject your livid lipstick. It may be the fashion in good old Ladore. It is not done in Man or London."

"*Ladno* (Okay)," said Ada and, baring her big teeth, rubbed fiercely her lips with a tiny handkerchief produced from her bosom.

"That's also provincial. You should carry a black silk purse. And now I'll show what a diviner I am: your dream is to be a concert pianist!"

"It is not," said Van indignantly. "What perfect nonsense. She can't play a note!"

"Well, no matter," said Demon. "Observation is not always the mother of deduction. However, there is nothing improper about a hanky dumped on a Bechstein. You don't have, my love, to blush so warmly. Let me quote for comic relief

> *"Lorsque son fi-ancé fut parti pour la guerre*
> *Irène de Grandfief, la pauvre et noble enfant*
> *Ferma son pi-ano . . . vendit son éléphant*

"The gobble *enfant* is genuine, but the elephant is mine."

"You don't say so," laughed Ada.

"Our great Coppée," said Van, "is awful, of course, yet he has one very fetching little piece which Ada de Grandfief here has twisted into English several times, more or less successfully."

"Oh, Van!" interjected Ada with unusual archness, and scooped up a handful of salted almonds.

"Let's hear it, let's hear it," cried Demon as he borrowed a nut from her cupped hand.

The neat interplay of harmonious motions, the candid gayety of family reunions, the never-entangling marionette strings—all this is easier described than imagined.

"Old storytelling devices," said Van, "may be parodied only by very great and inhuman artists, but only close relatives can be forgiven for paraphrasing illustrious poems. Let me preface the effort of a cousin—anybody's cousin—by a snatch of Pushkin, for the sake of rhyme—"

"For the *snake* of rhyme!" cried Ada. "A paraphrase, even my paraphrase, is like the corruption of 'snakeroot' into 'snagrel'—all that remains of a delicate little birthwort."

"Which is amply sufficient," said Demon, "for my little needs, and those of my little friends."

"So here goes," continued Van (ignoring what he felt was an indecent allusion, since the unfortunate plant used to be considered by the ancient inhabitants of the Ladore region not so much as a remedy for the bite of a reptile, as the token of a very young woman's easy delivery; but no matter). "By chance preserved has been the poem. In fact, I have it. Here it is: *Leur chute est lente* and one can know 'em . . ."

"Oh, *I* know 'em," interrupted Demon:

> *"Leur chute est lente. On peut les suivre*
> *Du regard en reconnaissant*
> *Le chêne à sa feuille de cuivre*
> *L'érable à sa feuille de sang*

"Grand stuff!"

"Yes, that was Coppée and now comes the cousin," said Van, and he recited:

> "Their fall is gentle. The leavesdropper
> Can follow each of them and know
> The oak tree by its leaf of copper,
> The maple by its blood-red glow."

"Pah!" uttered the versionist.

"Not at all!" cried Demon. "That 'leavesdropper' is a splendid trouvaille, girl." He pulled the girl to him, she landing on the arm of his *Klubsessel,* and he glued himself with thick moist lips to her hot red ear through the rich black strands. Van felt a shiver of delight.

It was now Marina's turn to make her entrée, which she did in excellent chiaroscuro circumstances, wearing a spangled dress, her face in the soft focus sought by ripe stars, holding out both arms and followed by Jones who carried two flambeaux and kept trying to keep within the limits of decorum the odd little go-away kicks he was aiming backwards at a brown flurry in the shadows.

"Marina!" cried Demon with perfunctory enthusiasm, and patted her hand as he joined her on a settee.

Puffing rhythmically, Jones set one of his beautiful dragon-entwined flambeaux on the low-boy with the gleaming drinks and was about to bring over its fellow to the spot where Demon and Marina were winding up affable preliminaries but was quickly motioned by Marina to a pedestal near the striped fish. Puffing, he drew the curtains, for nothing but picturesque ruins remained of the day. Jones was new, very efficient, solemn and slow, and one had to get used gradually to his ways and wheeze. Years later he rendered me a service that I will never forget.

"She's a *jeune fille fatale*, a pale, heart-breaking beauty," Demon confided to his former mistress without bothering to discover whether the subject of his praise could hear him (she did) from the other end of the room where she was helping Van to corner the dog—and showing much too much leg in the process. Our old friend, being quite as excited as the rest of the reunited family, had scampered in after Marina with an old miniver-furred slipper in his merry mouth. The slipper belonged to Blanche, who had been told to whisk Dack to her room but, as usual, had not incarcerated him properly. Both children experienced a chill of *déjà-vu* (a two-fold *déjà-vu*, in fact, when contemplated in artistic retro-spect).

"*Pozhalsta bez glupostey* (please, no silly things), especially *devant les gens*," said deeply flattered Marina (sound-ing the final "s" as her granddams had done); and when the slow fish-mouthed footman had gone carrying away, supine, high-chested Dack and his poor plaything, she continued: "Really, in comparison to the local girls, to Grace Erminin, for example, or Cordula de Prey, Ada is a Turgenevian maiden or even a Jane Austen miss."

[262]

"I'm Fanny Price, actually," commented Ada.

"In the staircase scene," added Van.

"Let's not bother about their private jokes," said Marina to Demon. "I never can understand their games and little secrets. Mlle Larivière, however, has written a wonderful screenplay about mysterious children doing strange things in old parks—but don't let her start talking of her literary successes tonight, that would be fatal."

"I hope your husband won't be *too* late," said Demon. "He is not at his best after eight P.M., summertime, you know. By the way, how's Lucette?"

At this moment both battants of the door were flung open by Bouteillan in the grand manner, and Demon offered *kalachikom* (in the form of a Russian crescent loaf) his arm to Marina. Van, who in his father's presence was prone to lapse into a rather dismal sort of playfulness, proposed taking Ada in, but she slapped his wrist away with a sisterly *sans-gêne*, of which Fanny Price might not have approved.

Another Price, a typical, too typical, old retainer whom Marina (and G. A. Vronsky, during their brief romance) had dubbed, for unknown reasons, "Grib," placed an onyx ashtray at the head of the table for Demon, who liked to smoke between courses—a puff of Russian ancestry. A side table supported, also in the Russian fashion, a collection of red, black, gray, beige hors-d'oeuvres, with the serviette caviar (*salfetochnaya ikra*) separated from the pot of Graybead (*ikra svezhaya*) by the succulent pomp of preserved boletes, "white," and "subbetuline," while the pink of smoked salmon vied with the incarnadine of Westphalian ham. The variously flavored *vodochki* glittered, on a separate tray. The French cuisine had contributed its *chaudfroids* and *foie gras*. A window was open, and the crickets were stridulating at an ominous speed in the black motionless foliage.

It was—to continue the novelistic structure—a long, joyful, delicious dinner, and although the talk consisted mainly of family quips and bright banalities, that reunion was to remain suspended in one's memory as a strangely significant, not wholly pleasant, experience. One treasured it in the same way as when falling in love with a picture in a pinacoteca or remembering a dream style, the dream detail, the meaningful richness of color and contour in an otherwise meaningless vision. It should be observed that nobody, not even the reader, not even Bouteillan (who crumbled, alas, a precious cork), was at his or her best at that particular party. A faint element of farce and falsity flawed it, preventing an angel—if angels could visit Ardis—from being completely at ease; and yet it was a marvelous show which no artist would have wanted to miss.

The tablecloth and the candle blaze attracted timorous or impetuous moths among which Ada, with a ghost pointing them out to her, could not help recognizing many old "flutterfriends." Pale intruders, anxious only to spread out their delicate wings on some lustrous surface; ceiling-bumpers in guildman furs; thick-set rake-hells with bushy antennae; and party-crashing hawkmoths with red black-belted bellies, sailed or shot, silent or humming, into the dining room out of the black hot humid night.

It was a black hot humid night in mid-July, 1888, at Ardis, in Ladore county, let us not forget, let us never forget, with a family of four seated around an oval dinner table, bright with flowers and crystal—not a scene in a play, as might have seemed—nay, *must* have seemed—to a spectator (with a camera or a program) placed in the velvet pit of the garden. Sixteen years had elapsed from the end of Marina's three-year affair with Demon. Intermissions of various length—a break of two months in the spring of 1870, another, of almost four, in the middle of 1871—had at the time only increased the tenderness and the torture. Her singularly coarsened features, her attire, that sequin-spangled dress, the glittering net over her strawberry-blond dyed hair, her red sunburnt chest and melodramatic make-up, with too much ochre and maroon in it, did not even vaguely remind the man, who had loved her more keenly than any other woman in his philanderings, of the dash, the glamour, the lyricism of Marina Durmanov's beauty. It aggrieved him—that complete collapse of the past, the dispersal of its itinerant court and music-makers, the logical impossibility to relate the dubious reality of the present to the unquestionable one of remembrance. Even these hors-d'oeuvres on the *zakusochnïy stol* of Ardis Manor and its painted dining room did not link up with their *petits soupers*, although, God knows, the triple staple to start with was always much the same—pickled young boletes in their tight-fitting glossy fawn helmets, the gray beads of fresh caviar, the goose liver paste, pique-aced with Perigord truffles.

Demon popped into his mouth a last morsel of black bread with elastic samlet, gulped down a last pony of vodka and took his place at the table with Marina facing him across its oblong length, beyond the great bronze bowl with carved-looking Calville apples and elongated Persty grapes. The alcohol his vigorous system had already imbibed was instrumental, as usual, in reopening what he gallicistically called condemned doors, and now as he gaped involuntarily as all men do while spreading a napkin, he considered Marina's pretentious *ciel-étoilé* hairdress and tried to *realize* (in the rare full sense of the word), tried to *possess* the reality of a fact by forcing it into the sensuous center, that here was a woman whom he had intolerably loved, who had loved him hysterically and skittishly, who insisted they make love on rugs and cushions laid on the floor ("as respectable people do in the Tigris-Euphrates valley"), who would woosh down fluffy slopes on a bobsleigh a fortnight after parturition, or arrive by the Orient Express with five trunks, Dack's grandsire, and a maid, to Dr. Stella Ospenko's *ospedale* where he was recovering from a scratch received in a sword duel (and still visible as a white weal under his eighth rib after a lapse of nearly seventeen years). How strange that when one met after a long separation a chum or fat aunt whom one had been fond of as a child the unimpaired human warmth of the friendship was rediscovered at once, but with an old mistress this never happened—the human part of one's affection seemed to be swept away with the dust of the inhuman passion, in a wholesale operation of demolishment. He looked at her and acknowledged the perfection of the potage, but she, this rather thick-set woman, goodhearted, no doubt, but restive and sour-faced, glazed over, nose, forehead and all, with a sort of brownish oil that she considered to be more "juvenizing" than powder, was more of a stranger to him than Bouteillan who had once carried her in his arms, in a feigned faint, out of a Ladore villa and into a cab, after a final, quite final row, on the eve of her wedding.

Marina, essentially a dummy in human disguise, experienced no such qualms, lacking as she did that *third sight* (individual, magically detailed imagination) which many otherwise ordinary and conformant people may also possess, but without which memory (even that of a profound "thinker" or technician of genius) is, let us face it, a stereotype or a tear-sheet. We do not wish to be too hard on Marina; after all, her blood throbs in our wrists and temples, and many of our megrims are hers, not his. Yet we cannot condone the grossness of her soul. The man sitting at the head of the table and joined to her by a pair of cheerful youngsters, the "juvenile" (in movie parlance) on her right, the "ingénue" on her left, differed in no way from the same Demon in much the same black jacket (minus perhaps the carnation he had evidently purloined from a vase Blanche had been told to bring from the gallery) who sat next to her at the Praslin's last Christmas. The dizzy chasm he felt every time he met her, that awful "wonder of life" with its extravagant jumble of geological faults, could not be bridged by what *she* accepted as a dotted line of humdrum encounters: "poor old" Demon (all her pillow mates being retired with that title) appeared before her like a harmless ghost, in the foyers of theaters "between mirror and fan," or in the drawing rooms of common friends, or once in Lincoln Park, indicating an indigo-buttocked ape with his cane and not saluting her, according to the rules of the *beau monde*, because he was with a courtesan. Somewhere, further back, much further back, safely transformed by her screen-corrupted mind into a stale melodrama was her three-year-long period of hectically spaced love-meetings with Demon, A *Torrid Affair* (the title of her only cinema hit), passion in *palaces*, the palms and larches, his Utter Devotion, his impossible temper, separations, reconciliations, Blue Trains, tears, treachery, terror, an insane sister's threats, helpless, no doubt, but leaving their tiger-marks on the drapery of dreams, especially when dampness and dark affect one with fever. And the shadow of retribution on the backwall (with ridiculous legal innuendoes). All this was mere scenery, easily packed, labeled "Hell" and freighted away; and only very infrequently some reminder would come—say, in the trick-work closeup of two left hands belonging to different sexes—doing what? Marina could no longer recall (though only *four* years had elapsed!)—playing *à quatre mains?*—no, neither took piano lessons—casting bunny-shadows on a wall?—closer, warmer, but still wrong; measuring something?

But what? Climbing a tree? The polished trunk of a tree? But where, when? Someday, she mused, one's past must be put in order. Retouched, retaken. Certain "wipes" and "inserts" will have to be made in the picture; certain telltale abrasions in the emulsion will have to be corrected; "dissolves" in the sequence discreetly combined with the trimming out of unwanted, embarrassing "footage," and definite guarantees obtained; yes, someday—before death with its clapstick closes the scene.

Tonight she contented herself with the automatic ceremony of giving him what she remembered, more or less correctly, when planning the menu, as being his favorite food —*zelyonïya shchi*, a velvety green sorrel-and-spinach soup, containing slippery hard-boiled eggs and served with finger-burning, irresistibly soft, meat-filled or carrot-filled or cabbage-filled *pirozhki*—peer-rush-KEY, thus pronounced, thus celebrated here, for ever and ever. After that, she had decided, there would be bread-crumbed sander (*sudak*) with boiled potatoes, hazel-hen (*ryabchiki*) and that special asparagus (*bezukhanka*) which does not produce Proust's After-effect, as cookbooks say.

"Marina," murmured Demon at the close of the first course. "Marina," he repeated louder. "Far from me" (a locution he favored) "to criticize Dan's taste in white wines or the manners *de vos domestiques*. You know me, I'm above all that rot, I'm . . ." (gesture); "but, my dear," he continued, switching to Russian, "the *chelovek* who brought me the *pirozhki*—the new man, the plumpish one with the eyes (*s glazami*)—"

"Everybody has eyes," remarked Marina drily.

"Well, *his* look as if they were about to octopus the food he serves. But that's not the point. He pants, Marina! He suffers from some kind of *odïshka* (shortness of breath). He

[268]

should see Dr. Krolik. It's depressing. It's a rhythmic pumping pant. It made my soup ripple."

"Look, Dad," said Van, "Dr. Krolik can't do much, because, as you know quite well, he's dead, and Marina can't tell her servants not to breathe, because, as you also know, they're alive."

"The Veen wit, the Veen wit," murmured Demon.

"Exactly," said Marina. "I simply refuse to do anything about it. Besides poor Jones is not at all asthmatic, but only nervously eager to please. He's as healthy as a bull and has rowed me from Ardisville to Ladore and back, and enjoyed it, many times this summer. You are cruel, Demon. I can't tell him '*ne pïkhtite*,' as I can't tell Kim, the kitchen boy, not to take photographs on the sly—he's a regular snap-shooting fiend, that Kim, though otherwise an adorable, gentle, honest boy; nor can I tell my little French maid to stop getting invitations, as she somehow succeeds in doing, to the most exclusive *bals masqués* in Ladore."

"That's interesting," observed Demon.

"He's a dirty old man!" cried Van cheerfully.

"Van!" said Ada.

"I'm a dirty *young* man," sighed Demon.

"Tell me, Bouteillan," asked Marina, "what other good white wine do we have—what can you recommend?" The butler smiled and whispered a fabulous name.

"Yes, oh, yes," said Demon. "Ah, my dear, you should not think up dinners all by yourself. Now about rowing—you mentioned rowing . . . Do you know that *moi, qui vous parle*, was a Rowing Blue in 1858? Van prefers football, but he's only a College Blue, aren't you Van? I'm also better than he at tennis—not lawn tennis, of course, a game for parsons, but 'court tennis' as they say in Manhattan. What else, Van?"

"You still beat me at fencing, but I'm the better shot. That's not real *sudak*, *papa*, though it's tops, I assure you."

(Marina, having failed to obtain the European product in time for the dinner, had chosen the nearest thing, wall-eyed pike, or "dory," with Tartar sauce and boiled young potatoes.)

"Ah!" said Demon, tasting Lord Byron's Hock. "This redeems Our Lady's Tears."

"I was telling Van a moment ago," he continued, raising his voice (he labored under the delusion that Marina had grown rather deaf), "about your husband. My dear, he overdoes the juniper vodka stuff, he's getting, in fact, a mite fuzzy and odd. The other day I chanced to walk through Pat Lane on the Fourth Avenue side, and there he was coming, at quite a spin, in his horrid town car, that primordial petrol two-seater he's got, with the tiller. Well, he saw me, from quite a distance, and waved, and the whole contraption began to shake down, and finally stopped half a block away, and there he sat trying to budge it with little jerks of his haunches, you know, like a child who can't get his tricycle unstuck, and as I walked up to him I had the definite impression that it was *his* mechanism that had stalled, not the Hardpan's." But what Demon, in the goodness of his crooked heart, omitted to tell Marina was that the imbecile, in secret from his art adviser, Mr. Aix, had acquired for a few thousand dollars from a gaming friend of Demon's, and with Demon's blessings, a couple of fake Correggios—only to resell them by some unforgivable fluke to an equally imbecile collector, for half a million which Demon considered henceforth as a loan his cousin should certainly refund him if sanity counted for something on this gemel planet. And, conversely, Marina refrained from telling Demon about the young hospital nurse Dan had been monkeying with ever since his last illness (it was, by the way, she, busybody Bess, whom Dan has asked on a memorable occasion to help him get "something nice for a half-Russian child interested in biology").

"*Vous me comblez,*" said Demon in reference to the burgundy, "though, *pravda,* my maternal grandfather would have left the table rather than see me drinking red wine instead of champagne with *gelinotte.* Superb, my dear (blowing a kiss through the vista of flame and silver)."

The roast hazel-hen (or rather its New World representative, locally called "mountain grouse") was accompanied by preserved lingonberries (locally called "mountain cranberries"). An especially succulent morsel of one of those brown little fowls yielded a globule of birdshot between Demon's red tongue and strong canine: "*La fève de Diane,*" he remarked, placing it carefully on the edge of his plate. "How is the car situation, Van?"

"Vague. I ordered a Roseley like yours but it won't be delivered before Christmas. I tried to find a Silentium with a side car and could not, because of the war, though what connection exists between wars and motorcycles is a mystery. But we manage, Ada and I, we manage, we ride, we bike, we even jikker."

"I wonder," said sly Demon, "why I'm reminded all at once of our great Canadian's lovely lines about blushing Irène:

"*Le feu si délicat de la virginité*
Qui something *sur son front . . .*

"All right. You can ship mine to England, provided—"

"By the way, Demon," interrupted Marina, "where and how can I obtain the kind of old roomy limousine with an old professional chauffeur that Praskovia, for instance, has had for years?"

"Impossible, my dear, they are all in heaven or on Terra. But what would Ada like, what would my silent love like for her birthday? It's next Saturday, *po razschyotu po moemu* (by my reckoning), isn't it? *Une rivière de diamants?*"

"*Protestuyu!*" cried Marina. "Yes, I'm speaking *seriozno*. I object to your giving her *kvaka sesva* (*quoi que ce soit*), Dan and I will take care of all that."

"Besides you'll forget," said Ada laughing, and very deftly showed the tip of her tongue to Van who had been on the look-out for her conditional reaction to "diamonds."

Van asked: "Provided what?"

"Provided you don't have one waiting already for you in George's Garage, Ranta Road."

"Ada, you'll be jikkering alone soon," he continued, "I'm going to have Mascodagama round out his vacation in Paris. *Qui* something *sur son front, en accuse la beauté!*"

So the trivial patter went. Who does not harbor in the darkest gulf of his mind such bright recollections? Who has not squirmed and covered his face with his hands as the dazzling past leered at him? Who, in the terror and solitude of a long night—

"What was that?" exclaimed Marina, whom certicle storms terrified even more than they did the Antiamberians of Ladore County.

"Sheet lightning," suggested Van.

"If you ask me," said Demon, turning on his chair to consider the billowing drapery, "I'd guess it was a photographer's flash. After all, we have here a famous actress and a sensational acrobat."

Ada ran to the window. From under the anxious magnolias a white-faced boy flanked by two gaping handmaids stood aiming a camera at the harmless, gay family group. But it was only a nocturnal mirage, not unusual in July. Nobody was taking pictures except Perun, the unmentionable god of thunder. In expectation of the rumble, Marina started to count under her breath, as if she were praying or checking the pulse of a very sick person. One heartbeat was supposed to span one mile of black night between the living heart and a doomed herdsman, felled somewhere—oh, very far—on the top of a mountain. The rumble came—but sounded rather subdued. A second flash revealed the structure of the French window.

Ada returned to her seat. Van picked up her napkin from under her chair and in the course of his brief plunge and ascent brushed the side of her knee with his temple.

"Might I have another helping of Peterson's Grouse, *Tetrastes bonasia windriverensis?*" asked Ada loftily.

Marina jangled a diminutive cowbell of bronze. Demon placed his palm on the back of Ada's hand and asked her to pass him the oddly evocative object. She did so in a staccato arc. Demon inserted his monocle and, muffling the tongue of memory, examined the bell; but it was not the one that had once stood on a bed-tray in a dim room of Dr. Lapiner's chalet; was not even of Swiss make; was merely one of those sweet-sounding translations which reveal a paraphrast's crass counterfeit as soon as you look up the original.

Alas, the bird had not survived "the honor one had made to it," and after a brief consultation with Bouteillan a somewhat incongruous but highly palatable bit of saucisson d'Arles added itself to the young lady's fare of *asperges en branches* that everybody was now enjoying. It almost awed one to see the pleasure with which she and Demon distorted their shiny-lipped mouths in exactly the same way to introduce orally from some heavenly height the voluptuous ally of the prim lily of the valley, holding the shaft with an identical bunching of the fingers, not unlike the reformed "sign of the cross" for protesting against which (a ridiculous little schism measuring an inch or so from thumb to index) so many Russians had been burnt by other Russians only two centuries earlier on the banks of the Great Lake of Slaves. Van remembered that his tutor's great friend, the learned but prudish Semyon Afanasievich Vengerov, then a young associate professor but already a celebrated Pushkinist (1855–1954), used to say that the only vulgar passage in his author's work was the cannibal joy of young gourmets tearing "plump and live" oysters out of their "cloisters" in an unfinished canto of *Eugene Onegin*. But then "everyone has his own taste," as the British writer Richard Leonard Churchill mistranslates a trite French phrase (*chacun à son gout*) twice in the course of his novel about a certain Crimean Khan once popular with reporters and politicians. "A Great Good Man"—according, of course, to the cattish and prejudiced Guillaume Monparnasse about whose new celebrity Ada, while dipping the reversed corolla of one hand in a bowl, was now telling Demon, who was performing the same rite in the same graceful fashion.

Marina helped herself to an Albany from a crystal box of Turkish cigarettes tipped with red rose petal and passed the box on to Demon. Ada, somewhat self-consciously, lit up too.

"You know quite well," said Marina, "that your father disapproves of your smoking at table."

"Oh, it's all right," murmured Demon.

"I had Dan in view," explained Marina heavily. "He's very prissy on that score."

"Well, and I'm not," answered Demon.

Ada and Van could not help laughing. All that was banter —not of a high order, but still banter.

A moment later, however, Van remarked: "I think I'll take an Alibi—I mean an Albany—myself."

"Please note, everybody," said Ada, "how *voulu* that slip was! I like a smoke when I go mushrooming, but when I'm back, this horrid tease insists I smell of some romantic Turk or Albanian met in the woods."

"Well," said Demon, "Van's quite right to look after your morals."

The real *profitrol'* (very soft "l") of the Russians, as first made by their cooks in Gavana before 1700, consists of larger puffs coated with creamier chocolate than the dark and puny "profit rolls" served in European restaurants. Our friends had finished that rich sweetmeat flooded with *chocolat-au-lait* sauce, and were ready for some fruit, when Bout followed by his father and floundering Jones made a sensational entry.

All the toilets and waterpipes in the house had been suddenly seized with borborygmic convulsions. This always signified, and introduced, a long-distance call. Marina, who had been awaiting for several days a certain message from California in response to a torrid letter, could now hardly contain her passionate impatience and had been on the point of running to the dorophone in the hall at the first bubbling spasm, when young Bout hurried in dragging the long green cord (visibly palpitating in a series of swells and contractions rather like a serpent ingesting a field mouse) of the ornate, brass-and-nacre receiver, which Marina with a wild "A *l'eau!*" pressed to her ear. It was, however, only fussy old Dan ringing her up to inform everybody that Miller could not make it that night after all and would accompany him to Ardis bright and early on the following morning.

"Early but hardly bright," observed Demon, who was now glutted with family joys and slightly annoyed he had missed

[275]

the first half of a gambling night in Ladore for the sake of all that well-meant but not *quite* first-rate food.

"We'll have coffee in the yellow drawing room," said Marina as sadly as if she were evoking a place of dreary exile. "Jones, *please*, don't walk on that phonecord. You have no idea, Demon, how I dread meeting again, after all those years, that dislikable Norbert von Miller, who has probably become even more arrogant and obsequious, and moreover does not realize, I'm sure, that Dan's wife is me. He's a Baltic Russian" (turning to Van) "but really *echt deutsch*, though his mother was born Ivanov or Romanov, or something, who owned a calico factory in Finland or Denmark. I can't imagine how he got his barony; when I knew him twenty years ago he was plain Mr. Miller."

"He is still that," said Demon drily, "because you've got two Millers mixed up. The lawyer who works for Dan is my old friend Norman Miller of the Fainley, Fehler and Miller law firm and physically bears a striking resemblance to Wilfrid Laurier. Norbert, on the other hand, has, I remember, a head like a *kegelkugel*, lives in Switzerland, knows perfectly well whom you married and is an unmentionable blackguard."

After a quick cup of coffee and a drop of cherry liqueur Demon got up.

"*Partir c'est mourir un peu, et mourir c'est partir un peu trop.* Do tell Dan and Norman I can give them tea-and-cake any time tomorrow at the Bryant. By the way, how's Lucette?"

Marina knitted her brows and shook her head acting the fond, worried mother though, in point of fact, she bore her daughters even less affection than she had for cute Dack and pathetic Dan.

"Oh, we had quite a scare," she replied finally, "quite a nasty scare. But now, apparently—"

"Van," said his father, "be a good scout. I did not have a hat but I did have gloves. Ask Bouteillan to look in the gallery, I may have dropped them there. No. Stay! It's all right. I left them in the car, because I recall the cold of this flower, which I took from a vase in passing . . ."

He now threw it away, discarding with it the shadow of his fugitive urge to plunge both hands in a soft bosom.

"I had hoped you'd sleep here," said Marina (not really caring one way or another). "What is your room number at the hotel—not 222 by any chance?"

She liked romantic coincidences. Demon consulted the tag on his key: 221—which was good enough, fatidically and anecdotically speaking. Naughty Ada, of course, stole a glance at Van, who tensed up the wings of his nose in a grimace that mimicked the slant of Pedro's narrow, beautiful nostrils.

"They make fun of an old woman," said Marina, not without coquetry, and in the Russian manner kissed her guest on his inclined brow as he lifted her hand to his lips: "You'll forgive me," she added, "for not going out on the terrace. I've grown allergic to damp and darkness; I'm sure my temperature has already gone up to thirty-seven and seven, at least."

Demon tapped the barometer next to the door. It had been tapped too often to react in any intelligible way and remained standing at a quarter past three.

Van and Ada saw him off. The night was very warm and dripping with what Ladore farmers called green rain. Demon's black sedan glinted elegantly among the varnished laurels in the moth-flaked porchlight. He tenderly kissed the children, the girl on one cheek, the boy on the other, then Ada again—in the hollow of the white arm that clasped his neck. Nobody paid much attention to Marina, who waved from a tangelo-colored oriel window a spangled shawl although all she could see was the sheen of the car's bonnet and the rain slanting in the light of its lamps.

Demon pulled on his gloves and sped away with a great growl of damp gravel.

"That last kiss went a little too far," remarked Van, laughing.

"Oh well—his lips sort of slipped," laughed Ada and, laughing, they embraced in the dark as they skirted the wing of the house.

They stopped for a moment under the shelter of an indulgent tree, where many a cigar-smoking guest had stopped after dinner. Tranquilly, innocently, side by side in their separately ordained attitudes, they added a trickle and a gush to the more professional sounds of the rain in the night, and then lingered, hand in hand, in a corner of the latticed gallery waiting for the lights in the windows to go out.

"What was faintly off-key, *ne tak*, about the whole evening?" asked Van softly. "You noticed?"

"Of course, I did. And yet I adore him. I think he's quite crazy, and with no place or occupation in life, and far from happy, and philosophically irresponsible—and there is absolutely nobody like him."

"But what went wrong tonight? You were tongue-tied, and everything we said was *fal'shivo*. I wonder if some inner nose in him smelled you in me, and me in you. He tried to ask me . . . Oh it was not a nice family reunion. What exactly went wrong at dinner?"

"My love, my love, as if you don't know! We'll manage, perhaps, to wear our masks always, till dee do us part, but we shall never be able to marry—while they're both alive. We simply can't swing it, because he's more conventional in his own way than even the law and the social lice. One can't bribe one's parents, and waiting forty, fifty years for them to die is too horrible to imagine—I mean the mere thought of *anybody* waiting for such a thing is not in our nature, is mean and monstrous!"

He kissed her half-closed lips, gently and "morally" as they defined moments of depth to distinguish them from the despair of passion.

"Anyway," he said, "it's fun to be two secret agents in an alien country. Marina has gone upstairs. Your hair is wet."

"Spies from Terra? You believe, you believe in the existence of Terra? Oh, you do! You accept it. I know you!"

"I accept it as a state of mind. That's not quite the same thing."

"Yes, but you want to prove it *is* the same thing."

He brushed her lips with another religious kiss. Its edge, however, was beginning to catch fire.

"One of these days," he said, "I will ask you for a repeat performance. You will sit as you did four years ago, at the same table, in the same light, drawing the same flower, and I shall go through the same scene with such joy, such pride, such—I don't know—gratitude! Look, all the windows are dark now. I, too, can translate when I simply have to. Listen to this:

> Lights in the rooms were going out.
> Breathed fragrantly the *rozï.*
> We sat together in the shade
> Of a wide-branched *beryozï.*"

"Yes, 'birch' is what leaves the translator in the 'lurch,' doesn't it? That's a terrible little poem by Konstantin Romanov, right? Just elected president of the Lyascan Academy of Literature, right? Wretched poet and happy husband. Happy husband!"

"You know," said Van, "I really think you should wear *something* underneath on formal occasions."

"Your hands are cold. Why formal? You said yourself it was a family affair."

"Even so. You were in peril whenever you bent or sprawled."

"I never *sprawl!*"

"I'm quite sure it's not hygienic, or perhaps it's a kind of jealousy on my part. Memoirs of a Happy Chair. Oh, my darling."

"At least," whispered Ada, "it pays off now, doesn't it? Croquet room? *Ou comme ça?*"

"*Comme ça,* for once," said Van.

39

Although fairly eclectic in 1888, Ladore fashions were not quite as free as taken for granted at Ardis.

For the grand picnic on her birthday sixteen-year-old Ada wore a plain linen blouse, maize-yellow slacks and scuffed moccasins. Van had wanted her to let her hair down; she demurred, saying it was too long for country comfort, but finally compromised by tying it midway behind with a rumpled ribbon of black silk. Van's only observance of summer elegancies consisted of a blue polo jersey, knee-length gray flannel trousers, and sport "creepers."

While the rustic feast was being prepared and distributed among the sun gouts of the traditional pine glade, the wild girl and her lover slipped away for a few moments of ravenous ardor in a ferny ravine where a rill dipped from ledge to ledge between tall burnberry bushes. The day was hot and breathless. The smallest pine had its cicada.

She said: "Speaking as a character in an old novel, it seems so long, long ago, *davnïm davno*, since I used to play word-games here with Grace and two other lovely girls. 'Insect, incest, nicest.'"

Speaking as a botanist and a mad woman, she said, the most extraordinary word in the English language was "husked," because it stood for opposite things, covered and uncovered, tightly husked but easily husked, meaning they peel off quite easily, you don't have to tear the waistband, you brute. "Carefully husked brute," said Van tenderly. The passage of time could only enhance his tenderness for the creature he clasped, this adored creature, whose motion was now more supple, whose haunches had grown more lyrate, whose hair-ribbon he had undone.

As they crouched on the brink of one of the brook's crystal shelves, where, before falling, it stopped to have its picture taken and take pictures itself, Van, at the last throb, saw the reflection of Ada's gaze in the water flash a warning. Something of the sort had happened somewhere before: he did not have time to identify the recollection that, nonetheless, led him to identify at once the sound of the stumble behind him.

Among the rugged rocks they found and consoled poor little Lucette, whose foot had slipped on a granite slab in a tangle of bushes. Flushed and flustered, the child rubbed her thigh in much-overdone agony. Van and Ada gaily grasped one little hand each and ran Lucette back to the glade, where she laughed, where she flopped, where she made for her favorite tarts awaiting her on one of the unfolded tables. There she husked out of her sweat shirt, hitched up her green shorts and, asquat on the russet ground, attacked the food she had collected.

Ada had declined to invite anybody except the Erminin twins to her picnic; but she had had no intention of inviting the brother without the sister. The latter, it turned out, could not come, having gone to New Cranton to see a young drummer, her first boy friend, sail off into the sunrise with his regiment. But Greg had to be asked to come after all: on the previous day he had called on her bringing a "talisman" from his very sick father, who wanted Ada to treasure as much as his grandam had a little camel of yellow ivory carved in Kiev, five centuries ago, in the days of Timur and Nabok.

Van did not err in believing that Ada remained unaffected by Greg's devotion. He now met him again with pleasure— the kind of pleasure, immoral in its very purity, which adds its icy tang to the friendly feelings a successful rival bears toward a thoroughly decent fellow.

Greg, who had left his splendid new black Silentium motorcycle in the forest ride, observed:

"We have company."

"Indeed we do," assented Van. "*Kto sii* (who are they)? Do you have any idea?"

Nobody had. Raincoated, unpainted, morose, Marina came over and peered through the trees the way Van pointed.

After reverently inspecting the Silentium, a dozen elderly townsmen, in dark clothes, shabby and uncouth, walked into the forest across the road and sat down there to a modest *colazione* of cheese, buns, salami, sardines and Chianti. They were quite sufficiently far from our picnickers not to bother them in any way. They had no mechanical music boxes with them. Their voices were subdued, their movements could not have been more discreet. The predominant gesture seemed to be ritually limited to this or that fist crumpling brown paper or coarse gazette paper or baker's paper (the very lightweight and inefficient sort), and discarding the crumpled bit in quiet, abstract fashion, while other sad apostolic hands unwrapped the victuals or for some reason or other wrapped them up again, in the noble shade of the pines, in the humble shade of the false acacias.

[283]

"How odd," said Marina, scratching her sunlit bald patch.

She sent a footman to investigate the situation and tell those Gipsy politicians, or Calabrian laborers, that Squire Veen would be *furious* if he discovered trespassers camping in his woods.

The footman returned, shaking his head. They did not speak English. Van went over:

"Please go away, this is private property," said Van in Vulgar Latin, French, Canadian French, Russian, Yukonian Russian, very low Latin again: *proprieta privata.*

He stood looking at them, hardly noticed by them, hardly shade-touched by the foliage. They were ill-shaven, blue-jowled men in old Sunday suits. One or two wore no collar but had kept the thyroid stud. One had a beard and a humid squint. Patent boots, with dust in the cracks, or orange-brown shoes either very square or very pointed had been taken off and pushed under the burdocks or placed on the old tree stumps of the rather drab clearing. How odd indeed! When Van repeated his request, the intruders started to mutter among themselves in a totally incomprehensible jargon, making small flapping motions in his direction as if half-heartedly chasing away a gnat.

He asked Marina—did she want him to use force, but sweet, dear Marina said, patting her hair, one hand on her hip, no, let us ignore them—especially as they were now drawing a little deeper into the trees—look, look—some dragging *à reculons* the various parts of their repast upon what resembled an old bedspread, which receded like a fishing boat pulled over pebbly sand, while others politely removed the crumpled wrappings to other more distant hiding places in keeping with the general relocation: a most melancholy and meaningful picture—but meaning what, what?

Gradually their presence dissolved from Van's mind. Eve-

rybody was now having a wonderful time. Marina threw off
the pale raincoat or rather "dustcoat" she had put on for the
picnic (after all, with one thing and another, her domestic
gray dress with the pink fichu was quite gay enough, she declared, for an old lady) and raising an empty glass she sang,
with brio and very musically, the Green Grass aria: "Replenish, replenish the glasses with wine! Here's a toast to love!
To the rapture of love!" With awe and pity, and no love, Van
kept reverting to that poor bald patch on Traverdiata's poor
old head, to the scalp burnished by her hairdye an awful pine
rust color much shinier than her dead hair. He attempted, as
so many times before, to squeeze out some fondness for her
but as usual failed and as usual told himself that Ada did
not love her mother either, a vague and cowardly consola-
tion.

Greg, assuming with touching simplicity that Ada would
notice and approve, showered Mlle Larivière with a thousand little attentions—helping her out of her mauve jacket,
pouring out for her the milk into Lucette's mug from a
thermos bottle, passing the sandwiches, replenishing, replenishing Mlle Larivière's wineglass and listening with a
rapt grin to her diatribes against the English, whom she said
she disliked even more than the Tartars, or the, well,
Assyrians.

"England!" she cried, "England! The country where for
every poet, there are ninety-nine *sales petits bourgeois*, some
of suspect extraction! England dares ape France! I have in
that hamper there an English novel of high repute in which
a lady is given a perfume—an expensive perfume!—called
'*Ombre Chevalier*,' which is really nothing but a fish—a
delicious fish, true, but hardly suitable for scenting one's
handkerchief with. On the very next page, a soi-disant philosopher mentions '*une acte gratuite*' as if all acts were feminine,

[285]

and a soi-disant Parisian hotel-keeper in the story says '*je me regrette*' for '*je regrette*'!"

"*D'accord*," interjected Van, "but what about such atrocious bloomers in French translations from the English as for example—"

Unfortunately, or maybe fortunately, at that very moment Ada emitted a Russian exclamation of utmost annoyance as a steel-gray convertible glided into the glade. No sooner had it stopped than it was surrounded by the same group of townsmen, who now seemed to have multiplied in strange consequence of having shed coats and waistcoats. Thrusting his way through their circle, with every sign of wrath and contempt, young Percy de Prey, frilled-shirted and white-trousered, strode up to Marina's deckchair. He was invited to join the party despite Ada's trying to stop her silly mother with an admonishing stare and a private small shake of the head.

"I dared not hope . . . Oh, I accept with great pleasure," answered Percy, whereupon—very much whereupon—the seemingly forgetful but in reality calculating bland bandit marched back to his car (near which a last wonderstruck admirer lingered) to fetch a bouquet of longstemmed roses stored in the boot.

"What a shame that I should loathe roses," said Ada, accepting them gingerly.

The muscat wine was uncorked, Ada's and Ida's healths drunk. "The conversation became general," as Monparnasse liked to write.

Count Percy de Prey turned to Ivan Demianovich Veen: "I'm told you like abnormal positions?"

The half-question was half-mockingly put. Van looked through his raised lunel at the honeyed sun.

"Meaning what?" he enquired.

"Well—that walking-on-your-hands trick. One of your aunt's servants is the sister of one of our servants and two pretty gossips form a dangerous team" (laughing). "The legend has it that you do it all day long, in every corner, congratulations!" (bowing).

Van replied: "The legend makes too much of my specialty. Actually, I practice it for a few minutes every other night, don't I, Ada?" (looking around for her). "May I give you, Count, some more of the mouse-and-cat—a poor pun, but mine."

"Vahn dear," said Marina, who was listening with delight to the handsome young men's vivacious and carefree prattle, "tell him about your success in London. *Zhe tampri* (please)!"

"Yes," said Van, "it all started as a rag, you know, up at Chose, but then—"

"Van!" called Ada shrilly. "I want to say something to you, Van, come here."

Dorn (flipping through a literary review, to Trigorin): "Here, a couple of months ago, a certain article was printed . . . a Letter from America, and I wanted to ask you, incidentally" (taking Trigorin by the waist and leading him to the front of the stage), "because I'm very much interested in that question . . ."

Ada stood with her back against the trunk of a tree, like a beautiful spy who has just rejected the blindfold.

"I wanted to ask you, incidentally, Van" (continuing in a whisper, with an angry flick of the wrist)—"stop playing the perfect idiot host; he came drunk as a welt, can't you see?"

The execution was interrupted by the arrival of Uncle Dan. He had a remarkably reckless way of driving, as happens so often, goodness knows why, in the case of many dour, dreary men. Weaving rapidly between the pines, he brought the little red runabout to an abrupt stop in front of Ada and presented her with the perfect gift, a big box of mints, white, pink and, oh boy, green! He had also an aerogram for her, he said, winking.

Ada tore it open—and saw it was not for her from dismal Kalugano, as she had feared, but for her mother from Los Angeles, a much gayer place. Marina's face gradually assumed an expression of quite indecent youthful beatitude as she scanned the message. Triumphantly, she showed it to Larivière-Monparnasse, who read it twice and tilted her head with a smile of indulgent disapproval. Positively stamping her feet with joy:

"Pedro is coming again," cried (gurgled, rippled) Marina to her calm daughter.

"And, I suppose, he'll stay till the end of the summer," remarked Ada—and sat down with Greg and Lucette, for a game of Snap, on a laprobe spread over the little ants and dry pine needles.

"Oh no, *da net zhe*, only for a fortnight" (girlishly giggling). "After that we shall go to Houssaie, *Gollivud-tozh*" (Marina was really in great form)—"yes, we shall all go, the author, and the children, and Van—if he wishes."

"I wish but I can't," said Percy (sample of *his* humor).

In the meantime, Uncle Dan, very dapper in cherry-striped blazer and variety-comic straw hat, feeling considerably intrigued by the presence of the adjacent picnickers, walked over to them with his glass of Hero wine in one hand and a caviar canapé in the other.

"The Accursed Children," said Marina in answer to something Percy wanted to know.

Percy, you were to die very soon—and not from that pellet in your fat leg, on the turf of a Crimean ravine, but a couple of minutes later when you opened your eyes and felt relieved and secure in the shelter of the macchie; you were to die very soon, Percy; but that July day in Ladore County, lolling under the pines, royally drunk after some earlier festivity, with lust in your heart and a sticky glass in your strong blond-haired hand, listening to a literary bore, chatting with an aging actress and ogling her sullen daughter, you reveled in the spicy situation, old sport, chin-chin, and no wonder. Burly, handsome, indolent and ferocious, a crack Rugger player, a cracker of country girls, you combined the charm of the off-duty athlete with the engaging drawl of a fashionable ass. I think what I hated most about your handsome moon face was that baby complexion, the smooth-skinned jaws of the easy shaver. I had begun to bleed every time, and was going to do so for seven decades.

"In a birdhouse fixed to that pine trunk," said Marina to her young admirer, "there was once a 'telephone.' How I'd welcome its presence right now! Ah, here he is, *enfin!*"

Her husband, minus the glass and the canapé, strolled back bringing wonderful news. They were an "exquisitely polite group." He had recognized at least a dozen Italian words. It was, he understood, a collation of shepherds. They thought, he thought, he was a shepherd too. A canvas from Cardinal Carlo de Medici's collection, author unknown, may have been at the base of that copy. Excitedly, overexcitedly, the little man said he insisted the servants take viands and wine to his excellent new friends; he got busy himself, seizing an empty bottle and a hamper that contained knitting equipment, an English novel by Quigley and a roll of toilet paper. Marina explained, however, that professional obligations demanded she call up California without delay; and, forgetting his project, he readily consented to drive her home.

Mists have long since hidden the links and loops of consecutive events, but—approximately while that departure took place, or soon after—Van found himself standing on the brink of the brook (which had reflected two pair of superposed eyes earlier in the afternoon) and chucking pebbles with Percy and Greg at the remnants of an old, rusty, indecipherable signboard on the other side.

"*Okh, nado* (I must) *passati!*" exclaimed Percy in the Slavic slang he affected, blowing out his cheeks and fumbling frantically at his fly. In all his life, said stolid Greg to Van, he had never seen such an ugly engine, surgically circumcised, terrifically oversized and high-colored, with such a phenomenal *coeur de boeuf*; nor had either of the fascinated, fastidious boys ever witnessed the like of its sustained, strongly arched, practically everlasting stream. "Phoeh!" uttered the young man with relief, and repacked.

How did the scuffle start? Did all three cross the brook stepping on slimy stones? Did Percy push Greg? Did Van jog Percy? Was there something—a stick? Twisted out of a fist? A wrist gripped and freed?

"Oho," said Percy, "you are playful, my lad!"

Greg, one bag of his plus-fours soaked, watched them helplessly—he was fond of both—as they grappled on the brink of the brook.

Percy was three years older, and a score of kilograms heavier than Van, but the latter had handled even burlier brutes with ease. Almost at once the Count's bursting face was trapped in the crook of Van's arm. The grunting Count toured the turf in a hunched-up stagger. He freed one scarlet ear, was retrapped, was tripped and collapsed under Van, who instantly put him "on his omoplates," *na lopatki*, as King Wing used to say in his carpet jargon. Percy lay panting like a dying gladiator, both shoulder blades pressed to the ground by his tormentor, whose thumbs now started to manipulate horribly that heaving thorax. Percy with a sudden bellow of pain intimated he had had enough. Van requested a more articulate expression of surrender, and got it. Greg, fearing Van had not caught the muttered plea for mercy, repeated it in the third person interpretative. Van released the unfortunate Count, whereupon he sat up, spitting, palpating his throat, rearranging the rumpled shirt around his husky torso and asking Greg in a husky voice to find a missing cufflink.

Van washed his hands in a lower shelf-pool of the brook and recognized, with amused embarrassment, the transparent, tubular thing, not unlike a sea-squirt, that had got caught in its downstream course in a fringe of forget-me-nots, good name, too.

He had started to walk back to the picnic glade when a mountain fell upon him from behind. With one violent heave he swung his attacker over his head. Percy crashed and lay supine for a moment or two. Van, his crab claws on the ready, contemplated him, hoping for a pretext to inflict a certain special device of exotic torture that he had not yet had the opportunity to use in a real fight.

"You've broken my shoulder," grumbled Percy, half-rising and rubbing his thick arm. "A little more self-control, young devil."

"Stand up!" said Van. "Come on, stand up! Would you like more of the same or shall we join the ladies? The ladies? All right. But, if you please, walk in front of me now."

As he and his captive drew near the glade Van cursed himself for feeling rattled by that unexpected additional round; he was secretly out of breath, his every nerve twanged, he caught himself limping and correcting the limp—while Percy de Prey, in his magically immaculate white trousers and casually ruffled shirt, marched, buoyantly exercising his arms and shoulders, and seemed quite serene and in fact rather cheerful.

Presently Greg overtook them, bringing the cufflink—a little triumph of meticulous detection; and with a trite "Atta-boy!" Percy closed his silk cuff, thus completing his insolent restoration.

Their dutiful companion, still running, got first to the site of the finished feast; he saw Ada, facing him with two stipple-stemmed red boletes in one hand and three in the other; and, mistaking her look of surprise at the sound of his thud-ding hooves for one of concern, good Sir Greg hastened to cry out from afar: "He's all right! He's all right, Miss Veen" —blind compassion preventing the young knight from real-izing that she could not possibly have known yet what a clash had occurred between the beau and the beast.

"Indeed I am," said the former, taking from her a couple of her toadstools, the girl's favorite delicacy, and stroking their smooth caps. "And why shouldn't I be? Your cousin has treated Greg and your humble servant to a most bracing ex-hibition of Oriental Skrotomoff or whatever the name may be."

He called for wine—but the remaining bottles had been given to the mysterious pastors whose patronage the adjacent clearing had already lost: they might have dispatched and buried one of their comrades, if the stiff collar and reptilian tie left hanging from a locust branch were his. Gone also was the bouquet of roses which Ada had ordered to be put back into the boot of the Count's car—better than waste them on her, let him give them, she said, to Blanche's lovely sister.

And now Mlle Larivière clapped her hands to rouse from their siesta, Kim, the driver of her gig, and Trofim, the children's fair-bearded coachman. Ada reclenched her boletes and all Percy could find for his *Handkuss* was a cold fist.

"Jolly nice to have seen you, old boy," he said, tapping Van lightly on the shoulder, a forbidden gesture in their milieu. "Hope to play with you again soon. I wonder," he added in a lower voice, "if you shoot as straight as you wrestle."

Van followed him to the convertible.

"Van, Van come here, Greg wants to say good-bye," cried Ada, but he did not turn.

"Is that a challenge, *me faites-vous un duel?*" inquired Van.

Percy, at the wheel, smiled, slit his eyes, bent toward the dashboard, smiled again, but said nothing. Click-click went the motor, then broke into thunder and Percy drew on his gloves.

"*Quand tu voudras, mon gars,*" said Van, slapping the fender and using the terrible second person singular of duelists in old France.

The car leapt forward and disappeared.

Van returned to the picnic ground, his heart stupidly thumping; he waved in passing to Greg who was talking to Ada a little way off on the road.

"Really, I assure you," Greg was saying to her, "your cousin is not to blame. Percy started it—and was defeated in a clean match of Korotom wrestling, as used in Teristan and Sorokat—my father, I'm sure, could tell you all about it."

"You're a dear," answered Ada, "but I don't think your brain works too well."

"It never does in your presence," remarked Greg, and mounted his black silent steed, hating it, and himself, and the two bullies.

He adjusted his goggles and glided away. Mlle Larivière, in

her turn, got into her gig and was borne off through the speckled vista of the forest ride.

Lucette ran up to Van and, almost kneeling, cosily embraced her big cousin around the hips, and clung to him for a moment. "Come along," said Van, lifting her, "don't forget your jersey, you can't go naked."

Ada strolled up. "My hero," she said, hardly looking at him, with that inscrutable air she had that let one guess whether she expressed sarcasm or ecstasy, or a parody of one or the other.

Lucette, swinging her mushroom basket, chanted:

> "He screwed off a nipple,
> He left him a cripple . . ."

"Lucy Veen, stop that!" shouted Ada at the imp; and Van with a show of great indignation, shook the little wrist he held, while twinkling drolly at Ada on his other side.

Thus, a carefree-looking young trio, they moved toward the waiting victoria. Slapping his thighs in dismay, the coachman stood berating a tousled footboy who had appeared from under a bush. He had concealed himself there to enjoy in peace a tattered copy of *Tattersalia* with pictures of tremendous, fabulously elongated race horses, and had been left behind by the charabanc which had carried away the dirty dishes and the drowsy servants.

He climbed onto the box, beside Trofim, who directed a vibrating "tpprr" at the backing bays, while Lucette considered with darkening green eyes the occupation of her habitual perch.

"You'll have to take her on your half-brotherly knee," said Ada in a neutral apart.

"But won't *La maudite rivière* object," he said absently, trying to catch by its tail the sensation of fate's rerun.

"Larivière can go and" (and Ada's sweet pale lips repeated Gavronski's crude crack) . . . "That goes for Lucette too," she added.

"V*os 'vyragences' sont assez lestes*," remarked Van. "Are you very mad at me?"

"Oh Van, I'm not! In fact, I'm delighted you won. But I'm sixteen today. Sixteen! Older than grandmother at the time of her first divorce. It's my last picnic, I guess. Childhood is scrapped. I love you. You love me. Greg loves me. Everybody loves me. I'm glutted with love. Hurry up or she'll pull that cock off—Lucette, leave him alone at once!"

Finally the carriage started on its pleasant homeward journey.

"Ouch!" grunted Van as he received the rounded load—explaining wrily that he had hit his right patella against a rock.

"Of course, if one goes in for horseplay . . ." murmured Ada—and opened, at its emerald ribbon, the small brown, gold-tooled book (a great success with the passing sun flecks) that she had been already reading during the ride to the picnic.

"I do fancy a little horseplay," said Van. "It has left me with quite a tingle, for more reasons than one."

"I saw you—horseplaying," said Lucette, turning her head.

"Sh-sh," uttered Van.

"I mean you and him."

"We are not interested in your impressions, girl. And don't look back all the time. You know you get carriage-sick when the road—"

"Coincidence: '*Jean qui tâchait de lui tourner la tête . . . ,*'" surfaced Ada briefly.

"—when the road 'runs out of you,' as your sister once said when she was your age."

"True," mused Lucette tunefully.

She had been prevailed upon to clothe her honey-brown body. Her white jersey had filched a lot from its recent background—pine needles, a bit of moss, a cake crumb, a baby caterpillar. Her remarkably well-filled green shorts were stained with burnberry purple. Her ember-bright hair flew into his face and smelt of a past summer. Family smell; yes, coincidence: a set of coincidences slightly displaced; the artistry of asymmetry. She sat in his lap, heavily, dreamily, full of *foie gras* and peach punch, with the backs of her brown iridescent bare arms almost touching his face—touching it when he glanced down, right and left, to check if the mushrooms had been taken. They had. The little footboy was reading and picking his nose—judging by the movements of his elbow. Lucette's compact bottom and cool thighs seemed to sink deeper and deeper in the quicksand of the dreamlike, dream-rephrased, legend-distorted past. Ada, sitting next to him, turning her smaller pages quicker than the boy on the box, was, of course, enchanting, obsessive, eternal and lovelier, more somberly ardent than four summers ago— but it was that other picnic which he now relived and it was Ada's soft haunches which he now held as if she were present in duplicate, in two different color prints.

Through strands of coppery silk he looked aslant at Ada, who puckered her lips at him in the semblance of a transmitted kiss (pardoning him at last for his part in that brawl!) and presently went back to her vellum-bound little volume, *Ombres et couleurs,* an 1820 edition of Chateaubriand's short stories with hand-painted vignettes and the flat mummy of a pressed anemone. The gouts and glooms of the woodland passed across her book, her face and Lucette's right arm, on which he could not help kissing a mosquito bite in pure tribute to the duplication. Poor Lucette stole a languorous look at him and looked away again—at the red neck of the coachman—of that other coachman who for several months had haunted her dreams.

We do not care to follow the thoughts troubling Ada, whose attention to her book was far shallower than might seem; we will not, nay, cannot follow them with any success, for thoughts are much more faintly remembered than shadows or colors, or the throbs of young lust, or a green snake in a dark paradise. Therefore we find ourselves more comfortably sitting within Van while his Ada sits within Lucette, and both sit within Van (and all three in me, adds Ada).

He remembered with a pang of pleasure the indulgent skirt Ada had been wearing then, so swoony-baloony as the Chose young things said, and he regretted (smiling) that Lucette had those chaste shorts on today, and Ada, husked-corn (laughing) trousers. In the fatal course of the most painful ailments, sometimes (nodding gravely), sometimes there occur sweet mornings of perfect repose—and that not owing to some blessed pill or potion (indicating the bedside clutter) or at least without our knowing that the loving hand of despair slipped us the drug.

Van closed his eyes in order better to concentrate on the golden flood of swelling joy. Many, oh many, many years later he recollected with wonder (how could one have endured such rapture?) that moment of total happiness, the complete eclipse of the piercing and preying ache, the logic of intoxication, the circular argument to the effect that the most eccentric girl cannot help being faithful if she loves one as one loves her. He watched Ada's bracelet flash in rhythm with the swaying of the victoria and her full lips, parted slightly in profile, show in the sun the red pollen of a remnant of salve drying in the transversal thumbnail lines of their texture. He opened his eyes: the bracelet was indeed flashing but her lips had lost all trace of rouge, and the certainty that in another moment he would touch their hot pale pulp threatened to touch off a private crisis under the solemn load of another child. But the little proxy's neck, glistening with sweat, was pathetic, her trustful immobility, sobering, and after all no furtive friction could compete with what awaited him in Ada's bower. A twinge in his kneecap also came to the rescue, and honest Van chided himself for having attempted to use a little pauper instead of the princess in the fairy tale—"whose precious flesh must not blush with the impression of a chastising hand," says Pierrot in Peterson's version.

With the fading of that fugitive flame his mood changed. Something should be said, a command should be given, the matter was serious or might become serious. They were now about to enter Gamlet, the little Russian village, from which a birch-lined road led quickly to Ardis. A small procession of kerchiefed peasant nymphs, unwashed, no doubt, but adorably pretty with naked shiny shoulders and high-divided plump breasts tuliped up by their corsets, walked past through a coppice, singing an old ditty in their touching English:

> Thorns and nettles
> For silly girls:
> Ah, torn the petals,
> Ah, spilled the pearls!

"You have a little pencil in your back pocket," said Van to Lucette. "May I borrow it, I want to write down that song."

"If you don't tickle me there," said the child.

Van reached for Ada's book and wrote on the fly leaf, as she watched him with odd wary eyes:

I don't wish to see him again.
It's serious.
Tell M. not to receive him or I leave.
No answer required.

She read it, and slowly, silently erased the lines with the top of the pencil which she passed back to Van, who replaced it where it had been.

"You're awfully fidgety," Lucette observed without turning. "Next time," she added, "I won't have him dislodge me."

They now swept up to the porch, and Trofim had to cuff the tiny blue-coated reader in order to have him lay his book aside and jump down to hand Ada out of the carriage.

40

Van was lying in his netted nest under the liriodendrons, reading Antiterrenus on Rattner. His knee had troubled him all night; now, after lunch, it seemed a bit better. Ada had gone on horseback to Ladore, where he hoped she would forget to buy the messy turpentine oil Marina had told her to bring him.

His valet advanced toward him across the lawn, followed by a messenger, a slender youth clad in black leather from neck to ankle, chestnut curls escaping from under a vizored cap. The strange child glanced around with an amateur thespian's exaggeration of attitude, and handed a letter, marked "confidential," to Van.

Dear Veen,

In a couple of days I must leave for a spell of military service abroad. If you desire to see me before I go I shall be glad to entertain you (and any other gentleman you might wish to bring along) at dawn tomorrow where the Maidenhair road crosses Tourbière Lane. If not, I beg you to confirm in a brief note that you

*bear me no grudge, just as no grudge is cherished in
regard to you, sir, by your obedient servant*
                                        Percy de Prey

No, Van did not desire to see the Count. He said so to
the pretty messenger, who stood with one hand on the hip
and one knee turned out like an extra, waiting for the signal
to join the gambaders in the country dance after Calabro's
aria.

"*Un moment*," added Van. "I would be interested to
know—this could be decided in a jiffy behind that tree—what
you are, stable boy or kennel girl?"

The messenger did not reply and was led away by the
chuckling Bout. A little squeal suggestive of an improper
pinch came from behind the laurels screening their exit.

It was hard to decide whether that clumsy and pretentious
missive had been dictated by the fear that one's sailing off
to fight for one's country might be construed as running away
from more private engagements, or whether its conciliatory
gist had been demanded from Percy by somebody—perhaps
a woman (for instance his mother, born Praskovia Lanskoy);
anyway, Van's honor remained unaffected. He limped to the
nearest garbage can and, having burnt the letter with its
crested blue envelope, dismissed the incident from his mind,
merely noting that now, at least, Ada would cease to be
pestered by the fellow's attentions.

She returned late in the afternoon—without the embrocation, thank goodness. He was still lolling in his low-slung
hammock, looking rather forlorn and sulky, but having
glanced around (with more natural grace than the brown-
locked messenger had achieved), she raised her veil, kneeled
down by him and soothed him.

When lightning struck two days later (an old image that

is meant to intimate a flash-back to an old barn), Van became aware that it brought together, in livid confrontation,
two secret witnesses; they had been hanging back in his
mind since the first day of his fateful return to Ardis: One
had been murmuring with averted gaze that Percy de Prey
was, and would always be, only a dance partner, a frivolous
follower; the other had kept insinuating, with spectral insistence, that some nameless trouble was threatening the very
sanity of Van's pale, faithless mistress.

On the morning of the day preceding the most miserable
one in his life, he found he could bend his leg without wincing, but he made the mistake of joining Ada and Lucette in an
impromptu lunch on a long-neglected croquet lawn and
walked home with difficulty. A swim in the pool and a
soak in the sun helped, however, and the pain had practically
gone when in the mellow heat of the long afternoon Ada
returned from one of her long "brambles" as she called her
botanical rambles, succinctly and somewhat sadly, for the
florula had ceased to yield much beyond the familiar favorites.
Marina, in a luxurious peignoir, with a large oval mirror hinged
before her, sat at a white toilet table that had been carried
out onto the lawn where she was having her hair dressed by
senile but still wonderworking Monsieur Violette of Lyon
and Ladore, an unusual outdoor activity which she explained
and excused by the fact of her grandmother's having also
liked *qu'on la coiffe au grand air* so as to forestall the zephyrs
(as a duelist steadies his hand by walking about with a poker).

"That's our best performer," she said, indicating Van to
Violette who mistook him for Pedro and bowed with *un air
entendu.*

Van had been looking forward to a little walk of convales-
cence with Ada before dressing for dinner, but she said, as she
drooped on a garden chair, that she was exhausted and filthy

and had to wash her face and feet, and prepare for the ordeal of helping her mother entertain the movie people who were expected later in the evening.

"I've seen him in *Sexico*," murmured Monsieur Violette to Marina, whose ears he had shut with both hands as he moved the reflection of her head in the glass this way and that.

"No, it's getting late," muttered Ada, "and, moreover, I promised Lucette—"

He insisted in a fierce whisper—fully knowing, however, how useless it was to attempt to make her change her mind, particularly in amorous matters; but unaccountably and marvelously her dazed look melted into one of gentle glee, as if in sudden perception of new-found release. Thus a child may stare into space, with a dawning smile, upon realizing that the bad dream is over, or that a door has been left unlocked, and that one can paddle with impunity in thawed sky. Ada rid her shoulder of the collecting satchel and, under Violette's benevolent gaze following them over Marina's mirrored head, they strolled away and sought the comparative seclusion of the park alley where she had once demonstrated to him her sun-and-shade games. He held her, and kissed her, and kissed her again as if she had returned from a long and perilous journey. The sweetness of her smile was something quite unexpected and special. It was not the sly demon smile of remembered or promised ardor, but the exquisite human glow of happiness and helplessness. All their passionate pump-joy exertions, from Burning Barn to Burnberry Brook, were nothing in comparison to this *zaychik*, this "sun blick" of the smiling spirit. Her black jumper and black skirt with apron pockets lost its "in-mourning-for-a-lost-flower" meaning that Marina had fancifully attached to her dress ("*nemedlenno pereodet'sya*, change immediately!" she had yelped into the

[303]

green-shimmering looking-glass); instead, it had acquired the charm of a Lyaskan, old-fashioned schoolgirl uniform. They stood brow to brow, brown to white, black to black, he supporting her elbows, she playing her limp light fingers over his collarbone, and how he "ladored," he said, the dark aroma of her hair blending with crushed lily stalks, Turkish cigarettes and the lassitude that comes from "lass." "No, no, don't," she said, I must wash, quick-quick, Ada must wash; but for yet another immortal moment they stood embraced in the hushed avenue, enjoying, as they had never enjoyed before, the "happy-forever" feeling at the end of never-ending fairy tales.

That's a beautiful passage, Van. I shall cry all night (late interpolation).

As a last sunbeam struck Ada, her mouth and chin shone drenched with his poor futile kisses. She shook her head saying they must really part, and she kissed his hands as she did only in moments of supreme tenderness, and then quickly turned away, and they really parted.

One common orchid, a Lady's Slipper, was all that wilted in the satchel which she had left on a garden table and now dragged upstairs. Marina and the mirror had gone. He peeled off his training togs and took one last dip in the pool over which the butler stood, looking meditatively into the false-blue water with his hands behind his back.

"I wonder," he said, "if I haven't just seen a tadpole."

The novelistic theme of written communications has now really got into its stride. When Van went up to his room he noticed, with a shock of grim premonition, a slip of paper sticking out of the heart pocket of his dinner jacket. Penciled in a large hand, with the contour of every letter deliberately whiffled and rippled, was the anonymous injunction: "One must not berne you." Only a French-speaking person would use that word for "dupe." Among the servants, fifteen at least were of French extraction—descendants of immigrants who had settled in America after England had annexed their beautiful and unfortunate country in 1815. To interview them all—torture the males, rape the females—would be, of course, absurd and degrading. With a puerile wrench he broke his best black butterfly on the wheel of his exasperation. The pain from the fang bite was now reaching his heart. He found another tie, finished dressing and went to look for Ada.

He found both girls and their governess in one of the "nursery parlors," a delightful sitting room with a balcony on which Mlle Larivière was sitting at a charmingly ornamented Pembroke table and reading with mixed feelings and furious annotations the third shooting script of *Les Enfants Maudits*. At a larger round table in the middle of the inner room, Lucette under Ada's direction was trying to learn to draw flowers; several botanical atlases, large and small, were lying about. Everything appeared as it always used to be, the little nymphs and goats on the painted ceiling, the mellow light of the day ripening into evening, the remote dreamy rhythm of Blanche's "linen-folding" voice humming "Malbrough" (. . . *ne sait quand reviendra, ne sait quand reviendra*) and the two lovely heads, bronze-black and copper-red, inclined over the table. Van realized that he must simmer down before consulting Ada—or indeed before telling her he wished to consult her. She looked gay and elegant; she was wearing his diamonds for the first time; she had put on a new evening dress with jet gleams, and—also for the first time—transparent silk stockings.

He sat down on a little sofa, took at random one of the open volumes and stared in disgust at a group of brilliantly pictured gross orchids whose popularity with bees depended, said the text, "on various attractive odors ranging from the smell of dead workers to that of a tomcat." Dead soldiers might smell even better.

In the meantime obstinate Lucette kept insisting that the easiest way to draw a flower was to place a sheet of transparent paper over the picture (in the present case a red-bearded pogonia, with indecent details of structure, a plant peculiar to the Ladoga bogs) and trace the outline of the thing in colored inks. Patient Ada wanted her to copy not mechanically but "from eye to hand and from hand to eye," and to use for model a live specimen of another orchid that had a brown wrinkled pouch and purple sepals; but after a while she gave in cheerfully and set aside the crystal vaselet holding the Lady's Slipper she had picked. Casually, lightly, she went on to explain how the organs of orchids work—but all Lucette wanted to know, after her whimsical fashion, was: could a boy bee impregnate a girl flower *through* something, through his gaiters or woolies or whatever he wore?

"You know," said Ada in a comic nasal voice, turning to Van, "you know, that child has the dirtiest mind imaginable and now she is going to be mad at me for saying this and sob on the Larivière bosom, and complain she has been pollinated by sitting on your knee."

"But I can't speak to Belle about dirty things," said Lucette quite gently and reasonably.

"What's the matter with you, Van?" inquired sharp-eyed Ada.

"Why do you ask?" inquired Van in his turn.

"Your ears wiggle and you clear your throat."

"Are you through with those horrible flowers?"

"Yes. I'm now going to wash my hands. We'll meet downstairs. Your tie is all crooked."

"All right, all right," said Van.

"Mon page, mon beau page,
—Mironton-mironton-mirontaine—
Mon page, mon beau page . . ."

Downstairs, Jones was already taking down the dinner gong from its hook in the hall.

"Well, what's the matter?" she asked when they met a minute later on the drawing-room terrace.

"I found this in my jacket," said Van.

Rubbing her big front teeth with a nervous forefinger, Ada read and reread the note.

"How do you know it's meant for you?" she asked, giving him back the bit of copybook paper.

"Well, I'm telling you," he yelled.

"*Tishe* (quiet!)!" said Ada.

"I'm telling you I found it *here*," (pointing at his heart).

"Destroy and forget," said Ada.

"Your obedient servant," replied Van.

41

Pedro had not yet returned from California. Hay fever and dark glasses did not improve G. A. Vronsky's appearance. Adorno, the star of *Hate*, brought his new wife, who turned out to have been one of the old (and most beloved) wives of another guest, a considerably more important comedian, who after supper bribed Bouteillan to simulate the arrival of a message necessitating his immediate departure. Grigoriy Akimovich went with him (having come with him in the same rented limousine), leaving Marina, Ada, Adorno and his ironically sniffing Marianne at a card table. They played *biryuch*, a variety of whist, till a Ladore taxi could be obtained, which was well after 1:00 A.M.

In the meantime Van changed back to shorts, cloaked himself in the tartan plaid and retired to his bosquet, where the bergamask lamps had not been lit at all that night which had not proved as festive as Marina had expected. He climbed into his hammock and drowsily started reviewing such French-speaking domestics as could have slipped him that ominous but according to Ada meaningless note. The first, obvious, choice was hysterical and fantastic Blanche—had there not been her timidity, her fear of being "fired" (he recalled a dreadful scene when she groveled, pleading for mercy, at the feet of Larivière, who accused her of "stealing" a bauble that eventually turned up in one of Larivière's own shoes). The ruddy face of Bouteillan and his son's grin next appeared in the focus of Van's fancy; but presently he fell asleep, and saw himself on a mountain smothered in snow, with people, trees, and a cow carried down by an avalanche.

Something roused him from that state of evil torpor. At first he thought it was the chill of the dying night, then recognized the slight creak (that had been a scream in his confused nightmare), and raising his head saw a dim light in between the shrubs where the door of the toolroom was being pushed ajar from the inside. Ada had never once come there without their prudently planning every step of their infrequent nocturnal trysts. He scrambled out of his hammock and padded toward the lighted doorway. Before him stood the pale wavering figure of Blanche. She presented an odd sight: bare armed, in her petticoat, one stocking gartered, the other down to her ankle; no slippers; armpits glistening with sweat; she was loosening her hair in a wretched simulacrum of seduction.

"*C'est ma dernière nuit au château*," she said softly, and rephrased it in her quaint English, elegiac and stilted, as spoken only in obsolete novels. "'Tis my last night with thee."

"Your last night? With me? What do you mean?" He considered her with the eerie uneasiness one feels when listening to the utterances of delirium or intoxication.

But despite her demented look, Blanche was perfectly lucid. She had made up her mind a couple of days ago to leave Ardis Hall. She had just slipped her demission, with a footnote on the young lady's conduct, under the door of Madame. She would go in a few hours. She loved him, he was her "folly and fever," she wished to spend a few secret moments with him.

He entered the toolroom and slowly closed the door. The slowness had its uncomfortable cause. She had placed her lantern on the rung of a ladder and was already gathering up and lifting her skimpy skirt. Compassion, courtesy and some assistance on her part might have helped him to work up the urge which she took for granted and whose total absence he carefully concealed under his tartan cloak; but quite aside from the fear of infection (Bout had hinted at some of the poor girl's troubles), a graver matter engrossed him. He diverted her bold hand and sat down on the bench beside her.

Was it she who had placed that note in his jacket?

It was. She had been unable to face departure if he was to remain fooled, deceived, betrayed. She added, in naive brackets, that she had been sure he always desired her, they could talk afterwards. *Je suis à toi, c'est bientôt l'aube,* your dream has come true.

"*Parlez pour vous,*" answered Van. "I am in no mood for love-making. And I will strangle you, I assure you, if you do not tell me the whole story in every detail, at once."

She nodded, fear and adoration in her veiled eyes. When and how had it started? Last August, she said. V*otre demoiselle* picking flowers, he squiring her through the tall grass, a flute in his hand. Who he? What flute? *Mais le musicien allemand, Monsieur Rack.* The eager informer had her own swain lying upon her on the other side of the hedge. How anybody could do it with *l'immonde Monsieur Rack*, who once forgot his waistcoat in a haystack, was beyond the informer's comprehension. Perhaps because he made songs for her, a very pretty one was once played at a big public ball at the Ladore Casino, it went . . . Never mind how it went, go on with the story. Monsieur Rack, one starry night, in a boat on the river, was heard by the informer and two gallants in the willow bushes, recounting the melancholy tale of his childhood, of his years of hunger and music and loneliness, and his sweetheart wept and threw her head back and he fed on her bare throat, *il la mangeait de baisers dégoûtants*. He must have had her not more than a dozen times, he was not as strong as another gentleman—oh, cut it out, said Van—and in winter the young lady learnt he was married, and hated his cruel wife, and in April when he began to give piano lessons to Lucette the affair was resumed, but then—

"That will do!" he cried and, beating his brow with his fist, stumbled out into the sunlight.

It was a quarter to six on the wristwatch hanging from the net of the hammock. His feet were stone cold. He groped for his loafers and walked aimlessly for some time among the trees of the coppice where thrushes were singing so richly, with such sonorous force, such fluty fioriture that one could not endure the agony of consciousness, the filth of life, the loss, the loss, the loss. Gradually, however, he regained a semblance of self-control by the magic method of not allowing the image of Ada to come anywhere near his awareness of himself. This created a vacuum into which rushed a multitude of trivial reflections. A pantomime of rational thought.

He took a tepid shower in the poolside shed, doing everything with comic deliberation, very slowly and cautiously, lest he break the new, unknown, brittle Van born a moment ago. He watched his thoughts revolve, dance, strut, clown a little. He found it delightful to imagine, for instance, that a cake of soap must be solid ambrosia to the ants swarming over it, and what a shock to be drowned in the midst of that orgy. The code, he reflected, did not allow to challenge a person who was not born a gentleman but exceptions might be made for artists, pianists, flutists, and if a coward refused, you could make his gums bleed with repeated slaps or, still better, thrash him with a strong cane—must not forget to choose one in the vestibule closet before leaving forever, forever. Great fun! He relished as something quite special the kind of one-legged jig a naked fellow performs when focusing on the shorts he tries to get into. He sauntered through a side gallery. He ascended the grand staircase. The house was empty, and cool, and smelled of carnations. Good morning, and good-bye, little bedroom. Van shaved, Van pared his toe-nails, Van dressed with exquisite care: gray socks, silk shirt, gray tie, dark-gray suit newly pressed—shoes, ah yes, shoes, mustn't forget shoes, and without bothering to sort out the rest of his belongings, crammed a score of twenty-dollar gold coins into a chamois purse, distributed handkerchief, checkbook, passport, what else? nothing else, over his rigid person and pinned a note to the pillow asking to have his things packed and forwarded to his father's address. Son killed by avalanche, no hat found, contraceptives donated to Old Guides' Home. After the passage of about eight decades all this sounds very amusing and silly—but at the time he was a dead man going through the motions of an imagined dreamer. He bent down with a grunt, cursing his knee, to fix his skis, in the driving snow, on the brink of the slope, but the skis had vanished, the bindings were shoelaces, and the slope, a staircase.

He walked down to the mews and told a young groom, who was almost as drowsy as he, that he wished to go to the railway station in a few minutes. The groom looked perplexed, and Van swore at him.

Wristwatch! He returned to the hammock where it was strapped to the netting. On his way back to the stables, around the house, he happened to look up and saw a black-haired girl of sixteen or so, in yellow slacks and a black bolero, standing on a third-floor balcony and signaling to him. She signaled telegraphically, with expansive linear gestures, indicating the cloudless sky (what a cloudless sky!), the jacaranda summit in bloom (blue! bloom!) and her own bare foot raised high and placed on the parapet (have only to put on my sandals!). Van, to his horror and shame, saw Van wait for her to come down.

She walked swiftly toward him across the iridescently glistening lawn. "Van," she said, "I must tell you my dream before I forget. You and I were high up in the Alps—Why on earth are you wearing townclothes?"

"Well, I'll tell you," drawled dreamy Van. "I'll tell you why. From a humble but reliable sauce, I mean source, excuse my accent, I have just learned *qu'on vous culbute* behind every hedge. Where can I find your tumbler?"

"Nowhere," she answered quite calmly, ignoring or not even perceiving his rudeness, for she had always known that disaster would come today or tomorrow, a question of time or rather timing on the part of fate.

"But he exists, he exists," muttered Van, looking down at a rainbow web on the turf.

"I suppose so," said the haughty child, "however, he left yesterday for some Greek or Turkish port. Moreover, he was going to do everything to get killed, if that information helps. Now listen, listen! Those walks in the woods meant nothing. Wait, Van! I was weak only twice when you had hurt him so hideously, or perhaps three times in all. Please! I can't explain in one gush, but eventually you will understand. Not everybody is as happy as we are. He's a poor, lost, clumsy boy. We are all doomed, but some are more doomed than others. He is nothing to me. I shall never see him again.

He is nothing, I swear. He adores me to the point of insanity."

"I think," said Van, "we've got hold of the wrong lover. I was asking about Herr Rack, who has such delectable gums and also adores you to the point of insanity."

He turned, as they say, on his heel, and walked toward the house.

He could swear he did not look back, could not—by any optical chance, or in any prism—have seen her physically as he walked away; and yet, with dreadful distinction, he retained forever a composite picture of her standing where he left her. The picture—which penetrated him, through an eye in the back of his head, through his vitreous spinal canal, and could never be lived down, never—consisted of a selection and blend of such random images and expressions of hers that had affected him with a pang of intolerable remorse at various moments in the past. Tiffs between them had been very rare, very brief, but there had been enough of them to make up the enduring mosaic. There was the time she stood with her back against a tree trunk, facing a traitor's doom; the time he had refused to show her some silly Chose snapshots of punt girls and had torn them up in fury and she had looked away knitting her brows and slitting her eyes at an invisible view in the window. Or that time she had hesitated, blinking, shaping a soundless word, suspecting him of a sudden revolt against her odd prudishness of speech, when he challenged her brusquely to find a rhyme to "patio" and she was not quite sure if he had in mind a certain foul word and if so what was its correct pronunciation. And perhaps, worst of all, that time when she stood fiddling with a bunch of wild flowers, a gentle half-smile hanging back quite neutrally in her eyes, her lips pursed, her head making imprecise little movements as if punctuating with self-directed nods secret decisions and silent clauses in some sort of contract with herself, with him, with unknown parties hereinafter called Comfortless, Inutile, Unjust—while he indulged in a brutal outburst triggered by her suggesting—quite sweetly and casually (as she might suggest walking a little way on the edge of a bog to see if a certain orchid was out)—that they visit the late Krolik's grave in a churchyard by which they were passing—and he had suddenly started to shout ("You know I abhor churchyards, I despise, I denounce death, dead bodies are burlesque, I refuse to stare at a stone under which a roly-poly old Pole is rotting, let him feed his maggots in peace, the entomologies of death leave me cold, I detest, I despise—"); he went on ranting that way for a couple of minutes and then literally fell at her feet, kissing her feet, imploring her pardon, and for a little while longer she kept gazing at him pensively.

Those were the fragments of the tesselation, and there were others, even more trivial; but in coming together the harmless parts made a lethal entity, and the girl in yellow slacks and black jacket, standing with her hands behind her back, slightly rocking her shoulders, leaning her back now closer now less closely against the tree trunk, and tossing her hair—a definite picture that he knew he had never seen in reality—remained within him more real than any actual memory.

Marina, in kimono and curlers, stood surrounded by servants before the porch and was asking questions that nobody seemed to answer.

Van said:

"I'm not eloping with your maid, Marina. It's an optical illusion. Her reasons for leaving you do not concern me. There's a bit of business I had been putting off like a fool but now must attend to before going to Paris."

"Ada is causing me a lot of worry," said Marina with a downcast frown and a Russian wobble of the cheeks. "Please come back as soon as you can. You have such a good influence upon her. *Au revoir.* I'm very cross with everybody."

Holding up her robe she ascended the porch steps. The tame silver dragon on her back had an ant-eater's tongue according to her eldest daughter, a scientist. What did poor mother know about P's and R's? Next to nothing.

Van shook hands with the distressed old butler, thanked Bout for a silver-knobbed cane and a pair of gloves, nodded to the other servants and walked toward the carriage and pair. Blanche, standing by in a long gray skirt and straw hat, with her cheap valise painted mahogany red and secured with a crisscrossing cord, looked exactly like a young lady setting out to teach school in a Wild West movie. She offered to sit on the box next to the Russian coachman but he ushered her into the *calèche.*

They passed undulating fields of wheat speckled with the confetti of poppies and bluets. She talked all the way about the young chatelaine and her two recent lovers in melodious low tones as if in a trance, as if *en rapport* with a dead minstrel's spirit. Only the other day from behind that row of thick firs, look there, to your right (but he did not look—sitting silent, both hands on the knob of his cane), she and her sister Madelon, with a bottle of wine between them, watched Monsieur le Comte courting the young lady on the moss, crushing her like a grunting bear as he also had crushed —many times!—Madelon who said she, Blanche, should warn him, Van, because she was a wee bit jealous but she also said—for she had a good heart—better put it off until "Malbrook" *s'en va t'en guerre*, otherwise they would fight; he had been shooting a pistol at a scarecrow all morning and that's why she waited so long, and it was in Madelon's hand, not in hers. She rambled on and on until they reached Tour-bière; two rows of cottages and a small black church with stained-glass windows. Van let her out. The youngest of the three sisters, a beautiful chestnut-curled little maiden with lewd eyes and bobbing breasts (where had he seen her before?—recently, but where?) carried Blanche's valise and birdcage into a poor shack smothered in climbing roses, but for the rest, dismal beyond words. He kissed Cendrillon's shy hand and resumed his seat in the carriage, clearing his throat and plucking at his trousers before crossing his legs. Vain Van Veen.

"The express does not stop at Torfyanka, does it, Trofim?"

"I'll take you five versts across the bog," said Trofim, "the nearest is Volosyanka."

His vulgar Russian word for Maidenhair; a whistle stop; train probably crowded.

Maidenhair. Idiot! Percy boy might have been buried by now! Maidenhair. Thus named because of the huge spreading Chinese tree at the end of the platform. Once, vaguely, confused with the Venus'-hair fern. She walked to the end of the platform in Tolstoy's novel. First exponent of the inner monologue, later exploited by the French and the Irish. N'est vert, n'est vert, n'est vert. L'arbre aux quarante écus d'or, at least in the fall. Never, never shall I hear again her "botanical" voice fall at biloba, "sorry, my Latin is showing." Ginkgo, gingko, ink, inkog. Known also as Salisbury's adiantofolia, Ada's infolio, poor Salisburia: sunk; poor Stream of Consciousness, marée noire by now. Who wants Ardis Hall!

"Barin, a barin," said Trofim, turning his blond-bearded face to his passenger.

"Da?"

"Dazhe skvoz' kozhanïy fartuk ne stal-bï ya trogat' etu frantsuzskuyu devku."

Bárin: master. *Dázhe skvoz' kózhanïy fártuk:* even through a leathern apron. *Ne stal-bï ya trógat':* I would not think of touching. *Étu:* this (that). *Frantsúzskuyu:* French (adj., accus.). *Dévku:* wench. *Úzhas, otcháyanie:* horror, despair. *Zhálost':* pity. *Kóncheno, zagázheno, rastérzano:* finished, fouled, torn to shreds.

42

Aqua used to say that only a very cruel or very stupid person, or innocent infants, could be happy on Demonia, our splendid planet. Van felt that for him to survive on this terrible Antiterra, in the multicolored and evil world into which he was born, he had to destroy, or at least to maim for life, two men. He had to find them immediately; delay itself might impair his power of survival. The rapture of their destruction would not mend his heart, but would certainly rinse his brain. The two men were in two different spots and neither spot represented an exact location, a definite street number, an identifiable billet. He hoped to punish them in an honorable way, if Fate helped. He was not prepared for the comically exaggerated zeal Fate was to display in leading him on and then muscling in to become an over-cooperative agent.

First, he decided to go to Kalugano to settle accounts with Herr Rack. Out of sheer misery he fell asleep in a corner of a compartment, full of alien legs and voices, in the crack express tearing north at a hundred miles per hour. He dozed till noon and got off at Ladoga, where after an incalculably long wait he took another, even more jerky and crowded train. As he was pushing his unsteady way through one corridor after another, cursing under his breath the window-gazers who did not draw in their bottoms to let him pass, and hopelessly seeking a comfortable nook in one of the first-class cars consisting of four-seat compartments, he saw Cordula and her mother facing each other on the window side. The two other places were occupied by a stout, elderly gentleman in an old-fashioned brown wig with a middle parting, and a bespectacled boy in a sailor suit sitting next to Cordula, who was in the act of offering him one half of her chocolate bar. Van entered, moved by a sudden very bright thought, but Cordula's mother did not recognize him at once, and the flurry of reintroductions combined with a lurch of the train caused Van to step on the prunella-shod foot of the elderly passenger, who uttered a sharp cry and said, indistinctly but not impolitely: "Spare my gout (or "take care" or "look out"), young man!"

"I do not like being addressed as 'young man,'" Van told the invalid in a completely uncalled-for, brutal burst of voice.

"Has he hurt you, Grandpa?" inquired the little boy.

"He has," said Grandpa, "but I did not mean to offend anybody by my cry of anguish."

"Even anguish should be civil," continued Van (while the better Van in him tugged at his sleeve, aghast and ashamed).

"Cordula," said the old actress (with the same apropos with which she once picked up and fondled a fireman's cat that had strayed into *Fast Colors* in the middle of her best speech), "why don't you go with this angry young demon to the tea-car? I think I'll take my thirty-nine winks now."

"What's wrong?" asked Cordula as they settled down in

the very roomy and rococo "crumpeter," as Kalugano College students used to call it in the 'Eighties and 'Nineties.

"Everything," replied Van, "but what makes you ask?"

"Well, we know Dr. Platonov slightly, and there was absolutely no reason for you to be so abominably rude to the dear old man."

"I apologize," said Van. "Let us order the traditional tea."

"Another queer thing," said Cordula, "is that you actually noticed me today. Two months ago you snubbed me."

"You had changed. You had grown lovely and languorous. You are even lovelier now. Cordula is no longer a virgin! Tell me—do you happen to have Percy de Prey's address? I mean we all know he's invading Tartary—but where could a letter reach him? I don't care to ask your snoopy aunt to forward anything."

"I daresay the Frasers have it, I'll find out. But where is V*an* going? Where shall I find Van?"

"At home—5 Park Lane, in a day or two. Just now I'm going to Kalugano."

"That's a gruesome place. Girl?"

"Man. Do you know Kalugano? Dentist? Best hotel? Concert hall? My cousin's music teacher?"

She shook her short curls. No—she went there very seldom. Twice to a concert, in a pine forest. She had not been aware that Ada took music lessons. How was Ada?

"Lucette," he said, "Lucette takes or took piano lessons. Okay. Let's dismiss Kalugano. These crumpets are very poor relatives of the Chose ones. You're right, *j'ai des ennuis*. But you can make me forget them. Tell me something to distract me, though you distract me as it is, *un petit topinambour* as the Teuton said in the story. Tell me about your affairs of the heart."

She was not a bright little girl. But she was a loquacious

and really quite exciting little girl. He started to caress her under the table, but she gently removed his hand, whispering "womenses," as whimsically as another girl had done in some other dream. He cleared his throat loudly and ordered half-a-bottle of cognac, having the waiter open it in his presence as Demon advised. She talked on and on, and he lost the thread of her discourse, or rather it got enmeshed in the rapid landscape, which his gaze followed over her shoulder, with a sudden ravine recording what Jack said when his wife 'phoned, or a lone tree in a clover field impersonating abandoned John, or a romantic stream running down a cliff and reflecting her brief bright affair with Marquis Quizz Quisana.

A pine forest fizzled out and factory chimneys replaced it. The train clattered past a roundhouse, and slowed down, groaning. A hideous station darkened the day.

"Good Lord," cried Van, "that's my stop."

He put money on the table, kissed Cordula's willing lips and made for the exit. Upon reaching the vestibule he glanced back at her with a wave of the glove he held—and crashed into somebody who had stooped to pick up a bag: "*On n'est pas goujat à ce point*," observed the latter: a burly military man with a reddish mustache and a staff captain's insignia.

Van brushed past him, and when both had come down on the platform, glove-slapped him smartly across the face.

The captain picked up his cap and lunged at the white-faced, black-haired young fop. Simultaneously Van felt somebody embrace him from behind in well-meant but unfair restraint. Not bothering to turn his head he abolished the invisible busybody with a light "piston blow" delivered by the left elbow, while he sent the captain staggering back into his own luggage with one crack of the right hand. By now several free-show amateurs had gathered around them; so, breaking their circle, Van took his man by the arm and marched him into the waiting room. A comically gloomy porter with a copiously bleeding nose came in after them carrying the captain's three bags, one of them under his arm. Cubistic labels of remote and fabulous places color-blotted the newer of the valises. Visiting cards were exchanged. "Demon's son?" grunted Captain Tapper, of Wild Violet Lodge, Kalugano. "Correct," said Van. "I'll put up, I guess, at the Majestic; if not, a note will be left for your second or seconds. You'll have to get me one, I can't very well ask the concierge to do it."

While speaking thus, Van chose a twenty dollar piece from a palmful of gold, and gave it with a grin to the damaged old porter. "Yellow cotton," Van added: "Up each nostril. Sorry, chum."

With his hands in his trouser pockets, he crossed the square to the hotel, causing a motor car to swerve stridently on the damp asphalt. He left it standing transom-wise in regard to its ordained course, and clawed his way through the revolving door of the hotel, feeling if not happier, at least more buoyant, than he had within the last twelve hours.

The Majestic, a huge old pile, all grime outside, all leather inside, engulfed him. He asked for a room with a bath, was told all were booked by a convention of contractors, tipped the desk clerk in the invincible Veen manner, and got a passable suite of three rooms with a mahogany paneled bathtub, an ancient rocking chair, a mechanical piano and a purple canopy over a double bed. After washing his hands, he immediately went down to inquire about Rack's whereabouts. The Racks had no telephone; they probably rented a room in the suburbs; the concierge looked up at the clock and called some sort of address bureau or lost person department. It proved closed till next morning. He suggested Van ask at a music store on Main Street.

On the way there he acquired his second walking stick: the Ardis Hall silver-knobbed one he had left behind in the Maidenhair station café. This was a rude, stout article with a convenient grip and an alpenstockish point capable of gouging out translucent bulging eyes. In an adjacent store he got a suitcase, and in the next, shirts, shorts, socks, slacks, pajamas, handkerchiefs, a lounging robe, a pullover and a pair of saffian bedroom slippers fetally folded in a leathern envelope. His purchases were put into the suitcase and sent at once to the hotel. He was about to enter the music shop when he remembered with a start that he had not left any message for Tapper's seconds, so he retraced his steps.

He found them sitting in the lounge and requested them to settle matters rapidly—he had more important business than that. "*Ne grubit' sekundantam*" (never be rude to seconds), said Demon's voice in his mind. Arwin Birdfoot, a lieutenant in the Guards, was blond and flabby, with moist pink lips and a foot-long cigarette holder. Johnny Rafin, Esq., was small, dark and dapper and wore blue suede shoes with a dreadful tan suit. Birdfoot soon disappeared, leaving Van to work out details with Johnny, who, though loyally eager to assist Van, could not conceal that his heart belonged to Van's adversary.

The Captain was a first-rate shot, Johnny said, and member of the Do-Re-La country club. Bloodthirsty brutishness did not come with his Britishness, but his military and academic standing demanded he defend his honor. He was an expert on maps, horses, horticulture. He was a wealthy landlord. The merest adumbration of an apology on Baron

Veen's part would clinch the matter with a token of gracious finality.

"If," said Van, "the good Captain expects *that*, he can go and stick his pistol up his gracious anality."

"That is not a nice way of speaking," said Johnny, wincing. "My friend would not approve of it. We must remember he is a very refined person."

Was Johnny Van's second, or the Captain's?

"I'm yours," said Johnny with a languid look.

Did he or the refined Captain know a German-born pianist, Philip Rack, married, with three babies (probably)?

"I'm afraid," said Johnny, with a note of disdain, "that I don't know many people with babies in Kalugano."

Was there a good whorehouse in the vicinity?

With increasing disdain Johnny answered he was a confirmed bachelor.

"Well, all right," said Van. "I have now to go out again before the shops close. Shall I acquire a brace of dueling pistols or will the Captain lend me an army 'bruger'?"

"We can supply the weapons," said Johnny.

When Van arrived in front of the music shop, he found it locked. He stared for a moment at the harps and the guitars and the flowers in silver vases on consoles receding in the dusk of looking-glasses, and recalled the schoolgirl whom he had longed for so keenly half a dozen years ago—Rose? Roza? Was that her name? Would he have been happier with her than with his pale fatal sister?

He walked for a while along Main Street—one of a million Main Streets—and then, with a surge of healthy hunger, entered a passably attractive restaurant. He ordered a beefsteak with roast potatoes, apple pie and claret. At the far end of the room, on one of the red stools of the burning bar, a graceful harlot in black—tight bodice, wide skirt, long black gloves, black-velvet picture hat—was sucking a golden drink through a straw. In the mirror behind the bar, amid colored glints, he caught a blurred glimpse of her russety blond beauty; he thought he might sample her later on, but when he glanced again she had gone.

He ate, drank, schemed.

He looked forward to the encounter with keen exhilaration. Nothing more invigorating could have been imagined. Shooting it out with that incidental clown furnished unhoped-for relief, particularly since Rack would no doubt accept a plain thrashing in lieu of combat. Designing and re-designing various contingencies pertaining to that little duel might be compared to those helpful hobbies which polio patients, lunatics and convicts are taught by generous institutions, by enlightened administrators, by ingenious psychiatrists— such as bookbinding, or putting blue beads into the orbits of dolls made by other criminals, cripples and madmen.

At first he toyed with the idea of killing his adversary: quantitatively, it would afford him the greatest sense of release; qualitatively, it suggested all sorts of moral and legal complications. Inflicting a wound seemed an inept half-measure. He decided to do something artistic and tricky, such as shooting the pistol out of the fellow's hand, or parting for him his thick brushy hair in the middle.

On his way back to the gloomy Majestic he acquired various trifles: three round cakes of soap in an elongated box, shaving cream in its cold resilient tube, ten safety-razor blades, a large sponge, a smaller soaping sponge of rubber, hair lotion, a comb, Skinner's Balsam, a toothbrush in a plastic container, toothpaste, scissors, a fountain pen, a pocket diary—what else?—yes, a small alarm clock—whose comforting presence, however, did not prevent him from telling the concierge to have him called at five A.M.

It was only nine P.M. in late summer; he would not have been surprised if told it was midnight in October. He had had an unbelievably long day. The mind could hardly grasp the fact that this very morning, at dawn, a fey character out of some Dormilona novel for servant maids had spoken to him, half-naked and shivering, in the toolroom of Ardis Hall. He wondered if the other girl still stood, arrow straight, adored and abhorred, heartless and heartbroken, against the trunk of a murmuring tree. He wondered if in view of tomorrow's *partie de plaisir* he should not prepare for her a when-you-receive-this-note, flippant, cruel, as sharp as an icicle. No. Better write to Demon.

Dear Dad,

in consequence of a trivial altercation with a Captain Tapper, of Wild Violet Lodge, whom I happened to step upon in the corridor of a train, I had a pistol duel this morning in the woods near Kalugano and am now no more. Though the manner of my end can be regarded as a kind of easy suicide, the encounter and the ineffable Captain are in no way connected with the Sorrows of Young Veen. In 1884, during my first summer at Ardis, I seduced your daughter, who was then twelve. Our torrid affair lasted till my return to Riverlane; it was resumed last June, four years later. That happiness has been the greatest event in my life, and I have no regrets. Yesterday, though, I discovered she had been unfaithful to me, so we parted. Tapper, I think, may be the chap who was thrown out of one of your gaming clubs for attempting oral intercourse with the washroom attendant, a toothless old cripple, veteran of the first Crimean War. Lots of flowers, please!

Your loving son, Van

He carefully reread his letter—and carefully tore it up. The note he finally placed in his coat pocket was much briefer.

Dad,
I had a trivial quarrel with a stranger whose face I slapped and who killed me in a duel near Kalugano. Sorry!

Van

Van was roused by the night porter who put a cup of coffee with a local "eggbun" on his bedside table, and expertly palmed the expected *chervonetz*. He resembled somewhat Bouteillan as the latter had been ten years ago and as he had appeared in a dream, which Van now retrostructed as far as it would go: in it Demon's former valet explained to Van that the "dor" in the name of an adored river equaled the corruption of hydro in "dorophone." Van often had word dreams.

He shaved, disposed of two blood-stained safety blades by leaving them in a massive bronze ashtray, had a structurally perfect stool, took a quick bath, briskly dressed, left his bag with the concierge, paid his bill and at six punctually squeezed himself next to blue-chinned and malodorous Johnny into the latter's Paradox, a cheap "semi-racer." For two or three miles they skirted the dismal bank of the lake—coal piles, shacks, boathouses, a long strip of black pebbly mud and, in the distance, over the curving bank of autumnally misted water, the tawny fumes of tremendous factories.

"Where are we now, Johnny dear?" asked Van as they

[328]

swung out of the lake's orbit and sped along a suburban avenue with clapboard cottages among laundry-linked pines.

"Dorofey Road," cried the driver above the din of the motor. "It abuts at the forest."

It abutted. Van felt a faint twinge in his knee where he had hit it against a stone when attacked from behind a week ago, in another wood. At the moment his foot touched the pine-needle strewn earth of the forest road, a transparent white butterfly floated past, and with utter certainty Van knew that he had only a few minutes to live.

He turned to his second and said:

"This stamped letter, in this handsome Majestic Hotel envelope, is addressed, as you see, to my father. I am transferring it to the back pocket of my pants. Please post it at once if the Captain, who I see has arrived in a rather funerary-looking limousine, accidentally slaughters me."

They found a convenient clearing, and the principals, pistol in hand, faced each other at a distance of some thirty paces, in the kind of single combat described by most Russian novelists and by practically all Russian novelists of gentle birth. As Arwin clapped his hands, informally signaling the permission to fire at will, Van noticed a speckled movement on his right: two little spectators—a fat girl and a boy in a sailorsuit, wearing glasses, with a basket of mushrooms between them. It was not the chocolate-muncher in Cordula's compartment, but a boy very much like him, and as this flashed through Van's mind he felt the jolt of the bullet ripping off, or so it felt, the entire left side of his torso. He swayed, but regained his balance, and with nice dignity discharged his pistol in the sun-hazy air.

His heart beat steadily, his spit was clear, his lungs felt intact, but a fire of pain raged somewhere in his left armpit. Blood oozed through his clothes and trickled down his trouserleg. He sat down, slowly, cautiously, and leaned on his right arm. He dreaded losing consciousness, but, maybe, did faint briefly, because next moment he became aware that Johnny had relieved him of the letter and was in the act of pocketing it.

"Tear it up, you idiot," said Van with an involuntary groan.

The Captain strolled up and muttered rather gloomily: "I bet you are in no condition to continue, are you?"

"I bet you can't wait—" began Van: he intended to say: "you can't wait to have me slap you again," but happened to laugh on "wait" and the muscles of mirth reacted so excruciatingly that he stopped in mid-sentence and bowed his sweating brow.

Meanwhile, the limousine was being transformed into an ambulance by Arwin. Newspapers were dismembered to protect the upholstery, and the fussy Captain added to them what looked like a potato bag or something rotting in a locker, and then after rummaging again in the car trunk and muttering about the "bloody mess" (quite a literal statement) decided to sacrifice the ancient and filthy macintosh on which a decrepit dear dog had once died on the way to the veterinary.

For half a minute Van was sure that he still lay in the car, whereas actually he was in the general ward of Lakeview (Lakeview!) Hospital, between two series of variously bandaged, snoring, raving and moaning men. When he understood this, his first reaction was to demand indignantly that he be transferred to the best private *palata* in the place and that his suitcase and alpenstock be fetched from the Majestic. His next request was that he be told how seriously he was hurt and how long he was expected to remain incapacitated. His third action was to resume what constituted the sole reason of his having to visit Kalugano (visit Kalugano!). His new quarters, where heartbroken kings had tossed in transit, proved to be a replica in white of his hotel apartment—white furniture, white carpet, white sparver. Inset, so to speak, was Tatiana, a remarkably pretty and proud young nurse, with black hair and diaphanous skin (some of her attitudes and gestures, and that harmony between neck and eyes which is the special, scarcely yet investigated secret of feminine grace fantastically and agonizingly reminded him of Ada, and he sought escape from that image in a powerful response to the charms of Tatiana, a torturing angel in her own right. Enforced immobility forbade the chase and grab of common cartoons. He begged her to massage his legs but she tested him with one glance of her grave, dark eyes—and delegated the task to Dorofey, a beefy-handed male nurse, strong enough to lift him bodily out of bed, with the sick child clasping the massive nape. When Van managed once to twiddle her breasts, she warned him she would complain if he ever repeated what she dubbed more aptly than she thought "that soft dangle." An exhibition of his state with a humble appeal for a healing caress resulted in her drily remarking that distinguished gentlemen in public parks got quite lengthy prison terms for that sort of thing. However, much later, she wrote him a charming and melancholy letter in red ink on pink paper; but other emotions and events had intervened, and he never met her again). His suitcase promptly arrived from the hotel; the stick, however, could not be located (it must be climbing nowadays Wellington Mountain, or perhaps, helping a lady to go "brambling" in Oregon); so the hospital supplied him with the Third Cane, a rather nice, knotty, cherry-dark thing with a crook and a solid black-rubber heel. Dr. Fitzbishop congratulated him on having escaped with a superficial muscle wound, the bullet having lightly grooved or, if he might say so, grazed the greater *serratus*. Doc Fitz commented on Van's wonderful recuperational power which was already in evidence, and promised to have him out of disinfectants and bandages in ten days or so if for the first three he remained as motionless as a felled treetrunk. Did Van like music? Sportsmen usually did, didn't they? Would he care to have a Sonorola by his bed? No, he disliked music, but did the doctor, being a concert-goer, know perhaps where a musician called Rack could be found? "Ward Five," answered the doctor promptly. Van misunderstood this as the title of some piece of music and repeated his question. Would he find Rack's address at Harper's music shop? Well, they used to rent a cottage way down Dorofey Road, near the forest, but now some other people had moved in. Ward Five was where hopeless cases were kept. The poor guy had always had a bad liver and a very indifferent heart, but on top of that a poison had seeped into his system; the local "lab" could not identify it and they were now waiting for a report, on those curiously frog-green faeces, from the Luga people. If Rack had administered it to himself by his own hand, he kept "mum"; it was more likely the work of his wife who dabbled in Hindu-Andean voodoo stuff and had just had a complicated miscarriage in the maternity ward. Yes, triplets—how did he guess? Anyway, if Van was so eager to visit his old pal it would have to be as soon as he could be rolled to Ward Five in a wheelchair by Dorofey, so he'd better apply a bit of voodoo, ha-ha, on his own flesh and blood.

That day came soon enough. After a long journey down corridors where pretty little things tripped by, shaking thermometers, and first an ascent and then a descent in two different lifts, the second of which was very capacious with a metal-handled black lid propped against its wall and bits of holly or laurel here and there on the soap-smelling floor,

Dorofey, like Onegin's coachman, said *priehali* ("we have arrived") and gently propelled Van, past two screened beds, toward a third one near the window. There he left Van, while he seated himself at a small table in the door corner and leisurely unfolded the Russian-language newspaper *Golos* (*Logos*).

"I am Van Veen—in case you are no longer lucid enough to recognize somebody you have seen only twice. Hospital records put your age at thirty; I thought you were younger, but even so that is a very early age for a person to die—whatever he be *tvoyu mat'*—half-baked genius or full-fledged scoundrel, or both. As you may guess by the plain but thoughtful trappings of this quiet room, you are an incurable case in one lingo, a rotting rat in another. No oxygen gadget can help you to eschew the 'agony of agony'—Professor Lamort's felicitous pleonasm. The physical torments you will be, or indeed are, experiencing, must be prodigious, but are nothing in comparison to those of a probable hereafter. The mind of man, by nature a monist, cannot accept *two* nothings; he knows there has been *one* nothing, his biological inexistence in the infinite past, for his memory is utterly blank, and *that* nothingness, being, as it were, past, is not too hard to endure. But a second nothingness—which perhaps might not be so hard to bear either—is logically unacceptable. When speaking of space we can imagine a live speck in the limitless oneness of space; but there is no analogy in such a concept with our brief life in time, because however brief (a thirty-year span is really obscenely brief!), our awareness of being is not a dot in eternity, but a slit, a fissure, a chasm running along the entire breath of metaphysical time, bisecting it and shining—no matter how narrowly—between the back panel and fore panel. Therefore, Mr. Rack, we can speak of past time, and in a vaguer, but familiar sense, of future time, but we simply cannot expect a *second* nothing, a second void, a second blank. Oblivion is a one-night performance; we have been to it once, there will be no repeat. We must face therefore the possibility of some prolonged form of disorganized consciousness and this brings me to my main point, Mr. Rack. Eternal Rack, infinite 'Rackness' may not be much but one thing is certain: the only consciousness that persists in the hereafter is the consciousness of pain. The little Rack of today is the infinite rack of tomorrow—*ich bin ein unverbesserlicher Witzbold*. We can imagine—I think we should imagine—tiny clusters of particles still retaining Rack's personality, gathering here and there in the here-and-there-after, clinging to each other, somehow, somewhere, a web of Rack's toothaches here, a bundle of Rack's nightmares there—rather like tiny groups of obscure refugees from some obliterated country huddling together for a little smelly warmth, for dingy charities or shared recollections of nameless tortures in Tartar camps. For an old man one special little torture must be to wait in a long long queue before a remote urinal. Well, Herr Rack, I submit that the surviving cells of aging Rackness will form such lines of torment, never, never reaching the coveted filth hole in the panic and pain of infinite night. You may answer, of course, if you are versed in contemporary novelistics, and if you fancy the jargon of English writers, that a 'lower-middle-class' piano tuner who falls in love with a fast 'upper-class' girl, thereby destroying his own family, is not committing a crime deserving the castigation which a chance intruder—"

With a not unfamiliar gesture, Van tore up his prepared speech and said:

"Mr. Rack, open your eyes. I'm Van Veen. A visitor."

The hollow-cheeked, long-jawed face, wax-pale, with a fattish nose and a small round chin, remained expressionless for a moment; but the beautiful, amber, liquid, eloquent eyes with pathetically long lashes had opened. Then a faint smile glimmered about his mouth parts, and he stretched one hand, without raising his head from the oil-cloth-covered pillow (why oil-cloth?).

Van, from his chair, extended the end of his cane, which the weak hand took, and palpated politely, thinking it was a well-meant offer of support. "No, I am not yet able to walk a few steps," Rack said quite distinctly, with the German accent which would probably constitute his most durable group of ghost cells.

Van drew in his useless weapon. Controlling himself, he thumped it against the footboard of his wheelchair. Dorofey glanced up from his paper, then went back to the article that engrossed him—"A Clever Piggy (from the memoirs of an animal trainer)," or else "The Crimean War: Tartar Guerillas Help Chinese Troops." A diminutive nurse simultaneously stepped out from behind the farther screen and disappeared again.

Will he ask me to transmit a message? Shall I refuse? Shall I consent—and not transmit it?

"Have they all gone to Hollywood already? Please, tell me, Baron von Wien."

"I don't know," answered Van, "they probably have. I really—"

"Because I sent my last flute melody, and a letter for *all* the family, and no answer has come. I must vomit now. I ring myself."

The diminutive nurse on tremendously high white heels pulled forward the screen of Rack's bed, separating him from the melancholy, lightly wounded, stitched-up, clean-shaven young dandy; who was rolled out and away by efficient Dorofey.

[335]

Upon returning to his cool bright room, with the rain and the sun mingling in the half-open window, Van walked on rather ephemeral feet to the looking-glass, smiled to himself in welcome, and without Dorofey's assistance went back to bed. Lovely Tatiana glided in, and asked if he wanted some tea.

"My darling," he said, "I want *you*. Look at this tower of strength!"

"If you knew," she said, over her shoulder, "how many prurient patients have insulted me—exactly that way."

He wrote Cordula a short letter, saying he had met with a little accident, was in the suite for fallen princes in Lakeview Hospital, Kalugano, and would be at her feet on Tuesday. He also wrote an even shorter letter to Marina, in French, thanking her for a lovely summer. This, on second thought, he decided to send from Manhattan to the Pisang Palace Hotel in Los Angeles. A third letter he addressed to Bernard Rattner, his closest friend at Chose, the great Rattner's nephew. "Your uncle has most honest standards," he wrote, in part, "but I am going to demolish him soon."

On Monday around noon he was allowed to sit in a deck-chair, on the lawn, which he had avidly gazed at for some days from his window. Dr. Fitzbishop had said, rubbing his hands, that the Luga laboratory said it was the not always lethal "*arethusoides*" but it had no practical importance now, because the unfortunate music teacher, and composer, was not expected to spend another night on Demonia, and would be on Terra, ha-ha, in time for evensong. Doc Fitz was what Russians call a *poshlyak* ("pretentious vulgarian") and in some obscure counterfashion Van was relieved not to be able to gloat over the wretched Rack's martyrdom.

A large pine tree cast its shadow upon him and his book. He had borrowed it from a shelf holding a medley of medical manuals, tattered mystery tales, the *Rivière de Diamants* collection of Monparnasse stories, and this odd volume of the *Journal of Modern Science* with a difficult essay by Ripley, "The Structure of Space." He had been wrestling with its phoney formulas and diagrams for several days now and saw he would not be able to assimilate it completely before his release from Lakeview Hospital on the morrow.

A hot sunfleck reached him, and tossing the red volume aside, he got up from his chair. With the return of health the image of Ada kept rising within him like a bitter and brilliant wave, ready to swallow him. His bandages had been removed; nothing but a special vest-like affair of flannel enveloped his torso, and though it was tight and thick it did not protect him any longer from the poisoned point of Ardis. Arrowhead Manor. *Le Château de la Flèche*, Flesh Hall.

He strolled on the shade-streaked lawn feeling much too warm in his black pajamas and dark-red dressing gown. A brick wall separated his part of the garden from the street and a little way off an open gateway allowed an asphalt drive to curve toward the main entrance of the long hospital building. He was on the point of returning to his deckchair when a smart, pale-gray four-door sedan glided in and stopped before him. The door flew open, before the chauffeur, an elderly man in tunic and breeches, had time to hand out Cordula, who now ran like a ballerina toward Van. He hugged her in a frenzy of welcome, kissing her rosy hot face and kneading her soft cat-like body through her black silk dress: what a delicious surprise!

She had come all the way from Manhattan, at a hundred kilometers an hour, fearing he might have already left, though he said it would be tomorrow.

"Idea!" he cried. "Take me back with you, right away. Yes, just as I am!"

"Okay," she said, "come and stay at my flat, there's a beautiful guest room for you."

She was a good sport—little Cordula de Prey. Next moment he was sitting beside her in the car, which was backing gateward. Two nurses came running and gesturing toward them, and the chauffeur asked in French if the Countess wished him to stop.

"*Non, non, non!*" cried Van in high glee and they sped away.

Panting, Cordula said:

"My mother rang me up from Malorukino" (their country estate at Malbrook, Mayne): "the local papers said you had fought a duel. You look a tower of health, I'm so glad. I knew something nasty must have happened because little Russel, Dr. Platonov's grandson—remember?—saw you from his side of the train beating up an officer on the station platform. But, first of all, Van, *net, pozhaluysta, on nas vidit* (no, please, he sees us), I have some very bad news for you. Young Fraser, who has just been flown back from Yalta, saw Percy killed on the second day of the invasion, less than a week after they had left Goodson airport. He will tell you the whole story himself, it accumulates more and more dreadful details with every telling, Fraser does not seem to have shined in the confusion, that's why, I suppose, he keeps straightening things out."

(Bill Fraser, the son of Judge Fraser, of Wellington, witnessed Lieutenant de Prey's end from a blessed ditch overgrown with cornel and medlar, but, of course, could do nothing to help the leader of his platoon and this for a number of reasons which he conscientiously listed in his report but which it would be much too tedious and embarrassing to itemize here. Percy had been shot in the thigh during a skirmish with Khazar guerillas in a ravine near Chew-Foot-Calais, as the American troops pronounced "Chufutkale," the name of a fortified rock. He had immediately assured himself, with the odd relief of the doomed, that he had got away with a flesh wound. Loss of blood caused him to faint, as we fainted, too, as soon as he started to crawl or rather squirm toward the shelter of the oak scrub and spiny bushes, where another casualty was resting comfortably. When a couple of minutes later, Percy—still Count Percy de Prey—regained consciousness he was no longer alone on his rough bed of gravel and grass. A smiling old Tartar, incongruously but somehow assuagingly wearing American blue-jeans with his *beshmet*, was squatting by his side. "*Bednïy, bednïy*" (you poor, poor fellow), muttered the good soul, shaking his shaven head and clucking: "*Bol'no* (it hurts)?" Percy answered in his equally primitive Russian that he did not feel too badly wounded: "*Karasho, karasho ne bol'no* (good, good)," said the kindly old man and, picking up the automatic pistol which Percy had dropped, he examined it with naive pleasure and then shot him in the temple. (One wonders, one always wonders, what had been the executed individual's brief, rapid series of impressions, as preserved somewhere, somehow, in some vast library of microfilmed last thoughts, between two moments: between, in the present case, our friend's becoming aware of those nice, quasi-Red Indian little wrinkles beaming at him out of a serene sky not much different from Ladore's, and then feeling the mouth of steel violently push through tender skin and exploding bone. One supposes it might have been a kind of suite for flute, a series of "movements" such as, say: I'm alive—who's that?—civilian—sympathy—thirsty—daughter with pitcher—that's my damned gun—don't . . . *et cetera* or rather no *cetera* . . . while Broken-Arm Bill prayed his Roman deity in a frenzy of fear for the Tartar to finish his job and go. But, of course, an invaluable detail in that strip of

thought would have been—perhaps, next to the pitcher peri—
a glint, a shadow, a stab of Ardis.)

"How strange, how strange," murmured Van when Cordula had finished her much less elaborate version of the report Van later got from Bill Fraser.

What a strange coincidence! Either Ada's Lethal shafts
were at work, or he, Van, had somehow managed to dispatch
her two wretched lovers in a duel with a dummy.

Strange, too, that he felt nothing special, except, perhaps,
a kind of neutral wonder, as he listened to little Cordula. A
one-track man in matters of soft passion, strange Van, strange
Demon's son, was at the moment much more anxious to enjoy Cordula as soon as humanly and humanely possible, as
soon as satanically and viatically feasible, than to keep de-
ploring the fate of a fellow he hardly knew; and although
Cordula's blue eyes flashed with tears once or twice, he knew
perfectly well that she had never seen much of her second
cousin and, in point of fact, had rather disliked him.

Cordula told Edmond: "*Arrêtez près de* what's-it-called,
yes, Albion, *le* store *pour messieurs*, in Luga"; and as peeved
Van remonstrated: "You can't go back to civilization in pajamas," she said firmly. "I shall buy you some clothes, while
Edmond has a mug of coffee."

She bought him a pair of trousers, and a raincoat. He had
been waiting impatiently in the parked car and now under
the pretext of changing into his new clothes asked her to
drive him to some secluded spot, while Edmond, wherever
he was, had another mug.

As soon as they reached a suitable area he transferred Cordula to his lap and had her very comfortably, with such howls
of enjoyment that she felt touched and flattered.

"Reckless Cordula," observed reckless Cordula cheerfully;
"this will probably mean another abortion—*encore un petit*

enfantôme, as my poor aunt's maid used to wail every time it happened to her. Did I say anything wrong?"

"Nothing wrong," said Van, kissing her tenderly; and they drove back to the diner.

43

Van spent a medicinal month in Cordula's Manhattan flat on Alexis Avenue. She dutifully visited her mother at their Malbrook castle two or three times a week, unescorted by Van either there or to the numerous social "flits" she attended in town, being a frivolous fun-loving little thing; but some parties she canceled, and resolutely avoided seeing her latest lover (the fashionable psychotechnician Dr. F. S. Fraser, a cousin of the late P. de P.'s fortunate fellow soldier). Several times Van talked on the dorophone with his father (who pursued an extensive study of Mexican spas and spices) and did several errands for him in town. He often took Cordula to French restaurants, English movies, and Varangian tragedies, all of which was most satisfying, for she relished every morsel, every sip, every jest, every sob, and he found ravishing the velvety rose of her cheeks and the azure-pure iris of her festively painted eyes to which indigo-black thick lashes, lengthening and upcurving at the outer canthus, added what fashion called the "harlequin slant."

One Sunday, while Cordula was still lolling in her perfumed bath (a lovely, oddly unfamiliar sight, which he delighted in twice a day), Van, "in the nude" (as his new sweetheart drolly genteelized "naked"), attempted for the first time after a month's abstinence to walk on his hands. He felt strong, and fit, and blithely turned over to the "first position" in the middle of the sun-drenched terrace. Next moment he was sprawling on his back. He tried again and lost his balance at once. He had the terrifying, albeit illusionary, feeling that his left arm was now shorter than his right, and Van wondered wrily if he ever would be able to dance on his hands again. King Wing had warned him that two or three months without practice might result in an irretrievable loss of the rare art. On the same day (the two nasty little incidents thus remained linked up in his mind forever) Van happened to answer the 'phone—a deep hollow voice which he thought was a man's wanted Cordula, but the caller turned out to be an old schoolmate, and Cordula feigned limpid delight, while making big eyes at Van over the receiver, and invented a number of unconvincing engagements.

"It's a gruesome girl!" she cried after the melodious adieux. "Her name is Vanda Broom, and I learned only recently what I never suspected at school—she's a regular *tribadka*—poor Grace Erminin tells me Vanda used to make constant passes at her and at—at another girl. There's her picture here," continued Cordula with a quick change of tone, producing a daintily bound and prettily printed graduation album of Spring, 1887, which Van had seen at Ardis, but in which he had not noticed the somber beetle-browed unhappy face of that particular girl, and now it did not matter any more, and Cordula quickly popped the book back into a drawer; but he remembered very well that among the various more or less coy contributions it contained a clever pastiche by Ada Veen mimicking Tolstoy's paragraph rhythm and chapter closings;

[343]

he saw clearly in mind her prim photo under which she had
added one of her characteristic jingles:

> In the old manor, I've parodied
> Every veranda and room,
> And jacarandas at Arrowhead
> In supernatural bloom.

It did not matter, it did not matter. Destroy and forget!
But a butterfly in the Park, an orchid in a shop window,
would revive everything with a dazzling inward shock of
despair.

His main industry consisted of research at the great
granite-pillared Public Library, that admirable and formi-
dable palace a few blocks from Cordula's cosy flat. One is irresistibly tempted to compare the strange longings and
nauseous qualms that enter into the complicated ecstasies
accompanying the making of a young writer's first book with
childbearing. Van had only reached the bridal stage; then, to
develop the metaphor, would come the sleeping car of
messy defloration; then the first balcony of honeymoon
breakfasts, with the first wasp. In no sense could Cordula
be compared to a writer's muse but the evening stroll back to
her apartment was pleasantly saturated with the afterglow
and afterthought of the accomplished task and the expectation of her caresses; he especially looked forward to those
nights when they had an elaborate repast sent up from "Monaco," a good restaurant in the entresol of the tall building
crowned by her penthouse and its spacious terrace. The sweet
banality of their little ménage sustained him much more securely than the company of his constantly agitated and fiery
father did at their rare meetings in town or was to do during
a fortnight in Paris before the next term at Chose. Except

gossip—gossamer gossip—Cordula had no conversation and that also helped. She had instinctively realized very soon that she should never mention Ada or Ardis. He, on his part, accepted the evident fact that she did not really love him. Her small, clear, soft, well-padded and rounded body was delicious to stroke, and her frank amazement at the variety and vigor of his love-making anointed what still remained of poor Van's crude virile pride. She would doze off between two kisses. When he could not sleep, as now often happened, he retired to the sitting room and sat there annotating his authors or else he would walk up and down the open terrace, under a haze of stars, in severely restricted meditation, till the first tramcar jangled and screeched in the dawning abyss of the city.

When in early September Van Veen left Manhattan for Lute, he was pregnant.

PART TWO

PART TWO

1

At the Goodson Airport, in one of the gilt-framed mirrors of its old-fashioned waiting room, Van glimpsed the silk hat of his father who sat awaiting him in an armchair of imitation marblewood, behind a newspaper that said in reverse characters: "Crimea Capitulates." At the same moment a raincoated man with a pleasant, somewhat porcine, pink face accosted Van. He represented a famous international agency, known as the VPL, which handled Very Private Letters. After a first flash of surprise, Van reflected that Ada Veen, a recent mistress of his, could not have chosen a smarter (in all senses of the word) way of conveying to him a message whose fantastically priced, and prized, process of transmission insured an absoluteness of secrecy which neither torture nor mesmerism had been able to break down in the evil days of 1859. It was rumored that even Gamaliel on his (no longer frequent, alas) trips to Paris, and King Victor during his still fairly regular visits to Cuba or Hecuba, and, of course, robust Lord Goal, Viceroy of France, when enjoying his randonnies all over Canady, preferred the phenomenally discreet, and in fact rather creepy, infallibility of the VPL

[349]

organization to such official facilities as sexually starved potentates have at their disposal for deceiving their wives. The present messenger called himself James Jones, a formula whose complete lack of connotation made an ideal pseudonym despite its happening to be his real name. A flurry and flapping had started in the mirror but Van declined to act hastily. In order to gain time (for, on being shown Ada's crest on a separate card, he felt he had to decide whether or not to accept her letter), he closely examined the badge resembling an ace of hearts which J.J. displayed with pardonable pride. He requested Van to open the letter, satisfy himself of its authenticity, and sign the card that then went back into some secret pit or pouch within the young detective's attire or anatomy. Cries of welcome and impatience from Van's father (wearing for the flight to France a scarlet-silk-lined black cape) finally caused Van to interrupt his colloquy with James and pocket the letter (which he read a few minutes later in the lavatory before boarding the airliner).

"Stocks," said Demon, "are on the zoom. Our territorial triumphs, et cetera. An American governor, my friend Bessborodko, is to be installed in Bessarabia, and a British one, Armborough, will rule Armenia. I saw you enlaced with your little Countess near the parking lot. If you marry her I will disinherit you. They're quite a notch below our set."

"In a couple of years," said Van, "I'll slide into my own little millions" (meaning the fortune Aqua had left him). "But you needn't worry, sir, we have interrupted our affair for the time being—till the next time I return to live in her *girlinière*" (Canady slang).

Demon, flaunting his flair, desired to be told if Van or his *poule* had got into trouble with the police (nodding toward Jim or John who having some other delivery to make sat glancing through Crime Copulate Bessarmenia).

"*Poule*," replied Van with the evasive taciturnity of the Roman rabbi shielding Barabbas.

"Why gray?" asked Demon, alluding to Van's overcoat. "Why that military cut? It's too late to enlist."

"I couldn't—my draft board would turn me down anyway."

"How's the wound?"

"*Komsi-komsa*. It now appears that the Kalugano surgeon messed up his job. The rip seam has grown red and raw, without any reason, and there's a lump in my armpit. I'm in for another spell of surgery—this time in London, where butchers carve so much better. Where's the *mestechko* here? Oh, I see it. Cute (a gentian painted on one door, a lady fern on the other: have to go to the herbarium)."

He did not answer her letter, and a fortnight later John James, now got up as a German tourist, all pseudo-tweed checks, handed Van a second message, in the Louvre right in front of Bosch's *Bâteau Ivre*, the one with a jester drinking in the riggings (poor old Dan thought it had something to do with Brant's satirical poem!). There would be no answer—though answers were included, with the return ticket, in the price, as the honest messenger pointed out.

It was snowing, yet James in a fit of abstract rakishness stood fanning himself with a third letter at the front door of Van's *cottage orné* on Ranta River, near Chose, and Van asked him to stop bringing him messages.

In the course of the next two years two more letters were handed to him, both in London, and both in the hall of the Albania Palace Hotel, by another VPL agent, an elderly gent in a bowler, whose matter-of-fact, undertakerish aspect might irritate Mr. Van Veen less, thought modest and sensitive Jim, than that of a romanesque private detective. A sixth came by natural means to Park Lane. The lot (minus the last, which dealt exclusively with Ada's stage & screen ventures) is given below. Ada ignored dates, but they can be approximatively determined.

[Los Angeles, early September, 1888]
You must pardon me for using such a posh (and also *poshliy*) means of having a letter reach you, but I'm unable to find any safer service.

When I said I could not speak and would write, I meant I could not utter the proper words at short notice. I implore you. I felt that I could not produce them and arrange them orally in the necessary order. I implore you. I felt that one wrong or misplaced word would be fatal, you would simply turn away, as you did, and walk off again, and again, and again. I implore you for breath [*sic*. Ed.] of understanding. But now I think that I should have taken the risk of speaking, of stammering, for I see now that it is just as dreadfully hard to put my heart and honor in script—even more so because in speaking one can use a stutter as a shutter, and plead a chance slurring of words, like a bleeding hare with one side of its mouth shot off, or twist back, and improve; but against a background of snow, even the blue snow of this notepaper, the blunders are red and final. I implore you.

One thing should be established once for all, indefeasibly. I loved, love, and shall love only you. I implore you and love you with everlasting pain and passion, my darling. *Ti tut stoyal* (you stayed here), in this *karavansaray*, you in the middle of everything, always, when I must have been seven or eight, didn't you?

[Los Angeles, mid-September, 1888]
This is a second howl *iz ada* (out of Hades). Strangely, I learned on the same day, from three different sources, of your duel in K.; of P's death; and of your recuperating at his

[352]

cousin's (congs, as she and I used to say). I rang her up, but she said that you had left for Paris and that R. had also died —not through your intervention, as I had thought for a moment, but through that of his wife. Neither he nor P. was technically my lover, but both are on Terra now, so it does not matter.

[Los Angeles, 1889]

We are still at the candy-pink and pisang-green albergo where you once stayed with your father. He is awfully nice to me, by the way. I enjoy going places with him. He and I have gamed at Nevada, my rhyme-name town, but you are also there, as well as the legendary river of Old Rus. *Da.* Oh, write me, one tiny note, I'm trying so hard to please you! Want some more (desperate) little topics? Marina's new director of artistic conscience defines Infinity as the farthest point from the camera which is still in fair focus. She has been cast as the deaf nun Varvara (who, in some ways, is the most interesting of Chekhov's Four Sisters). She sticks to Stan's principle of having lore and rôle overflow into everyday life, insists on keeping it up at the hotel restaurant, drinks tea *v prikusku* ("biting sugar between sips"), and feigns to misunderstand every question in Varvara's quaint way of feigning stupidity—a double imbroglio, which annoys strangers but which somehow makes me feel I'm her daughter much more distinctly than in the Ardis era. She's a great hit here, on the whole. They gave her (not quite gratis, I'm afraid) a special bungalow, labeled Marina Durmanova, in Universal City. As for me, I'm only an incidental waitress in a fourth-rate Western, hip-swinging between table-slapping drunks, but I rather enjoy the *Houssaie* atmosphere, the dutiful art, the winding hill roads, the reconstructions of streets, and the obligatory square, and a mauve shop sign on an

[353]

ornate wooden façade, and around noon all the extras in period togs queuing before a glass booth, but I have nobody to call.

Speaking of calls, I saw a truly marvelous ornithological film the other night with Demon. I had never grasped the fact that the paleotropical sunbirds (look them up!) are "mimotypes" of the New World hummingbirds, and all my thoughts, oh, my darling, are mimotypes of yours. I know, I know! I even know that you stopped reading at "grasped"— as in the old days.

[California? 1890]
I love only you, I'm happy only in dreams of you, you are my joy and my world, this is as certain and real as being aware of one's being alive, but . . . oh, I don't accuse you!—but, Van, you *are* responsible (or Fate through you is responsible, *ce qui revient au même*) of having let loose something mad in me when we were only children, a physical hankering, an insatiable itch. The fire you rubbed left its brand on the most vulnerable, most vicious and tender point of my body. Now I have to pay for your rasping the red rash too strongly, too soon, as charred wood has to pay for burning. When I remain without your caresses, I lose all control of my nerves, nothing exists any more than the ecstasy of friction, the abiding effect of your sting, of your delicious poison. I do not accuse you, but this is why I crave and cannot resist the impact of alien flesh; this is why our joint past radiates ripples of boundless betrayals. All this you are free to diagnose as a case of advanced erotomania, but there is more to it, because there exists a simple cure for all my *maux* and *throes* and that is an extract of scarlet aril, the flesh of yew, just only yew. *Je réalise*, as your sweet Cinderella de Torf (now Madame Trofim Fartukov) used to say, that I'm being coy and

obscene. But it all leads up to an important, important suggestion! Van, *je suis sur la verge* (Blanche again) of a revolting amorous adventure. I could be instantly saved by you. Take the fastest flying machine you can rent straight to El Paso, your Ada will be waiting for you there, waving like mad, and we'll continue, by the New World Express, in a suite I'll obtain, to the burning tip of Patagonia, Captain Grant's Horn, a Villa in Verna, my jewel, my agony. Send me an aerogram with one Russian word—the end of my name and wit.

[Arizona, summer, 1890]

Mere pity, a Russian girl's *zhalost'*, drew me to R. (whom musical critics have now "discovered"). He knew he would die young and was always, in fact, mostly corpse, never once, I swear, rising to the occasion, even when I showed openly my compassionate non-resistance because I, alas, was brimming with Van-less vitality, and had even considered buying the services of some rude, the ruder the better, young muzhik. As to P., I could explain my submitting to his kisses (first tender and plain, later growing fiercely expert, and finally tasting of me when he returned to my mouth—a vicious circle set spinning in early Thargelion, 1888) by saying that if I stopped seeing him he would divulge my affair with my cousin to my mother. He did say he could produce witnesses, such as the sister of your Blanche, and a stable boy who, I suspect, was impersonated by the youngest of the three demoiselles de Tourbe, witches all—but enough. Van, I could make much of those threats in explaining my conduct to you. I would not mention, naturally, that they were made in a bantering tone, hardly befitting a genuine blackmailer. Nor would I mention that even if he had proceeded to recruit anonymous messengers and informers, it might have ended in his wrecking his own reputation as soon as his motives and actions were exposed, as they were bound to be in the long ruin [sic! "run" in her blue stocking. Ed.]. I would conceal, in a word, that I knew the coarse banter was meant only to drill-jar your poor brittle Ada—because, despite the coarseness, he had a keen sense of honor, odd though it may seem to you and me. No. I would concentrate entirely on the effect of the threat upon one ready to submit to any infamy rather than face the shadow of disclosure, for (and this, of course, neither he nor his informers could know), shocking as an affair between first cousins might have seemed to a law-abiding family, I refused to imagine (as you and I have always done) how Marina and Demon would have reacted in "our" case. By the jolts and skids of my syntax you will see that I cannot logically explain my behavior. I do not deny that I experienced a strange weakness during the perilous assignations I granted him, as if his brutal desire kept fascinating not only my inquisitive senses but also my reluctant intellect. I can swear, however, solemn Ada can swear that in the course of our "sylvan trysts" I successfully evaded if not pollution, at least possession before and after your return to Ardis—except for one messy occasion when he half-took me by force—the over-eager dead man.

I'm writing from Marina Ranch—not very far from the little gulch in which Aqua died and into which I myself feel like creeping some day. For the time being, I'm returning for a while to the Pisang Hotel.

I salute the good auditor.

When Van retrieved in 1940 this thin batch of five letters, each in its VPL pink silk-paper case, from the safe in his Swiss bank where they had been preserved for exactly one half of a century, he was baffled by their small number. The expansion of the past, the luxuriant growth of memory had magnified that number to at least fifty. He recalled that he had also used as a cache the desk in his Park Lane studio, but he knew he had kept there only the innocent sixth letter (Dreams of Drama) of 1891, which had perished, together with her coded notes (of 1884–88) when the irreplaceable little palazzo burnt down in 1919. Rumor attributed the bright deed to the city fathers (three bearded elders and a blue-eyed young Mayor with a fabulous amount of front teeth), who could no longer endure their craving for the space that the solid dwarf occupied between two alabaster colossi; but instead of selling them the blackened area as expected, Van gleefully erected there his famous Lucinda Villa, a miniature museum just two stories high, with a still growing collection of microphotographed paintings from all public and private galleries in the world (not excluding Tartary) on one floor and a honeycomb of projection cells on the other: a most appetizing little memorial of Parian marble, administered by a considerable staff, guarded by three heavily armed stalwarts, and open to the public only on Mondays for a token fee of one gold dollar regardless of age or condition.

No doubt the singular multiplication of those letters in retrospect could be explained by each of them casting an excruciating shadow, similar to that of a lunar volcano, over several months of his life, and tapering to a point only when the no less pangful precognition of the next message began to dawn. But many years later, when working on his *Texture of Time*, Van found in that phenomenon additional proof of real time's being connected with the interval between events, not with their "passage," not with their blending, not with their shading the gap wherein the pure and impenetrable texture of time transpires.

He told himself he would be firm and suffer in silence. Self-esteem was satisfied: the dying duelist dies a happier man than his live foe ever will be. We must not blame Van, however, for failing to persevere in his resolution, for it is not hard to understand why a seventh letter (transmitted to him by Ada's and his half-sister, at Kingston, in 1892) could make him succumb. Because he knew it was the last in the series. Because it had come from the blood-red *érable* arbors of Ardis. Because a sacramental four-year period equaled that of their first separation. Because Lucette turned out to be, against all reason and will, the impeccable paranymph.

2

Ada's letters breathed, writhed, lived; Van's *Letters from Terra*, "a philosophical novel," showed no sign of life whatsoever.

(I disagree, it's a nice, nice little book! Ada's note.)

He had written it involuntarily, so to speak, not caring a dry fig for literary fame. Neither did pseudonymity tickle him in reverse—as it did when he danced on his hands. Though "Van Veen's vanity" often cropped up in the drawing-room prattle among fan-wafting ladies, this time his long blue pride feathers remained folded. What, then, moved him to contrive a romance around a subject that had been worried to extinction in all kinds of "Star Rats," and "Space Aces"? We —whoever "we" are—might define the compulsion as a pleasurable urge to express through verbal imagery a compendium of certain inexplicably correlated vagaries observed by him in mental patients, on and off, since his first year at Chose. Van had a passion for the insane as some have for arachnids or orchids.

There were good reasons to disregard the technological details involved in delineating intercommunication between

Terra the Fair and our terrible Antiterra. His knowledge of physics, mechanicalism and that sort of stuff had remained limited to the scratch of a prep-school blackboard. He consoled himself with the thought that no censor in America or Great Britain would pass the slightest reference to "magnetic" gewgaws. Quietly, he borrowed what his greatest forerunners (Counterstone, for example) had imagined in the way of a manned capsule's propulsion, including the clever idea of an initial speed of a few thousand miles per hour increasing, under the influence of a Counterstonian type of intermediate environment between sibling galaxies, to several trillions of light-years per second, before dwindling harmlessly to a parachute's indolent descent. Elaborating anew, in irrational fabrications, all that Cyraniana and "physics fiction" would have been not only a bore but an absurdity, for nobody knew how far Terra, or other innumerable planets with cottages and cows, might be situated in outer or inner space: "inner," because why not assume their microcosmic presence in the golden globules ascending quick-quick in this flute of Moët or in the corpuscles of my, Van Veen's—

(or my, Ada Veen's)

—bloodstream, or in the pus of a Mr. Nekto's ripe boil newly lanced in Nektor or Neckton. Moreover, although reference works existed on library shelves in available, and redundant, profusion, no direct access could be obtained to the banned, or burned, books of the three cosmologists, Xertigny, Yates and Zotov (pen names), who had recklessly started the whole business half a century earlier, causing, and endorsing, panic, demency and execrable *romanchiks*. All three scientists had vanished now: X had committed suicide; Y had been kidnapped by a laundryman and transported to Tartary; and Z, a ruddy, white-whiskered old sport, was driving his Yakima jailers crazy by means of incomprehensible crepitations, ceaseless invention of invisible inks, chameleonizations, nerve signals, spirals of outgoing light and feats of ventriloquism that imitated pistol shots and sirens.

Poor Van! In his struggle to keep the writer of the letters from Terra strictly separate from the image of Ada, he gilt and carmined Theresa until she became a paragon of banality. This Theresa maddened with her messages a scientist on our easily maddened planet; his anagram-looking name, Sig Leymanski, had been partly derived by Van from that of Aqua's last doctor. When Leymanski's obsession turned into love, and one's sympathy got focused on his enchanting, melancholy, betrayed wife (née Antilia Glems), our author found himself confronted with the distressful task of now stamping out in Antilia, a born brunette, all traces of Ada, thus reducing yet another character to a dummy with bleached hair.

After beaming to Sig a dozen communications from her planet, Theresa flies over to him, and he, in his laboratory, has to place her on a slide under a powerful microscope in order to make out the tiny, though otherwise perfect, shape of his minikin sweetheart, a graceful microorganism extending transparent appendages toward his huge humid eye. Alas, the testibulus (test tube—never to be confused with *testiculus*, orchid), with Theresa swimming inside like a micromermaid, is "accidentally" thrown away by Professor Leyman's (he had trimmed his name by that time) assistant, Flora, initially an ivory-pale, dark-haired funest beauty, whom the author transformed just in time into a third bromidic dummy with a dun bun.

(Antilia later regained her husband, and Flora was weeded out. Ada's addendum.)

On Terra, Theresa had been a Roving Reporter for an American magazine, thus giving Van the opportunity to describe the sibling planet's political aspect. This aspect gave him the least trouble, presenting as it did a mosaic of painstakingly collated notes from his own reports on the "transcendental delirium" of his patients. Its acoustics were poor, proper names often came out garbled, a chaotic calendar messed up the order of events but, on the whole, the colored dots did form a geomantic picture of sorts. As earlier experimentators had conjectured, our annals lagged by about half a century behind Terra's along the bridges of time, but overtook some of its underwater currents. At the moment of our sorry story, the king of Terra's England, yet another George (there had been, apparently, at least half-a-dozen bearing that name before him) ruled, or had just ceased to rule, over an empire that was somewhat patchier (with alien blanks and blots between the British Islands and South Africa) than the solidly conglomerated one on our Antiterra. Western Europe presented a particularly glaring gap: ever since the eighteenth century, when a virtually bloodless revolution had dethroned the Capetians and repelled all invaders, Terra's France flourished under a couple of emperors and a series of bourgeois presidents, of whom the present one, Doumercy, seemed considerably more lovable than Milord Goal, Governor of Lute! Eastward, instead of Khan Sosso and his ruthless Sovietnamur Khanate, a super Russia, dominating the Volga region and similar watersheds, was governed by a Sovereign Society of Solicitous Republics (or so it came through) which had superseded the Tsars, conquerors of Tartary and Trst. Last but not least, Athaulf the Future, a fair-haired giant in a natty uniform, the secret flame of many a British nobleman, honorary captain of the French police, and benevolent ally of Rus and Rome, was said to be in the act of transforming a gingerbread Germany into a great country of speedways, immaculate soldiers, brass bands and modernized barracks for misfits and their young.

No doubt much of that information, gleaned by our terrapists (as Van's colleagues were dubbed), came in a botched form; but the strain of sweet happiness could be always distinguished as an all-pervading note. Now the purpose of the novel was to suggest that Terra cheated, that all was not paradise there, that perhaps in some ways human minds and human flesh underwent on that sibling planet worse torments than on our much maligned Demonia. In her first letters, before leaving Terra, Theresa had nothing but praise for its rulers—especially Russian and German rulers. In her later messages from space she confessed that she had exaggerated the bliss; had been, in fact, the instrument of "cosmic propaganda"—a brave thing to admit, as agents on Terra might have yanked her back or destroyed her in flight had they managed to intercept her undissembling ondulas, now mostly going one way, our way, don't ask Van by what method or principle. Unfortunately, not only mechanicalism, but also moralism, could hardly be said to constitute something in which he excelled, and what we have rendered here in a few leisurely phrases took him two hundred pages to develop and adorn. We must remember that he was only twenty; that his young proud soul was in a state of grievous disarray; that he had read too much and invented too little; and that the brilliant mirages, which had risen before him when he felt the first pangs of book-birth on Cordula's terrace, were now fading under the action of prudence, as did those wonders which medieval explorers back from Cathay were afraid to reveal to the Venetian priest or the Flemish philistine.

He devoted a couple of months at Chose to copying in a clean hand his scarecrow scribblings and then heavily recorrecting the result, so that his final copy looked like a first draft when he took it to an obscure agency in Bedford to have it secretly typed in triplicate. This he disfigured again during his voyage back to America on board the *Queen Guinevere*. And in Manhattan the galleys had to be reset twice, owing not only to the number of new alterations but also to the eccentricity of Van's proofreading marks.

Letters from Terra, by Voltemand, came out in 1891 on Van's twenty-first birthday, under the imprint of two bogus houses, "Abencerage" in Manhattan, and "Zegris" in London.

(Had I happened to see a copy I would have recognized Chateaubriand's *lapochka* and hence your little paw, *at once*.)

His new laywer, Mr. Gromwell, whose really beautiful floral name suited somehow his innocent eyes and fair beard, was a nephew of the great Grombchevski, who for the last thirty years or so had managed some of Demon's affairs with good care and acumen. Gromwell nursed Van's personal fortune no less tenderly; but he had little experience in the intricacies of book-publishing matters, and Van was an absolute ignoramus there, not knowing, for example, that "review copies" were supposed to go to the editors of various periodicals or that advertisements should be purchased and not be expected to appear by spontaneous generation in full-page adulthood between similar blurbs boosting *The Possessed* by Miss Love and *The Puffer* by Mr. Dukes.

For a fat little fee, Gwen, one of Mr. Gromwell's employees, was delegated not only to entertain Van, but also to supply Manhattan bookstores with one-half of the printed copies, whilst an old lover of hers in England was engaged to place the rest in the bookshops of London. The notion that anybody kind enough to sell his book should not keep the ten dollars or so that every copy had cost to manufacture seemed unfair and illogical to Van. Therefore he felt sorry for all the trouble that underpaid, tired, bare-armed, brunette-pale shopgirls had no doubt taken in trying to tempt dour homosexuals with his stuff ("Here's a rather fancy novel about a girl called Terra"), when he learned from a careful study of a statement of sales, which his stooges sent him in February, 1892, that in twelve months only six copies had been sold—two in England and four in America. Statistically speaking, no reviews could have been expected, given the unorthodox circumstances in which poor Terra's correspondence had been handled. Curiously enough, as many as two did appear. One, by the First Clown in *Elsinore*, a distinguished London weekly, popped up in a survey entitled, with a British journalist's fondness for this kind of phoney wordplay, "*Terre à terre*, 1891," and dealt with the year's "Space Romances," which by that time had begun to fine off. He sniffed Voltemand's contribution as the choicest of the lot, calling it (alas, with unerring flair) "a sumptuously fripped up, trite, tedious and obscure fable, with a few absolutely marvelous metaphors marring the otherwise total ineptitude of the tale."

The only other compliment was paid to poor Voltemand in a little Manhattan magazine (*The Village Eyebrow*) by the poet Max Mispel (another botanical name—"medlar" in English), member of the German Department at Goluba University. Herr Mispel, who liked to air his authors, discerned in *Letters from Terra* the influence of Osberg (Spanish writer of pretentious fairy tales and mystico-allegoric anecdotes, highly esteemed by short-shift thesialists) as well as that of an obscene ancient Arab, expounder of anagrammatic dreams, Ben Sirine, thus transliterated by Captain de Roux, according to Burton in his adaptation of Nefzawi's treatise on the best method of mating with obese or hunchbacked females (*The Perfumed Garden*, Panther edition, p. 187, a copy given to ninety-three-year-old Baron Van Veen by his ribald physician Professor Lagosse). His critique ended as follows: "If Mr. Voltemand (or Voltimand or Mandalatov) is a psychiatrist, as I think he might be, then I pity his patients, while admiring his talent."

Upon being cornered, Gwen, a fat little *fille de joie* (by inclination if not by profession), squealed on one of her new admirers, confessing she had begged him to write that article because she could not bear to see Van's "crooked little smile" at finding his beautifully bound and boxed book so badly neglected. She also swore that Max not only did not know who Voltemand really was, but had not read Van's novel. Van toyed with the idea of challenging Mr. Medlar (who, he hoped, would choose swords) to a duel at dawn in a secluded corner of the Park whose central green he could see from the penthouse terrace where he fenced with a French coach twice a week, the only exercise, save riding, that he still indulged in; but to his surprise—and relief (for he was a little ashamed to defend his "novelette" and only wished to forget it, just as another, unrelated, Veen might have denounced—if allowed a longer life—his pubescent dream of ideal bordels) Max Mushmula (Russian for "medlar") answered Van's tentative cartel with the warm-hearted promise of sending him his next article, "The Weed Exiles the Flower" (Melville & Marvell).

A sense of otiose emptiness was all Van derived from those contacts with Literature. Even while writing his book, he had become painfully aware how little he knew his own planet while attempting to piece together another one from jagged bits filched from deranged brains. He decided that after completing his medical studies at Kingston (which he found more congenial than good old Chose) he would undertake long travels in South America, Africa, India. As a boy of fifteen (Eric Veen's age of florescence) he had studied with a poet's passion the timetables of three great American transcontinental trains that one day he would take—not alone (now alone). From Manhattan, via Mephisto, El Paso, Meksikansk and the Panama Chunnel, the dark-red New World Express reached Brazilia and Witch (or Viedma, founded by a Russian admiral). There it split into two parts, the eastern one continuing to Grant's Horn, and the western returning north through Valparaiso and Bogota. On alternate days the fabulous journey began in Yukonsk, a two-way section going to the Atlantic seaboard, while another, via California and Central America, roared into Uruguay. The dark-blue African Express began in London and reached the Cape by three different routes, through Nigero, Rodosia or Ephiopia. Finally, the brown Orient Express joined London to Ceylon and Sydney, via Turkey and several Chunnels. It is not clear, when you are falling asleep, why all continents except you begin with an A.

Those three admirable trains included at least two carriages in which a fastidious traveler could rent a bedroom with bath and water closet, and a drawing room with a piano or a harp. The length of the journey varied according to Van's predormient mood, when at Eric's age he imagined the landscapes unfolding all along his comfortable, too comfortable, fauteuil. Through rain forests and mountain canyons and other fascinating places (oh, name them! Can't—falling asleep), the room moved as slowly as fifteen miles per hour but across desertorum or agricultural drearies it attained seventy, ninety-seven, night-nine, one hund, red dog—

3

In the spring of 1869, David van Veen, a wealthy architect of Flemish extraction (in no way related to the Veens of our rambling romance), escaped uninjured when the motorcar he was driving from Cannes to Calais blew a front tire on a frost-glazed road and tore into a parked furniture van; his daughter sitting beside him was instantly killed by a suitcase sailing into her from behind and breaking her neck. In his London studio her husband, an unbalanced, unsuccessful painter (ten years older than his father-in-law whom he envied and despised) shot himself upon receiving the news by cablegram from a village in Normandy called, dreadfully, Deuil.

The momentum of disaster lost none of its speed, for neither did Eric, a boy of fifteen, despite all the care and adoration which his grandfather surrounded him with, escape a freakish fate: a fate strangely similar to his mother's.

After being removed from Note to a small private school in Vaud Canton and then spending a consumptive summer in the Maritime Alps, he was sent to Ex-en-Valais, whose crystal air was supposed at the time to strengthen young lungs; instead of which its worst hurricane hurled a roof tile at him, fatally fracturing his skull. Among the boy's belongings David van Veen found a number of poems and the draft of an essay entitled "Villa Venus: an Organized Dream."

To put it bluntly, the boy had sought to solace his first sexual torments by imagining and detailing a project (derived from reading too many erotic works found in a furnished house his grandfather had bought near Vence from Count Tolstoy, a Russian or Pole): namely, a chain of palatial brothels that his inheritance would allow him to establish all over "both hemispheres of our callipygian globe." The little chap saw it as a kind of fashionable club, with branches, or, in his poetical phrase, "Floramors," in the vicinity of cities and spas. Membership was to be restricted to noblemen, "handsome and healthy," with an age limit of fifty (which must be praised as very broadminded on the poor kid's part), paying a yearly fee of 3650 guineas not counting the cost of bouquets, jewels and other gallant donations. Resident female physicians, good-looking and young ("of the American secretarial or dentist-assistant type"), would be there to check the intimate physical condition of "the caresser and the caressed" (another felicitous formula) as well as their own if "the need arose." One clause in the Rules of the Club seemed to indicate that Eric, though frenziedly heterosexual, had enjoyed some tender *ersatz* fumblings with schoolmates at Note (a notorious preparatory school in that respect): at least two of the maximum number of fifty inmates in the major floramors might be pretty boys, wearing frontlets and short smocks, not older than fourteen if fair, and not more than twelve if dark. However, in order to exclude a regular flow of "inverterate pederasts," boy love could be dabbled in by the jaded guest only between two sequences of three girls each, all possessed in the course of the same week—a somewhat comical, but not unshrewd, stipulation.

The candidates for every floramor were to be selected by a Committee of Club Members who would take into consideration the annual accumulation of impressions and desiderata, jotted down by the guests in a special Shell Pink Book. "Beauty and tenderness, grace and docility" composed the main qualities required of the girls, aged from fifteen to twenty-five in the case of "slender Nordic dolls," and from ten to twenty in that of "opulent Southern charmers." They would gambol and loll in "boudoirs and conservatories," invariably naked and ready for love; not so their attendants, attractively dressed handmaids of more or less exotic extraction, "unavailable to the fancy of members except by special permission from the Board." My favorite clause (for I own a photostat of that poor boy's calligraph) is that any girl in her floramor could be Lady-in-Chief by acclamation during her menstrual period. (This of course did not work, and the committee compromised by having a good-looking female homosexual head the staff and adding a bouncer whom Eric had overlooked.)

Eccentricity is the greatest grief's greatest remedy. The boy's grandfather set at once to render in brick and stone, concrete and marble, flesh and fun, Eric's fantasy. He resolved to be the first sampler of the first houri he would hire for his last house, and to live until then in laborious abstinence.

It must have been a moving and magnificent sight—that of the old but still vigorous Dutchman with his rugged reptilian face and white hair, designing with the assistance of Leftist decorators the thousand and one memorial floramors he resolved to erect all over the world—perhaps even in brutal Tartary, which he thought was ruled by "Americanized Jews," but then "Art redeemed Politics"—profoundly original concepts that we must condone in a lovable old crank. He began with rural England and coastal America, and was engaged in a Robert Adam-like composition (cruelly referred to by local wags as the Madam-I'm-Adam House), not far from Newport, Rodos Island, in a somewhat senile style, with marble columns dredged from classical seas and still encrusted with Etruscan oyster shells—when he died from a stroke while helping to prop up a propylon. It was only his hundredth house!

His nephew and heir, an honest but astoundingly stuffy clothier in Ruinen (somewhere near Zwolle, I'm told), with a large family and a small trade, was not cheated out of the millions of guldens, about the apparent squandering of which he had been consulting mental specialists during the last ten years or so. All the hundred floramors opened simultaneously on September 20, 1875 (and by a delicious coincidence the old Russian word for September, "ryuen'," which might have spelled "ruin," also echoed the name of the ecstatic Neverlander's hometown). By the beginning of the new century the Venus revenues were pouring in (their final gush, it is true). A tattling tabloid reported, around 1890, that out of gratitude and curiosity "Velvet" Veen traveled once—and only once—to the nearest floramor with his entire family—and it is also said that Guillaume de Monparnasse indignantly rejected an offer from Hollywood to base a screenplay on that dignified and hilarious excursion. Mere rumors, no doubt.

Eric's grandfather's range was wide—from dodo to dada, from Low Gothic to Hoch Modern. In his parodies of paradise he even permitted himself, just a few times, to express the rectilinear chaos of Cubism (with "abstract" cast in "concrete") by imitating—in the sense described so well in Vulner's paperback *History of English Architecture* given me by good Dr. Lagosse—such ultra-utilitarian boxes of brick as the *maisons closes* of El Freud in Lubetkin, Austria, or the great-necessity houses of Dudok in Friesland.

But on the whole it was the idyllic and the romantic that he favored. English gentlemen of parts found many pleasures in Letchworth Lodge, an honest country house plastered up to its bulleyes, or Itchenor Chat with its battered chimney breasts and hipped gables. None could help admiring David van Veen's knack of making his brand-new Regency mansion look like a renovated farmhouse or of producing a converted convent on a small offshore island with such miraculous effect that one could not distinguish the arabesque from the arbutus, ardor from art, the sore from the rose. We shall always remember Little Lemantry near Rantchester or the Pseudotherm in the lovely cul-de-sac south of the viaduct of fabulous Palermontovia. We appreciated greatly his blending local banality (that château girdled with chestnuts, that castello guarded by cypresses) with interior ornaments that pandered to all the orgies reflected in the ceiling mirrors of little Eric's erogenetics. Most effective, in a functional sense, was the protection the architect distilled, as it were, from the ambitus of his houses. Whether nestling in woodland dells or surrounded by a many-acred park, or overlooking terraced groves and gardens, access to Venus began by a private road and continued through a labyrinth of hedges and walls with inconspicuous doors to which only the guests and the guards had keys. Cunningly distributed spotlights followed the wandering of the masked and caped grandees through dark mazes of coppices; for one of the stipulations imagined by Eric was that "every establishment should open only at nightfall and close at sunrise." A system of bells that Eric may have thought up all by himself (it was really as old as the *bautta* and the *vyshibala*) prevented visitors from running into each other on the premises, so that no matter how many noblemen were waiting or wenching in any part of the floramor, each felt he was the only cock in the coop, because the bouncer, a silent and courteous person resembling a Manhattan shopwalker, did not count, of course: you sometimes saw him when a hitch occurred in connection with your credentials or credit but he was seldom obliged to apply vulgar force or call in an assistant.

According to Eric's plan, Councils of Elderly Noblemen were responsible for mustering the girls. Delicately fashioned phalanges, good teeth, a flawless epiderm, undyed hair, impeccable buttocks and breasts, and the unfeigned vim of avid venery were the absolute prerequisites demanded by the Elders as they had been by Eric. Intactas were tolerated only if very young. On the other hand, no woman who had ever borne a child (even in her own childhood) could be accepted, no matter how free she was of mammilary blemishes.

Their social rank had been left unspecified but the Committees were inclined, initially and theoretically, to recruit girls of more or less gentle birth. Daughters of artists were preferred, on the whole, to those of artisans. Quite an unexpected number turned out to be the children of peeved peers in cold castles or of ruined baronesses in shabby hotels. In a list of about two thousand females working in all the floramors on January 1, 1890 (the greatest year in the annals of Villa Venus), I counted as many as twenty-two directly connected with the royal families of Europe, but at least one-quarter of all the girls belonged to plebeian groups. Owing to some nice *vstryaska* (shake-up) in the genetic kaleidoscope, or mere poker luck, or no reason at all, the daughters of peasants and peddlers and plumbers were not seldom more stylish than their middle-middle-class or upper-upper-class companions, a curious point that will please my non-gentle readers no less than the fact that the servant-girls "below" the Oriental charmers (who assisted in various rituals of silver basins, embroidered towels and dead-end smiles the client and his clickies) not seldom descended from emblazoned princely heights.

Demon's father (and very soon Demon himself), and Lord Erminin, and a Mr. Ritcov, and Count Peter de Prey, and Mire de Mire, Esq., and Baron Azzuroscudo were all members of the first Venus Club Council; but it was bashful, obese, big-nosed Mr. Ritcov's visits that really thrilled the girls and filled the vicinity with detectives who dutifully impersonated hedgecutters, grooms, horses, tall milkmaids, new statues, old drunks and so forth, while His Majesty dallied, in a special chair built for his weight and whims, with this or that sweet subject of the realm, white, black or brown.

Because the particular floramor that I visited for the first time on becoming a member of the Villa Venus Club (not long before my second summer with my Ada in the arbors of Ardis) is today, after many vicissitudes, the charming country house of a Chose don whom I respect, and his charming family (a charming wife and a triplet of charming twelve-year-old daughters, Ala, Lolá and Lalage—especially Lalage), I cannot name it—though my dearest reader insists I *have* mentioned it somewhere before.

I had frequented bordels since my sixteenth year, but although some of the better ones, especially in France and Ireland, rated a triple red symbol in Nugg's guidebook, nothing about them pre-announced the luxury and mollitude of my first Villa Venus. It was the difference between a den and an Eden.

Three Egyptian squaws, dutifully keeping in profile (long ebony eye, lovely snub, braided black mane, honey-hued

faro frock, thin amber arms, Negro bangles, doughnut ear-
ring of gold bisected by a pleat of the mane, Red Indian
hairband, ornamental bib), lovingly borrowed by Eric
Veen from a reproduction of a Theban fresco (no doubt
pretty banal in 1420 B.C.), printed in Germany (*Künstler-
postkarte* Nr. 6034, says cynical Dr. Lagosse), prepared me
by means of what parched Eric called "exquisite manipula-
tions of certain nerves whose position and power are known
only to a few ancient sexologists," accompanied by the no
less exquisite application of certain ointments, not too spe-
cifically mentioned in the pornolore of Eric's Orientalia, for
receiving a scared little virgin, the descendant of an Irish
king, as Eric was told in his last dream in Ex, Switzerland,
by a master of funerary rather than fornicatory ceremonies.

Those preparations proceeded in such sustained, unendur-
ably delicious rhythms that Eric dying in his sleep and Van
throbbing with foul life on a rococo couch (three miles
south of Bedford) could not imagine how those three
young ladies, now suddenly divested of their clothes (a well-
known oneirotic device), could manage to draw out a prel-
ude that kept one so long on the very lip of its resolution.
I lay supine and felt twice the size I had ever been (senescent
nonsense, says science!) when finally six gentle hands attempted to ease *la gosse*, trembling Adada, upon the terrible
tool. Silly pity—a sentiment I rarely experience—caused my
desire to droop, and I had her carried away to a feast of peach
tarts and cream. The Egypsies looked disconcerted, but very
soon perked up. I summoned all the twenty hirens of the
house (including the sweet-lipped, glossy-chinned darling)
into my resurrected presence. After considerable examination, after much flattering of haunches and necks, I chose a
golden Gretchen, a pale Andalusian, and a black belle from
New Orleans. The handmaids pounced upon them like pards

and, having empasmed them with not unlesbian zest, turned the three rather melancholy graces over to me. The towel given me to wipe off the sweat that filmed my face and stung my eyes could have been cleaner. I raised my voice, I had the reluctant accursed casement wrenched wide open. A lorry had got stuck in the mud of a forbidden and unfinished road, and its groans and exertions dissipated the bizarre gloom. Only one of the girls stung me right in the soul, but I went through all three of them grimly and leisurely, "changing mounts in midstream" (Eric's advice) before ending every time in the grip of the ardent Ardillusian, who said as we parted, after one last spasm (although non-erotic chit-chat was against the rules), that her father had constructed the swimming pool on the estate of Demon Veen's cousin.

It was now all over. The lorry had gone or had drowned, and Eric was a skeleton in the most expensive corner of the Ex cemetery ("but then, all cemeteries are ex," remarked a jovial 'protestant' priest), between an anonymous alpinist and my stillborn double.

Cherry, the only lad in our next (American) floramor, a little Salopian of eleven or twelve, looked so amusing with his copper curls, dreamy eyes and elfin cheekbones that two exceptionally sportive courtesans, entertaining Van, prevailed upon him one night to try the boy. Their joint efforts failed, however, to arouse the pretty catamite, who had been exhausted by too many recent engagements. His girlish crupper proved sadly defaced by the varicolored imprints of bestial clawings and flesh-twistings; but worst of all, the little fellow could not disguise a state of acute indigestion, marked by unappetizing dysenteric symptoms that coated his lover's shaft with mustard and blood, the result, no doubt, of eating too many green apples. Eventually, he had to be destroyed or given away.

[376]

Generally speaking, the adjunction of boys had to be discontinued. A famous French floramor was never the same after the Earl of Langburn discovered his kidnapped son, a green-eyed frail faunlet, being examined by a veterinary whom the Earl shot dead by mistake.

In 1905 a glancing blow was dealt Villa Venus from another quarter. The personage we have called Ritcov or Vrotic had been induced by the ailings of age to withdraw his patronage. However, one night he suddenly arrived, looking again as ruddy as the proverbial fiddle; but after the entire staff of his favorite floramor near Bath had worked in vain on him till an ironic Hesperus rose in a milkman's humdrum sky, the wretched sovereign of one-half of the globe called for the Shell Pink Book, wrote in it a line that Seneca had once composed:

subsidunt montes et juga celsa ruunt,

—and departed, weeping. About the same time a respectable Lesbian who conducted a Villa Venus at Sovenir, the beautiful Missouri spa, throttled with her own hands (she had been a Russian weightlifter) two of her most beautiful and valuable charges. It was all rather sad.

When the deterioration of the club set in, it proceeded with amazing rapidity along several unconnected lines. Girls of flawless pedigree turned out to be wanted by the police as the "molls" of bandits with grotesque jaws, or to have been criminals themselves. Corrupt physicians passed faded blondes who had had half a dozen children, some of them being already prepared to enter remote floramors themselves. Cosmeticians of genius restored forty-year-old matrons to look and smell like schoolgirls at their first prom. Highborn gentlemen, magistrates of radiant integrity, mild-mannered scholars, proved to be such violent copulators that some of their younger victims had to be hospitalized and removed to ordinary lupanars. The anonymous protectors of courtesans bought medical inspectors, and the Rajah of Cachou (an impostor) was infected with a venereal disease by a (genuine) great-grandniece of Empress Josephine. Simultaneously, economic disasters (beyond the financial or philosophical ken of invulnerable Van and Demon but affecting many persons of their set) began to restrict the esthetic assets of Villa Venus. Disgusting pimps with obsequious grins disclosing gaps in their tawny teeth popped out of rosebushes with illustrated pamphlets, and there were fires and earthquakes, and quite suddenly, out of the hundred original palazzos, only a dozen remained, and even those soon sank to the level of stagnant stews, and by 1910 all the dead of the English cemetery at Ex had to be transferred to a common grave.

Van never regretted his last visit to one last Villa Venus. A cauliflowered candle was messily burning in its tin cup on the window ledge next to the guitar-shaped paper-wrapped bunch of long roses for which nobody had troubled to find, or could have found, a vase. On a bed, some way off, lay a pregnant woman, smoking, looking up at the smoke mingling its volutes with the shadows on the ceiling, one knee raised, one hand dreamily scratching her brown groin. Far beyond her, a door standing ajar gave on what appeared to be a moonlit gallery but was really an abandoned, half-demolished, vast reception room with a broken outer wall, zigzag fissures in the floor, and the black ghost of a gaping grand piano, emitting, as if all by itself, spooky glissando twangs in the middle of the night. Through a great rip in the marbleized brick and plaster, the naked sea, not seen but heard as a panting space separated from time, dully boomed, dully withdrew its platter of pebbles, and, with the crumbling sounds, indolent gusts of warm wind reached the unwalled rooms, disturbing the volutes of shadow above the woman, and a bit of dirty fluff that had drifted down onto her pale belly, and even the reflection of the candle in a cracked pane of the bluish casement. Beneath it, on a rump-tickling coarse couch, Van reclined, pouting pensively, pensively caressing the pretty head on his chest, flooded by the black hair of a much younger sister or cousin of the wretched florinda on the tumbled bed. The child's eyes were closed, and whenever he kissed their moist convex lids the rhythmic motion of her blind breasts changed or stopped altogether, and was presently resumed.

He was thirsty, but the champagne he had brought, with the softly rustling roses, remained sealed and he had not the heart to remove the silky dear head from his breast so as to begin working on the explosive bottle. He had fondled and fouled her many times in the course of the last ten days, but was not sure if her name was really Adora, as everybody maintained—she, and the other girl, and a third one (a maidservant, Princess Kachurin), who seemed to have been born in the faded bathing suit she never changed and would die in, no doubt, before reaching majority or the first really cold winter on the beach mattress which she was moaning on now in her drugged daze. And if the child really was called Adora, then what was she?—not Rumanian, not Dalmatian, not Sicilian, not Irish, though an echo of brogue could be discerned in her broken but not too foreign English. Was she eleven or fourteen, almost fifteen perhaps? Was it really her birthday—this twenty-first of July, nineteen-four or eight or even several years later, on a rocky Mediterranean peninsula?

A very distant church clock, never audible except at night, clanged twice and added a quarter.

"*Smorchiama la secandela,*" mumbled the bawd on the bed in the local dialect that Van understood better than Italian. The child in his arms stirred and he pulled his opera cloak over her. In the grease-reeking darkness a faint pattern of moonlight established itself on the stone floor, near his forever discarded half-mask lying there and his pump-shod foot. It was not Ardis, it was not the library, it was not even a human room, but merely the squalid recess where the bouncer had slept before going back to his Rugby-coaching job at a public school somewhere in England. The grand piano in the otherwise bare hall seemed to be playing all by itself but actually was being rippled by rats in quest of the succulent refuse placed there by the maid who fancied a bit of music when her cancered womb roused her before dawn with its first familiar stab. The ruinous Villa no longer bore any resemblance to Eric's "organized dream," but the soft little creature in Van's desperate grasp was Ada.

4

What are dreams? A random sequence of scenes, trivial or tragic, viatic or static, fantastic or familiar, featuring more or less plausible events patched up with grotesque details, and recasting dead people in new settings.

In reviewing the more or less memorable dreams I have had during the last nine decades I can classify them by subject matter into several categories among which two surpass the others in generic distinctiveness. There are the professional dreams and there are the erotic ones. In my twenties the first kind occurred about as frequently as the second, and both had their introductory counterparts, insomnias conditioned either by the overflow of ten hours of vocational work or by the memory of Ardis that a thorn in my day had maddeningly revived. After work I battled against the might of the mind-set: the stream of composition, the force of the phrase demanding to be formed could not be stopped for hours of darkness and discomfort, and when some result had been achieved, the current still hummed on and on behind the wall, even if I locked up my brain by an act of self-hypnosis (plain will, or pill, could no longer help) within some other image or meditation—but not Ardis, not Ada, for that would mean drowning in a cataract of worse wakefulness, with rage and regret, desire and despair sweeping me into an abyss where sheer physical extenuation stunned me at last with sleep.

In the professional dreams that especially obsessed me when I worked on my earliest fiction, and pleaded abjectly with a very frail muse ("kneeling and wringing my hands" like the dusty-trousered Marmlad before his Marmlady in Dickens), I might see for example that I was correcting galley proofs but that somehow (the great "somehow" of dreams!) the book had already come out, had come out literally, being proffered to me by a human hand from the wastepaper basket in its perfect, and dreadfully imperfect, stage—with a typo on every page, such as the snide "bitterly" instead of "butterfly" and the meaningless "nuclear" instead of "unclear." Or I would be hurrying to a reading I had to give— would feel exasperated by the sight of the traffic and people blocking my way, and then realize with sudden relief that all I had to do was to strike out the phrase "crowded street" in my manuscript. What I might designate as "skyscape" (not "skyscrape," as two-thirds of the class will probably take it down) dreams belongs to a subdivision of my vocational visions, or perhaps may represent a preface to them, for it was in my early pubescence that hardly a night would pass without some old or recent waketime impression's establishing a soft deep link with my still-muted genius (for we are "van," rhyming with and indeed signifying "one" in Marina's double-you-less deep-voweled Russian pronunciation). The presence, or promise, of art in that kind of dream would come in the image of an overcast sky with a manifold lining of cloud, a motionless but hopeful white, a hopeless but gliding gray, showing artistic signs of clearing, and presently the glow of a pale sun grew through the leaner layer only to be recowled by the scud, for I was not yet ready.

Allied to the professional and vocational dreams are "dim-doom" visions: fatidic-sign nightmares, thalamic calamities, menacing riddles. Not infrequently the menace is well concealed, and the innocent incident will turn out to possess, if jotted down and looked up later, the kind of precognitive flavor that Dunne has explained by the action of "reverse memory"; but for the moment I am not going to enlarge upon the uncanny element particular to dreams—beyond observing that some law of logic should fix the number of coincidences, in a given domain, after which they cease to be coincidences, and form, instead, the living organism of a new truth ("Tell me," says Osberg's little gitana to the Moors, El Motela and Ramera, "what is the precise minimum of hairs on a body that allows one to call it 'hairy'?").

Between the dim-doom and the poignantly sensual I would place "melts" of erotic tenderness and heart-rending enchantment, chance *frôlements* of anonymous girls at vague parties, half-smiles of appeal or submission—forerunners or echoes of the agonizing dreams of regret when series of receding Adas faded away in silent reproach; and tears, even hotter than those I would shed in waking life, shook and scalded poor Van, and were remembered at odd moments for days and weeks.

Van's sexual dreams are embarrassing to describe in a family chronicle that the very young may perhaps read after a very old man's death. Two samples, more or less euphemistically worded, should suffice. In an intricate arrangement of thematic recollections and automatic phantasmata, Aqua impersonating Marina or Marina made-up to look like Aqua, arrives to inform Van, joyfully, that Ada has just been delivered of a girl-child whom he is about to know carnally on a hard garden bench while under a nearby pine, his father, or his dress-coated mother, is trying to make a transatlantic call for an ambulance to be sent from Vence at once. Another dream, recurring in its basic, unmentionable form, since 1888 and well into this century, contained an essentially triple and, in a way, tribadic, idea. Bad Ada and lewd Lucette had found a ripe, very ripe ear of Indian corn. Ada held it at both ends as if it were a mouth organ and now it *was* an organ, and she moved her parted lips along it, varnishing its shaft, and while she was making it trill and moan, Lucette's mouth engulfed its extremity. The two sisters' avid lovely young faces were now close together, doleful and wistful in their slow, almost languid play, their tongues meeting in flicks of fire and curling back again, their tumbled hair, red-bronze and black-bronze, delightfully commingling and their sleek hindquarters lifted high as they slaked their thirst in the pool of his blood.

I have some notes here on the general character of dreams. One puzzling feature is the multitude of perfect strangers with clear features, but never seen again, accompanying, meeting, welcoming me, pestering me with long tedious tales about other strangers—all this in localities familiar to me and in the midst of people, deceased or living, whom I knew well; or the curious tricks of an agent of Chronos—a very exact clock-time awareness, with all the pangs (possibly full-bladder pangs in disguise) of not getting somewhere in time, and with that clock hand before me, numerically meaningful, mechanically plausible, but combined—and that is the curious part—with an extremely hazy, hardly existing passing-of-time feeling (this theme I will also reserve for a later chapter). All dreams are affected by the experiences and impressions of the present as well as by memories of childhood; reflect, in images or sensations, a draft, a light, a rich meal or a grave internal disorder. Perhaps the most typical trait of practically all dreams, unimportant or portentous—and this despite the presence, in stretches or patches, of fairly logical (within special limits) cogitation and awareness (often absurd) of dream-past events—should be understood by my students as a dismal weakening of the intellectual faculties of the dreamer, who is not really shocked to run into a long-dead friend. At his best the dreamer wears semi-opaque blinkers; at his worst he's an imbecile. The class (1891, 1892, 1893, 1894, et cetera) will carefully note (rustle of bluebooks) that, owing to their very nature, to that mental mediocrity and bumble, dreams cannot yield any semblance of morality or symbol or allegory or Greek myth, unless, naturally, the dreamer is a Greek or a mythicist. Metamorphoses in dreams are as common as metaphors in poetry. A writer who likens, say, the fact of imagination's weakening less rapidly than memory, to the lead of a pencil getting used up more slowly than its erasing end, is comparing two real, concrete, existing things. Do you want me to repeat that? (cries of "yes! yes!") Well, the pencil I'm holding is still conveniently long though it has served me a lot, but its rubber cap is practically erased by the very action it has been performing too many times. My imagination is still strong and serviceable but my memory is getting shorter and shorter. I compare that real experience to the condition of this real commonplace object. Neither is a symbol of the other. Similarly, when a teashop humorist says that a little conical titbit with a comical cherry on top resembles this or that (titters in the audience) he is turning a pink cake into a pink breast (tempestuous laughter) in a fraise-like frill or frilled phrase (silence). Both objects are real, they are not interchangeable, not tokens of something else, say, of Walter Raleigh's decapitated trunk still topped by the image of his wetnurse (one lone chuckle). Now the mistake—the lewd, ludicrous and vulgar mistake of the Signy-Mondieu analysts consists in their regarding a real object, a pompon, say, or a pumpkin (actually seen in a dream by the patient) as a significant abstraction of the real object, as a bumpkin's bonbon or one-half of the bust if you see what I mean (scattered giggles). There can be no emblem or parable in a village idiot's hallucinations or in last night's dream of any of us in this hall. In those random visions nothing—underscore "nothing" (grating sound of horizontal strokes)—can be construed as allowing itself to be deciphered by a witch doctor who can then cure a madman or give comfort to a killer by laying the blame on a too fond, too fiendish or too indifferent parent —secret festerings that the foster quack feigns to heal by expensive confession fests (laughter and applause).

5

Van spent the fall term of 1892 at Kingston University, Mayne, where there was a first-rate madhouse, as well as a famous Department of Terrapy, and where he now went back to one of his old projects, which turned on the Idea of Dimension & Dementia ("You will 'sturb,' Van, with an alliteration on your lips," jested old Rattner, resident pessimist of genius, for whom life was only a "disturbance" in the rattnerterological order of things—from "*nertoros*," not "*terra*").

Van Veen [as also, in his small way, the editor of *Ada*] liked to change his abode at the end of a section or chapter or even paragraph, and he had almost finished a difficult bit dealing with the divorce between time and the contents of time (such as action on matter, in space, and the nature of space itself) and was contemplating moving to Manhattan (that kind of switch being a reflection of mental rubrication rather than a concession to some farcical "influence of environment" endorsed by Marx *père*, the popular author of "historical" plays), when he received an unexpected dorophone call which for a moment affected violently his entire pulmonary and systemic circulation.

Nobody, not even his father, knew that Van had recently bought Cordula's penthouse apartment between Manhattan's Library and Park. Besides its being the perfect place to work in, with that terrace of scholarly seclusion suspended in a celestial void, and that noisy but convenient city lapping below at the base of his mind's invulnerable rock, it was, in fashionable parlance, a "bachelor's folly" where he could secretly entertain any girl or girls he pleased. (One of them dubbed it "your wing à terre"). But he was still in his rather dingy Chose-like rooms at Kingston when he consented to Lucette's visiting him on that bright November afternoon.

He had not seen her since 1888. In the fall of 1891 she had sent him from California a rambling, indecent, crazy, almost savage declaration of love in a ten-page letter, which shall not be discussed in this memoir [See, however, a little farther. Ed.]. At present, she was studying the History of Art ("the second-rater's last refuge," she said) in nearby Queenston College for Glamorous and *Glupovatïh* ("dumb") Girls. When she rang him up and pleaded for an interview (in a new, darker voice, agonizingly resembling Ada's), she intimated that she was bringing him an important message. He suspected it would be yet another installment of her unrequited passion, but he also felt that her visit would touch off infernal fires.

As he awaited her, walking the whole length of his brown-carpeted suite and back again, now contemplating the emblazed trees, that defied the season, through the northeast casement at the end of the passage, then returning to the sitting room which gave on sun-bordered Greencloth Court, he kept fighting Ardis and its orchards and orchids, bracing himself for the ordeal, wondering if he should not cancel her visit, or have his man convey his apologies for the suddenness of an unavoidable departure, but knowing all the time he would go through with it. With Lucette herself, he was only obliquely concerned: she inhabited this or that dapple of drifting sunlight, but could not be wholly dismissed with the rest of sun-flecked Ardis. He recalled, in passing, the sweetness in his lap, her round little bottom, her prasine eyes as she turned toward him and the receding road. Casually he wondered whether she had become fat and freckled, or had joined the graceful Zemski group of nymphs. He had left the parlor door that opened on the landing slightly ajar, but somehow missed the sound of her high heels on the stairs (or did not distinguish them from his heartbeats) while he was in the middle of his twentieth trudge "back to the ardors and arbors! Eros *qui prend son essor!* Arts that our marblery harbors: Eros, the rose and the sore." I am ill at these numbers, but e'en rhymery is easier "than confuting the past in mute prose." Who wrote that? Voltimand or Voltemand? Or the Burning Swine? A pest on his anapest! "All our old loves are corpses or wives." All our sorrows are virgins or whores.

A black bear with bright russet locks (the sun had reached its first parlor window) stood awaiting him. Yes—the Z gene had won. She was slim and strange. Her green eyes had grown. At sixteen she looked considerably more dissolute than her sister had seemed at that fatal age. She wore black furs and no hat.

"My joy (*moya radost'*)," said Lucette—just like that; he had expected more formality: all in all he had hardly known her before—except as an embered embryo.

Eyes swimming, coral nostrils distended, red mouth perilously disclosing her tongue and teeth in a preparatory half-open skew (tame animal signaling by that slant the semblance of a soft bite), she advanced in the daze of a commencing trance, of an unfolding caress—the aurora, who knows (*she* knew), of a new life for both.

"Cheekbone," Van warned the young lady.

"You prefer *skeletiki* (little skeletons)," she murmured, as Van applied light lips (which had suddenly become even drier than usual) to his half-sister's hot hard pommette. He could not help inhaling briefly her Degrasse, smart, though decidedly "paphish," perfume and, through it, the flame of her Little Larousse as he and the other said when they chose to emprison her in bath water. Yes, very nervous and fragrant. Indian summer too sultry for furs. The cross (*krest*) of the best-groomed redhead (*rousse*). Its four burning ends. Because one can't stroke (as he did now) the upper copper without imagining at once the lower fox cub and the paired embers.

"This is where he lives," she said, looking around, turning around, as he helped her with wonder and sorrow out of her soft, deep, dark coat, side-thinking (he liked furs): sea bear (*kotik*)? No, desman (*vïhuhol'*). Assistant Van admired her elegant slenderness, the gray tailor-made suit, the smoky fichu and as it wafted away, her long white neck. Take your jacket off, he said or thought he said (standing with extended hands, in his charcoal suit, spontaneous combustion, in his bleak parlor, in the bleak house anglophilically named Voltemand Hall at Kingston University, fall term 1892, around four P.M.).

"I think I'll take off my jacket," she said with the usual flitting frown of feminine fuss that fits the "thought." "You've got central heating; we girls have tiny fireplaces."

She threw it off, revealing a sleeveless frilly white blouse. She raised her arms to pass her fingers through her bright curls, and he saw the expected bright hollows.

Van said, "All three casements *pourtant* are open and can

open wider; but they can do it only westward and that green yard down below is the evening sun's praying rug, which makes this room even warmer. Terrible for a window not to be able to turn its paralyzed embrasure and see what's on the other side of the house."

Once a Veen, always a Veen.

She unclicked her black-silk handbag, fished out a handkerchief and, leaving the gaping bag on the edge of the sideboard, went to the farthest window and stood there, her fragile shoulders shaking unbearably.

Van noticed a long, blue, violet-sealed envelope protruding from the bag.

"Lucette, don't cry. That's too easy."

She walked back, dabbing her nose, curbing her childishly humid sniffs, still hoping for the decisive embrace.

"Here's some brandy," he said. "Sit down. Where's the rest of the family?"

She returned the balled handkerchief of many an old romance to her bag, which, however, remained unclosed. Chows, too, have blue tongues.

"Mamma dwells in her private Samsara. Dad has had another stroke. Sis is revisiting Ardis."

"Sis! *Cesse*, Lucette! We don't want any baby serpents around."

"This baby serpent does not quite know what tone to take with Dr. V. V. Sector. You have not changed one bit, my pale darling, except that you look like a ghost in need of a shave without your summer *Glanz*."

And summer *Mädel*. He noticed that the letter, in its long blue envelope, lay now on the mahogany sideboard. He stood in the middle of the parlor, rubbing his forehead, not daring, not daring, because it was Ada's notepaper.

"Like some tea?"

She shook her head. "I can't stay long. Besides, you said something about a busy day over the phone. One can't help being dreadfully busy after four absolutely blank years" (he would start sobbing too if she did not stop).

"Yes. I don't know. I have an appointment around six."

Two ideas were locked up in a slow dance, a mechanical menuet, with bows and curtseys: one was "We-have-so-much-to say"; the other was "We have absolutely nothing to say." But that sort of thing can change in one instant.

"Yes, I have to see Rattner at six-thirty," murmured Van, consulting a calendar he did not see.

"Rattner on Terra!" ejaculated Lucette. "Van is reading Rattner on Terra. Pet must never, never disturb him and me when we are reading Rattner!"

"I implore, my dear, no impersonations. Let us not transform a pleasant reunion into mutual torture."

What was she doing at Queenston? She had told him before. Of course. Tough course? No. Oh. From time to time both kept glancing askance at the letter to see if it was behaving itself—not dangling its legs, not picking its nose.

Return it sealed?

"Tell Rattner," she said, gulping down her third brandy as simply as if it were technicolored water. "Tell him" (the liquor was loosening her pretty viper tongue)—

(Viper? Lucette? My dead dear darling?)

—"Tell him that when in the old days you and Ada—"

The name yawned like a black doorway, then the door banged.

"—left me for him, and then came back, I knew every time that you *vsyo sdelali* (had appeased your lust, had allayed your fire)."

"One remembers those little things much too clearly, Lucette. Please, stop."

"One remembers, Van, those little things much more clearly than the big fatal ones. As for example the clothes you wore at any given moment, at a generously given moment, with the sun on the chairs and the floor. I was practically naked, of course, being a neutral pure little child. But she wore a boy's shirt and a short skirt, and all you had on were those wrinkled, soiled shorts, shorter because wrinkled, and they smelled as they always did after you'd been on Terra with Ada, with Rattner on Ada, with Ada on Antiterra in Ardis Forest—oh, they positively stank, you know, your little shorts, of lavendered Ada, and her catfood, and your caked algarroba!"

Should that letter, now next to the brandy, listen to all this? Was it from Ada after all (there was no address)? Because it was Lucette's mad, shocking letter of love that was doing the talking.

"Van, it will make you smile" [thus in the MS. Ed.].

"Van," said Lucette, "it will make you smile" (it did not: that prediction is seldom fulfilled), "but if you posed the famous Van Question, I would answer in the affirmative."

What he had asked little Cordula. In that bookshop behind the revolving paperbacks' stand, *The Gitanilla, Our Laddies, Clichy Clichés, Six Pricks, The Bible Unabridged, Mertvago Forever, The Gitanilla* . . . He was known in the *beau monde* for asking that question the very first time he met a young lady.

"Oh, to be sure, it was not easy! In parked automobiles and at rowdy parties, thrusts had to be parried, advances fought off! And only last winter, on the Italian Riviera, there was a youngster of fourteen or fifteen, an awfully precocious but terribly shy and neurotic young violinist, who reminded Marina of her brother . . . Well, for almost three months, every blessed afternoon, I had him touch me, and I reciprocated, and after that I could sleep at last without pills, but otherwise I haven't once kissed male epithelia in all my love —I mean, life. Look, I can swear I never have, by—by William Shakespeare" (extending dramatically one hand toward a shelf with a set of thick red books).

"Hold it!" cried Van. "That's the *Collected Works of Falknermann*, dumped by my predecessor."

"Pah!" uttered Lucette.

"And, please, don't use that expletive."

"Forgive me—oh, I know, oh, I shan't."

"Of course, you know. All the same, you are very sweet. I'm glad you came."

"I'm glad, too," she said. "But Van! Don't you dare think I 'relanced' you to reiterate that I'm madly and miserably in love with you and that you can do anything you want with me. If I didn't simply press the button and slip that note into the burning slit and cataract away, it was because I *had* to see you, because there is something else you must know, even if it makes you detest and despise Ada and me. *Otvratitel'no trudno* (it is disgustingly hard) to explain, especially for a virgin—well, technically, a virgin, a *kokotische* virgin, half *poule*, half *puella*. I realize the privacy of the subject, mysterious matters that one should not discuss even with a vaginal brother—mysterious, not merely in their moral and mystical aspect—"

Uterine—but close enough. It certainly came from Lucette's sister. He knew that shade and that shape. "That shade of blue, that shape of you" (corny song on the Sonorola). Blue in the face from pleading RSVP.

"—but also in a direct physical sense. Because, darling Van, in that direct physical sense I know as much about our Ada as you."

"Fire away," said Van, wearily.

"She never wrote you about it?"

Negative Throat Sound.

"Something we used to call Pressing the Spring?"

"We?"

"She and I."

N.T.S.

"Do you remember Grandmother's scrutoir between the globe and the gueridon? In the library?"

"I don't even know what a scrutoir is; and I do not visualize the gueridon."

"But you remember the globe?"

Dusty Tartary with Cinderella's finger rubbing the place where the invader would fall.

"Yes, I do; and a kind of stand with golden dragons painted all over it."

"That's what I meant by 'gueridon.' It was really a Chinese stand japanned in red lacquer, and the scrutoir stood in between."

"China or Japan? Make up your mind. And I still don't know how your inscrutable looks. I mean, looked in 1884 or 1888."

Scrutoir. Almost as bad as the other with her Blemolopias and Molospermas.

"Van, Vanichka, we are straying from the main point. The point is that the writing desk or if you like, secretaire—"

"I hate both, but it stood at the opposite end of the black divan."

Now mentioned for the first time—though both had been tacitly using it as an orientator or as a right hand painted on a transparent signboard that a philosopher's orbitless eye, a peeled hard-boiled egg cruising free, but sensing which of its ends is proximal to an imaginary nose, sees hanging in infinite space; whereupon, with Germanic grace, the free eye

[395]

sails around the glass sign and sees a left hand shining through
—*that*'s the solution! (Bernard said six-thirty but I may be a
little late.) The mental in Van always rimmed the sensuous:
unforgettable, roughish, villous, Villaviciosa velour.

"Van, you are deliberately sidetracking the issue—"

"One can't do that with an issue."

"—because at the other end, at the *heel* end of the Vaniada
divan—remember?—there was only the closet in which you
two locked me up at least ten times."

"*Nu uzh i desyat'* (exaggeration). Once—and *never* more.
It had a keyless hole as big as Kant's eye. Kant was famous
for his cucumicolor iris."

"Well, that secretaire," continued Lucette, considering her
left shoe, her very chic patent-leather Glass shoe, as she
crossed her lovely legs, "that secretaire enclosed a folded card
table and a top-secret drawer. And you thought, I think, it
was crammed with our grandmother's love letters, written
when she was twelve or thirteen. And our Ada knew, oh, she
knew, the drawer was there but she had forgotten how to release the orgasm or whatever it is called in card tables and
bureaus."

Whatever it is called.

"She and I challenged you to find the secret *chuvstvilishche*
(sensorium) and make it work. It was the summer Belle
sprained her backside, and we were left to our own devices,
which had long lost the *particule* in your case and Ada's, but
were touchingly pure in mine. You groped around, and felt,
and felt for the little organ, which turned out to be a yielding
roundlet in the rosewood under the felt you felt—I mean,
under the felt you were feeling: it was a felted thumb spring,
and Ada laughed as the drawer shot out."

"And it was empty," said Van.

"Not quite. It contained a minuscule red pawn that high"

[396]

(showing its barleycorn-size with her finger—above what? Above Van's wrist). "I kept it for luck; I must still have it somewhere. Anyway, the entire incident pre-emblematized, to quote my Professor of Ornament, the depravation of your poor Lucette at fourteen in Arizona. Belle had returned to Canady, because Vronsky had defigured *The Doomed Children*; her successor had eloped with Demon; *papa* was in the East, *maman* hardly ever came home before dawn, the maids joined their lovers at star-rise, and I hated to sleep alone in the corner room assigned to me, even if I did not put out the pink night-light of porcelain with the transparency picture of a lost lamb, because I was afraid of the cougars and snakes" [quite possibly, this is not remembered speech but an extract from her letter or letters. Ed.], "whose cries and rattlings Ada imitated admirably, and, I think, designedly, in the desert's darkness under my first-floor window. Well [here, it would seem, taped speech is re-turned-on], to make a short story sort of longish—"

Old Countess de Prey's phrase in praise of a lame mare in her stables in 1884, thence passed on to her son, who passed it on to his girl who passed it on to her half-sister. Thus instantly reconstructed by Van sitting with tented hands in a red-plush chair.

"—I took my pillow to Ada's bedroom where a similar night-light transparency thing showed a blond-bearded faddist in a toweling robe embracing the found lamb. The night was oven-hot and we were stark naked except for a bit of sticking plaster where a doctor had stroked and pricked my arm, and she was a dream of white and black beauty, *pour cogner une fraise*, touched with fraise in four places, a symmetrical queen of hearts."

Next moment they grappled and had such delicious fun

[397]

that they knew they would be doing it always together, for hygienic purposes, when boyless and boiling.

"She taught me practices I had never imagined," confessed Lucette in rerun wonder. "We interweaved like serpents and sobbed like pumas. We were Mongolian tumblers, monograms, anagrams, adalucindas. She kissed my *krestik* while I kissed hers, our heads clamped in such odd combinations that Brigitte, a little chambermaid who blundered in with her candle, thought for a moment, though naughty herself, that we were giving birth simultaneously to baby girls, your Ada bringing out *une rousse*, and no one's Lucette, *une brune*. Fancy that."

"Side-splitting," said Van.

"Oh, it went on practically every night at Marina Ranch, and often during siestas; otherwise, in between those *vanouissements* (her expression), or when she and I had the flow, which, believe it or not—"

"I can believe anything," said Van.

"—took place at coincident dates, we were just ordinary sisters, exchanging routine nothings, having little in common, she collecting cactuses or running through her lines for the next audition in Sterva, and I reading a lot, or copying beautiful erotic pictures from an album of Forbidden Masterpieces that we found, *apropos*, in a box of *korsetov i khrestomatiy* (corsets and chrestomathies) which Belle had left behind, and I can assure you, they were far more realistic than the scroll-painting by Mong Mong, very active in 888, a millennium before Ada said it illustrated Oriental calisthenics when I found it by chance in the corner of one of my ambuscades. So the day passed, and then the star rose, and tremendous moths walked on all sixes up the window panes, and we tangled until we fell asleep. And that's when I learnt—" concluded Lucette, closing her eyes and making

Van squirm by reproducing with diabolical accuracy Ada's demure little whimper of ultimate bliss.

At this point, as in a well-constructed play larded with comic relief, the brass campophone buzzed and not only did the radiators start to cluck but the uncapped soda water fizzed in sympathy.

Van (crossly): "I don't understand the first word . . . What's that? *L'adorée?* Wait a second" (to Lucette). "Please, stay where you are." (Lucette whispers a French child-word with two "p"s.). "Okay" (pointing toward the corridor). "Sorry, Polly. Well, is it *l'adorée?* No? Give me the context. Ah—*la durée. La durée* is not . . . sin on what? Synonymous with duration. Aha. Sorry again, I must stopper that orgiastic soda. Hold the line." (Yells down the 'cory door,' as they called the long second-floor passage at Ardis.) "Lucette, *let* it run over, who cares!"

He poured himself another glass of brandy and for a ridiculous moment could not remember what the hell he had been —yes, the polliphone.

It had died, but buzzed as soon as he recradled the receiver, and Lucette knocked discreetly at the same time.

"*La durée* . . . For goodness sake, come in without knocking . . . No, Polly, knocking does not concern you—it's my little cousin. All right. *La durée* is not synonymous with duration, being saturated—yes, as in Saturday—with that particular philosopher's thought. What's wrong now? You don't know if it's *dorée* or *durée?* D, U, R. I thought you knew French. Oh, I see. So long.

"My typist, a trivial but always available blonde, could not make out *durée* in my quite legible hand because, she says, she knows French, but not scientific French."

"Actually," observed Lucette, wiping the long envelope which a drop of soda had stained, "Bergson is only for very

[399]

young people or very unhappy people, such as this available *rousse*."

"Spotting Bergson," said the assistant lecher, "rates a B minus *dans ton petit cas*, hardly more. Or shall I reward you with a kiss on your *krestik*—whatever that is?"

Wincing and rearranging his legs, our young Vandemonian cursed under his breath the condition in which the image of the four embers of a vixen's cross had now solidly put him. One of the synonyms of "condition" is "state," and the adjective "human" may be construed as "manly" (since L'Humanité means "Mankind"!), and that's how, my dears, Lowden recently translated the title of the *malheureux* Pompier's cheap novel *La Condition Humaine*, wherein, incidentally, the term "Vandemonian" is hilariously glossed as "*Koulak tasmanien d'origine hollandaise*." Kick her out before it is too late.

"If you are serious," said Lucette, passing her tongue over her lips and slitting her darkening eyes, "then, my darling, you can do it right now. But if you are making fun of me, then you're an abominably cruel Vandemonian."

"Come, come, Lucette, it means 'little cross' in Russian, that's all, what else? Is it some amulet? You mentioned just now a little red stud or pawn. Is it something you wear, or used to wear, on a chainlet round your neck? a small acorn of coral, the *glandulella* of vestals in ancient Rome? What's the matter, my dear?"

Still watching him narrowly, "I'll take a chance," she said. "I'll explain it, though it's just one of our sister's 'tender-turret' words and I thought you were familiar with her vocabulary."

"Oh, I know," cried Van (quivering with evil sarcasm, boiling with mysterious rage, taking it out on the redhaired scapegoatling, naive Lucette, whose only crime was to be suffused with the phantasmata of the other's innumerable lips). "Of course, I remember now. A foul taint in the singular can be a sacred mark in the plural. You are referring of course to the stigmata between the eyebrows of pure sickly young nuns whom priests had over-anointed there and elsewhere with cross-like strokes of the myrrherabol brush."

"No, it's much simpler," said patient Lucette. "Let's go back to the library where you found that little thing still erect in its drawer—"

"Z for Zemski. As I had hoped, you do resemble Dolly, still in her pretty pantelets, holding a Flemish pink in the library portrait above her inscrutable."

"No, no," said Lucette, "that indifferent oil presided over your studies and romps at the other end, next to the closet, above a glazed bookcase."

When will this torture end? I can't very well open the letter in front of her and read it aloud for the benefit of the audience. I have not art to reckon my groans.

"One day, in the library, kneeling on a yellow cushion placed on a Chippendale chair before an oval table on lion claws—"

[The epithetic tone strongly suggests that this speech has an epistolary source. Ed.]

"—I got stuck with six *Buchstaben* in the last round of a Flavita game. Mind you, I was eight and had not studied anatomy, but was doing my poor little best to keep up with two *Wunderkinder*. You examined and fingered my groove and quickly redistributed the haphazard sequence which made, say, LIKROT or ROTIKL and Ada flooded us both with her raven silks as she looked over our heads, and when you had completed the rearrangement, you and she came simultaneously, *si je puis le mettre comme ça* (Canady French), came falling on the black carpet in a paroxysm of

incomprehensible merriment; so finally I quietly composed
ROTIK ("little mouth") and was left with my own cheap
initial. I hope I've thoroughly got you mixed up, Van, because *la plus laide fille au monde peut donner beaucoup plus
qu'elle n'a,* and now let us say adieu, yours ever."

"Whilst the machine is to him," murmured Van.

"Hamlet," said the assistant lecturer's brightest student.

"Okay, okay," replied her and his tormentor, "but, you
know, a medically minded *English* Scrabbler, having two
more letters to cope with, could make, for example, STIR-
COIL, a well-known sweat-gland stimulant, or CITROILS,
which grooms use for rubbing fillies."

"Please stop, Vandemonian," she moaned. "Read her letter and bring me my coat."

But he continued, his features working:

"I'm amazed! I never imagined that a hand-reared scion
of Scandinavian kings, Russian grand princes and Irish barons
could use the language of the proverbial gutter. Yes, you're
right, you behave as a cocotte, Lucette."

In sad meditation Lucette said: "As a rejected cocotte,
Van."

"O *moya dushen'ka* (my dear darling)," cried Van, struck
by his own coarseness and cruelty. "Please, forgive me! I'm
a sick man. I've been suffering for these last four years from
consanguineocanceroformia—a mysterious disease described
by Coniglietto. Don't put your little cold hand on my paw—
that could only hasten your end and mine. On with your
story."

"Well, after teaching me simple exercises for one hand
that I could practice alone, cruel Ada abandoned me. True,
we never really stopped doing it together every now and then
—in the ranchito of some acquaintances after a party, in a
white saloon she was teaching me to drive, in the sleeping

[402]

car tearing across the prairie, at sad, sad Ardis where I spent one night with her before coming to Queenston. Oh, I love her hands, Van, because they have the same *rodinka* (small birthmark), because the fingers are so long, because, in fact, they are Van's in a reducing mirror, in tender diminutive, *v laskatel'noy forme*" (the talk—as so often happened at emotional moments in the Veen-Zemski branch of that strange family, the noblest in Estotiland, the grandest on Antiterra —was speckled with Russian, an effect not too consistently reproduced in this chapter—the readers are restless tonight).

"She abandoned me," continued Lucette, tchucking on one side of the mouth and smoothing up and down with an abstract palm her flesh-pale stocking. "Yes, she started a rather sad little affair with Johnny, a young star from Fuerteventura, *c'est dans la famille,* her exact *odnoletok* (coeval), practically her twin in appearance, born the same year, the same day, the same instant—"

That was a mistake on silly Lucette's part.

"Ah, that cannot be," interrupted morose Van and after rocking this side and that with clenched hands and furrowed brow (how one would like to apply a boiling-water-soaked *Wattebausch,* as poor Rack used to call her limp arpeggiation, to that ripe pimple on his right temple), "that simply cannot be. No damned twin can do that. Not even those seen by Brigitte, a cute little number I imagine, with that candle flame flirting with her exposed nipples. The usual difference in age between twins"—he went on in a madman's voice so well controlled that it sounded overpedantic—"is seldom less than a quarter of an hour, the time a working womb needs to rest and relax with a woman's magazine, before resuming its rather unappetizing contractions. In very rare cases, when the matrix just goes on pegging away automatically, the doctor can take advantage of that and ease out the second brat who then can be considered to be, say, three minutes younger, which in dynastic happy events—doubly happy events—with all Egypt agog—may be, and has been, even more important than in a marathon finish. But the creatures, no matter how numerous, never come out *à la queue-leu-leu*. 'Simultaneous twins' is a contradiction in terms."

"*Nu uzh ne znayu* (well, I don't know)," muttered Lucette (echoing faithfully her mother's dreary intonation in that phrase, which seemingly implied an admission of error and ignorance, but tended somehow—owing to a hardly perceptible nod of condescension rather than consent—to dull and dilute the truth of her interlocutor's corrective retort).

"I only meant," she continued, "that he was a handsome Hispano-Irish boy, dark and pale, and people mistook them for twins. I did not say they were really twins. Or 'driblets.'"

Driblets? Driplets? Now who pronounced it that way? Who? Who? A dripping ewes-dropper in a dream? Did the orphans live? But we must listen to Lucette.

"After a year or so she found out that an old pederast kept him and she dismissed him, and he shot himself on a beach at high tide but surfers and surgeons saved him, and now his brain is damaged; he will never be able to speak."

"One can always fall back on mutes," said Van gloomily. "He could act the speechless eunuch in 'Stambul, my bulbul' or the stable boy disguised as a kennel girl who brings a letter."

"Van, I'm boring you?"

"Oh, nonsense, it's a gripping and palpitating little case history."

Because that was really not bad: bringing down three in as many years—besides winging a fourth. Jolly good shot—Adiana! Wonder whom she'll bag next.

"You must not press me for the details of our sweet torrid

and horrid nights together, before and between that poor guy and the next intruder. If my skin were a canvas and her lips a brush, not an inch of me would have remained unpainted and vice versa. Are you horrified, Van? Do you loathe us?"

"On the contrary," replied Van, bringing off a passable imitation of bawdy mirth. "Had I not been a heterosexual male, I would have been a Lesbian."

His trite reaction to her set piece, to her desperate cunning, caused Lucette to give up, to dry up, as it were, before a black pit with people dismally coughing here and there in the invisible and eternal audience. He glanced for the hundredth time at the blue envelope, its near long edge not quite parallel to that of the glossy mahogany, its left upper corner half hidden behind the tray with the brandy and soda, its right lower corner pointing at Van's favorite novel *The Slat Sign* that lay on the sideboard.

"I want to see you again soon," said Van, biting his thumb, brooding, cursing the pause, yearning for the contents of the blue envelope. "You must come and stay with me at a flat I now have on Alex Avenue. I have furnished the guest room with *bergères* and *torchères* and rocking chairs; it looks like your mother's boudoir."

Lucette curtseyed with the wicks of her sad mouth, *à l'Américaine.*

"Will you come for a few days? I promise to behave properly. All right?"

"My notion of propriety may not be the same as yours. And what about Cordula de Prey? She won't mind?"

"The apartment is mine," said Van, "and besides, Cordula is now Mrs. Ivan G. Tobak. They are making follies in Florence. Here's her last postcard. Portrait of Vladimir Christian

[405]

of Denmark, who, she claims, is the dead spit of her Ivan Giovanovich. Have a look."

"Who cares for Sustermans," observed Lucette, with something of her uterine sister's knight move of specious response, or a Latin footballer's *rovesciata*.

No, it's an elm. Half a millennium ago.

"His ancestor," Van pattered on, "was the famous or *fameux* Russian admiral who had an *épée* duel with Jean Nicot and after whom the Tobago Islands, or the Tobakoff Islands, are named, I forget which, it was so long ago, half a millennium."

"I mentioned her only because an old sweetheart is easily annoyed by the wrong conclusions she jumps at like a cat not quite making a fence and then running off without trying again, and stopping to look back."

"Who told you about that lewd cordelude—I mean, interlude?"

"Your father, *mon cher*—we saw a lot of him in the West. Ada supposed, at first, that Tapper was an invented name—that you fought your duel with another person—but that was before anybody heard of the other person's death in Kalugano. Demon said you should have simply cudgeled him."

"I could not," said Van, "the rat was rotting away in a hospital bed."

"I meant the real Tapper," cried Lucette (who was making a complete mess of her visit), "not my poor, betrayed, poisoned, innocent teacher of music, whom not even Ada, unless she fibs, could cure of his impotence."

"Driblets," said Van.

"Not necessarily *his*," said Lucette. "His wife's lover played the triple viol. Look, I'll borrow a book" (scanning on the nearest bookshelf *The Gitanilla, Clichy Clichés, Mertvago Forever, The Ugly New Englander*) "and curl up, *komondi*, in the next room for a few minutes, while you—Oh, I adore *The Slat Sign.*"

"There's no hurry," said Van.

Pause (about fifteen minutes to go to the end of the act).

"At the age of ten," said Lucette to say something, "I was at the Vieux-Rose Stopchin stage, but our (using, that day, that year, the unexpected, thronal, authorial, jocular, technically loose, forbidden, possessive plural in speaking of her to him) sister had read at that age, in three languages, many more books than I did at twelve. However! After an appalling illness in California, I recouped myself: the Pioneers vanquished the Pyogenes. I'm not showing off but do you happen to know a great favorite of mine: Herodas?"

"Oh yes," answered Van negligently. "A ribald contemporary of Justinus, the Roman scholar. Yes, great stuff. Blinding blend of subtility and brilliant coarseness. You read it, dear, in the literal French translation with the Greek *en regard*—didn't you?—but a friend of mine here showed me a scrap of new-found text, which you could not have seen, about two children, a brother and sister, who did it so often that they finally died in each other's limbs, and could not be separated—it just stretched and stretched, and snapped back in place every time the perplexed parents let go. It is all very obscene, and very tragic, and terribly funny."

"No, I don't know that passage," said Lucette. "But Van, why are you—"

"Hay fever, hay fever!" cried Van, searching five pockets at once for a handkerchief. Her stare of compassion and the fruitless search caused such a swell of grief that he preferred to stomp out of the room, snatching the letter, dropping it, picking it up, and retreating to the farthest room (redolent of her Degrasse) to read it in one gulp.

"*O dear Van, this is the last attempt I am making. You*

may call it a document in madness or the herb of repentance,
but I wish to come and live with you, wherever you are, for
ever and ever. If you scorn the maid at your window I will
aerogram my immediate acceptance of a proposal of marriage
that has been made to your poor Ada a month ago in Valen-
tine State. He is an Arizonian Russian, decent and gentle,
not overbright and not fashionable. The only thing we have
in common is a keen interest in many military-looking desert
plants, especially various species of agave, hosts of the larvae
of the most noble animals in America, the Giant Skippers
(Krolik, you see, is burrowing again). He owns horses, and
Cubistic pictures, and 'oil wells' (whatever they are—our
father in hell who has some too, does not tell me, getting
away with off-color allusions as is his wont). I have told my
patient Valentinian that I shall give him a definite answer
after consulting the only man I have ever loved or shall love.
Try to ring me up tonight. Something is very wrong with
the Ladore line, but I am assured that the trouble will be
grappled with and eliminated before rivertide. Tvoya, tvoya,
tvoya (thine). A."

Van took a clean handkerchief from a tidy pile in a drawer,
an action he analogized at once by plucking a leaf from a
writing pad. It is wonderful how helpful such repetitive
rhythms on the part of coincidental (white, rectangular) objects can be at such chaotic moments. He wrote a short
aerogram and returned to the parlor. There he found Lucette
putting on her fur coat, and five uncouth scholars, whom his
idiot valet had ushered in, standing in a silent circle around
the bland graceful modeling of the coming winter's fashions.
Bernard Rattner, a heavily bespectacled black-haired, red-
cheeked thick-set young man greeted Van with affable relief.

"Good Log!" exclaimed Van, "I had understood we were
to meet at your uncle's place."

With a quick gesture he centrifuged them to waiting-room chairs, and despite his pretty cousin's protests ("It's a twenty minute's walk; don't accompany me") campophoned for his car. Then he clattered, in Lucette's wake, down the cataract of the narrow staircase, *katrakatra* (*quatre à quatre*). Please, children not *katrakatra* (Marina).

"I also know," said Lucette as if continuing their recent exchange, "who *he* is."

She pointed to the inscription "Voltemand Hall" on the brow of the building from which they now emerged.

Van gave her a quick glance—but she simply meant the courtier in *Hamlet*.

They passed through a dark archway, and as they came out into the colored air of a delicate sunset, he stopped her and gave her the note he had written. It told Ada to charter a plane and be at his Manhattan flat any time tomorrow morning. He would leave Kingston around midnight by car. He still hoped the Ladore dorophone would be in working order before his departure. *Le château que baignait le Dorophone.* Anyway, he assumed the aerogram would reach her in a couple of hours. Lucette said "uhn-uhn," it would first fly to Mont-Dore—sorry, Ladore—and if marked "urgent" would arrive at sunrise by dazzled messenger, galloping east on the postmaster's fleabitten nag, because on Sundays you could not use motorcycles, old local law, *l'ivresse de la vitesse, conceptions dominicales*; but even so, she would have ample time to pack, find the box of Dutch crayons Lucette wanted her to bring *if* she came, and be in time for breakfast in Cordula's recent bedroom. Neither half-sibling was at her or his best that day.

"By the way," he said, "let's fix the date of your visit. Her letter changes my schedule. Let's have dinner at Ursus next weekend. I'll get in touch with you."

[409]

"I knew it was hopeless," she said, looking away. "I did my best. I imitated all her *shtuchki* (little stunts). I'm a better actress than she but that's not enough, I know. Go back now, they are getting dreadfully drunk on your cognac."

He thrust his hands into the warm vulvas of her mole-soft sleeves and held her for a moment on the inside by her thin bare elbows, looking down with meditative desire at her painted lips.

"*Un baiser, un seul!*" she pleaded.

"You promise not to open your mouth? not to melt? not to flutter and flick?"

"I won't, I swear!"

He hesitated. "No," said Van, "it is a mad temptation but I must not succumb. I could not live through another disaster, another sister, even one-half of a sister."

"*Takoe otchayanie* (such despair)!" moaned Lucette, wrapping herself closely in the coat she had opened instinctively to receive him.

"Might it console you to know that I expect only torture from her return? That I regard you as a bird of paradise?"

She shook her head.

"That my admiration for you is painfully strong?"

"I want Van," she cried, "and not intangible admiration—"

"Intangible? You goose. You may gauge it, you may brush it once very lightly, with the knuckles of your gloved hand. I said knuckles. I said once. That will do. I can't kiss you. Not even your burning face. Good-bye, pet. Tell Edmond to take a nap after he returns. I shall need him at two in the morning."

6

The matter of that important discussion was a comparison of notes regarding a problem that Van was to try to resolve in another way many years later. Several cases of acrophobia had been closely examined at the Kingston Clinic to determine if they were combined with any traces or aspects of time-terror. Tests had yielded completely negative results, but what seemed particularly curious was that the only available case of acute chronophobia differed by its very nature—metaphysical flavor, psychological stamp and so forth—from that of space-fear. True, one patient maddened by the touch of time's texture presented too small a sample to compete with a great group of garrulous acrophobes, and readers who have been accusing Van of rashness and folly (in young Rattner's polite terminology) will have a higher opinion of him when they learn that our young investigator did his best not to let Mr. T.T. (the chronophobe) be cured too hastily of his rare and important sickness. Van had satisfied himself that it had nothing to do with clocks or calendars, or any measurements or contents of time, while he suspected and hoped (as only a discoverer, pure and passionate, and profoundly inhuman, can hope) that the dread of heights would be found by his colleagues to depend mainly on the misestimation of distances and that Mr. Arshin, their best acrophobe, who could not step down from a footstool, could be made to step down into space from the top of a tower if persuaded by some optical trick that the fire net spread fifty yards below was a mat one inch beneath him.

Van had cold cuts brought up for them, and a gallon of Gallows Ale—but his mind was elsewhere, and he did not shine in the discussion which forever remained in his mind as a grisaille of inconclusive tedium.

They left around midnight; their clatter and chatter still came from the stairs when he began ringing up Ardis Hall— vainly, vainly. He kept it up intermittently till daybreak, gave up, had a structurally perfect stool (its cruciform symmetry reminding him of the morning before his duel) and, without bothering to put on a tie (all his favorite ones were awaiting him in his new apartment), drove to Manhattan, taking the wheel when he found that Edmond had needed forty-five minutes instead of half an hour to cover one fourth of the way.

All he had wanted to say to Ada over the dumb dorophone amounted to three words in English, contractable to two in Russian, to one and a half in Italian; but Ada was to maintain that his frantic attempts to reach her at Ardis had only resulted in such a violent rhapsody of "eagre" that finally the basement boiler gave up and there was no hot water—no water at all, in fact—when she got out of bed, so she pulled on her warmest coat, and had Bouteillan (discreetly rejoicing old Bouteillan!) carry her valises down and drive her to the airport.

In the meantime Van had arrived at Alexis Avenue, had lain in bed for an hour, then shaved and showered, and almost torn off with the brutality of his pounce the handle of the door leading to the terrace as there came the sound of a celestial motor.

Despite an athletic strength of will, ironization of excessive emotion, and contempt for weepy weaklings, Van was aware of his being apt to suffer uncurbable blubbering fits (rising at times to an epileptic-like pitch, with sudden howls that shook his body, and inexhaustible fluids that stuffed his nose) ever since his break with Ada had led to agonies, which his self-pride and self-concentration had never foreseen in the hedonistic past. A small monoplane (chartered, if one judged by its nacreous wings and illegal but abortive attempts to settle on the central green oval of the Park, after which it melted in the morning mist to seek a perch elsewhere) wrenched a first sob from Van as he stood in his short "terry" on the roof terrace (now embellished by shrubs of blue spiraea in invincible bloom). He stood in the chill sun until he felt his skin under the robe turn to an armadillo's pelvic plates. Cursing and shaking both fists at breast level, he returned into the warmth of his flat and drank a bottle of champagne, and then rang for Rose, the sportive Negro maid whom he shared in more ways than one with the famous, recently decorated cryptogrammatist, Mr. Dean, a perfect gentleman, dwelling on the floor below. With jumbled feelings, with unpardonable lust, Van watched her pretty behind roll and tighten under its lacy bow as she made the bed, while her lower lover could be heard through the radiator pipes humming to himself happily (he had decoded again a Tartar dorogram telling the Chinese where we planned to land next time!). Rose soon finished putting the room in order, and flirted off, and the Pandean hum had hardly had time to be replaced (rather artlessly for a person of Dean's profession) by a crescendo of international creaks that a child could decipher, when the hallway bell dingled, and next moment whiter-faced, redder-mouthed, four-year-older Ada stood before a convulsed, already sobbing, ever-adolescent Van, her flowing hair blending with dark furs that were even richer than her sister's.

He had prepared one of those phrases that sound right in dreams but lame in lucid life: "I saw you circling above me on libelulla wings"; he broke down on ". . . ulla," and fell at her feet—at her bare insteps in glossy black Glass slippers—precisely in the same attitude, the same heap of hopeless tenderness, self-immolation, denunciation of demoniac life, in which he would drop in backthought, in the innermost bower of his brain every time he remembered her impossible semismile as she adjusted her shoulder blades to the trunk of the final tree. An invincible stagehand now slipped a seat under her, and she wept, and stroked his black curls as he went through his fit of grief, gratitude and regret. It might have persisted much longer had not another, physical frenzy, that had been stirring his blood since the previous day, offered a blessed distraction.

As if she had just escaped from a burning palace and a perishing kingdom, she wore over her rumpled nightdress a deep-brown, hoar-glossed coat of sea-otter fur, the famous *kamchatstkiy bobr* of ancient Estotian traders, also known as "lutromarina" on the Lyaska coast: "my natural fur," as Marina used to say pleasantly of her own cape, inherited from a Zemski granddam, when, at the dispersal of a winter ball, some lady wearing vison or coypu or a lowly *manteau de castor* (beaver, *nemetskiy bobr*) would comment with a rapturous moan on the *bobrovaya shuba*. "*Staren'kaya* (old little thing)," Marina used to add in fond deprecation (the usual counterpart of the Bostonian lady's coy "thank you" ventriloquizing her banal mink or nutria in response to polite

praise—which did not prevent her from denouncing afterwards the "swank" of that "stuck-up actress," who, actually,
was the least ostentatious of souls). Ada's *bobri* (princely
plural of *bobr*) were a gift from Demon, who as we know, had
lately seen in the Western states considerably more of her
than he had in Eastern Estotiland when she was a child.
The bizarre enthusiast had developed the same *tendresse* for
her as he had always had for Van. Its new expression in regard to Ada looked sufficiently fervid to make watchful fools
suspect that old Demon "slept with his niece" (actually, he
was getting more and more occupied with Spanish girls who
were getting more and more youthful every year until by the
end of the century, when he was sixty, with hair dyed a midnight blue, his flame had become a difficult nymphet of ten).
So little did the world realize the real state of affairs that
even Cordula Tobak, born de Prey, and Grace Wellington,
born Erminin, spoke of Demon Veen, with his fashionable
goatee and frilled shirtfront, as "Van's successor."

Neither sibling ever could reconstruct (and all this, including the sea-otter, must not be regarded as a narrator's eva-
sion—we have done, in our time, much more difficult things)
what they said, how they kissed, how they mastered their
tears, how he swept her couch-ward, gallantly proud to mani-
fest his immediate reaction to her being as scantily gowned
(under her hot furs) as she had been when carrying her
candle through that magic picture window.

After feasting fiercely on her throat and nipples he was
about to proceed to the next stage of demented impatience,
but she stopped him, explaining that she must first of all take
her morning bath (this, indeed, was a new Ada) and that,
moreover, she expected her luggage would be brought up any
moment now by the louts of the "Monaco" lounge (she had
taken the wrong entrance—yet Van had bribed Cordula's

devoted janitor to practically carry Ada upstairs). "Quick, quick," said Ada, "da, da, Ada'll be out of the foam in two secs!" But mad, obstinate Van shed his terry and followed her into the bathroom, where she strained across the low tub to turn on both taps, and then bent over to insert the bronze chained plug; it got sucked in by itself, however, while he steadied her lovely lyre and next moment was at the suede-soft root, was gripped, was deep between the familiar, in-comparable, crimson-lined lips. She caught at the twin cock crosses, thus involuntarily increasing the sympathetic volume of the water's noise, and Van emitted a long groan of deliver-ance, and now their four eyes were looking again into the azure brook of Pinedale, and Lucette pushed the door open with a perfunctory knuckle knock and stopped, mesmerized by the sight of Van's hairy rear and the dreadful scar all along his left side.

Ada's hands stopped the water. Luggage was being bumped down all over the flat.

"I'm not looking," said Lucette idiotically, "I only dropped in for my box."

"Please, tip them, pet," said Van, a compulsive tipper— "And pass me that towel," added Ada, but the ancilla was picking up coins she had spilled in her haste, and Ada now saw in her turn Van's scarlet ladder of sutures—"Oh my poor darling," she cried, and out of sheer compassion allowed him the repeat performance which Lucette's entrance had threat-ened to interrupt.

"I'm not sure I did bring her damned Cranach crayons," said Ada a moment later, making a frightened frog face. He watched her with a sense of perfect pine-fragrant bliss, as she squeezed out spurts of gem-like liquid from a tube of Pennsil-vestris lotion into the bath water.

Lucette had gone (leaving a curt note with her room num-ber at the Winster Hotel for Young Ladies) when our two lovers, now weak-legged and decently robed, sat down to a beautiful breakfast (Ardis' crisp bacon! Ardis' translucent honey!) brought up in the lift by Valerio, a ginger-haired elderly Roman, always ill-shaven and gloomy, but a dear old boy (he it was who, having procured neat Rose last June, was being paid to keep her strictly for Veen and Dean).

What laughs, what tears, what sticky kisses, what a tumult of multitudinous plans! And what safety, what freedom of love! Two unrelated gypsy courtesans, a wild girl in a gaudy lolita, poppy-mouthed and black-downed, picked up in a café between Grasse and Nice, and another, a part-time model (you have seen her fondling a virile lipstick in Fellata ads), aptly nicknamed Swallowtail by the patrons of a Norfolk Broads floramor, had both given our hero exactly the same reason, unmentionable in a family chronicle, for considering him absolutely sterile despite his prowesses. Amused by the Hecatean diagnose, Van underwent certain tests, and although pooh-poohing the symptom as coincidental, all the doctors agreed that Van Veen might be a doughty and durable lover but could never hope for an offspring. How merrily little Ada clapped her hands!

Would she like to stay in this apartment till Spring Term (he thought in terms of Terms now) and then accompany him to Kingston, or would she prefer to go abroad for a couple of months—anywhere, Patagonia, Angola, Gululu in the New Zealand mountains? Stay in this apartment? So, she liked it? Except some of Cordula's stuff which should be ejected—as, for example, that conspicuous Brown Hill Alma Mater of Almehs left open on poor Vanda's portrait. She had been shot dead by the girlfriend of a girlfriend on a starry night, in Ragusa of all places. It was, Van said, sad. Little Lucette no doubt had told him about a later escapade? Punning in an Ophelian frenzy on the feminine glans? Raving about the delectations of clitorism? *"N'exagérons pas, tu sais*," said Ada, patting the air down with both palms. "Lucette affirmed," he said, "that she (Ada) imitated mountain lions."

He was omniscient. Better say, omni-incest.

"That's right," said the other total-recaller.

And, by the way, Grace—yes, Grace—was Vanda's real favorite, *pas petite moi* and my little crest. She (Ada) had, hadn't she, a way of always smoothing out the folds of the past—making the flutist practically impotent (except with his wife) and allowing the gentleman farmer only one embrace, with a premature *eyakulyatsiya*, one of those hideous Russian loanwords? Yes, wasn't it hideous, but she'd love to play Scrabble again when they'd settled down for good. But where, how? Wouldn't Mr. and Mrs. Ivan Veen do quite nicely anywhere? What about the "single" in each passport? They'd go to the nearest Consulate and with roars of indignation and/or a fabulous bribe have it corrected to married, for ever and ever.

"I'm a good, good girl. Here are her special pencils. It was very considerate and altogether charming of you to invite her next weekend. I think she's even more madly in love with you than with me, the poor pet. Demon got them in Strassburg. After all she's a demi-vierge now" ("I hear you and Dad—" began Van, but the introduction of a new subject was swamped) "and we shan't be afraid of her witnessing our *ébats*" (pronouncing on purpose, with triumphant hooliganism, for which my prose, too, is praised, the first vowel *à la Russe*).

"You do the puma," he said, "but she does—to perfection! —my favorite *viola sordina*. She's a wonderful imitatrix, by the way, and if you are even better—"

"We'll speak about my talents and tricks some other time," said Ada. "It's a painful subject. Now let's look at these snapshots."

7

During her dreary stay at Ardis, a considerably changed and enlarged Kim Beauharnais called upon her. He carried under his arm an album bound in orange-brown cloth, a dirty hue she had hated all her life. In the last two or three years she had not seen him, the light-footed, lean lad with the sallow complexion had become a dusky colossus, vaguely resembling a janizary in some exotic opera, stomping in to announce an invasion or an execution. Uncle Dan, who just then was being wheeled out by his handsome and haughty nurse into the garden where coppery and blood-red leaves were falling, clamored to be given the big book, but Kim said "Perhaps later," and joined Ada in the reception corner of the hall.

He had brought her a present, a collection of photographs he had taken in the good old days. He had been hoping the good old days would resume their course, but since he understood that *mossio votre cossin* (he spoke a thick Creole thinking that its use in solemn circumstances would be more proper than his everyday Ladore English) was not expected to revisit the castle soon—and thus help bring the album up to date—the best procedure *pour tous les cernés* ("the shadowed ones," the "encircled" rather than "concerned")

[419]

might be for her to keep (or destroy and forget, so as not to hurt anybody) the illustrated document now in her pretty hands. Wincing angrily at the *jolies*, Ada opened the album at one of its maroon markers meaningly inserted here and there, glanced once, reclicked the clasp, handed the grinning blackmailer a thousand-dollar note that she happened to have in her bag, summoned Bouteillan and told him to throw Kim out. The mud-colored scrapbook remained on a chair, under her Spanish shawl. With a shuffling kick the old retainer expelled a swamp-tulip leaf swept in by the draft and closed the front door again.

"*Mademoiselle n'aurait jamais dû recevoir ce gredin,*" he grumbled on his way back through the hall.

"That's just what I was on the point of observing," said Van when Ada had finished relating the nasty incident. "Were the photos pretty filthy?"

"Ach!" exhaled Ada.

"That money might have furthered a worthier cause— Home for Blind Colts or Aging Ashettes."

"Odd, your saying that."

"Why?"

"Never mind. Anyway, the beastly thing is now safe. I *had* to pay for it, lest he show poor Marina pictures of Van seducing his little cousin Ada—which would have been bad enough; actually, as a hawk of genius, he may have suspected the whole truth."

"So you really think that because you bought his album for a paltry thousand all evidence has been disposed of and everything is in order?"

"Why, yes. Do you think the sum was too mean? I might send him more. I know where to reach him. He lectures, if you please, on the Art of Shooting Life at the School of Photography in Kalugano."

"Good place for shooting," said Van. "So you are quite sure you own the 'beastly thing'?"

"Of course, I do. It's with me, at the bottom of that trunk; I'll show it to you in a moment."

"Tell me, my love, what was your so-called I.Q. when we first met?"

"Two hundred and something. A sensational figure."

"Well, by now it has shrunk rather badly. Peeking Kim has kept all the negatives plus lots of pictures he will paste or post later."

"Would you say it has dropped to Cordula's level?"

"Lower. Now let's look at those snapshots—before settling his monthly salary."

The first item in the evil series had projected one of Van's initial impressions of Ardis Manor at an angle that differed from that of his own recollection. Its area lay between the shadow of a calèche darkening the gravel and the white step of a pillared porch shining in the sun. Marina, one arm still in the sleeve of the dust coat which a footman (Price) was helping her to remove, stood brandishing her free arm in a theatrical gesture of welcome (entirely at variance with the grimace of helpless beatitude twisting her face), while Ada in a black hockey blazer—belonging really to Vanda— spilled her hair over her bare knees as she flexed them and flipped Dack with her flowers to check his nervous barks.

Then came several preparatory views of the immediate grounds: the colutea circle, an avenue, the grotto's black O, and the hill, and the big chain around the trunk of the rare oak, *Quercus ruslan* Chât., and a number of other spots meant to be picturesque by the compiler of the illustrated pamphlet but looking a little shabby owing to inexperienced photography.

It improved gradually.

Another girl (Blanche!) stooping and squatting exactly like Ada (and indeed not unlike her in features) over Van's valise opened on the floor, and "eating with her eyes" the silhouette of Ivory Revery in a perfume advertisement. Then the cross and the shade of boughs above the grave of Marina's dear housekeeper, Anna Pimenovna Nepraslinov (1797–1883).

Let's skip nature shots—of skunklike squirrels, of a striped fish in a bubble tank, of a canary in its pretty prison.

A photograph of an oval painting, considerably diminished, portrayed Princess Sophia Zemski as she was at twenty, in 1775, with her two children (Marina's grandfather born in 1772, and Demon's grandmother, born in 1773).

"I don't seem to remember it," said Van, "where did it hang?"

"In Marina's boudoir. And do you know who this bum in the frock coat is?"

"Looks to me like a poor print cut out of a magazine. Who's he?"

"Sumerechnikov! He took sumerographs of Uncle Vanya years ago."

"The Twilight before the Lumières. Hey, and here's Alonso, the swimming-pool expert. I met his sweet sad daughter at a Cyprian party—she felt and smelt and melted like you. The strong charm of coincidence."

"I'm not interested. Now comes a little boy."

"*Zdraste*, Ivan Dementievich," said Van, greeting his fourteen-year-old self, shirtless, in shorts, aiming a conical missile at the marble fore-image of a Crimean girl doomed to offer an everlasting draught of marble water to a dying marine from her bullet-chipped jar.

Skip Lucette skipping rope.

Ah, the famous first finch.

"No, that's a *kitayskaya punochka* (Chinese Wall Bunting). It has settled on the threshold of a basement door. The door is ajar. There are garden tools and croquet mallets inside. You remember how many exotic, alpine and polar, animals mixed with ordinary ones in our region."

Lunchtime. Ada bending low over the dripping peach improperly peeled that she is devouring (shot from the garden through the french window).

Drama and comedy. Blanche struggling with two amorous *tsigans* in the Baguenaudier Bower. Uncle Dan calmly reading a newspaper in his little red motorcar, hopelessly stuck in black mud on the Ladore road.

Two huge common Peacock moths, still connected. Grooms and gardeners brought Ada that species every blessed year; which, in a way, reminds us of you, sweet Marco d'Andrea, or you, red-haired Domenico Benci, or you, dark and broody Giovanni del Brina (who thought they were bats) or the one I dare not mention (because it is Lucette's scholarly contribution—so easily botched after the scholar's death) who likewise might have picked up, at the foot of an orchard wall, not overhung with not-yet-imported wisteria (her half-sister's addition), on a May morning in 1542, near Florence, a pair of the Pear Peacock *in copula*, the male with the feathery antennae, the female with the plain threads, to depict them faithfully (among wretched, unvisualized insects) on one side of a fenestral niche in the so-called "Elements Room" of the Palazzo Vecchio.

Sunrise at Ardis. Congs: naked Van still cocooned in his hammock under the "lidderons" as they called in Ladore the liriodendrons, not exactly a *lit d'édredon*, though worth an auroral pun and certainly conducive to the physical expression of a young dreamer's fancy undisguised by the network.

"Congratulations," repeated Van in male language. "The

[423]

first indecent postcard. Bewhorny, no doubt, has a blown-up copy in his private stock."

Ada examined the pattern of the hammock through a magnifying glass (used by Van for deciphering certain details of his lunatics' drawings).

"I'm afraid there's more to come," she remarked with a catch in her voice; and taking advantage of their looking at the album in bed (which we now think lacked taste) odd Ada used the reading loupe on live Van, something she had done many times as a scientifically curious and artistically depraved child in that year of grace, here depicted.

"I'll find a *mouche* (patch) to conceal it," she said, returning to the leering caruncula in the unreticent reticulation. "By the way, you have quite a collection of black masks in your dresser."

"For masked balls (*bals-masqués*)," murmured Van.

A comparison piece: Ada's very-much-exposed white thighs (her birthday skirt had got entangled with twigs and leaves) straddling a black limb of the tree of Eden. Thereafter: several shots of the 1884 picnic, such as Ada and Grace dancing a Lyaskan fling and reversed Van nibbling at pine starworts (conjectural identification).

"That's finished," said Van, "a precious sinistral sinew has stopped functioning. I can still fence and deliver a fine punch but hand-walking is out. You shall not sniffle, Ada. Ada is not going to sniffle and wail. King Wing says that the great Vekchelo turned back into an ordinary *chelovek* at the age I'm now, so everything is perfectly normal. Ah, drunken Ben Wright trying to rape Blanche in the mews—she has quite a big part in this farrago."

"He's doing nothing of the sort. You see quite well they are dancing. It's like the Beast and the Belle at the ball where Cinderella loses her garter and the Prince his beautiful codpiece of glass. You can also make out Mr. Ward and Mrs. French in a bruegelish *kimbo* (peasant prance) at the farther end of the hall. All those rural rapes in our parts have been grossly exaggerated. *D'ailleurs*, it was Mr. Ben Wright's last petard at Ardis."

Ada on the balcony (photographed by our acrobatic *voyeur* from the roof edge) drawing one of her favorite flowers, a Ladore satyrion, silky-haired, fleshy, erect. Van thought he recalled that particular sunny evening, the excitement, the softness, and some casual words she had muttered (in connection with an inane botanical comment of his): "My flower opens only at dusk." The one she was moistly mauving.

A formal photograph, on a separate page: Adochka, pretty and impure in her flimsy, and Vanichka in gray-flannel suit, with slant-striped school tie, facing the *kimera* (chimera, camera) side by side, at attention, he with the shadow of a forced grin, she, expressionless. Both recalled the time (between the first tiny cross and a whole graveyard of kisses) and the occasion: it was ordered by Marina, who had it framed and set up in her bedroom next to a picture of her brother at twelve or fourteen clad in a *bayronka* (open shirt) and cupping a guinea pig in his gowpen (hollowed hands); the three looked like siblings, with the dead boy providing a vivisectional alibi.

Another photograph was taken in the same circumstances but for some reason had been rejected by capricious Marina: at a tripod table, Ada sat reading, her half-clenched hand covering the lower part of the page. A very rare, radiant, seemingly uncalled-for smile shone on her practically Moorish lips. Her hair flowed partly across her collarbone and partly down her back. Van stood inclining his head above her and looked, unseeing, at the opened book. In full, deliberate consciousness, at the moment of the hooded click, he bunched the recent past with the imminent future and thought to himself that this would remain an objective perception of the real present and that he must remember the flavor, the flash, the flesh of the present (as he, indeed, remembered it half a dozen years later—and now, in the second half of the next century).

But what about the rare radiance on those adored lips? Bright derision can easily grade, through a cline of glee, into a look of rapture:

"Do you know, Van, *what* book lay there—next to Marina's hand mirror and a pair of tweezers? I'll tell you. One of the most tawdry and *réjouissants* novels that ever 'made' the front page of the Manhattan *Times*' Book Review. I'm sure your Cordula still had it in her cosy corner where you sat temple to temple after you jilted me."

"Cat," said Van.

"Oh, much worse. Old Beckstein's *Tabby* was a masterpiece in comparison to this—this *Love under the Lindens* by one Eelmann transported into English by Thomas Gladstone, who seems to belong to a firm of Packers & Porters, because on the page which Adochka, *adova dochka* (Hell's daughter) happens to be relishing here, 'automobile' is rendered as 'wagon.' And to think, to think, that little Lucette had to study Eelmann, and three terrible Toms in her Literature course at Los!"

"You remember that trash but I remember our nonstop three-hour kiss Under the Larches immediately afterwards."

"See next illustration," said Ada grimly.

"The scoundrel!" cried Van; "He must have been creeping after us on his belly with his entire apparatus. I will have to destroy him."

"No more destruction, Van. Only love."

[426]

"But look, girl, here I'm glutting your tongue, and there I'm glued to your epiglottis, and—"

"Intermission," begged Ada, "quick-quick."

"I'm ready to oblige till I'm ninety," said Van (the vulgarity of the peep show was catchy), "ninety times a month, roughly."

"Make it even more roughly, oh much more, say a hundred and fifty, that would mean, that would mean—"

But, in the sudden storm, calculations went to the canicular devils.

"Well," said Van, when the mind took over again, "let's go back to our defaced childhood. I'm anxious"—(picking up the album from the bedside rug)—"to get rid of this burden. Ah, a new character, the inscription says: Dr. Krolik."

"Wait a sec. It may be the best Vanishing Van but it's terribly messy all the same. Okay. Yes, that's my poor nature teacher."

Knickerbockered, panama-hatted, lusting for his *babochka* (Russian for "lepidopteron"). A passion, a sickness. What could Diana know about *that* chase?

"How curious—in the state Kim mounted him here, he looks much less furry and fat than I imagined. In fact, darling, he's a big, strong, handsome old March Hare! Explain!"

"There's nothing to explain. I asked Kim one day to help me carry some boxes there and back, and here's the visual proof. Besides, that's not *my* Krolik but his brother, Karol, or Karapars, Krolik. A doctor of philosophy, born in Turkey."

"I love the way your eyes narrow when you tell a lie. The remote mirage in Effrontery Minor."

"I'm not lying!"—(with lovely dignity): "He *is* a doctor of philosophy."

"Van *ist auch* one," murmured Van, sounding the last word as "*wann.*"

"Our fondest dream," she continued, "Krolik's and my fondest dream, was to describe and depict the early stages, from ova to pupa, of all the known Fritillaries, Greater and Lesser, beginning with those of the New World. I would have been responsible for building an argynninarium (a pestproof breeding house, with temperature patterns, and other refinements—such as background night smells and night-animal calls to create a natural atmosphere in certain difficult cases) —a caterpillar needs exquisite care! There are hundreds of species and good subspecies in both hemispheres but, I repeat, we'd begin with America. Live egg-laying females and live food plants, such as violets of numerous kinds, airmailed from everywhere, starting, for the heck of it, with arctic habitats—Lyaska, Le Bras d'Or, Victor Island. The magnanery would be also a violarium, full of fascinating flourishing plants, from the *endiconensis* race of the Northern Marsh Violet to the minute but magnificent *Viola kroliki* recently described by Professor Hall from Goodson Bay. I would contribute colored figures of all the instars, and line drawings of the perfect insect's genitalia and other structures. It would be a wonderful work."

"A work of love," said Van, and turned the page.

"Unfortunately, my dear collaborator died intestate, and all his collections, including my own little part, were surrendered by a regular warren of collateral Kroliks to agents in Germany and dealers in Tartary. Disgraceful, unjust, and so sad!"

"We'll find you another director of science. Now what do we have here?"

Three footmen, Price, Norris, and Ward dressed up as grotesque firemen. Young Bout devotedly kissing the veined instep of a pretty bare foot raised and placed on a balustrade. Nocturnal outdoor shot of two small white ghosts pressing their noses from the inside to the library window.

Artistically *éventail*-ed all on one page were seven *fotochki* (diminutive stills) taken within as many minutes—from a fairly distant lurk—in a setting of tall grass, wild flowers, and overhanging foliage. Its shade, and the folly of peduncles, delicately camouflaged the basic details, suggesting little more than a tussle between two incompletely clad children.

In the central miniature, Ada's only limb in sight was her thin arm holding aloft, in a static snatch, like a banner, her discarded dress above the daisy-starred grass. The magnifier (now retrieved from under the bed sheet) clearly showed, topping the daisies in an upper picture, the type of tight-capped toadstool called in Scots law (ever since witching was banned) "the Lord of Erection." Another interesting plant, Marvel's Melon, imitating the backside of an occupied lad, could be made out on the floral horizon of a third photo. In the next three stills *la force des choses* ("the fever of intercourse") had sufficiently disturbed the lush herbage to allow one to distinguish the details of a tangled composition consisting of clumsy Romany clips and illegal nelsons. Finally, in the last picture, the lower one in the fanlike sequence, Ada was represented by her two hands rearranging her hair while her Adam stood over her, a frond or inflorescence veiling his thigh with the deliberate casualness of an Old Master's device to keep Eden chaste.

In an equally casual tone of voice Van said: "Darling, you smoke too much, my belly is covered with your ashes. I suppose Bouteillan knows Professor Beauharnais's exact address in the Athens of Graphic Arts."

"You shall not slaughter him," said Ada. "He is subnormal, he is, perhaps, blackmailerish, but in his sordidity there is an *istoshnïy ston* ("visceral moan") of crippled art. Furthermore, this page is the only really naughty one. And let's not forget that a copperhead of eight was also ambushed in the brush."

"Art my *foute*. This is the hearse of *ars*, a toilet roll of the Carte du Tendre! I'm sorry you showed it to me. That ape has vulgarized our own mind-pictures. I will either horsewhip his eyes out or redeem our childhood by making a book of it: *Ardis*, a family chronicle."

"Oh do!" said Ada (skipping another abominable glimpse —apparently, through a hole in the boards of the attic). "Look, here's our little Caliph Island!"

"I don't want to look any more. I suspect you find that filth titillating. Some nuts get a kick from motor-bikini comics."

"Please, Van, do glance! These are our willows, remember?"

> " 'The castle bathed by the Adour:
> The guidebooks recommend that tour.' "

It happens to be the only one in color. The willows look sort of greenish because the twigs are greenish, but actually they are leafless here, it's early spring, and you can see our red boat *Souvenance* through the rushes. And here's the last one: Kim's apotheosis of Ardis.

The entire staff stood in several rows on the steps of the pillared porch behind the Bank President Baroness Veen and the Vice President Ida Larivière. Those two were flanked by the two prettiest typists, Blanche de la Tourberie (ethereal, tearstained, entirely adorable) and a black girl who had been hired, a few days before Van's departure, to help French, who towered rather sullenly above her in the second row, the focal point of which was Bouteillan, still wearing the *costume sport* he had on when driving off with Van (*that* picture had been muffed or omitted). On the butler's right side stood three footmen; on his left, Bout (who had valeted Van), the fat, flour-pale cook (Blanche's father) and, next to French, a terribly tweedy gentleman with sightseeing strappings athwart one shoulder: actually (according to Ada), a tourist, who, having come all the way from England to see Bryant's Castle, had bicycled up the wrong road and was, in the picture, under the impression of accidentally being conjoined to a group of fellow tourists who were visiting some other old manor quite worth inspecting too. The back rows consisted of less distinguished menservants and scullions, as well as of gardeners, stableboys, coachmen, shadows of columns, maids of maids, aids, laundresses, dresses, recesses—getting less and less distinct as in those bank ads where limited little employees dimly dimidiated by more fortunate shoulders, but still asserting themselves, still smile in the process of humble dissolve.

"Isn't that wheezy Jones in the second row? I always liked the old fellow."

"No," answered Ada, "that's Price. Jones came four years later. He is now a prominent policeman in Lower Ladore. Well, that's all."

Nonchalantly, Van went back to the willows and said:

"Every shot in the book has been snapped in 1884, except this one. I never rowed you down Ladore River in early spring. Nice to note you have not lost your wonderful ability to blush."

"It's *his* error. He must have thrown in a *fotochka* taken later, maybe in 1888. We can rip it out if you like."

"Sweetheart," said Van, "the whole of 1888 has been ripped out. One need not be a sleuth in a mystery story to see that at least as many pages have been removed as retained. *I* don't mind—I mean *I* have no desire to see the *Knabenkräuter* and other pendants of your friends botanizing with you; but 1888 has been withheld and he'll turn up with it when the first grand is spent."

"I destroyed 1888 myself," admitted proud Ada; "but I swear, I solemnly swear, that the man behind Blanche, in the *perron* picture, was, and has always remained, a complete stranger."

"Good for him," said Van. "Really it has no importance. It's our entire past that has been spoofed and condemned. On second thoughts, I will not write that Family Chronicle. By the way, where is my poor little Blanche now?"

"Oh, she's all right. She's still around. You know, she came back—after you abducted her. She married our Russian coachman, the one who replaced Bengal Ben, as the servants called him."

"Oh she did? That's delicious. Madame Trofim Fartukov. I would never have thought it."

"They have a blind child," said Ada.

"Love is blind," said Van.

"She tells me you made a pass at her on the first morning of your first arrival."

"Not documented by Kim," said Van. "Will their child *remain* blind? I mean, did you get them a really first-rate physician?"

"Oh yes, hopelessly blind. But speaking of love and its myths, do you realize—because I never did before talking to her a couple of years ago—that the people around our affair had very good eyes indeed? Forget Kim, he's only the necessary clown—but do you realize that a veritable legend was growing around you and me while we played and made love?"

She had never realized, she said again and again (as if intent to reclaim the past from the matter-of-fact triviality of

the album), that their first summer in the orchards and or-
chidariums of Ardis had become a sacred secret and creed,
throughout the countryside. Romantically inclined handmaids, whose reading consisted of *Gwen de Vere* and *Klara
Mertvago*, adored Van, adored Ada, adored Ardis's ardors in
arbors. Their swains, plucking ballads on their seven-stringed
Russian lyres under the racemosa in bloom or in old rose
gardens (while the windows went out one by one in the
castle), added freshly composed lines—naive, lackey-daisical,
but heartfelt—to cyclic folk songs. Eccentric police officers
grew enamored with the glamour of incest. Gardeners paraphrased iridescent Persian poems about irrigation and the
Four Arrows of Love. Nightwatchmen fought insomnia and
the fire of the clap with the weapons of *Vaniada's Adventures*. Herdsmen, spared by thunderbolts on remote hillsides,
used their huge "moaning horns" as ear trumpets to catch the
lilts of Ladore. Virgin châtelaines in marble-floored manors
fondled their lone flames fanned by Van's romance. And another century would pass, and the painted word would be
retouched by the still richer brush of time.

"All of which," said Van, "only means that our situation is
desperate."

8

Knowing how fond his sisters were of Russian fare and Russian floor shows, Van took them Saturday night to "Ursus," the best Franco-Estotian restaurant in Manhattan Major. Both young ladies wore the very short and open evening gowns that Vass "miraged" that season—in the phrase of that season: Ada, a gauzy black, Lucette, a lustrous cantharid green. Their mouths "echoed" in tone (but not tint) each other's lipstick; their eyes were made up in a "surprised bird-of-paradise" style that was as fashionable in Los as in Lute. Mixed metaphors and double-talk became all three Veens, the children of Venus.

The *uha*, the shashlik, the *Ai* were facile and familiar successes; but the old songs had a peculiar poignancy owing to the participation of a Lyaskan contralto and a Banff bass, renowned performers of Russian "romances," with a touch of heart-wringing *tsiganshchina* vibrating through Grigoriev and Glinka. And there was Flora, a slender, hardly nubile, half-naked music-hall dancer of uncertain origin (Rumanian? Romany? Ramseyan?) whose ravishing services Van had availed himself of several times in the fall of that year. As a "man of the world," Van glanced with bland (perhaps too bland) unconcern at her talented charms, but they certainly added a secret bonus to the state of erotic excitement tingling in him from the moment that his two beauties had been unfurred and placed in the colored blaze of the feast before him; and that thrill was somehow augmented by his awareness (carefully profiled, diaphanely blinkered) of the furtive, jealous, intuitive suspicion with which Ada *and* Lucette watched, unsmilingly, his facial reactions to the demure look of professional recognition on the part of the passing and repassing *blyadushka* (cute whorelet), as our young misses referred to (*very* expensive and altogether delightful) Flora with ill-feigned indifference. Presently, the long sobs of the violins began to affect and almost choke Van and Ada: a juvenile conditioning of romantic appeal, which at one moment forced tearful Ada to go and "powder her nose" while Van stood up with a spasmodic sob, which he cursed but could not control. He went back to whatever he was eating, and cruelly stroked Lucette's apricot-bloomed forearm, and she said in Russian "I'm drunk, and all that, but I adore (*obozhayu*), I adore, I adore, I adore more than life you, you (*tebya, tebya*), I ache for you unbearably (*ya toskuyu po tebe nevïnosimo*), and, please, don't let me swill (*hlestat'*) champagne any more, not only because I will jump into Goodson River if I can't hope to have you, and not only because of the physical red thing—your heart was almost ripped out, my poor *dushen'ka* ('darling,' more than 'darling'), it looked to me at least eight inches long—"

"Seven and a half," murmured modest Van, whose hearing the music impaired.

"—but because you are Van, all Van, and nothing but Van, skin and scar, the only truth of our only life, of *my* accursed life, Van, Van, Van."

Here Van stood up again, as Ada, black fan in elegant motion, came back followed by a thousand eyes, while the opening bars of a *romance* (on Fet's glorious *Siyala noch'*) started to run over the keys (and the bass coughed *à la russe* into his fist before starting).

A radiant night, a moon-filled garden. Beams
Lay at our feet. The drawing room, unlit;
Wide open, the grand piano; and our hearts
Throbbed to your song, as throbbed the strings in it . . .

Then Banoffsky launched into Glinka's great amphibrachs (Mihail Ivanovich had been a summer guest at Ardis when their uncle was still alive—a green bench existed where the composer was said to have sat under the pseudoacacias especially often, mopping his ample brow):

Subside, agitation of passion!

Then other singers took over with sadder and sadder ballads—"The tender kisses are forgotten," and "The time was early in the spring, the grass was barely sprouting," and "Many songs have I heard in the land of my birth: Some in sorrow were sung, some in gladness," and the spuriously populist

There's a crag on the Ross, overgrown with wild moss
On all sides, from the lowest to highest . . .

and a series of viatic plaints such as the more modestly anapestic:

In a monotone tinkles the yoke-bell,
And the roadway is dusting a bit. . . .

[436]

And that obscurely corrupted soldier dit of singular genius

Nadezhda, I shall then be back
When the true batch outboys the riot . . .

and Turgenev's only memorable lyrical poem beginning

Morning so nebulous, morning gray-dawning,
Reaped fields so sorrowful under snow coverings

and naturally the celebrated pseudo-gipsy guitar piece by
Apollon Grigoriev (another friend of Uncle Ivan's)

O you, at least, do talk to me,
My seven-stringed companion,
Such yearning ache invades my soul,
Such moonlight fills the canyon!

"I declare we are satiated with moonlight and strawberry
soufflé—the latter, I fear, has not quite 'risen' to the occasion," remarked Ada in her archest, Austen-maidenish manner. "Let's all go to bed. You have seen our huge bed, pet?
Look, our cavalier is yawning 'fit to declansh his masher'"
(vulgar Ladore cant).

"How (ascension of Mt. Yawn) true," uttered Van, ceas-
ing to palpate the velvet cheek of his Cupidon peach, which
he had bruised but not sampled.

The captain, the *vinocherpiy*, the shashlikman, and a crew
of waiters had been utterly entranced by the amount of
zernistaya ikra and *Ai* consumed by the vaporous-looking
Veens and were now keeping a multiple eye on the tray that
had flown back to Van with a load of gold change and bank
notes.

"Why," asked Lucette, kissing Ada's cheek as they both rose (making swimming gestures behind their backs in search of the furs locked up in the vault or somewhere), "why did the first song, *Uzh gasli v komnatah ogni*, and the 'redolent roses,' upset you more than your favorite Fet and the other, about the bugler's sharp elbow?"

"Van, too, was upset," replied Ada cryptically and grazed with freshly rouged lips tipsy Lucette's fanciest freckle.

Detachedly, merely tactually, as if he had met those two slow-moving, hip-swaying graces only that night, Van, while steering them through a doorway (to meet the sinchilla mantillas that were being rushed toward them by numerous, new, eager, unfairly, inexplicably impecunious, humans), placed one palm, the left, on Ada's long bare back and the other on Lucette's spine, quite as naked and long (had she meant the lad or the ladder? Lapse of the lisping lips?). Detachedly, he sifted and tasted this sensation, then that. His girl's ensellure was hot ivory; Lucette's was downy and damp. He too had had just about his "last straw" of champagne, namely four out of half a dozen bottles minus a rizzom (as we said at old Chose) and now, as he followed their bluish furs, he inhaled like a fool his right hand before gloving it.

"I say, Veen," whinnied a voice near him (there were lots of lechers around), "you don't rally need two, d'you?"

Van veered, ready to cuff the gross speaker—but it was only Flora, a frightful tease and admirable mimic. He tried to give her a banknote, but she fled, bracelets and breast stars flashing a fond farewell.

As soon as Edmund (not Edmond, who for security reasons—he knew Ada—had been sent back to Kingston) brought them home, Ada puffed out her cheeks, making big eyes, and headed for Van's bathroom. Hers had been turned over to the tottering guest. Van, at a geographical point a shade nearer to the elder girl, stood and used in a sustained stream the amenities of a little *vessie* (Canady form of W.C.) next to his dressing room. He removed his dinner jacket and tie, undid the collar of his silk shirt and paused in virile hesitation: Ada, beyond their bedroom and sitting room, was running her bath; to its gush a guitar rhythm, recently heard, kept adapting itself aquatically (the rare moments when he remembered her and her quite rational speech at her last sanatorium in Agavia).

He licked his lips, cleared his throat and, deciding to kill two finches with one fircone, walked to the other, southern, extremity of the flat through a boudery and manger hall (we always tend to talk Canady when *haut*). In the guest bedroom, Lucette stood with her back to him, in the process of slipping on her pale green nightdress over her head. Her narrow haunches were bare, and our wretched rake could not help being moved by the ideal symmetry of the exquisite twin dimples that only very perfect young bodies have above the buttocks in the sacral belt of beauty. Oh, they were even more perfect than Ada's! Fortunately, she turned around, smoothing her tumbled red curls while her hem dropped to knee level.

"My dear," said Van, "do help me. She told me about her Valentian *estanciero* but now the name escapes me and I hate bothering her."

"Only she never told you," said loyal Lucette, "so nothing could escape. Nope. I can't do that to your sweetheart and mine, because we know you could hit that keyhole with a pistol."

"Please, little vixen! I'll reward you with a very special kiss."

"Oh, Van," she said over a deep sigh. "You promise you won't tell her I told you?"

"I promise. No, no, no," he went on, assuming a Russian accent, as she, with the abandon of mindless love, was about to press her abdomen to his. "*Nikak-s net*: no lips, no philtrum, no nosetip, no swimming eye. Little vixen's axilla, just that—unless"—(drawing back in mock uncertainty)— "you *shave* there?"

"I stink worse when I do," confided simple Lucette and obediently bared one shoulder.

"Arm up! Point at Paradise! Terra! Venus!" commanded Van, and for a few synchronized heartbeats, fitted his working mouth to the hot, humid, perilous hollow.

She sat down with a bump on a chair, pressing one hand to her brow.

"Turn off the footlights," said Van. "I want the name of that fellow."

"Vinelander," she answered.

He heard Ada Vinelander's voice calling for her Glass bed slippers (which, as in Cordulenka's princessdom too, he found hard to distinguish from dance footwear), and a minute later, without the least interruption in the established tension, Van found himself, in a drunken dream, making violent love to Rose—no, to Ada, but in the rosacean fashion, on a kind of lowboy. She complained he hurt her "like a Tiger Turk." He went to bed and was about to doze off for good when she left his side. Where was she going? Pet wanted to see the album.

"I'll be back in a rubby," she said (tribadic schoolgirl slang), "so keep awake. From now on by the way, it's going to be *Chère-amie-fait-morata*"—(play on the generic and specific names of the famous fly)—"until further notice."

"But no sapphic *vorschmacks*," mumbled Van into his pillow.

"Oh, Van," she said, turning to shake her head, one hand

[440]

on the opal doorknob at the end of an endless room. "We've been through that so many times! You admit yourself that I am only a pale wild girl with gipsy hair in a deathless ballad, in a nulliverse, in Rattner's 'menald world' where the only principle is random variation. You cannot demand," she continued—somewhere between the cheeks of his pillow (for Ada had long vanished with her blood-brown book)—"you cannot demand pudicity on the part of a delphinet! You know that I really love only males and, alas, only one man."

There was always something colorfully impressionistic, but also infantile, about Ada's allusions to her affairs of the flesh, reminding one of baffle painting, or little glass labyrinths with two peas, or the Ardis throwing-trap—you remember?— which tossed up clay pigeons and pine cones to be shot at, or cockamaroo (Russian *"biks"*), played with a toy cue on the billiard cloth of an oblong board with holes and hoops, bells and pins among which the ping-pong-sized eburnean ball zigzagged with bix-pix concussions.

Tropes are the dreams of speech. Through the boxwood maze and bagatelle arches of Ardis, Van passed into sleep. When he reopened his eyes it was nine A.M. She lay curved away from him, with nothing beyond the opened parenthesis, its contents not yet ready to be enclosed, and the beloved, beautiful, treacherous, blue-black-bronze hair smelt of Ardis, but also of Lucette's "Oh-de-grâce."

Had she cabled him? Canceled or Postponed? Mrs. Viner —no, Vingolfer, no, Vinelander—first Russki to taste the labruska grape.

"Mne snitsa saPERnik SHCHASTLEEVOY!" (Mihail Ivanovich arcating the sand with his cane, humped on his bench under the creamy racemes).

"I dream of a fortunate rival!"

In the meantime it's Dr. Hangover for me, and his strong-est Kaffeina pill.

Ada, being at twenty a long morning sleeper, his usual practice, ever since their new life together had started, was to shower before she awoke and, while shaving, ring from the bathroom for their breakfast to be brought by Valerio, who would roll in the laid table out of the lift into the sitting room next to their bedroom. But on this particular Sunday, not knowing what Lucette might like (he remembered her old craving for cocoa) and being anxious to have an engage-ment with Ada before the day began, even if it meant in-truding upon her warm sleep, Van sped up his ablutions, robustly dried himself, powdered his groin, and without both-ering to put anything on re-entered the bedroom in full pride, only to find a tousled and sulky Lucette, still in her willow green nightie, sitting on the far edge of the concubital bed, while fat-nippled Ada, already wearing, for ritual and fatidic reasons, his river of diamonds, was inhaling her first smoke of the day and trying to make her little sister decide whether she would like to try the Monaco's pancakes with Potomac syrup, or, perhaps, their incomparable amber-and-ruby bacon. Upon seeing Van, who without a flinch in his imposing de-portment proceeded to place a rightful knee on the near side of the tremendous bed (Mississippi Rose had once brought there, for progressive visual-education purposes, her two small toffee-brown sisters, and a doll almost their size but white), Lucette shrugged her shoulders and made as if to leave, but Ada's avid hand restrained her.

"Pop in, pet (it all started with the little one letting wee winds go free at table, *circa* 1882). And you, Garden God, ring up room service—three coffees, half a dozen soft-boiled eggs, lots of buttered toast, loads of—"

"Oh no!" interrupted Van. "Two coffees, four eggs, *et*

cetera. I refuse to let the staff know that I have two girls in my bed, one (*teste* Flora) is enough for my little needs."

"*Little* needs!" snorted Lucette. "Let me go, Ada. *I* need a bath, and *he* needs you."

"Pet stays right here," cried audacious Ada, and with one graceful swoop plucked her sister's nightdress off. Involuntarily Lucette bent her head and frail spine; then she lay back on the outer half of Ada's pillow in a martyr's pudibund swoon, her locks spreading their orange blaze against the black velvet of the padded headboard.

"Uncross your arms, silly," ordered Ada and kicked off the top sheet that partly covered six legs. Simultaneously, without turning her head, she slapped furtive Van away from her rear, and with her other hand made magic passes over the small but very pretty breasts, gemmed with sweat, and along the flat palpitating belly of a seasand nymph, down to the firebird seen by Van once, fully fledged now, and as fascinating in its own way as his favorite's blue raven. Enchantress! Acrasia!

What we have now is not so much a Casanovanic situation (that double-wencher had a definitely monochromatic pencil—in keeping with the memoirs of his dingy era) as a much earlier canvas, of the Venetian (*sensu largo*) school, reproduced (in "Forbidden Masterpieces") expertly enough to stand the scrutiny of a bordel's *vue d'oiseau*.

Thus seen from above, as if reflected in the ciel mirror that Eric had naively thought up in his Cyprian dreams (actually all is shadow up there, for the blinds are still drawn, shutting out the gray morning), we have the large island of the bed illumined from our left (Lucette's right) by a lamp burning with a murmuring incandescence on the west-side bedtable. The top sheet and quilt are tumbled at the footboardless south of the island where the newly landed eye starts on its northern trip, up the younger Miss Veen's pried-open legs. A dewdrop on russet moss eventually finds a sty-listic response in the aquamarine tear on her flaming cheekbone. Another trip from the port to the interior reveals the central girl's long white left thigh; we visit souvenir stalls: Ada's red-lacquered talons, which lead a man's reasonably recalcitrant, pardonably yielding wrist out of the dim east to the bright russet west, and the sparkle of her diamond neck-lace, which, for the nonce, is not much more valuable than the aquamarines on the other (west) side of Novelty Novel lane. The scarred male nude on the island's east coast is half-shaded, and, on the whole, less interesting, though con-siderably more aroused than is good for him or a certain type of tourist. The recently repapered wall immediately west of the now louder-murmuring (*et pour cause*) doro-cene lamp is ornamented in the central girl's honor with Peru-vian "honeysuckle" being visited (not only for its nectar, I'm afraid, but for the animalcules stuck in it) by marvelous Lod-digesia Hummingbirds, while the bedtable on that side bears a lowly box of matches, a *karavanchik* of cigarettes, a Monaco ashtray, a copy of Voltemand's poor thriller, and a Lurid Oncidium Orchid in an amethystine vaselet. The companion piece on Van's side supports a similar superstrong but unlit lamp, a dorophone, a box of Wipex, a reading loupe, the re-turned Ardis album, and a separatum "Soft music as cause of brain tumors," by Dr. Anbury (young Rattner's waggish pen-name). Sounds have colors, colors have smells. The fire of Lucette's amber runs through the night of Ada's odor and ardor, and stops at the threshold of Van's lavender goat. Ten eager, evil, loving, long fingers belonging to two different young demons caress their helpless bed pet. Ada's loose black hair accidentally tickles the local curio she holds in her left fist, magnanimously demonstrating her acquisition. Unsigned and unframed.

That about summed it up (for the magical gewgaw liquefied all at once, and Lucette, snatching up her nightdress, escaped to her room). It was only the sort of shop where the jeweler's fingertips have a tender way of enhancing the preciousness of a trinket by something akin to a rubbing of hindwings on the part of a settled lycaenid or to the frottage of a conjurer's thumb dissolving a coin; but just in such a shop the anonymous picture attributed to Grillo or Obieto, caprice or purpose, *ober-* or *unterart,* is found by the ferreting artist.

"She's terribly nervous, the poor kid," remarked Ada stretching across Van toward the Wipex. "You can order that breakfast now—unless . . . Oh, what a good sight! Orchids. I've never seen a man make such a speedy recovery."

"Hundreds of whores and scores of cuties more experienced than the future Mrs. Vinelander have told me that."

"I may not be as bright as I used to be," sadly said Ada, "but I know somebody who is not simply a cat, but a polecat, and that's Cordula Tobacco alias Madame Perwitsky. I read in this morning's paper that in France ninety percent of cats die of cancer. I don't know what the situation is in Poland."

After a while he adored [*sic!* Ed.] the pancakes. No Lucette, however, turned up, and when Ada, still wearing her diamonds (in sign of at least one more *caro* Van and a Camel before her morning bath) looked into the guest room, she found the white valise and blue furs gone. A note scrawled in Arlen Eyelid Green was pinned to the pillow.

> *Would go mad if remained one more night shall ski at Verma with other poor woolly worms for three weeks or so miserable*
>
> Pour Elle

Van walked over to a monastic lectern that he had acquired for writing in the vertical position of vertebrate thought and wrote what follows:

> Poor L.
>
> *We are sorry you left so soon. We are even sorrier to have inveigled our Esmeralda and mermaid in a naughty prank. That sort of game will never be played again with you, darling firebird. We apollo [apologize]. Remembrance, embers and membranes of beauty make artists and morons lose all self-control. Pilots of tremendous airships and even coarse, smelly coachmen are known to have been driven insane by a pair of green eyes and a copper curl. We wished to admire and amuse you, BOP (bird of paradise). We went too far. I, Van, went too far. We regret that shameful, though basically innocent scene. These are times of emotional stress and reconditioning. Destroy and forget.*
>
> *Tenderly yours A & V.*
> *(in alphabetic order).*

"I call this pompous, puritanical rot," said Ada upon scanning Van's letter. "Why *should* we apollo for her having experienced a delicious *spazmochka*? I love her and would never allow you to harm her. It's curious—you know, something in the tone of your note makes me really jealous for the first time in my fire [thus in the manuscript, for 'life.' Ed.] Van, Van, somewhere, some day, after a sunbath or dance, you will sleep with her, Van!"

"Unless you run out of love potions. Do you allow me to send her these lines?"

[446]

"I do, but I want to add a few words."

Her P.S. read:

> *The above declaration is Van's composition which I sign reluctantly. It is pompous and puritanical. I adore you*, mon petit, *and would never allow him to hurt you, no matter how gently or madly. When you're sick of Queen, why not fly over to Holland or Italy?*
>
> A.

"Now let's go out for a breath of crisp air," suggested Van. "I'll order Pardus and Peg to be saddled."

"Last night two men recognized me," she said. "Two separate Californians, but they didn't dare bow—with that silk-tuxedoed *bretteur* of mine glaring around. One was Anskar, the producer, and the other, with a cocotte, Paul Whinnier, one of your father's London pals. I sort of hoped we'd go back to bed."

"We shall now go for a ride in the park," said Van firmly, and rang, first of all, for a Sunday messenger to take the letter to Lucette's hotel—or to the Verma resort, if she had already left.

"I suppose you know what you're doing?" observed Ada.

"Yes," he answered.

"You are breaking her heart," said Ada.

"Ada girl, adored girl," cried Van, "I'm a radiant void. I'm convalescing after a long and dreadful illness. You cried over my unseemly scar, but now life is going to be nothing but love and laughter, and corn in cans. I cannot brood over broken hearts, mine is too recently mended. You shall wear a blue veil, and I the false mustache that makes me look like Pierre Legrand, my fencing master."

"*Au fond*," said Ada, "first cousins have a perfect right to ride together. And even dance or skate, if they want. After all, first cousins are almost brother and sister. It's a blue, icy, breathless day."

She was soon ready, and they kissed tenderly in their hallway, between lift and stairs, before separating for a few minutes.

"Tower," she murmured in reply to his questioning glance, just as she used to do on those honeyed mornings in the past, when checking up on happiness: "And you?"

"A regular ziggurat."

9

After some exploration, they tracked down a rerun of *The Young and the Doomed* (1890) to a tiny theater that specialized in Painted Westerns (as those deserts of nonart used to be called). Thus had Mlle Larivière's *Enfants Maudits* (1887) finally degenerated! She had had two adolescents, in a French castle, poison their widowed mother who had seduced a young neighbor, the lover of one of her twins. The author had made many concessions to the freedom of the times, and the foul fancy of scriptwriters; but both she and the leading lady disavowed the final result of multiple tamperings with the plot that had now become the story of a murder in Arizona, the victim being a widower about to marry an alcoholic prostitute, whom Marina, quite sensibly, refused to impersonate. But poor little Ada had clung to her bit part, a two-minute scene in a *traktir* (roadside tavern). During the rehearsals she felt she was doing not badly as a serpentine barmaid—until the director blamed her for moving like an angular "backfish." She had not deigned to see the final product and was not overeager to have Van see it now, but he reminded her that the same director, G. A.

Vronsky, had told her she was always pretty enough to serve one day as a stand-in for Lenore Colline, who at twenty had been as attractively *gauche* as she, raising and tensing forward her shoulders in the same way, when crossing a room. Having sat through a preliminary P.W. short, they finally got to *The Young and the Doomed* only to discover that the barmaid scene of the barroom sequence had been cut out—except for a perfectly distinct shadow of Ada's elbow, as Van kindly maintained.

Next day, in their little drawing room, with its black divan, yellow cushions, and draftproof bay whose new window seemed to magnify the slow steady straight-falling snowflakes (coincidentally stylized on the cover of the current issue of *The Beau & the Butterfly* which lay on the window ledge), Ada discussed her "dramatic career." The whole matter secretly nauseated Van (so that, by contrast, her Natural History passion acquired a nostalgic splendor). For him the written word existed only in its abstract purity, in its unrepeatable appeal to an equally ideal mind. It belonged solely to its creator and could not be spoken or enacted by a mime (as Ada insisted) without letting the deadly stab of another's mind destroy the artist in the very lair of his art. A written play was intrinsically superior to the best performance of it, even if directed by the author himself. Otherwise, Van agreed with Ada that the talking screen was certainly preferable to the live theater for the simple reason that with the former a director could attain, and maintain, his own standards of perfection throughout an unlimited number of performances.

Neither of them could imagine the partings that her professional existence "on location" might necessitate, and neither could imagine their traveling together to Argus-eyed destinations and living together in Hollywood, U.S.A., or

Ivydell, England, or the sugar-white Cohnritz Hotel in Cairo. To tell the truth they did not imagine any other life at all beyond their present *tableau vivant* in the lovely dove-blue Manhattan sky.

At fourteen, Ada had firmly believed she would shoot to stardom and there, with a grand bang, break into prismatic tears of triumph. She studied at special schools. Unsuccessful but gifted actresses, as well as Stan Slavsky (no relation, and not a stage name), gave her private lessons of drama, despair, hope. Her debut was a quiet little disaster; her subsequent appearances were sincerely applauded only by close friends.

"One's first love," she told Van, "is one's first standing ovation, and *that* is what makes great artists—so Stan and his girl friend, who played Miss Spangle Triangle in *Flying Rings*, assured me. Actual recognition may come only with the last wreath."

"Bosh!" said Van.

"Precisely—he too was hooted by hack hoods in much older Amsterdams, and look how three hundred years later every Poppy Group pup copies him! I still think I have talent, but then maybe I'm confusing the right *podhod* (approach) with talent, which does not give a dry fig for rules deduced from past art."

"Well, at least you know that," said Van; "and you've dwelt at length upon it in one of your letters."

"I seem to have always felt, for example, that acting should be focused not on 'characters,' not on 'types' of something or other, not on the *fokus-pokus* of a social theme, but exclusively on the subjective and unique poetry of the author, because playwrights, as the greatest among them has shown, are closer to poets than to novelists. In 'real' life we are creatures of chance in an absolute void—unless we be artists ourselves, naturally; but in a good play I feel authored, I feel passed by the board of censors, I feel secure, with only a breathing blackness before me (instead of our Fourth-Wall Time), I feel cuddled in the embrace of puzzled Will (he thought I was you) or in that of the much more normal Anton Pavlovich, who was always passionately fond of long dark hair."

"That you also wrote to me once."

The beginning of Ada's limelife in 1891 happened to coincide with the end of her mother's twenty-five-year-long career. What is more, both appeared in Chekhov's *Four Sisters*. Ada played Irina on the modest stage of the Yakima Academy of Drama in a somewhat abridged version which, for example, kept only the references to Sister Varvara, the garrulous *originalka* ("odd female"—as Marsha calls her) but eliminated her actual scenes, so that the title of the play might have been *The Three Sisters*, as indeed it appeared in the wittier of the local notices. It was the (somewhat expanded) part of the nun that Marina acted in an elaborate film version of the play; and the picture and she received a goodly amount of undeserved praise.

"Ever since I planned to go on the stage," said Ada (we are using her notes), "I was haunted by Marina's mediocrity, *au dire de la critique*, which either ignored her or lumped her in the common grave with other 'adequate sustainers'; or, if the role had sufficient magnitude, the gamut went from 'wooden' to 'sensitive' (the highest compliment her accomplishments had ever received). And here she was, at the most delicate moment of *my* career, multiplying and sending out to friends and foes such exasperating comments as 'Durmanova is superb as the neurotic nun, having transferred an essentially static and episodical part into *et cetera, et cetera, et cetera.*'

"Of course, the cinema has no language problems," continued Ada (while Van swallowed, rather than stifled, a yawn). "Marina and three of the men did not need the excellent dubbing which the other members of the cast, who lacked the lingo, were provided with; but our wretched Yakima production could rely on only two Russians, Stan's protégé Altshuler in the role of Baron Nikolay Lvovich Tuzenbach-Krone-Altschauer, and myself as Irina, *la pauvre et noble enfant*, who is a telegraph operator in one act, a town-council employee in another, and a schoolteacher in the end. All the rest had a macedoine of accents—English, French, Italian—by the way what's the Italian for 'window'?"

"*Finestra, sestra*," said Van, mimicking a mad prompter.

"Irina (sobbing): 'Where, where has it all gone? Oh, dear, oh, dear! All is forgotten, forgotten, muddled up in my head—I don't remember the Italian for "ceiling" or, say, "window."'"

"No, 'window' comes first in that speech," said Van, "because she looks around, and then up; in the natural movement of thought."

"Yes, of course: still wrestling with 'window,' she looks up and is confronted by the equally enigmatic 'ceiling.' In fact, I'm sure I played it your psychological way, but what does it matter, what did it matter?—the performance was perfectly odious, my baron kept fluffing every other line—but Marina, Marina was *marvelous* in her world of shadows! 'Ten years and one have gone by-abye since I left Moscow'"—(Ada, now playing Varvara, copied the nun's "singsongy devotional tone" (*pevuchiy ton bogomolki*, as indicated by Chekhov and as rendered so irritatingly well by Marina). "'Nowadays, Old Basmannaya Street, where you (turning to Irina) were born a score of yearkins (*godkov*) ago, is Busman Road, lined on both sides with workshops and garages (Irina tries to control

[453]

her tears). Why, then, should you want to go back, Arin-ushka? (Irina sobs in reply).' Naturally, as would every fine player, mother improvised quite a bit, bless her soul. And moreover her voice—in young tuneful Russian!—is substituted for Lenore's corny brogue."

Van had seen the picture and had liked it. An Irish girl, the infinitely graceful and melancholy Lenore Colline—

> *Oh! qui me rendra ma colline*
> *Et le grand chêne* and my colleen!

—harrowingly resembled Ada Ardis as photographed with her mother in *Belladonna,* a movie magazine which Greg Ermi-nin had sent him, thinking it would delight him to see aunt and cousin, together, on a California patio just before the film was released. Varvara, the late General Sergey Prozorov's eldest daughter, comes in Act One from her remote nunnery, Tsitsikar Convent, to Perm (also called Permwail), in the back woods of Akimsk Bay, North Canady, to have tea with Olga, Marsha, and Irina on the latter's name day. Much to the nun's dismay, her three sisters dream only of one thing—leaving cool, damp, mosquito-infested but otherwise nice and peaceful "Permanent" as Irina mockingly dubs it, for high life in remote and sinful Moscow, Id., the former capital of Estoti-land. In the first edition of his play, which never quite man-ages to heave the soft sigh of a masterpiece, Tchechoff (as he spelled his name when living that year at the execrable Pension Russe, 9, rue Gounod, Nice) crammed into the two pages of a ludicrous expository scene all the information he wished to get rid of, great lumps of recollections and calendar dates—an impossible burden to place on the fragile shoulders of three unhappy Estotiwomen. Later he redistributed that information through a considerably longer scene in which the arrival of the *monashka* Varvara provides all the speeches needed to satisfy the restless curiosity of the audience. This was a neat stroke of stagecraft, but unfortunately (as so often occurs in the case of characters brought in for disingenuous purposes) the nun stayed on, and not until the third, penultimate, act was the author able to bundle her off, back to her convent.

"I assume," said Van (knowing his girl), "that you did not want any tips from Marina for your Irina?"

"It would have only resulted in a row. I always resented her suggestions because they were made in a sarcastic, insulting manner. I've heard mother birds going into neurotic paroxysms of fury and mockery when their poor little tailless ones (*bezkhvostïe bednyachkí*) were slow in learning to fly. I've had enough of that. By the way, here's the program of *my* flop."

Van glanced through the list of players and D.P.'s and noticed two amusing details: the role of Fedotik, an artillery officer (whose comedy organ consists of a constantly clicking camera), had been assigned to a "Kim (short for Yakim) Eskimossoff" and somebody called "John Starling" had been cast as Skvortsov (a *sekundant* in the rather amateurish duel of the last act) whose name comes from *skvorets*, starling. When he communicated the latter observation to Ada, she blushed as was her Old World wont.

"Yes," she said, "he was quite a lovely lad and I sort of flirted with him, but the strain and the split were too much for him—he had been, since pubescence, the *puerulus* of a fat ballet master, Dangleleaf, and he finally committed suicide. You see ('the blush now replaced by a *matovaya* pallor') I'm not hiding one stain of what rhymes with Perm."

"I see. And Yakim—"

"Oh, he was nothing."

"No, I mean, Yakim, at least, did not, as *his* rhymesake did, take a picture of your brother embracing his girl. Played by Dawn de Laire."

"I'm not sure. I seem to recall that our director did not mind some comic relief."

"Dawn *en robe rose et verte,* at the end of Act One."

"I think there was a click in the wings and some healthy mirth in the house. All poor Starling had to do in the play was to hollo off stage from a rowboat on the Kama River to give the signal for my fiancé to come to the dueling ground."

But let us shift to the didactic metaphorism of Chekhov's friend, Count Tolstoy.

We all know those old wardrobes in old hotels in the Old World subalpine zone. At first one opens them with the utmost care, very slowly, in the vain hope of hushing the excruciating creak, the growing groan that the door emits midway. Before long one discovers, however, that if it is opened or closed with celerity, in one resolute sweep, the hellish hinge is taken by surprise, and triumphant silence achieved. Van and Ada, for all the exquisite and powerful bliss that engulfed and repleted them (and we do not mean here the rose sore of Eros alone), knew that certain memories had to be left closed, lest they wrench every nerve of the soul with their monstrous moan. But if the operation is performed swiftly, if indelible evils are mentioned between two quick quips, there is a chance that the anesthetic of life itself may allay unforgettable agony in the process of swinging its door.

Now and then she poked fun at his sexual peccadilloes, though generally she tended to ignore them as if demanding, by tacit implication, a similar kind of leniency in regard to her frailty. He was more inquisitive than she but hardly managed to learn more from her lips than he had from her letters. To her past admirers Ada attributed all the features and faults we have already been informed of: incompetence of performance, inanity and nonentity, and to her own self nothing beyond easy feminine compassion and such considerations of hygiene and sanity as hurt Van more than would a defiant avowal of passionate betrayal. Ada had made up her mind to transcend his and her sensual sins: the adjective being a near synonym of "senseless" and "soulless"; therefore not represented in the ineffable hereafter that both our young people mutely and shyly believed in. Van endeavored to follow the same line of logic but could not forget the shame and the agony even while reaching heights of happiness he had not known at his brightest hour before his darkest one in the past.

10

They took a great many precautions—all absolutely useless, for nothing can change the end (written and filed away) of the present chapter. Only Lucette and the agency that forwarded letters to him and to Ada knew Van's address. Through an amiable lady in waiting at Demon's bank, Van made sure that his father would not turn up in Manhattan before March 30. They never came out or went in together, arranging a meeting place at the Library or in an emporium whence to start the day's excursions—and it so happened that the only time they broke that rule (she having got stuck in the lift for a few panicky moments and he having blithely trotted downstairs from their common summit), they issued right into the visual field of old Mrs. Arfour who happened to be passing by their front door with her tiny tan-and-gray long-silked Yorkshire terrier. The simultaneous association was immediate and complete: she had known both families for years and was now interested to learn from chattering (rather than chatting) Ada that Van had happened to be in town just when she, Ada, had happened to return from the West; that Marina was fine; that Demon was in Mexico or

Oxmice; and that Lenore Colline had a similar adorable pet with a similar adorable parting along the middle of the back. That same day (February 3, 1893) Van rebribed the already gorged janitor to have him answer all questions which any visitor, and especially a dentist's widow with a caterpillar dog, might ask about any Veens, with a brief assertion of utter ignorance. The only personage they had not reckoned with was the old scoundrel usually portrayed as a skeleton or an angel.

Van's father had just left one Santiago to view the results of an earthquake in another, when Ladore Hospital cabled that Dan was dying. He set off at once for Manhattan, eyes blazing, wings whistling. He had not many interests in life.

At the airport of the moonlit white town we call Tent, and Tobakov's sailors, who built it, called Palatka, in northern Florida, where owing to engine trouble he had to change planes, Demon made a long-distance call and received a full account of Dan's death from the inordinately circumstantial Dr. Nikulin (grandson of the great rodentiologist Kunikulinov—we can't get rid of the lettuce). Daniel Veen's life had been a mixture of the ready-made and the grotesque; but his death had shown an artistic streak because of its reflecting (as his cousin, not his doctor, instantly perceived) the man's latterly conceived passion for the paintings, and faked paintings, associated with the name of Hieronymus Bosch.

Next day, February 5, around nine P.M., Manhattan (winter) time, on the way to Dan's lawyer, Demon noted—just as he was about to cross Alexis Avenue, an ancient but insignificant acquaintance, Mrs. Arfour, advancing toward him, with her toy terrier, along his side of the street. Unhesitatingly, Demon stepped off the curb, and having no hat to raise (hats were not worn with raincloaks and besides he had just taken a very exotic and potent pill to face the day's ordeal on top of a sleepless journey), contented himself—quite properly—with a wave of his slim umbrella; recalled with a paint dab of delight one of the gargle girls of her late husband; and smoothly passed in front of a slow-clopping horse-drawn vegetable cart, well out of the way of Mrs. R4. But precisely in regard to such a contingency, Fate had prepared an alternate continuation. As Demon rushed (or, in terms of the pill, sauntered) by the Monaco, where he had often lunched, it occurred to him that his son (whom he had been unable to "contact") might still be living with dull little Cordula de Prey in the penthouse apartment of that fine building. He had never been up there—or had he? For a business consultation with Van? On a sun-hazed terrace? And a clouded drink? (He had, that's right, but Cordula was not dull and had not been present.)

With the simple and, combinationally speaking, neat, thought that, after all, there was but one sky (white, with minute, multicolored optical sparks), Demon hastened to enter the lobby and catch the lift which a ginger-haired waiter had just entered, with breakfast for two on a wiggle-wheel table and the Manhattan *Times* among the shining, ever so slightly scratched, silver cupolas. Was his son still living up there, automatically asked Demon, placing a piece of nobler metal among the domes. *Si*, conceded the grinning imbecile, he had lived there with his lady all winter.

"Then we are fellow travelers," said Demon inhaling not without gourmand anticipation the smell of Monaco's coffee, exaggerated by the shadows of tropical weeds waving in the breeze of his brain.

On that memorable morning, Van, after ordering breakfast, had climbed out of his bath and donned a strawberry-red terrycloth robe when he thought he heard Valerio's voice from the adjacent parlor. Thither he padded, humming tunelessly, looking forward to another day of increasing happiness (with yet another uncomfortable little edge smoothed away, another raw kink in the past so refashioned as to fit into the new pattern of radiance).

Demon, clothed entirely in black, black-spatted, black-scarved, his monocle on a broader black ribbon than usual, was sitting at the breakfast table, a cup of coffee in one hand, and a conveniently folded financial section of the *Times* in the other.

He gave a slight start and put down his cup rather jerkily on noting the coincidence of color with a persistent detail in an illumined lower left-hand corner of a certain picture reproduced in the copiously illustrated catalogue of his immediate mind.

All Van could think of saying was "I am not alone" (*je ne suis pas seul*), but Demon was brimming too richly with the bad news he had brought to heed the hint of the fool who should have simply walked on into the next room and come back one moment later (locking the door behind him—locking out years and years of lost life), instead of which he remained standing near his father's chair.

According to Bess (which is "fiend" in Russian), Dan's buxom but otherwise disgusting nurse, whom he preferred to all others and had taken to Ardis because she managed to extract orally a few last drops of "play-zero" (as the old whore called it) out of his poor body, he had been complaining for some time, even before Ada's sudden departure, that a devil combining the characteristics of a frog and a rodent desired to straddle him and ride him to the torture house of eternity. To Dr. Nikulin Dan described his rider as black, pale-bellied, with a black dorsal buckler shining like a dung beetle's back and with a knife in his raised forelimb. On a very cold morning in late January Dan had somehow escaped, through a basement maze and a toolroom, into the brown shrubbery of Ardis; he was naked except for a red bath towel which trailed from his rump like a kind of caparison, and, despite the rough going, had crawled on all fours, like a crippled steed under an invisible rider, deep into the wooded landscape. On the other hand, had he attempted to warn her she might have made her big Ada yawn and uttered something irrevocably cozy at the moment he opened the thick protective door.

"I beg you, sir," said Van, "go down, and I'll join you in the bar as soon as I'm dressed. I'm in a delicate situation."

"Come, come," retorted Demon, dropping and replacing his monocle. "Cordula won't mind."

"It's another, much more impressionable girl"—yet another awful fumble!). "Damn Cordula! Cordula is now Mrs. Tobak."

"Oh, of course!" cried Demon. "How stupid of me! I remember Ada's fiancé telling me—he and young Tobak worked for a while in the same Phoenix bank. Of *course*. Splendid broad-shouldered, blue-eyed, blond chap. Backbay Tobakovich!"

"I don't care," said clenched Van, "if he looks like a crippled, crucified, albino toad. Please, Dad, I really must—"

"Funny your saying that. I've dropped in only to tell you poor cousin Dan has died an odd Boschean death. He thought a fantastic rodent sort of rode him out of the house. They found him too late, he expired in Nikulin's clinic, raving about that detail of the picture. I'm having the deuce of a time rounding up the family. The picture is now preserved in the Vienna Academy of Art."

"Father, I'm sorry—but I'm trying to tell you—"

"If I could write," mused Demon, "I would describe, in too many words no doubt, how passionately, how incandes-

cently, how incestuously—*c'est le mot*—art and science meet
in an insect, in a thrush, in a thistle of that ducal bosquet.
Ada is marrying an outdoor man, but her mind is a closed
museum, and she, and dear Lucette, once drew my attention,
by a creepy coincidence, to certain details of that other
triptych, that tremendous garden of tongue-in-cheek de-
lights, circa 1500, and, namely, to the butterflies in it—a
Meadow Brown, female, in the center of the right panel, and
a Tortoiseshell in the middle panel, placed there as if settled
on a flower—mark the 'as if,' for here we have an example of
exact knowledge on the part of those two admirable little
girls, because they say that actually the *wrong* side of the bug
is shown, it should have been the underside, if seen, as it is,
in profile, but Bosch evidently found a wing or two in the
corner cobweb of his casement and showed the prettier upper
surface in depicting his incorrectly folded insect. I mean I
don't give a hoot for the esoteric meaning, for the myth behind the moth, for the masterpiece-baiter who makes Bosch
express some bosh of his time, I'm allergic to allegory and
am quite sure he was just enjoying himself by crossbreeding
casual fancies just for the fun of the contour and color, and
what we have to study, as I was telling your cousins, is the
joy of the eye, the feel and the taste of the woman-sized
strawberry that you embrace *with* him, or the exquisite surprise of an unusual orifice—but you are not following me,
you want me to go, so that you may interrupt her beauty
sleep, lucky beast! A *propos*, I have not been able to alert
Lucette, who is somewhere in Italy, but I've managed to
trace Marina to Tsitsikar—flirting there with the Bishop of
Belokonsk—she will arrive in the late afternoon, wearing, no
doubt, *pleureuses*, very becoming, and we shall then travel
à trois to Ladore, because I don't think—"

Was he perhaps under the influence of some bright Chilean

drug? That torrent was simply unstoppable, a crazy spectrum, a talking palette—

"—no really, I don't think we should bother Ada in her Agavia. He is—I mean, Vinelander is—the scion, s,c,i,o,n, of one of those great Varangians who had conquered the Copper Tartars or Red Mongols—or whoever they were—who had conquered some earlier Bronze Riders—before *we* introduced our Russian roulette and Irish loo at a lucky moment in the history of Western casinos."

"I am extremely, I am hideously sorry," said Van, "what with Uncle Dan's death and your state of excitement, sir, but my girl friend's coffee is getting cold, and I can't very well stumble into our bedroom with all that infernal paraphernalia."

"I'm leaving, I'm leaving. After all we haven't seen each other—since when, August? At any rate, I hope she's prettier than the Cordula you had here before, volatile boy!"

Volatina, perhaps? Or dragonara? He definitely smelled of ether. Please, please, please, go.

"My gloves! Cloak! Thank you. Can I use your W.C.? No? All right. I'll find one elsewhere. Come over as soon as you can, and we'll meet Marina at the airport around four and then whizz to the wake, and—"

And here Ada entered. Not naked—oh no; in a pink peignoir so as not to shock Valerio—comfortably combing her hair, sweet and sleepy. She made the mistake of crying out "*Bozhe moy!*" and darting back into the dusk of the bedroom. All was lost in that one chink of a second.

"Or better—come at once, both of you, because I'll cancel my appointment and go home right now." He spoke, or thought he spoke, with the self-control and the clarity of enunciation which so frightened and mesmerized blunderers, blusterers, a voluble broker, a guilty schoolboy. Especially so now—when everything had gone to the hell curs, *k chertyam sobach'im,* of Jeroen Anthniszoon van Äken and the *molti aspetti affascinati* of his *enigmatica arte,* as Dan explained with a last sigh to Dr. Nikulin and to nurse Bellabestia ("Bess") to whom he bequeathed a trunkful of museum catalogues and his second-best catheter.

11

The dragon drug had worn off: its aftereffects are not pleasant, combining as they do physical fatigue with a certain starkness of thought as if all color were drained from the mind. Now clad in a gray dressing gown, Demon lay on a gray couch in his third-floor study. His son stood at the window with his back to the silence. In a damask-padded room on the second floor, immediately below the study, waited Ada, who had arrived with Van a couple of minutes ago. In the skyscraper across the lane a window was open exactly opposite the study and an aproned man stood there setting up an easel and cocking his head in search of the right angle.

The first thing Demon said was:

"I insist that you face me when I'm speaking to you."

Van realized that the fateful conversation must have already started in his father's brain, for the admonishment had the ring of a self-interruption, and with a slight bow he took a seat.

"However, before I advise you of those two facts, I would like to know how long this—how long this has been . . ." ('going on,' one presumes, or something equally banal, but then all ends are banal—hangings, the Nuremberg Old Maid's iron sting, shooting oneself, last words in the brand-new Ladore hospital, mistaking a drop of thirty thousand feet for the airplane's washroom, being poisoned by one's wife, expecting a bit of Crimean hospitality, congratulating Mr. and Mrs. Vinelander—)

"It will be nine years soon," replied Van. "I seduced her in the summer of eighteen eighty-four. Except for a single occasion, we did not make love again until the summer of eighteen eighty-eight. After a long separation we spent one winter together. All in all, I suppose I have had her about a thousand times. She is my whole life."

A longish pause not unlike a fellow actor's dry-up, came in response to his well-rehearsed speech.

Finally, Demon: "The second fact may horrify you even more than the first. I know it caused me much deeper worry—moral of course, not monetary—than Ada's case—of which eventually her mother informed Cousin Dan, so that, in a sense—"

Pause, with an underground trickle.

"Some other time I'll tell you about the Black Miller; not now; too trivial."

(Dr. Lapiner's wife, born Countess Alp, not only left him, in 1871, to live with Norbert von Miller, amateur poet, Russian translator at the Italian Consulate in Geneva, and professional smuggler of neonegrine—found only in the Valais —but had imparted to her lover the melodramatic details of the subterfuge which the kindhearted physician had considered would prove a boon to one lady and a blessing to the other. Versatile Norbert spoke English with an extravagant accent, hugely admired wealthy people and, when name-dropping, always qualified such a person as "enawmously rich" with awed amorous gusto, throwing himself back in his chair and spreading tensely curved arms to enfold an invisible fortune. He had a round head as bare as a knee, a corpse's button nose, and very white, very limp, very damp hands adorned with rutilant gems. His mistress soon left him. Dr. Lapiner died in 1872. About the same time, the Baron married an innkeeper's innocent daughter and began to blackmail Demon Veen; this went on for almost twenty years, when aging Miller was shot dead by an Italian policeman on a little-known border trail, which had seemed to get steeper and muddier every year. Out of sheer kindness, or habit, Demon bade his lawyer continue to send Miller's widow—who mistook it naively for insurance money—the trimestrial sum which had been swelling with each pregnancy of the robust Swissess. Demon used to say that he would publish one day "Black Miller's" quatrains which adorned his letters with the jingle of verselets on calendarial leaves:

> My spouse is thicker, I am leaner.
> Again it comes, a new bambino.
> You must be good like I am good.
> Her stove is big and wants more wood.

We may add, to complete this useful parenthesis, that in early February, 1893, not long after the poet's death, two other less successful blackmailers were waiting in the wings: Kim who would have bothered Ada again had he not been carried out of his cottage with one eye hanging on a red thread and the other drowned in its blood; and the son of one of the former employees of the famous clandestine-message agency after it had been closed by the U.S. Government in 1928, when the past had ceased to matter, and nothing but the straw of a prison cell could reward the optimism of second-generation rogues.)

The most protracted of the several pauses having run its dark course, Demon's voice emerged to say, with a vigor that it had lacked before:

"Van, you receive the news I impart with incomprehensible calmness. I do not recall any instance, in factual or fictional life, of a father's having to tell his son that particular kind of thing in these particular circumstances. But you play with a pencil and seem as unruffled as if we were discussing your gaming debts or the demands of a wench knocked up in a ditch."

Tell him about the herbarium in the attic? About the indiscretions of (anonymous) servants? About a forged wedding date? About everything that two bright children had so gaily gleaned? I will. He did.

"She was twelve," Van added, "and I was a male primatal of fourteen and a half, and we just did not care. And it's too late to care now."

"Too late?" shouted his father, sitting up on his couch.

"Please, Dad, do not lose your temper," said Van. "Nature, as I informed you once, has been kind to me. We can afford to be careless in every sense of the word."

"I'm not concerned with semantics—or semination. One thing, and only one, matters. It is *not* too late to stop that ignoble affair—"

"No shouting and no philistine epithets," interrupted Van.

"All right," said Demon. "I take back the adjective, and I ask you instead: Is it too late to prevent your affair with your sister from wrecking her life?"

Van knew this was coming. He knew, he said, this was coming. "Ignoble" had been taken care of; would his accuser define "wrecking"?

The conversation now took a neutral turn that was far more terrible than its introductory admission of faults for which our young lovers had long pardoned their parents. How did Van imagine his sister's pursuing a scenic career? Would he admit it would be wrecked if they persisted in their relationship? Did he envisage a life of concealment in luxurious exile? Was he ready to deprive her of normal interests and a normal marriage? Children? Normal amusements?

"Don't forget 'normal adultery,'" remarked Van.

"How much better that would be!" said grim Demon, sitting on the edge of the couch with both elbows propped on his knees, and nursing his head in his hands: "The awfulness of the situation is an abyss that grows deeper the more I think of it. You force me to bring up the tritest terms such as 'family,' 'honor,' 'set,' 'law.' . . . All right, I have bribed many officials in my wild life but neither you nor I can bribe a whole culture, a whole country. And the emotional impact of learning that for almost ten years you and that charming child have been deceiving their parents—"

Here Van expected his father to take the "it-would-kill-your-mother" line, but Demon was wise enough to keep clear of it. Nothing could "kill" Marina. If any rumors of incest did come her way, concern with her "inner peace" would help her to ignore them—or at least romanticize them out of reality's reach. Both men knew all that. Her image appeared for a moment and accomplished a facile fade-out.

Demon spoke on: "I cannot disinherit you: Aqua left you enough 'ridge' and real estate to annul the conventional punishment. And I cannot denounce you to the authorities without involving my daughter, whom I mean to protect at all cost. But I can do the next proper thing, I can curse you, I can make this our last, our last—"

Van, whose finger had been gliding endlessly to and fro along the mute but soothingly smooth edge of the mahogany desk, now heard with horror the sob that shook Demon's entire frame, and then saw a deluge of tears flowing down those hollow tanned cheeks. In an amateur parody, at Van's birthday party fifteen years ago, his father had made himself up as Boris Godunov and shed strange, frightening, jet-black tears before rolling down the steps of a burlesque throne in death's total surrender to gravity. Did those dark streaks, in the present show, come from his blackening his orbits, eyelashes, eyelids, eyebrows? The funest gamester . . . the pale fatal girl, in another well-known melodrama. . . . In this one. Van gave him a clean handkerchief to replace the soiled rag. His own marble calm did not surprise Van. The ridicule of a good cry with Father adequately clogged the usual ducts of emotion.

Demon regained his composure (if not his young looks) and said:

"I believe in you and your common sense. You must not allow an old debaucher to disown an only son. If you love her, you wish her to be happy, and she will not be as happy as she could be once you gave her up. You may go. Tell her to come here on your way down."

Down. My first is a vehicle that twists dead daisies around its spokes; my second is Oldmanhattan slang for "money"; and my whole makes a hole.

As he traversed the second-floor landing, he saw, through the archway of two rooms, Ada in her black dress standing, with her back to him, at the oval window in the boudoir. He told a footman to convey her father's message to her and passed almost at a run through the familiar echoes of the stone-flagged vestibule.

My second is also the meeting place of two steep slopes. Right-hand lower drawer of my practically unused new desk —which is quite as big as Dad's, with Sig's compliments.

He judged it would take him as much time to find a taxi at this hour of the day as to walk, with his ordinary swift swing, the ten blocks to Alex Avenue. He was coatless, tieless, hatless; a strong sharp wind dimmed his sight with salty frost and played Medusaean havoc with his black locks. Upon letting himself in for the last time into his idiotically cheerful apartment, he forthwith sat down at that really magnificent desk and wrote the following note:

Do what he tells you. His logic sounds preposterous, prepsupposing [*sic*] a vague kind of "Victorian" era, as they have on Terra according to 'my mad' [?], but in a paroxysm of [illegible] I suddenly realized he was right. Yes, right, here and there, not neither here, nor there, as most things are. You see, girl, how it is and must be. In the last window we shared we both saw a man painting [us?] but your second-floor level of vision probably prevented your seeing that he wore what looked like a butcher's apron, badly smeared. Goodbye, girl.

Van sealed the letter, found his Thunderbolt pistol in the place he had visualized, introduced one cartridge into the magazine, and translated it into its chamber. Then, standing before a closet mirror, he put the automatic to his head, at the point of the pterion, and pressed the comfortably concaved trigger. Nothing happened—or perhaps everything happened, and his destiny simply forked at that instant, as it probably does sometimes at night, especially in a strange bed, at stages of great happiness or great desolation, when we happen to die in our sleep, but continue our normal existence, with no perceptible break in the faked serialization, on the following, neatly prepared morning, with a spurious past discreetly but firmly attached behind. Anyway, what he held in his right hand was no longer a pistol but a pocket comb which he passed through his hair at the temples. It was to gray by the time that Ada, then in her thirties, said, when they spoke of their voluntary separation:

"I would have killed myself too, had I found Rose wailing over your corpse. 'Secondes pensées sont les bonnes,' as your other, white, bonne used to say in her pretty patois. As to the apron, you are quite right. And what *you* did not make out was that the artist had about finished a large picture of your meek little palazzo standing between its two giant guards. Perhaps for the cover of a magazine, which rejected that picture. But, you know, there's one thing I regret," she added: "Your use of an alpenstock to release a brute's fury—not yours, not my Van's. I should never have told you about the Ladore policeman. You should never have taken him into your confidence, never connived with him to burn those files —and most of Kalugano's pine forest. *Eto unizitel'no* (it is humiliating)."

"Amends have been made," replied fat Van with a fat man's chuckle. "I'm keeping Kim safe and snug in a nice Home for Disabled Professional People, where he gets from me loads of nicely brailled books on new processes in chromophotography."

There are other possible forkings and continuations that occur to the dream-mind, but these will do.

PART THREE

PART THREE

1

He traveled, he studied, he taught.

He contemplated the pyramids of Ladorah (visited mainly because of its name) under a full moon that silvered the sands inlaid with pointed black shadows. He went shooting with the British Governor of Armenia, and his niece, on Lake Van. From a hotel balcony in Sidra his attention was drawn by the manager to the wake of an orange sunset that turned the ripples of a lavender sea into goldfish scales and was well worth the price of enduring the quaintness of the small striped rooms he shared with his secretary, young Lady Scramble. On another terrace, overlooking another fabled bay, Eberthella Brown, the local Shah's pet dancer (a naive little thing who thought "baptism of desire" meant something sexual), spilled her morning coffee upon noticing a six-inch-long caterpillar, with fox-furred segments, *qui rampait*, was tramping, along the balustrade and curled up in a swoon when picked up by Van—who for hours, after removing the beautiful animal to a bush, kept gloomily plucking itchy bright hairs out of his fingertips with the girl's tweezers.

He learned to appreciate the singular little thrill of following dark byways in strange towns, knowing well that he would discover nothing, save filth, and ennui, and discarded "merry-cans" with "Billy" labels, and the jungle jingles of exported jazz coming from syphilitic cafés. He often felt that the famed cities, the museums, the ancient torture house and the suspended garden, were but places on the map of his own madness.

He liked composing his works (*illegible Signatures*, 1895; *Clairvoyeurism*, 1903; *Furnished Space*, 1913; *The Texture of Time*, begun 1922), in mountain refuges, and in the drawing rooms of great expresses, and on the sundecks of white ships, and on the stone tables of Latin public parks. He would uncurl out of an indefinitely lengthy trance, and note with wonder that the ship was going the other way or that the order of his left-hand fingers was reversed, now beginning, clockwise, with his thumb as on his right hand, or that the marble Mercury that had been looking over his shoulder had been transformed into an attentive arborvitae. He would realize all at once that three, seven, thirteen years, in one cycle of separation, and then four, eight, sixteen, in yet another, had elapsed since he had last embraced, held, bewept Ada.

Numbers and rows and series—the nightmare and malediction harrowing pure thought and pure time—seemed bent on mechanizing his mind. Three elements, fire, water, and air, destroyed, in that sequence, Marina, Lucette, and Demon. Terra waited.

For seven years, after she had dismissed her life with her husband, a successfully achieved corpse, as irrelevant, and retired to her still dazzling, still magically well-staffed Côte d'Azur villa (the one Demon had once given her), Van's mother had been suffering from various "obscure" illnesses, which everybody thought she made up, or talentedly simulated, and which she contended could be, and partly were,

cured by willpower. Van visited her less often than dutiful
Lucette, whom he glimpsed there on two or three occasions;
and once, in 1899, he saw, as he entered the arbutus-and-
laurel garden of Villa Armina, a bearded old priest of the
Greek persuasion, clad in neutral black, leaving on a motor
bicycle for his Nice parish near the tennis courts. Marina
spoke to Van about religion, and Terra, and the Theater, but
never about Ada, and just as he did not suspect she knew
everything about the horror and ardor of Ardis, none suspected *what* pain in her bleeding bowels she was trying to
allay by incantations, and "self-focusing" or its opposite device, "self-dissolving." She confessed with an enigmatic and
rather smug smile that much as she liked the rhythmic blue
puffs of incense, and the *dyakon*'s rich growl on the ambon,
and the oily-brown ikon coped in protective filigree to receive
the worshipper's kiss, her soul remained irrevocably conse-
crated, *naperekor* (in spite of) Dasha Vinelander, to the ultimate wisdom of Hinduism.

Early in 1900, a few days before he saw Marina, for the
last time, at the clinic in Nice (where he learned for the *first*
time the name of her illness), Van had a "verbal" nightmare,
caused, maybe, by the musky smell in the Miramas (Bouches
Rouges-du-Rhône) Villa Venus. Two formless fat transparent creatures were engaged in some discussion, one repeating "I can't!" (meaning "can't die"—a difficult procedure to
carry out voluntarily, without the help of the dagger, the
ball, or the bowl), and the other affirming "You can, sir!"
She died a fortnight later, and her body was burnt, according to her instructions.

Van, a lucid soul, considered himself less brave morally
than physically. He was always (meaning well into the
nineteen-sixties) to recollect with reluctance, as if wishing
to suppress in his mind a petty, timorous, and stupid deed

(for, actually, who knows, the later antlers might have been set right then, with green lamps greening green growths before the hotel where the Vinelanders stayed) his reacting from Kingston to Lucette's cable from Nice ("Mother died this morning the funeral dash cremation dash is to be held after tomorrow at sundown") with the request to advise him ("please advise") who else would be there, and upon getting her prompt reply that Demon had already arrived with Andrey and Ada, his cabling back: *Désolé de ne pouvoir être avec vous.*

He had roamed in Kingston's Cascadilla Park, in the active sweet-swarming spring dusk, so much more seraphic than that flurry of cables. The last time he had seen mummy-wizened Marina and told her he must return to America (though actually there was no hurry—only the smell in her hospital room that no breeze could dislodge), she had asked, with her new, tender, myopic, because inward, expression: "Can't you wait till I'm gone?"; and his reply had been "I'll be back on the twenty-fifth. I have to deliver an address on the Psychology of Suicide"; and she had said, stressing, now that everything was *tripitaka* (safely packed), the exact kinship: "Do tell them about your silly aunt Aqua," whereupon he had nodded, with a smirk, instead of answering: "Yes, mother." Hunched up in a last band of low sun, on the bench where he had recently fondled and fouled a favorite, lanky, awkward, black girl student, Van tortured himself with thoughts of insufficient filial affection—a long story of unconcern, amused scorn, physical repulsion, and habitual dismissal. He looked around, making wild amends, willing her spirit to give him an unequivocal, and indeed all-deciding, sign of continued being behind the veil of time, beyond the flesh of space. But no response came, not a petal fell on his bench, not a gnat touched his hand. He wondered what really kept him alive on terrible Antiterra, with Terra a myth and all art a game, when nothing mattered any more since the day he slapped Valerio's warm bristly cheek; and whence, from what deep well of hope, did he still scoop up a shivering star, when everything had an edge of agony and despair, when another man was in every bedroom with Ada.

2

On a bleak morning between the spring and summer of 1901, in Paris, as Van, black-hatted, one hand playing with the warm loose change in his topcoat pocket and the other, fawn-gloved, upswinging a furled English umbrella, strode past a particularly unattractive sidewalk café among the many lining the Avenue Guillaume Pitt, a chubby bald man in a rumpled brown suit with a watch-chained waistcoat stood up and hailed him.

Van considered for a moment those red round cheeks, that black goatee.

"*Ne uznayosh'* (You don't recognize me)?"

"Greg! Grigoriy Akimovich!" cried Van tearing off his glove.

"I grew a regular *vollbart* last summer. You'd never have known me then. Beer? Wonder what you do to look so boyish, Van."

"Diet of champagne, not beer," said Professor Veen, putting on his spectacles and signaling to a waiter with the crook of his 'umber.' "Hardly stops one adding weight, but keeps the scrotum crisp."

"I'm also very fat, yes?"

"What about Grace, I can't imagine *her* getting fat?"

"Once twins, always twins. My wife is pretty portly, too."

"*Tak ti zhenat* (so you are married)? Didn't know it. How long?"

"About two years."

"To whom?"

"Maude Sween."

"The daughter of the poet?"

"No, no, her mother is a Brougham."

Might have replied "Ada Veen," had Mr. Vinelander not been a quicker suitor. I think I met a Broom somewhere. Drop the subject. Probably a dreary union: hefty, high-handed wife, he more of a bore than ever.

"I last saw you thirteen years ago, riding a black pony—no, a black Silentium. *Bozhe moy!*"

"Yes—*Bozhe moy*, you can well say that. Those lovely, lovely agonies in lovely Ardis! Oh, I was *absolyutno bezumno* (madly) in love with your cousin!"

"You mean Miss Veen? I did not know it. How long—"

"Neither did she. I was terribly—"

"How long are you staying—"

"—terribly shy, because, of course, I realized that I could not compete with her numerous boy friends."

Numerous? Two? Three? Is it possible he never heard about the main one? All the rose hedges knew, all the maids knew, in all three manors. The noble reticence of our bedmakers.

"How long will you be staying in Lute? No, Greg, I ordered it. You pay for the next bottle. Tell me—"

"So odd to recall! It was frenzy, it was fantasy, it was reality in the *x* degree. I'd have consented to be beheaded by a Tartar, I declare, if in exchange I could have kissed her instep.

You were her cousin, almost a brother, you can't understand that obsession. Ah, those picnics! And Percy de Prey who boasted to me about her, and drove me crazy with envy and pity, and Dr. Krolik, who, they said, also loved her, and Phil Rack, a composer of genius—dead, dead, all dead!"

"I really know very little about music but it was a great pleasure to make your chum howl. I have an appointment in a few minutes, alas. *Za tvoyo zdorovie, Grigoriy Akimovich*."

"Arkadievich," said Greg, who had let it pass once but now mechanically corrected Van.

"*Ach* yes! Stupid slip of the slovenly tongue. How *is* Arkadiy Grigorievich?"

"He died. He died just before your aunt. I thought the papers paid a very handsome tribute to her talent. And where is Adelaida Danilovna? Did she marry Christopher Vinelander or his brother?"

"In California or Arizona. Andrey's the name, I gather. Perhaps I'm mistaken. In fact, I never knew my cousin very well: I visited Ardis only twice, after all, for a few weeks each time, years ago."

"Somebody told me she's a movie actress."

"I've no idea, I've never seen her on the screen."

"Oh, that would be terrible, I declare—to switch on the dorotelly, and suddenly see her. Like a drowning man seeing his whole past, and the trees, and the flowers, and the wreathed dachshund. She must have been terribly affected by her mother's terrible death."

Likes the word "terrible," I declare. A terrible suit of clothes, a terrible tumor. Why must I stand it? Revolting— and yet fascinating in a weird way: my babbling shadow, my burlesque double.

Van was about to leave when a smartly uniformed chauffeur came up to inform "my lord" that his lady was parked at the corner of rue Saïgon and was summoning him to appear.

"Aha," said Van. "I see you are using your British title. Your father preferred to pass for a Chekhovian colonel."

"Maude is Anglo-Scottish and, well, likes it that way. Thinks a title gets one better service abroad. By the way, somebody told me—yes, Tobak!—that Lucette is at the Alphonse Four. I haven't asked you about your father? He's in good health?" (Van bowed.) "And how is the *guvernantka belletristka?*"

"Her last novel is called *L'ami Luc.* She just got the Lebon Academy Prize for her copious rubbish."

They parted laughing.

A moment later, as happens so often in farces and foreign cities, Van ran into another friend. With a surge of delight he saw Cordula in a tight scarlet skirt bending with baby words of comfort over two unhappy poodlets attached to the waitingpost of a sausage shop. Van stroked her with his fingertips, and as she straightened up indignantly and turned around (indignation instantly replaced by gay recognition), he quoted the stale but appropriate lines he had known since the days his schoolmates annoyed him with them:

> The Veens speak only to Tobaks
> But Tobaks speak only to dogs.

The passage of years had but polished her prettiness and though many fashions had come and gone since 1889, he happened upon her at a season when hairdos and skirtlines had reverted briefly (another much more elegant lady was already ahead of her) to the style of a dozen years ago, abolishing the interruption of remembered approval and pleasure. She plunged into a torrent of polite questions—but he had a more important matter to settle at once—while the flame still flickered.

"Let's not squander," he said, "the tumescence of retrieved time on the gush of small talk. I'm bursting with energy, if that's what you want to know. Now look; it may sound silly and insolent but I have an urgent request. Will you cooperate with me in cornuting your husband? It's a must!"

"Really, Van!" exclaimed angry Cordula. "You go a bit far. I'm a happy wife. My Tobachok adores me. We'd have ten children by now if I'd not been careful with him and others."

"You'll be glad to learn that this other has been found utterly sterile."

"Well, I'm anything but. I guess I'd cause a mule to foal by just looking on. Moreover, I'm lunching today with the Goals."

"*C'est bizarre*, an exciting little girl like you who can be so tender with poodles and yet turns down a poor paunchy stiff old Veen."

"The Veens are much too gay as dogs go."

"Since you collect adages," persisted Van, "let me quote an Arabian one. Paradise is only one assbaa south of a pretty girl's sash. *Eh bien?*"

"You are impossible. Where and when?"

"Where? In that drab little hotel across the street. When? Right now. I've never seen you on a hobbyhorse yet, because that's what *tout confort* promises—and not much else."

"I must be home not later than eleven-thirty, it's almost eleven now."

"It will take five minutes. Please!"

Astraddle, she resembled a child braving her first merry-go-round. She made a rectangular *moue* as she used that vulgar contraption. Sad, sullen streetwalkers do it with expressionless faces, lips tightly closed. She rode it twice. Their brisk nub and its repetition lasted fifteen minutes in all, not five. Very pleased with himself, Van walked with her for a stretch through the brown and green Bois de Belleau in the direction of her *osobnyachyok* (small mansion).

"That reminds me," he said, "I no longer use our Alexis apartment. I've had some poor people live there these last seven or eight years—the family of a police officer who used to be a footman at Uncle Dan's place in the country. My policeman is dead now and his widow and three boys have gone back to Ladore. I want to relinquish that flat. Would you like to accept it as a belated wedding present from an admirer? Good. We shall do it again some day. Tomorrow I have to be in London and on the third my favorite liner, *Admiral Tobakoff*, will take me to Manhattan. *Au revoir*. Tell him to look out for low lintels. Antlers can be very sensitive when new. Greg Erminin tells me that Lucette is at the Alphonse Four?"

"That's right. And where's the other?"

"I think we'll part here. It's twenty minutes to twelve. You'd better toddle along."

"*Au revoir*. You're a very bad boy and I'm a very bad girl. But it was fun—even though you've been speaking to me not as you would to a lady friend but as you probably do to little whores. Wait. Here's a top secret address where you can always"—(fumbling in her handbag)—"reach me"—(finding a card with her husband's crest and scribbling a postal cryptograph)—"at Malbrook, Mayne, where I spend every August."

She looked around, rose on her toes like a ballerina, and kissed him on the mouth. Sweet Cordula!

3

The Bourbonian-chinned, dark, sleek-haired, ageless concierge, dubbed by Van in his blazer days "Alphonse Cinq," believed he had just seen Mlle Veen in the Récamier room where Vivian Vale's golden veils were on show. With a flick of coattail and a swing-gate click, Alphonse dashed out of his lodge and went to see. Van's eye over his umbrella crook traveled around a carousel of Sapsucker paperbacks (with that wee striped woodpecker on every spine): *The Gitanilla, Salzman, Salzman, Salzman, Invitation to a Climax, Squirt, The Go-go Gang, The Threshold of Pain, The Chimes of Chose, The Gitanilla*—here a Wall Street, very "patrician" colleague of Demon's, old Kithar K. L. Sween, who wrote verse, and the still older real-estate magnate Milton Eliot, went by without recognizing grateful Van, despite his being betrayed by several mirrors.

The concierge returned shaking his head. Out of the goodness of his heart Van gave him a Goal guinea and said he'd call again at one-thirty. He walked through the lobby (where the author of *Agonic Lines* and Mr. Eliot, *affalés*, with a great amount of jacket over their shoulders, *dans des fauteuils*, were comparing cigars) and, leaving the hotel by a side exit, crossed the rue des Jeunes Martyres for a drink at Ovenman's.

Upon entering, he stopped for a moment to surrender his coat; but he kept his black fedora and stick-slim umbrella as he had seen his father do in that sort of bawdy, albeit smart, place which decent women did not frequent—at least, un-escorted. He headed for the bar, and as he was in the act of wiping the lenses of his black-framed spectacles, made out, through the optical mist (Space's recent revenge!), the girl whose silhouette he recalled having seen now and then (much more distinctly!) ever since his pubescence, passing alone, drinking alone, always alone, like Blok's *Incognita*. It was a queer feeling—as of something replayed by mistake, part of a sentence misplaced on the proof sheet, a scene run prematurely, a repeated blemish, a wrong turn of time. He hastened to reequip his ears with the thick black bows of his glasses and went up to her in silence. For a minute he stood behind her, sideways to remembrance and reader (as she, too, was in regard to us and the bar), the crook of his silk-swathed cane lifted in profile almost up to his mouth. There she was, against the aureate backcloth of a sakarama screen next to the bar, toward which she was sliding, still upright, about to be seated, having already placed one white-gloved hand on the counter. She wore a high-necked, long-sleeved romantic black dress with an ample skirt, fitted bodice and ruffy collar, from the black soft corolla of which her long neck gracefully rose. With a rake's morose gaze we follow the pure proud line of that throat, of that tilted chin. The glossy red lips are parted, avid and fey, offering a side gleam of large upper teeth. We know, we love that high cheekbone (with an atom of powder puff sticking to the hot pink skin), and the forward upsweep of black lashes and the painted feline eye—

[489]

all this in profile, we softly repeat. From under the wavy wide brim of her floppy hat of black faille, with a great black bow surmounting it, a spiral of intentionally disarranged, expertly curled bright copper descends her flaming cheek, and the light of the bar's "gem bulbs" plays on her *bouffant* front hair, which, as seen laterally, convexes from beneath the extravagant brim of the picture hat right down to her long thin eyebrow. Her Irish profile sweetened by a touch of Russian softness, which adds a look of mysterious expectancy and wistful surprise to her beauty, must be seen, I hope, by the friends and admirers of my memories, as a natural masterpiece incomparably finer and younger than the portrait of the similarly postured lousy jade with her Parisian *gueule de guenon* on the vile poster painted by that wreck of an artist for Ovenman.

"Hullo there, Ed," said Van to the barman, and she turned at the sound of his dear rasping voice.

"I didn't expect you to wear glasses. You almost got *le paquet*, which I was preparing for the man supposedly 'goggling' my hat. Darling Van! *Dushka moy!*"

"Your hat," he said, "is positively lautréamontesque—I mean, lautrecaquesque—no, I can't form the adjective."

Ed Barton served Lucette what she called a Chambéryzette.

"Gin and bitter for me."

"I'm so happy and sad," she murmured in Russian. "*Moyo grustnoe schastie!* How long will you be in old Lute?"

Van answered he was leaving next day for England, and then on June 3 (this was May 31) would be taking the *Admiral Tobakoff* back to the States. She would sail with him, she cried, it was a marvelous idea, she didn't mind whither to drift, really, West, East, Toulouse, Los Teques. He pointed out that it was far too late to obtain a cabin (on that not very grand ship so much shorter than *Queen Guinevere*), and changed the subject.

"The last time I saw you," said Van, "was two years ago, at a railway station. You had just left Villa Armina and I had just arrived. You wore a flowery dress which got mixed with the flowers you carried because you moved so fast—jumping out of a green calèche and up into the Ausonian Express that had brought me to Nice."

"*Très expressioniste*. I did not see you or I would have stopped to tell you what I had just learned. Imagine, mother knew everything—your garrulous dad told her everything about Ada and you!"

"But not about you and her."

Lucette asked him not to mention that sickening, maddening girl. She was furious with Ada and jealous by proxy. Her Andrey, or rather his sister on his behalf, he was too stupid even for that, collected progressive philistine Art, bootblack blotches and excremental smears on canvas, imitations of an imbecile's doodles, primitive idols, aboriginal masks, *objets trouvés*, or rather *troués*, the polished log with its polished hole à la Heinrich Heideland. His bride found the ranch yard adorned with a sculpture, if that's the right word, by old Heinrich himself and his four hefty assistants, a huge hideous lump of bourgeois mahogany ten feet high, entitled "Maternity," the mother (in reverse) of all the plaster gnomes and pig-iron toadstools planted by former Vinelanders in front of their dachas in Lyaska.

The barman stood wiping a glass in endless slow motion as he listened to Lucette's denunciation with the limp smile of utter enchantment.

"And yet (*odnako*)," said Van in Russian, "you enjoyed your stay there, in 1896, so Marina told me."

"I did not (*nichego podobnago*)! I left Agavia minus my

[491]

luggage in the middle of the night, with sobbing Brigitte. I've never seen such a household. Ada had turned into a dumb *brune.* The table talk was limited to the three C's—cactuses, cattle, and cooking, with Dorothy adding her comments on cubist mysticism. He's one of those Russians who *shlyopayut* (slap) to the toilet barefoot, shave in their underwear, wear garters, consider hitching up one's pants indecent, but when fishing out coins hold their right trouser pocket with the left hand or vice versa, which is not only indecent but vulgar. Demon is, perhaps, disappointed they don't have children, but really he 'engripped' the man after the first flush of father-in-law-hood. Dorothy is a prissy and pious monster who comes to stay for months, orders the meals, and has a private collection of keys to the servants' rooms—which our dumb brunette should have known—and other little keys to open people's hearts—she has tried, by the way, to make a practicing Orthodox not only of every American Negro she can catch, but of our sufficiently *pravoslavnaya* mother—though she only succeeded in making the Trimurti stocks go up. One beautiful, nostalgic night—"

"*Po-russki,*" said Van, noticing that an English couple had ordered drinks and settled down to some quiet auditing.

"*Kak-to noch'yu* (one night), when Andrey was away having his tonsils removed or something, dear watchful Dorochka went to investigate a suspicious noise in my maid's room and found poor Brigitte fallen asleep in the rocker and Ada and me *tryahnuvshih starinoy* (reshaking old times) on the bed. That's when I told Dora I would not stand her attitude, and immediately left for Monarch Bay."

"Some people are certainly odd," said Van. "If you've finished that sticky stuff let's go back to your hotel and get some lunch."

She wanted fish, he stuck to cold cuts and salad.

"You know whom I ran into this morning? Good old Greg Erminin. It was he who told me you were around. His wife *est un peu snob*, what?"

"Everybody is *un peu snob*," said Lucette. "Your Cordula, who is also around, cannot forgive Shura Tobak, the violinist, for being her husband's neighbor in the telephone book. Immediately after lunch, we'll go to my room, a numb twenty-five, my age. I have a fabulous Japanese divan and lots of orchids just supplied by one of my beaux. Ach, *Bozhe moy* —it has just occurred to me—I shall have to look into this— maybe they are meant for Brigitte, who is marrying after tomorrow, at three-thirty, a head waiter at the Alphonse Trois, in Auteuil. Anyway they are greenish, with orange and purple blotches, some kind of delicate *Oncidium*, 'cypress frogs,' one of those silly commercial names. I'll stretch out upon the divan like a martyr, remember?"

"Are you still half-a-martyr—I mean half-a-virgin?" inquired Van.

"A quarter," answered Lucette. "Oh, try me, Van! My divan is black with yellow cushions."

"You can sit for a minute in my lap."

"No—unless we undress and you ganch me."

"My dear, as I've often reminded you, you belong to a princely family but you talk like the loosest Lucinda imaginable. Is it a fad in your set, Lucette?"

"I have no set, I'm a loner. Once in a while, I go out with two diplomats, a Greek and an Englishman, who are allowed to paw me and play with each other. A corny society painter is working on my portrait and he and his wife caress me when I'm in the mood. Your friend Dick Cheshire sends me presents and racing tips. It's a dull life, Van.

"I enjoy—oh, loads of things," she continued in a melancholy, musing tone of voice, as she poked with a fork at her blue trout which, to judge by its contorted shape and bulging eyes, had boiled alive, convulsed by awful agonies. "I love Flemish and Dutch oils, flowers, food, Flaubert, Shakespeare, shopping, sheeing, swimming, the kisses of beauties and beasts—but somehow all of it, this sauce and all the riches of Holland, form only a kind of *tonen'kiy-tonen'kiy* (thin little) layer, under which there is absolutely nothing, except, of course, your image, and that only adds depth and a trout's agonies to the emptiness. I'm like Dolores—when she says she's 'only a picture painted on air.'"

"Never could finish that novel—much too pretentious."

"Pretentious but true. It's exactly my sense of existing—a fragment, a wisp of color. Come and travel with me to some distant place, where there are frescoes and fountains, why can't we travel to some distant place with ancient fountains? By ship? By sleeping car?"

"It's safer and faster by plane," said Van. "And for Log's sake, speak Russian."

Mr. Sween, lunching with a young fellow who sported a bullfighter's sideburns and other charms, bowed gravely in the direction of their table; then a naval officer in the azure uniform of the Gulfstream Guards passed by in the wake of a dark, ivory-pale lady and said: "Hullo Lucette, hullo, Van."

"Hullo, Alph," said Van, whilst Lucette acknowledged the greeting with an absent smile: over her propped-up entwined hands she was following with mocking eyes the receding lady. Van cleared his throat as he gloomily glanced at his half-sister.

"Must be at least thirty-five," murmured Lucette, "yet still hopes to become his queen."

(His father, Alphonse the First of Portugal, a puppet potentate manipulated by Uncle Victor, had recently abdicated upon Gamaliel's suggestion in favor of a republican re-

[494]

gime, but Lucette spoke of fragile beauty, not fickle politics.)

"That was Lenore Colline. What's the matter, Van?"

"Cats don't stare at stars, it's not done. The resemblance is much less close than it used to be—though, of course, I've not kept up with counterpart changes. A *propos*, how's the career been progressing?"

"If you mean Ada's career, I hope it's also a flop, the same as her marriage. So my getting you will be all Demon gains. I don't go often to movies, and I refused to speak to Dora and her when we met at the funeral and haven't the remotest idea of what her stage or screen exploits may have been lately."

"Did that woman tell her brother about your innocent frolics?"

"Of course not! She *drozhit* (trembles) over his bliss. But I'm sure it was she who forced Ada to write me that I 'must never try again to wreck a successful marriage'—and this I forgive Daryushka, a born blackmailer, but not Adochka. I don't care for your cabochon. I mean it's all right on your dear hairy hand, but Papa wore one like that on his hateful pink paw. He belonged to the silent-explorer type. Once he took me to a girls' hockey match and I had to warn him I'd yell for help if he didn't call off the search."

"*Das auch noch,*" sighed Van, and pocketed the heavy dark-sapphire ring. He would have put it into the ashtray had it not been Marina's last present.

"Look, Van," she said (finishing her fourth flute). "Why not risk it? Everything is quite simple. You marry me. You get my Ardis. We live there, you write there. I keep melting into the background, never bothering you. We invite Ada— alone, of course—to stay for a while on *her* estate, for I had always expected mother to leave Ardis to her. While she's there, I go to Aspen or Gstaad, or Schittau, and you live with her in solid crystal with snow falling as if forever all around *pendant que je* shee in Aspenis. Then I come back like a shot, but she can stay on, she's welcome, I'll hang around in case you two want me. And then she goes back to her husband for a couple of dreary months, see?"

"Yes, magnificent plan," said Van. "The only trouble is: she will never come. It's now three o'clock, I have to see a man who is to renovate Villa Armina which *I* inherited and which will house one of my harems. Slapping a person's wrist that way is not your prettiest mannerism on the Irish side. I shall now escort you to your apartment. You are plainly in need of some rest."

"I have an important, important telephone call to make, but I don't want you to listen," said Lucette searching for the key in her little black handbag.

They entered the hall of her suite. There, firmly resolved to leave in a moment, he removed his glasses and pressed his mouth to her mouth, and she tasted exactly as Ada at Ardis, in the early afternoon, sweet saliva, salty epithelium, cherries, coffee. Had he not sported so well and so recently, he might not have withstood the temptation, the impardonable thrill. She plucked at his sleeve as he started to back out of the hallway.

"Let us kiss again, let us kiss again!" Lucette kept repeating, childishly, lispingly, barely moving her parted lips, in a fussy incoherent daze, doing her best to prevent him from thinking it over, from saying no.

He said that would do.

"Oh but why? Oh please!"

He brushed away her cold trembling fingers.

"Why, Van? Why, why, why?"

"You know perfectly well why. I love her, not you, and I

simply refuse to complicate matters by entering into yet another incestuous relationship."

"That's rich," said Lucette, "you've gone far enough with me on several occasions, even when I was a kid; your refusing to go further is a mere quibble on your part; and besides, besides you've been unfaithful to her with a thousand girls, you dirty cheat!"

"You shan't talk to me in that tone," said Van, meanly turning her poor words into a pretext for marching away.

"I apollo, I love you," she whispered frantically, trying to *cry* after him in a *whisper* because the corridor was all door and ears, but he walked on, waving both arms in the air without looking back, quite forgivingly, though, and was gone.

4

A teasy problem demanded Dr. Veen's presence in England. Old Paar of Chose had written him that the "Clinic" would like him to study a singular case of chromesthesia, but that given certain aspects of the case (such as a faint possibility of trickery) Van should come and decide for himself whether he thought it worth the trouble to fly the patient to Kingston for further observation. One Spencer Muldoon, born eyeless, aged forty, single, friendless, and the third blind character in this chronicle, had been known to hallucinate during fits of violent paranoia, calling out the names of such shapes and substances as he had learned to identify by touch, or thought he recognized through the awfulness of stories about them (falling trees, extinct saurians) and which now pressed on him from all sides, alternating with periods of stupor, followed invariably by a return to his normal self, when for a week or two he would finger his blind books or listen, in red-lidded bliss, to records of music, bird songs, and Irish poetry.

His ability to break space into ranks and files of "strong" and "weak" things in what seemed a wallpaper pattern remained a mystery until one evening, when a research student

(R.S.—he wished to remain that way), who intended to trace certain graphs having to do with the metabasis of another patient, happened to leave within Muldoon's reach one of those elongated boxes of new, unsharpened, colored-chalk pencils whose mere evocation (Dixon Pink Anadel!) make one's memory speak in the language of rainbows, the tints of their painted and polished woods being graded spectrally in their neat tin container. Poor Muldoon's childhood could not come to him with anything like *such* iridian recall, but when his groping fingers opened the box and palpated the pencils, a certain expression of sensual relish appeared on his parchment-pale face. Upon observing that the blind man's eyebrows went up slightly at red, higher at orange, still higher at the shrill scream of yellow and then stepped down through the rest of the prismatic spectrum, R.S. casually told him that the woods were dyed differently—"red," "orange," "yellow," et cetera, and quite as casually Muldoon rejoined that they also felt different one from another.

In the course of several tests conducted by R.S. and his colleagues, Muldoon explained that by stroking the pencils in turn he perceived a gamut of "stingles," special sensations somehow allied to the tingling aftereffects of one's skin contact with stinging nettles (he had been raised in the country somewhere between Ormagh and Armagh, and had often tumbled, in his adventurous boyhood, the poor thick-booted soul, into ditches and even ravines), and spoke eerily of the "strong" green stingle of a piece of blotting paper or the wet weak pink stingle of nurse Langford's perspiring nose, these colors being checked by himself against those applied by the researchers to the initial pencils. In result of the tests, one was forced to assume that the man's fingertips could convey to his brain "a tactile transcription of the prismatic specter" as Paar put it in his detailed report to Van.

When the latter arrived, Muldoon had not quite come out of a state of stupor more protracted than any preceding one. Van, hoping to examine him on the morrow, spent a delightful day conferring with a bunch of eager psychologists and was interested to spot among the nurses the familiar squint of Elsie Langford, a gaunt girl with a feverish flush and protruding teeth, who had been obscurely involved in a "poltergeist" affair at another medical institution. He had dinner with old Paar in his rooms at Chose and told him he would like to have the poor fellow transferred to Kingston, *with* Miss Langford, as soon as he was fit to travel. The poor fellow died that night in his sleep, leaving the entire incident suspended in midair within a nimbus of bright irrelevancy.

Van, in whom the pink-blooming chestnuts of Chose always induced an amorous mood, decided to squander the sudden bounty of time before his voyage to America on a twenty-four-hour course of treatment at the most fashionable and efficient of all the Venus Villas in Europe; but during the longish trip in the ancient, plushy, faintly perfumed (musk? Turkish tobacco?) limousine which he usually got from the Albania, his London hotel, for travels in England, other restless feelings joined, without dispelling it, his sullen lust. Rocking along softly, his slippered foot on a footrest, his arm in an armloop, he recalled his first railway journey to Ardis and tried—what he sometimes advised a patient doing in order to exercise the "muscles of consciousness"—namely putting oneself back not merely into the frame of mind that had preceded a radical change in one's life, but into a state of complete ignorance regarding that change. He knew it could not be done, that not the achievement, but the obstinate attempt was possible, because he would not have remembered the preface to Ada had not life turned the next page, causing now its radiant text to flash through all the tenses of the mind. He wondered if he would remember the present commonplace trip. An English late spring with literary associations lingered in the evening air. The built-in "canoreo" (an old-fashioned musical gadget which a joint Anglo-American Commission had only recently unbanned) transmitted a heart-wounding Italian song. What was he? Who was he? Why was he? He thought of his slackness, clumsiness, dereliction of spirit. He thought of his loneliness, of its passions and dangers. He saw through the glass partition the fat, healthy, reliable folds of his driver's neck. Idle images queued by—Edmund, Edmond, simple Cordula, fantastically intricate Lucette, and, by further mechanical association, a depraved little girl called Lisette, in Cannes, with breasts like lovely abscesses, whose frail favors were handled by a smelly big brother in an old bathing machine.

He turned off the canoreo and helped himself to the brandy stored behind a sliding panel, drinking from the bottle, because all three glasses were filthy. He felt surrounded by crashing great trees, and the monstrous beasts of unachieved, perhaps unachievable tasks. One such task was Ada whom he knew he would never give up; to her he would surrender the remnants of his self at the first trumpet blast of destiny. Another was his philosophic work, so oddly impeded by its own virtue—by that originality of literary style which constitutes the only real honesty of a writer. He had to do it his own way, but the cognac was frightful, and the history of thought bristled with clichés, and it was that history he had to surmount.

He knew he was not quite a savant, but completely an artist. Paradoxically and unnecessarily it had been in his "academic career," in his nonchalant and arrogant lectures, in his conduct of seminars, in his published reports on sick minds, that, starting as something of a prodigy before he was twenty, he had gained by the age of thirty-one "honors" and a "position" that many unbelievably laborious men do not reach at fifty. In his sadder moments, as now, he attributed at least part of his "success" to his rank, to his wealth, to the numerous donations, which (in a kind of extension of his overtipping the haggard beggars who cleaned rooms, manned lifts, smiled in hotel corridors) he kept showering upon worthwhile institutions and students. Maybe Van Veen did not err too widely in his wry conjecture; for on our Antiterra (and on Terra as well, according to his own writings) a powerfully plodding Administration prefers, unless moved by the sudden erection of a new building or the thunder of torrential funds, the safe drabness of an academic mediocrity to the suspect sparkle of a V.V.

Nightingales sang, when he arrived at his fabulous and ignoble destination. As usual, he experienced a surge of brutal elation as the car entered the oak avenue between two rows of phallephoric statues presenting arms. A welcome habitué of fifteen years' standing, he had not bothered to "telephone" (the new official term). A searchlight lashed him: Alas, he had come on a "gala" night!

Members usually had their chauffeurs park in a special enclosure near the guardhouse, where there was a pleasant canteen for servants, with nonalcoholic drinks and a few inexpensive and homely whores. But that night several huge police cars occupied the garage boxes and overflowed into an adjacent arbor. Telling Kingsley to wait a moment under the oaks, Van donned his *bautta* and went to investigate. His favorite walled walk soon took him to one of the spacious lawns velveting the approach to the manor. The grounds were lividly illuminated and as populous as Park Avenue—an association that came very readily, since the disguises of the astute sleuths belonged to a type which reminded Van of his native land. Some of those men he even knew by sight—they used to patrol his father's club in Manhattan whenever good Gamaliel (not reelected after his fourth term) happened to dine there in his informal gagality. They mimed what they were accustomed to mime—grapefruit vendors, black hawkers of bananas and banjoes, obsolete, or at least untimely, "copying clerks" who hurried in circles to unlikely offices, and peripatetic Russian newspaper readers slowing down to a trance stop and then strolling again behind their wide open *Estotskiya Vesti*. Van remembered that Mr. Alexander Screepatch, the new president of the United Americas, a plethoric Russian, had flown over to see King Victor; and he correctly concluded that both were now sunk in mollitude. The comic side of the detectives' display (befitting, perhaps, their dated notion of an American sidewalk, but hardly suiting a weirdly illumined maze of English hedges) tempered his disappointment as he shuddered squeamishly at the thought of sharing the frolics of historical personages or contenting himself with the brave-faced girlies they had started to use and rejected.

Here a bedsheeted statue attempted to challenge Van from its marble pedestal but slipped and landed on its back in the bracken. Ignoring the sprawling god, Van returned to the still-throbbing jolls-joyce. Purple-jowled Kingsley, an old tried friend, offered to drive him to another house, ninety miles north; but Van declined upon principle and was taken back to the Albania.

5

At five P.M., June 3, his ship had sailed from Le Havre-de-Grâce; on the evening of the same day Van embarked at Old Hantsport. He had spent most of the afternoon playing court tennis with Delaurier, the famous Negro coach, and felt very dull and drowsy as he watched the low sun's ardency break into green-golden eye-spots a few sea-serpent yards to starboard, on the far-side slope of the bow wave. Presently he decided to turn in, walked down to the A deck, devoured some of the still-life fruit prepared for him in his sitting room, attempted to read in bed the proofs of an essay he was contributing to a festschrift on the occasion of Professor Counterstone's eightieth birthday, gave it up, and fell asleep. A tempest went into convulsions around midnight, but despite the lunging and creaking (*Tobakoff* was an embittered old vessel) Van managed to sleep soundly, the only reaction on the part of his dormant mind being the dream image of an aquatic peacock, slowly sinking before somersaulting like a diving grebe, near the shore of the lake bearing his name in the ancient kingdom of Arrowroot. Upon reviewing that bright dream he traced its source to his recent visit to Armenia where he had gone fowling with Armborough and that gentleman's extremely compliant and accomplished niece. He wanted to make a note of it—and was amused to find that all three pencils had not only left his bed table but had neatly aligned themselves head to tail along the bottom of the outer door of the adjacent room, having covered quite a stretch of blue carpeting in the course of their stopped escape.

The steward brought him a "Continental" breakfast, the ship's newspaper, and the list of first-class passengers. Under "Tourism in Italy," the little newspaper informed him that a Domodossola farmer had unearthed the bones and trappings of one of Hannibal's elephants, and that two American Psychiatrists (names not given) had died an odd death in the Bocaletto range: the older fellow from heart failure and his boy friend by suicide. After pondering the Admiral's morbid interest in Italian mountains, Van clipped the item and picked up the passenger list (pleasingly surmounted by the same crest that adorned Cordula's notepaper) in order to see if there was anybody to be avoided during the next days. The list yielded the Robinson couple, Robert and Rachel, old bores of the family (Bob had retired after directing for many years one of Uncle Dan's offices). His gaze, traveling on, tripped over Dr. Ivan Veen and pulled up at the next name. What constricted his heart? Why did he pass his tongue over his thick lips? Empty formulas befitting the solemn novelists of former days who thought they could explain everything.

The level of the water slanted and swayed in his bath imitating the slow seesaw of the bright-blue, white-flecked sea in the porthole of his bedroom. He rang up Miss Lucinda Veen, whose suite was on the Main Deck amidships exactly above his, but she was absent. Wearing a white polo-neck sweater and tinted glasses, he went to look for her. She was not on the Games Deck from where he looked down at some other redhead, in a canvas chair on the Sun Deck: the girl sat writing a letter at passionate speed and he thought that if ever he switched from ponderous factitude to light fiction he would have a jealous husband use binoculars to decipher from where he stood that outpour of illicit affection.

She was not on the Promenade Deck where blanket-swathed old people were reading the number-one best seller *Salzman* and awaiting with borborygmic forebubbles the eleven o'clock bouillon. He betook himself to the Grill, where he reserved a table for two. He walked over to the bar and warmly greeted bald fat Toby who had served on the *Queen Guinevere* in 1889, and 1890, and 1891, when she was still unmarried and he a resentful fool. They could have eloped to Lopadusa as Mr. and Mrs. Dairs or Sardi!

He espied their half-sister on the forecastle deck, looking perilously pretty in a low-cut, brightly flowered, wind-worried frock, talking to the bronzed but greatly aged Robinsons. She turned toward him, brushing back the flying hair from her face with a mixture of triumph and embarrassment in her expression, and presently they took leave of Rachel and Robert who beamed after them, waving similarly raised hands to her, to him, to life, to death, to the happy old days when Demon paid all the gambling debts of their son, just before he was killed in a head-on car collision.

She dispatched the *pozharskiya kotleti* with gratitude: he was not scolding her for popping up as some sort of transcendental (rather than transatlantic) stowaway; and in her eagerness to see him she had botched her breakfast after having gone dinnerless on the eve. She who enjoyed the hollows and hills of the sea, when taking part in nautical sports, or the ups and oops, when flying, had been ignominiously sick aboard this, her first liner; but the Robinsons had given her a marvelous medicine, she had slept ten hours, in Van's arms all the time, and now hoped that both he and she were tolerably awake except for the fuzzy edge left by the drug.

Quite kindly he asked where she thought she was going.

To Ardis, with him—came the prompt reply—for ever and ever. Robinson's grandfather had died in Araby at the age of one hundred and thirty-one, so Van had still a whole century before him, she would build for him, in the park, several pavilions to house his successive harems, they would gradually turn, one after the other, into homes for aged ladies, and then into mausoleums. There hung, she said, a steeplechase picture of "Pale Fire with Tom Cox Up" above dear Cordula's and Tobak's bed, in the suite "wangled in one minute flat" from them, and she wondered how it affected the Tobaks' love life during sea voyages. Van interrupted Lucette's nervous patter by asking her if her bath taps bore the same inscriptions as his: Hot Domestic, Cold Salt. Yes, she cried, Old Salt, Old Salzman, Ardent Chambermaid, Comatose Captain!

They met again in the afternoon.

To most of the Tobakoff's first-class passengers the afternoon of June 4, 1901, in the Atlantic, on the meridian of Iceland and the latitude of Ardis, seemed little conducive to open-air frolics: the fervor of its cobalt sky kept being cut by glacial gusts, and the wash of an old-fashioned swimming pool rhythmically flushed the green tiles, but Lucette was a hardy girl used to bracing winds no less than to the detestable sun. Spring in Fialta and a torrid May on Minataor, the famous artificial island, had given a nectarine hue to her limbs, which looked lacquered with it when wet, but re-evolved their natural bloom as the breeze dried her skin. With glowing cheekbones and that glint of copper showing from under her tight rubber cap on nape and forehead, she evoked the

Helmeted Angel of the Yukonsk Ikon whose magic effect was said to change anemic blond maidens into *konskie deti*, freckled red-haired lads, children of the Sun Horse.

She returned after a brief swim to the sun terrace where Van lay and said:

"You can't imagine"—("I can imagine anything," he insisted)—"you *can* imagine, okay, what oceans of lotions and streams of creams I am compelled to use—in the privacy of my balconies or in desolate sea caves—before I can exhibit myself to the elements. I always teeter on the tender border between sunburn and suntan—or between lobster and *Obst* as writes Herb, my beloved painter—I'm reading his diary published by his last duchess, it's in three mixed languages and lovely, I'll lend it to you. You see, darling, I'd consider myself a pied cheat if the small parts I conceal in public were not of the same color as those on show."

"You looked to me kind of sandy all over when you were inspected in 1892," said Van.

"I'm a brand-new girl now," she whispered. "A happy new girl. Alone with you on an abandoned ship, with ten days at least till my next flow. I sent you a silly note to Kingston, just in case you didn't turn up."

They were now reclining on a poolside mat face to face, in symmetrical attitudes, he leaning his head on his right hand, she propped on her left elbow. The strap of her green breast-cups had slipped down her slender arm, disclosing drops and streaks of water at the base of one nipple. An abyss of a few inches separated the jersey he wore from her bare midriff, the black wool of his trunks from her soaked green pubic mask. The sun glazed her hipbone; a shadowed dip led to the five-year-old trace of an appendectomy. Her half-veiled gaze dwelt upon him with heavy, opaque greed, and she was right, they were really quite alone, he had possessed Marion Armborough behind her uncle's back in much more complex circumstances, what with the motorboat jumping like a flying fish and his host keeping a shotgun near the steering wheel. Joylessly, he felt the stout snake of desire weightily unwind; grimly, he regretted not having exhausted the fiend in Villa Venus. He accepted the touch of her blind hand working its way up his thigh and cursed nature for having planted a gnarled tree bursting with vile sap within a man's crotch. Suddenly Lucette drew away, exhaling a genteel *"merde."* Eden was full of people.

Two half-naked children in shrill glee came running toward the pool. A Negro nurse brandished their diminutive bras in angry pursuit. Out of the water a bald head emerged by spontaneous generation and snorted. The swimming coach appeared from the dressing room. Simultaneously, a tall splendid creature with trim ankles and repulsively fleshy thighs stalked past the Veens, all but treading on Lucette's emerald-studded cigarette case. Except for a golden ribbon and a bleached mane, her long, ripply, beige back was bare all the way down to the tops of her slowly and lusciously rolling buttocks, which divulged, in alternate motion, their nether bulges from under the lamé loincloth. Just before disappearing behind a rounded white corner, the Titanesque Titaness half-turned her brown face and greeted Van with a loud "hullo!"

Lucette wanted to know: *kto siya pava?* (who's that stately dame?)

"I thought she addressed *you*," answered Van. "I did not distinguish her face and do not remember that bottom."

"She gave you a big jungle smile," said Lucette, readjusting her green helmet, with touchingly graceful movements of her raised wings, and touchingly flashing the russet feathering of her armpits.

"Come with me, hm?" she suggested, rising from the mat.

He shook his head, looking up at her: "You rise," he said, "like Aurora."

"His first compliment," observed Lucette with a little cock of her head as if speaking to an invisible confidant.

He put on his tinted glasses and watched her stand on the diving board, her ribs framing the hollow of her intake as she prepared to ardis into the amber. He wondered, in a mental footnote that might come handy some day, if sunglasses or any other varieties of vision, which certainly twist our concept of "space," do not also influence our style of speech. The two well-formed lassies, the nurse, the prurient merman, the natatorium master, all looked on with Van.

"Second compliment ready," he said as she returned to his side. "You're a divine diver. I go in with a messy plop."

"But you swim faster," she complained, slipping off her shoulder straps and turning into a prone position; "*Mezhdu prochim* (by the way), is it true that a sailor in Tobakoff's day was not taught to swim so he wouldn't die a nervous wreck if the ship went down?"

"A common sailor, perhaps," said Van. "When *michman* Tobakoff himself got shipwrecked off Gavaille, he swam around comfortably for hours, frightening away sharks with snatches of old songs and that sort of thing, until a fishing boat rescued him—one of those miracles that require a minimum of cooperation from all concerned, I imagine."

Demon, she said, had told her, last year at the funeral, that he was buying an island in the Gavailles ("incorrigible dreamer," drawled Van). He had "wept like a fountain" in Nice, but had cried with even more abandon in Valentina, at an earlier ceremony, which poor Marina did not attend either. The wedding—in the Greek-faith style, if you please—looked like a badly faked episode in an old movie, the priest was gaga and the *dyakon* drunk, and—perhaps, fortunately—Ada's thick white veil was as impervious to light as a widow's weeds. Van said he would not listen to that.

"Oh, you must," she rejoined, "*hotya bï potomu* (if only because) one of her *shafer*'s (bachelors who take turns holding the wedding crown over the bride's head) looked momentarily, in impassive profile and impertinent attitude (he kept raising the heavy metallic *venets* too high, too athletically high as if trying on purpose to keep it as far as possible from her head), exactly like you, like a pale, ill-shaven twin, delegated by you from wherever you were."

At a place nicely called Agony, in Terra del Fuego. He felt an uncanny tingle as he recalled that when he received there the invitation to the wedding (airmailed by the groom's sinister sister) he was haunted for several nights by dream after dream, growing fainter each time (much as her movie he was to pursue from flick-house to flick-house at a later stage of his life) of his holding that crown over her.

"Your father," added Lucette, "paid a man from *Belladonna* to take pictures—but of course, real fame begins only when one's name appears in that cine-magazine's crossword puzzle. We all know it will never happen, never! Do you hate me now?"

"I don't," he said, passing his hand over her sun-hot back and rubbing her coccyx to make pussy purr. "Alas, I don't! I love you with a brother's love and maybe still more tenderly. Would you like me to order drinks?"

"I'd like you to go on and on," she muttered, her nose buried in the rubber pillow.

"There's that waiter coming. What shall we have—Honoloolers?"

"You'll have them with Miss Condor" (nasalizing the first syllable) "when I go to dress. For the moment I want only

[511]

tea. Mustn't mix drugs and drinks. Have to take the famous Robinson pill sometime tonight. Sometime tonight."

"Two teas, please."

"And lots of sandwiches, George. Foie gras, ham, anything."

"It's very bad manners," remarked Van, "to invent a name for a poor chap who can't answer: 'Yes, Mademoiselle Condor.' Best Franco-English pun I've ever heard, incidentally."

"But his name *is* George. He was awfully kind to me yesterday when I threw up in the middle of the tearoom."

"For the sweet all is sweet," murmured Van.

"And so were the old Robinsons," she rambled on. "Not much chance, is there, they might turn up here? They've been sort of padding after me, rather pathetically, ever since we happened to have lunch at the same table on the boat-train, and I realized who they were but was sure they would not recognize the little fat girl seen in eighteen eighty-five or -six, but they were hypnotically talkative—at first we thought you were French, this salmon is really delicious, what's your home town?—and I'm a weak fool, and one thing led to another. Young people are less misled by the passage of time than the established old who have not much changed lately and are not used to the long-unseen young changing."

"That's very clever, darling," said Van "—except that time itself is motionless and changeless."

"Yes, it's always *I* in your lap and the receding road. Roads move?"

"Roads move."

After tea Lucette remembered an appointment with the hairdresser and left in a hurry. Van peeled off his jersey and stayed on for a while, brooding, fingering the little green-gemmed case with five Rosepetal cigarettes, trying to enjoy the heat of the platinum sun in its aura of "film-color" but only managing to fan, with every shiver and heave of the ship, the fire of evil temptation.

A moment later, as if having spied on his solitude the *pava* (peahen) reappeared—this time with an apology.

Polite Van, scrambling up to his feet and browing his spectacles, started to apologize in his turn (for misleading her innocently) but his little speech petered out in stupefaction as he looked at her face and saw in it a gross and grotesque caricature of unforgettable features. That mulatto skin, that silver-blond hair, those fat purple lips, reinacted in coarse negative *her* ivory, *her* raven, *her* pale pout.

"I was told," she explained, "that a great friend of mine, Vivian Vale, the cootooriay—voozavay *entendue?*—had shaved his beard, in which case he'd look rather like you, right?"

"Logically, no, ma'am," replied Van.

She hesitated for the flirt of a second, licking her lips, not knowing whether he was being rude or ready—and here Lucette returned for her Rosepetals.

"See you aprey," said Miss Condor.

Lucette's gaze escorted to a good-riddance exit the indolent motion of those gluteal lobes and folds.

"You deceived me, Van. It is, it *is* one of your gruesome girls!"

"I swear," said Van, "that she's a perfect stranger. I wouldn't deceive you."

"You deceived me many, many times when I was a little girl. If you're doing it now *tu sais que j'en vais mourir*."

"You promised me a harem," Van gently rebuked her.

"Not today, not today! Today is sacred."

The cheek he intended to kiss was replaced by her quick mad mouth.

"Come and see my cabin," she pleaded as he pushed her

away with the very spring, as it were, of his animal reaction to the fire of her lips and tongue. "I simply must show you their pillows and piano. There's Cordula's smell in all the drawers. I beseech you!"

"Run along now," said Van. "You've no right to excite me like that. I'll hire Miss Condor to chaperone me if you do not behave yourself. We dine at seven-fifteen."

In his bedroom he found a somewhat belated invitation to the Captain's table for dinner. It was addressed to Dr. and Mrs. Ivan Veen. He had been on the ship once before, in between the *Queens*, and remembered Captain Cowley as a bore and an ignoramus.

He called the steward and bade him carry the note back, with the penciled scrawl: "no such couple." He lay in his bath for twenty minutes. He attempted to focus on something else besides a hysterical virgin's body. He discovered an insidious omission in his galleys where an entire line was wanting, with the vitiated paragraph looking, however, quite plausible—to an automatic reader—since the truncated end of one sentence, and the lower-case beginning of the other, now adjacent, fitted to form a syntactically correct passage, the insipidity of which he might never have noticed in the present folly of his flesh, had he not recollected (a recollection confirmed by his typescript) that at this point should have come a rather apt, all things considered, quotation: *Insiste, anime meus, et adtende fortiter* (courage, my soul and press on strongly).

"Sure you'd not prefer the restaurant?" he inquired when Lucette, looking even more naked in her short evening frock than she had in her "bickny," joined him at the door of the grill. "It's crowded and gay down there, with a masturbating jazzband. No?"

Tenderly she shook her jeweled head.

[514]

They had huge succulent "grugru shrimps" (the yellow larvae of a palm weevil) and roast bearlet à la Tobakoff. Only half-a-dozen tables were occupied, and except for a nasty engine vibration, which they had not noticed at lunch, everything was subdued, soft, and cozy. He took advantage of her odd demure silence to tell her in detail about the late pencil-palpating Mr. Muldoon and also about a Kingston case of glossolalia involving a Yukonsk woman who spoke several Slavic-like dialects which existed, maybe, on Terra, but certainly not in Estotiland. Alas, another case (with a quibble on *cas*) engaged his attention subverbally.

She asked questions with pretty co-ed looks of doelike devotion, but it did not require much scientific training on a professor's part to perceive that her charming embarrassment and the low notes furring her voice were as much contrived as her afternoon effervescence had been. Actually she thrashed in the throes of an emotional disarray which only the heroic self-control of an American aristocrat could master. Long ago she had made up her mind that by forcing the man whom she absurdly but irrevocably loved to have intercourse with her, even once, she would, somehow, with the help of some prodigious act of nature, transform a brief tactile event into an eternal spiritual tie; but she also knew that if it did not happen on the first night of their voyage, their relationship would slip back into the exhausting, hopeless, hopelessly familiar pattern of banter and counterbanter, with the erotic edge taken for granted, but kept as raw as ever. He understood her condition or at least believed, in despair, that he *had* understood it, retrospectively, by the time no remedy except Dr. Henry's oil of Atlantic prose could be found in the medicine chest of the past with its banging door and toppling toothbrush.

As he gloomily looked at her thin bare shoulders, so mobile

and tensile that one wondered if she could not cross them in front of her like stylized angel wings, he reflected abjectly that he would have to endure, if conforming to his innermost code of honor, five such days of ruttish ache—not only because she was lovely and special but because he could never go without girl pleasure for more than forty-eight hours. He feared precisely that which she wanted to happen: that once he had tasted her wound and its grip, she would keep him insatiably captive for weeks, maybe months, maybe more, but that a harsh separation would inevitably come, with a new hope and the old despair never able to strike a balance. But worst of all, while aware, and ashamed, of lusting after a sick child, he felt, in an obscure twist of ancient emotions, his lust sharpened by the shame.

They had sweet, thick Turkish coffee and surreptitiously he looked at his wrist watch to check—what? How long the torture of self-denial could still be endured? How soon were certain events coming such as a ballroom dance competition? Her age? (Lucinda Veen was only five hours old if one reversed the human "time current.")

She was such a pathetic darling that, as they proceeded to leave the grill, he could not help, for sensuality is the best breeding broth of fatal error, caressing her glossy young shoulder so as to fit for an instant, the happiest in her life, its ideal convexity bilboquet-wise within the hollow of his palm. Then she walked before him as conscious of his gaze as if she were winning a prize for "poise." He could describe her dress only as struthious (if there existed copper-curled ostriches), accentuating as it did the swing of her stance, the length of her legs in ninon stockings. Objectively speaking, her chic was keener than that of her "vaginal" sister. As they crossed landings where velvet ropes were being hastily stretched by Russian sailors (who glanced with sympathy at the handsome pair speaking their incomparable tongue) or walked this or that deck, Lucette made him think of some acrobatic creature immune to the rough seas. He saw with gentlemanly displeasure that her tilted chin and black wings, and free stride, attracted not only blue innocent eyes but the bold stare of lewd fellow passengers. He loudly exclaimed that he would slap the next jackanapes, and involuntarily walked backward with ridiculous truculent gestures into a folded deck chair (he also running the reel of time backward, in a minor way), which caused her to emit a yelp of laughter. Feeling now much happier, enjoying his gallant champagne-temper, she steered Van away from the mirage of her admirers, back to the lift.

They examined without much interest the objects of pleasure in a display window. Lucette sneered at a gold-threaded swimsuit. The presence of a riding crop and a pickax puzzled Van. Half a dozen glossy-jacketed copies of *Salzman* were impressively heaped between a picture of the handsome, thoughtful, now totally forgotten, author and a Mingo-Bingo vase of immortelles.

He clutched at a red rope and they entered the lounge.

"Whom did she look like?" asked Lucette. "*En laid et en lard?*"

"I don't know," he lied. "Whom?"

"Skip it," she said. "You're mine tonight. Mine, mine, mine!"

She was quoting Kipling—the same phrase that Ada used to address to Dack. He cast around for a straw of Procrustean procrastination.

"Please," said Lucette, "I'm tired of walking around, I'm frail, I'm feverish, I hate storms, let's all go to bed!"

"Hey, look!" he cried, pointing to a poster. "They're show-

ing something called *Don Juan's Last Fling*. It's prerelease
and for adults only. Topical *Tobakoff!*"

"It's going to be an unmethylated bore," said Lucy
(Houssaie School, 1890) but he had already pushed aside the
entrance drapery.

They came in at the beginning of an introductory picture,
featuring a cruise to Greenland, with heavy seas in gaudy
technicolor. It was a rather irrelevant trip since their *Tobakoff*
did not contemplate calling at Godhavn; moreover, the cinema theater was swaying in counterrhythm to the cobalt-
and-emerald swell on the screen. No wonder the place was
emptovato, as Lucette observed, and she went on to say
that the Robinsons had saved her life by giving her on the eve
a tubeful of Quietus Pills.

"Want one? One a day keeps 'no shah' away. Pun. You
can chew it, it's sweet."

"Jolly good name. No, thank you, my sweet. Besides you
have only five left."

"Don't worry, I have it all planned out. There may be less
than five days."

"More in fact, but no matter. Our measurements of time
are meaningless; the most accurate clock is a joke; you'll read
all about it someday, you just wait."

"Perhaps, not. I mean, perhaps I shan't have the patience.
I mean, his charwoman could never finish reading Leonardo's
palm. I may fall asleep before I get through your next book."

"An art-class legend," said Van.

"That's the final iceberg, I know by the music. Let's go,
Van! Or you want to see Hoole as Hooan?"

She brushed his cheek with her lips in the dark, she took
his hand, she kissed his knuckles, and he suddenly thought:
after all, why not? Tonight? Tonight.

He enjoyed her impatience, the fool permitted himself to

be stirred by it, the cretin whispered, prolonging the free, new, apricot fire of anticipation:

"If you're a good girl we'll have drinks in my sitting room at midnight."

The main picture had now started. The three leading parts —cadaverous Don Juan, paunchy Leporello on his donkey, and not too irresistible, obviously forty-year-old, Donna Anna —were played by solid stars, whose images passed by in "semi-stills," or as some say "translucencies," in a brief introduction. Contrary to expectations, the picture turned out to be quite good.

On the way to the remote castle where the difficult lady, widowed by his sword, has finally promised him a long night of love in her chaste and chilly chamber, the aging libertine nurses his potency by spurning the advances of a succession of robust belles. A *gitana* predicts to the gloomy cavalier that before reaching the castle he will have succumbed to the wiles of her sister, Dolores, a dancing girl (lifted from Osberg's novella, as was to be proved in the ensuing lawsuit). She also predicted something to Van, for even before Dolores came out of the circus tent to water Juan's horse, Van knew who she would be.

In the magic rays of the camera, in the controlled delirium of ballerina grace, ten years of her life had glanced off and she was again that slip of a girl *qui n'en porte pas* (as he had jested once to annoy her governess by a fictitious Frenchman's mistranslation): a remembered triviality that intruded upon the chill of his present emotion with the jarring stupidity of an innocent stranger's asking an absorbed voyeur for directions in a labyrinth of mean lanes.

Lucette recognized Ada three or four seconds later, but then clutched his wrist:

"Oh, how awful! It was bound to happen. That's she! Let's

go, please, let's go. You must not see her *debasing* herself. She's terribly made up, every gesture is childish and wrong—"

"Just another minute," said Van.

Terrible? Wrong? She was absolutely perfect, and strange, and poignantly familiar. By some stroke of art, by some enchantment of chance, the few brief scenes she was given formed a perfect compendium of her 1884 and 1888 and 1892 looks.

The *gitanilla* bends her head over the live table of Leporello's servile back to trace on a scrap of parchment a rough map of the way to the castle. Her neck shows white through her long black hair separated by the motion of her shoulder. It is no longer another man's Dolores, but a little girl twisting an aquarelle brush in the paint of Van's blood, and Donna Anna's castle is now a bog flower.

The Don rides past three windmills, whirling black against an ominous sunset, and saves her from the miller who accuses her of stealing a fistful of flour and tears her thin dress. Wheezy but still game, Juan carries her across a brook (her bare toe acrobatically tickling his face) and sets her down, top up, on the turf of an olive grove. Now they stand facing each other. She fingers voluptuously the jeweled pommel of his sword, she rubs her firm girl belly against his embroidered tights, and all at once the grimace of a premature spasm writhes across the poor Don's expressive face. He angrily disentangles himself and staggers back to his steed.

Van, however, did not understand until much later (when he saw—*had* to see; and then see again and again—the entire film, with its melancholy and grotesque ending in Donna Anna's castle) that what seemed an incidental embrace constituted the Stone Cuckold's revenge. In fact, being upset beyond measure, he decided to go even before the olive-grove sequence dissolved. Just then three old ladies with stony faces showed their disapproval of the picture by rising from beyond Lucette (who was slim enough to remain seated) and brushing past Van (who stood up) in three jerky shuffles. Simultaneously he noticed two people, the long-lost Robinsons, who apparently had been separated from Lucette by those three women, and were now moving over to her. Beaming and melting in smiles of benevolence and self-effacement, they sidled up and plumped down next to Lucette, who turned to them with her last, last, last free gift of staunch courtesy that was stronger than failure and death. They were craning already across her, with radiant wrinkles and twittery fingers toward Van when he pounced upon their intrusion to murmur a humorous bad-sailor excuse and leave the cinema hall to its dark lurching.

In a series of sixty-year-old actions which now I can grind into extinction only by working on a succession of words until the rhythm is right, I, Van, retired to my bathroom, shut the door (it swung open at once, but then closed of its own accord) and using a temporary expedient less far-fetched than that hit upon by Father Sergius (who chops off the wrong member in Count Tolstoy's famous anecdote), vigorously got rid of the prurient pressure as he had done the last time seventeen years ago. And how sad, how significant that the picture projected upon the screen of his paroxysm, while the unlockable door swung open again with the movement of a deaf man cupping his ear, was not the recent and pertinent image of Lucette, but the indelible vision of a bent bare neck and a divided flow of black hair and a purple-tipped paint brush.

Then, for the sake of safety, he repeated the disgusting but necessary act.

He saw the situation dispassionately now and felt he was doing right by going to bed and switching off the "ectric" light (a surrogate creeping back into international use). The blue ghost of the room gradually established itself as his eyes got used to the darkness. He prided himself on his willpower. He welcomed the dull pain in his drained root. He welcomed the thought which suddenly seemed so absolutely true, and new, and as lividly real as the slowly widening gap of the sitting room's doorway, namely, that on the morrow (which was at least, and at best, seventy years away) he would explain to Lucette, as a philosopher and another girl's brother, that he knew how agonizing and how absurd it was to put all one's spiritual fortune on one physical fancy and that his plight closely resembled hers, but that he managed, after all, to live, to work, and not pine away because he refused to wreck her life with a brief affair and because Ada was still a child. At that point the surface of logic began to be affected by a ripple of sleep, but he sprang back into full consciousness at the sound of the telephone. The thing seemed to squat for each renewed burst of ringing and at first he decided to let it ring itself out. Then his nerves surrendered to the insisting signal, and he snatched up the receiver.

No doubt he was morally right in using the first pretext at hand to keep her away from his bed; but he also knew, as a gentleman and an artist, that the lump of words he brought up was trite and cruel, and it was only because she could not accept him as being either, that she believed him:

"*Mozhno pridti teper'* (can I come now)?" asked Lucette.

"*Ya ne odin* (I'm not alone)," answered Van.

A small pause followed; then she hung up.

After he had stolen away, she had remained trapped between the cozy Robinsons (Rachel, dangling a big handbag, had squeezed by immediately to the place Van had vacated, and Bob had moved one seat up). Because of a sort of *pudeur* she did not inform them that the actress (obscurely and fleetingly billed as "Theresa Zegris" in the "going-up" lift-list at the end of the picture) who had managed to obtain the small but not unimportant part of the fatal gipsy was none other than the pallid schoolgirl they might have seen in Ladore. They invited Lucette to a Coke with them—proselytical teetotalists—in their cabin, which was small and stuffy and badly insulated, one could hear every word and whine of two children being put to bed by a silent seasick nurse, so late, so late—no, not children, but probably very young, very much disappointed honeymooners.

"We understand," said Robert Robinson going for another supply to his portable fridge, "we understand perfectly that Dr. Veen is deeply immersed in his Inter Resting Work —personally, I sometimes regret having retired—but do you think, Lucy, *prosit!*, that he might accept to have dinner tomorrow with you and us and maybe Another Couple, whom he'll certainly enjoy meeting? Shall Mrs. Robinson send him a formal invitation? Would you sign it, too?"

"I don't know, I'm very tired," she said, "and the rock and roll are getting worse. I guess I'll go up to my hutch and take your Quietus. Yes, by all means, let's have dinner, all of us. I really needed that lovely cold drink."

Having cradled the nacred receiver she changed into black slacks and a lemon shirt (planned for tomorrow morning); looked in vain for a bit of plain notepaper without caravelle or crest; ripped out the flyleaf of Herb's Journal, and tried to think up something amusing, harmless, and scintillating to say in a suicide note. But she had planned everything except that note, so she tore her blank life in two and disposed of the pieces in the W.C.; she poured herself a glass of dead water from a moored decanter, gulped down one by one four green pills, and, sucking the fifth, walked to the lift which took her one click up from her three-room suite straight to the red-carpeted promenade-deck bar. There, two sluglike young men were in the act of sliding off their red toadstools, and the older one said to the other as they turned to leave: "You may fool his lordship, my dear, but not me, oh, no."

She drank a "Cossack pony" of Klass vodka—hateful, vulgar, but potent stuff; had another; and was hardly able to down a third because her head had started to swim like hell. Swim like hell from sharks, Tobakovich!

She had no purse with her. She almost fell from her convex ridiculous seat as she fumbled in her shirt pocket for a stray bank note.

"Beddydee," said Toby the barman with a fatherly smile, which she mistook for a leer. "Bedtime, miss," he repeated and patted her ungloved hand.

Lucette recoiled and forced herself to retort distinctly and haughtily:

"Mr. Veen, my cousin, will pay you tomorrow and bash your false teeth in."

Six, seven—no, more than that, about ten steps up. *Dix marches.* Legs and arms. *Dimanche. Déjeuner sur l'herbe. Tout le monde pue. Ma belle-mère avale son râtelier. Sa petite chienne,* after too much exercise, gulps twice and quietly vomits, a pink pudding onto the picnic *nappe. Après quoi* she waddles off. These steps are something.

While dragging herself up she had to hang onto the rail. Her twisted progress was that of a cripple. Once on the open deck she felt the solid impact of the black night, and the mobility of the accidental home she was about to leave.

Although Lucette had never died before—no, *dived* before, Violet—from such a height, in such a disorder of shadows and snaking reflections, she went with hardly a splash through the wave that humped to welcome her. That perfect end was spoiled by her instinctively surfacing in an immediate sweep—instead of surrendering under water to her drugged lassitude as she had planned to do on her last night ashore if it ever did come to this. The silly girl had not rehearsed the technique of suicide as, say, free-fall parachutists do every day in the element of another chapter. Owing to the tumultuous swell and her not being sure which way to peer through the spray and the darkness and her own tenta-clinging hair—t,a,c,l—she could not make out the lights of the liner, an easily imagined many-eyed bulk mightily receding in heartless triumph. Now I've lost my next note.

Got it.

The sky was also heartless and dark, and her body, her head, and particularly those damned thirsty trousers, felt clogged with Oceanus Nox, n,o,x. At every slap and splash of cold wild salt, she heaved with anise-flavored nausea and there was an increasing number, okay, or numbness, in her neck and arms. As she began losing track of herself, she thought it proper to inform a series of receding Lucettes—telling them to pass it on and on in a trick-crystal regression —that what death amounted to was only a more complete assortment of the infinite fractions of solitude.

She did not see her whole life flash before her as we all were afraid she might have done; the red rubber of a favorite doll remained safely decomposed among the myosotes of an unanalyzable brook; but she did see a few odds and ends as she swam like a dilettante Tobakoff in a circle of brief panic and merciful torpor. She saw a pair of new vair-furred bedroom slippers, which Brigitte had forgotten to pack; she saw Van wiping his mouth before answering, and then, still withholding the answer, throwing his napkin on the table as they both got up; and she saw a girl with long black hair quickly bend in passing to clap her hands over a dackel in a half-torn wreath.

A brilliantly illumined motorboat was launched from the not-too-distant ship with Van and the swimming coach and the oilskin-hooded Toby among the would-be saviors; but by that time a lot of sea had rolled by and Lucette was too tired to wait. Then the night was filled with the rattle of an old but still strong helicopter. Its diligent beam could spot only the dark head of Van, who, having been propelled out of the boat when it shied from its own sudden shadow, kept bobbing and bawling the drowned girl's name in the black, foam-veined, complicated waters.

6

Father:

  enclosed is a self-explanatory letter which, please, read and, if unobjectionable in your opinion, forward to Mrs. Vinelander, whose address I don't know. For your own edification—although it hardly matters at this stage—Lucette never was my mistress, as an obscene ass, whom I cannot trace, implies in the "write-up" of the tragedy.

  I'm told you'll be back East next month. Have your current secretary ring me up at Kingston, if you care to see me.

Ada:

  I wish to correct and amplify the accounts of her death published here even before I arrived. We were not "traveling together." We embarked at two different ports and I did not know that she was aboard. Our relationship remained what it had always been. I spent the next day (June 4) entirely with her, except for a couple of hours before dinner. We basked in the sun.

[527]

She enjoyed the brisk breeze and the bright brine of the pool. She was doing her best to appear carefree but I saw how wrong things were. The romantic attachment she had formed, the infatuation she cultivated, could not be severed by logic. On top of that, somebody she could not compete with entered the picture. The Robinsons, Robert and Rachel, who, I know, planned to write to you through my father, were the penultimate people to talk to her that night. The last was a bartender. He was worried by her behavior, followed her up to the open deck and witnessed but could not stop her jump.

I suppose it is inevitable that after such a loss one should treasure its every detail, every string that snapped, every fringe that frayed, in the immediate precession. I had sat with her through the greater part of a movie, Castles in Spain (or some title like that), and its liberal villain was being directed to the last of them, when I decided to abandon her to the auspices of the Robinsons, who had joined us in the ship's theater. I went to bed—and was called around 1 A.M. mariTime, a few moments after she had jumped overboard. Attempts to rescue her were made on a reasonable scale, but, finally, the awful decision to resume the voyage, after an hour of confusion and hope, had to be taken by the Captain. Had I found him bribable, we would still be circling today the fatal spot.

As a psychologist, I know the unsoundness of speculations as to whether Ophelia would not have drowned herself after all, without the help of a treacherous sliver, even if she had married her Voltemand. Impersonally I believe she would have died in her bed, *gray and serene, had V. loved her; but since he did not really love the wretched little virgin, and since no amount of carnal tenderness could or can pass for true love, and since, above all, the fatal Andalusian wench who had come, I repeat, into the picture, was unforgettable, I am bound to arrive, dear Ada and dear Andrey, at the conclusion that whatever the miserable man could have thought up, she would have* pokonchila soboy *("put an end to herself") all the same. In other more deeply moral worlds than this pellet of muck, there might exist restraints, principles, transcendental consolations, and even a certain pride in making happy someone one does not really love; but on this planet Lucettes are doomed.*

Some poor little things belonging to her—a cigarette case, a tulle evening frock, a book dog's-eared at a French picnic—have had to be destroyed, because they stared at me. I remain your obedient servant.

Son:

I have followed your instructions, anent that letter, to the letter. Your epistolary style is so involute that I should suspect the presence of a code, had I not known you belonged to the Decadent School of writing, in company of naughty old Leo and consumptive Anton. I do not give a damn whether you slept or not with Lucette; but I know from Dorothy Vinelander that the child had been in love with you. The film you saw was, no doubt, Don Juan's Last Fling *in which Ada, indeed, impersonates (very beautifully) a Spanish girl. A jinx has been cast on our poor girl's career. Howard Hool argued after the release that he had been made to play an impossible cross between two*

*Dons; that initially Yuzlik (the director) had meant
to base his "fantasy" on Cervantes's crude romance;
that some scraps of the basic script stuck like dirty
wool to the final theme; and that if you followed
closely the sound track you could hear a fellow reveler
in the tavern scene address Hool twice as "Quicks."
Hool managed to buy up and destroy a number of
copies while others have been locked up by the lawyer of the writer Osberg, who claims the gitanilla sequence was stolen from one of his own concoctions. In
result it is impossible to purchase a reel of the picture which will vanish like the proverbial smoke once
it has fizzled out on provincial screens. Come and have
dinner with me on July 10. Evening dress.*

Cher ami,

Nous fûmes, mon mari et moi, profondément boule-
versés par l'effroyable nouvelle. C'est à moi—et je
m'en souviendrai toujours!—que presqu'à la veille
de sa mort cette pauvre fille s'est adressée pour ar-
ranger les choses sur le *Tobakoff* qui est toujours
bondé, et que désormais je ne prendrai plus, par
un peu de superstition et beaucoup de sympathie
pour la douce, la tendre Lucette. J'étais si heur-
euse de faire mon possible, car quelqu'un m'avait dit
que vous aussi y seriez; d'ailleurs, elle m'en a parlé
elle-même: elle semblait tellement joyeuse de passer
quelques jours sur le "pont des gaillards" avec son cher
cousin! La psychologie du suicide est un mystère que
nul savant ne peut expliquer.

Je n'ai jamais versé tant de larmes, la plume m'en
tombe des doigts. Nous revenons à Malbrook vers la
mi-août. Bien à vous,

Cordula de Prey-Tobak

Van:

Andrey and I were deeply moved by the additional data you provide in your dear (i.e., insufficiently stamped!) letter. We had already received, through Mr. Grombchevski, a note from the Robinsons, who cannot forgive themselves, poor well-meaning friends, for giving her that seasickness medicine, an overdoze of which, topped by liquor, must have impaired her capacity to survive—if she changed her mind in the cold dark water. I cannot express, dear Van, how unhappy I am, the more so as we never learned in the arbors of Ardis that such unhappiness could exist.

My only love:

This letter will never be posted. It will lie in a steel box buried under a cypress in the garden of Villa Armina, and when it turns up by chance half a millennium hence, nobody will know who wrote it and for whom it was meant. It would not have been written at all if your last line, your cry of unhappiness, were not my cry of triumph. The burden of that excitement must be . . . [The rest of the sentence was found to be obliterated by a rusty stain when the box was dug up in 1928. The letter continues as follows]: . . . back in the States, I started upon a singular quest. In Manhattan, in Kingston, in Ladore, in dozens of other towns, I kept pursuing the picture which I had not [badly discolored] on the boat, from cinema to cinema, every time discovering a new item of glorious torture, a new convulsion of beauty in your performance. That [illegible] is a complete refutation of odious Kim's odious stills. Artistically, and ardisiacally, the best moment is one of the last—when you follow barefoot the Don who walks down a marble gallery to his doom, to the scaffold of Dona Anna's black-curtained bed, around which you flutter, my Zegris butterfly, straightening a comically drooping candle, whispering delightful but futile instructions into the frowning lady's ear, and then peering over that mauresque screen and suddenly dissolving in such natural laughter, helpless and lovely, that one wonders if any art could do without that erotic gasp of schoolgirl mirth. And to think, Spanish orange-tip, that all in all your magic gambol lasted but eleven minutes of stopwatch time in patches of two- or three-minute scenes!

Alas, there came a night, in a dismal district of workshops and bleary shebeens, when for the very last time, and only halfway, because at the seduction scene the film black-winked and shriveled, I managed to catch [the entire end of the letter is damaged].

7

He greeted the dawn of a placid and prosperous century (more than half of which Ada and I have now seen) with the beginning of his second philosophic fable, a "denunciation of space" (never to be completed, but forming, in rear vision, a preface to his Texture of Time). Part of that treatise, a rather mannered affair, but nasty and sound, appeared in the first issue (January, 1904) of a now famous American monthly, *The Artisan*, and a comment on the excerpt is preserved in one of the tragically formal letters (all destroyed save this one) that his sister sent him by public post now and then. Somehow, after the interchange occasioned by Lucette's death such nonclandestine correspondence had been established with the tacit sanction of Demon:

> And o'er the summits of the Tacit
> He, banned from Paradise, flew on:
> Beneath him, like a brilliant's facet,
> Mount Peck with snows eternal shone.

It would seem indeed that continued ignorance of each

other's existence might have looked more suspicious than the following sort of note:

Agavia Ranch
February 5, 1905

I have just read Reflections in Sidra, *by Ivan Veen, and I regard it as a grand piece, dear Professor. The "lost shafts of destiny" and other poetical touches reminded me of the two or three times you had tea and muffins at our place in the country about twenty years ago. I was, you remember (presumptuous phrase!), a petite fille modèle practicing archery near a vase and a parapet and you were a shy schoolboy (with whom, as my mother guessed, I may have been a wee bit in love!), who dutifully picked up the arrows I lost in the lost shrubbery of the lost castle of poor Lucette's and happy, happy Adette's childhood, now a "Home for Blind Blacks"—both my mother and L., I'm sure, would have backed Dasha's advice to turn it over to her Sect. Dasha, my sister-in-law (you must meet her soon, yes, yes, yes, she's dreamy and lovely, and lots more intelligent than I), who showed me your piece, asks me to add she hopes to "renew" your acquaintance—maybe in Switzerland, at the Bellevue in Mont Roux, in October. I think you once met pretty Miss "Kim" Blackrent, well, that's exactly dear Dasha's type. She is very good at perceiving and pursuing originality and all kinds of studies which I can't even name! She finished Chose (where she read History—our Lucette used to call it "Sale Histoire," so sad and funny!). For her you're le beau ténébreux, because once upon a time, once upon libellula wings, not long before my marriage, she attended—I mean at that time, I'm stuck in my "turn-*

[534]

style"—one of your public lectures on dreams, after which she went up to you with her latest little nightmare all typed out and neatly clipped together, and you scowled darkly and refused to take it. Well, she's been after Uncle Dementiy to have him admonish le beau ténébreux to come to Mont Roux Bellevue Hotel, in October, around the seventeenth, I guess, and he only laughs and says it's up to Dashenka and me to arrange matters.

So "congs" again, dear Ivan! You are, we both think, a marvelous, inimitable artist who should also "only laugh," if cretinic critics, especially lower-upper-middle-class Englishmen, accuse his turnstyle of being "coy" and "arch," much as an American farmer finds the parson "peculiar" because he knows Greek.

P.S.

Dushevno klanyayus' (*"am souledly bowing"* an incorrect and vulgar construction evoking the image of a *"bowing soul"*) nashemu zaochno dorogomu professoru (*"to our 'unsight-unseen' dear professor"*), o kotorom mnogo slïshal (*about whom have heard much*) ot dobrago Dementiya Dedalovicha i sestritsï (*from good Demon and my sister*).

S uvazheniem (*with respect*),
Andrey Vaynlender

Furnished Space, *l'espace meublé* (known to us only as furnished and full even if its contents be "absence of substance"—which seats the mind, too), is mostly watery so far as this globe is concerned. In that form it destroyed Lucette. Another variety, more or less atmospheric, but no less gravitational and loathsome, destroyed Demon.

Idly, one March morning, 1905, on the terrace of Villa

Armina, where he sat on a rug, surrounded by four or five lazy nudes, like a sultan, Van opened an American daily paper published in Nice. In the fourth or fifth worst airplane disaster of the young century, a gigantic flying machine had inexplicably disintegrated at fifteen thousand feet above the Pacific between Lisiansky and Laysanov Islands in the Gavaille region. A list of "leading figures" dead in the explosion comprised the advertising manager of a department store, the acting foreman in the sheet-metal division of a facsimile corporation, a recording firm executive, the senior partner of a law firm, an architect with heavy aviation background (a first misprint here, impossible to straighten out), the vice president of an insurance corporation, another vice president, this time of a board of adjustment whatever that might be—

"I'm hongree," said a *maussade* Lebanese beauty of fifteen sultry summers.

"Use bell," said Van, continuing in a state of odd fascination to go through the compilation of labeled lives:

—the president of a wholesale liquor-distributing firm, the manager of a turbine equipment company, a pencil manufacturer, two professors of philosophy, two newspaper reporters (with nothing more to report), the assistant controller of a wholesome liquor distribution bank (misprinted and misplaced), the assistant controller of a trust company, a president, the secretary of a printing agency—

The names of those big shots, as well as those of some eighty other men, women, and silent children who perished in blue air, were being withheld until all relatives had been reached; but the tabulatory preview of commonplace abstractions had been thought to be too imposing not to be given at once as an appetizer; and only on the following morning did Van learn that a bank president lost in the closing garble was his father.

"The lost shafts of every man's destiny remain scattered all around him," etc. (*Reflections in Sidra*).

The last occasion on which Van had seen his father was at their house, in the spring of 1904. Other people had been present: old Eliot, the real-estate man, two lawyers (Gromb-chevski and Gromwell), Dr. Aix, the art expert, Rosalind Knight, Demon's new secretary, and solemn Kithar Sween, a banker who at sixty-five had become an *avant-garde* author; in the course of one miraculous year he had produced *The Waistline*, a satire in free verse on Anglo-American feeding habits, and *Cardinal Grishkin*, an overtly subtle yarn extolling the Roman faith. The poem was but the twinkle in an owl's eye; as to the novel it had already been pronounced "seminal" by celebrated young critics (Norman Girsh, Louis Deer, many others) who lauded it in reverential voices pitched so high that an ordinary human ear could not make much of that treble volubility; it seemed, however, all very exciting, and after a great bang of obituary essays in 1910 ("Kithar Sween: the man and the writer," "Sween as poet and person," "Kithar Kirman Lavehr Sween: a tentative biography") both the satire and the romance were to be forgotten as thoroughly as that acting foreman's control of background adjustment—or Demon's edict.

The table talk dealt mainly with business matters. Demon had recently bought a small, perfectly round Pacific island, with a pink house on a green bluff and a sand beach like a frill (as seen from the air), and now wished to sell the precious little palazzo in East Manhattan that Van did not want. Mr. Sween, a greedy practitioner with flashy rings on fat fingers, said he might buy it if some of the pictures were thrown in. The deal did not come off.

Van pursued his studies in private until his election (at thirty-five!) to the Rattner Chair of Philosophy in the University of Kingston. The Council's choice had been a consequence of disaster and desperation; the two other candidates, solid scholars much older and altogether better than he, esteemed even in Tartary where they often traveled, starry-eyed, hand-in-hand, had mysteriously vanished (perhaps dying under false names in the never-explained accident above the smiling ocean) at the "eleventh hour," for the Chair was to be dismantled if it remained vacant for a legally limited length of time, so as to give another, less-coveted but perfectly good seat the chance to be brought in from the back parlor. Van neither needed nor appreciated the thing, but accepted it in a spirit of good-natured perversity or perverse gratitude, or simply in memory of his father who had been somehow involved in the whole affair. He did not take his task too seriously, reducing to a strict minimum, ten or so per year, the lectures he delivered in a nasal drone mainly produced by a new and hard to get "voice recorder" concealed in his waistcoat pocket, among anti-infection Venus pills, while he moved his lips silently and thought of the lamplit page of his sprawling script left unfinished in his study. He spent in Kingston a score of dull years (variegated by trips abroad), an obscure figure around which no legends collected in the university or the city. Unbeloved by his austere colleagues, unknown in local pubs, unregretted by his male students, he retired in 1922, after which he resided in Europe.

8

arriving mont roux bellevue sunday
dinnertime adoration sorrow rainbows

Van got this bold cable with his breakfast on Saturday, October 10, 1905, at the Manhattan Palace in Geneva, and that same day moved to Mont Roux at the opposite end of the lake. He put up there at his usual hotel, Les Trois Cygnes. Its small, frail, but almost mythically ancient concierge had died during Van's stay four years earlier, and instead of wizened Julien's discreet smile of mysterious complicity that used to shine like a lamp through parchment, the round rosy face of a recent bellboy, who now wore a frockcoat, greeted fat old Van.

"Lucien," said Dr. Veen, peering over his spectacles, "I may have—as your predecessor would know—all kinds of queer visitors, magicians, masked ladies, madmen—*que sais-je?* and I expect miracles of secrecy from all three mute swans. Here's a prefatory bonus."

"*Merci infiniment,*" said the concierge, and, as usual, Van felt infinitely touched by the courteous hyperbole provoking no dearth of philosophical thought.

He engaged two spacious rooms, 509 and 510: an Old World salon with golden-green furniture, and a charming bed chamber joined to a square bathroom, evidently converted from an ordinary room (around 1875, when the hotel was renovated and splendified). With thrilling anticipation, he read the octagonal cardboard sign on its dainty red string: Do not disturb. *Prière de ne pas déranger.* Hang this notice on the doorhandle outside. Inform Telephone Exchange. *Avisez en particulier la téléphoniste* (no emphasis, no limpid-voiced girl in the English version).

He ordered an orgy of orchids from the *rez-de-chaussée* flower shop, and one ham sandwich from Room Service. He survived a long night (with Alpine Choughs heckling a cloudless dawn) in a bed hardly two-thirds the size of the tremendous one at their unforgettable flat twelve years ago. He breakfasted on the balcony—and ignored a reconnoitering gull. He allowed himself an opulent siesta after a late lunch; took a second bath to drown time; and with stops at every other bench on the promenade spent a couple of hours strolling over to the new Bellevue Palace, just half a mile southeast.

One red boat marred the blue mirror (in Casanova's days there would have been hundreds!). The grebes were there for the winter but the coots had not yet returned.

Ardis, Manhattan, Mont Roux, our little rousse is dead. Vrubel's wonderful picture of Father, those demented diamonds staring at me, painted *into* me.

Mount Russet, the forested hill behind the town, lived up to its name and autumnal reputation, with a warm glow of curly chestnut trees; and on the opposite shore of Leman, Leman meaning Lover, loomed the crest of Sex Noir, Black Rock.

He felt hot and uncomfortable in silk shirt and gray flannels

—one of his older suits that he had chosen because it happened to make him look slimmer; but he should have omitted its tightish waistcoat. Nervous as a boy at his first rendezvous! He wondered what better to hope for—that her presence should be diluted at once by that of other people or that she should manage to be alone, for the first minutes, at least? Did his glasses and short black mustache really make him look younger, as polite whores affirmed?

When he reached at long last the whitewashed and blue-shaded Bellevue (patronized by wealthy Estotilanders, Rheinlanders, and Vinelanders, but not placed in the same superclass as the old, tawny and gilt, huge, sprawling, lovable Trois Cygnes), Van saw with dismay that his watch still lagged far behind 7:00 p.m., the earliest dinner hour in local hotels. So he recrossed the lane and had a double kirsch, with a lump of sugar, in a pub. A dead and dry hummingbird moth lay on the window ledge of the lavatory. Thank goodness, symbols did not exist either in dreams or in the life in between.

He pushed through the revolving door of the Bellevue, tripped over a gaudy suitcase, and made his entrée at a ridiculous run. The concierge snapped at the unfortunate green-aproned *cameriere*, who had left the bag there. Yes, they were expecting him in the lounge. A German tourist caught up with him, to apologize, effusively, and not without humor, for the offending object, which, he said, was his.

"If so," remarked Van, "you should not allow spas to slap their stickers on your private appendages."

His reply was inept, and the whole episode had a faint paramnesic tang—and next instant Van was shot dead from behind (such things happen, some tourists are very unbalanced) and stepped into his next phase of existence.

He stopped on the threshold of the main lounge, but

hardly had he begun to scan the distribution of its scattered human contents, than an abrupt flurry occurred in a distant group. Ada, spurning decorum, was hurrying toward him. Her solitary and precipitate advance consumed in reverse all the years of their separation as she changed from a dark-glittering stranger with the high hair-do in fashion to the pale-armed girl in black who had always belonged to him. At that particular twist of time they happened to be the only people conspicuously erect and active in the huge room, and heads turned and eyes peered when the two met in the middle of it as on a stage; but what should have been, in culmination of her headlong motion, of the ecstasy in her eyes and fiery jewels, a great explosion of voluble love, was marked by incongruous silence; he raised to his unbending lips and kissed her cygneous hand, and then they stood still, staring at each other, he playing with coins in his trouser pockets under his "humped" jacket, she fingering her necklace, each reflecting, as it were, the uncertain light to which all that radiance of mutual welcome had catastrophically decreased. She was more Ada than ever, but a dash of new elegancy had been added to her shy, wild charm. Her still blacker hair was drawn back and up into a glossy chignon, and the Lucette line of her exposed neck, slender and straight, came as a heartrending surprise. He was trying to form a succinct sentence (to warn her about the device he planned for securing a rendezvous), but she interrupted his throat clearing with a muttered injunction: *Sbrit' uśi!* (that mustache must go) and turned away to lead him to the far corner from which she had taken so many years to reach him.

The first person whom she introduced him to, at that island of fauteuils and androids, now getting up from around a low table with a copper ashbowl for hub, was the promised *belle-soeur*, a short plumpish lady in governess gray, very oval-faced, with bobbed auburn hair, a sallowish complexion, smoke-blue unsmiling eyes, and a fleshy little excrescence, resembling a ripe maize kernel, at the side of one nostril, added to its hypercritical curve by an afterthought of nature as not seldom happens when a Russian's face is mass-produced. The next outstretched hand belonged to a handsome, tall, remarkably substantial and cordial nobleman who could be none other than the Prince Gremin of the preposterous libretto, and whose strong honest clasp made Van crave for a disinfecting fluid to wash off contact with any of her husband's public parts. But as Ada, beaming again, made fluttery introductions with an invisible wand, the person Van had grossly mistaken for Andrey Vinelander was transformed into Yuzlik, the gifted director of the ill-fated Don Juan picture. "Vasco de Gama, I presume," Yuzlik murmured. Beside him, ignored by him, unknown by name to Ada, and now long dead of dreary anonymous ailments, stood in servile attitudes the two agents of Lemorio, the flamboyant comedian (a bearded boor of exceptional, and now also forgotten, genius, whom Yuzlik passionately wanted for his next picture). Lemorio had stood him up twice before, in Rome and San Remo, each time sending him for "preliminary contact" those two seedy, incompetent, virtually insane, people with whom by now Yuzlik had nothing more to discuss, having exhausted everything, topical gossip, Lemorio's sex life, Hoole's hooliganism, as well as the hobbies of his, Yuzlik's, three sons and those of their, the agents', adopted child, a lovely Eurasian lad, who had recently been slain in a night-club fracas—which closed *that* subject. Ada had welcomed Yuzlik's unexpected reality in the lounge of the Bellevue not only as a counterpoise to the embarrassment and the deceit, but also because she hoped to sidle into *What*

Daisy Knew; however, besides having no spells left in the turmoil of her spirit for business blandishments, she soon understood that if Lemorio were finally engaged, he would want her part for one of his mistresses.

Finally Van reached Ada's husband.

Van had murdered good Andrey Andreevich Vinelander so often, so thoroughly, at all the dark crossroads of the mind, that now the poor chap, dressed in a hideous, funereal, double-breasted suit, with those dough-soft features slapped together anyhow, and those sad-hound baggy eyes, and the dotted lines of sweat on his brow, presented all the depressing features of an unnecessary resurrection. Through a not-too-odd oversight (or rather "undersight") Ada omitted to introduce the two men. Her husband enunciated his name, patronymic, and surname with the didactic intonations of a Russian educational-film narrator. *"Obnimemsya, dorogoy"* (let us embrace, old boy), he added in a more vibrant voice but with his mournful expression unchanged (oddly remindful of that of Kosygin, the mayor of Yukonsk, receiving a girl scout's bouquet or inspecting the damage caused by an earthquake). His breath carried the odor of what Van recognized with astonishment as a strong tranquilizer on a neocodein base, prescribed in the case of psychopathic pseudobronchitis. As Andrey's crumpled forlorn face came closer, one could distinguish various wartlets and lumps, none of them, however, placed in the one-sided jaunty position of his kid sister's naric codicil. He kept his dun-colored hair as short as a soldier's by means of his own clippers. He had the *korrektnïy*, and neat appearance of the one-bath-per-week Estotian *hobereau*.

We all flocked to the dining room. Van brushed against the past as he shot an arm out to forestall a door-opening waiter, and the past (still fingering *his* necklace) recompensed him with a sidelong "Dolores" glance.

Chance looked after the seating arrangement.

Lemorio's agents, an elderly couple, unwed but having lived as man and man for a sufficiently long period to warrant a silver-screen anniversary, remained unsplit at table between Yuzlik, who never once spoke to them, and Van, who was being tortured by Dorothy. As to Andrey (who made a thready "sign of the cross" over his un-unbuttonable abdomen before necking in his napkin), he found himself seated between sister and wife. He demanded the "cart de van" (affording the real Van mild amusement), but, being a hard-liquor man, cast only a stunned look at the "Swiss White" page of the wine list before "passing the buck" to Ada who promptly ordered champagne. He was to inform her early next morning that her "*Kuzen proizvodit* (produces) *udivitel'no simpatichnoe vpechatlenie* (a remarkably sympathetic, in the sense of 'fetching,' impression)." The dear fellow's verbal apparatus consisted almost exclusively of remarkably sympathetic Russian commonplaces of language, but—not liking to speak of himself—he spoke little, especially since his sister's sonorous soliloquy (lapping at Van's rock) mesmerized and childishly engrossed him. Dorothy preambled her long-delayed report on her pet nightmare with a humble complaint ("Of course, I know that for your patients to have bad dreams is a *zhidovskaya prerogativa*"), but her reluctant analyst's attention every time it returned to her from his plate fixed itself so insistently on the Greek cross of almost ecclesiastical size shining on her otherwise unremarkable chest that she thought fit to interrupt her narrative (which had to do with the eruption of a dream volcano) to say: "I gather from your writings that you are a terrible cynic. Oh, I quite agree with Simone Traser that a dash of cynicism adorns a real man; yet I'd like to warn you that I object to anti-Orthodox jokes in case you intend making one."

By now Van had more than enough of his mad, but not interestingly mad, convive. He just managed to steady his glass, which a gesture he made to attract Ada's attention had almost knocked down, and said, without further ado, in what Ada termed afterwards a mordant, ominous and altogether inadmissible tone:

"Tomorrow morning, *je veux vous accaparer, ma chère*. As my lawyer, or yours, or both, have, perhaps, informed you, Lucette's accounts in several Swiss banks—" and he trotted out a prepared version of a state of affairs invented *in toto*. "I suggest," he added, "that if you have no other engagements"—(sending a questioning glance that avoided the Vinelanders by leaping across and around the three cinematists, all of whom nodded in idiotic approval)—"you and I go to see Maître Jorat, or Raton, name escapes me, my adviser, *enfin*, in Luzon, half an hour drive from here—who has given me certain papers which I have at my hotel and which I must have you sigh—I mean sign with a sigh—the matter is tedious. All right? All right."

"But, Ada," clarioned Dora, "you forget that tomorrow morning we wanted to visit the Institute of Floral Harmony in the Château Piron!"

"You'll do it after tomorrow, or Tuesday, or Tuesday week," said Van. "I'd gladly drive all three of you to that fascinating *lieu de méditation* but my fast little Unseretti seats only one passenger, and that business of untraceable deposits is terribly urgent, I think."

Yuzlik was dying to say something. Van yielded to the well-meaning automaton.

"I'm delighted and honored to dine with Vasco de

Gama," said Yuzlik holding up his glass in front of his handsome facial apparatus.

The same garbling—and this gave Van a clue to Yuzlik's source of recondite information—occurred in *The Chimes of Chose* (a memoir by a former chum of Van's, now Lord Chose, which had climbed, and still clung to, the "best seller" trellis—mainly because of several indecent but very funny references to the Villa Venus in Ranton Brooks). While he munched the marrow of an adequate answer, with a mouthful of *sharlott* (not the charlatan "*charlotte russe*" served in most restaurants, but the hot toasty crust, with apple filling, of the authentic castle pie made by Takomin, the hotel's head cook, who hailed from California's Rose Bay), two urges were cleaving Van asunder: one to insult Yuzlik for having placed his hand on Ada's when asking her to pass him the butter two or three courses ago (he was incomparably more jealous of that liquid-eyed male than of Andrey and remembered with a shiver of pride and hate how on New Year's Eve, 1893, he had lashed out at a relative of his, foppish Van Zemski, who had permitted himself a similar caress when visiting their restaurant table, and whose jaw he had broken later, under some pretext or other, at the young prince's club); and the other—to tell Yuzlik how much he had admired *Don Juan's Last Fling*. Not being able, for obvious reasons, to satisfy urge number one he dismissed number two as secretly smacking of a poltroon's politeness and contented himself with replying, after swallowing his amber-soaked mash:

"Jack Chose's book is certainly most entertaining—especially that bit about apples and diarrhea, and the excerpts from the Venus Shell Album"—(Yuzlik's eyes darted aside in specious recollection, whereupon he bowed in effusive tribute to a common memory)—"but the rascal should have neither divulged my name nor botched my thespionym."

During that dismal dinner (enlivened only by the *sharlott* and five bottles of Moët, out of which Van consumed more than three), he avoided looking at that part of Ada which is called "the face"—a vivid, divine, mysteriously shocking part, which, in that essential form, is rarely met with among human beings (pasty and warty marks do not count). Ada, on the other hand could not help her dark eyes from turning to him every other moment, as if, with each glance, she regained her balance; but when the company went back to the lounge and finished their coffee there, difficulties of focalization began to beset Van, whose *points de repère* disastrously decreased after the three cinematists had left.

ANDREY: *Adochka, dushka* (darling), *razskazhi zhe pro rancho, pro skot* (tell about the ranch, the cattle), *emu zhe lyubopïtno* (it cannot fail to interest him).

ADA (*as if coming out of a trance*): *O chyom ti* (you were saying something)?

ANDREY: *Ya govoryu, razskazhi emu pro tvoyo zhit'yo bït'yo* (I was saying, tell him about your daily life, your habitual existence). *Avos' zaglyanet k nam* (maybe he'd look us up).

ADA: *Ostav', chto tam interesnago* (what's so interesting about it)?

DASHA (*turning to Ivan*): Don't listen to her. *Massa interesnago* (heaps of interesting stuff). *Delo brata ogromnoe, volnuyushchee delo, trebuyushchee ne men'she truda, chem uchyonaya dissertatsiya* (his business is a big thing, quite as demanding as a scholar's). *Nashi sel'skohozyaystvennïya mashinï i ih teni* (our agricultural machines and their shadows)—*eto tselaya kollektsiya predmetov modernoy skul'pturï i zhivopisi* (is a veritable collection of modern art) which I suspect you adore as I do.

IVAN (*to Andrey*): I know nothing about farming but thanks all the same.

(*A pause.*)

IVAN (*not quite knowing what to add*): Yes, I would certainly like to see your machinery some day. Those things always remind me of long-necked prehistoric monsters, sort of grazing here and there, you know, or just brooding over the sorrows of extinction—but perhaps I'm thinking of excavators—

DOROTHY: Andrey's machinery is anything but prehistoric! (*laughs cheerlessly*).

ANDREY: *Slovom, milosti prosim* (anyway, you are most welcome). *Budete zharit' verhom s kuzinoy* (you'll have a rollicking time riding on horseback with your cousin).

(*Pause.*)

IVAN (*to Ada*): Half-past nine tomorrow morning won't be too early for you? I'm at the Trois Cygnes. I'll come to fetch you in my tiny car—not on horseback (smiles like a corpse at Andrey).

DASHA: *Dovol'no skuchno* (rather a pity) that Ada's visit to lovely Lake Leman need be spoiled by sessions with lawyers and bankers. I'm sure you can satisfy most of those needs by having her come a few times *chez vous* and not to Luzon or Geneva.

[549]

The madhouse babble reverted to Lucette's bank accounts, Ivan Dementievich explained that she had been mislaying one checkbook after another, and nobody knew exactly in how many different banks she had dumped considerable amounts of money. Presently, Andrey who now looked like the livid Yukonsk mayor after opening the Catkin Week Fair or fighting a Forest Fire with a new type of extinguisher, grunted out of his chair, excused himself for going to bed so early, and shook hands with Van as if they were parting forever (which, indeed, they were). Van remained with the two ladies in the cold and deserted lounge where a thrifty subtraction of faraday-light had imperceptibly taken place.

"How did you like my brother?" asked Dorothy. "*On red-chayshiy chelovek* (he's a most rare human being). I can't tell you how profoundly affected he was by the terrible death of your father, and, of course, by Lucette's bizarre end. Even he, the kindest of men, could not help disapproving of her Parisian *sans-gêne*, but he greatly admired her looks—as I think you also did—no, no, do not negate it!—because, as I always said, her prettiness seemed to complement Ada's, the two halves forming together something like perfect beauty, in the Platonic sense" (that cheerless smile again). "Ada is certainly a 'perfect beauty,' a real *muirninochka*—even when she winces like that—but she is beautiful only in our little human terms, within the quotes of our social esthetics—right, Professor?—in the way a meal or a marriage or a little French tramp can be called perfect."

"Drop her a curtsey," gloomily remarked Van to Ada.

"Oh, my Adochka knows how devoted I am to her"— (opening her palm in the wake of Ada's retreating hand). "I've shared all her troubles. How many *podzharïh* (tight-crotched) cowboys we've had to fire because they *delali ey glazki* (ogled her)! And how many bereavements we've gone through since the new century started! Her mother and my mother; the Archbishop of Ivankover and Dr. Swissair of Lumbago (where mother and I reverently visited him in 1888); three distinguished uncles (whom, fortunately, I hardly knew); and your father, who, I've always maintained, resembled a Russian aristocrat much more than he did an Irish Baron. Incidentally, in her deathbed delirium—you don't mind, Ada, if I divulge to him *ces potins de famille?*— our splendid Marina was obsessed by two delusions, which mutually excluded each other—that you were married to Ada and that you and she were brother and sister, and the clash between those two ideas caused her intense mental anguish. How does your school of psychiatry explain that kind of conflict?"

"I don't attend school any longer," said Van, stifling a yawn; "and, furthermore, in my works, I try not to 'explain' anything, I merely describe."

"Still, you cannot deny that certain insights—"

It went on and on like that for more than an hour and Van's clenched jaws began to ache. Finally, Ada got up, and Dorothy followed suit but continued to speak standing:

"Tomorrow dear Aunt Beloskunski-Belokonski is coming to dinner, a delightful old spinster, who lives in a villa above Valvey. *Terriblement grande dame et tout ça. Elle aime taquiner* Andryusha *en disant qu'un simple cultivateur comme lui n'aurait pas dû épouser la fille d'une actrice et d'un marchand de tableaux.* Would you care to join us— Jean?"

Jean replied: "Alas, no, dear Daria Andrevna: *Je dois 'surveiller les kilos.'* Besides, I have a business dinner tomorrow."

"At least"—(smiling)—"you could call me Dasha."

"I do it for Andrey," explained Ada, "actually the grand' *dame* in question is a vulgar old skunk."

"Ada!" uttered Dasha with a look of gentle reproof.

Before the two ladies proceeded toward the lift, Ada glanced at Van—and he—no fool in amorous strategy—refrained to comment on her "forgetting" her tiny black silk handbag on the seat of her chair. He did not accompany them beyond the passage leading liftward and, clutching the token, awaited her planned return behind a pillar of hotel-hall mongrel design, knowing that in a moment she would say to her accursed companion (by now revising, no doubt, her views on the "*beau ténébreux*") as the lift's eye turned red under a quick thumb: "*Akh, sumochku zabïla* (forgot my bag)!"—and instantly flitting back, like Vere's Ninon, she would be in his arms.

Their open mouths met in tender fury, and then he pounced upon her new, young, divine, Japanese neck which he had been coveting like a veritable Jupiter Olorinus throughout the evening.

"We'll vroom straight to my place as soon as you wake up, don't bother to bathe, jump into your lenclose—" and, with the burning sap brimming, he again devoured her, until (Dorothy must have reached the sky!) she danced three fingers on his wet lips—and escaped.

"Wipe your neck!" he called after her in a rapid whisper (who, and where in this tale, in this life, had also attempted a *whispered cry?*)

That night, in a post-Moët dream, he sat on the talc of a tropical beach full of sun-baskers, and one moment was rubbing the red, irritated shaft of a writhing boy, and the next was looking through dark glasses at the symmetrical shading on either side of a shining spine with fainter shading between the ribs belonging to Lucette or Ada sitting on a towel at some distance from him. Presently, she turned and lay prone, and she, too, wore sunglasses, and neither he nor she could perceive the exact direction of each other's gaze through the black amber, yet he knew by the dimple of a faint smile that she was looking at his (it had been *his* all the time) raw scarlet. Somebody said, wheeling a table nearby: "It's one of the Vane sisters," and he awoke murmuring with professional appreciation the oneiric word-play combining his name and surname, and plucked out the wax plugs, and, in a marvelous act of rehabilitation and link-up, the breakfast table clanked from the corridor across the threshold of the adjacent room, and, already munching and honey-crumbed, Ada entered his bedchamber. It was only a quarter to eight!

"Smart girl!" said Van; "but first of all I must go to the *petit endroit* (W.C.)"

That meeting, and the nine that followed, constituted the highest ridge of their twenty-one-year-old love: its complicated, dangerous, ineffably radiant coming of age. The somewhat Italianate style of the apartment, its elaborate wall lamps with ornaments of pale caramel glass, its white knobbles that produced indiscriminately light or maids, the slat-stayed, veiled, heavily curtained windows which made the morning as difficult to disrobe as a crinolined prude, the convex sliding doors of the huge white "Nuremberg Virgin"-like closet in the hallway of their suite, and even the tinted engraving by Randon of a rather stark three-mast ship on the zigzag green waves of Marseilles Harbor—in a word, the alberghian atmosphere of those new trysts added a novelistic touch (Aleksey and Anna may have asterisked here!) which Ada welcomed as a frame, as a form, something supporting and guarding life, otherwise unprovidenced on Desdemonia, where artists are the only gods. When after three or four hours of frenetic love Van and Mrs. Vinelander would abandon their sumptuous retreat for the blue haze of an extraor-

dinary October which kept dreamy and warm throughout
the duration of adultery, they had the feeling of still being
under the protection of those painted Priapi that the Romans once used to set up in the arbors of Rufomonticulus.

"I shall walk you home—we have just returned from a conference with the Luzon bankers and I'm walking you back to
your hotel from mine"—this was the *phrase consacrée* that
Van invariably uttered to inform the fates of the situation.
One little precaution they took from the start was to strictly
avoid equivocal exposure on their lakeside balcony which
was visible to every yellow or mauve flowerhead on the plat-
bands of the promenade.

They used a back exit to leave the hotel.

A boxwood-lined path, presided over by a nostalgic-looking
sempervirent sequoia (which American visitors mistook for a
"Lebanese cedar"—if they remarked it at all) took them to
the absurdly misnamed rue du Mûrier, where a princely
paulownia ("mulberry tree!" snorted Ada), standing in state
on its incongruous terrace above a public W.C., was shedding generously its heart-shaped dark green leaves, but retained enough foliage to cast arabesques of shadow onto the
south side of its trunk. A ginkgo (of a much more luminous
greenish gold than its neighbor, a dingily yellowing local
birch) marked the corner of a cobbled lane leading down to
the quay. They followed southward the famous Fillietaz
Promenade which went along the Swiss side of the lake from
Valvey to the Château de Byron (or "She Yawns Castle").
The fashionable season had ended, and wintering birds, as
well as a number of knickerbockered Central Europeans, had
replaced the English families as well as the Russian noblemen
from Nipissing and Nipigon.

"My upper-lip space feels indecently naked." (He had

shaved his mustache off with howls of pain in her presence). "And I cannot keep sucking in my belly all the time."

"Oh, I like you better with that nice overweight—there's more of you. It's the maternal gene, I suppose, because Demon grew leaner and leaner. He looked positively Quixotic when I saw him at Mother's funeral. It was all very strange. He wore blue mourning. D'Onsky's son, a person with only one arm, threw his remaining one around Demon and both wept *comme des fontaines*. Then a robed person who looked like an extra in a technicolor incarnation of Vishnu made an incomprehensible sermon. Then she went up in smoke. He said to me, sobbing: "*I* will not cheat the poor grubs!" Practically a couple of hours after he broke that promise we had sudden visitors at the ranch—an incredibly graceful moppet of eight, black-veiled, and a kind of duenna, also in black, with two bodyguards. The hag demanded certain fantastic sums—which Demon, she said, had not had time to pay, for 'popping the hymen'—whereupon I had one of our strongest boys throw out *vsyu* (the entire) *kompaniyu*."

"Extraordinary," said Van, "they had been growing younger and younger—I mean the girls, not the strong silent boys. His old Rosalind had a ten-year-old niece, a primed chickabiddy. Soon he would have been poaching them from the hatching chamber."

"You never loved your father," said Ada sadly.

"Oh, I did and do—tenderly, reverently, understandingly, because, after all, that minor poetry of the flesh is something not unfamiliar to me. But as far as we are concerned, I mean you and I, he was buried on the same day as our uncle Dan."

"I know, I know. It's pitiful! And what use was it? Perhaps I oughtn't to tell you, but his visits to Agavia kept getting rarer and shorter every year. Yes, it was pitiful to hear him and Andrey talking. I mean, Andrey *n'a pas le verbe*

facile, though he greatly appreciated—without quite understanding it—Demon's wild flow of fancy and fantastic fact,
and would often exclaim, with his Russian 'tssk-tssk' and a
shake of the head—complimentary and all that—'what a
balagur (wag) you are!'—And then, one day, Demon warned
me that he would not come any more if he heard again poor
Andrey's poor joke (*Nu i balagur-zhe vï, Dementiy Labirinto-
vich*) or what Dorothy, *l'impayable* ('priceless for impudence
and absurdity') Dorothy, thought of my camping out in the
mountains with only Mayo, a cowhand, to protect me from
lions."

"Could one hear more about that?" asked Van.

"Well, nobody did. All this happened at a time when I
was not on speaking terms with my husband and sister-in-
law, and so could not control the situation. Anyhow, Demon
did not come even when he was only two hundred miles away
and simply mailed instead, from some gaming house, your
lovely, lovely letter about Lucette and my picture."

"One would also like to know some details of the actual
coverture—frequence of intercourse, pet names for secret
warts, favorite smells—"

"*Platok momental'no* (handkerchief quick)! Your right
nostril is full of damp jade," said Ada, and then pointed to a
lawn-side circular sign, rimmed with red, saying: *Chiens
interdits* and depicting an impossible black mongrel with a
white ribbon around its neck: Why, she wondered should the
Swiss magistrates forbid one to cross highland terriers with
poodles?

The last butterflies of 1905, indolent Peacocks and Red
Admirables, one Queen of Spain and one Clouded Yellow,
were making the most of the modest blossoms. A tram on
their left passed close to the promenade, where they rested
and cautiously kissed when the whine of wheels had sub-

sided. The rails hit by the sun acquired a beautiful cobalt sheen—the reflection of noon in terms of bright metal.

"Let's have cheese and white wine under that pergola," suggested Van. "The Vinelanders will lunch *à deux* today."

Some kind of musical gadget played jungle jingles; the open bags of a Tirolese couple stood unpleasantly near—and Van bribed the waiter to carry their table out, onto the boards of an unused pier. Ada admired the waterfowl population: Tufted Ducks, black with contrasty white flanks making them look like shoppers (this and the other comparisons are all Ada's) carrying away an elongated flat carton (new tie? gloves?) under each arm, while the black tuft recalled Van's head when he was fourteen and wet, having just taken a dip in the brook. Coots (which *had* returned after all), swimming with an odd pumping movement of the neck, the way horses walk. Small grebes and big ones, with crests, holding their heads erect, with something heraldic in their demeanor. They had, she said, wonderful nuptial rituals, closely facing each other—so (putting up her index fingers bracketwise)— rather like two bookends and no books between, and, shaking their heads in turn, with flashes of copper.

"I asked you about Andrey's rituals."

"Ach, Andrey is so excited to see all those European birds! He's a great sportsman and knows our Western game remarkably well. We have in the West a very cute little grebe with a black ribbon around its fat white bill. Andrey calls it *pestroklyuvaya chomga*. And that big *chomga* there is *hohlushka*, he says. If you scowl like that once again, when I say something innocent and on the whole rather entertaining, I'm going to kiss you on the tip of the nose, in front of everybody."

Just a tiny mite artificial, not in her best Veen. But she recovered instantly:

"Oh, look at those sea gulls playing chicken."

Several *rieuses*, a few of which were still wearing their tight black summer bonnets, had settled on the vermilion railing along the lakeside, with their tails to the path and watched which of them would stay staunchily perched at the approach of the next passerby. The majority flapped waterward as Ada and Van neared; one twitched its tail feathers and made a movement analogous to "bending one's knees" but saw it through and remained on the railing.

"I think we noticed that species only once in Arizona—at a place called Saltsink—a kind of man-made lake. Our common ones have quite different wing tips."

A Crested Grebe, afloat some way off, slowly, very slowly started to sink, then abruptly executed a jumping fish plunge, showing its glossy white underside, and vanished.

"Why on earth," asked Van, "didn't you let her know, in one way or another, that you were not angry with her? Your phoney letter made her most unhappy!"

"Pah!" uttered Ada. "She put me in a most embarrassing situation. I can quite understand her being mad at Dorothy (who meant well, poor stupid thing—stupid enough to warn me against possible 'infections' such as 'labial lesbianitis.' *Labial lesbianitis!*) but that was no reason for Lucette to look up Andrey in town and tell him she was great friends with the man I had loved before my marriage. He didn't dare annoy me with his revived curiosity, but he complained to Dorothy of Lucette's *neopravdannaya zhestokost'* (unjustified cruelty)."

"Ada, Ada," groaned Van, "I want you to get rid of that husband of yours, *and* his sister, right *now!*"

"Give me a fortnight," she said, "I have to go back to the ranch. I can't bear the thought of her poking among my things."

At first everything seemed to proceed according to the instructions of some friendly genius.

Much to Van's amusement (the tasteless display of which his mistress neither condoned nor condemned), Andrey was laid up with a cold for most of the week. Dorothy, a born nurser, considerably surpassed Ada (who, never being ill herself, could not stand the sight of an ailing stranger) in readiness of sickbed attendance, such as reading to the sweating and suffocating patient old issues of the *Golos Feniksa*; but on Friday the hotel doctor bundled him off to the nearby American Hospital, where even his sister was not allowed to visit him "because of the constant necessity of routine tests" —or rather because the poor fellow wished to confront disaster in manly solitude.

During the next days, Dorothy used her leisure to spy upon Ada. The woman was sure of three things: that Ada had a lover in Switzerland; that Van was her brother; and that he was arranging for his irresistible sister secret trysts with the person she had loved before her marriage. The delightful phenomenon of all three terms being true, but making nonsense when hashed, provided Van with another source of amusement.

The Three Swans overwinged a bastion. Anyone who called, flesh or voice, was told by the concierge or his acolytes that Van was out, that Madame André Vinelander was unknown, and that all they could do was to take a message. His car, parked in a secluded bosquet, could not betray his presence. In the forenoon he regularly used the service lift that communicated directly with the backyard. Lucien, something of a wit, soon learned to recognize Dorothy's contralto: *"La voix cuivrée a téléphoné,"* *"La Trompette n'était pas contente ce matin,"* et cetera. Then the friendly Fates took a day off.

Andrey had had a first copious hemorrhage while on a business trip to Phoenix sometime in August. A stubborn, independent, not overbright optimist, he had ascribed it to a nosebleed having gone the wrong way and concealed it from everybody so as to avoid "stupid talks." He had had for years a two-pack smoker's fruity cough, but when a few days after that first "postnasal blood drip" he spat a scarlet gob into his washbasin, he resolved to cut down on cigarettes and limit himself to *tsigarki* (cigarillos). The next *contretemps* occurred in Ada's presence, just before they left for Europe; he managed to dispose of his bloodstained handkerchief before she saw it, but she remembered him saying "V*ot te na*" (well, that's odd) in a bothered voice. Believing with most other Estotians that the best doctors were to be found in Central Europe, he told himself he would see a Zurich specialist whose name he got from a member of his "lodge" (meeting place of brotherly moneymakers), if he again coughed up blood. The American hospital in Valvey, next to the Russian church built by Vladimir Chevalier, his granduncle, proved to be good enough for diagnosing advanced tuberculosis of the left lung.

On Wednesday, October 22, in the early afternoon, Dorothy, "frantically" trying to "locate" Ada (who after her usual visit to the Three Swans was spending a couple of profitable hours at Paphia's "Hair and Beauty" Salon) left a message for Van, who got it only late at night when he returned from a trip to Sorcière, in the Valais, about one hundred miles east, where he bought a villa for himself *et ma cousine,* and had supper with the former owner, a banker's widow, amiable Mme Scarlet and her blond, pimply but pretty, daughter Eveline, both of whom seemed erotically moved by the rapidity of the deal.

He was still calm and confident; after carefully studying

Dorothy's hysterical report, he still believed that nothing threatened their destiny; that at best Andrey would die right now, sparing Ada the bother of a divorce; and that at worst the man would be packed off to a mountain sanatorium in a novel to linger there through a few last pages of epilogical mopping up far away from the reality of *their* united lives. Friday morning, at nine o'clock—as bespoken on the eve—he drove over to the Bellevue, with the pleasant plan of motoring to Sorcière to show her the house.

At night a thunderstorm had rather patly broken the back of the miraculous summer. Even more patly the sudden onset of her flow had curtailed yesterday's caresses. It was raining when he slammed the door of his car, hitched up his velveteen slacks, and, stepping across puddles, passed between an ambulance and a large black Yak, waiting one behind the other before the hotel. All the wings of the Yak were spread open, two bellboys had started to pile in luggage under the chauffeur's supervision, and various parts of the old hackney car were responding with discreet creaks to the grunts of the loaders.

He suddenly became aware of the rain's reptile cold on his balding head and was about to enter the glass revolvo, when it produced Ada, somewhat in the manner of those carved-wood barometers whose doors yield either a male puppet or a female one. Her attire—that mackintosh over a high-necked dress, the fichu on her upswept hair, the crocodile bag slung across her shoulder—formed a faintly old-fashioned and even provincial ensemble. "On her there was no face," as Russians say to describe an expression of utter dejection.

She led him around the hotel to an ugly rotunda, out of the miserable drizzle, and there she attempted to embrace him but he evaded her lips. She was leaving in a few minutes. Heroic, helpless Andrey had been brought back to the hotel

[561]

in an ambulance. Dorothy had managed to obtain three seats on the Geneva-Phoenix plane. The two cars were taking him, her and the heroic sister straight to the helpless airport.

She asked for a handkerchief, and he pulled out a blue one from his windjacket pocket, but her tears had started to roll and she shaded her eyes, while he stood before her with outstretched hand.

"Part of the act?" he inquired coldly.

She shook her head, took the handkerchief with a childish "*merci,*" blew her nose and gasped, and swallowed, and spoke, and next moment all, all was lost.

She could not tell her husband while he was ill. Van would have to wait until Andrey was sufficiently well to bear the news and that might take some time. Of course, she would have to do everything to have him completely cured, there was a wondermaker in Arizona—

"Sort of patching up a bloke before hanging him," said Van.

"And to think," cried Ada with a kind of square shake of stiff hands as if dropping a lid or a tray, "to think that he dutifully concealed everything! Oh, of course, I can't leave him now!"

"Yes, the old story—the flute player whose impotence has to be treated, the reckless ensign who may never return from a distant war!"

"*Ne ricane pas!*" exclaimed Ada. "The poor, poor little man! How dare you sneer?"

As had been peculiar to his nature even in the days of his youth, Van was apt to relieve a passion of anger and disappointment by means of bombastic and arcane utterances which hurt like a jagged fingernail caught in satin, the lining of Hell.

"Castle True, Castle Bright!" he now cried, "Helen of

Troy, Ada of Ardis! You have betrayed the Tree and the Moth!"

"*Perestagne* (stop, *cesse*)!"

"Ardis the First, Ardis the Second, Tanned Man in a Hat, and now Mount Russet—"

"*Perestagne!*" repeated Ada (like a fool dealing with an epileptic).

"*Oh! Qui me rendra mon Hélène—*"

"Ach, *perestagne!*"

"*—et le phalène.*"

"*Je t'emplie* ('*prie*' and '*supplie*'), stop, Van. *Tu sais que j'en vais mourir.*"

"But, but, but"—(slapping every time his forehead)—"to be on the very brink of, of, of—and then have that idiot turn Keats!"

"*Bozhe moy*, I must be going. Say something to me, my darling, my only one, something that might help!"

There was a narrow chasm of silence broken only by the rain drumming on the eaves.

"Stay with me, girl," said Van, forgetting everything—pride, rage, the convention of everyday pity.

For an instant she seemed to waver—or at least to consider wavering; but a resonant voice reached them from the drive and there stood Dorothy, gray-caped and mannish-hatted, energetically beckoning with her unfurled umbrella.

"I can't, I can't, I'll write you," murmured my poor love in tears.

Van kissed her leaf-cold hand and, letting the Bellevue worry about his car, letting all Swans worry about his effects and Mme Scarlet worry about Eveline's skin trouble, he walked some ten kilometers along soggy roads to Rennaz and thence flew to Nice, Biskra, the Cape, Nairobi, the Basset range—

And o'er the summits of the Basset—

Would she write? Oh, she did! Oh, every old thing turned out superfine! Fancy raced fact in never-ending rivalry and girl giggles. Andrey lived only a few months longer, *po pal'tzam* (finger counting) one, two, three, four—say, five. Andrey was doing fine by the spring of nineteen six or seven, with a comfortably collapsed lung and a straw-colored beard (nothing like facial vegetation to keep a patient busy). Life forked and reforked. Yes, she told him. He insulted Van on the mauve-painted porch of a Douglas hotel where Van was awaiting his Ada in a final version of *Les Enfants Maudits*. Monsieur de Tobak (an earlier cuckold) and Lord Erminin (a second-time second) witnessed the duel in the company of a few tall yuccas and short cactuses. Vinelander wore a cutaway (he would); Van, a white suit. Neither man wished to take any chances, and both fired simultaneously. Both fell. Mr. Cutaway's bullet struck the outsole of Van's left shoe (white, black-heeled), tripping him and causing a slight *four-millement* (excited ants) in his foot—that was all. Van got his adversary plunk in the underbelly—a serious wound from which he recovered in due time, if at all (here the forking swims in the mist). Actually it was all much duller.

So she did write as she had promised? Oh, yes, yes! In seventeen years he received from her around a hundred brief notes, each containing around one hundred words, making around thirty printed pages of insignificant stuff—mainly about her husband's health and the local fauna. After helping her to nurse Andrey at Agavia Ranch through a couple of acrimonious years (she begrudged Ada every poor little hour devoted to collecting, mounting, and rearing!), and then taking exception to Ada's choosing the famous and excellent Grotonovich Clinic (for her husband's endless periods of treatment) instead of Princess Alashin's select sanatorium, Dorothy Vinelander retired to a subarctic monastery town (Ilemna, now Novostabia) where eventually she married a Mr. Brod or Bred, tender and passionate, dark and handsome, who traveled in eucharistials and other sacramental objects throughout the Severnïya Territorii and who subsequently was to direct, and still may be directing half a century later, archeological reconstructions at Goreloe (the "Lyaskan Herculanum"); what treasures he dug up in matrimony is another question.

Steadily but very slowly Andrey's condition kept deteriorating. During his last two or three years of idle existence on various articulated couches, whose every plane could be altered in hundreds of ways, he lost the power of speech, though still able to nod or shake his head, frown in concentration, or faintly smile when inhaling the smell of food (the origin, indeed, of our first beatitudes). He died one spring night, alone in a hospital room, and that same summer (1922) his widow donated her collections to a National Park museum and traveled by air to Switzerland for an "exploratory interview" with fifty-two-year-old Van Veen.

PART FOUR

1

Here a heckler asked, with the arrogant air of one wanting to see a gentleman's driving license, how did the "Prof" reconcile his refusal to grant the future the status of Time with the fact that it, the future, could hardly be considered nonexistent, since "it possessed at least one future, I mean, feature, involving such an important idea as that of absolute necessity."

Throw him out. Who said *I* shall die?

Refuting the determinist's statement more elegantly: unconsciousness, far from awaiting us, with flyback and noose, somewhere ahead, envelops both the Past and the Present from all conceivable sides, being a character not of Time itself but of organic decline natural to all things whether conscious of Time or not. That I know others die is irrelevant to the case. I also know that you, and, probably, I, were born, but that does not *prove* we went through the chronal phase called the Past: my Present, my brief span of consciousness, tells me I did, not the silent thunder of the infinite unconsciousness proper to my birth fifty-two years and 195 days ago. My first recollection goes back to mid-July, 1870, i.e., my seventh month of life (with most people, of course, retentive consciousness starts somewhat later, at three or four years of age) when, one morning, in our Riviera villa, a chunk of green plaster ornament, dislodged from the ceiling by an earthquake, crashed into my cradle. The 195 days preceding that event being indistinguishable from infinite unconsciousness, are not to be included in perceptual time, so that, insofar as my mind and my pride of mind are concerned, I am today (mid-July, 1922) quite exactly fifty-two, *et trêve de mon style plafond peint.*

In the same sense of individual, perceptual time, I can put my Past in reverse gear, enjoy this moment of recollection as much as I did the horn of abundance whose stucco pineapple just missed my head, and postulate that next moment a cosmic or corporeal cataclysm might—not kill me, but plunge me into a permanent state of stupor, of a type sensationally new to science, thus depriving natural dissolution of any logical or chronal sense. Furthermore, this reasoning takes care of the much less interesting (albeit important, important) Universal Time ("we had a thumping time chopping heads") also known as Objective Time (really, woven most coarsely of private times), the history, in a word, of humanity and humor, and that kind of thing. Nothing prevents mankind as such from having no future at all—if for example our genus evolves by imperceptible (this is the ramp of my argument) degrees a *novo-sapiens* species or another subgenus altogether, which will enjoy other varieties of being and dreaming, beyond man's notion of Time. Man, in that sense, will never die, because there may never be a taxonomical point in his evolutionary progress that could be determined as the last stage of man in the cline turning him into Neohomo, or some horrible, throbbing slime. I think our friend will not bother us any further.

My purpose in writing my *Texture of Time*, a difficult, delectable and blessed work, a work which I am about to place on the dawning desk of the still-absent reader, is to purify my own notion of Time. I wish to examine the essence of Time, not its lapse, for I do not believe that its essence can be reduced to its lapse. I wish to caress Time.

One can be a lover of Space and its possibilities: take, for example, speed, the smoothness and sword-swish of speed; the aquiline glory of ruling velocity; the joy cry of the curve; and one can be an amateur of Time, an epicure of duration. I delight sensually in Time, in its stuff and spread, in the fall of its folds, in the very impalpability of its grayish gauze, in the coolness of its continuum. I wish to do something about it; to indulge in a simulacrum of possession. I am aware that all who have tried to reach the charmed castle have got lost in obscurity or have bogged down in Space. I am also aware that Time is a fluid medium for the culture of metaphors.

Why is it so difficult—so degradingly difficult—to bring the notion of Time into mental focus and keep it there for inspection? What an effort, what fumbling, what irritating fatigue! It is like rummaging with one hand in the glove compartment for the road map—fishing out Montenegro, the Dolomites, paper money, a telegram—everything except the stretch of chaotic country between Ardez and Something-soprano, in the dark, in the rain, while trying to take advantage of a red light in the coal black, with the wipers functioning metronomically, chronometrically: the blind finger of space poking and tearing the texture of time. And Aurelius Augustinus, too, he, too, in his tussles with the same theme, fifteen hundred years ago, experienced this oddly physical torment of the shallowing mind, the *shchekotiki* (tickles) of approximation, the evasions of cerebral exhaustion—but he, at least, could replenish his brain with God-dispensed energy (have a footnote here about how delightful it is to watch him pressing on and interspersing his cogitations, between sands and stars, with vigorous little fits of prayer).

Lost again. Where was I? Where am I? Mud road. Stopped car. Time is rhythm: the insect rhythm of a warm humid night, brain ripple, breathing, the drum in my temple—these are our faithful timekeepers; and reason corrects the feverish beat. A patient of mine could make out the rhythm of flashes succeeding one another every three milliseconds (0.003!). On.

What nudged, what comforted me, a few minutes ago at the stop of a thought? Yes. Maybe the only thing that hints at a sense of Time is rhythm; not the recurrent beats of the rhythm but the gap between two such beats, the gray gap between black beats: the Tender Interval. The regular throb itself merely brings back the miserable idea of measurement, but in between, something like true Time lurks. How can I extract it from its soft hollow? The rhythm should be neither too slow nor too fast. One beat per minute is already far beyond my sense of succession and five oscillations per second make a hopeless blur. The ample rhythm causes Time to dissolve, the rapid one crowds it out. Give me, say, three seconds, then I can do both: perceive the rhythm and probe the interval. A hollow, did I say? A dim pit? But that is only Space, the comedy villain, returning by the back door with the pendulum he peddles, while I grope for the meaning of Time. What I endeavor to grasp is precisely the Time that Space helps me to measure, and no wonder I fail to grasp Time, since knowledge-gaining itself "takes time."

If my eye tells me something about Space, my ear tells me something about Time. But while Space can be contemplated, naively, perhaps, yet directly, I can listen to Time only between stresses, for a brief concave moment warily and worriedly, with the growing realization that I am listening not to Time itself but to the blood current coursing through my brain, and thence through the veins of the neck heartward, back to the seat of private throes which have no relation to Time.

The direction of Time, the ardis of Time, one-way Time, here is something that looks useful to me one moment, but dwindles the next to the level of an illusion obscurely related to the mysteries of growth and gravitation. The irreversibility of Time (which is not heading anywhere in the first place) is a very parochial affair: had our organs and orgitrons not been asymmetrical, our view of Time might have been amphitheatric and altogether grand, like ragged night and jagged mountains around a small, twinkling, satisfied hamlet. We are told that if a creature loses its teeth and becomes a bird, the best the latter can do when needing teeth again is to evolve a serrated beak, never the real dentition it once possessed. The scene is Eocene and the actors are fossils. It is an amusing instance of the way nature cheats but it reveals as little relation to essential Time, straight or round, as the fact of my writing from left to right does to the course of my thought.

And speaking of evolution, can we imagine the origin and stepping stones and rejected mutations of Time? Has there ever been a "primitive" form of Time in which, say, the Past was not yet clearly differentiated from the Present, so that past shadows and shapes showed through the still soft, long, larval "now"? Or did that evolution only refer to timekeeping, from sandglass to atomic clock and from that to portable pulsar? And *what* time did it take for Old Time to become

Newton's? Ponder the Egg, as the French cock said to his hens.

Pure Time, Perceptual Time, Tangible Time, Time free of content, context, and running commentary—this is *my* time and theme. All the rest is numerical symbol or some aspect of Space. The texture of Space is not that of Time, and the piebald four-dimensional sport bred by relativists is a quadruped with one leg replaced by the ghost of a leg. My time is also Motionless Time (we shall presently dispose of "flowing" time, water-clock time, water-closet time).

The Time I am concerned with is only the Time stopped by me and closely attended to by my tense-willed mind. Thus it would be idle and evil to drag in "passing" time. Of course, I shave longer when my thought "tries on" words; of course, I am not aware of the lag until I look at my watch; of course, at fifty years of age, one year seems to pass faster because it is a smaller fraction of my increased stock of existence and also because I am less often bored than I was in childhood between dull game and duller book. But that "quickening" depends precisely upon one's not being attentive to Time.

It is a queer enterprise—this attempt to determine the nature of something consisting of phantomic phases. Yet I trust that my reader, who by now is frowning over these lines (but ignoring, at least, his breakfast), will agree with me that there is nothing more splendid than lone thought; and lone thought must plod on, or—to use a less ancient analogy—drive on, say, in a sensitive, admirably balanced Greek car that shows its sweet temper, and road-holding assurance at every turn of the alpine highway.

Two fallacies should be dealt with before we go any further. The first is the confusion of temporal elements with spatial ones. Space, the impostor, has been already denounced in these notes (which are now being set down during half a day's break in a crucial journey); his trial will take place at a later stage of our investigation. The second dismissal is that of an immemorial habit of speech. We regard Time as a kind of stream, having little to do with an actual mountain torrent showing white against a black cliff or a dull-colored great river in a windy valley, but running invariably through our chronographical landscapes. We are so used to that mythical spectacle, so keen upon liquefying every lap of life, that we end up by being unable to speak of Time without speaking of physical motion. Actually, of course, the sense of its motion is derived from many natural, or at least familiar, sources—the body's innate awareness of its own bloodstream, the ancient vertigo caused by rising stars, and, of course, our methods of measurement, such as the creeping shadow line of a gnomon, the trickle of an hourglass, the trot of a second hand—and here we are back in Space. Note the frames, the receptacles. The idea that Time "flows" as naturally as an apple thuds down on a garden table implies that it flows in and through something else and if we take that "something" to be Space then we have only a metaphor flowing along a yardstick.

But beware, *anime meus*, of the marcel wave of fashionable art; avoid the Proustian bed and the assassin pun (itself a suicide—as those who know their Verlaine will note).

We are now ready to tackle Space. We reject without qualms the artificial concept of space-tainted, space-parasited time, the space-time of relativist literature. Anyone, if he likes, may maintain that Space is the outside of Time, or the body of Time, or that Space is suffused with Time and vice versa, or that in some peculiar way Space is merely the waste product of Time, even its corpse, or that in the long, infinitely long, run Time *is* Space; that sort of gossip may be pleasing, especially when we are young; but no one shall make

[575]

me believe that the movement of matter (say, a pointer) across a carved-out area of Space (say, a dial) is by nature identical with the "passing" of time. Movement of matter merely spans an extension of some other palpable matter, against which it is measured, but tells us nothing about the actual structure of impalpable Time. Similarly, a graduated tape, even of infinite length, is not Space itself, nor can the most exact odometer represent the road which I see as a black mirror of rain under turning wheels, hear as a sticky rustle, smell as a damp July night in the Alps, and feel as a smooth basis. We, poor Spatians, are better adapted, in our three-dimensional Lacrimaval, to Extension rather than to Duration: our body is capable of greater stretching than volitional recall can boast of. I cannot memorize (though I sought only yesterday to resolve it into mnemonic elements) the number of my new car but I feel the asphalt under my front tires as if they were parts of my body. Yet Space itself (like Time) is nothing I can comprehend: a place where motion occurs. A plasm in which matter—concentrations of Space plasm—is organized and enclosed. We can measure the globules of matter and the distances between them, but Space plasm itself is incomputable.

We measure Time (a second hand trots, or a minute hand jerks, from one painted mark to another) in terms of Space (without knowing the nature of either), but the spanning of Space does not always require Time—or at least does not require more time than the "now" point of the specious present contains in its hollow. The perceptual possession of a unit of space is practically instantaneous when, for example, an expert driver's eye takes in a highway symbol—the black mouth and neat archivolt within a red triangle (a blend of color and shape recognized in "no time," when properly seen, as meaning a road tunnel) or something of less immediate importance such as the delightful Venus sign ♀ , which might be misunderstood as permitting whorelets to thumb rides, but actually tells the worshipper or the sightseer that a church is reflected in the local river. I suggest adding a pilcrow for persons who read while driving.

Space is related to our senses of sight, touch, and muscular effort; Time is vaguely connected with hearing (still, a deaf man would perceive the "passage" of time incomparably better than a blind limbless man would the idea of "passage"). "Space is a swarming in the eyes, and Time a singing in the ears," says John Shade, a modern poet, as quoted by an invented philosopher ("Martin Gardiner") in *The Ambidextrous Universe*, page 165. Space flutters to the ground, but Time remains between thinker and thumb, when Monsieur Bergson uses his scissors. Space introduces its eggs into the nests of Time: a "before" here, an "after" there—and a speckled clutch of Minkowski's "world-points." A stretch of Space is organically easier to measure mentally than a "stretch" of Time. The notion of Space must have been formed before that of Time (Guyau in Whitrow). The indistinguishable inane (Locke) of infinite space is mentally distinguishable (and indeed could not be imagined otherwise) from the ovoid "void" of Time. Space thrives on surds, Time is irreducible to blackboard roots and birdies. The same section of Space may seem more extensive to a fly than to S. Alexander, but a moment to him is *not* "hours to a fly," because if that were true flies would know better than wait to get swapped. I cannot imagine Space without Time, but I can very well imagine Time without Space. "Space-Time"— that hideous hybrid whose very hyphen looks phoney. One can be a hater of Space, and a lover of Time.

There are people who can fold a road map. Not this writer. At this point, I suspect, I should say something about my attitude to "Relativity." It is not sympathetic. What many cosmogonists tend to accept as an objective truth is really the flaw inherent in mathematics which parades as truth. The body of the astonished person moving in Space is shortened in the direction of motion and shrinks catastrophically as the velocity nears the speed beyond which, by the fiat of a fishy formula, no speed can be. That is his bad luck, not mine—but I sweep away the business of his clock's slowing down. Time, which requires the utmost purity of consciousness to be properly apprehended, is the most rational element of life, and my reason feels insulted by those flights of Technology Fiction. One especially grotesque inference, drawn (I think by Engelwein) from Relativity Theory—and destroying it, if drawn correctly—is that the galactonaut and his domestic animals, after touring the speed spas of Space, would return younger than if they had stayed at home all the time. Imagine them filing out of their airark—rather like those "Lions," juvenilified by romp suits, exuding from one of those huge chartered buses that stop, horribly blinking, in front of a man's impatient sedan just where the highway wizens to squeeze through the narrows of a mountain village.

Perceived events can be regarded as simultaneous when they belong to the same span of attention; in the same way (insidious simile, unremovable obstacle!) as one can visually possess a unit of space—say, a vermilion ring with a frontal view of a toy car within its white kernel, forbidding the lane into which, however, I turned with a furious *coup de volant*. I know relativists, hampered by their "light signals" and "traveling clocks," try to demolish the idea of simultaneity on a cosmic scale, but let us imagine a gigantic hand with its thumb on one star and its minimus on another—will it not be touching both at the same time—or are tactile coincidences even more misleading than visual ones? I think I had better back out of this passage.

Such a drought affected Hippo in the most productive months of Augustine's bishopric that clepsydras had to be replaced by sandglasses. He defined the Past as what is no longer and the future as what is not yet (actually the future is a fantasm belonging to another category of thought essentially different from that of the Past which, at least, was here a moment ago—where did I put it? Pocket? But the search itself is already "past").

The Past is changeless, intangible, and "never-to-be-revisited"—terms that do not fit this or that section of Space which I see, for instance, as a white villa and its whiter (newer) garage with seven cypresses of unequal height, tall Sunday and short Monday, watching over the private road that loops past scrub oak and briar down to the public one connecting Sorcière with the highway to Mont Roux (still one hundred miles apart).

I shall now proceed to consider the Past as an accumulation of sensa, not as the dissolution of Time implied by immemorial metaphors picturing transition. The "passage of time" is merely a figment of the mind with no objective counterpart, but with easy spatial analogies. It is seen only in rear view, shapes and shades, arollas and larches silently tumbling away: the perpetual disaster of receding time, *éboulements*, landslides, mountain roads where rocks are always falling and men always working.

We build models of the past and then use them spatiologically to reify and measure Time. Let us take a familiar example. Zembre, a quaint old town on the Minder River, near Sorcière, in the Valais, was being lost by degrees among new buildings. By the beginning of this century it had acquired a definitely modern look, and the preservation people decided to act. Today, after years of subtle reconstruction, a replica of the old Zembre, with its castle, its church, and its mill extrapolated onto the other side of the Minder, stands opposite the modernized town and separated from it by the length of a bridge. Now, if we replace the spatial view (as seen from a helicopter) by the chronal one (as seen by a retrospector), and the material model of old Zembre by the mental model of it in the Past (say, around 1822), the modern town and the model of the old turn out to be something else than two points in the same place at different times (in spatial perspective they *are* at the same time in different places). The space in which the modern town coagulates is immediately real, while that of its retrospective image (as seen apart from material restoration) shimmers in an imaginary space and we cannot use any bridge to walk from the one to the other. In other words (as one puts it when both writer and reader flounder at last in hopeless confusion of thought), by making a model of the old town in one's mind (and on the Minder) all we do is to spatialize it (or actually drag it out of its own element onto the shore of Space). Thus the term "one century" does *not* correspond in any sense to the hundred feet of steel bridge between modern and model towns, and *that* is what we wished to prove and have now proven.

The Past, then, is a constant accumulation of images. It can be easily contemplated and listened to, tested and tasted at random, so that it ceases to mean the orderly alternation of linked events that it does in the large theoretical sense. It is now a generous chaos out of which the genius of total recall, summoned on this summer morning in 1922, can pick anything he pleases: diamonds scattered all over the parquet in 1888; a russet blackhatted beauty at a Parisian bar in 1901; a humid red rose among artificial ones in 1883; the pensive

half-smile of a young English governess, in 1880, neatly re-
closing her charge's prepuce after the bedtime treat; a little
girl, in 1884, licking the breakfast honey off the badly bitten nails of her spread fingers; the same, at thirty-three,
confessing, rather late in the day, that she did not like flowers in vases; the awful pain striking him in the side while
two children with a basket of mushrooms looked on in the
merrily burning pine forest; and the startled quonk of a
Belgian car, which he had overtaken and passed yesterday on
a blind bend of the alpine highway. Such images tell us
nothing about the texture of time into which they are woven
—except, perhaps, in one matter which happens to be hard to
settle. Does the coloration of a recollected object (or anything else about its visual effect) differ from date to date?
Could I tell by its tint if it comes earlier or later, lower or
higher, in the stratigraphy of my past? Is there any mental
uranium whose dream-delta decay might be used to measure
the age of a recollection? The main difficulty, I hasten to
explain, consists in the experimenter not being able to use
the *same* object at different times (say, the Dutch stove
with its little blue sailing boats in the nursery of Ardis
Manor in 1884 and 1888) because of the two or more impressions borrowing from one another and forming a com-
pound image in the mind; but if different objects are to be
chosen (say, the faces of two memorable coachmen: Ben
Wright, 1884, and Trofim Fartukov, 1888), it is impossible,
insofar as my own research goes, to avoid the intrusion not
only of different characteristics but of different emotional
circumstances, that do not allow the two objects to be considered essentially equal before, so to speak, their being exposed to the action of Time. I am not sure that such objects
cannot be discovered. In my professional work, in the labora-
tories of psychology, I have devised myself many a subtle test

(one of which, the method of determining female virginity without physical examination, today bears my name). Therefore we can assume that the experiment *can* be performed—and how tantalizing, then, the discovery of certain exact levels of decreasing saturation or deepening brilliance—so exact that the "something" which I vaguely perceive in the image of a remembered but unidentifiable person, and which assigns it "somehow" to my early boyhood rather than to my adolescence, can be labeled if not with a name, at least with a definite date, e.g., January 1, 1908 (eureka, the "e.g." worked —*he* was my father's former house tutor, who brought me *Alice in the Camera Obscura* for my eighth birthday).

Our perception of the Past is not marked by the link of succession to as strong a degree as is the perception of the Present and of the instants immediately preceding its point of reality. I usually shave every morning and am accustomed to change the blade in my safety razor after every second shave; now and then I happen to skip a day, have to scrape off the next a tremendous growth of loud bristle, whose obstinate presence my fingers check again and again between strokes, and in such cases I use a blade only once. Now, when I visualize a recent series of shaves, I ignore the element of succession: all I want to know is whether the blade left in my silver plough has done its work once or twice; if it was once, the order of the two bristle-growing days in my mind has no importance—in fact, I tend to hear and feel the second, grittier, morning first, and *then* to throw in the shaveless day, in consequence of which my beard grows in reverse, so to speak.

If now, with some poor scraps of teased-out knowledge relating to the colored contents of the Past, we shift our view and regard it simply as a coherent reconstruction of elapsed events, some of which are retained by the ordinary mind less clearly, if at all, than the others, we can indulge in an easier game with the light and shade of its avenues. Memory-images include after-images of sound, regurgitated, as it were, by the ear which recorded them a moment ago while the mind was engaged in avoiding hitting schoolchildren, so that actually we can replay the message of the church clock after we have left Turtsen and its hushed but still-echoing steeple behind. Reviewing those last steps of the immediate Past involves less physical time than was needed for the clock's mechanism to exhaust its strokes, and it is this mysterious "less" which is a special characteristic of the still-fresh Past into which the Present slipped during that instant inspection of shadow sounds. The "less" indicates that the Past is in no need of clocks and the succession of its events is not clock time, but something more in keeping with the authentic rhythm of Time. We have suggested earlier that the dim intervals between the dark beats have the *feel* of the texture of Time. The same, more vaguely, applies to the impressions received from perceiving the gaps of unremembered or "neutral" time between vivid events. I happen to remember in terms of color (grayish blue, purple, reddish gray) my three farewell lectures—public lectures—on Mr. Bergson's Time at a great university a few months ago. I recall less clearly, and indeed am able to suppress in my mind completely, the six-day intervals between blue and purple and between purple and gray. But I visualize with perfect clarity the circumstances attending the actual lectures. I was a little late for the first (dealing with the Past) and observed with a not-unpleasant thrill, as if arriving at my own funeral, the brilliantly lighted windows of Counterstone Hall and the small figure of a Japanese student who, being also late, overtook me at a wild scurry, and disappeared in the doorway long before I reached its semicircular steps. At the second lecture

—the one on the Present—during the five seconds of silence
and "inward attention" which I requested from the audience
in order to provide an illustration for the point I, or rather
the speaking jewel in my waistcoat pocket, was about to
make regarding the true perception of time, the behemoth
snores of a white-bearded sleeper filled the house—which, of
course, collapsed. At the third and last lecture, on the Future
("Sham Time"), after working perfectly for a few minutes,
my secretly recorded voice underwent an obscure mechanical
disaster, and I preferred simulating a heart attack and being
carried out into the night forever (insofar as lecturing was
concerned) to trying to decipher and sort out the batch of
crumpled notes in pale pencil which poor speakers are obsessed with in familiar dreams (attributed by Dr. Froid of
Signy-Mondieu-Mondieu to the dreamer's having read in infancy his adulterous parents' love letters). I give these ludicrous but salient details to show that the events to be
selected for the test should be not only gaudy and graduated
(three lectures in three weeks), but related to each other by
their main feature (a lecturer's misadventures). The two intervals of five days each are seen by me as twin dimples, each
brimming with a kind of smooth, grayish mist, and a faint
suggestion of shed confetti (which, maybe, might leap into
color if I allowed some casual memory to form in between
the diagnostic limits). Because of its situation among dead
things, that dim continuum cannot be as sensually groped
for, tasted, harkened to, as Veen's Hollow between rhythmic beats; but it shares with it one remarkable indicium: the
immobility of perceptual Time. Synesthetia, to which I am
inordinately prone, proves to be of great help in this type of
task—a task now approaching its crucial stage, the flowering
of the Present.

Now blows the wind of the Present at the top of the Past

—at the top of the passes I have been proud to reach in my life, the Umbrail, the Fluela, the Furka, of my clearest consciousness! The moment changes at the point of perception only because I myself am in a constant state of trivial metamorphosis. To give myself time to time Time I must move my mind in the direction opposite to that in which I am moving, as one does when one is driving past a long row of poplars and wishes to isolate and stop one of them, thus making the green blur reveal and offer, yes, offer, its every leaf. Cretin behind me.

This act of attention is what I called last year the "Deliberate Present" to distinguish it from its more general form termed (by Clay in 1882) the "Specious Present." The conscious construction of one, and the familiar current of the other give us three or four seconds of what can be felt as nowness. This nowness is the only reality we know; it follows the colored nothingness of the no-longer and precedes the absolute nothingness of the future. Thus, in a quite literal sense, we may say that conscious human life lasts always only one moment, for at any moment of deliberate attention to our own flow of consciousness we cannot know if that moment will be followed by another. As I shall later explain, I do not believe that "anticipation" ("looking forward to a promotion or fearing a social blunder" as one unfortunate thinker puts it) plays any significant part in the formation of the specious present, nor do I believe that the future is transformed into a third panel of Time, even if we do anticipate something or other—a turn of the familiar road or the picturesque rise of two steep hills, one with a castle, the other with a church, for the more lucid the forevision the less prophetic it is apt to be. Had that rascal behind me decided to risk it just now he would have collided head-on with the truck that came from beyond the bend, and I and the view might have been eclipsed in the multiple smash.

Our modest Present is, then, the time span that one is directly and actually aware of, with the lingering freshness of the Past still perceived as part of the nowness. In regard to everyday life and the habitual comfort of the body (reasonably healthy, reasonably strong, breathing the green breeze, relishing the aftertaste of the most exquisite food in the world—a boiled egg), it does not matter that we can never enjoy the *true* Present, which is an instant of zero duration, represented by a rich smudge, as the dimensionless point of geometry is by a sizable dot in printer's ink on palpable paper. The normal motorist, according to psychologists and policemen, can perceive, visually, a unit of time as short in extension as one tenth of a second (I had a patient, a former gambler, who could identify a playing card in a five-times-faster flash!). It would be interesting to measure the instant we need to become aware of disappointed or fulfilled expectation. Smells can be very sudden, and in most people the ear and sense of touch work quicker than the eye. Those two hitchhikers really smelled—the male one revoltingly.

Since the Present is but an imaginary point without an awareness of the immediate past, it is necessary to define that awareness. Not for the first time will Space intrude if I say that what we are aware of as "Present" is the constant building up of the Past, its smoothly and relentlessly rising level. How meager! How magic!

Here they are, the two rocky ruin-crowned hills that I have retained for seventeen years in my mind with decalcomaniac romantic vividness—though not quite exactly, I confess; memory likes the *otsebyatina* ("what one contributes oneself"); but the slight discrepancy is now corrected and the act of artistic correction enhances the pang of the Present.

The sharpest feeling of nowness, in visual terms, is the deliberate possession of a segment of Space collected by the eye. This is Time's only contact with Space, but it has a far-reaching reverberation. To be eternal the Present must depend on the conscious spanning of an infinite expansure. Then, and only then, is the Present equatable with Timeless Space. I have been wounded in my duel with the Impostor.

And now I drive into Mont Roux, under garlands of heart-rending welcome. Today is Monday, July 14, 1922, five-thirteen P.M. by my wrist watch, eleven fifty-two by my car's built-in clock, four-ten by all the timepieces in town. The author is in a confused state of exhilaration, exhaustion, expectancy and panic. He has been climbing with two Austrian guides and a temporarily adopted daughter in the incomparable Balkan mountains. He spent most of May in Dalmatia, and June in the Dolomites, and got letters in both places from Ada telling him of her husband's death (April 23, in Arizona). He started working his way west in a dark-blue Argus, dearer to him than sapphires and morphos because she happened to have ordered an exactly similar one to be ready for her in Geneva. He collected three additional villas, two on the Adriatic and one at Ardez in the Northern Grisons. Late on Sunday, July 13, in nearby Alvena, the concierge of the Alraun Palace handed him a cable that had waited for him since Friday.

ARRIVING MONT ROUX TROIS CYGNES MONDAY DINNER-TIME I WANT YOU TO WIRE ME FRANKLY IF THE DATE AND THE WHOLE TRALALA ARE INCONVENIENT.

He transmitted by the new "instantogram," flashed to the Geneva airport, a message ending in the last word of her 1905 cable; and despite the threats of a torrential night set out by

car for the Vaud. Traveling too fast and too wildly, he somehow missed the Oberhalbstein road at the Sylvaplana fork
(150 kilometers south of Alvena); wriggled back north, via
Chiavenna and Splügen, to reach in apocalyptic circumstances Highway 19 (an unnecessary trip of 100 kilometers);
veered by mistake east to Chur; performed an unprintable
U-turn, and covered in a couple of hours the 175-kilometer
stretch westward to Brig. The pale flush of dawn in his rear-
vision mirror had long since turned to passionately bright
daylight when he looped south, by the new Pfynwald road,
to Sorcière, where seventeen years ago he had bought a house
(now Villa Jolana). The three or four servants he had left
there to look after it had taken advantage of his lengthy absence to fade away; so, with the enthusiastic help of two
hitch-hikers stranded in the vicinity—a disgusting youth from
Hilden and his long-haired, slatternly, languorous Hilda—
he had to break into his own house. His accomplices were
mistaken if they expected to find loot and liquor there. After
throwing them out he vainly courted sleep on a sheetless bed
and finally betook himself to the bird-mad garden, where his
two friends were copulating in the empty swimming pool and
had to be shooed off again. It was now around noon. He
worked for a couple of hours on his *Texture of Time*, begun
in the Dolomites at the Lammermoor (not the best of his
recent hotels). The utilitarian impulse behind the task was
to keep him from brooding on the ordeal of happiness awaiting him 150 kilometers west; it did not prevent a healthy
longing for a hot breakfast from making him interrupt his
scribbling to seek out a roadside inn on his way to Mont
Roux.

The Three Swans where he had reserved rooms 508-509-510
had undergone certain changes since 1905. A portly, plum-
nosed Lucien did not recognize him at once—and then

remarked that Monsieur was certainly not "deperishing"—although actually Van had almost reverted to his weight of seventeen years earlier, having shed several kilos in the Balkans rock-climbing with crazy little Acrazia (now dumped in a fashionable boarding school near Florence). No, Madame Vinn Landère had not called. Yes, the hall had been renovated. Swiss-German Louis Wicht now managed the hotel instead of his late father-in-law Luigi Fantini. In the lounge, as seen through its entrance, the huge memorable oil—three ample-haunched Ledas swapping lacustrine impressions—had been replaced by a neoprimitive masterpiece showing three yellow eggs and a pair of plumber's gloves on what looked like wet bathroom tiling. As Van stepped into the "elevator" followed by a black-coated receptionist, it acknowledged his footfall with a hollow clank and then, upon moving, feverishly began transmitting a fragmentary report on some competition—possibly a tricycle race. Van could not help feeling sorry that this blind functional box (even smaller than the slop-pail lift he had formerly used at the back) now substituted for the luxurious affair of yore—an ascentive hall of mirrors—whose famous operator (white whiskers, eight languages) had become a button.

In the hallway of 509, Van recognized the *Bruslot à la sonde* picture next to the pregnant-looking white closet (under whose round sliding doors the corner of the carpet, now gone, would invariably catch). In the salon itself, only a lady's bureau and the balcony view were familiar. Everything else —the semi-transparent shredded-wheat ornaments, the glass flowerheads, the silk-covered armchairs—had been superseded by *Hochmodern* fixtures.

He showered and changed, and finished the flask of brandy in his dressing case, and called the Geneva airport and was told that the last plane from America had just arrived. He went for a stroll—and saw that the famous "mûrier," that spread its great limbs over a humble lavatory on a raised terrace at the top of a cobbled lane, was now in sumptuous purple-blue bloom. He had a beer at the café opposite the railway station, and then, automatically, entered the flower shop next door. He must be gaga to have forgotten what she said the last time about her strange anthophobia (somehow stemming from that debauche à trois thirty years ago). Roses she never liked anyway. He stared and was easily outstared by small Carols from Belgium, long-stemmed Pink Sensations, vermilion Superstars. There were also zinnias, and chrysanthemums, and potted aphelandras, and two graceful fringetails in an inset aquarium. Not wishing to disappoint the courteous old florist, he bought seventeen odorless Baccara roses, asked for the directory, opened it at Ad-Au, Mont Roux, lit upon "Addor, Yolande, Mlle secrét., rue des Délices, 6," and with American presence of mind had his bouquet sent there.

People were already hurrying home from work. Mademoiselle Addor, in a sweat-stained frock, was climbing the stairs. The streets had been considerably quieter in the sourdine Past. The old Morris pillar, upon which the present Queen of Portugal figured once as an actress, no longer stood at the corner of Chemin de Mustrux (old corruption of the town's name). Must Trucks roar through Must Rux?

The chambermaid had drawn the curtains. He wrenched them all open as if resolved to prolong to its utmost limit the torture of that day. The ironwork balcony jutted out far enough to catch the slanting rays. He recalled his last glimpse of the lake on that dismal day in October, 1905, after parting with Ada. Fuligula ducks were falling and rising upon the rain-pocked swell in concentrated enjoyment of doubled water; along the lake walk scrolls of froth curled over the ridges of advancing gray waves and every now and then a welter heaved sufficiently high to splash over the parapet. But now, on this radiant summer evening, no waves foamed, no birds swam; only a few seagulls could be seen, fluttering white over their black reflections. The wide lovely lake lay in dreamy serenity, fretted with green undulations, ruffed with blue, patched with glades of lucid smoothness between the ackers; and, in the lower right corner of the picture, as if the artist had wished to include a very special example of light, the dazzling wake of the westering sun pulsated through a lake-side lombardy poplar that seemed both liquefied and on fire.

A distant idiot leaning backward on waterskis behind a speedboat started to rip the canvas; fortunately, he collapsed before doing much harm, and at the same instant the drawing-room telephone rang.

Now it so happened that she had never—never, at least, in adult life—spoken to him by phone; hence the phone had preserved the very essence, the bright vibration, of her vocal cords, the little "leap" in her larynx, the laugh clinging to the contour of the phrase, as if afraid in girlish glee to slip off the quick words it rode. It was the timbre of their past, as if the past had put through that call, a miraculous connection ("Ardis, one eight eight six"—*comment? Non, non, pas huitante-huit—huitante-six*). Goldenly, youthfully, it bubbled with all the melodious characteristics he knew—or better say recollected, at once, in the sequence they came: that *entrain*, that whelming of quasi-erotic pleasure, that assurance and animation—and, what was especially delightful, the fact that she was utterly and innocently unaware of the modulations entrancing him.

There had been trouble with her luggage. There still was. Her two maids, who were supposed to have flown over the day before on a Laputa (freight airplane) with her trunks, had got stranded somewhere. All she had was a little valise. The concierge was in the act of making some calls for her. Would Van come down? She was *neveroyatno golodnaya* (incredibly hungry).

That telephone voice, by resurrecting the past and linking it up with the present, with the darkening slate-blue mountains beyond the lake, with the spangles of the sun wake dancing through the poplar, formed the centerpiece in his deepest perception of tangible time, the glittering "now" that was the only reality of Time's texture. After the glory of the summit there came the difficult descent.

Ada had warned him in a recent letter that she had "changed considerably, in contour as well as in color." She wore a corset which stressed the unfamiliar stateliness of her body enveloped in a black-velvet gown of a flowing cut both eccentric and monastic, as their mother used to favor. She had had her hair bobbed page-boy-fashion and dyed a brilliant bronze. Her neck and hands were as delicately pale as ever but showed unfamiliar fibers and raised veins. She made lavish use of cosmetics to camouflage the lines at the outer corners of her fat carmined lips and dark-shadowed eyes whose opaque iris now seemed less mysterious than myopic owing to the nervous flutter of her painted lashes. He noted that her smile revealed a gold-capped upper premolar; he had a similar one on the other side of his mouth. The metallic sheen of her fringe distressed him less than that velvet gown, full-skirted, square-shouldered, of well-below-the-calf length, with hip-padding which was supposed both to diminish the waist and disguise by amplification the outline of the now buxom pelvis. Nothing remained of her gangling grace, and the new mellowness, and the velvet stuff, had an irritatingly dignified air of obstacle and defense. He loved her much too tenderly, much too irrevocably, to be unduly depressed by sexual misgivings; but his senses certainly remained stirless—so stirless in fact, that he did not feel at all anxious (as she and he raised their flashing champagne glasses in parody of the crested-grebe ritual) to involve his masculine pride in a half-hearted embrace immediately after dinner. If he was expected to do so, that was too bad; if he was not, that was even worse. At their earlier reunions the constraint, subsisting as a dull ache after the keen agonies of Fate's surgery, used to be soon drowned in sexual desire, leaving life to pick up by and by. Now they were on their own.

The utilitarian trivialities of their table talk—or, rather, of his gloomy monologue—seemed to him positively degrading. He explained at length—fighting her attentive silence, sloshing across the puddles of pauses, abhorring himself—that he had a long and hard journey; that he slept badly; that he was working on an investigation of the nature of Time, a theme that meant struggling with the octopus of one's own brain. She looked at her wrist watch.

"What I'm telling you," he said harshly, "has nothing to do with timepieces." The waiter brought them their coffee. She smiled, and he realized that her smile was prompted by a conversation at the next table, at which a newcomer, a stout sad Englishman, had begun a discussion of the menu with the maître d'hôtel.

"I'll start," said the Englishman, "with the bananas."

"That's not bananas, sir. That's *ananas*, pineapple juice."

"Oh, I see. Well, give me some clear soup."

Young Van smiled back at young Ada. Oddly, that little exchange at the next table acted as a kind of delicious release.

"When I was a kid," said Van, "and stayed for the first—or rather, second—time in Switzerland, I thought that 'Verglas' on roadway signs stood for some magical town, always around the corner, at the bottom of every snowy slope, never seen, but biding its time. I got your cable in the Engadine where there are *real* magical places, such as Alraun or Alruna—which means a tiny Arabian demon in a German wizard's mirror. By the way, we have the old apartment upstairs with an additional bedroom, number five-zero-eight."

"Oh dear. I'm afraid you must cancel poor 508. If I stayed for the night, 510 would do for both of us, but I've got bad news for you. I can't stay. I must go back to Geneva directly after dinner to retrieve my things and maids, whom the authorities have apparently put in a Home for Stray Females because they could not pay the absolutely medieval new *droits de douane*—isn't Switzerland in Washington State, sort of, *après tout*? Look, don't scowl"—(patting his brown blotched hand on which their shared birthmark had got lost among the freckles of age, like a babe in autumn woods, *on peut les suivre en reconnaissant* only Mascodagama's disfigured thumb and the beautiful almond-shaped nails)—"I promise to get in touch with you in a day or two, and then we'll go on a cruise to Greece with the Baynards—they have a yacht and three adorable daughters who still swim in the tan, okay?"

"I don't know what I loathe more," he replied, "yachts or Baynards; but can I help you in Geneva?"

He could not. Baynard had married his Cordula, after a sensational divorce—Scotch veterinaries had had to saw off her husband's antlers (last call for that joke).

Ada's Argus had not yet been delivered. The gloomy black gloss of the hackney Yak and the old-fashioned leggings of its driver reminded him of her departure in 1905.

He saw her off—and ascended, like a Cartesian glassman, like spectral Time standing at attention, back to his desolate fifth floor. Had they lived together these seventeen wretched years, they would have been spared the shock and the humiliation; their aging would have been a gradual adjustment, as imperceptible as Time itself.

His Work-in-Progress, a sheaf of notes tangling with his pajamas, came to the rescue as it had done at Sorcière. Van swallowed a favodorm tablet and, while waiting for it to relieve him of himself, a matter of forty minutes or so, sat down at a lady's bureau to his "lucubratiuncula."

Does the ravage and outrage of age deplored by poets tell the naturalist of Time anything about Time's essence? Very little. Only a novelist's fancy could be caught by this small oval box, once containing Duvet de Ninon (a face powder, with a bird of paradise on the lid), which has been forgotten in a not-quite-closed drawer of the bureau's arc of triumph—not, however, triumph over Time. The blue-green-orange thing looked as if he were meant to be deceived into thinking it had been waiting there seventeen years for the bemused, smiling finder's dream-slow hand: a shabby trick of feigned restitution, a planted coincidence—and a bad blunder, since it had been Lucette, now a mermaid in the groves of Atlantis (and not Ada, now a stranger somewhere near Morges in a black limousine) who had favored that powder. Throw it away lest it mislead a weaker philosopher; what I am concerned with is the delicate texture of Time, void of all embroidered events.

Let us recapitulate.

Physiologically the sense of Time is a sense of continuous becoming, and if "becoming" has a voice, the latter might be, not unnaturally, a steady vibration; but for Log's sake, let us not confuse Time with Tinnitus, and the seashell hum of duration with the throb of our blood. Philosophically, on the other hand, Time is but memory in the making. In every individual life there goes on from cradle to deathbed the gradual shaping and strengthening of that *backbone of con-*

sciousness, which is the Time of the strong. "To be" means to know one "has been." "Not to be" implies the only "new" kind of (sham) time: the future. I dismiss it. Life, love, libraries, have no future.

Time is anything but the popular triptych: a no-longer existing Past, the durationless point of the Present, and a "not-yet" that may never come. No. There are only two panels. The Past (ever-existing in my mind) and the Present (to which my mind gives duration and, therefore, reality). If we make a third compartment of fulfilled expectation, the foreseen, the foreordained, the faculty of prevision, perfect forecast, we are still applying our mind to the Present.

If the Past is perceived as a storage of Time, and if the Present is the process of that perception, the future, on the other hand, is not an item of Time, has nothing to do with Time and with the dim gauze of its physical texture. The future is but a quack at the court of Chronos. Thinkers, social thinkers, feel the Present as pointing beyond itself toward a not yet realized "future"—but that is topical utopia, progressive politics. Technological Sophists argue that by taking advantage of the Laws of Light, by using new telescopes revealing ordinary print at cosmic distances through the eyes of our nostalgic agents on another planet, we can actually see our own past (Goodson discovering the Goodson and that sort of thing) including documentary evidence of our not knowing what lay in store for us (and our knowing *now*), and that consequently the Future did exist yesterday and by inference does exist today. This may be good physics but is execrable logic, and the Tortoise of the Past will never overtake the Achilles of the future, no matter how we parse distances on our cloudy blackboards.

What we do at best (at worst we perform trivial tricks) when postulating the future, is to expand enormously the specious present causing it to permeate any amount of time with all manner of information, anticipation and precognition. At best, the "future" is the idea of a hypothetical present based on our experience of succession, on our faith in logic and habit. Actually, of course, our hopes can no more bring it into existence than our regrets change the Past. The latter has at least the taste, the tinge, the tang, of our individual being. But the future remains aloof from our fancies and feelings. At every moment it is an infinity of branching possibilities. A determinate scheme would abolish the very notion of time (here the pill floated its first cloudlet). The unknown, the not yet experienced and the unexpected, all the glorious "x" intersections, are the inherent parts of human life. The determinate scheme by stripping the sunrise of its surprise would erase all sunrays—

The pill had really started to work. He finished changing into his pajamas, a series of fumbles, mostly unfinished, which he had begun an hour ago, and fumbled into bed. He dreamed that he was speaking in the lecturing hall of a transatlantic liner and that a bum resembling the hitch-hiker from Hilden was asking sneeringly how did the lecturer explain that in our dreams we know we shall awake, is not that analogous to the certainty of death and if so, the future—

At daybreak he sat up with an abrupt moan, and trembling: if he did not act *now*, he would lose her forever! He decided to drive at once to the Manhattan in Geneva.

Van welcomed the renewal of polished structures after a week of black fudge fouling the bowl slope so high that no amount of flushing could dislodge it. Something to do with olive oil and the Italian type water closets. He shaved, bathed, rapidly dressed. Was it too early to order breakfast? Should he ring up her hotel before starting? Should he rent a plane? Or might it, perhaps, be simpler—

The door-folds of his drawing room balcony stood wide open. Banks of mist still crossed the blue of the mountains beyond the lake, but here and there a peak was tipped with ocher under the cloudless turquoise of the sky. Four tremendous trucks thundered by one after another. He went up to the rail of the balcony and wondered if he had ever satisfied the familiar whim by going platch—had he? had he? You could never know, really. One floor below, and somewhat adjacently, stood Ada engrossed in the view.

He saw her bronze bob, her white neck and arms, the pale flowers on her flimsy peignoir, her bare legs, her high-heeled silver slippers. Pensively, youngly, voluptuously, she was scratching her thigh at the rise of the right buttock: Ladore's pink signature on vellum at mosquito dusk. Would she look up? All her flowers turned up to him, beaming, and she made the royal-grant gesture of lifting and offering him the mountains, the mist and the lake with three swans.

He left the balcony and ran down a short spiral staircase to the fourth floor. In the pit of his stomach there sat the suspicion that it might not be room 410, as he conjectured, but 412 or even 414. What would happen if she had not understood, was not on the lookout? She had, she was.

When, "a little later," Van, kneeling and clearing his throat, was kissing her dear cold hands, gratefully, gratefully, in full defiance of death, with bad fate routed and her dreamy afterglow bending over him, she asked:

"Did you really think I had gone?"

"*Obmanshchitsa* (deceiver), *obmanshchitsa*," Van kept repeating with the fervor and gloat of blissful satiety.

"I told him to turn," she said, "somewhere near Morzhey ("morses" or "walruses," a Russian pun on "Morges"—maybe a mermaid's message). And *you* slept, you could sleep!"

"I worked," he replied, "my first draft is done."

She confessed that on coming back in the middle of the night she had taken to her room from the hotel bookcase (the night porter, an avid reader, had the key) the British Encyclopedia volume, here it was, with this article on Space-Time: " 'Space' (it says here, rather suggestively) 'denotes the property, you are my property, in virtue of which, you are my virtue, rigid bodies can occupy different positions' Nice? Nice."

"Don't laugh, my Ada, at our philosophic prose," remonstrated her lover. "All that matters just now is that I have given new life to Time by cutting off Siamese Space and the false future. My aim was to compose a kind of novella in the form of a treatise on the Texture of Time, an investigation of its veily substance, with illustrative metaphors gradually increasing, very gradually building up a logical love story, going from past to present, blossoming as a concrete story, and just as gradually reversing analogies and disintegrating again into bland abstraction."

"I wonder," said Ada, "I wonder if the attempt to discover those things is worth the stained glass. We can know the time, we can know a time. We can never know Time. Our senses are simply not meant to perceive it. It is like—"

PART FIVE

PART FIVE

1

I, Van Veen, salute you, life, Ada Veen, Dr. Lagosse, Stepan Nootkin, Violet Knox, Ronald Oranger. Today is my ninety-seventh birthday, and I hear from my wonderful new Everyrest chair a spade scrape and footsteps creak in the snow-sparkling garden, and my old Russian valet, who is deafer than he thinks, pull out and push in nose-ringed drawers in the dressing room. This Part Five is not meant as an epilogue; it is the true introduction of my ninety-seven percent true, and three percent likely, *Ada or Ardor, a family chronicle*.

Of all their many houses, in Europe and in the Tropics, the château recently built at Ex, in the Swiss Alps, with its pillared front and crenelated turrets, became their favorite, especially in midwinter, when the famous glittering air, *le cristal d'Ex*, "matches the highest forms of human thought —pure mathematics & decipherment" (unpublished ad).

At least twice a year our happy couple indulged in fairly long travels. Ada did not breed or collect butterflies any more, but throughout her healthy and active old age loved to film them in their natural surroundings, at the bottom of her garden or the end of the world, flapping and flitting, settling on flowers or filth, gliding over grass or granite, fighting or mating. Van accompanied her on picture-shooting journeys to Brazil, the Congo, New Guinea, but secretly preferred a long drink under a tent to a long wait under a tree for some rarity to come down to the bait and be taken in color. One would need another book to describe Ada's adventures in Adaland. The films—and the crucified actors (Identification Mounts)—can be seen by arrangement at the Lucinda Museum, 5, Park Lane, Manhattan.

2

He had lived up to the ancestral motto: "As healthy a Veen as father has been." At fifty he could look back at the narrowing recession of only one hospital corridor (with a pair of white-shod trim feet tripping away), along which he had ever been wheeled. He now noticed, however, that furtive, furcating cracks kept appearing in his physical well-being, as if inevitable decomposition were sending out to him, across static gray time, its first emissaries. A stuffed nose caused a stifling dream, and, at the door of the slightest cold, intercostal neuralgia waited with its blunt spear. The more spacious his bedside table grew the more cluttered it became with such absolute necessities of the night as nose drops, eucalyptic pastilles, wax earplugs, gastric tablets, sleeping pills, mineral water, zinc ointment, a spare cap for its tube lest the original escape under the bed, and a large handkerchief to wipe the sweat accumulating between right jaw and right clavicle, neither being accustomed to his new fleshiness and insistence to sleep on one side only, so as not to hear his heart: he had made the mistake one night in 1920 of calculating the maximal number of its remaining beats (allowing for another half-century), and now the preposterous hurry of the countdown irritated him and increased the rate at which he could hear himself dying. During his solitary and quite superfluous peregrinations, he had developed a morbid sensitivity to night noises in luxury hotels (the gogophony of a truck rated three distressibles; the Saturday-night gawky cries exchanged by young apprentices in the empty street, thirty; a radiator-relayed snore from downstairs, three hundred); but, though indispensable at times of total despair, earplugs had the disadvantage (especially after too much wine) of magnifying the throbbing in his temples, the weird squeaks in his inexplored nasal cavity, and the atrocious creak of his neck vertebras. To an echo of that creak, transmitted vascularly to the brain before the system of sleep took over, he put down the eerie detonation that took place somewhere in his head at the instant that his senses played false to his consciousness. Antacid mints and the like proved sometimes insufficient to relieve the kind of good old-fashioned heartburn, which invariably afflicted him after certain rich sauces; but on the other hand, he looked forward with juvenile zest to the delightful effect of a spoonful of sodium bicarbonate dissolved in water that was sure to release three or four belches as big as the speech balloons in the "funnies" of his boyhood.

Before he met (at eighty) tactful and tender, ribald and learned, Dr. Lagosse who thenceforth resided and traveled with him and Ada, he had detested physicians. Notwithstanding his own medical training, he could not shake off a sneaky, credulous feeling, befitting a yokel, that the doctor who pumped up a sphygmomanometer or listened in to his wheeze already knew (but still kept secret) what fatal illness had been diagnosed with the certainty of death itself. He wryly remembered his late brother-in-law, when he caught himself concealing from Ada that his bladder troubled him on and off or that he had had another spell of dizziness after paring his toenails (a task he performed himself, being unable to endure any human hand to touch his bare feet).

As if doing his best to avail himself of his body, soon to be removed like a plate wherefrom one collects the last sweet crumbs, he now prized such small indulgences as squeezing out the vermicule of a blackhead, or obtaining with the long nail of his little finger the gem of an itch from the depths of his left ear (the right one was less interesting), or permitting himself what Bouteillan used to brand as *le plaisir anglais*— holding one's breath, and making one's own water, smooth and secret, while lying chin-deep in one's bath.

On the other hand, the pains of life affected him more acutely than in the past. He groaned, on the tympanic rack, when a saxophone blared, or when a subhuman young moron let loose the thunder of an infernal motorcycle. The obstructive behavior of stupid, inimical things—the wrong pocket, the ruptured shoestring, the idle hanger toppling with a shrug and a hingle-tingle in the darkness of a wardrobe—made him utter the Oedipean oath of his Russian ancestry.

He had stopped aging at about sixty-five but by sixty-five he had changed in muscle and bone more sharply than people who had never gone in for such a variety of athletic pursuits as he had enjoyed in his prime. Squash and tennis gave way to ping-pong; then, one day, a favorite paddle, still warm from his grip, was forgotten in the playroom of a club, and the club was never revisited. During his sixth decade some punching-bag exercise had done duty for the wrestling and pugilistics of his earlier years. Gravitational surprises now made skiing grotesque. He could still click foils at sixty, but a few minutes of practice blinded him with sweat; so fencing soon shared the fate of the table tennis. He could never overcome his snobbish prejudice against golf; it was too late to begin, anyway. At seventy, he tried jogging before breakfast in a secluded lane, but the clacking and bouncing of his breasts reminded him too dreadfully that he was thirty kilograms heavier than in his youth. At ninety, he still danced on his hands—in a recurrent dream.

Normally, one or two sleeping pills helped him to hold at bay the monster of insomnia for three or four hours in one blessed blur, but sometimes, particularly after he had completed a mental task, a night of excruciating restlessness would grade into morning migraine. No pill could cope with that torment. There he sprawled, curled up, uncurled, turned off and turned on the bedside light (a gurgling new surrogate —real lammer having been forbidden again by 1930), and physical despair pervaded his unresolvable being. Steady and strong struck his pulse; supper had been adequately digested; his daily ration of one bottle of burgundy had not been exceeded—and yet that wretched restlessness continued to make of him an outcast in his own home: Ada was fast asleep, or comfortably reading, a couple of doors away; the various domestics in their more remote quarters had long passed over to the inimical multitude of local sleepers that seemed to blanket the surrounding hills with the blackness of their repose; he alone was denied the unconsciousness he so fiercely scorned and so assiduously courted.

3

During the years of their last separation, his libertinism had remained essentially as implacable as before; but sometimes the score of love-making would drop to once in four days, and sometimes he would realize with a shock that a whole week had passed in unruffled chastity. The series of exquisite harlots might still alternate with runs of amateur charmers at chance resorts and might still be broken by a month of inventive love in the company of some frivolous women of fashion (there was one red-haired English virgin, Lucy Manfristan, seduced June 4, 1911, in the walled garden of her Norman manor and carried away to Fialta, on the Adriatic, whom he recalled with a special little shiver of lust); but those false romances only fatigued him; the indifferently plumbed *palazzina* would soon be given away, the badly sunburnt girl sent back—and he would need something really nasty and tainted to revive his manhood.

Upon starting in 1922 a new life with Ada, Van firmly resolved to be true to her. Save for a few discreet, and achingly draining, surrenders to what Dr. Lena Wien has so aptly termed "onanistic voyeurism," he somehow managed to stick to his resolution. The ordeal was morally rewarding, physically preposterous. As pediatricians are often cursed with impossible families, so our psychologist presented a not uncommon case of subdivided personality. His love for Ada was a condition of being, a steady hum of happiness unlike anything he had met with professionally in the lives of the singular and the insane. He would have promptly plunged into boiling pitch to save her just as he would have sprung to save his honor at the drop of a glove. Their life together responded antiphonally to their first summer in 1884. She never refused to help him achieve the more and more precious, because less and less frequent, gratification of a fully shared sunset. He saw reflected in her everything that his fastidious and fierce spirit sought in life. An overwhelming tenderness impelled him to kneel suddenly at her feet in dramatic, yet utterly sincere attitudes, puzzling to anyone who might enter with a vacuum cleaner. And on the same day his other compartments and subcompartments would be teeming with longings and regrets, and plans of rape and riot. The most hazardous moment was when he and she moved to another villa, with a new staff and new neighbors, and his senses would be exposed in icy, fantastic detail, to the gipsy girl poaching peaches or the laundry woman's bold daughter.

In vain he told himself that those vile hankerings did not differ, in their intrinsic insignificance, from the anal pruritis which one tries to relieve by a sudden fit of scratching. Yet he knew that by daring to satisfy the corresponding desire for a young wench he risked wrecking his life with Ada. How horribly and gratuitously it might hurt her, he foreglimpsed one day in 1926 or '27 when he caught the look of proud despair she cast on nothing in particular before walking away to the car that was to take her on a trip in which, at the last moment, he had declined to join her. He had declined—and had simulated the grimace and the limp of podagra—because he had just realized, what she, too, had realized—that the beautiful native girl smoking on the back porch would offer her mangoes to Master as soon as Master's housekeeper had left for the Film Festival in Sindbad. The chauffeur had already opened the car door, when, with a great bellow, Van overtook Ada and they rode off together, tearful, voluble, joking about his foolishness.

"It's funny," said Ada, "what black, broken teeth they have hereabouts, those *blyadushki*."

("Ursus," Lucette in glistening green, "Subside, agitation of passion," Flora's bracelets and breasts, the whelk of Time.)

He discovered that a touch of subtle sport could be derived from constantly fighting temptation while constantly dreaming of somehow, sometime, somewhere, yielding to it. He also discovered that whatever fire danced in those lures, he could not spend one day without Ada; that the solitude he needed to sin properly did not represent a matter of a few seconds behind an evergreen bush, but a comfortable night in an impregnable fortress; and that, finally, the temptations, real or conjured up before sleep, were diminishing in frequency. By the age of seventy-five fortnightly intimacies with cooperative Ada, mostly *Blitzpartien*, sufficed for perfect contentment. The successive secretaries he engaged got plainer and plainer (culminating in a coconut-haired female with a horse mouth who wrote love notes to Ada); and by the time Violet Knox broke the lackluster series Van Veen was eighty-seven and completely impotent.

4

Violet Knox [now Mrs. Ronald Oranger. Ed.], born in 1940, came to live with us in 1957. She was (and still is—ten years later) an enchanting English blonde with doll eyes, a velvet carnation and a tweed-cupped little rump [.....]; but such designs, alas, could no longer flesh my fancy. She has been responsible for typing out this memoir—the solace of what are, no doubt, my last ten years of existence. A good daughter, an even better sister, and half-sister, she had supported for ten years her mother's children from two marriages, besides laying aside [something]. I paid her [generously] per month, well realizing the need to ensure unembarrassed silence on the part of a puzzled and dutiful maiden. Ada called her *"Fialochka"* and allowed herself the luxury of admiring "little Violet" 's cameo neck, pink nostrils, and fair pony-tail. Sometimes, at dinner, lingering over the liqueurs, my Ada would consider my typist (a great lover of Koo-Ahn-Trow) with a dreamy gaze, and then, quick-quick, peck at her flushed cheek. The situation might have been considerably more complicated had it arisen twenty years earlier.

I do not know why I should have devoted so much attention to the hoary hairs and sagging apparatus of the venerable Veen. Rakes never reform. They burn, sputter a few last green sparks, and go out. Far greater importance must be attached by the self-researcher and his faithful companion to the unbelievable intellectual surge, to the creative explosion, that occurred in the brain of this strange, friendless, rather repulsive nonagenarian (cries of "no, no!" in lectorial, sororial, editorial brackets).

More fiercely than ever he execrated all sham art, from the crude banalities of junk sculpture to the italicized passages meant by a pretentious novelist to convey his fellow hero's cloudbursts of thought. He had even less patience than before with the "Sig" (Signy-M.D.-M.D.) school of psychiatry. Its founder's epoch-making confession ("In my student days I became a *deflowerer* because I failed to pass my botany examination") he prefixed, as an epigraph, to one of his last papers (1959) entitled *The Farce of Group Therapy in Sexual Maladjustment*, the most damaging and satisfying blast of its kind (the Union of Marital Counselors and Catharticians at first wanted to sue but then preferred to detumify).

Violet knocks at the library door and lets in plump, short, bow-tied Mr. Oranger, who stops on the threshold, clicks his heels, and (as the heavy hermit turns with an awkward sweep of frieze robe) darts forward almost at a trot not so much to stop with a masterful slap the avalanche of loose sheets which the great man's elbow has sent sliding down the lectern-slope, as to express the eagerness of his admiration.

Ada, who amused herself by translating (for the Oranger editions *en regard*) Griboyedov into French and English, Baudelaire into English and Russian, and John Shade into Russian and French, often read to Van, in a deep mediumesque voice, the published versions made by other workers in that field of semiconsciousness. The verse translations in English were especially liable to distend Van's face in a grotesque grin which made him look, when he was not wearing his dental plates, exactly like a Greek comedial mask. He could not tell who disgusted him more: the well-meaning mediocrity, whose attempts at fidelity were thwarted by lack of artistic insight as well as by hilarious errors of textual interpretation, or the professional poet who embellished with his own inventions the dead and helpless author (whiskers here, private parts there)—a method that nicely camouflaged the paraphrast's ignorance of the From language by having the bloomers of inept scholarship blend with the whims of flowery imitation.

As Ada, Mr. Oranger (a born catalyzer), and Van were discussing those matters one afternoon in 1957 (Van's and Ada's book *Information and Form* had just come out), it suddenly occurred to our old polemicist that all his published works—even the extremely abstruse and specialized *Suicide and Sanity* (1912), *Compitalia* (1921), and *When an Alienist Cannot Sleep* (1932), to cite only a few—were not epistemic tasks set to himself by a savant, but buoyant and bellicose exercises in literary style. He was asked why, then, did he not let himself go, why did he not choose a big playground for a match between Inspiration and Design; and with one thing leading to another it was resolved that he would write his memoirs—to be published posthumously.

He was a very slow writer. It took him six years to write the first draft and dictate it to Miss Knox, after which he revised the typescript, rewrote it entirely in long hand (1963–1965) and redictated the entire thing to indefatigable Violet, whose pretty fingers tapped out a final copy in 1967. E, p, i— why "*y*," my dear?

5

Ada, who resented the insufficiency of her brother's fame, felt
soothed and elated by the success of *The Texture of Time*
(1924). That work, she said, always reminded her, in some
odd, delicate way, of the sun-and-shade games she used to
play as a child in the secluded avenues of Ardis Park. She
said she had been somehow responsible for the metamorphoses of the lovely larvae that had woven the silk of "Veen's
Time" (as the concept was now termed in one breath, one
breeze, with "Bergson's Duration," or "Whitehead's Bright
Fringe"). But a considerably earlier and weaker work, the
poor little *Letters from Terra*, of which only half a dozen
copies existed—two in Villa Armina and the rest in the stacks
of university libraries—was even closer to her heart because
of its nonliterary associations with their 1892–93 sojourn in
Manhattan. Sixty-year-old Van crustily and contemptuously
dismissed her meek suggestion to the effect that it should be
republished, together with the Sidra reflections and a very
amusing anti-Signy pamphlet on Time in Dreams. Seventy-
year-old Van regretted his disdain when Victor Vitry, a brilliant French director, based a completely unauthorized

picture on *Letters from Terra* written by "Voltemand" half a century before.

Vitry dated Theresa's visit to Antiterra as taking place in 1940, but 1940 by the Terranean calendar, and about 1890 by ours. The conceit allowed certain pleasing dips into the modes and manners of our past (did you remember that horses wore hats—yes, *hats*—when heat waves swept Manhattan?) and gave the impression—which physics-fiction literature had much exploited—of the capsulist traveling backward in terms of time. Philosophers asked nasty questions, but were ignored by the wishing-to-be-gulled movie-goers.

In contrast to the cloudless course of Demonian history in the twentieth century, with the Anglo-American coalition managing one hemisphere, and Tartary, behind her Golden Veil, mysteriously ruling the other, a succession of wars and revolutions were shown shaking loose the jigsaw puzzle of Terrestrial autonomies. In an impressive historical survey of Terra rigged up by Vitry—certainly the greatest cinematic genius ever to direct a picture of such scope or use such a vast number of extras (some said more than a million, others, half a million men and as many mirrors)—kingdoms fell and dictatordoms rose, and republics half-sat, half-lay in various attitudes of discomfort. The conception was controversial, the execution flawless. Look at all those tiny soldiers scuttling along very fast across the trench-scarred wilderness, with explosions of mud and things going *pouf-pouf* in silent French now here, now there!

In 1905, Norway with a mighty heave and a long dorsal ripple unfastened herself from Sweden, her unwieldy co-giantess, while in a similar act of separation the French parliament, with parenthetical outbursts of *vive émotion*, voted a divorce between State and Church. Then, in 1911, Norwegian troops led by Amundsen reached the South Pole and simultaneously the Italians stormed into Turkey. In 1914 Germany invaded Belgium and the Americans tore up Panama. In 1918 they and the French defeated Germany while she was busily defeating Russia (who had defeated her own Tartars some time earlier). In Norway there was Siegrid Mitchel, in America Margaret Undset, and in France, Sidonie Colette. In 1926 Abd-el-Krim surrendered, after yet another photogenic war, and the Golden Horde again subjugated Rus. In 1933, Athaulf Hindler (also known as Mittler—from "to mittle," mutilate) came to power in Germany, and a conflict on an even more spectacular scale than the 1914–1918 war was under way, when Vitry ran out of old documentaries and Theresa, played by his wife, left Terra in a cosmic capsule after having covered the Olympic Games held in Berlin (the Norwegians took most of the prizes, but the Americans won the fencing event, an outstanding achievement, and beat the Germans in the final football match by three goals to one).

Van and Ada saw the film nine times, in seven different languages, and eventually acquired a copy for home use. They found the historical background absurdly farfetched and considered starting legal proceedings against Vitry—not for having stolen the L.F.T. idea, but for having distorted Terrestrial politics as obtained by Van with such diligence and skill from extrasensorial sources and manic dreams. But fifty years had elapsed, and the novella had not been copyrighted; in fact, Van could not even prove that "Voltemand" was he. Reporters, however, ferreted out his authorship, and in a magnanimous gesture, he allowed it to be publicized.

Three circumstances contributed to the picture's exceptional success. One factor was, of course, that organized religion, disapproving of Terra's appeal to sensation-avid sects, attempted to have the thing banned. A second attraction came from a little scene that canny Vitry had not cut out: in a flashback to a revolution in former France, an unfortunate extra, who played one of the under-executioners, got accidentally decapitated while pulling the comedian Steller, who played a reluctant king, into a guillotinable position. Finally, the third, and even more human reason, was that the lovely leading lady, Norwegian-born Gedda Vitry, after titillating the spectators with her skimpy skirts and sexy rags in the existential sequences, came out of her capsule on Antiterra stark naked, though, of course, in miniature, a millimeter of maddening femininity dancing in "the charmed circle of the microscope" like some lewd elf, and revealing, in certain attitudes, I'll be damned, a pinpoint glint of pubic floss, gold-powdered!

L.F.T. tiny dolls, L.F.T. breloques of coral and ivory, appeared in souvenir shops, from Agony, Patagonia, to Wrinkleballs, Le Bras d'Or. L.F.T. clubs sprouted. L.F.T. girlies minced with mini-menus out of roadside snackettes shaped like spaceships. From the tremendous correspondence that piled up on Van's desk during a few years of world fame, one gathered that thousands of more or less unbalanced people believed (so striking was the visual impact of the Vitry-Veen film) in the secret Government-concealed identity of Terra and Antiterra. Demonian reality dwindled to a casual illusion. Actually, we had passed through all that. Politicians, dubbed Old Felt and Uncle Joe in forgotten comics, had really existed. Tropical countries meant, not only Wild Nature Reserves but famine, and death, and ignorance, and shamans, and agents from distant Atomsk. Our world *was*, in fact, mid-twentieth-century. Terra convalesced after enduring the rack and the stake, the bullies and beasts that Germany inevitably generates when fulfilling her dreams of glory. Russian peasants and poets had not been transported to Estotiland, and the Barren Grounds, ages ago—they were dying, at this very moment, in the slave camps of Tartary. Even the governor of France was not Charlie Chose, the suave nephew of Lord Goal, but a bad-tempered French general.

6

Nirvana, Nevada, Vaniada. By the way, should I not add, my Ada, that only at the very last interview with poor dummy-mummy, soon after my premature—I mean, premonitory—nightmare about "You can, Sir," she employed *mon petit nom*, Vanya, Vanyusha—never had before, and it sounded so odd, so tend . . . (voice trailing off, radiators tinkling).

"Dummy-mum"—(laughing). "Angels, too, have brooms—to sweep one's soul clear of horrible images. My black nurse was Swiss-laced with white whimsies."

Sudden ice hurtling down the rain pipe: brokenhearted stalactite.

Recorded and replayed in their joint memory was their early preoccupation with the strange idea of death. There is one exchange that it would be nice to enact against the green moving backdrop of one of our Ardis sets. The talk about "double guarantee" in eternity. Start just before that.

"I know there's a Van in Nirvana. I'll be with him in the depths *moego ada*, of my Hades," said Ada.

"True, true" (bird-effects here, and acquiescing branches, and what you used to call "golden gouts").

[620]

"As lovers *and* siblings," she cried, "we have a double chance of being together in eternity, in terrarity. Four pairs of eyes in paradise!"

"Neat, neat," said Van.

Something of the sort. One great difficulty. The strange mirage-shimmer standing in for death should not appear too soon in the chronicle and yet it should permeate the first amorous scenes. Hard but not insurmountable (I can do anything, I can tango and tap-dance on my fantastic hands). By the way, who dies first?

Ada. Van. Ada. Vaniada. Nobody. Each hoped to go first, so as to concede, by implication, a longer life to the other, and each wished to go last, in order to spare the other the anguish, or worries, of widowhood. One solution would be for you to marry Violet.

"Thank you. *J'ai tâté de deux tribades dans ma vie, ça suffit.* Dear Emile says '*terme qu'on évite d'employer.*' How right he is!"

"If not Violet, then a local Gauguin girl. Or Yolande Kickshaw."

Why? Good question. Anyway, Violet must not be given this part to type. I'm afraid we're going to wound a lot of people (openwork American lilt)! Oh come, art cannot hurt. It can, and how!

Actually the question of mortal precedence has now hardly any importance. I mean, the hero and heroine should get so close to each other by the time the horror begins, so *organically* close, that they overlap, intergrade, interache, and even if Vaniada's end is described in the epilogue we, writers and readers, should be unable to make out (myopic, myopic) who exactly survives, Dava or Vada, Anda or Vanda.

I had a schoolmate called Vanda. And *I* knew a girl called Adora, little thing in my last floramor. What makes me see

[621]

that bit as the purest *sanglot* in the book? What is the worst part of dying?

For you realize there are three facets to it (roughly corresponding to the popular tripartition of Time). There is, first, the wrench of relinquishing forever all one's memories—that's a commonplace, but what courage man must have had to go through that commonplace again and again and not give up the rigmarole of accumulating again and again the riches of consciousness that will be snatched away! Then we have the second facet—the hideous physical pain—for obvious reasons let us not dwell upon that. And finally, there is the featureless pseudo-future, blank and black, an everlasting nonlastingness, the crowning paradox of our boxed brain's eschatologies!

"Yes," said Ada (aged eleven and a great hair-tosser), "yes —but take a paralytic who forgets the entire past gradually, stroke by stroke, who dies in his sleep like a good boy, and who has believed all his life that the soul is immortal—isn't that desirable, isn't that a quite comfortable arrangement?"

"Cold comfort," said Van (aged fourteen and dying of other desires). "You lose your immortality when you lose your memory. And if you land then on Terra Caelestis, with your pillow and chamberpot, you are made to room not with Shakespeare or even Longfellow, but with guitarists and cretins."

She insisted that if there were no future, then one had the right of making up a future, and in that case one's very own future did exist, insofar as one existed oneself. Eighty years quickly passed—a matter of changing a slide in a magic lantern. They had spent most of the morning reworking their translation of a passage (lines 569–572) in John Shade's famous poem:

>   . . . Sovetï mï dayom
> Kak bït' vdovtsu: on poteryal dvuh zhyon;
> On ih vstrechaet—lyubyashchih, lyubimïh,
> Revnuyushchih ego drug k druzhke . . .

>   (. . . *We give advice*
> *To widower. He has been married twice:*
> *He meets his wives; both loved, both loving, both*
> *Jealous of one another . . .*)

Van pointed out that here was the rub—one is free to imagine any type of hereafter, of course: the generalized paradise promised by Oriental prophets and poets, or an individual combination; but the work of fancy is handicapped—to a quite hopeless extent—by a logical ban: you cannot bring your friends along—or your enemies for that matter—to the party. The transposition of all our remembered relationships into an Elysian life inevitably turns it into a second-rate continuation of our marvelous mortality. Only a Chinaman or a retarded child can imagine being met, in that Next-Installment World, to the accompaniment of all sorts of tail-wagging and groveling of welcome, by the mosquito executed eighty years ago upon one's bare leg, which has been amputated since then and now, in the wake of the gesticulating mosquito, comes back, stomp, stomp, stomp, here I am, stick me on.

She did not laugh; she repeated to herself the verses that had given them such trouble. The Signy brain-shrinkers would gleefully claim that the reason the three "boths" had been skipped in the Russian version was not at all, oh, not at all, because cramming three cumbersome amphibrachs into the pentameter would have necessitated adding at least one more verse for carrying the luggage:

"Oh, Van, oh Van, we did not love her enough. *That's* whom you should have married, the one sitting feet up, in ballerina black, on the stone balustrade, and then everything would have been all right—I would have stayed with you both in Ardis Hall, and instead of that happiness, handed out gratis, instead of all that we *teased* her to death!"

Was it time for the morphine? No, not yet. Time-and-pain had not been mentioned in the *Texture*. Pity, since an element of pure time enters into pain, into the thick, steady, solid duration of I-can't-bear-it pain; nothing gray-gauzy about it, solid as a black bole, I can't, oh, call Lagosse.

Van found him reading in the serene garden. The doctor followed Ada into the house. The Veens had believed for a whole summer of misery (or made each other believe) that it was a touch of neuralgia.

Touch? A giant, with an effort-contorted face, clamping and twisting an engine of agony. Rather humiliating that physical pain makes one supremely indifferent to such moral issues as Lucette's fate, and rather amusing, if that is the right word, to constate that one bothers about problems of style even at those atrocious moments. The Swiss doctor, who had been told everything (and had even turned out to have known at medical school a nephew of Dr. Lapiner) displayed an intense interest in the almost completed but only partly corrected book and drolly said it was not a person or persons but *le bouquin* which he wanted to see *guéri de tous ces accrocs* before it was too late. It was. What everybody thought would be Violet's supreme achievement, ideally clean, produced on special Atticus paper in a special cursive type (the glorified version of Van's hand), with the master copy bound in purple calf for Van's ninety-seventh birthday, had been immediately blotted out by a regular inferno of alterations in red ink and blue pencil. One can even surmise that if our time-racked, flat-lying couple ever intended to die they would die, as it were, *into* the finished book, into Eden or Hades, into the prose of the book or the poetry of its blurb.

Their recently built castle in Ex was inset in a crystal winter. In the latest *Who's Who* the list of his main papers included by some bizarre mistake the title of a work he had never written, though planned to write many pains: *Unconsciousness and the Unconscious*. There was no pain to do it now—and it was high pain for *Ada* to be completed. *"Quel livre, mon Dieu, mon Dieu,"* Dr. [Professor. Ed.] Lagosse exclaimed, weighing the master copy which the flat pale parents of the future Babes, in the brown-leaf Woods, a little book in the Ardis Hall nursery, could no longer prop up in the mysterious first picture: two people in one bed.

Ardis Hall—the Ardors and Arbors of Ardis—this is the leitmotiv rippling through *Ada*, an ample and delightful chronicle, whose principal part is staged in a dream-bright America—for are not our childhood memories comparable to Vineland-born caravelles, indolently encircled by the white birds of dreams? The protagonist, a scion of one of our most illustrious and opulent families, is Dr. Van Veen, son of Baron "Demon" Veen, that memorable Manhattan and Reno figure. The end of an extraordinary epoch coincides with Van's no less extraordinary boyhood. Nothing in world literature, save maybe Count Tolstoy's reminiscences, can vie in pure joyousness and Arcadian innocence with the "Ardis" part of the book. On the fabulous country estate of his art-collecting uncle, Daniel Veen, an ardent childhood romance develops in a series of fascinating scenes between Van and pretty Ada, a truly unusual *gamine*, daughter of Marina, Daniel's stage-struck wife. That the relationship is not simply dangerous *cousinage*, but possesses an aspect prohibited by law, is hinted in the very first pages.

In spite of the many intricacies of plot and psychology, the story proceeds at a spanking pace. Before we can pause to take breath and quietly survey the new surroundings into which the writer's magic carpet has, as it were, spilled us, another attractive girl, Lucette Veen, Marina's younger daughter, has also been swept off her feet by Van, the irresistible rake. Her tragic destiny constitutes one of the highlights of this delightful book.

The rest of Van's story turns frankly and colorfully upon his long love-affair with Ada. It is interrupted by her marriage to an Arizonian cattle-breeder whose fabulous ancestor discovered our country. After her husband's death our lovers are reunited. They spend their old age traveling together and dwelling in the various villas, one lovelier than another, that Van has erected all over the Western Hemisphere.

Not the least adornment of the chronicle is the delicacy of pictorial detail: a latticed gallery; a painted ceiling; a pretty plaything stranded among the forget-me-nots of a brook; butterflies and butterfly orchids in the margin of the romance; a misty view described from marble steps; a doe at gaze in the ancestral park; and much, much more.